Emma Blair Omnibus

EMMA BLAIR OMNIBUS

Nellie Wildchild
Jessie Gray

EMMA BLAIR

WARNER BOOKS

A *Warner* Book

This omnibus edition first published in Great Britain by Warner Books in 2001

Emma Blair Omnibus Copyright © Emma Blair 2001

Previously published separately:

Nellie Wildchild
First published in Great Britain by Arrow Books in 1983
Published by Warner Books in 1996
Reprinted 1996 (twice), 1999

Copyright © 1983 Emma Blair

Jessie Gray
First published in Great Britain in 1986 by Arrow Books Ltd
Published by Warner Books in 1997
Reprinted 1997 (twice), 1999

Copyright © Emma Blair, 1986

The moral right of the author has been asserted.

A CIP catalogue record for this book
is available from the British Library.

ISBN 0 7515 3169 3

Printed and bound in Great Britain by Clays Ltd, St Ives plc

Warner Books
A Division of
Little, Brown and Company (UK)
Brettenham House
Lancaster Place
London WC2E 7EN

www.littlebrown.co.uk

Nellie Wildchild

ACKNOWLEDGEMENTS

The author wishes to thank the copyright-holders for permission to reproduce the lyrics of the following songs:

'The Parisien Pierrot' by Noël Coward © 1923 Keith Prowse Music Publishing Co. Ltd and 'I Belong to Glasgow' by Will Fyffe © 1921 Francis Day and Hunter Ltd, both songs used by kind permission of E.M.I. Publishing Ltd.

'Boy! What Love Has Done for Me!' and 'In the Mandarin's Orchard Garden' by George Gershwin, both © New World Music Corp. (Warner Brothers) Chappell Music Ltd, for territories of the British Commonwealth (excluding Canada). Used by kind permission of Chappell Music Ltd.

I went doon by the sweetie work and my heart began to beat,
seeing all the factory lasses coming doon the street
with their flashy dashy petticoats and their flashy dashy shawls,
five and tanner guttie boots,
oh, we're big gallus molls!

Old Glasgow street song

1

Nellie sang as she combed her long, yellow hair. Her voice was like an angel's, her father often said. An angel come to earth.

'Nellie, it's five past seven! Babs will have been waiting for you down at the close mouth five minutes since!' Betty Thompson, Nellie's mother, shouted from ben the kitchen.

'I'm ready!' Nellie shouted back. And, after a final inspection of her face, shrugged herself into her coat, picked up her handbag and hurried through to the kitchen where she found Betty washing up the tea dishes at the sink and her da sitting slumped in his chair before the fire reading the evening paper. Her wee brother Roddy was sitting in the other fireside chair facing her da with his head buried in a comic. He was a great one for the comics.

'Will I do?' Nellie demanded, her eyes bright with anticipation at the evening lying ahead. For it was Friday night, time for fun and a few laughs.

Davey Thompson glanced up from his paper. 'Come closer so I can get a better look at you,' he commanded.

Nellie took a few steps forward.

Davey shook his head. 'I don't know why you lassies have to wear make-up,' he said. 'You're just spoiling the natural beauty the good God gave you.'

Nellie sighed. Ever since she'd started wearing make-up it had been a bone of contention between her father and herself. Over-gilding the lily was how he usually put it.

'I'm wearing hardly any at all,' she defended. 'Less than half what Babs and the other girls at work wear.'

'I'm not interested in Babs or the girls at work,' Davey said. 'You're my daughter. You're the one I'm interested in.'

'Ma?' Nellie appealed.

'It's the fashion for lassies to be made up,' Betty said from the sink. Drying her workworn hands on a tea cloth, she came to her husband's side. 'She looks all right to me,' she added.

Davey grumbled under his breath, a look of uncertainty still on his face.

Nellie was impatient now, desperate to get on her way. But she curbed her impatience knowing full well that unless her father was placated she'd be ordered back through to the house's one bedroom to wipe her make-up off and start afresh.

'Come on, Davey, she's late as it is,' Betty cajoled.

Nellie silently blessed her mother whom she knew she could always rely on. Luckily Ma wasn't an old stick-in-the-mud like her da. Ma understood about things like this.

'I think the eyes are a bit heavy but aye, all right, away you go then,' Davey said reluctantly, adding sharply, as Nellie hurried to the door, 'And mind you're home by eleven. Any later and you're for it my lass. It's bad enough you go out looking like a painted Jezebel. What I'll not stand for is you coming in at God knows what hour when you think we're asleep and don't know.'

Nellie stopped at the door. 'That only happened once, Da, because Babs and I missed the last bus and had to walk.'

'Well see you don't miss it again, that's all.'

'I promise.'

'Enjoy yourself, lass,' Betty said, an understanding smile hovering round her lips.

'Cheerio,' said Nellie. And then she was gone, the

sound of her high heels clattering down the stone close steps.

'And no smoking!' Davey called out. But he was too late. She was well out of hearing.

'She thinks I'm daft but I'm not,' he said to his wife. 'Comes in here smelling like an ashtray and tells me she's not smoking. Well, I know better. I didn't come up the Clyde on a bicycle after all.'

'What did you come up in, Da?' Roddy asked, his eyes twinkling mischievously as he looked up for the first time.

Fast as a striking snake Davey's hand lashed out to clip Roddy's ear.

'And I'll have no cheek from you either,' Davey said, settling himself back into his chair while Roddy howled.

'You asked for that,' Betty said, before turning on her heel and returning to the dishes piled high in the sink.

'Youngsters nowadays think they can get away with murder. Well I've got news for them, they can't in my house,' Davey said, having, as usual, the last word.

'What kept you?' Babs Boyd demanded when Nellie appeared at the close mouth. She and Nellie had been great pals since their schooldays and now worked together side by side at Harrison's sweet factory.

'Och, it was my da wittering on as usual,' Nellie replied.

Babs sighed. 'I know what you mean. Mine's just the same, as you well know. If it isn't one thing he finds to go on about it's another.'

The two girls nodded in sympathy.

'So where's it to be then? Up the town or local?' Babs asked.

Nellie had been swithering about that for the last hour. 'What do you fancy?'

'I'm easy.'

'Me too.'

'There's a new band at the Roxy. Big Jessie at work has heard them before and says they're good.' The Roxy was a dance-hall in the centre of Govan, the area where they both lived, less than a quarter of a mile away.

'Shall we take a chance on that then?' Nellie asked.

'Why not?'

'Then the Roxy it is,' Nellie said, slipping her arm through Babs's, adding as they started down the street, 'I didn't really fancy going too far away in case it buckets which I'm sure it's going to do later.'

Babs glanced up at the heavy, lowering sky which was so close as to seem to be resting on the tenement roofs. 'Aye, I think you're right,' she said, unconsciously touching her brolly to make sure she'd brought it with her.

'Tram or walk?' Nellie demanded.

'May as well walk. It's hardly worth the tram.'

'Right.'

Arm in arm they strode past the tram stop and into the grey, sooty night.

For a while they walked in silence and then, giggling suddenly, Babs said, 'Do you think he'll be there the night?'

'Who?'

'*Him. Mr Right.*'

Nellie smiled. Babs was always going on about her *Fate*. The man, the one and only Babs was convinced destiny had earmarked for her.

'He might well be. You never know do you?' Nellie replied.

Babs's face lit up. This was her favourite subject and one she never tired of talking about or speculating upon. 'What do you think yours will look like?' she asked. It was a question she'd asked Nellie at least a thousand times before.

Nellie's answer always depended upon her mood, or the last man she'd seen whom she'd fancied. 'Tall,' she said.

'Aye, tall,' Babs breathed. A tall man was always the first prerequisite, the vast majority of Glasgow men being under six foot six.

'Good looking –'

'That goes without saying. A real dreamboat.'

'With a wee tache like William Powell.'

'You don't fancy a wee tache surely?' Babs said in horror. 'They tickle when you kiss.'

'Maybe so but they make a man look more debonair, sophisticated. Don't you fancy William Powell?'

'Oh aye. But without the tache.'

'And he must have broad shoulders,' Nellie went on. 'I can't stand those skinnymalinks you run into. Most of them look like a good puff of wind would knock them over.'

Babs giggled. 'I know what you mean. But I'm not against the skinny ones. Some of them can be awful affectionate, as though they're trying to make up for being so wee and runty.'

Like a lot of Glasgow women, Babs was well-fleshed and rounded, and would have made two of the skinnymalinks they were talking about.

'And he has to be kind,' Nellie said.

'None of your cruel sods for me either,' said Babs. 'Especially those who come home and beat the hell out of you whenever they've had a bucket. And believe me, there's plenty of that kind about.'

Both girls nodded knowingly at one another. Brought up in the tenements, they knew only too well what went on at night, especially on a Friday after the boozers shut and the drunks staggered home with what remained of their pay packets in their pockets. Those were the times when wives, and sometimes children, were likely to be beaten.

Nellie thanked God her da had never been like that. Sure he often took a good drink and came home the worse for wear, but she could never remember him lifting his hand against her ma. It was the same with Babs's da.

Their conversation about Mr Right stopped on reaching the Roxy where they had to stand in a queue.

'It looks like a good turnout the night,' Babs said as they shuffled forward. But then Friday and Saturday nights invariably were at the dancing, Glasgow being the most dancing-mad city in the whole Empire.

Once inside they made straight for the cloakroom where they immediately lit up. 'Jesus, but I was gasping for that,' Babs said, drawing smoke deep into her lungs. She'd been dying for a fag since leaving home but would never have dreamt of smoking in the street. Only a tart would ever do that.

As soon as they had their cigarettes they took themselves out on to the floor where Nellie was asked if she was for up?

She made sure the boy who'd done the asking

seemed acceptable before assenting to his roughly made request.

'Do you come here often?' the boy asked as they glided round the floor.

Nellie groaned inwardly. It was the clichéd, standard opening. If only some of them could be at least a little original!

'Now and again,' she replied, resisting his attempts to pull her close.

At the end of the dance he asked if she'd like a lemonade.

'No thanks,' she smiled and excused herself, leaving him standing there looking after her. She'd quickly decided he wasn't her type at all.

She found Babs eyeing the unmatched males lining the opposite wall.

'The talent's not bad,' Babs said. 'One or two right lookers among them.'

Nellie took a quick glance across at the male line-up. Babs was right, there were one or two who weren't half bad.

'Are you dancing?'

Babs flashed what she hoped was a winning smile. 'Are you asking?'

'No, I'm here trying to get a couple of pints.'

'A wit!' Babs exclaimed. Then to Nellie, 'Glasgow's full of them.'

'That's not all Glasgow's full of,' the boy retorted.

'What do you mean by that?'

'Come on the floor and I'll tell you.'

Babs laughed. 'You sound like a right patter merchant. Come on then, let's see if your feet are as quick as your tongue.'

Babs and the young man melted into the dancing throng where they were quickly lost to view.

Three times in a row Nellie turned down offers of a partner. She didn't fancy any of them and besides, Babs had been right, the band was good, so for the moment she was content just to stand and listen.

A little later Babs reappeared by her side. 'I thought you'd got a click there,' Nellie said.

'Maybe. Maybe not,' Babs shrugged. 'I think he's gone away to consider the idea. I get the impression he's not exactly the impulsive type.'

Both girls laughed.

'How about a drink?' Nellie asked a few minutes later. Babs agreed and they trooped off to the refreshment bar, but as she drank her lemonade Nellie became aware of a young man watching her covertly from a spot a dozen or so feet away. Glancing boldly in his direction she laughed inwardly when he coloured and hurriedly looked elsewhere. But Babs began to chat again, and the young man was instantly forgotten.

The night passed and they both danced a number of times, Nellie more than Babs as was almost always the case when they went out together. But the fact that Nellie was far prettier than she was never bothered Babs. It was something she accepted and, in fact, secretly enjoyed, basking in a sort of reflected glory.

It had just gone twenty past ten and Nellie was thinking of saying she thought it was time they were for off, when out of the crowd materialized a smallish, dark-haired young man who, stammering, asked her to dance.

She was about to refuse, thinking he wasn't her type at all, when it suddenly came to her that this was the same chap whom she'd caught watching her earlier on at the refreshment bar. Not quite knowing why she changed her mind, she accepted his invitation.

He was clumsy, tripping over his own feet and hers. 'I'm awful sorry,' he mumbled after he'd nipped her toe for the second time. They'd been dancing less than a minute.

His hair was dark brown and curly; his eyebrows thick as ropes; the eyes beneath them brown and liquid.

'My name's Frank,' he said.

'I'm Nellie.'

'I know.'

'Oh, do you now?'

He blushed again, the way he had earlier on. 'I heard somebody mention it,' he said.

'Are you sure you didn't ask?'

He laughed, a deep, warm sound, which was the last thing she'd been expecting. 'Well, maybe I did,' he confessed.

The hand in hers tightened fractionally and his feet became more sure of themselves as though, somehow, that small confession had given him confidence.

'You were watching me earlier on,' she said boldly. 'Why?'

'You'll think I'm soft.'

'Try me.'

'I saw you come into the hall and I just . . . well I just fancied you. Something rotten,' he added hurriedly and looked away.

Nellie found this amusing. And not just a little touching. 'Why didn't you ask me up earlier?' she smiled.

'Now you really will think me soft.'

'Go on.'

He licked his lips and cleared his throat. He was about to reply when the music stopped and they had to applaud along with everybody else.

'Will you stay up?' he asked, a hint of pleading in his voice.

'All right,' she said softly, and coming into his arms they moved off again as the music began.

'You were about to say?' she prodded.

'I was too feart,' he replied after a pause of a few seconds.

She'd known that was the answer, of course, but it impressed her that he'd admitted to it. It was rare for a Glasgow man to admit fear in any form – especially to or about a woman.

'Are you usually shy?' she asked.

He shook his head.

'Only with me?'

'A dozen times I was about to come over and ask you up but every time I tried my legs started to shake. I felt a proper fool I can tell you.'

Nellie was warming rapidly to this dark-haired lad called Frank. There was a different quality about him, something which made him stand out from the others. He'd caught her interest.

'You're the best-looking bird here. Do you know that?' he said.

'You're only saying that,' she replied coyly.

'No, no. It's true!'

She allowed herself to be drawn a little closer to him. The extreme heat in the hall had caused him to sweat. A not unpleasant smell, she thought – surprised at herself.

As they birled round she suddenly caught sight of the clock above the main entrance, it was twenty to the hour and if she didn't leave right that instant she risked being late home. She couldn't bear to think of the scene that would follow should that happen. It just wasn't worth it.

Pulling away from him she said, 'Look, I'm awful sorry, Frank, but I really must fly.'

He looked bewildered. 'But I thought –'

'It's not you. It's my da. He'll kill me if I'm not in by eleven.' Then she added mischievously, 'See, you should have asked me up earlier,' and, turning, she hurried across to where Babs was waiting for her.

They were just coming out of the cloakroom when Nellie found her arm being grasped. Anger flared in her but that vanished instantly when she saw it was Frank who had accosted her.

'Can I take you home?' he asked.

She shook her head. 'Thanks for asking but it really isn't worth it. I'll have to run as it is.'

He looked crestfallen. 'Will you be here tomorrow night?' he asked.

'I've already arranged to go to the pictures with some of my pals. Sorry.' Thinking she was giving him the brush off, he started to move away only to be stopped by her hand reaching out to touch him. 'I could come next Friday night,' she said.

'I'll be here waiting,' he replied, a smile lighting up his face.

Long after she was gone he was still staring at the door through which she'd vanished.

*

Nellie hated the alarm clock whose strident jangling announced it was time for her to get up. Monday morning again. The start of another working week. God, what a life!

Opening her eyes she stared across at the kitchen window, through which she could see that it was a grey, dreich morning. Although still warm in bed, she shivered.

In the bedroom her parents' alarm went off. Her mother would make an appearance in a minute to light the fire and put the kettle on, but her da would wait until she'd washed herself at the sink and got dressed before he got up.

Yawning, she swung herself out of the cavity bed she shared with her brother Roddy. The yawn turned to a sharp intake of breath as her feet made contact with the cold linoleum floor.

Hastily she pulled her dressing gown around her and slid her feet into her slippers. Crossing to the sink she began to wash herself, a lick really more than a proper wash, in the icy water from the tap.

Betty bustled in and set about bringing the house to life. Soon a cheery fire was crackling in the grate and the smell of porridge filled the room. Nellie dressed hurriedly, calling to her father when she was finished.

Sitting at the table drinking her first cup of tea, she thought of the dream she'd had the night before. A knight in shining armour, just like the one in the story book she'd had as a child, had come on a white horse to save her from a horrible dragon, and when the dragon was dead the knight had lifted his visor to reveal himself as Frank, the lad she'd met at the Roxy on Friday night. The dream amused Nellie. Her dreams weren't usually that fanciful.

Perhaps she should have gone back to the Roxy on the Saturday night instead of saying she was going to the pictures, which had been a lie. But no, that would have made it too easy for him. Let him wait a week. Her feminine instincts told her that was the right tack to take.

'Time you weren't here,' Betty said glancing across at the alarm clock standing on a chair by the cavity bed.

'Aye, right,' replied Nellie.

'And hap up warm. It may be April, but it's like the middle of winter out there.'

At the door Betty kissed Nellie on the cheek and then handed her her lunchtime piece. 'See you the night,' Betty said.

Down at the front close Nellie found Babs waiting for her as she did every working morning. 'Another blinking Monday,' Babs sniffed.

'Aye. It would sicken your kidneys so it would,' Nellie agreed.

'You can say that again.'

Arm in arm and with heads bent against the biting wind, the two girls hurried on their way. Thanks to the wind the air was clean and fresh, not filled with its usual stench of cat urine and human waste.

How she hated this place, Nellie thought. The street was like a tipped midden, as were all its neighbours. Soot, dust, grime and just general filth were everywhere. The tenements lining either side were weighed down with countless years of neglect. Once tall, proud edifices, they were now raddled, diseased shells. Someday, somehow, I'll escape all this, Nellie thought to herself, knowing at the same time that very few of her kind ever did. Except to the graveyard, that is.

Harrison's sweet factory, where both girls worked, was a squat building with nearly a century of starling droppings covering its roof. Like a great, grey cake with icing on its top, as it had once been described. To those who worked there it was known as the Bastille.

Nellie and Babs clocked on, then took themselves through to the long, soulless room where coats were exchanged for overalls. From there the 150 women who worked for Harrison's made their way to their various positions. Promptly on the hour the hooter sounded and the machinery ground into motion.

Every Monday morning was the same for Nellie. Coming back afresh to the heavy, sickly, sugar smell that pervaded everything made her stomach turn over.

On starting at the factory two years previously, having left school at fifteen, she'd vomited every morning for a month. If work hadn't been so desperately hard to come by she'd have chucked the job and gone elsewhere. Trouble was, there wasn't really an elsewhere to go to.

She was damn lucky to be grafting and appreciated the fact. But that didn't make the job any easier to live with.

At half past ten, the hooter sounded again announcing a ten minute tea break. Ladies with trolleys were already in position, the workers helping themselves to the poured out cups of tea.

The girls in Nellie's section assembled as they always did, but although all of them smoked not one lit up; to have done so and been caught would have meant instant dismissal.

'You should have seen the one I got off with on Saturday night,' Big Jessie, the section's self-appointed leader bragged. 'What a maddie, but nice looking with it.'

'What happened then?' Daisy demanded. 'Did he lumber you?'

'Oh aye, he took me home all right. But when he asked me, he said he'd run me there so I thought that he had a car.'

'And didn't he?'

'Don't tell me he produced a pair of sandshoes?' Agnes said, and everyone laughed. It was an old Glasgow joke.

'No, a motorbike. An old rattly affair that I thought was going to fall apart right there under me. Up and down Sauchiehall Street we went, giving me a wee hurl as he put it, and then back to my house with all the neighbours coming to their windows and gawping because of the noise the damn thing made.'

'Are you seeing him again?' Daisy demanded eagerly.

Big Jessie shook her head. 'No fear. He was a university student. What would I want with the likes of that? Oil and water, we just wouldn't mix.' Looking a trifle wistful she added, 'But he was good-looking. No denying that.'

'What about you, Babs?' Agnes asked.

'Aye, what about you?' Big Jessie chimed in. 'Weren't you and Nellie going to the jigging? Did you go into town?'

'We went to the Roxy,' Babs said.

'Bloody dump that place,' Big Jessie said. 'I much prefer the town dances myself.'

'We like it,' Nellie said. She wasn't going to let Jessie turn up her nose at her. The Roxy wasn't *that* bad after all.

'Did you get a lumber then, Babs?' Daisy asked.

'I nearly did. I met this chap who I thought had taken a notion, but he went away to think about it and that was the last I saw of him.'

Big Jessie rolled her eyes. 'If you fancied him you shouldn't have let him go. Never give them time to think, that's always a mistake.'

'Some of us prefer it that way, having enough confidence in ourselves,' Nellie said sweetly.

Jessie glared at Nellie. There was a rivalry between them that nothing ever changed.

'What was I supposed to do, twist his arm or something?' Babs demanded.

'There are ways and means,' Big Jessie replied knowingly.

'Such as? Throw him to the floor and sit on him?'

The group erupted with laughter at the image of Babs sitting on top of a struggling lad in the middle of a dancehall.

'What about you, Nellie? Did you meet anyone nice?' Agnes asked when the hilarity had subsided.

'Possibly. I'm not quite sure yet,' Nellie replied mysteriously.

'You either did or you didn't,' said Big Jessie.

'Was he tall and handsome?' demanded Daisy.

'Not too tall. But he was certainly handsome. That right, Babs?'

Babs nodded to the company that that was so.

'Are you seeing him again?' Agnes went on.

'Maybe.'

'What does that mean exactly?' Jessie demanded.

'It means maybe. I haven't made up my mind yet. We left things sort of open.'

'In other words you're meeting him in the hall,' Big Jessie said. 'Too mean is he to pay your way in?'

Nellie stared at her coldly. 'I made that particular arrangement because that's the way I want it. Some of us like to pick and choose you know, and not just be swept along by whoever will have us.'

'You're a right cheeky bitch!' hissed Jessie.

'If I am then that makes two of us,' retorted Nellie.

'I wish I could pick and choose,' said Daisy, trying to change the subject. 'But no such luck.'

'You and me both,' added Babs.

Big Jessie was about to make another barbed remark to Nellie when the hooter indicated that the tea break was over.

'What about you, Agnes?' asked Nellie as they made their way back to their stations.

Agnes was exceptionally short and fat with legs that would have done credit to a rugby fullback.

'I went dancing on Friday and stood there all night. I didn't have one offer for the floor,' Agnes said.

'Still, maybe next week,' said Nellie.

'Aye, maybe then,' replied Agnes.

The machinery, that had been stopped for the tea break, clanked into action putting paid to any further conversation.

The week dragged by for Nellie who found excitement mounting within her at the thought of her forthcoming rendezvous. It was rare for her to be so taken with a chap.

When Friday night finally arrived she left work to hurry to the public baths where she treated herself to a good long, piping-hot soak. They had a zinc tub at home which was used in front of the fire sometimes but it wasn't nearly as good as the luxury of the public baths.

Bath over she went swiftly home for her tea, then took herself into her parents' bedroom to get dressed.

The Thompsons lived in what was known as a room and kitchen, the room being the small flat's one bedroom. The toilet was a communal one on the stairs' half-landing and was shared by the three flats on the level above.

Nellie hated having to share the kitchen bed with her brother, desperately wanting a bedroom of her own and the privacy that it would give her. But there was no chance that they would ever be able to move to a larger, more comfortable flat.

Standing in her slip in front of the wardrobe mirror Nellie scraped her hair back behind her ears. With her face freshly scrubbed and free of make-up, she looked incredibly young and childlike. For the space of a few moments she stared critically at herself. Her figure was trim, her breasts neither large nor small. Her bottom stuck out rather pertly; enough to be noticed but not too much to make it look either peculiar or plump. Her legs were good and there was a nice, attractive curve to her belly.

But it was her face that was by far and away her best feature, the corn-yellow hair that was so unusual in Glasgow where the norm was brunette with the occasional redhead thrown in as a colourful relief. Then there were her eyes, which were a deep sea-green with a golden fleck in them.

Frank had been right when he'd said she was the prettiest lassie in the dance-hall that night. She had been, as she was well aware. In fact, she rarely came across anyone who could top her when it came to beauty.

Humming she got to work on her make-up. When that was finished, and she started dressing, she began to sing in a golden voice that never failed to capture the ears and hearts of anyone who listened to it.

Through in the kitchen, Davey Thompson closed his eyes in appreciation. An angel come to earth, he thought to himself. In a life that had been filled with poverty and hard graft, that description of his daughter's voice – which he'd first thought of years before – was the only poetic expression he would have in his entire life.

Nellie and Babs arrived at the Roxy at the same time as they had the previous Friday night. Trying to appear nonchalant, Nellie glanced around her, expecting Frank to materialize out of the throng and come rushing to her side. Ten minutes later she was still looking, more or less certain he wasn't in the hall yet.

'Are you for up?'

The lad doing the asking was rough and not at all to her fancy. 'Sorry, I'm waiting for someone,' Nellie smiled.

Shrugging his shoulders the lad moved on.

Three-quarters of an hour later, Nellie was still alone and fuming. Loose as the arrangement had been, it was the first time in her life she'd ever been stood up and she didn't like it one little bit.

'No sign?' asked Babs sympathetically, joining her on the sidelines.

Nellie shook her head.

'Maybe he took ill or something?'

'Aye, maybe,' Nellie said, not believing a word of it.

And then, suddenly, he was there as though he had come out of thin air. He was hot, flushed and his tie was slightly askew.

'I'm helluva sorry,' he said, afraid to look her in the eyes and afraid not to.

He looked like a wee boy who'd done wrong, Nellie thought, and despite herself her anger melted instantly.

'Have you been here long?' he asked.

'No,' Nellie lied.

Babs had opened her mouth to answer but hearing Nellie's reply she quickly shut it again.

'I got caught up,' Frank said.

'Oh?'

'I went into the pub for a pint, you see, and the next thing I knew I was involved with some mates. Well you know what it's like? You daren't leave before you've stood your round and, try as I might, I just couldn't seem to be able to stand mine. I had to practically fight those blokes to get away in the end.' Then, both contrite and pleading, he added, 'I came as soon as I could. Honest!'

Nellie knew only too well what Glasgow pubs were like. It was unthinkable to leave without standing your round. It was certainly an excuse she could understand and accept.

'You're looking great,' Frank said, his eyes shining as he stared at her.

'And you look like you've come through a hedge backwards,' she replied, gesturing to his tie.

Muttering more apologies he straightened the offending article.

'Well, are you two going to stand there all night or are you going to show me how it's done?' said Babs gesturing with a smile toward the dance floor.

'Do you want to cool off first?' Nellie asked.

'No,' Frank replied, and taking her hand in his led her on to the floor.

They moved easily together, two people naturally tuned to each other's rhythm. The first dance was completed in silence, each content merely to be in the other's company. During this time Frank glanced occasionally at Nellie's face, as though reassuring himself that she was actually there in his arms.

'Do you live round about?' he asked halfway through the second dance. The spell had been broken and they began to talk freely with one another.

'Neptune Street,' Nellie replied. 'And you?'

'I come from Drumoyne.'

'And what do you work at?'

'I'm an apprentice at the Langbank Yard.'

Nellie exclaimed, 'That's where my da works! He's a welder there. His name's Davey Thompson.'

Frank thought for a moment before shaking his head. 'It's an awful big place you understand,' he said. 'I'm afraid I don't know him.'

'Apprentice what?' she asked.

'Boilermaker.'

'And how long have you got to go before you're a journeyman?'

'Eighteen months,' he said. 'Then I'll be in the money.'

She grinned in sympathy. All apprentices were traditionally very poorly paid; one step above slave labour she'd once heard her father describe it as.

'And what about you, Nellie?'

She told him then about the sweetie factory, what she did there, and the lassies she worked beside.

'This Big Jessie sounds quite a character,' he said when she'd finished.

'She's that all right. And the bane of my life to boot. A proper madam and no mistake.'

Frank looked at Nellie in wonder, still not able to believe his luck that he'd managed to pull this gorgeous creature and that she seemed to like him as much as he liked her.

As they danced he became almost intoxicated by the smell and touch of her. He wanted to wrap her up and take her home with him and never ever let her out of his sight again.

Nellie, for her part, was thinking how funny Frank could be. He made her laugh and she liked that. She'd never before met a boy with whom she felt so empathetic. That realization made her insides tingle. It also scared her a little although she couldn't think why.

Later Frank asked if he could walk her home and Nellie agreed. He insisted they take Babs home first as that was only fair, and so, at the appropriate time, the three of them left the Roxy. Frank walked in the middle with Nellie on his arm and Babs a little apart on his other side. When they reached Babs's close they made their good-byes and Babs ran giggling up the gas-lit stairs.

Nellie's heart was beating quickly now that she and Frank were alone, and they fell silent again as they walked to her close where they stopped in the entranceway.

'Can I see you tomorrow night?' Frank asked in a rush.

Nellie stared at her feet as though she were thinking, but answered quickly, 'Yes.'

'Anywhere particular you fancy going?'

'There's a picture on I wouldn't mind seeing.'

'Then that's what we'll do.'

They fell silent again and in that silence she knew he desperately wanted to kiss her – and that she wanted to kiss him.

'Come down here a bit,' she said in a voice suddenly husky. Taking his arm she led him along the length of the close and round into the back stair where it was dark.

He took her in his arms and held her tightly as their mouths met in a kiss.

When the kiss was over Frank shuddered as though something had gone out of him.

'I like you,' he said.

'And I like you.'

'I mean I *really* like you.'

'And I *really* like you.'

They kissed again. This time he put his tongue into her mouth which she greedily accepted.

Later, after the final good-bye and the final kiss, she made her way upstairs. Arriving at her door she paused for a minute to allow herself to calm down a bit. Standing there in the flickering gaslight she thought about the fact that he hadn't once tried to touch her in any of her private places. She liked that. And how different from many of the boys who'd walked her home and who'd no sooner got her into the back close than they'd started pawing and mauling her.

Smiling to herself she opened the door and slipped inside.

She found her father, mother and a stranger sitting around the kitchen table. Her brother Roddy was fast asleep and snoring in the cavity bed.

Da was wearing his best suit with his tie undone. She remembered then that he'd been to a Masonic 'do' that night. He was a dedicated Mason.

'Come away in, lass,' called Davey, his words slurred by drink. 'I'd like you to meet a pal of mine. Jim Biles, this is my daughter, Nellie.'

Jim Biles rose. He was tall and fair with a good broad pair of shoulders on him, twinkling blue eyes and an easy smile and manner.

'Pleased to meet you, Nellie,' he said, eyeing her coolly.

Davey waved at the bottle of whisky and bottles of beer standing on the table. 'Jim had a wee win on the dogs today and pal that he is, he decided to share some of it with me.'

'It was a good win,' said Biles. 'And not the first I've had this week either.'

Betty pulled out a chair beside her and Nellie sat down.

'Do you gamble a great deal?' she asked politely.

'A fair amount.'

'And do you win a lot?'

'More often than not. I'm lucky.'

'Lucky my foot!' exclaimed Davey. 'It's skill the way he does it. Isn't it, Jim lad?'

Jim smiled modestly. 'Well let's just say I don't rely entirely on luck.'

'A glass of beer, hen?' Davey asked.

'I don't think –' Nellie started to reply but Jim Biles interjected.

'Och, you *must*, Nellie. I'm superstitious, you see, and if you don't have some of my winnings' drink I'll worry in case it breaks my winning streak.'

'A *wee* glass then,' Nellie said.

'Jim's a butcher,' Davey said as he poured out the beer and then retopped everyone else's glass. The whiskies he poured after that were very large ones.

'A butcher?'

'Aye, down the Gallowgate. I work for a man called Sanderson. So any time you're short of a few pounds of sausages, you know where to come.'

Davey laughed loudly at that.

Nellie stared at Jim's hands which she'd noticed for the first time. Unlike the rest of him, which was almost elegant, these were large, extremely thick-fingered and very red as though he had them in hot water all day. There was something about those hands she didn't like at all.

'You mentioned you had a lassie but not that she was so good-looking,' Biles said smoothly.

'And you should hear her sing. The voice of an angel,' Davey said.

'Is that so?'

'The voice of an angel,' Davey repeated.

A bit too smooth, Nellie thought. The compliment was no more than what Frank had said to her earlier but in his case it had come out as though he really meant it. Whereas with Biles it was as though it were something he'd said a thousand times or more.

'I love a good song,' said Jim. 'What about singing for us?'

Nellie glanced across at the sleeping Roddy. 'It's awful late and –'

'Don't you worry about any of that,' Davey cut in. 'I'd love a song, too, so what about it? For your old da's sake if nothing else?'

Put like that Nellie didn't see how she could refuse. 'If you're sure it's all right?'

Betty nodded which was the final seal of approval.

Nellie took a sip of her beer and then, rising, stepped back a few paces. It didn't bother or embarrass her to sing like this as her father often requested her to do so. If there had been any embarrassment at performing, it had long since died.

'Give us "The Skye Boat Song",' said Davey. Aside to Jim he added, 'Just wait till you hear this.'

'Speed bonny boat like a bird on the wing, over the sea to Skye,' Nellie sang.

Jim Biles didn't have much of an ear for music but he knew the voice he was listening to was a good one. And what a cracker it belonged to, he thought. A real jewel amongst the dross.

When Nellie had finished Davey led the clapping. 'What did I tell you, eh?' he said to Jim. 'Sheer magic!'

'I thought that was absolutely grand,' he said. 'A real treat.'

'How was the dancing?' Betty asked, as Nellie sat down.

'Fine.'

'And the lad you thought you might meet?'

Nellie noted that Jim Biles's eyes had suddenly become veiled as he watched her closely. It was as though her answer was important to him.

'I met the chap, his name's Frank, and we had a good time together,' Nellie said slowly.

'Seeing him again?'

'Tomorrow night.'

'Back to the dancing?'

'No. The pictures.'

'You like the pictures, do you?' Jim asked casually. Nellie nodded.

'So do I. Particularly Westerns. They're my favourite.'

'I prefer the love stories myself. But I suppose that's natural, being a woman.'

And what a one, Jim thought to himself.

'Have you been a Mason long?' Nellie asked. 'Or aren't you allowed to tell me?' She laughed softly. 'I swear I've never come across anyone or anything as secret as you lot!'

'I'm in the process of becoming fully fledged, so to speak,' replied Jim. 'Your father's very kindly been helping me with some of the things I have to learn.'

'And then you'll wear a wee pinny like the rest of them when you do the mumbo jumbo,' Nellie said, and despite herself a combination giggle and snigger burst from between her lips.

Davey frowned. 'That's enough,' he said warningly. He took the Masons very seriously.

'I was only –'

'I won't have the Masons mocked. Not by you or anyone. Is that clear?'

Nellie nodded and looked away, not wishing to continue meeting her father's threatening gaze.

'I think it's time I went,' said Jim Biles.

'Aye, it is getting on and you three have work in the morning,' Betty said.

'One last dram?' suggested Davey. 'It's your bottle after all.'

'Another time,' replied Jim. Turning his attention to the two women he said, 'It's been a great pleasure meeting you, Mrs Thompson –'

'Och, call me Betty.'

'All right. It's been a great pleasure meeting you, Betty. And you, Nellie.'

'Likewise,' Nellie replied.

Davey saw Jim Biles to the door, then took himself off to bed, leaving the women to themselves.

'A nice lad I thought,' Betty said, rinsing the glasses out at the sink.

'A bit of a smoothie.'

'Well mannered I'd say. I've always liked a man to be well mannered.'

Nellie thought of Frank as she started to undress. Now there was someone who was really well mannered, and without being smooth about it either. 'I know what you mean,' she said.

'Goodnight, lass,' Betty said at the kitchen door.

'Goodnight, Ma.'

Nellie wound the alarm clock before putting the lights out and crawling into bed aside Roddy who was still snoring. Smiling in the darkness she thought back over the evening and her time spent with Frank. '*Mr Right*,' she breathed aloud. And, using another of Babs's expressions, '*My Fate*!'

Was he that? It was far too early to tell. Goodness, she'd only had the one date with him so far. What could you tell from that? An awful lot she decided. An awful lot indeed.

Eventually, feeling warm, contented and at peace with the world, she fell asleep to dream of her knight in shining armour – who, when he wasn't killing dragons, made her laugh.

'There's three-quarters of an hour yet before the picture starts, so how about nipping in for a fly one?' Frank asked.

Nellie was undecided. Although, like most working-class Glasgow girls, she knew a great deal about pubs, the truth of the matter was she'd only actually been in one twice before.

Taking Frank's arm she whispered, 'I'm only seventeen. I'm under age.'

Seventeen? He'd been wondering what age she was. The childlike quality in her face had made him think that she might be younger.

'Och, just have a soft drink then and I'm sure they'll say nothing,' he replied.

'You sound like you're dying for a pint.'

'I could murder one.'

She laughed. 'All right, I'll chance it if you will.'

'Follow me,' he said, leading the way.

The pub was a huge, barnlike affair, smelling strongly of alcohol and cigarette smoke. Although still reasonably early, there were a number of drunks clustered round the bar. Nellie noticed that one of them was so bad he kept slipping to the floor, only to be hauled back on to his feet by the chap he was drinking with.

The pub was pretty busy and soon would become jam-packed, Friday and Saturday nights being the busiest of the week.

'Slainte!' said Frank when he'd rejoined her with the drinks, and, lifting his pint, he saw off nearly half of it.

'You *were* dry!' Nellie exclaimed.

'I told you I was. How's the orange juice?'

She sipped, and as she did so her eyes widened fractionally. 'You've put something in this.'

'You didn't think I was really going to give you a soft drink, did you? Help ma bob, what sort of Saturday night out would that be?'

'What is it then?'

'Gin. Haven't you had it before?'

She shook her head.

Leaning close to her he whispered, 'They call it mother's ruin.' And waggling his eyebrows up and down added, 'If you get my meaning.'

She laughed, really enjoying herself. 'My da gives me the odd whisky and beer at home. But that's all I've ever had.'

'I can see I'm going to have to educate you,' he teased. 'There's more to drinking life than just whisky and beer. For example, have you ever heard of vodka?'

'No.'

'Grand stuff from Russia. Clear like gin but tasteless.'

'If it's tasteless then why bother to drink it?' she asked.

'Only a lassie would ask that question,' he grinned. 'Why bother to drink it indeed!'

'Are you an awful boozer?'

'I like a drink, let's put it that way. Who in Glasgow doesn't? But I know when to stop if that's what you're getting at.'

'As long as you do,' she said primly, causing him to grin again.

They talked for a few minutes more and then Frank went back to the bar to get another round. While he was trying to attract one of the barmen's attention, a rowdy gang of football supporters invaded the pub, wearing the blue and white scarves of Rangers' fans.

'You on your own, hen?'

Nellie stared up at the supporter whom she hadn't notice approach.

'No, my fellow's at the bar,' she replied.

'Is that so? But you wouldn't mind another wee bit of company would you?'

Fear fluttered through Nellie. She didn't like this sort of situation at all. 'Please leave me alone,' she said firmly.

The man swayed on the spot, his eyes glassy and his breath reeking of alcohol. His teeth, when he grinned, were discoloured with decay.

'Now you don't really mean that, do you?' he leered.

'Yes she does,' said Frank, who'd come up quietly beside the man. He laid his pint and Nellie's fresh drink on the table in front of her without taking his eyes off the head above the blue and white scarf. 'On your bike,' he ordered now that his hands were free.

For a moment Nellie thought there was going to be a punch-up – but then the moment passed.

'Just a wee misunderstanding,' the supporter slurred.

'Sure, pal,' said Frank.

'No hard feelings?'

Frank shook his head.

'All right then,' said the other man, and, turning, lurched across to where his friends were standing.

When Frank sat down Nellie saw that his hands were trembling. 'Bloody animal,' he muttered.

Nellie didn't care that they were in public, after what had happened she wanted a cigarette. She lit two and passed one across to Frank.

'Never a dull moment,' Frank joked, grinning.

Nellie grinned back. 'He frightened the living daylights out of me.'

'Me too,' Frank confessed, sounding so relieved that they both laughed.

'He must have been on the booze all day from the state of him.' She shuddered. 'Those teeth! I could have nightmares about them.'

Frank stared across at the group of supporters who were swallowing whisky as though it was about to be banned come morning. They were all hard-

faced working men who had the air of trouble-
makers about them.

'When you get that down you we'll go,' he said.
'I'll just have a quick trip to the toilet before,' Frank
said apologetically. 'Sorry, but it's the beer, it's gone
straight through me.'

'Be as quick as you can, will you?'

'Not a second longer than I have to,' and rising he
hurried across to the door marked Gents.

Through the hustle and bustle Nellie saw that
the drunken footballers had gone and presumed
they'd moved on to another pub. She watched in
fascination as the drunk who'd kept slipping to the
floor earlier was dragged to the swing doors by one
of the barmen and ejected into the street beyond.
Nervously, she kept looking towards the door
through which Frank had disappeared, but when it
finally did open it was not Frank but the rowdy
football supporters who emerged. Nellie's heart
sank, and her whole body became cold with dread.
When the one who'd tried to pick her up leered
across at her she knew for certain what had
happened.

Noisily the supporters pushed their way through
the drinkers and out of the pub, the last one
through the doors shouting as though in defiance,
'Rangers are the boys!'

Numb inside, she rose and made her way to the

bar where she finally managed to attract the attention of one of the barmen.

'I'll have a look,' the barman said after she'd made her request.

She stood outside the door of the Gents, staring blankly, not even noticing the stink of stale urine that hung there like a pall. When the barman re-emerged he was supporting Frank under the arm.

Nellie caught her breath when she saw Frank. His face had been badly punched and one cheek was seeping blood from a gash down the side of his nose. His suit was filthy and stained and it was obvious they'd been kicking him.

'Come through the back and sit down for a wee while,' the barman said kindly.

Customers stopped to watch as the barman and Nellie helped Frank round behind the bar and into the room beyond. When Frank was sitting the barman said, 'I'll get you a towel and a dram.'

'Thank you,' said Nellie. After the barman had gone she sat beside Frank and took his hand.

'I walked right into the sods,' he said. 'I didn't have a chance. There were just too many of them.'

'I feel it's my fault.'

'Don't be silly, there was more to it than just you.'

'What do you mean?' she asked, puzzled.

'They were Rangers' supporters,' he said through lips that had already started to swell.

An uneasy feeling – as though she already knew the answer to her own question – suddenly overpowered her.

'So?'

'They recognized me for a Catholic,' Frank said softly, looking right at her.

Catholic. The word was a bombshell.

'Surely you realized?' His hand reached towards her.

How could she have been so dense as not to see it! Everything about him screamed Catholic. The curly black hair. The thick black eyebrows. Why he practically had the map of Ireland written all over his face.

'Nellie?'

But before she could reply the barman was back with a hot towel and a large glass of whisky. Frank's eyes never left hers as she wiped the blood from his face and then applied the sticking plaster the barman had also thoughtfully provided. When she made him as presentable as she could, he knocked back the whisky in one grateful swallow.

'Can you stand?' the barman asked.

Unsteadily, Frank came to his feet. His thighs were shaking from the kicking they'd taken and come morning, he knew, his body would be black and blue. 'I think I'll live. Just about,' he said, grimacing with the pain.

Once outside the pub he suggested they still go on

to the pictures, but Nellie replied that he wasn't to be so daft. The only thing for him to do was go home.

'I'll get a taxi and drop you off first,' he said.

Being Saturday night the town was chock-a-block and they had to wait nearly half an hour before being successful in flagging down a cab. During that time they barely spoke.

When they were settled in the back seat of the taxi and headed for Govan Frank said quietly, 'Well? What about us?'

'It's my fault for being so stupid. It was staring me right in the face and for some reason it just didn't dawn.'

Frank glanced out at the passing scenery. A grey landscape of stone and concrete. Damn this town for its bigotry he thought. The orange and the green, and never the twain shall meet.

'How do you feel?' she asked, changing the subject.

'A bit shaky. I'll be stiff as a board tomorrow but it could've been a lot worse. At least none of them was carrying a razor or any other kind of weapon.'

Nellie nodded. He had been lucky. Only the other week a boy in her street had got into a fight and ended up in hospital with a hatchet embedded in the back of his neck.

She tensed as his hand crept into hers. 'Will I see you again?' he asked.

'I don't know, Frank. Does it make that much difference?'

'You know it does. Now that I've found you, I don't want to lose you, Nellie.'

And the truth was she didn't want to lose him either. But a Catholic of all things! She dreaded to think what her da would say should he ever find out, he being the staunch Protestant and Mason that he was.

The taxi drew up at the kerb and they were outside her house in Neptune Street. Withdrawing her hand from his she opened the door and stepped out on to the pavement.

'Think about it if you have to. But next Friday night I'll be waiting for you outside the Roxy at eight o'clock. I'll wait all night if necessary,' he said.

His eyes were vulnerable and appealing. She felt as though she could fall in them and drown.

'Drumoyne,' he said to the taxi driver, and closed the door. She watched for a second as the cab moved off and then turned and hurried into her close. As she climbed the stairs she felt more lost than she'd ever done in her life before.

The house was asleep. Beside her in the cavity bed Roddy was snoring like a good one. His leg was thrown over hers which he did often and which usually annoyed her. Tonight she found it strangely comforting.

A Catholic! Why hadn't she noticed! She should have seen it the first time he'd asked her up to dance.

What a mess she'd landed herself in, she thought. For she'd meant it when she'd said she really liked him. In one short week he'd come to mean an awful lot to her.

But a Catholic! In any other Scottish city it might not have been quite so bad but in Glasgow the gulf between the two religions was both wide and bitter.

From birth the hatred was instilled into you. You might have to work with a Catholic but you never went to school with one – and as for intermarriage, that was the most heinous crime you could commit.

Let him go, she told herself. See him again and it could only lead to tears and trouble and God knows what. To continue their relationship was a sure path to disaster. And yet . . . and yet . . .

The week was interminable, each day seeming longer than the last.

Hour after hour she toiled at the machine she was in charge of which turned out sherbet boilings. But it wasn't boilings she saw when the machine spewed them forth. It was Frank's battered and torn features staring appealingly back at her.

During the tea breaks she was quiet and morose,

which at last prompted Big Jessie to ask what the hell was wrong with her. She replied that she wasn't feeling all that clever, which satisfied Jessie's curiosity and put a stop to any further probing questions.

Earlier in the week she'd taken Babs into her confidence. Babs had been surprised she hadn't realized right away that Frank was a left-footer. 'Obvious as a bloody doorpost,' Babs had said. Then added, in a romantic tone of voice, 'I suppose it was the true love that blinded you. They say it often does.'

She'd scoffed at that. But there was more in what Babs said than she cared to admit.

Babs was sworn to secrecy, of course. This was something she didn't want getting around. Not until she finally decided what was what anyway.

For, even as the week wore on, Nellie still hadn't made up her mind about Friday night. One moment she'd decided not to go, the next she was wondering what to wear.

At home, Betty noticed the change in her and asked what was wrong. To which Nellie replied she was just in a bit of a mood that's all and to ignore her as it was nothing important.

Her sleep was also affected. Night after night she lay staring at the ceiling thinking things through, trying to come to the right decision.

Viewed logically there was only one right decision, as well she knew. And yet . . . and yet . . .

She wasn't going to go. Her mind was made up. Slowly she buttered a slice of bread and listened to her father rattle on about some problem they'd been having down at the Yard.

Betty was also listening to Davey, and although she didn't reply, she nodded her head from time to time to show him she was paying attention.

Roddy was eating his second French cake, a box of which Davey often brought home on a Friday night as a special treat for Betty who had a sweet tooth.

Glancing up at the kitchen window Nellie saw that it had started to smir. Even as she watched, the smir became rain proper which within minutes was bucketing down.

They cleared the tea things away and she helped Betty wash and dry while Davey and Roddy ensconced themselves by the fire. Davey puffed contentedly at his pipe while Roddy buried himself in a new comic he'd bought that day with his pocket money.

'Is it the jigging the night?' Betty asked.

Nellie shook her head. 'I thought I'd stay in for a change.'

'Well, in that case, you can help me patch some of

the sheets that need mending,' Betty said. Then, loudly over her shoulder so Davey would hear, added, 'It would be a grand thing to have a sewing machine like Mrs McAllister two closes down. Would fair save on time and effort.'

'McAllister's a gaffer and earns more than me,' Davey retorted. 'That's why they can afford such luxuries while we can't.'

'You might not think it such a luxury if you had to do the sewing yourself,' Betty said tartly.

'No matter how much you give them they're never bloody satisfied,' Davey mumbled into his pipe.

While this exchange was going on Nellie stared out of the window watching a flash of lightning rend the sky. A few seconds later the thunder came.

'Looks like it's going to be quite a night,' said Betty peering over Nellie's shoulder. 'Just as well you're staying in.'

More lightning ripped its way across the heavens. 'Just as well,' Nellie echoed softly.

She thought the storm couldn't get worse but it did. As she sewed her eyes kept coming back again and again to the window.

After a while Davey fell asleep and Roddy took himself off into a corner of the room to play with some lead soldiers and a papier mâché fort that had been his present the previous Christmas.

Seven o'clock came and went, as did the half hour. Slowly the hands on the clock crept towards eight.

When the clock struck eight it was as though an electric current had been shot through her. In her mind's eye she could see Frank standing outside the Roxy. He'd promised to wait all night if necessary, even an hour in this appalling weather and he'd be a candidate for pneumonia.

Suddenly, as though a tap had been opened, her resolve drained from her. She had to go to him. She just couldn't leave him standing about on a night like this.

'I'm going out after all, Ma,' she said, laying her mending down and rising.

Betty looked up in surprise. 'But it's coming down cats and dogs!' she exclaimed.

Nellie decided she didn't have time to make up or change. She would just have to go the way she was. 'I'll be in by eleven,' she assured her, and without further ado hurried through to the hallway where she shrugged herself into her raincoat.

When the outside door had banged shut Betty sat open-mouthed in amazement. Now what on earth was all that about? she wondered. Young lassies, she thought, they were all the same. Daft as a brush. And hadn't she been the same way at Nellie's age? She smiled to herself at the memory.

Shrewdly she guessed it had something to do with this new boy Nellie had been seeing. Must be serious she thought. And mulled over that while she got on with her sewing.

Nellie ran all the way through the streets, awash with rain. The gutters she passed were miniature rivers in spate.

At first she didn't see him. Then she caught sight of his face reflected in the street gaslight. One of his eyes was black and his mouth and cheek were puffed out. That same damaged cheek was yellow and brown in patches. When she heard him coughing she was almost overcome with emotion.

'Nellie! You came after all!' he exclaimed, his expression one of absolute joy.

'You're soaked through.'

'A wee bit of rain water never hurt anyone,' he replied with a laugh.

She wanted to take him in her arms and hug him tightly.

For almost a full minute they stood staring at one another. And then, not giving a damn – the street was almost deserted anyway because of the weather – he drew her to him and kissed her on the mouth.

Normally she would have been scandalized. But as it was she didn't give a damn either.

'Shall we go inside?' he asked.

'I'm not dressed nor am I made-up.'

'What did you do? Change your mind at the last moment?'

Taking his hand in hers she said, 'I'm here now and that's all that matters.'

'Yes. That's all that matters,' he echoed softly. For a few moments they simply looked at one another. 'There's the fleapit down the road,' he suggested at last. 'I've already seen the picture that's on but who cares about that?'

She laughed. 'So have I but, as you say, who cares?'

Arm in arm and laughing together they walked into the night.

'Nellie?'

She'd just come out of the wee newsagent's on the corner having run down for some pipe tobacco for her da. At first she couldn't place the man smiling at her, but then the penny dropped.

'My da's masonic pal,' she said.

'Right first time,' he replied, and fell into step beside her as she began walking back to the house. 'How are you doing?' he asked.

'All right I suppose. Getting by like everybody else.'

She really was a cracker, he thought. As good-looking a piece as he'd seen in a long time. He could imagine her naked, the shape and colour of her, and the thought excited him. Women, what marvellous creatures they were. With some men it was drink, with others tobacco. But with him it was female flesh. Soft, yielding female flesh. He could never get enough of it.

'There's a good picture on in town this week,' he said. 'I was wondering if you'd like to come and see it with me?'

She could tell by the tone in his voice that this was no spur of the moment notion on his part. He'd been thinking about asking her out. 'It's kind of you to ask, Jim, but I'm afraid I'm already winching.'

'The boy at the dance?'

'That's right.'

'I see,' he replied and continued smiling. The smile hadn't wavered since he'd called out her name.

'I'm awful sorry,' she said.

'My loss.'

There was a hurt look in his eyes and suddenly she didn't think him such a smoothie after all. Maybe he's just shy and the smoothie thing is his way of getting over it, she thought.

At her front close they stopped. 'Are you coming up to see da?' she asked.

'I was on my way to your house but it wasn't Davey I wanted to see,' he said. Behind the smile his eyes probed into her, making her feel guilty and uneasy –

as though she was being unreasonable in some way. She shuffled her feet, not quite sure what to say next or how to terminate the conversation.

He was drinking her in. Itching to lay hands on her. Her long yellow hair fascinated him, and he wondered if it was the same colour in other places. Just thinking about it excited him even more. God, he could've done it to her right there against the front close wall.

'I'll have to go. Da's waiting for his baccy,' she said. She was about to turn away when he reached out and caught her by the arm. 'Sure you won't change your mind?' he asked, his voice thicker with the lust raging through him.

'I don't two-time, Jim,' she answered softly.

He nodded. 'If sometime in the future you broke up with this lad and I was to ask you out, then would you go?'

'I might do.'

She was young he thought. At her age boyfriends must come and go with great rapidity. With a bit of luck his wait wouldn't be a long one.

'We'll leave it at that then,' he said, releasing her.

Nellie shivered, and didn't know why she'd done so. 'Someone walking over my grave,' she said.

He waited till the yellow hair had vanished round the gloomy turning on the first-floor landing before turning and walking swiftly away.

There was a bird over in Luath Street whose husband was at sea with the Royal Navy. He'd pick up a half bottle and go chapping her door as he'd done a number of times in the past. His need for a woman was great at the moment and she would happily oblige.

Starting to whistle he increased his pace.

2

Months passed and Nellie and Frank continued seeing each other as often as they could, which meant every Friday and Saturday night. And, as time went by, so did their friendship deepen and strengthen. When September arrived they were hopelessly in love with one another.

It was the Friday afternoon tea break before the long Bank Holiday weekend when Big Jessie said, 'So how are you getting on with this new click of yours, Nellie? You keep helluva quiet about him.'

'It must be love right enough,' added Daisy, causing all the girls present, with the exception of Nellie and Babs, to laugh.

'I'm getting on with him fine enough,' replied Nellie, glancing sideways at Babs. All the girls present were staunch Protestants; to say they would be

55

upset had they known she was going out with a Catholic would be putting it mildly.

Big Jessie had a suspicion there was something fishy about Nellie's boyfriend, or why else was Nellie so close-mouthed about him? That just wasn't like Nellie at all. Especially as she herself hadn't had a boyfriend for some time now and Nellie hadn't even bothered to crow once. No rubbing of salt into the wound. No long accounts of how clever or good-looking or whatever that this Frank was; his name being about the only thing they'd found out about him. No, something was queer all right.

'What are you doing at the weekend then?' Big Jessie asked.

'We thought of going away for the day. Down the coast maybe or perhaps a trip to Loch Lomond. We haven't made up our minds yet,' Nellie replied.

'Just the day and not the weekend?' Jessie asked with an innocent air.

'The *day*,' Nellie replied firmly.

'I suppose you'll be giving him his rights now you've been together this long?' Jessie said.

Daisy, Agnes and a new girl, called Lena, who'd joined their group stared expectantly at Nellie. Was she or wasn't she? That was what they were all dying to know.

'I wouldn't judge everyone by your own stand-ards,' replied Nellie tartly.

Babs grinned and buried her face in her teacup. Good for you, Nellie, she thought. That was telling the big one.

Jessie glowered, then stuck her nose in the air. 'I'll have you know I'm a virgin,' she sniffed.

'You're also a comedienne,' Nellie replied.

Anger flared across Big Jessie's face and for a moment it seemed she was going to fly at Nellie. The only thing that stopped her was the thought of getting the sack, which was automatic for fighting.

'I'm just not that sort of girl,' Nellie said lightly. 'When I get married I'll be in white. And what's more, the white won't be a lie.'

Big Jessie glared and chewed her lip. She would have given almost anything, except of course her precious job, to be able to go across and sock Nellie.

'I'd love to go down the coast myself,' said Daisy. 'Or should I say I'd love to go with a man.' She sighed. 'That must be nice.'

'Especially if the man's your *Fate*,' added Babs.

'Is your Frank that?' asked Lena.

Nellie shrugged her shoulders, 'Too soon to tell.' It was a lie. She knew Frank was the only man for her.

'It'll probably rain all day Monday,' said Jessie viciously.

'When you're with a man who cares?' said Daisy.

'Amen to that,' added Agnes.

'What did you say his last name was?' asked Lena.

Babs glanced up at her friend. That was a loaded question if ever there was one. A Catholic could be identified just as easily by his surname as by his features.

'I didn't,' smiled Nellie. 'If you think I'm going to tell you his full name so you can look him up and try to steal him away, then you're daft.'

'You think I'd have a chance then?' asked Lena.

'No. But why should I take the risk?' Next to Nellie Lena was the best looking girl in the group.

'Maybe he's got a brother?' suggested Lena.

'And maybe you should away and raffle your head,' retorted Nellie, which raised a laugh, Lena joining in against herself.

The hooter sounded.

'Back to bloody work,' said Big Jessie sourly. 'Still, only a few hours to go and that's it till Tuesday morning.'

Nellie returned to her boiling making machine, having successfully fended off the probing questions one more time. But that was something she wouldn't be able to go on doing for ever. The longer she went out with Frank, the more curious people became. At home as well as work.

The Bank Holiday dawned a scorcher. Nellie met Frank down at the red bus station where they queued for the Balmaha bus, Balmaha being on the shores of Loch Lomond.

Frank's mother had made up some sandwiches which he'd brought along with some bottles of beer. Their plan was to find a nice spot and have a picnic.

At Balmaha they started walking north, wanting to get well away from the other day-trippers. After a mile over undulating countryside they came to a beautiful little inlet where the waters of the loch were lapping gently.

Nelli stretched out on the grass and stared up at the duck-blue sky. There was a soft wind stirring which took the edge off the intense heat blazing down. September is nearly always a good month in Scotland, far better than July or August, which are often cold and wet.

'Like the South of France,' said Frank lying down beside Nellie.

'Oh, you know it, do you?' she teased.

'Och, aye. I'm always going there on my holidays. Makes a change from down the Clyde.'

Nellie laughed. 'Daftie!'

She closed her eyes and let the heat sink through her. What a change from the grey, griminess of Glasgow. It was amazing to think the city was so close, just over an hour's bus-drive away. The contrast between the city and Loch Lomondside was so startling that she might have been on another planet.

'Fancy a paddle?' asked Frank.

'No, but you away in.'

He grinned at her as he stripped off his shoes and socks, rolling up his trouser legs before striding down to the water's edge.

Nellie sat up to watch him. She felt so at peace, so together with him. There was no doubt at all in her mind that he was the right man for her. In a lifetime she'd never meet another more right for her, or her for him.

'It's blinking freezing,' he said pulling a face.

'It looks warm enough.'

'You come in and you'll find out differently,' he retorted. A few seconds later he yelped, saying, 'There's a bloody fish down here having a chew at my toes.'

Nellie laughed at the comical, outraged expression on his face. 'You'd better come out before you poison it,' she said.

'Very funny!'

'Is it still there?'

'Aye, and it's got a wee pal with it now as well. I think you're right. It's time I came out before there's a whole shoal of them here having a go at me.' And having said that he beat a hasty retreat for the bank.

Nellie set out the sandwiches while he opened the beer. 'This was kind of your ma,' she said.

'She's not a bad old stick.'

'Does she know I'm a Protestant?'

He glanced sideways at her. 'Ma assumes you're one of the green, just like us. For the moment I thought it best not to shatter her illusions.'

'And what'll she say when she finds out?'

'She'll have a knipshit, as will my da. They'll probably disown me. Ordered out of the house never to return and all that bunk.'

Nellie shook her head. So much energy and emotion wasted on what was such a little thing after all. Only the green and the orange didn't see the differences between them as being little. And as time went by, rather than trying to bring their two sides closer together, the factions built on the existing hatred and bigotry so that the gulf separating them became wider and wider.

After the sandwiches and beer they lit cigarettes and lay side by side smoking. Nellie was so happy she felt she could have stayed there till the end of time. Or till hell froze over as her da would have put it.

He came into her arms and they kissed. A languorous, indulged-in kiss, very different from the frantic, passionate ones of the back close. The kiss went on and on and it seemed to Nellie it would never stop. Nor did she want it to.

His hand crept up to her breast, cupping and squeezing it. She made no resistance when the same hand undid the top buttons of her dress and slipped inside. He didn't undo her bra, but rather pulled it out and over so that her breasts fell free. Having exposed them he buried his face in their softness.

Nellie stroked the back of his head while he kissed and nibbled her nipples. They'd gone this far before in the back close but it was so much nicer here in the open air with the sun beating down.

'Oh, Frank,' she murmured.

He was like a little boy, she thought. But then weren't all men when like this? They certainly were in her experience. A little boy sucking greedily at her breast. She liked the idea.

His breath was coming in short, laboured gasps. He brought his hand up the bottom of her dress to tug at the cotton knickers she wore. He jerked when his hand came into contact with downy pubic hair. Then it was her turn to jerk as his finger went inside her.

Nellie groaned and writhed. It was such a marvellous, marvellous sensation. His finger was like a column of fire. Probing, touching, exploring what, for the moment, was the very centre of her universe.

She was suddenly aware that he was using his free hand to undo his trousers. 'No, Frank!' She grabbed hold of the hand to stop it.

'But, Nellie –'

'It's my fault for letting you go this far,' she broke in, pulling herself free.

'Please?' he pleaded, desperation in his voice.

'Do you think I don't want to?' she said, tugging her knickers into place.

'Then why not, for God's sake?'

She sat up readjusting her bra and buttoning her dress.

'Nellie?'

'Not until I'm married,' she said firmly. 'What if I was to get pregnant?'

'There are things you can use, you know.'

'I'm well aware of that. Just as I'm well aware they're never a hundred per cent certain. Anyway, being a Catholic you're not supposed to use those.'

'You sound like the priest now,' he said, and laughed.

'Have you got some with you?'

'Some what?' he asked, feigning innocence.

'What we've just been talking about.'

'I might have,' he replied coyly.

Her eyes narrowed fractionally. 'Were they bought especially for the occasion?'

'Could be. Then again they might be something I carry around in my wallet all the time.'

'Have you . . .' She was embarrassed to ask the question and it showed by the blush that crept across her face. 'Have you . . .?'

'Oh lots,' he said, guessing her question.

Mixed emotions sparked in her eyes. 'How many are lots?'

He put his hand to his mouth and pretended to think. 'Twenty, maybe twenty-five. You lose count after a while.'

'What!'

'Then again it could be more. I have that effect on women, you see. They just can't keep their hands off me.'

Nellie was scandalized and shocked. Twenty-five. She'd thought maybe one or two. But twenty-five!

Then she noticed the amused glint that escaped his otherwise fixed expression and knew he was having her on.

'You bugger!' she exclaimed and launched herself at him.

He laughed as they rolled on the ground, she pummelling his chest with clenched fists.

To stop her he encircled her with his arms and hugged her tight. With her breasts pressing into him he kissed her.

'You're rotten, you know that?' she said breaking away.

'Will I tell you how many there have really been, Nellie?' he asked softly.

She stared at him, waiting.

'None. Not one.'

'Maybe I shouldn't have let the cat out the bag,' he went on, suddenly unsure of himself. 'Women like to think their man has been around a wee bit. That he's got some experience.'

Her man, it was an expression she liked. Her man. Yes, that was exactly what he was.

'Well this is one woman who doesn't,' she replied. 'I like you just as you are. I wouldn't want to change anything at all about you.'

'Nor I you.'

He felt awkward, clumsy; wishing he could find the words to express what was in his mind and the emotions he felt for her.

'You sure you won't do it till you get married?' he asked, looking at the ground.

'No, Frank. And nothing you can say will make me change my mind. That's the way it's going to be with me.'

'You're scared of getting in the club?'

'That's got a lot to do with it. But it's more than that. Can't you understand?'

'Aye. Although I don't really want to.'

She grinned. He was now looking even more like a little boy.

The words came out in a rush. 'Well, I suppose that's what we'll just have to do then,' he said.

She wasn't quite sure if she'd understood him properly. 'What exactly do you mean?'

'We'll just have to get married. What do you think I meant?'

For a moment or two she forgot to breathe as the enormity of what he'd just said sunk in. 'Are you proposing?' she asked huskily.

'Well, I'm sure as hell not asking you to pass what's left of the bloody sandwiches!'

Although she was already hot from the sun, a different kind of heat enveloped her. She wanted to leap to her feet and sing and dance but she restrained herself.

'We can't. Not yet anyway,' she said quietly.

He blushed. 'Are you turning me down?'

Immediately she was in his arms, resting her head on his shoulder. 'Of course I'm not. I love you, Frank Connelly. And I have done since the night we first met.'

He wanted to say he loved her too but it just wasn't in him to utter the word. He would've felt a prize idiot had he done so. A man just didn't say that word. Not in the daylight, anyway.

'Is it the religious thing that's bothering you?' he asked.

'That, and other things. To marry you now I'd need my da's permission and there's certainly no way he's going to give me that when he finds out you're a left-footer. And then there's the fact you're still an apprentice. We'll have to wait till you're time served before we get married. We're going to have to move away from Glasgow, there's just no two ways about that. And besides these other problems we just couldn't live on what we earn now. Together we don't earn a full man's wage.'

What she said was true. Even skimping and scraping in the extreme, their combined wages wouldn't cover the cost of a house and the other necessities. He had no choice but to accept the facts.

'How long till you finish your apprenticeship?'

'Fifteen months,' he replied.

'By which time I'll be well eighteen and not have to ask anyone's permission to get wed.'

'Near the time I could start writing away, Newcastle maybe. And when I line myself up with a job then we could elope.'

Elope! It was so romantic.

But he went on, 'That way there'll be no problem from anyone here in Glasgow. No priest screaming in my ear, or da in yours. We'll leave them all to stew in their own bloody juice.'

It was a marvellous idea. An inspiration. She kissed him deeply and considered giving in. But no, she would do what she'd always said she would do – wait until her wedding night.

'Does that mean we're engaged?' she teased.

'I suppose it does. But we'll have to keep it secret, mind. You know as well as I do, if it gets out there'll be hell to pay.'

'Will you buy me a ring?'

'Do you think that's wise? In the circumstances, I mean.'

'I wouldn't feel properly engaged without a ring, Frank. And I don't have to wear it as such. I could just keep it for times like this when we're alone.'

He thought about the wee bit of money he had put by. It wasn't much, but it was enough to buy her a ring of some sort.

'It'll be an awful wee diamond. You'll probably need a microscope to see it,' he joked.

She snuggled close. 'The fact that it'll be from you will be the important thing. The size of the stone won't matter at all,' she whispered.

'We'll go into town and get it Saturday afternoon,' he replied. He brought his hands down to encircle her bottom. 'Now that we're engaged and almost married, how about it then?'

'Frank!'

He sighed. He was going to have to wait – but at the moment fifteen months seemed like two eternities. 'Is there any of that beer left?' he asked at last, resigned.

Nellie broke away. 'I'll get it for you,' she said.

After the beer he went back for another paddle. As he explained, he needed cooling down.

So did Nellie, but she didn't tell him that.

Arm in arm they strolled along Sauchiehall Street,

gazing in jewellers' windows until at last they came to one that Nellie decided she fancied.

Frank had already been to the bank to withdraw every penny he possessed. Although little enough he'd never had so much money on him before and the thought of it bulging out his wallet made him feel ten feet tall.

There were only two trays of rings within their budget, but even so Nellie spent over an hour poring over them, each ring being tried on and considered at least half a dozen times. Finally the choice was made, and as no adjustment had to be made to the band, Nellie was able to wear it away with her.

Outside the shop again a beaming Nellie said she had a spot at the back of her drawer at home where she would plank it. But in the meantime was it all right to wear it till they got on the tram?

'Och, aye, there'll be no harm in that,' smiled Frank.

Before slipping her arm into his, Nellie held the ring up to have yet another look at it. 'It's a right smasher,' she said.

'Just like you.' Laughing, they continued down the street.

If Nellie hadn't been so caught up in her ring she might have seen Big Jessie standing across the road, staring open-mouthed at her and Frank. There was nothing wrong with Big Jessie's eyesight, nor her powers of deduction. Nellie and her bloke had obviously been buying a ring, and the fact that it was the left hand Nellie was wearing it on could only mean it was an engagement one.

But the real turn-up for the book, as far as Jessie was concerned, was Frank himself. He just had to be a Fenian, everything about him screamed it.

Suddenly it all clicked into place. No wonder Nellie had been so reticent to talk about her man. He was a bloody Catholic. That was why they'd never got his surname, or any other facts out of her.

'A Fenian,' Jessie breathed aloud. That really was something. She stared after the departing couple till they'd been swallowed up in the Saturday throng. Then, turning, she hurried in the opposite direction. She was meeting up with Daisy and Agnes for coffee. Did she have something to tell them!

She couldn't wait to see their faces.

Monday morning Nellie teamed up with Babs at the close mouth, and, as they did every working morning, they trudged off to the Bastille together.

For a change Nellie had been down before Babs arrived. She was dying to show Babs the ring which Babs had known she and Frank were off to buy the previous Saturday.

With the ring duly admired, Nellie recounted

every detail about the jeweller's shop and the other rings she'd had to choose from, and why she'd preferred this particular one over the others. Babs hung on every syllable. In her mind she saw herself choosing a ring with the man who was *her Fate* – and whom she'd still to meet.

When they reached the factory Nellie put the ring back in its box, which she then stuffed into her coat pocket. Later she would transfer the box to her overalls, so it would be on her and safe for the working day.

It wasn't till the break that she realized something was up. Agnes, Daisy and Lena were studiously avoiding looking her straight in the eye. Big Jessie on the other hand had a curious exultant glint in hers.

She glanced at the other groups of lassies standing and sitting around. Two, who were usually quite chummy, turned their heads away when she started to smile at them. And Bella Murcheson, who was another out of the Big Jessie mould, positively glowered at her.

She brought her attention back to her own group, where Lena and Agnes were talking about the dancing they'd gone to on the Saturday night. It was an ordinary enough conversation of the sort they were always having, only this time there was something forced about it, as though they were somehow talking for talking's sake. Were they talking to one another so they wouldn't have to talk to her? Then there was that glint in Big Jessie's eye. What did that mean?

Suddenly she knew with absolute certainty what it meant. Big Jessie, as well as the others, had found out about Frank. She didn't know how, but guessed that they must have been seen together.

Well, what did she expect, after all? She and Frank had been going out long enough. It was a miracle they'd gone on this long without being spotted. Glasgow might seem a sizeable place but it wasn't really. There was no way you could get lost in it like she was told you could in London.

Mind you, they'd done their best not to be seen together. After their first few dates in Govan they'd met in town or an area where the odds against them running into someone they knew were greatly diminished.

Their lovemaking in the back close was surreptitiously conducted: she going in first to be followed shortly after by him, having trailed her from the tram.

The hooter sounded, rousing her from her reverie. On the way back to her machine she saw Bella Murcheson was still glowering hate at her, and remembered then that Bella's father was a fanatical Orangeman. She shivered. Bella's look of hate was only a foretaste of what she could expect to come.

*

Two days later, on the Wednesday night, the Thompson family was sitting round the table having tea. Normally a good eater, eight-year-old Roddy was playing with his food, pushing it with his fork round his plate.

'Will you stop that and get on with it,' Betty said with a frown.

Roddy muttered something unintelligible and stuck some egg into his mouth. He chewed it slowly as though it was something distasteful.

'Are you not feeling well, son?' she asked.

'I'm fine, Ma,' Roddy replied morosely.

'Well, there's something wrong. It's not like you to lose your appetite.'

'Have you had an upset at school?' asked Davey.

Roddy pulled a face.

'Well?' Betty demanded.

'One of my pals said if you're a pageboy you have to dress up in a velvet suit. Is that right, Ma?'

The question caught Betty by surprise. 'Pageboys don't *have* to wear velvet suits but it's often the done thing.'

'You'll not make me wear one then? Please, Nellie.'

Nellie's fork stopped halfway to her mouth. She was acutely aware of her mother's and father's gazes coming to rest on her. For years she'd been telling Roddy that when she got married he'd be a pageboy at her wedding.

'Please, Nellie?' Roddy pleaded. 'All my pals would laugh at me if I had to dress up like that.'

'I'm sure you'll be far too old for a velvet suit by the time Nellie gets married,' Davey said with a grin. Then to Nellie, 'Eh, lass?'

Nellie was about to reply when Roddy said, 'And you'll not make me go to the chapel either, will you, Nellie? My pals at school would make my life a misery if you did.'

Oh, Jesus! Nellie thought. He'd landed her right in it now.

Very slowly and carefully, Davey put down his knife and fork. 'What are you talking about?' he asked his son.

'Nellie marrying a Catholic.'

'Who told you that?'

'Tam Gray in my class. He heard his sister Fiona talking about it. She works at the sweetie factory same as Nellie.'

Fear and apprehension had tied a knot in Nellie's stomach. The look Davey turned on her caused her to shrink in on herself.

'Well, girl?' Davey demanded.

'Tell us it's not true,' coaxed Betty.

'I eh . . . I . . . Yes it is,' she whispered.

A long hiss of breath escaped from Davey. His daughter marry a Catholic! The very thought made his skin crawl. Catholics were little better than vermin.

Betty had gone quite pale, looking at Nellie as though seeing her for the first time.

'*Will* I have to go to the chapel, Nellie?' Roddy asked.

She wanted to reach across the table and slap his face. Don't take it out on him, she chided herself. He was too young to realize what it was he'd just done.

'The boy you've been going out with all these months?' asked Davey.

Nellie nodded.

'A Catholic?'

Nellie nodded again.

'What's his name?'

'Frank Connelly.'

'Frank Connelly,' Davey said, tasting the words as though they were something nasty that had found their way into his mouth. 'I suppose amongst his own kind they call him Francey?'

'I don't know.'

'He's asked you to marry him?'

'You didn't accept, did you?' Betty put in quickly.

'He bought me an engagement ring last Saturday,' Nellie said slowly.

Betty caught her breath and put her hand to her mouth.

'Behind our backs, eh?' Davey said. 'Like a couple of thieves in the night.'

'I knew you would be upset and that's why I didn't tell you,' Nellie defended.

'Upset! That's putting it mildly!'

'Are you going to turn?' Betty asked anxiously.

Nellie opened her mouth to reply but before she could do so Davey's clenched fist came crashing down on the table causing everything on it to jump, and a teacup and saucer to fall to the floor and shatter. 'There'll be no bloody turning in my family!' he roared.

'I hadn't planned to,' Nellie said.

'What *had* you planned to do?'

'We were going to wait till I was eighteen and he'd served his apprenticeship – he's at Langbank Yard same as you – and then we were going to elope to somewhere religion didn't matter so much.'

'Oh, were you now?' mocked Davey.

'I love him, Ma,' Nellie pleaded. 'He's the only man for me.'

Tears came into Betty's eyes. 'But he's a Catholic, lass. He's not one of us. He's a different kind altogether.'

'I don't care what he is. I love him and that's all that matters.'

'Love? What do you know about it at your age?' Davey said scornfully. Coming to his feet he started unbuckling his belt.

Originally brown, the belt was now black with age.

Nellie stared at it in fascination. It was years since her father had used it on her.

'Ma?' But when she looked at Betty her mother averted her gaze.

The expression on Davey's face was terrifying. At that moment he looked quite capable of murder.

'You're going to tell this Connelly that your so called engagement's off. Understand?'

'No,' Nellie breathed more than said.

Davey came slowly round the table. 'In the other room,' he said.

'No.'

She screamed when he grabbed hold of her hair and yanked her from her chair. She screamed all the way to the bedroom as he dragged her stumbling through. He closed the door behind them before throwing her from him. His nostrils were dilated and his eyes hooded as he wrapped a section of the belt around his fist. 'Now, you're going to break off this engagement,' he commanded.

Nellie stared at her father in terror. Her legs had started to shake so much she thought she was going to lose control of them.

'You haven't answered me, girl.'

She had never seen her father so angry; his anger so intense it seemed to be sparking off him like electricity.

'I won't,' she whispered.

She screamed as the belt curled viciously round her backside raising an ugly red weal under the material of her dress.

'I'll never give him up,' she said defiantly and screamed again as the belt struck her a second time.

Again and again the belt lashed her buttocks and legs till she thought she must surely faint from the pain. But she didn't. Even that release was denied her. She lay on the floor with her father towering above her, her bottom and legs covered with blood.

Davey paused. 'Will you break it off?' he demanded.

Her face was drenched with sweat and tears, her long yellow hair matted and sticking to her cheeks and neck. From the waist downward she felt as though she'd been skinned alive. She made a fist and screwed it into her mouth, her body convulsed with uncontrollable sobs.

Davey reached down and grabbed her arm, 'Well?'

'No,' the word so faint as to be almost inaudible.

Even in his rage he knew he couldn't leather her any more. 'I'll have my way over this. One way or the other, Nellie, you'll break with that Catholic.'

He strode to the door where he paused to stare back at her. 'You'll stay in here till you come to your senses. Your mother and I will sleep in the cavity bed with Roddy until you do.'

He went out closing the door hard behind him. Nellie listened to the key turning in the lock. She wouldn't give in, she wouldn't, she swore to herself. There was nothing he could do to her that would make her give up Frank.

Groaning in pain, she crawled across the linoleum floor to the bed. It took her long, agonizing minutes to heave herself up on to it, and she collapsed, face down, burying her tears in the cool softness of the feather quilt.

She'd had some beltings in her life but nothing to compare with this. Da had behaved like a man possessed. But then he was possessed, she told herself. Possessed with hatred and bigotry.

'Oh, Frank,' she cried into the quilt, her eyes filling again with hot, salty tears. 'Oh, Frank, what can we do?'

Sunlight was flooding the room when she came to, her position on the bed exactly as it had been when she'd fallen asleep.

She whimpered when she tried to move. It was well after going to work time, though it would have been impossible for her to go anyway.

Gritting her teeth, she forced herself up on to her arms and legs. Then, with a monumental effort, she got off the bed and on to her feet. She removed her dress, having to pull it away in places where it was stuck to her with her own dried blood. Then she took off her petticoat, stockings and pants. Clad only in her bra, she forced herself over to the wardrobe to look at herself in the mirror.

Her bottom was puffed up and swollen, and beneath the blood were large areas of flesh already turning black and blue.

The key twisted in the lock and the door opened. Betty came in carrying a jug of water and a plate on which were several slices of unbuttered bread. 'God Almighty!' she exclaimed. Setting the jug and plate down she hurried over to Nellie's side.

'Pretty, isn't it?' Nellie said bitterly.

'You've no one to blame but yourself,' Betty snapped back, adding, with a shake of her head, 'but he shouldn't have gone that far.'

'I hate him! I hate him! I hate him!' Nellie suddenly burst out, her cheeks flaming with anger. Then with a strangled sob she threw herself into Betty's arms where she rested her head on her mother's bosom.

Betty stroked her hair and made soothing noises while Nellie wept. When the crying fit was finally over she said, 'I'll away through and get some hot water and antiseptic. I'll soon have you washed and cleaned.'

'Wouldn't it be easier if I came through to the kitchen with you?'

Betty's face hardened. 'Your da said you're to stay in here, and that's what you'll have to do. He also says you're on bread and water till you see sense.'

'Then I'll be on it for the rest of my life.'

'You really love him, eh?' said Betty, softening.

'He's the only one for me, Ma. And please don't say that because I'm only seventeen I don't know my own mind, for I do.'

She'd always had her father's stubborn streak, Betty thought. Nellie and Davey were more alike than they knew. As much as Nellie swore she wouldn't break off this engagement, Davey was equally determined that she would.

'Lie on the bed and I'll get the hot water,' Betty sighed, and left the room.

Nellie hobbled to the door which her mother had left unlocked. Silently, she went out into the hallway to where her coat was hanging. It took only a moment to slip the box containing her engagement ring from her coat pocket.

She had told Frank that she was going to hide the ring in a secret place of hers in the kitchen, but she'd changed her mind about that. Instead, she'd taken it with her to work so that she could have it with her during the day. She might not have been able to wear it, but she'd found great comfort and pleasure in being able to reach down and touch its box from time to time.

Back in the bedroom, she took the ring from its box and slipped it on to her finger. The time for secrecy was over. From now on she'd wear it for all the world to see.

Nellie was lying on the bed reading a book when she heard the front door slam, followed by the sound of her father's footsteps in the hall. She cringed involuntarily, wondering if he was going to come in and belt her again. Surely Betty wouldn't allow it?

Still, she winced when the key turned in the lock and her father entered the room. It was something of a relief to see his belt was round his waist and not in his hand.

His face was rock hard as he came to the bed to stand beside her. 'Have you anything to say to me?' he asked.

'No.'

'You won't change your mind?'

'Never.'

His lips thinned and his eyes flashed fire. 'Well I've got something to say to you,' he said. 'I looked up this Frank Connelly with the intention of having it out with him. But then I had a better idea, and one which will solve this nonsense once and for all.'

Having said that he seemed to relax a little. Crossing to the fireplace he placed his baccy tin on top of it and proceeded to fill his pipe. When his pipe had been puffed into life he went on. 'Shipbuilding yards are dangerous places as you well know. Despite safety precautions and regulations, accidents happen all the time. Bad accidents that maim and cripple people.' He paused before adding ominously, 'Kill them even.'

Nellie was rigid, her eyes never leaving her father's.

'You say you love this boy?'

She nodded.

'Then you wouldn't want anything to happen to him, would you?'

'You're not capable of that,' she challenged. Or so she'd thought until last night.

'Oh, but I am, lass. I'll do anything to stop a daughter of mine marrying a Fenian. And you'd better believe me.'

Despair welled in her and her resolve began to crumble.

'It would be a fall, probably. Or a heavy weight dropped on him. Something substantial like a girder.'

'I'd go to the police.'

He gave a terrible smile. 'That wouldn't do you any good. When it happens I'll be somewhere else and with plenty of company to vouch for me. No, I wouldn't be doing it personally, not when you could put the finger on me. I've been at Langbank an awful long time and have many pals there. Pals who'd do anything for me. And do it happily when they knew a Catholic was involved.'

This wasn't the father she knew. It was a monster she'd never seen before. She couldn't match this man making such dreadful threats with the kind, but strict, dad she'd known all her life.

It came to her that she'd finally stepped through the door into adulthood. No more was there to be the protection afforded children. She was now in the harsh world of reality where she had to stand on her own two feet without support.

'What do you say now?' he asked.

She had to capitulate. There was nothing else for it. The alternative was simply too horrible to contemplate. 'I'll give him his ring back when I see him on Friday.'

Davey nodded. 'You'll not only give him his ring back, but you'll tell him you never want to see him again. You'll say you made a mistake, that you thought you cared for him but you don't. You'll tell him he's never to contact you again.'

Like hell, she thought. She'd tell Frank the truth and then they'd just have not to see one another till his time was out when they could elope as planned. 'All right,' she lied.

But Davey wasn't stupid. 'Furthermore, when you

do tell him, I'll be within earshot,' he said. 'I want to make sure you get your story just right.' He held her chin so that her eyes met his. 'And I want you to be quite clear about this. If you do see him again, or contact him to try and arrange something between you, then he'll still be for the high jump. The accident will take place and that *will* be the end of it. Understand?'

She wanted to be sick. He'd thought of everything. But she'd find a way. Somehow or another she'd let Frank know the truth.

'You say you're seeing him Friday night?'

Nellie nodded.

'Then you can stay locked up in here till then. Where does he live?'

'Drumoyne.'

'Which street?'

'I don't know, and that's the truth. He was never able to invite me to his house for the same reason I was never able to invite him here.'

'You're sure you don't know?'

'Yes!'

He was satisfied she wasn't trying to put one over on him. 'That'll rule out letters then.'

A cloud of smoke wafted behind him as he walked to the door.

'Can I get something decent to eat now?' she asked.

'No.'

Nor did she until Friday dinner time.

Frank was waiting for her when she got off the tram. Smiling, he came straight to her and took her arm. 'Hello,' he said.

She'd been crying all morning, and her eyes were rimmed in red. She wanted to take him in her arms, to kiss him, to smother him with love. Instead she nodded towards a shop entranceway. 'We have to talk,' she said.

'What is it, Nellie?' he asked once they were in the relative privacy of the entranceway.

Through the glass window she could see her father out in the street, pretending to be studying the window's contents. It was a position from which he'd be able to overhear every word that was about to be said.

'I've changed my mind about the engagement. In fact, I've changed my mind about us. We're finished, Frank.' Taking the box containing her engagement ring from her handbag, she pressed it into his hand.

Frank was dumbfounded. 'What?'

She was close to tears but fought them back. 'It just wouldn't work,' she choked.

He looked at the box then back at her. 'You can't mean it, surely?'

Of course she didn't mean it, she screamed inside herself! In her mind's eye she saw a falling girder with Frank below it. She shuddered. 'I'm afraid I do.'

'But just last weekend you said –'

'I know what I said, but I was wrong.'

'You don't love me?'

A sideways flick of her eyes told her Davey was watching her intently. The hard face nodded.

'I thought I did, but I don't. I'm sorry. I don't want to see or hear from you ever again.'

His face had gone grey, his shoulders slumped – as though he were suddenly beginning to age.

I do love you! I do! she desperately wanted to shout. And I'll go on loving you till the end of time!

Frank pulled himself together. 'That's it then,' he said. His initial shock was now giving way to anger. Anger against Nellie, against himself, against the world in general.

'Good-bye,' she said, and hurriedly kissed him on the cheek.

Her high heels clattered on the ground as she rushed out of the entranceway.

When she was gone, Frank touched the mark of her kiss with the fingers of one hand. He'd been suckered, taken for a ride. The mark of the kiss was cold on his cheek. Slowly he rubbed the flesh warm again.

Back out on the street, he saw she was gone. 'And good riddance,' he said out loud.

It was later, when he was well in his cups and feeling sorry for himself, that the idea came to him. He knew as soon as he thought of it that it was what he was going to do.

Babs listened wide-eyed as Nellie told her what had happened, on the way to work the following Monday morning.

'So it's all off then?' she said when Nellie had finally come to the end of her tale.

'I'll find a way of letting Frank know I was forced into doing what I did. He'll understand once I've explained.'

'It's a right mess and no mistake,' Babs said. They were walking at half the pace they usually did as Nellie was still stiff and sore.

'You should have seen his face when I told him. It was terrible,' Nellie whispered, seeing again that face, that look.

'I can imagine.'

'And in a shop entranceway too. But my da insisted it was done somewhere he could overhear. When I left Frank I got halfway along Sauchiehall Street before my da caught up with me. He said I was running, but I wasn't aware of it. The ride home in the tram is a complete blank as well.'

They arrived at the factory and after clocking on went through to change into their overalls. Nellie found herself beside Big Jessie.

'And how was your weekend? Did you see your boyfriend?' Jessie asked with a smirk.

She didn't reply.

'And when are we going to see the engagement ring he bought you? Or are you ashamed to wear it seeing as how it came from a Mick?'

Nellie glanced at Babs, who shook her head. 'How did you know about that?'

Big Jessie's smirk became even wider. 'There I was, minding my own business, when who do I see coming out the jeweller's shop but you and him. The way you were goggling at your left hand it wasn't hard to put two and two together.'

So it was Jessie who'd seen her. Now she knew. And thanks to Jessie she'd lost Frank.

Fury blazed inside of Nellie. And the centre point of that fury was Big Jessie.

The lassies came streaming out the factory gates, all of them eager to get away home. Many of them were laughing and chatting gaily, now that the working day was done.

Nellie stood waiting with Babs by her side. She'd already confided to Babs what she intended to do.

'There she is,' said Babs out the side of her mouth, nodding with her head.

Raucously, Big Jessie's voice rose above those of the others she was with. She swaggered as she walked.

Nellie was icy cold inside. All day she'd been thinking about this and looking forward to it. It didn't matter at all that Jessie was taller and carried considerably more weight than she did. Her strength lay in the fact she didn't care what happened to her as long as she got a good few in on her enemy.

Quietly she stepped forward in front of Jessie. 'I want a word with you,' she said.

That infuriating smirk came back on Jessie's face. 'If it isn't the Fenian lover,' she said spitefully. 'And what can I do for you?'

'Your mouth is as big as your arse, which is saying something,' Nellie said clearly.

The chatter from the girls crowding round stilled instantly.

'What did you say?' Big Jessie demanded. Her smirk was gone.

'You're a born troublemaker of the worst kind. And what's more, you've got a head on you that's as thick as your ankles.'

Jessie coloured. 'You mind your tongue,' she warned.

'No, Jessie, it's you should've minded yours.' Having said that, she suddenly leapt forward.

Jessie screeched as Nellie's nails raked her face. The screech became an anguished howl as Nellie yanked at her hair.

Jessie got Nellie into a bear hug and started to squeeze. Finding her hand close to Jessie's breast Nellie sought out the nipple and pulled it viciously. It was a massacre. Jessie was completely unable to cope with this hissing, spitting ball of venom.

'I give in! I give in!' she screamed.

The two were on the ground, with Nellie sitting astride Jessie, banging her head on the pavement.

'She'll bloody murder her,' yelled a voice from the crowd of onlookers.

Babs knew it was up to her to stop this before it got completely out of hand. Certainly none of the others was going to try. None of them wanted to tackle the hellcat that Nellie had become.

'It's all over. You've beaten her,' Babs said taking hold of Nellie's arms.

At first Nellie didn't hear her friend's voice, so overcome was she with fury. It was as though a red curtain had descended in front of her eyes.

'Nellie! Nellie, stop it! Stop it! You've won.'

Big Jessie was crying, the tears streaming down her face.

Slowly, Nellie stood to stare down at Jessie. Her chest was heaving and her bottom was throbbing again from her unhealed cuts.

'Let's go home,' Babs said gently.

The crowd parted for them. With Babs's arm hooked in Nellie's, they continued on their way.

'That showed her,' said Nellie.

Babs thought of the battered, bleeding Jessie they'd left lying back there on the pavement. 'Aye, it certainly did that,' she agreed. 'Just promise me one thing though?'

'What's that?'

'If you ever get upset with me, let me know so I can get well out of town.'

They were still laughing when they reached Nellie's close.

A month passed and Nellie still hadn't been able to get in touch with Frank. If only she knew his address or a special friend she could contact. But she knew neither.

Her efforts were further hampered by the fact she was now indefinitely confined to the house after work and at weekends.

Babs had tried to help her by going to the Roxy several times in the hope that Frank would show up there, but so far she had failed to meet him.

Then, one night, the family had finished tea and Davey had settled into his chair with the evening paper, when he discovered his tobacco tin was empty. 'Nellie!' he called, reaching into his trouser pocket. 'Away down to the newsagent's and get me half an ounce.'

Nellie, who had been helping Betty with the dishes, wiped her hands on the tea towel before taking the money from him. 'Are you sure you trust me out for five minutes?' she asked bitterly, the abhorrence she felt for her father burning in her eyes.

'Less of your cheek, girl. And five minutes is all you've got. Any longer and I'll want to know why.'

'It's like being in jail,' she snapped.

She was emerging from the newsagent's when she saw a chap who'd taken her out several times in the past. His name was Colin Cunningham, and at one time he'd been rather keen on her.

'Colin!' she called suddenly. She'd just remembered that she'd pointed him out to Frank one night at the pictures, and Frank had said he knew him from Langbank.

'Hello, Nellie, how are you?' Colin greeted her.

'Listen, I've only got a moment. Will you do me a favour?'

'Aye, sure. What is it?'

'If I was to send you a letter with another letter inside would you pass the inside one on to Frank Connelly at the Yard? I haven't time to explain, but you'd have to promise to keep it secret. Would you do that for me?'

'I would if I could Nellie, but I can't.'

'Why not?'

'Was Frank a friend of yours?'

There was a sharp, constricting pain in her chest. 'What do you mean *was*?'

'He just didn't turn up for work one day and no one has seen him since. The rumour is he upped and left for Canada or New Zealand.'

The world reeled and Nellie staggered where she stood. It wasn't true! It couldn't be!

'Are you all right?' he asked, taking her arm to steady her.

'Are you sure about what you've just told me?' She could barely speak.

'I'm sure that he hasn't been to work in weeks and that his card's been removed from the time clock. As for him going abroad, well that's what's being said.'

'Canada or New Zealand,' she repeated, shaking her head. It was so unexpected.

'A queer business right enough. No one knows what caused him to go charging off like that.'

Colin looked at her expectantly but all she said was 'Thanks', in a voice that was little above a whisper.

So Davey had got his way after all. She'd had it all planned, too. Fifteen months of lying doggo and then on a prearranged day it would be goodbye to

Glasgow and a train south to marriage and a happy life together.

She'd never see him again her father had said. And he had been right. Frank Connelly would never come back to the city or the woman who'd betrayed him.

Damn you, Father! she raged. I'll never forgive you as long as I live.

Never.

3

Nellie sat staring into the fire while her mother ironed and Davey dozed in his chair.

Although allowed out at nights again, it had been months since Nellie had been anywhere, the last time being a trip to the pictures with Babs. Since Frank, she wasn't interested in enjoying herself or meeting anyone new.

'Cheer up, for Pete's sake!' said Betty. 'You look like you lost a pound and found a tanner.'

Nellie glanced up at her mother. 'I'm all right.'

'No you're not. Your face is tripping you.'

'I'm sorry if it bothers you. I'll try to be more cheerful, but I haven't exactly got a lot to be cheerful about, have I?'

'Och, lassie that's just not true. You're bonny, you're healthy and you've got your whole life stretching ahead of you. What more could you want?'

Nellie went back to staring into the fire. But it wasn't coal and dancing flames she saw; it was a knight in shining armour whose face was Frank Connelly's.

She never had found out exactly where it was he'd gone. She'd even heard later that it wasn't Canada or New Zealand at all but South Africa. No matter where, really. Wherever it was it was far away from her – and that was what mattered.

She glanced across at her father's sleeping form. She'd never have believed it possible to hate anyone so much.

'Nellie? Is that a knock at the door?'

With a sigh Nellie stood. It must be Roddy back from his pal's she thought, as the outside door was lightly chapped again.

But it wasn't Roddy.

'Hello. Remember me?' Jim Biles said with a smile.

'Of course I do. Come away in.'

Betty exclaimed with pleasure as Jim entered the kitchen. 'Davey! Davey!' she called out. 'There's someone here to see you!'

Davey woke with a snort, blinking open his eyes and elbowing himself up in the chair. When he saw it was Jim Biles who was calling his face broke into a warm smile.

'I hope I'm not intruding?'

'Och, no, no, it's good to see you,' Davey answered, waving Jim to the other fireside chair.

Jim produced a half bottle and placed it on the table. 'A wee something I bought on the way up,' he said.

Davey's eyes shone. He was a man who enjoyed his drink. 'Is it a special occasion then?'

Jim shook his head. 'I just thought a bevy would go down a treat.'

'You can say that again. Nellie, get some glasses.'

Still smiling, Jim watched Nellie as she moved to the sideboard. She was the reason for his visit. He'd asked after her a few days earlier and, in great confidence, Davey had told him the story of her and Frank Connelly.

So, she was now free again and as desirable as ever as far as he was concerned. He stared hungrily at her slim body and long yellow hair. And those green eyes – they were magic.

Nellie poured drinks for the two men.

'Grand stuff, right enough,' said Davey, sipping appreciatively.

Nellie sat at the table while Betty got on with the ironing. Jim and Davey chatted for a while about this and that, and then Jim turned his attention to her. 'And how are you?' he asked.

'Fine, thanks.'

'You're looking well.'

Davey saw the gleam in Jim's eyes. So that's how the land lies, he mused to himself. Well, he certainly had no objection. He was a good man, Jim Biles. One of the best. And a Protestant.

'Are you still going to the jigging?' Jim asked.

'Not of late. I haven't bothered going out much recently.'

Jim nodded, as if it were news to him.

'And how about yourself?'

He thought of his bird in Luath Street. Thank God for the Royal Navy! And then there was the widow in Penilee he saw from time to time. Now, she was nice. But neither she nor Luath Street were in the same league as Nellie.

'I'm not much for the jigging myself, but I get around,' he replied casually. Then, conversationally, to Betty, 'What are you planning to have for your Christmas dinner?' Christmas was only a fortnight away.

'I'm hoping for a nice chicken but they're awful expensive and difficult to come by besides.'

'Aye, there's a shortage of them right enough. But you leave it to me. I'll see you get one at a price that won't dint the housekeeping too much.'

Betty beamed. 'That's right kind of you, Jim. We fair appreciate it.'

'What else are friends for?' he laughed.

When the bottle was empty and it was almost time

to go Jim said, 'I've had an idea, Nellie. I've been asked to a butchers' Christmas do next week and I was wondering . . . Are you still winching?'

'No,' she said slowly, averting her eyes from his.

'Well why don't you come along as my partner? Should be a good night with lots of food and drink. What do you say?'

'I –'

'Sounds like a great idea to me,' Davey broke in. 'Why don't you go, lass? It would do you good.'

Jim's eyes flicked across at Davey. He'd found himself an ally.

Nellie was uncertain. Her initial reaction was to refuse. But she had to start going out again sometime. She could hardly stay at home for the rest of her life.

'Aye, all right then,' she sighed. 'I'd like that.'

'I'll look forward to it,' Jim smiled.

Together they made the arrangements.

Nellie was enjoying herself for the first time since Frank. She'd never seen so much food and drink! And the band was a right laugh that did crazy novelty numbers every so often.

'Do you fancy getting up again?' Jim asked. They'd already danced a number of times.

'Lovely,' she replied, really smiling at last.

He took her into his arms and they moved off

into a foxtrot. 'Are you enjoying yourself?'

'Isn't it obvious?'

He grinned. 'Just making sure.' He'd already decided how he was going to play the Frank Connelly business. He reckoned the time had come to bring it up.

'You broke with your lad then?'

She looked up at him. 'Has my da not said anything to you?'

He shook his head. 'Should he have done?'

'Frank was a Catholic,' she said simply.

'I see.' He paused for a few seconds. 'I can imagine how upset Davey must've been.'

The hate Nellie felt for her father welled up inside her. 'And what about you? How do you feel about Catholics?' she demanded.

Jim shrugged. 'I may be a Mason, but that doesn't mean I'm against them. There's nothing in the Masonic Order that specifies we hate Catholics. I suppose I take them as I find them. Some are all right, others I wouldn't give the time of day. In other words they're just like any other people as far as I'm concerned.'

And what would you do if you had a daughter who wanted to marry one?'

Jim pretended to furrow his brow in thought. 'I think, at least I'd like to think, that I'd tend to let them get on with it.'

Nellie's face softened. It was the answer she'd wanted to hear. Which, of course, was why Jim had said it.

'We were going to go to Newcastle or somewhere like that when he'd finished his apprenticeship,' she said. 'Anywhere away from this town and its prejudices.'

He could see how deeply hurt she still was. He was going to have to continue playing this very coolly indeed if he was going to get anywhere. Well, he could be patient when the prize was Nellie Thompson. She was worth waiting for.

As he walked her home, he didn't attempt to take her arm as he'd normally have done. When they stopped at her close he could sense her tensing, worried that he was going to try and take her into the back.

'I really have enjoyed myself. Thank you, Jim,' she said formally.

'I know how you feel about Frank, you've made that quite plain.' Gently, he took her hand. 'But I'd still like to take you out again. What do you say?'

'Could we just be friends?'

'We'll be whatever you want us to be, Nellie. I'm just happy to be in your company.'

She stared at him. He was quite nice really. A bit too smooth, perhaps, but that might just be his manner.

'There's a new picture on at Green's in the town that I wouldn't mind seeing,' she answered hesitantly.

'Right, then. I'll chap your door half past six Friday night.'

And without waiting for a reply he turned and strode off quickly down the street.

It was a Sunday afternoon and the thirteenth time he'd taken her out. He knew it was thirteen because he'd counted them. Being a Sunday everything was shut, even the swing parks remained locked. They were sitting in an Italian café sipping coffee, Italian cafés being the only establishments to break the Protestant Sabbath.

He'd kissed her by now and had a few cuddles, but that had only whetted his appetite. What he really wanted was her in bed with him.

Nellie stared into her coffee, her mind a million miles away.

'Nellie?'

She looked up and smiled. 'Sorry, I was dreaming.'

'About Frank?'

She looked back into her cup.

'He's left Glasgow, you know. Gone abroad according to your da.'

'I didn't know,' she lied. This was the first time

she'd officially been told, his name never having been mentioned again in the house.

'It's time to try and forget him, Nellie. This way you'll only keep on hurting yourself, and what's the good in that? He's gone and you'll never see him again. Accept the fact.'

'Have you ever been in love, Jim?'

'Yes.'

'Was she pretty?'

'Very.'

'What happened?'

'Oh, I haven't given up hope yet. The trouble is, you see, she's still in love with someone else.'

He was talking about her. 'Let's just not go too fast,' she said.

'At whatever speed you like, Nellie. That'll be all right with me.'

She reached out and held his hand. 'Thank you.'

It was the first time she'd ever voluntarily touched him in a tender way. Progress, he thought. Small, maybe, but progress all the same.

They were on their way to the pictures one Saturday night when their path was suddenly blocked by a man who must have been waiting for them. He had a razor scar running from his ear to the corner of his mouth.

'Hello, Jim,' he said almost politely.

Jim came up short: for a brief moment fear showed on his face. 'Hello.'

Scarface looked from Jim to Nellie and then back again. 'Wee Mo would like to see you,' he said slowly.

'Right,' Jim tried to sound cheerful. 'Tell him I'll be round next week.'

'Now,' the stranger said shortly, steel creeping into his voice.

Jim knew any further protestations were useless. 'It won't take long,' he said to Nellie. 'Do you mind?'

She didn't like the man's look – he sent shivers racing up and down her spine. How had Jim come to be acquainted with a man like this?

Without a further word, Scarface led the way to a car parked nearby. A jerk of his thumb told them they were to get in the back. They then drove up west to a posh part of the city.

'Wee' Mo was well over six feet tall and must have weighed all of twenty stone. 'Glad you could come,' he said politely as they entered the room where he was holding court. There were two more hardmen present, neither of whom was introduced.

'My girlfriend, Nellie Thompson,' Jim said when Mo raised an enquiring eyebrow.

'Pleased to meet you, Miss Thompson,' Mo said, shaking her hand.

It was a curious handshake, she thought. Light and sensitive, almost like shaking hands with another woman. Except that the hand which enveloped hers was of massive proportions.

'Now how about a dram?' invited Mo.

'We're really in a hurry,' said Jim.

Wee Mo smiled, the effect being more sinister than pleasant. 'I'm having one myself. I'm sure our business together won't take long.'

'Then a dram would be grand,' Jim said quickly. Although he, too, was smiling there was sweat under his armpits and in the small of his back. He had noticed that one of the hardmen was openly carrying razors in his waistcoat pocket.

'And you, Miss Thompson?'

'Please.'

Nellie's eyes glanced round the room while Mo poured the drinks. There were lovely pictures on the walls, and the furniture and furnishings were far nicer than anything she'd ever seen except in magazines.

She sat close beside Jim on a pink, satin-covered sofa. Wee Mo eased his huge bulk into a very large armchair facing them.

'You lost again on the dogs today, I'm told,' said Mo.

Jim licked his lips. 'I'm having a bad run. It happens.'

'Oh, it does that. Which is how people like me make money.'

The penny dropped for Nellie. The man was a bookie, Jim's bookie by the sound of things.

'You've been a good client, Jim. A very good one over the years, which is why you're one of the couple dozen I allow credit.'

Jim shifted uncomfortably.

'What you dropped today brings it up to two hundred pounds. An awful lot of money for a butcher to find.'

'You'll get your money. There's no need to worry about that,' Jim assured him.

'I'm not worried. I always get what's due me – one way or another. Eh, boys?'

The two hardmen stared gravely back at their boss, one of them giving the slightest of nods.

The threat wasn't lost. Jim knew what to expect should he fail to pay up. Sweat beaded on his forehead at the thought of himself razor-scarred for life. And it would be a terrible scarring too, they'd make sure of that.

'Now, about what you owe,' said Mo. 'I'm going to have to ask you to settle that before I accept any more of your bets. That's fair, isn't it?'

Jim tried to regain his composure. 'Yes, entirely.'

'And as for the two hundred, when can I expect it?'

Jim's mind was whirling. Damn this losing streak he'd been on recently. Look where it had landed him. His back against the wall and Wee Mo's boys all set to jump on him from a great height. And all he had to his name was his week's wages. 'A month?' he asked hopefully.

'A fortnight,' Mo decided. 'As from today. In fact,' he glanced at his watch, 'as from now.'

Mo rose. Jim was free to go.

'It's been a pleasure meeting you,' Mo said to Nellie.

'Likewise,' she replied.

'I'll be in touch,' said Jim.

Mo's sinister, chilling smile returned. He didn't reply.

At the door to the room the man with the scarred face was waiting to see them out. There was no offer to drive them back.

Jim sat with Nellie's hand in his, staring up at the silver screen. The picture was an exciting swashbuckler but he was taking none of it in. Instead, he was feverishly trying to work out where he could lay his hands on £200.

He could tap his employer for twenty, twenty-five maybe. But that still left £175 to find. An absolute fortune.

Then he thought of the Masons. Surely he could expect some help there. For the first time all night he began to think there might be hope. But he would have to decide the best way to approach them.

'You all right?' whispered Nellie in the darkness.

'Yes,' he whispered back.

'Worried about Wee Mo?'

'I think I know how to sort that problem out now.' She squeezed his hand.

For the first time since entering the cinema he concentrated on the picture. It was rather a good one after all.

He had her pinned against the wall in the darkness of the back close, his tongue in her mouth and his hand on her breast.

Nellie pulled her mouth from his. 'I'll have to go on up,' she said quietly.

Jim was quite beside himself with passion. He wanted this woman like he'd never wanted any other. His hand travelled down the front of her dress.

'No, Jim,' Nellie said firmly.

She was proving amazingly stubborn. Far, far more than he'd ever imagined. 'Please.'

'It's your own fault for getting yourself all worked up.' She pulled away. 'I've told you, nothing's going to come of it.'

Desperate with wanting her, he took her hand and held it against him.

'No, Jim!' she hissed, jerking away.

'Nellie. Please.'

'Not in a back close, Jim. Is that all you think of me?'

'Of course not. I'd much rather we were at my place, but you'll never come.'

She smiled wryly. 'Do you blame me? If you're like this here what would you be like there?'

'Nellie you're driving me crazy. I swear to God, I'm going out of my mind with wanting you.'

'Then you'll just have to control yourself. You know how I feel.'

'Don't you fancy me, Nellie? Is that it?' He stood so close to her she could hear his heartbeat.

'No it isn't, as you well know,' she answered tenderly.

'What can I do?'

'Well, right now you can see me to my door.' Then, seeing the expression on his face, she had to smile.

'I'm glad you think it's funny!' he said bitterly.

'You're too serious about it, Jim, and that's a fact.'

'I only wish you would be,' he grumbled as they went through to the front close, where they stood bathed in the flickering gaslight.

'I have to see someone else tomorrow afternoon,' he said.

'Are you angry with me?'

'No. I've just got some things to see to.'

She touched his arm. 'Those men – that *will* be all right, won't it? They frightened me.'

'Don't you worry about me. I'll come up smelling of roses. You wait and see.'

'Till Friday then.'

'Aye. Till Friday.'

He gave her a final kiss, and stood watching as she ran up the stairs.

Outside the tenement he stood under a street lamp and lit up, deciding what to do next. It was a toss up between the widow in Penilee and the bird over in Luath Street.

The bird in Luath Street won for the simple reason that she was the closest. The silly cow thought he was in love with her. She'd murder him if she discovered he was using her to work off his frustrations with Nellie.

Jim hurried off into the night.

The next time they were out together, Nellie invited him up for a cup of tea when he took her back home.

They found Davey at home. Betty and Roddy were out visiting her sister who lived a few streets away.

As always, Davey was delighted to see Jim, immediately ushering him into the other fireside chair while Nellie put the kettle on.

Jim was morose and preoccupied, not wanting to

talk in front of Nellie, not sure how to say what he wanted to say. But Davey was full of conversation. Jim listened politely, trying to seem enthusiastic, until Nellie finally gave him his opportunity.

'I'm away downstairs a minute,' she said, meaning she was off to the landing toilet.

The instant she was out the house, Jim changed the conversation by saying, 'I'm in bad trouble, Davey, and was wondering if you could give me your advice?'

Davey frowned. 'If I can, son.'

Jim explained the position, ending up by saying, 'So do you know anyone in the lodge who could lend me that sort of money? I know it's an awful lot, but I just have to have it. And there'll be no risk involved. I swear to God I'll pay it back. It may take a while, mind, but they'll get back every ha'penny, I promise you.'

Davey tamped down his pipe and looked thoughtful. 'Aye, it is a lot indeed,' he agreed.

'But do you know anyone?'

An idea had come into Davey's mind. He was fond of this lad, as it seemed Nellie was. He knew how bitter she still was about the Frank Connelly affair. Perhaps this was his chance to make it up to her.

'I could lend you two hundred,' he said at last.

Jim was surprised. He would never have thought Davey would have that much.

Davey interpreted Jim's expression correctly. 'Och, I've been prudent, you understand. Putting a bit by every week. And it's amazing how it soon adds up.' He leaned forward, gesturing that Jim should lean forward also. In confidential, hushed tones he went on, 'I also have a wee fiddle going with a scrap man I know. There's me and another chap at work been pulling the same stroke for years. We split it like.'

'Well, well,' said Jim, nodding his admiration.

'You'll keep this strictly to yourself, of course.'

'You can trust me never to breathe a word of it, Davey. I'm not one for breaking a confidence.'

Davey cleared his throat and sat back in his chair to peer at Jim through a fug of acrid blue smoke. 'What was in my mind was to give it to you rather than lend it,' he said.

Jim was taken aback. 'Give it to me? What do you mean?'

Davey's eyes were sparkling. 'I was thinking two hundred pound would make an awful generous wedding present. And there would be something else forbye, so Nellie need never know about it, unless you want her to.'

Elation welled through Jim. Here was the chance he'd been praying for. This could get him off the hook once and for all. But marriage: that was something he'd never even considered.

Well, why not, he asked himself. At twenty-three he wasn't getting any younger. If he wasn't careful, he could end up with someone who'd make his life a misery.

And he'd told Nellie he loved her, which was true enough, he supposed. He certainly fancied her rotten. That yellow hair and those green eyes were driving him mad! And all along she'd made no bones about it: marriage was the price for having her. And he wanted her. He wanted her more than anything he'd ever wanted in his life before.

He was going to get married someday, wasn't he? That being the case, he'd be daft not to grab this opportunity: two hundred nicker and Nellie. Anyone who turned that down needed his head felt.

'I had intended asking her anyway when this trouble I'm in had sorted itself out,' he lied smoothly.

'I could see that's the way things were going,' said Davey. 'Knowing Nellie, she'd hardly have gone out with you this long if she hadn't thought awful highly of you.'

The door banged shut and Nellie was back. 'What are you two up to? You look like a right couple of conspirators,' she said, going right to the stove where the kettle had been boiling its head off for the last couple of minutes.

'Wouldn't you like to know?' replied Jim mysteriously, and laughed. He wouldn't ask her tonight; he'd set it up specially.

When Nellie's back was turned Davey nodded to Jim and winked. The deal had been made.

'You can sure think up places to take me that I've never been before,' Nellie said. She was staring up at a palm tree from which hung clusters of coconuts.

They were up west, not far from where Wee Mo lived, at the Botanical Gardens.

'Is it the first palm tree you've ever seen?' he asked.

'Course not. There are thousands of them in Govan. You can hardly move for bumping into the damn things,' she retorted.

He chided himself for asking a stupid question and leaving himself wide open, but his mind had been on working himself up to proposing.

It was extremely warm in the greenhouse, a complete contrast to the bitter cold outside.

'Nellie?' he began.

'Yes?'

'I eh . . . I . . . eh –'

'What is it?'

He couldn't remember ever being stuck for words like this before. But then, he'd never asked anyone to marry him before.

Nellie giggled. 'You've got the most amazingly

comical expression on your face. What is going on in that head of yours?'

In a sudden rush, he grabbed her hands and blurted out, 'Will you marry me?'

Nellie lowered her gaze to the floor. 'Can we walk a little?' she replied quietly.

They strolled side by side. Outside there was snow on the ground and in the distance they could see some wee boys sledging down a hill. Nellie thought of how strange it was to be amongst tropical lushness while staring out at such a landscape.

Was she going to turn him down? Jim wondered. He knew how deep her feelings still ran for Frank Connelly. Well, whatever her answer, he couldn't lose. Wee Mo was paid off with Davey's money. If her answer was in the negative then all it meant was he had to pay the money back as he would've had to do to Mo anyway. Only with Davey he could take his time without worrying about a razor in the face.

But the other side of the coin was how much he wanted her. If she turned him down he knew he'd have lost and would never have her.

Taking her by the arm he said, 'I'll be a good man to you, Nellie. You have my word on that. I'll see you want for nothing.'

Nellie had known for some time that he was going to propose. After all, he'd said he loved her, and a man didn't say that unless he had something permanent in mind. She should have made a decision before now, but had shied away from doing so. Now she would have to. Only not right here and now.

'Can I have a day to think it over?' she asked.

'If you like.'

'I want to be absolutely sure, Jim.'

'I understand.'

She smiled up at him. 'You've been awful patient with me. I appreciate that.'

He glanced around to make sure no one was watching. Catching her in his arms he said, 'I'll call round tomorrow night and we'll go out for a walk. You can give me your answer then.' Slowly, tenderly, he kissed her fully and deeply. And for the first time she responded with none of her usual initial hesitancy.

Out came the boilings in a steady flow. Hundreds a minute in a seemingly never ending stream.

Nellie glanced around. God, how she hated this place. The boredom, the smell, the sheer mindlessness of the job.

Day in, day out, five-and-a-half days a week, fifty weeks of the year. On and on and on till all she wanted to do was throw her head back and scream with frustration.

Up until a fortnight ago she'd thought her life at

the factory couldn't get any worse, but she'd been sadly wrong. For a fortnight ago Big Jessie had been appointed supervisor of this section, and after the hammering Nellie had given Jessie, the big one was out to make life for her an absolute hell.

She could see Jessie now, watching her from behind one of the machines further along. What would she find wrong with her work today she wondered? For she'd find something wrong all right. She always did.

Jessie, she knew, was out to get her the sack. It was only a matter of time before she succeeded. They both knew that.

Her mind came back to Jim Biles. She didn't love him, but she was fond of him. She didn't think she'd ever love a man again. All her love, that kind of love anyway, had gone to Frank whom she'd love to her dying day. No other relationship could even begin to approach that one.

But she had to face the fact that Frank was gone – probably never to return. So where did that leave her? Clinging to a memory, that's where. And beautiful as the memory was, she didn't want that to be all she had to sustain her for the rest of her life.

Then there was her father whom she hated for what he'd done to break up her and Frank. At the moment she was forcing herself to be friendly towards him. What else could she do in a house the size of theirs, where they practically lived on top of one another? Besides, she had her mother and brother to consider. Open warfare would have made their lives intolerable.

Marriage was the answer. Once out the house she could cut all ties with her father and have a life of her own.

Whichever way she looked at it, the odds were in favour of her marrying Jim. If she couldn't get Frank, then Jim was as decent a man as was likely to come her way. And once married she wouldn't have to worry about her job because Jim wouldn't expect her to continue working. A married woman's place was in the home looking after her family.

She smiled at the thought of children. She couldn't wait for a babe of her own. In fact, the more the merrier to fill the house with gaiety and laughter.

Yes, she told herself, if she couldn't have Frank – then why not Jim? If she didn't love him, at least he loved her. She could do an awful lot worse than that.

It was the first time Nellie had ever been in his house, which was no more than a one-room apartment.

She was impressed by how neat and tidy it was. She'd been expecting a bachelor tip but that just wasn't the case.

'Do you have someone come in?' she asked.

He grinned. 'You've found me out. There's a wifey upstairs who I pay a dollar to come in twice a week. For another two bob she takes my washing to the steamie when she goes.'

'And your ironing?'

'She does that as well.'

'You get your money's worth, don't you?'

'I try,' he replied, taking her in his arms.

'We'll need new curtains and I'm wondering what your bed linen's like?' she continued, ignoring his advances.

'And I'm wondering what you're like.'

She pushed his arms away, and, going to the bed, threw the covers back. The sheets were old and threadbare, the blankets as thin as she'd ever seen. 'We'll need new bedding,' she decided.

It was a lot better than Nellie had thought. The walls had been distempered fairly recently and underfoot the linoleum was almost new. Given a few improvements and a woman's hand here and there, she could soon have this a wee palace.

'You like it?' he asked.

'It'll do for the moment.'

'Now don't be too enthusiastic, will you?' he said sarcastically.

'All right then, Jim,' she laughed, giving him a hug, 'it's very nice. And in far better condition than I'd dared hope.'

'Aye, well I never could abide living in a pigsty. There's plenty that do around here, mind you, but not me. It doesn't take that much of an effort.'

'Especially when you can afford to get someone else to do the dirty work?'

He grinned. 'That's one of the big secrets in life, Nellie. Never forget it. Delegate when you can.'

He had a good brain on him and she admired that. He would go far in the butchering trade, getting his own shop one day, of that she had no doubt.

His only drawback that she could see was his addiction to gambling, which bothered her. But he'd got himself out of the scrape he was in with Wee Mo the bookie, though she never had found out how he'd pulled that one off, and was now back on a winning streak again.

He certainly seemed to know what he was doing when it came to the dogs and horses. Still, it worried her all the same. A wee flutter was one thing: wholesale addiction quite another. She was going to have to work on the gambling, she thought as she looked around her new home – but there was time for that.

'Nellie?'

She came out of her reverie to find him sitting on the bed staring at her. He had a look in his eye which she'd come to know only too well.

'No, Jim,' she said flatly.

'Why the hell not? We're going to be married, aren't we?'

'*Going* to be. We're not yet.'

'Does it make such a big difference?'

'To me it does.'

He sighed. She was the most exasperating woman he'd ever come across. And yet maybe she was right. He'd waited this long so why not a little longer? When he finally did have her he wanted her full co-operation and it was obvious that was only going to happen on the wedding night. Some things, he was sure, were worth waiting for.

'You win,' he said resignedly. Later, when he'd dropped her off home, he'd slip up to Luath Street and work off his itch there.

'How do I look, Ma?' Nellie spun slowly around in place.

Betty stood back to admire her daughter. 'A proper treat, lass. As beautiful as any bride I've ever seen and that's a fact.'

Indeed, even in the simple shop dress she looked like a princess, her hair so golden and her beauty so radiant.

'Are you excited?' Betty asked, fussing with the skirt.

'Yes, Ma. Yes, I am,' dismissing the phantom thought of Frank with a smile.

'I can remember our wedding –' Betty started, but trailed off. 'But never mind that. It's ancient history now.' Then, 'You're getting a right good chap, Nellie. I hope you appreciate that?'

'I appreciate it,' she whispered, though that would never mean that she had forgotten.

'Fine. As long as you do.'

Nellie turned around once more. 'Do you think the hem could do with coming up a fraction, Ma? It looked all right in the shop but now I'm not so sure.'

'Let me see,' said Betty, and bent to have a look.

Jim walked down the aisle with his best man, a chap called Phil Drummond who worked alongside him at the shop. He'd been drunk out of his skull the night before at the stag booze-up which had gone the round of all the local pubs, and, thanks to Phil, already had a goodly number of halves and chasers under his belt since getting up that morning. He was feeling no pain at all.

Until he saw Marj Henderson.

He came up short and his jaw fell open. What in the world was she doing here? God Almighty, he thought suddenly, surely she hadn't come to denounce him! What a showing up that would be. What would Nellie say? He daren't even think about that.

'What's up?' Phil whispered.

He watched in horror as Marj raised a hand and waved at him. If he could have wished himself a thousand miles away he would have done so.

'Jim?'

'Aye, it's all right, Phil. Just something that flashed through my mind that's all.'

Side by side, they continued walking toward the front of the church while around them none too expertly executed organ music rent the air.

Thankfully, Nellie didn't keep him waiting long as some might have done. The music changed to 'Here Comes The Bride' as she appeared at the top of the aisle with her father.

'Here you go,' whispered Phil.

Jim put a smile on his face and tried not to look as shocked as he felt.

When the ceremony reached the part where the minister asked the congregation if there was anyone who objected to this marriage he tensed, fully expecting Marj's voice to be raised saying, yes, she objected as he really loved her and had been seeing her secretly and frequently for the past year to prove it.

No voice came. If she wasn't here to object then what?

Phil handed him the ring which he slipped onto Nellie's finger. She was absolutely stunning, the perfect bride. He'd never fancied her more than he did at that moment – which was saying something.

'I now pronounce you man and wife,' said the minister. And that was that. They were wed.

'You may kiss the bride.'

It was a moment she'd dreamed of nearly all her life and yet she didn't feel at all as she'd imagined. She had the ghost of Frank Connelly to thank for that.

She put Frank from her mind as Jim's lips met hers. From now on the less she thought of Frank the better. Having married Jim she now had to give that marriage a chance. She had to forget about her lost love.

People crowded round them, shaking her hand and slapping Jim on the back.

'Congratulations, lass,' said Davey, pecking her on the cheek.

She wilted under the kiss, feeling as though she'd been scalded. God, how I loathe you and how marvellous it is to be rid of you, she thought, staring at her father.

Then her attention was diverted to Betty who was having a right good cry. She squeezed Betty's hand and said, 'It's a wedding, Ma, not a funeral. You're supposed to be happy for me.'

'But I am!' wailed Betty.

'Women! I'll never understand them,' said Davey pulling a face.

Cars were outside the church waiting to take them on to the reception which was being held directly after the ceremony in the local Co-operative Hall.

'What a day!' said Jim when they were in the car and driving away. Behind them a swarm of small boys were fighting for the scramble, the money the bridegroom traditionally throws from the car window.

'I could murder a drink,' he added.

'From the smell of your breath you've murdered quite a few already,' she said.

'Now you're not going to start our marriage off by nagging, are you?'

He was right. 'I'm sorry,' she apologized, leaning against him.

'If a man can't have a few bevvies on his wedding day, then when can he have them? After all, it only happens once.'

'You hope,' she said. And they both laughed.

They took a long detour round Govan so that when they arrived at the hall, most of the guests were already there waiting for them. They entered to applause and some ribald shouts from the back.

Phil Drummond immediately came forward to hand them each a glass of champagne. 'To the bride and groom!' he toasted.

While the guests toasted them they toasted one another.

A band had been hired which consisted of accordion, piano and saxophone. At a signal from Davey they started to play.

Those who wanted to dance danced; those to eat ate; and those to drink drank. It was an informal, neighbourly affair, the main criterion being to enjoy yourself.

Later speeches would be made, but not until most people would be too drunk to remember them.

Jim took the floor with Nellie to a round of applause and more ribald shouts from the back. They danced two dances and then decided to take a breather. Jim was at the makeshift bar, collecting some whisky, when a voice beside him said, 'Hello? And wasn't I surprised to find out you were the bridegroom.'

He nearly jumped out of his skin at the sound of that so familiar voice. He turned to find Marj Henderson smiling at him.

'What the hell are you doing here?' he hissed, drawing her to one side.

'I might ask you the same?'

'I'm getting married. What in the name of the Wee Man does it look like?'

'I didn't mean that. What I meant was, what are you doing here after all the things you've been telling me for the past year? "I *love* you Marj." "I'd do *anything* for you." Why only the other night –'

'Sssh! For God's sake!' he whispered, having just seen Nellie closing on them.

'Hello, Marj. It's good to see you,' Nellie said on joining them.

'You look marvellous, Nellie. May you have all the happiness in the world.'

Nellie turned to Jim. 'I didn't know you two knew one another?'

'We don't,' he replied hastily. 'We just got chatting.'

'Then let me introduce you. Marj, this is my husband Jim.'

'Hello.'

'And, Jim, this is my cousin, Marj Henderson. She lives over in Luath Street with her husband who's in the Royal Navy.'

'How do you do,' said Jim thickly.

He swallowed half his drink. Cousins! What a turn up for the book. They didn't look at all alike. Not even the hint of a family resemblance.

'Jack's at sea, I take it, otherwise he'd have been here the day?' Nellie said.

'Aye. But he'll be back soon. He's been out to the Indian Ocean and back. Last word I had they were steaming through the Med.'

Nellie shook her head. 'Wouldn't suit me being married to a sailor. Being left alone so much.'

'Och, you get used to it,' Marj replied, smiling as she caught Jim's look.

They talked for a few minutes more and then Jim took Nellie back on the floor. As they were excusing themselves from Marj he saw a mischievous glint in Marj's eyes. She'd enjoyed watching his discomfiture, knowing she could drop him right in it at any second. She was a cool one that, and no mistake. He was going to miss his visits to Luath Street.

An hour-and-a-half later Jim had nearly drunk his fill and was feeling decidedly unsteady. He'd danced with Betty and just about every other female he could lay his hands on. He was having a whale of a time. The air was rent with wheechs and cries as a reel got under way.

Blearily, he gazed round the floor to see that Nellie was up with Phil Drummond. He decided to go to the toilet.

Lurching down the dingy corridor that led him to the turn off where the toilets stood side by side, he was just about to enter the Gents when the door to the Ladies opened and Marj emerged.

'Well, if it isn't Romeo himself,' she said wickedly.

'Oh, come on, none of that now,' he coaxed. But secretly he was pleased. He liked the idea of being thought of as a notorious lover.

Marj had also had a fair amount of drink. Her cheeks were flushed and her eyes slightly watery. 'I've been watching you give everyone else a dance, but not me. What's wrong? Have I suddenly got the plague or something?'

He leaned against the wall to steady himself. 'I thought it best to leave you alone, in the circumstances.'

'Did you now?'

He suddenly laughed. 'It is helluva funny when you think about it. You and Nellie being cousins, I mean.'

'Very funny indeed.'

'Ah, well,' he sighed. 'Maybe you don't think so.'

'I really thought you cared, Jim,' she said in an accusatory tone.

'You're married, Marj.'

'Marriages have been broken before.'

He shook his head. 'I really am sorry the way things have turned out. I never meant to hurt you. I promise.'

'You should've seen your face in the church,' she said, her lips twitching upward.

'I thought you'd come to make a scene. I nearly died when the minister asked if there was anyone in the congregation who objected to our marriage. I was sure you were going to leap to your feet and give me a right sherricking.'

'I was tempted, I can tell you. But no, I wouldn't do that, if for no other reason than I've got my own marriage to consider. Divorcing Jack's one thing.

But standing up and making a spectacle of myself is quite another.'

'Aye, I understand,' he replied.

'I'm going to miss you, Jim.'

'And I'll miss you.'

'No you won't. You'll have Nellie to keep you warm.'

'I'll still miss you, Marj. I swear it.'

They were alone in the turn off and there was no one in the corridor. Putting his arm round her neck, he drew her face to his and kissed her. The kiss was full and luscious. As always happened when he kissed her, he was instantly aroused.

'Oh, Marj,' he whispered, all thoughts of Nellie momentarily forgotten.

'You should have told me what the situation really was,' she whispered back.

'You would have told me to take a running jump.'

'Maybe. Maybe not.' Through an alcoholic haze she thought of the awful, long lonely nights when Jack was away at sea. A body needed some comfort and you took it where you could. She'd lied to Nellie; you never got used to the long separations. Especially when you were a passionate, loving woman like herself.

Jim could smell her; the warm body he knew so well.

'Marj,' he sighed, and kissed her again.

*

It was time to be changed and be off, Nellie decided. Crossing to where Babs and Phil Drummond were deep in conversation she told them she thought it was time.

'Right. I'll away out to the car and get the things. Where are you going to change?' asked Phil.

'Nowhere else but the toilet.'

'All right, you and Babs away along there now and I'll be by with your things in a minute.'

Nellie glanced around. 'Have you seen Jim? I seem to have lost him.'

'He'll be around somewhere. Don't you worry about him, I'll root him out.'

Nellie smiled and squeezed his arm. 'Thanks, Phil.'

'Just doing my duty as best man.'

He was a really nice chap, Nellie thought. And from the way Babs was looking at him she wouldn't disagree with her. She'd keep her fingers crossed that something developed out of this meeting. They'd make a good couple together.

'Come on then,' said Babs as Phil left them for the hired car that had been patiently waiting outside all this while. In its boot were their suitcases for the honeymoon.

'Another hour and most of this lot will be flat on their backs,' said Babs as they made their way through the boisterous crowd.

'As long as they've enjoyed themselves, that's the main thing,' Nellie laughed.

'There's been some booze drunk I can tell you.' She stumbled and would have fallen if Nellie hadn't caught her round the shoulders. 'And I've had my fair share,' Babs added.

They were almost at the toilet when Nellie heard the noise which brought her to a halt.

Babs frowned; she'd heard it too.

A sort of moan, Nellie thought, as though someone was in pain.

But Babs knew differently. A grin spread across her face as it dawned on her what they were hearing. Gesturing Nellie close she whispered in her ear, 'There's more than one person in there.'

'No!' protested Nellie, understanding dawning.

Babs nodded. As if in confirmation, a female voice said clearly, 'Oh, that's lovely, lovely.'

The sound was coming from behind a door facing the toilets. Nellie placed her finger over her lips and nodded that they should move on into the toilet. They were about to do so when suddenly an unmistakable voice said, 'Christ, the feeling!'

Nellie froze, completely shocked. A glance at Babs's face told her she hadn't misheard.

Babs took Nellie by the arm. 'Come on, leave it,' she whispered.

Nellie jerked her arm away.

'Leave it, Nellie!' Babs said urgently.

Taking a deep breath, Nellie turned again to face the door from behind which the voices had come. She had to be absolutely certain. She had to see with her own two eyes. There must be no mistake.

She swallowed hard as she put her hand on the doorknob. Then, feeling so light inside that a decent puff of wind would blow her away, she opened the door.

It was a bucket and broom closet. But she didn't take that in right away. The scene that etched itself forever in her memory was that of Jim with his trousers down round his ankles and her cousin Marj with her knickers off and kicked to one side.

'Oh my God!' exclaimed Marj when through the light which had suddenly invaded the privacy of the closet she saw Nellie staring at her.

For a moment or two Jim wasn't aware of anything. He swore as Marj pulled herself off him to fumble with her skirt. And then, for the first time, he noticed the light and realized they weren't alone. Still dazed, he turned to find his wife of a few hours staring at him in horror.

Marj picked up her knickers and slipped into them, turning her back on the others as she did so. Her face and shoulders were beet coloured. Although not exactly sober, she was considerably more so than she'd been the moment before the door opened to reveal Nellie.

Anger and disgust raged through Nellie. She was both hot and cold in the same instant. She wanted to be sick.

'Nellie –' he began.

'Cover yourself,' she snapped, her voice like steel.

He did as he was told without a murmur.

'Nellie, don't do anything daft. It's not what you think,' Marj said.

'What do you mean, it's not what I think?'

Marj bit her tongue. She was genuinely fond of Nellie, although Nellie would hardly believe that after what she'd just witnessed.

'We'd both had too much to drink. It was one of these stupid things. Nothing more. I swear it,' Marj said.

'You lied when you said you'd never met her before, didn't you?' she accused.

For once words deserted him. He couldn't begin to think of a reply, and in failing to do so confirmed Nellie's accusation.

'It's time for us to go. Phil will be here any second with your change,' Nellie said. Then to Marj, 'Get back to the reception.'

'You won't tell Jack, will you? Please, Nellie?'

Nellie felt nothing but contempt for her cousin. 'Jack will never know from me. Nor Babs here. You have my word on that.'

'You're still going on the honeymoon?'

'Of course. It's all been paid for. I'm not going to waste that.'

'Forget it if you can, Nellie. It was the drink, nothing else.'

'Good-bye.'

Marj hurried out of the turn off and along the corridor in the direction of the reception.

'Someone's coming. Sounds like Phil,' said Babs who'd been spellbound ever since the door had been opened.

'Knock on the toilet door when you're ready,' Nellie said to Jim.

Phil arrived with the suitcase containing their change. 'There you are. I've been looking all over for you,' he said when he saw Jim.

Babs took the suitcase. 'I'll take Nellie's stuff out and then I'll pass it through.'

'Aye, fine,' replied Phil, wondering what had been going on. Half cut as he was, he still couldn't fail to be aware of the atmosphere he'd walked into.

Once in the toilet Nellie leaned on the washbasin, shaking with shame and revulsion. She still wanted to be sick but it wouldn't come.

Babs lit two cigarettes and passed her one. 'What are you going to do?' she asked quietly.

Nellie drew heavily on the cigarette. She felt dirty and unclean somehow. She also felt years older than when she'd got up that morning. 'I don't know. I'll have to think about it.'

'Don't go off half-cocked. I'm sure Marj was right and it was only the drink. We all do bloody stupid things when we've had too much. I'm positive it was no more than that.' Then, when Nellie didn't reply, 'It's your wedding day, Nellie. You can't end things before they've even begun.'

'I'll have to think about it. Long and hard,' Nellie said, wondering how their relationship could ever be the same again. It wouldn't, of course. Not after what she'd just witnessed. With her own cousin too!

'Let's get on with it then,' said Babs. And started to help Nellie to strip.

When Nellie was changed and combing her hair she said to Babs, 'You'll never breathe a word of this, will you?'

'You know better than that.'

There was a knock on the door and Phil's voice called out, 'Ready when you are, ladies.'

'Won't be a jiffy!' Babs called back.

Nellie lit another cigarette, her hands still shaking. 'Jim can wait,' she said.

All the folk from the reception came out to wave good-bye to them when they left for the station. Despite the fact that her world had just come crashing down around her, Nellie somehow managed to put on a brave and beautiful smile, waving back to the well-wishers until they were left far behind.

Settling back into her seat she gazed out at the passing scene. Beside her, Jim fidgeted.

The journey to the station was made in silence; he was desperate to speak, his emotions a combination of anger and guilt, but couldn't, because there was no partition between them and the driver. She did not even respond when she was offered a cigarette or acknowledge the offer in any way.

At the station Jim tipped the driver then lifted their suitcases. 'Platform 3,' he said.

Nellie strode off, leading the way.

He'd wanted an empty compartment but there were none to be had. They had to settle for one containing a blowsy, middle-aged woman and a wee girl who throughout the journey chattered non-stop about 'goin' doon ra watter', as going down to the Clyde Coast was often called by Glaswegians.

Troon was a sleepy little city on the Firth of Clyde. There they got off the train and hailed a taxi which took them to the hotel. The room was a nice double with a good view of the Clyde. Nellie took off her gloves and hat. Sitting on the bed she stared straight ahead.

'Please forgive me, Nellie,' he said.

She looked up at him. 'What I can't understand is why you'd even want to? And on our wedding day of all days?'

'We told you, it was the drink. Phil had been feeding me the stuff long before we even got to church. By the time the reception came round it only took a few halves to send me away with the fairies. And she was the same way.'

'Why didn't you admit to knowing her before?'

He sat in a wicker chair and twiddled his thumbs. He couldn't very well tell her the truth. 'I don't really know,' he hedged.

'I take it then you'd . . . well, made love to her before that incident in the closet?'

'I knew her before you,' he said, which in itself was true. 'We were gey close for a while. You understand?'

'Was she married to Jack at the time?'

He nodded.

'I see.'

'I packed in seeing her ages ago,' he lied. 'She never crossed my mind after we met.'

'And the wedding was the first time you've seen her since going out with me?'

'Yes.'

That seemed to mollify her a little.

'I suppose I denied knowing her because her turning up had caught me so much by surprise. And on top of that I felt guilty. I had no idea she was your cousin.'

Somewhere in the depths of the building a gong

sounded to announce the evening meal. The last thing she wanted was food.

'Nothing like it will ever happen again, Nellie. You have my solemn word on that,' he pleaded.

She regarded him thoughtfully. Babs was right. She couldn't allow this to be finished before it had even begun. Everyone was allowed one big mistake, after all. The pity was he'd made his so soon.

She'd forgive him. But not yet. He was going to have to suffer a little while longer. A couple of days at least.

'Let's away down,' she said rising.

'Nellie?'

'We'll talk about it over the meal,' she said.

He smiled inwardly, thinking he'd won the round.

It had been an excellent meal. At least they'd thought so. They'd even had a bottle of wine, which they'd considered very posh.

At the door to their room Jim excused himself saying he had to go to the toilet. Humming he went off down the corridor.

Nellie undressed and put on the special nightie she'd bought for the occasion. She wouldn't have worn it now except it was the only one she'd brought with her.

She took off her make-up and then tied her hair back. When that was done she took several blankets from the bed and arranged them on the floor. At their head she put one of the bed's two pillows.

Having crawled between the blankets she tucked herself in. The floor was hard and unyielding but she'd endure it.

Coming into the room, Jim gaped when he saw her. 'What the hell are you doing down there?' he demanded.

She regarded him coldly. 'This is where I'm sleeping.'

'But why?'

'You have the affrontery to ask me that after what you did the day?'

He walked over to stand glaring down at her. 'I thought we'd sorted that out?' he said.

'Surely you don't expect me to let you sleep with me only hours after you've been with my cousin? Oh no, you've another thing coming if that's what you had in mind.'

'Be reasonable, Nellie,' he pleaded. 'It's our honeymoon, after all.'

'You should have thought of that before you went into the broom closet with Marj.'

Squatting, he placed his hand on her shoulder. 'Please?'

'No!' she said, finality ringing in her voice. And closing her eyes willed herself to sleep.

Nostrils dilated and breathing heavily, he came to

his feet. Turning abruptly on his heel he strode from the room, banging the door behind him.

The bar was still open for residents so he ordered up a large whisky. He drank it off in a single gulp and immediately ordered another. Four large whiskies and quarter of an hour later found him sitting at a table overlooking the sea. Okay, he thought, so he'd been bloody stupid, but to do this to him! It was inhuman after all these months of waiting. To be denied like this on the first night of his honeymoon was just too much to bear.

He thought of her lying upstairs. That body he'd so desperately craved for so long. The hair, the eyes, the form he'd never seen unclothed.

By the time midnight struck he was the only one left in the bar. He was lolling at the table, having consumed a little over three-quarters of a bottle of whisky since coming down. From behind the bar the barman watched him anxiously.

By now he'd convinced himself Nellie was being completely unfair in denying him his rights. Her behaviour was totally out of order. Just not bloody fair at all.

'Are you all right, sir?'

Jim stared drunkenly up at the barman. 'Why, what's it to you?'

The barman took a step backward, only too familiar with Glasgow drunks. He knew how mean and nasty, not to mention violent, they could be.

'It's just that you look a working man yourself, sir, and you'll appreciate I have to be back on duty at six in the morning.'

Jim grunted. That seemed reasonable enough. Not like some bloody people he could think of.

'Do you know I got married the day?' he mumbled. The barman was now a friend rather than a foe.

'Congratulations.'

'One for the road, eh?'

The barman relented. It was the chap's wedding day after all. And at this late hour what was another five minutes?

'Coming up, sir.'

'And one for yourself, John. A large one, same as me.'

'Thank you very much.'

The large one became four before Jim finally staggered out of the bar and up the stairs to his room. He stumbled twice on the stairs and nearly fell but managed to save himself both times. Entering the room, he stood with his back against the door. He could see her lying there, yellow hair gleaming in the moonlight. Staring at her all the while, he slowly stripped in the darkness. When he was finally naked he crossed to stand staring down at her, swaying like a young tree in the wind.

All those months of waiting, wanting her. And here she was, his legal wife – and still denying him.

Nellie awoke with a start, only just managing to stifle a scream when she saw the swaying figure looming over her. 'Jim?' she breathed tremulously.

Suddenly he was on her, ripping the blankets away. Taking hold of her nightie he tore it straight down the middle so that her body was exposed and vulnerable. The body that had driven him nearly crazy all these months and for which he'd had to find a substitute in Marj Henderson.

Nellie couldn't cry out. That might have brought someone – the last thing she wanted. No! she screamed inside herself. Please God not like this!

Drink had never interfered with Jim's ability to get aroused, and it certainly didn't now. Forcing her thighs apart he rammed himself viciously into her.

She gasped, then whimpered with the shock and acute pain of his entry. Grabbing his hair she pulled; he slapped her viciously across the mouth.

He was far too strong for her. To continue struggling would only result in her getting hurt further. Oh, God, she silently prayed, just let him get it over with.

She lay with her head to one side so that she couldn't see the white shape pounding relentlessly into her. Tears trickled from her eyes to run hot and scalding down the length of her cheeks. Would it never finish? He was going on and on, oblivious to her, almost unaware that he was not alone.

With a grunt and final heave he came. 'That'll teach you, you bitch!' he snarled. Stumbling to the bed he fell face down across it. Within seconds he was snoring.

She lay in the darkness feeling completely violated. It was as though her very essence, the core of her being, had been beaten and betrayed.

To think she'd saved herself all these years for this to happen. She'd dreamed of it being gentle, loving, a thing of beauty. Instead, it had been a crime. A joyless and violent nightmare.

Come morning she'd be covered in bruises, but they would heal in time. Her heart never would. The experience would never fade. That would be with her, like some festering canker, for the rest of her life.

'Oh, Frank!' she whispered into the cold, still dark. If only she'd known. If only . . . if only . . .

4

Nellie started drying her hands on the tea towel the moment she heard the front door snick shut. It was Jim's second day back at work after their honeymoon. She made up, combed her hair, and put on one of her best dresses. Once outside she headed for Harrison's, the sweetie factory.

She was going to leave him. She'd made up her mind about that the night of the rape.

Nor had she any intentions of returning to her ma and da. Davey, as the saying went, could go and bile his can as far as she was concerned. If she never saw him again it would be too soon.

She wasn't sure how she was going to solve her living problem yet, but she would, somehow. Perhaps Babs's parents would take her in as a lodger. That was one of several possibilities running through her mind. But first she had to find a job.

Although she'd left the factory partly because of Jessie, she wasn't particularly worried about the big one now. It was highly unlikely she'd be put back in the section she'd been in before, which would mean Jessie would have nothing to do with her. She would have a new supervisor.

As she walked she thought of the nightmare that had been her honeymoon. There had been no apologies the next morning, not that she would've forgiven him anyway. Instead, on waking, he'd dragged her up on to the bed and taken her again.

She'd felt totally cold towards him then as she'd felt every time he'd had her since. When he approached her her body would go tense and rigid. She'd lie inert, giving no response and feeling none.

She'd come to hate his hands. During their courtship she'd forgotten how horrible they were, but now the very sight of them was enough to make her grue. Large, thick fingered and very red – as though they'd been skinned – she wanted to shriek every time he laid them on her flesh. She thought of them as the hands of a beast and not a man.

It might not have been so bad if he'd shown even a little tenderness. But he didn't. He was on her like an animal, whenever he wanted, and when he'd finished turn and walk away, as though, the act completed, she no longer interested him.

In those moments she felt like a whore. Degraded, defiled, humiliated in the extreme.

She put these thoughts from her mind as she entered the factory, amazed to find that it was as though she'd never been away.

The room she was ushered into was sparse and utilitarian. She sat there for nearly an hour before being seen.

'Why do you want to come back to us, Miss Thompson?' Mr Geddes asked. He had a hard face, like a slab of granite from his native Aberdeen.

'Mrs Biles,' she corrected. 'I'm married now. And that's why I left, to get married.'

He waited, his expression one of irritation. She hadn't answered his question.

'We need the money,' she said finally. It was none of his business she intended leaving Jim.

'I see. Didn't you realize that before you left?'

'Things have changed at home during the last few weeks. Family responsibilities you understand.' She hoped he wouldn't ask her to elaborate on the lie.

Geddes pursed his mouth. 'You're lucky, there is a vacancy. Wait here a minute.'

The minute became twenty. Then he was back and this time he didn't sit down.

'I'm sorry, Mrs Biles, we've nothing to offer you.'

'But you just said –'

'I was mistaken.'

She was bewildered. What had she done? If he'd said there was a job available there must be. No one else could've been taken on without his knowledge as he was solely responsible for all hiring and firing.

'Good-day, Mrs Biles,' he said, indicating the open door.

Suddenly she knew what had happened. He'd left her to go and have a word with her ex-supervisor. That had to be the case.

She could just imagine what Big Jessie would have said about her. Slack, lazy, a bad timekeeper. Oh, she would have had a field day! None of it true of course, but Geddes wouldn't know that. He'd have swallowed every lie Jessie fed him as gospel.

Geddes left her in the corridor, hurrying the opposite way on other business. She found her own way out.

It was raining, a drizzle that fell relentlessly out of an iron grey sky. For a moment or two she stood, undecided about what to do. That her guess about why Harrison's had turned her down was correct, she had no doubt. Her lips thinned in anger. She'd made a bad enemy in Big Jessie.

Well, Harrison's wasn't the only place of employment in Glasgow. She'd just keep on chapping doors till she found work somewhere.

She thought of Coates, the thread people. Now that was a possibility.

Hunching her shoulders against the rain she hurried down the street to the tram stop.

Nellie sat staring into the fire, while across from her Jim dozed in his chair. He'd gone out after his tea, coming in again only half an hour since. He'd said he had a wee bit of business to attend to. She presumed it had something to do with horses, dogs or bookies. His business always had.

She lit a Willy Woodbine, the last from the packet of five she bought herself every day. Their budget didn't stretch to more. Then she went back to staring into the dying coals of the fire. Her front was nice and toasty hot, but she wore a shawl to keep her back warm against the chill of the rest of the room.

She was filled with despair. Four months they'd been married now and she was no nearer to finding herself a job than she'd been that first day she'd gone to Harrison's.

She'd known things were bad but had been sure she'd have come up with something in this time. How wrong she'd been. God alone knew how many endless miles she'd trudged, how many doors she'd chapped, how many hard-faced men she'd asked for work, all to no avail.

The only offers she'd come up with were two part-time jobs, both working the same hours or she might have been able to dovetail them, paying so little money it would have been impossible for her to exist on her own.

Full of despair she might be, but she was still a long way from giving up hope. Somewhere there was a job for her. She just knew it. If she persevered she was bound to knock the right door one of these days.

With a snort Jim came awake. 'Bed,' he growled.

She sighed inwardly. *That* time had come round again. Morning and night without fail.

She'd hoped that, as time went by, she might come to find it less repugnant. But every time he touched her she found it as loathsome as the first.

She undressed quickly, with her back to him, slipping into a warm flannelette nightie that could never have been accused of being arousing.

Lying back, she waited for the hands to touch her. Those hands she'd come to have nightmares about. All day long they handled meat. At night and in the morning they handled her the same way.

'G'night,' he mumbled.

She couldn't believe her ears. 'Good night,' she replied in a whisper.

It was a game, she thought. He was teasing her. Making her think she'd got off before pouncing the way he always did.

She lay staring at the ceiling, rosily tinged with fire glow. Hurry up and get it over with so I can get my sleep, she thought. He started to snore.

Relief surged through Nellie. It was the first night since their marriage that he'd failed to want her, failed to take her.

She finally fell asleep praying that the cycle had been broken and that from now on he would leave her alone.

She laid the mince and potatoes on the table while he washed his hands at the sink. It was Friday night and he was just home from work. They ate in silence, as they usually did. A year they'd been married now. To Nellie it seemed like ten.

After they'd finished she cleared the dishes into the sink. As she put on her pinny she said, 'Well? Where is it then?' It was pay night.

Jim took a small, buff-coloured envelope from his pocket and threw it down on the table.

Nellie opened the envelope to count its contents, frowning as she did so. It was only a quarter of what she was usually given for the housekeeping.

'What's going on?' she demanded.

'I lost a few bob on the horses last week. I had to settle up the night before coming home.'

She spread the money on the table and stood staring at it. 'How in God's name am I supposed to manage on this?'

He shrugged. 'You'll manage somehow.'

His gambling had always been a bone of contention between them. There had been a time when she'd thought she could wean him away from it but she'd soon learned her mistake. He was addicted to gambling the way an alcoholic is to drink, and, since paying Wee Mo the £200 he'd owed, he'd been on a winning streak.

Not that she saw any of his winnings. She was given the housekeeping and that was that. They never went out together, they rarely spoke.

Her only pleasure in life was her cigarettes and the odd night, usually about once a month, when he allowed her to go off to the pictures either on her own or with Babs, who now was engaged and shortly to be married herself.

'Have you nothing put by? A wee fly something?' he asked.

She laughed. 'From what you give me? You must be joking!'

'Well you don't have to worry about meat. I'll see we're all right there.' He normally brought home the meat which he paid for at cost price. But that wasn't what he was talking about now.

'You mean you're going to steal it?' she demanded.

'I'll think of some story to cover the fact I'm not buying it as usual. I could say you've developed a sudden mania for fish and chips.'

She stared at him in contempt. 'Wouldn't it just

be a lot easier if you didn't lose what you can't afford?'

'Shut up!' he ordered.

Anger flared in her. 'Don't you speak like that to me. I won't have you coming in here taking out on me the fact you've lost nearly all your wage packet on some bloody horse!'

He glared at her, his hands automatically knotting into fists. 'Don't nag. I could never abide a nag!'

'Then don't give me anything to nag about.'

'I said we wouldn't go hungry next week!'

'And what about the rent? How am I going to pay that?'

'There's almost enough there. Tell them you'll pay the rest the following week.'

'Oh, aye. And if I give the factor what you say, how will I get coal in? Or bread, or potatoes?'

He had no answer to that.

'I can just imagine you getting up in the morning to a freezing cold room with no fire. You're going to love that.'

'Dry your eyes,' he said angrily. He ran his fingers through his hair. He knew damn well he was wrong. There was no need to go on and on about it.

'And another thing –'

But she got no further. 'Oh for God's sake!' he exploded, leaping to his feet to send his chair crashing to the floor behind him.

She tried to duck the fist that came punching toward her but wasn't quick enough. She cried out as it took her in the eye knocking her head backward and sideways.

'I said shut up!' he screamed.

Sobbing she held her hand over her eye. Already she could feel the flesh there puffing and closing.

He pulled his jacket from the peg behind the door and savagely thrust his arms into it, one after the other. 'I'm going out,' he said.

She didn't reply. What she was thinking was if only she'd have been born a man she could have stood up physically to Jim Biles. Just ten minutes of a man's strength and she would have thrashed him the way he'd so often thrashed her. Oh the glorious satisfaction there would be in that!

'And I don't know when I'll be back,' he added. He hesitated for a moment or two, turning something over in his mind. Then, coming to the table, he scooped two half-crowns into his hand before banging his way out of the house.

He's taken drinking money she thought bitterly. Now there was even less to get by on than there had been before.

Crossing to the sink she wet a flannel under the tap and held it to her eye. There was enough coal in the bin to see them through to the next day. And after that?

There was Barrie's coalyard not that far away where they bagged the coal and loaded the carts which brought it round the streets. The coal was kept in buildings under lock and key. But at night the yard was deserted and easy to get into.

She knew from playing around there as a child that if you were prepared to go along and pick it up there were always lumps to be found. That's what she would do tomorrow, after the men had gone off for the weekend.

The factor would just have to be put off with a story, for she needed what was left of Jim's pay for essentials. The factor fancied her, she knew that from the way he stared at her every week when she went to pay the rent. She'd play on that. Flirt with him a wee bit. Win him around.

Jim had been right. She'd manage. That was a woman's lot.

The other wives in the steamie were chattering nine-teen to the dozen. 'Have you heard about her down in Beresford Street?' 'You mean her with the ginger hair?' The chattering became a medley of whispers, punctuated every second or two by giggles and the odd raucous laugh.

Nellie waited patiently for the copper to come to the boil. She enjoyed steamie days. They were an escape from the incredible boredom of the house.

There were days when she was sure she'd end up screaming because of it! All day long on her own, and then at night *him*.

And he was certainly no company. When he was at home, which wasn't all that often nowadays, he would doze and read the paper exactly the same way her father had done. But most evenings he was out, on business as he called it.

And she knew all about that, didn't she just! This new losing streak of his seemed to be going on forever. She rarely got her full housekeeping money each week. She could hardly show her face down at the factor's, so behind were they with the rent.

Nor had she given up hope of finding a job and getting the hell away from him. But there were just no jobs to be had.

She would have been able to get something up the town if she could type or take dictation, but she had no skills at all. It would have to be a factory, boilings or thread or something of the like. She didn't care what. Anything would do.

The copper was bubbling now so she picked up the pile of clothes and the water received them, glugging them into its depths.

One of his shirts was the last item in. She was about to poke it under the surface with the large wooden tongs when a red smear on the shirt's tail caught her eye. Frowning, she pulled the shirt out again, draping it over the rim of the copper in such a way that she could examine the smear.

Lipstick. No doubt about it.

It could have been hers, of course. Even in such a queer place. Except for one thing. Her last lipstick had given out months ago and she hadn't had the money to replace it since.

She prodded the shirt back into the copper and pushed it down amongst the rest of the clothes. Putting the top on the copper she moved away to a work surface for folding clothes and sat. Sweat was running down her face and back. Her hair clung damply to her head and neck. She felt a hundred years old.

So, he had another woman. That explained why his sexual demands hadn't been nearly so great of late. She should have been able to put two and two together before now. A man like Jim demanded his full quota. If he wasn't bothering her for it then someone else just had to be involved.

But did she care? That was the question she asked herself. Shouldn't she be grateful to this other woman who'd taken the pressure off her?

As she sat thinking she again became aware of the hum of conversation from the other women present. A laugh rose stridently to saw the air.

'And her none the wiser!' a voice said.

Mocking laughter filled the steamie like a roll from a timpani.

'Poor bitch!' another voice said.

'And him the sort you wouldn't think to look at twice. Just goes to show you, you can never judge a book by its cover.'

'It's what's under the cover that counts,' the first voice said.

Again the laughter swelled, to die into whispers interspersed by chortles and giggles.

A thought had struck Nellie making her chill despite the heat. Were her neighbours talking about her and Jim like that? Laughing and sniggering behind her back? Had they realized before she herself had? Have you heard about Nellie Biles's man? Did you know that . . . ?

She could hear it all now. A short while married and already lost her man. Of course, maybe it's not his fault, they'd say. Could be he's got to look elsewhere for what he should be getting at home. The tongues clacking. The fingers pointing. The eyes watching behind curtains and blinds.

Gossip. There was nothing the women of the tenements liked more. And when sex or morality, or both, were involved they were in their element. She couldn't bear the thought of the neighbours talking about her like that. Scorn, derision and even pretended pity.

She couldn't mind that he had someone else, but he should be discreet about it. He owed her that. She'd make him promise. Make him swear.

'Are you going out the night?' she asked.

He was just finishing his tea. Without looking up he grunted a yes.

'With her?'

He threw his knife and fork clattering onto the plate, then regarded her biliously. 'Who?'

'Your fancy woman.'

His eyes hardened and shrunk to slits. Fear turned her stomach over. She'd learned to be scared of him when he looked like that.

'What are you talking about?' he demanded harshly.

'I know you're seeing someone else, so don't bother to lie about it.'

'How do you know?'

'Lipstick on your shirt. You should tell her to be more careful. And what the hell was she doing anyway to get it on your shirt-tail? Isn't that sort of thing a bit difficult up a back close?'

He let the jibe pass. She was only fishing for information.

'Who is she?'

'None of your bloody business.'

'I think it is.'

He stood, scraping the chair away from him. 'I haven't got time for a fight. I'm late as it is.'

'It's not Marj, is it?'

'No. You finding us in the broom closet scared the living daylights out of her. I haven't spoken to her since. I have seen her once or twice in the street, but seeing me coming she's ducked down a close or round a corner.'

Well that was something, Nellie thought. At least it wasn't her cousin he was two-timing her with.

'Why? Are you jealous?'

'Not me. Whoever she is, she's welcome to you.'

He decided to stick the knife in. Christ, to think how he'd once panted after this woman! He could hardly credit it now. For now she meant nothing to him. Nothing at all.

'At least she doesn't lie there like a stookie. She gives me a bit of come on, shows that she's enjoying it.'

'If I'm like that you've only yourself to blame,' she answered hotly.

'How so?'

She was flabbergasted he had to ask. 'What you did to me on our wedding night was enough to put anyone off for life.'

'I'd have thought you would have forgotten about that by now.'

'Forgotten about it? Forgotten?'

'I think you're just making that an excuse anyway. You'd have been the same whether that night happened or not. And it was your own bloody fault it did. Trying to refuse me my rights after keeping me at arm's length like you had all those months.'

'If I'd known what you were really like I'd never have married you. Not in a million years. I thought you cared.'

'Cared!' he spat contemptuously. 'Sure I cared. To get you into bed.'

'Was that all I meant to you? Bed?'

'No. You meant more than that. You meant two hundred quid which got me out of trouble with Wee Mo.'

'What?' she said, appalled.

'You heard me.'

'I don't understand. What two hundred quid?'

'The two hundred your father gave me for taking you off his hands.'

'This is the first I've heard of it.'

'It was between him and me. Nothing to do with you.'

'Nothing to do with me!' she laughed. 'It had everything to do with me, I'd say.'

'Well now you know,' he said.

'God you are an evil bastard!'

He laughed cruelly. She was devastated and that pleased him. If he'd had the time he'd have taken her there and then. Perhaps in her present state he'd get some response out of her.

She thought of her da, hating him, detesting him. He'd not only lost her Frank but he'd saddled her with Jim. Surely that man had a lot to answer for.

'Two hundred quid,' said Jim cruelly. 'And I've suffered for every penny of it. You're useless, you know that? Bloody useless. Pretty packaging with nothing underneath. Why, I'd be better off with a tailor's dummy than with you.'

He was close to her now, leering down at her. How she hated that face. She reached out to grasp hold of the bread knife.

'You would, would you!' he cried as the knife swept up in an arc aimed at his belly. He dodged to one side and then, using a chopping motion, hit her wrist to send the knife clattering to the floor.

Grabbing hold of the front of her dress, he half hauled her to her feet. His open hand smashed again and again into the face that once had mesmerised him.

When he let her go she slumped to the floor where she lay, sobbing. He picked up the knife and placed it on the table.

'No use bitch!' he said, and left the house slamming the door behind him.

If only she could run away! But she couldn't. Until she found a job she was trapped with this animal who was her husband.

Still sobbing, she brought herself into a sitting position. She knew Babs's parents would take her in for nothing until a job came up, but she couldn't ask that of them. Like everyone else their resources were stretched to the limit. Another mouth to feed would mean them getting less themselves.

No, she would just have to endure it for the time being.

Somehow.

'I'm sorry, Mrs Biles, but I can't put anything else on the slate for you. You owe me . . .' and here Mr Simpson consulted the book he kept account of the tick in, 'three pounds, nine and six as it is. That's a lot more than I allow most of my customers.'

Mr Simpson smiled kindly at her, but behind the smile he was resolute. He'd learned to be to stay in business.

'My husband will soon have –'

'Sorry, Mrs Biles,' he interjected firmly. 'Not another item out this shop until this bill's paid off.'

She sagged where she stood. How in God's name was she going to feed them for the rest of the week? It was only Tuesday and she hadn't a penny left to her name. It had been months since she'd had a full week's housekeeping money.

'I understand,' she said dully.

'I'm sorry, lass,' Mr Simpson replied.

Outside she stood for a few moments to gather herself. She felt like running screaming down the street. Instead, she set off home at her normal pace, even managing a smile on passing folk she knew.

Once in she sat in front of the lifeless fire. The scuttle was empty which meant she would have to go scrounging round Barrie's coal yard again that night. She hoped she could at least find a few lumps in the dark to bring home.

Her head rested in her hands. Jim was earning good money but she was seeing little of it. Wee Mo's runners were getting the lion's share and most of what was left he was holding on to to pay for his nights out.

Her stomach rumbled, reminding her of just how hungry she was. Her last bite had been yesterday dinnertime. Some fish she'd got cheap because it wasn't as fresh as it might be.

She thought of the meat he used to bring home from the shop: the chops, the sausages, the joints. Those had stopped now, too. For a while he'd helped himself without paying, but that had come to an end when he'd got the idea his boss was getting fly to him.

She was still sitting in the chair a little while later when there was a knock on the front door.

'Can I have a word with you, Mrs Biles?'

Her heart sank on seeing it was the factor. There

was only one thing he could have come about. She ushered him through.

In the kitchen he took off his bowler to reveal his balding head. He was a tall man, beaky and gaunt.

'I'm sorry, Mr Butter, but I'm still not in a position to give you anything,' she said.

'You're six months behind now.'

'That much?' She was genuinely surprised. She hadn't realized it had been so long.

'Aye, I'm afraid it is.'

She ran a hand over her face. 'What are you going to do?'

'Give you a week's notice of eviction, I'm afraid,' he said, apologetically.

'But you can't do that!'

'Oh, I can Mrs Biles, I assure you. The Corporation's not a charity, you know. We can't afford to let you live in our house for free.'

She bit her lip, thoroughly ashamed and thoroughly lost.

'Your man's working, isn't he?'

'Yes.'

'So,' he said, nodding his head. He'd seen it all before. 'Drink, is it?'

'Gambling.'

'I see.'

Tears filled her eyes. If the bailiffs came they'd be thrown out on to the street, lock, stock and barrel.

The shame and humiliation would be bad enough – but where would they go? What would they do? For he had no relatives that would put them up. None that would offer, anyway. Which left Betty and Davey. But no, she wouldn't go back there, she couldn't go back home. She'd sworn that much to herself.

'Please?' she pleaded.

Mr Butter's heart went out to Nellie. He pretended to be a hard man, but he wasn't really, and he'd always had a soft spot for Nellie.

'I can't extend any longer. It would be more than my job's worth.'

Those eyes, he thought. He'd never seen anything like them. What a contrast to the wife he had at home, who was fat and homely. Chalk to Nellie Biles's cheese. He'd fantasized a number of times about Nellie after she'd been to see him. He could imagine himself, twenty years younger and handsome, stepping out with her up to the town. And then he'd imagined making love to her.

Nellie took hold of his arm. 'I'll do anything,' she said.

Suddenly he was nervous, the insides of his legs trembling.

Nellie was well aware of what she was saying. But she meant it. She'd do anything rather than be thrown out in the street or have to go home to her da. Mr Butter had a kind face. What was one slice off a cut loaf, anyway?

She could see the indecision on his face and guessed that he was wanting to be absolutely certain about the offer and that he hadn't misinterpreted her meaning.

'*Anything,*' she repeated.

He licked his lips, unable suddenly to meet her gaze. 'Perhaps . . . I could put on your file that there were extenuating circumstances and because of this I was allowing you extra time to pay.'

'How long?'

'A month.'

'Two?'

'Six weeks.'

Crossing to the bed, she removed her dress, which she folded neatly before laying it to one side and then took off her bra and knickers to stand totally naked before him.

'Well, Mr Butter?' she asked.

She felt nothing while he was doing it to her, but, unlike with Jim, she pretended otherwise. He told her that she'd been absolutely marvellous.

When he was gone it surprised her that she didn't feel tainted in any way.

She just felt hungry.

Nellie huddled in her thin coat against the wind

cutting through her like a knife. The wind was off the sea and you could still smell the salt in it despite its corruption by city smoke and other odours.

She was on her way to see about yet another job. How many was this now she'd gone after? If it wasn't a thousand it certainly felt like it.

She was in the Gallowgate, not all that far from where Jim worked, when, looking up, she saw his boss, Mr Sanderson, coming towards her. She was preparing to nod and pass by when, in desperation, it occurred to her that he might be able to help her.

'Mister Sanderson?'

He stopped and smiled. From the expression in his eyes she knew he hadn't placed her.

'Nellie Biles. Jim's wife.'

'Oh, aye, of course,' he replied, his smile widening.

'You're probably in a hurry, but could you spare me a minute?'

'Certainly. What can I do for you?'

In a voice cracking with emotion she told him about Jim's gambling and how, with this losing streak he was going through which seemed to be going on forever, nearly all his wages were ending up in the pocket of Wee Mo the bookie.

'I'm desperate,' she ended, close to tears.

Sanderson was frowning. An elder of the kirk, he strongly disapproved of gambling and strong drink.

'Jim thinks an awful lot of you. I know, he's mentioned it a number of times,' she went on. 'And what I was wondering was, if you could have a word with him? Try to convince him that gambling's a mug's game and that the only person who wins in the long run is the bookie. He might just listen to you, Mister Sanderson. At least I think it's worth a try.'

Sanderson thought of the money he'd lent Jim in the past. Jim had always said it was for domestic matters, but he could see now that was a lie. 'I had no idea Jim was a gambler,' he said.

'Will you speak to him?'

Sanderson nodded. 'I consider it my duty.'

She took his hand and shook it. 'Thank you,' she said.

'I just hope it does some good.'

'It certainly won't do any harm.'

She looked drawn and haggard, he thought, but even so she was still beautiful. Jim Biles was a lucky man, in more ways than one. On an impulse he took two pound notes from his wallet and slipped them into Nellie's coat pocket.

She protested and tried to hand them back but he wouldn't accept them. 'Give yourself a treat,' he said. 'And don't worry, I can afford it.'

As she hurried on her way she thought of the meal she'd make when she got home. And to hell with Jim, he could go without. What she bought she'd eat herself.

*

'Does that mean I've got the job?' Nellie asked eagerly. The manager nodded. 'Provided you're here at eight sharp in the morning. We set a lot of store by good timekeeping at Goldman's. You're either on the dot or not at all.'

'I'll be early,' she said.

'That's the idea,' the manager replied, his lips smug with approval.

She could scarcely believe her luck. After all this time she'd done it. She'd landed a job! She'd leave Jim, find a room somewhere. Life was going to be marvellous at last.

The Gallowgate was abustle with people hurrying hither and yon. She passed among them; seeing nothing, hearing nothing.

What a day it was turning out to be! First of all there was the two pounds Mr Sanderson had given her, which meant she would be able to eat her fill, and now a job!

Nor was it a bad job either. Goldman's was a big china importers. She was to be employed downstairs in the packing room at a wage which was eight shillings more than she'd been getting at the sweet factory.

Her luck had changed. No doubt about it.

Tea was bread and scrape, and he was lucky to get that considering the amount of money he'd given her to get through the week on.

She was feeling gloriously happy. It was amazing what a full stomach and a job to start in the morning could do. Another ten days till she got her first full week's wages and then she was off. Jim Biles could hang as he grew for all she cared. Let his fancy woman look after him. She'd had enough.

She put the kettle on the moment she heard the key in the lock. When he entered the room he had a face like a thundercloud. He stood by the door, glowering at her.

'What is it?' she asked, already tensed.

He was so angry he had trouble speaking. 'Sanderson kept me back after work. He told me you'd been complaining to him about me.'

Fear exploded inside her. What a stupid thing Sanderson had done, putting it like that.

'Well?'

'You can't go on the way you are,' she pleaded. 'It's madness. We're months behind with the rent and when was the last time we had a decent meal? I can't manage on what you're giving me, Jim. I've told you that till I'm sick of telling you. You've got to give up gambling.'

'Got to, have I?'

'For your own good. It's become an illness with you.'

Slowly he stalked forward, his eyes, dark and evil, stabbing right through her.

She backed away. 'No, Jim,' she pleaded.

His hands knotted into fists. 'You'll not do the likes of that to me again,' he said.

He'd beaten her badly before but nothing like he did now. Finally, reluctantly, he forced himself to stop. Breathing heavily he stood staring down at the woman lying curled at his feet.

'You can't do this to me,' she gasped at last, painfully crawling away from him towards the bed.

'Who bloody can't?' he asked. 'I've just done it, haven't I?'

She stared at him, her body burning with pain, hating him.

'I'm going out,' he said. 'On business.'

She let the tears come after he'd gone. She ached all over. Every muscle, every joint, every inch of flesh. The crawl to the bed had been indescribable agony.

She felt so lost and alone. She thought of Frank and what life with him might have been like. Frank whom she loved and had never stopped loving. Frank who she had never let make love to her.

Frank, who . . .

She fell asleep, to dream.

The alarm clock burst into a strident jangle to bring her awake. Without thinking she reached to turn it off causing a wave of pain and nausea to sweep through her.

She had to make it to Goldman's, she told herself, and as early as she'd said she'd be. To lose a job after spending so long looking for one didn't bear thinking about.

Jim came out of bed, hardly bothering to glance in her direction as he got dressed. He drank his tea and ate his bread in silence. When he was finished he left the house without having spoken a word.

Every step was a torment. Every movement of her body the same. She couldn't walk a yard without having to stop for a breather.

She cleared up and then got herself into her coat. Taking tiny steps which seemed to minimise the pain she made her way out on to the landing and down half a flight of stairs. By the time she got to the end of the first flight she knew she wasn't going to be able to make it. And even if she had, how would she get through a day's work in this state? She could hardly move, far less cope with what would be expected of her.

Leaning against the wall she bent over. She had no control over her legs when they slowly gave way under her. She ended up sitting on the cold stone stair with her back against the wall.

Her chance had come and gone. She would have to stay on, and at that thought her heart filled with terrible despair. Was there to be no end?

There *will* be another job, she told herself as, gritting her teeth, she forced herself back up the stairs. There just has to be!

Please, God.

She sat staring into the empty grate. It was a week since Jim had beaten her and even now she still wasn't fully recovered. Not even enough to go down to Barrie's coal yard to scrounge some lumps for the fire. Because there was nothing else to do she started to sing, a soft crooning melody that warmed her heart and made her feel better. She often sang when she was alone. It was a pleasure and comfort that didn't cost anything.

She broke off when there was a chap on the door. Now who can that be she wondered, coming stiffly to her feet.

Betty smiled nervously when the door was opened. 'Hello, hen, it's me,' she said.

'Come in,' said Nellie, gesturing into the hallway.

Betty entered, looking round as she did so. It was the first time she'd been in Nellie's house.

Betty sat by the empty fireplace while Nellie made tea. 'How are you?'

'Stiff,' Nellie replied, not having intended to tell the truth.

'Why's that?' asked her mother, politely.

'Because I've a man who's forever beating the

living daylights out of me,' Nellie sobbed, her voice breaking.

Betty stared at her daughter, shocked, unable to think or speak.

Nellie pulled herself together, sweeping the hair back from her face. It was dull and lifeless of late. Like I am, she thought.

'What does he beat you for?' Betty asked gently.

'For the sheer pleasure of it, mainly. Other times it's because I've done something dreadful, like complain about not having any housekeeping money.'

'But he earns a good wage –'

'Oh, aye,' Nellie interjected. 'Only he's got a wee weakness that takes care of most of it. His gambling. Remember?'

'But he always won, I thought.'

'Used to, Ma. For a long time now he's been losing.' And, then, with her mother's arms around her, she spoke for the first time of what life was like with Jim Biles.

'Och, you're exaggerating a bit, surely?' Betty tried to soothe.

'I've not exaggerated anything, not one thing.'

Betty stared into her tea. 'Your da will go daft when he hears,' she said at last.

Nellie's laugh was sharp and mirthless. 'Will he, now? Will it annoy him because he'll think he hasn't got his money's worth?'

'What are you talking about?'

'Hasn't he told you either, then? He paid Jim Biles to take me off his hands.'

'I don't believe that!'

'It's true. Two hundred pounds that Jim needed to pay off a gambling debt. He and Da arranged it between them.'

There was an enormous pause and then Betty said, her voice half-dead, 'Is that why you haven't been to see us?'

'I never want to see him again. And that's why I got married. I couldn't stand being in the same house with him.'

'But he's your da, Nellie, no matter what he's done.'

'He lost me Frank Connelly. He lost me Frank, and, not content with that, he landed me with Jim. I wouldn't spit on him if he was on fire. As far as I'm concerned he doesn't exist.'

Betty's eyes were wet with tears. 'And me? What about me?'

'I've nothing against you, Ma,' holding her mother's trembling hand. 'You've always tried your best.'

Betty stared at her daughter in silence, noting how thin she'd become. And how pale. She looked like a half-starved animal. 'What are you going to do?' she finally asked.

'Leave him when I get the chance. It's getting the job to support myself that's the problem. Something always goes wrong.'

'You won't consider coming home, then?'

Nellie shook her head, averting her mother's eyes.

'Your da will want to come round when I tell him.'

'You tell him from me to go to hell first.'

'What he did he thought he was doing for your own good.'

'Then Heaven preserve me from my enemies,' Nellie sighed.

'I never knew about the money. I wouldn't have let him do that,' Betty said. 'It wasn't right.'

They talked for a little while longer and then Betty rose to go. 'Now that I know I'm welcome, can I come back?'

'Anytime you like, Ma.'

She opened her purse and took out four single pound notes and a ten shilling one, it was all the money she had.

'No, Ma,' said Nellie.

'Ach, away with you,' Betty replied, placing the money on the mantelpiece above the fire.

The two women stared at one another. Joined for the moment by more than the bond of flesh and blood. Each, in her own way, had experienced the hardness of life and it was the understanding of this which now flowed between them.

'I'd better be off,' said Betty at last.

At the door, with a hint of tears still in her eyes, she kissed Nellie on the cheek.

'Look after yourself, Ma.'

'And you, Nellie. And you.'

Nellie went back through to the kitchen, put on her coat, and took the money from where it was lying beside a china dog. Folding it carefully, she put it into her pocket.

A glance at the clock told her it was just gone 8 p.m. None of the shops would be open at this time, but the chippie would. That was where she'd go to treat herself.

It was foggy out, not too bad, but thick enough that you had to be careful how you went. As she walked, yellow-eyed cars passed her, and the fog caught in her throat making her cough. A line of Corporation buses, like arthritic dinosaurs, lumbered by. Somewhere in the distance a foghorn sounded.

There was a queue at the chippie, but the wait was worth it. Standing outside the blazing window, she ravenously dug into her fish supper. She was halfway through her feed when she saw them.

Disbelief stamped itself across her face. She was imagining things, she thought. She had to be!

But she wasn't. There was Jim coming towards her, holding hands with a woman. And the woman was Big Jessie.

Even as she watched Jim paused to kiss Jessie on the mouth. Then, laughing like a couple of school-children or newlyweds, they continued towards her.

He'd promised her. Given her his word he'd be discreet. And here he was, holding hands and canoodling for all the world to see. And not more than a few hundred yards from his own front door. And with *her*.

How long it had been going on she didn't know, but how Jessie must have laughed at her behind her back. How she must have enjoyed Nellie's shame.

In her mind's eye she saw Jim and Jessie, together, in a back close, behind a midgie, wherever, laughing at her, making a fool of her.

And Jessie wouldn't have wasted any time putting it round the sweetie factory. Hey, guess who I'm going out with? Jim Biles. That's right, Nellie's man. That's one in the eye for her, eh?

Why the hell hadn't Babs told her? For Babs must know. Babs must think she was protecting her in some way.

Big Jessie! Of all the women in the world, he had to pick her!

She wasn't aware when the remains of her supper slipped from her hand to fall messily on to the pavement. The red mist of rage had descended on her, an anger transcending anything she'd ever experienced before.

Her hands formed themselves into claws. She'd rip the witch's face to shreds. She'd gouge out her eyes.

Big Jessie saw her first. It was a moment she'd been anticipating for a long time, but the look of triumph that flashed across her face disappeared almost instantly, to be replaced by one of fear when she saw Nellie advancing on her like an avenging angel.

'Oh, my God!' Jessie whispered.

Eyes popping, hair flying, Nellie ran at Jessie who, with a screech, turned and fled.

Jim grabbed hold of Nellie as she tried to go past him, and taking her by the shoulders shook her vigorously. When he saw her hands coming at his face he hit her hard on the side of the head. Nellie fell, rolling into the gutter, lying there momentarily stunned amongst the refuse and dirt.

Whirling, Jim shouted, 'Jessie! Jessie!' and ran out into the street after her.

There was a split second when he might have saved himself. But the sight of the motorcycle – bursting out of the fog straight at him – made him freeze as if he'd taken root.

Nellie saw none of it. By the time she registered the sound and turned to look, it was all over.

A horrible wailing noise tore through the night. Jessie had come running back to find herself staring down at Jim's inert body.

Within seconds a crowd had gathered, one man galloping away for the police while others hauled the bike off Jim and the motorcyclist.

Jim was lying in a pool of blood, his face the colour of milk. He looked asleep.

Jessie, with several women trying to console her, continued wailing.

'This one's dead,' one of the men said, looking up from the body of the motorcyclist. Then he put his head to Jim's chest and listened. He screwed up his face as though not sure if he was hearing something or not. 'This one's still alive. Just,' he said finally.

Jessie had totally given herself over to hysterics. Breaking away from the women who'd been trying to console her, she threw herself down on her knees by Jim's side. Curiously detached, Nellie watched Jessie's wailing grief. Her gaze went from Jessie to Jim. She was unmoved to see him lying there, more so than if he had been a complete stranger.

'Are you his wife, missus?' a policeman asked quietly, hunching down beside Jessie.

Nellie stepped forward. 'No, I am,' she said, in a voice she didn't recognize. 'I'm his wife.'

It was a glorious feeling, having the bed to herself for the first time since she'd been married. The only glorious feeling she was likely to have. She yawned and stretched. It was past midnight and she wasn't long back from the hospital. Jim was going to make it after all, but he'd lost his right leg below the knee.

She felt no pity toward him. Try as she would, she felt he'd brought it on himself. She had no tears left for him.

Was she being too hard? No, he'd been nothing but cruel toward her, treating her the way she wouldn't treat a dog. How could she feel pity for a man like that?

Part of her wished he'd died out there on the street. For now she could never leave him. Now she was going to have to live with a cripple for the rest of her life, and God alone knew how they were going to manage. God alone knew how they would ever survive.

'It's bad news I'm afraid, Mrs Biles,' the doctor said. He'd taken her into the Sister's room at the head of the ward.

She looked at the doctor, waiting for him to continue. It was only the morning after the accident, but already it seemed so long ago.

'Your husband's paralysed down his entire left side,' the doctor said, in what he thought was his most consoling manner.

She was almost afraid to ask the only important question. 'Will he ever get better?'

The doctor shrugged. 'It has been known. But in

the majority of cases like this, the chances are very small. However, you mustn't give up hope,' he said, patting her on the shoulder.

She stared out of the window at the sandstone wall opposite. 'What happens to him?' she asked at last, from very far away.

'How do you mean?'

It was funny how all hospitals smelled the same she thought. Sharp and antiseptic, and something else. Fear perhaps.

'Will he be in hospital for the rest of his life?'

'He'll certainly be a few months with us. But then, we hope, he'll be able to go home.'

The old trapped feeling descended on her like a shroud. Home, and her having to look after him, for there was no one else. None of his family would take him on. In the eyes of the law, after all, *she* was his family.

'Aren't there special places? Institutions?'

She could see the doctor was looking at her strangely, wondering what sort of woman she was.

'Yes, there are,' he said slowly. 'But there's usually a long waiting list.'

'How do I get him on it?' she asked.

She didn't fail to notice the coldness in his voice during the remainder of their conversation. I wonder how you would have reacted in my place, she thought. But then men didn't know what it was like to be a woman. Or to have their bodies violated and their pride destroyed.

They just didn't know.

Later that day she opened the door to a man she'd never seen before.

'Mrs Biles?'

'Yes.'

'I was supposed to meet your husband last night but he never showed up. My name's Hendry, I work for Wee Mo.'

'If it's money you're wanting I haven't any,' she said harshly.

'No, no, you've got it all wrong. I've come to give you some.' And he pulled out a wad of notes from which he peeled off eight fivers.

Nellie took the money, hardly believing her eyes.

'I'm away through to Edinburgh this evening for a couple of weeks and I thought I'd better let Jim have his money before I went. He might think I'd done a moonlight with it otherwise,' said Hendry grinning.

'Aye, he might,' Nellie replied.

Hendry cocked his head. 'Give him my best and tell him I think his luck's changed at long last.'

With a wave of his hand Hendry went clattering down the stairs.

Nellie closed the door and leaned her back

against it. She clutched the fivers to her bosom.

A grin split her face. 'Tell him his luck's changed at long last,' she repeated.

Oh that was rich! That was bloody marvellous! His luck's *changed*. She started to laugh hysterically, holding herself tightly from the ache of it. She had a husband who'd beaten and abused her, and now she would have to look after him, waiting on him hand and foot. His luck had changed all right, but for the worse. As had hers. *Hers*.

She wasn't laughing anymore. Tears streamed down her face as she sobbed. What had she done to deserve all this? Why had she been given such a cross as Jim Biles to bear?

Filled with despair and self-pity she sank down to the floor and buried her head between her knees. She cursed the day she'd first met Jim Biles. And she cursed the day she'd become his wife.

She cried so hard, and so long, that, exhausted, she eventually fell asleep where she sat. But there was no peace in that sleep. For in it she was being pursued by a pair of large, red, raw hands.

Hands she knew so well.

Three months and one week later they brought Jim home.

The ambulancemen brought Jim up the stairs on a stretcher to which he had to be strapped. Because it was impossible to get the stretcher through the door they unstrapped him and brought him into the kitchen carrying him between them in a chair position.

The cavity bed he was laid on had been transformed from what it had been formerly. Workmen from the hospital had been to turn it into a sort of cocoon.

When Jim was tucked up, she bid the ambulancemen good-bye, then she put the kettle on.

When the tea was made she gave Jim his. He could still eat and drink by himself.

As she drank her tea, she studied him while he, in turn, studied her. He'd lost a considerable amount of weight, his face now almost emaciated. The once broad shoulders had shrunk and become bony.

'I take it they told you I've put you down for an institution? But a bed won't become available for some time as the waiting list is a lengthy one,' she said at last into the empty silence.

'They told me.' His speech was thick and slurred. He'd been fortunate not to have completely lost the power of speech. When he spoke it was out of the right side of his mouth only, the words he produced having a curious elliptical sound. But at least they were understandable.

'I've paid off the back rent and we're now up to date. I've enough money for a few weeks more and then that's it,' she said.

'What are you going to do?'

'Go on the parish till I can find work,' she replied.

'Aye, I suppose so,' he sighed. 'I take it Harrison's won't give you your old job back then?'

'Your friend Jessie put the mockers on that for me some time ago. Didn't she tell you?'

'No,' he replied, looking at her with his old loathing. 'I blame all this on you, you know,' he said carefully. 'You've been nothing but a Jonah ever since I married you.'

'And how I wish *that* had never happened.'

'That makes two of us, I can assure you.'

They glared at one another, only the hatred between them real. 'I'll give you your rub and then I'm going out for a wee while,' she said. She wanted some fresh air. She wanted to be away from him. She was finding his presence hard to bear after thirteen weeks on her own.

'And your husband will never work again?' one of the men asked. There were six of them on the Parish Board interviewing Nellie.

'There's a doctor's statement there confirming it,' she replied.

God, how she was hating this. Her neck was burning with embarrassment and shame. She felt totally humiliated.

All six men were looking at her as though she

were a prisoner in the dock. From their stern gazes you would've thought she was trying to lie to them. Make the facts worse than they were. Well that she certainly didn't have to do. They were bad enough as they were.

'Can't you get a job and support him?' another man asked. This one was the army-type with a monocle and clipped moustache.

'If you know of a job going, *any* job, I'll happily take it,' Nellie replied.

'Hmmh!' said the army-type, nodding. Her reply pleased him.

And so it went on. Question after question until it seemed her entire life had been laid bare before these inquisitors.

Later, when she'd left the room, they told her that she'd have their decision in a few days. It took every ounce of willpower she had to keep her head held high and stare those she met in the eye.

It was hours before her mortification began to fade.

Several months passed and she got into a routine for looking after Jim. They were scraping by, just, on the money the parish had awarded them.

The funny thing was, Nellie thought, they were actually marginally better off than when Jim had been on his losing streak and most of his wages had been going straight into Wee Mo's pocket.

Then, early one evening, just as she was thinking about making the tea, there came a rapping on the front door.

'Hello!' said Babs, kissing Nellie on the cheek. Then, indicating Phil Drummond who was standing behind her, 'We thought we'd pay you a visit.'

Nellie ushered them through, consciously grateful for the company. Most of the time she spent alone with Jim, her only alternative being to go out for a walk.

'We brought fish suppers. Thought you'd like a change,' said Phil.

'His idea,' said Babs, staring with unashamed love at him. They were now engaged, the wedding scheduled for later on in the year.

Nellie stuck on the kettle and put out plates. While she was doing this Babs said, 'After we've had this I thought you and I might go up the town and see a flick. Phil's only too happy to stay with Jim.'

Nellie's eyes shone with excitement. She couldn't remember the last time she'd been to the pictures.

'I'm paying, of course,' said Babs. 'And Phil will give us money for chocolates to take in with us.'

'Thanks for telling me,' exclaimed Phil, pretending to be put out.

Babs had been lucky with Phil, Nellie thought. A real nice, easy-going fellow who worshipped the ground Babs walked on. In many ways he reminded her of Frank Connelly. And, as usual when she thought of Frank, a small, black creature passed through her; despair and regret nibbling her insides.

They went into town on a tram, going upstairs so that they could have a smoke.

'We could've gone locally but I thought you'd enjoy the town more,' said Babs.

Nellie smiled and nodded.

'Any news of Jim going into an institution yet?'

'No.'

'Is it bad having to look after him?'

'Bad enough. I can think of a lot of other things I'd rather do.'

'Aye,' said Babs, her voice sympathetic.

'I'm still looking for a job, mind you, but it seems I'm fated never to find one.' And then, thinking of Goldman's, added, 'Or lose it again when I do.'

'Big Jessie's getting married. Have you heard?'

'No. Who to?'

'Some chap she met at the jigging. A sheet-metal worker from over Shieldhall way.'

'God help him for taking her on.'

'Exactly what we all said.'

They rode for a little while in silence, the tram rattling and swaying. Schoogling they would've called it.

'You should've told me about those two,' Nellie said, a little further on.

Babs pulled a face. 'How could I, Nellie? She was aye like a red rag to a bull where you were concerned.' Then, giving a sudden grin, 'Let's be nasty and hope she's marrying a right sod who beats hell out of her every week.'

Just like I married, thought Nellie bitterly. Well, at least one thing was certain. Jim Biles would never beat her again.

He'd been a bastard in his day. But by God he'd paid for it. And would continue to pay.

But even the grim satisfaction gave her no real comfort.

'A real smashing film,' said Babs as the lights came up for the interval. 'Now how about an ice cream?'

'If you can afford it.'

'Relax, you're out with your auntie,' replied Babs, causing Nellie to smile.

As Babs excused her way down the row of seats a man came on stage in front of the curtains.

'For those of you who don't know me, I'm Mr Nisbit, the theatre manager,' he explained. This news was greeted by several catcalls.

'I can see I've got some fans in tonight,' he said, which raised a laugh. 'As you're well aware, it's Friday night, therefore I'd like to introduce, for your entertainment, our guest singer Miss Moira Tinning. A big hand for Miss Tinning please, ladies and gentlemen!'

It had been so long since Nellie had been to the pictures she'd forgotten that at weekends in the larger town cinemas there was often a singer in the interval. It was a tradition that went back as long as she could remember.

'She's not bad,' said Babs rejoining Nellie and handing over a tub of ice cream.

Nellie agreed. Moira Tinning had a pleasant voice indeed.

'She's not a patch on you though.'

The idea came to Nellie like a thunderbolt from the blue. 'What did you just say, Babs?'

'I said she's not a patch on you. I think you've got the best singing voice I've ever heard.'

Nellie leaned forward to stare at Moira Tinning with renewed interest, her mind suddenly churning with ideas.

It wasn't a bad idea at all, and certainly one worth thinking about she decided as, having concluded her spot, Moira Tinning walked offstage to a warm round of applause.

The lights dimmed and the second feature started. But Nellie's mind was elsewhere.

She lay in bed listening to Jim snore. Her bed was a

fold-down one that she made up every night over by the window, which was about as far away from him as she could get in that room.

She hadn't shared a bed with him since he'd come home from hospital. Nor would she ever again.

Would she have the nerve to stand up in front of several hundred people and sing, she asked herself. She wasn't sure, but she thought so. Singing in front of people had certainly never bothered her in the past. But then, they had always been small groups, friends and relations. Going out in front of a mass of strangers would be a different matter entirely.

For a start, Glasgow audiences could be downright vicious if they didn't like you. She could remember one poor woman being pelted with all manner of things and all because she'd gone off key. On the other hand, of course, if Glasgow audiences took to you there was no one like them for warmth and appreciation.

Money, she thought. How much did someone like that Tinning lassie get paid? It must be fairly decent, surely? Perhaps even enough to take her and Jim off the parish.

God how she loathed and detested having to report every week for her money. They always succeeded in making her feel like a beggar or a parasite. That contemptuous look of the man who handed the money over. The way he had of looking down his nose at her, as though she was a bad smell suddenly wafted in his direction.

And always, always the feeling that she was some-how trying to put one over on them. That she was lazy, work-shy. And that they were, self-righteously, having to support her because of it.

And she did have a good voice. No doubt about that. The voice of an angel her da had always said. She made up her mind. She would have a go at it. After all, what did she have to lose? Nothing at all.

In the morning she would go round to the music shop and buy some sheet music. She couldn't really afford to, mind you, but it would have to be done. The sort of songs she knew weren't at all what would be required. And if she was going to have a bash at this she might as well do it properly.

The other problem was that she literally didn't have anything decent to wear, not having bought anything new since Jim's losing streak started. She'd have a word with Babs. Babs might have something she could borrow, or even give her.

Her head was spinning with plans when she finally fell asleep.

She was despondent. This was the fifth picture house she'd been to and so far no one even bothered to lis-ten to her.

'We're already fixed up, hen,' one of them had said. Two of them had said, 'Sorry,' and the fourth, had kept her waiting over half an hour before finally going off somewhere for the rest of the day, leaving her sitting there like a fool. Had he forgotten her, or was he just being nasty? She suspected the former, but she could be wrong.

'I'd like to see the manager please,' she said to a woman cleaner.

'Down that passage there and third door on the right,' the cleaner replied.

She knocked.

'Come in!'

He had a kind-looking face, she thought. 'Are you the manager?' she asked.

He laid down his pen and studied her. 'I am. What can I do for you?'

'I'm looking for a job singing at the weekend intervals. Have you anything going?'

'Not at the moment.'

Her heart sank. Another blank.

'But I'll listen to you and if I like what I hear I'll take your name and address in case something comes up. I'm afraid that's the best I can do.'

Well, at least she was making some progress, she thought. He was the first to show even a flicker of interest.

'Will I sing here?' she asked.

'In a wee room like this?' he laughed. 'No, I want to make sure you can hit the back of the circle.'

Once out the room she followed him down the corridor to a door that took them into the auditorium. They walked down to the front row of the stalls where he indicated a flight of steps running up the side of the proscenium arch that would take her on to the stage.

'Give me a minute to get up to the circle. I'll shout from there when to start,' he said, and, turning, strode away.

Once on stage she put down her handbag, but kept hold of her music. That for confidence more than anything else. There obviously wasn't going to be a pianist to accompany her. But no matter, she was used to singing on her own.

She stared out over the huge expanse of red plush, a sea of it, she thought. The walls were cream and gilt, further adorned in places with murals of Far Eastern scenes. High above was a glass dome that looked like it needed a good clean.

But what impressed her most was the sheer size of the place. It was so huge from up here, a veritable cavern.

'Are you ready?' the manager's voice bellowed from the back of the circle.

'Yes!' she shouted back.

'On you go, then!'

The song she'd chosen, thinking it appropriate for the occasion, was a number called 'At The Moving Picture Ball'.

Nervously, she began to sing, her voice hesitating but sweet.

She watched a couple of cleaners come in at the back of the stalls, rattling buckets, mops and brooms and talking to one another.

One of the cleaners laughed, then the other, the second having just delivered the tag line of a joke.

God Almighty! Nellie thought. She was accustomed to rapt audiences, not this sort of treatment. Well, she'd better get used to it, she told herself. For there would be a lot of it if she landed a job as an interval singer.

When she was finished she took a bow the way Moira Tinning had done. Up at the very back of the circle the manager had the graciousness to clap. She appreciated that.

The cleaners were now going about their business of sweeping between the seats. They hadn't once glanced in her direction.

She went back down into the auditorium and waited for the manager.

'Very good,' he said coming up to her. 'And clear as a bell.'

He ushered her back to his office where he sat behind his desk.

'Have you done this sort of thing before?' he asked.

'No.'

He raised an eyebrow. 'In that case you were even better than I thought. And you've got charisma. That counts for a lot.'

Nellie wondered what charisma was.

He took up his pen. 'Name and address?' he asked, carefully writing it down when she gave it to him.

When he'd filed that in his drawer he rose and, leaning across the desk, shook her hand. 'If anything comes up, I'll be in touch.'

At the door she turned to thank him but he was already lost in a sheaf of papers he'd started to read.

She closed the door quietly behind her.

It was six weeks since she'd done the rounds of the town picture houses and she was still as short of a job as ever. She sat gazing morosely into the fire.

'How about a cup of tea?' Jim demanded from his bed.

He was becoming more and more demanding of late. And petulant, too. 'In a minute.'

She glanced at the clock. Six o'clock on a Saturday night. All the young people would be home getting dressed ready to go out. God, how she envied them.

It was so incredibly boring being stuck at home for most of the day. Housework, cooking, body rubs, emptying Jim's pot – it was driving her crazy.

It might not have been so bad if she'd been a reader. There was a library nearby. But books had never really interested her all that much. Nine times out of ten she never got past the first chapter.

She started when the knock on the door came. She hoped it was Babs come visiting.

But it wasn't. It was a lad about fifteen years old.

'Are you Mrs Biles?' he asked.

'Aye.'

'Mister McRae sent me. He wants to know if you'll do the night?'

She was lost. 'Who's Mister McRae and what does he want me to do?'

'Who's Mister McRae!' the boy exclaimed, rolling his eyes upwards. 'He's only the manager. And he wants you to sing.'

Excitement gripped her. It had happened. At long last it had happened!

'Manager of which picture house?' she asked patiently.

'The Kingsway in West Nile Street.'

The Kingsway. Her mind flew back. Of course! He was the nice man who'd been the first to ask her to sing. He'd sat at the back of the circle while those dreadful cleaners made such a racket. She'd never even found out his name. Up until now.

'Well, will you come?' the lad demanded.

'What time does he want me there?'

'As soon as you can make it. The first singing interval's at five past eight.'

'Tell Mister McRae I'm on my way,' she said.

'Do you want me to wait for you?'

'No, no. You go ahead. I'll have to change first.'

'Aye, well don't take too long about it.'

She indicated her pinny. 'You don't expect me to go on and sing in this do you?'

He gave her a cheeky grin. 'See you again shortly then,' he called, running down the stairs.

For a moment or two she stood in the doorway, a dozen things tumbling through her mind at once.

'Who is it?' Jim shouted from the kitchen.

She ignored him. First thing to do was to get someone to look after him while she was out.

She hurried up the stairs, praying as she went that Myra Finlayson was home. From time to time, Myra had looked after Jim.

She rapped Myra's door and waited impatiently. She rapped again almost at once.

'Aye, what is it, Nellie?' Myra's mother asked, opening the door.

Nellie quickly explained her mission and Myra's ma said yes, Myra was home and would be only too happy to look after Jim while Nellie went into town.

'She'll be down in a minute,' Myra's ma said to Nellie's already retreating back.

'Right!' Nellie called back up the stair.

'What the hell's going on?' Jim demanded querulously when she burst into the kitchen.

She told him in a few short, terse sentences as she pulled her dress off and quickly washed herself at the sink.

Jim knew about her trying to get a job as an interval singer, and in fact had been rather scathing about it, asking if she didn't think she wasn't getting a wee bit above herself? After all, you had to be good to stand up in front of all those folk. The implication being that she wasn't as good as she thought she was.

She was making up when Myra chapped the door. 'Come away in,' she said, ushering Myra through. She'd just managed to afford the make-up out of their meagre income. It had lain new and untouched in its box against this very moment.

When her make-up was complete, she slipped into the dress Babs had given her and which she'd virtually remade. It fitted well and looked a treat.

It was the work of a moment to put on her best pair of shoes and get into her coat. Picking up her music she stuffed it into her pocket.

'Will I do?' she asked.

'You look right smashing,' said Myra.

Jim grunted.

'I'm away then,' she said. 'Wish me luck!'

'All the best, Nellie!' Myra called out as Nellie flew from the house. Jim remained silent.

Standing waiting for the tram Nellie thought of Myra Finlayson, or the daftie as some of the crueller children in the neighbourhood called her. She was a little mentally backward or eleven pence ha'penny in the shilling, as a neighbour had been heard to remark, but she was a good soul of whom Nellie was genuinely fond. Kind, warm hearted, nothing was ever too much trouble for Myra if you asked her to help you.

At nineteen, Myra was unemployed and had been since leaving school. Although she looked a lot simpler than she actually was, the natural slow way she had about her made employers reluctant to give her a job.

After all, why take a chance when there were far brighter sparks clamouring for work, any work, when it became available?

Nellie often thought of her as poor Myra upstairs.

'I'm glad you could make it, Mrs Biles,' Mr McRae said when she entered his office. A glance at his watch confirmed there was still plenty of time before the first singing interval.

'Were you let down by your regular?' she asked.

He picked up a letter from his desk and waved it

at her. 'This came in this morning but I never got round to reading it until early evening. Says she's had a better offer from elsewhere and has to start there the night, which, of course, well and truly lumbered me. Till I remembered you, that is. Now how about a cup of tea before you go on?'

'Yes please,' she replied. She had butterflies in her stomach and her brain felt as though it had been partially anaesthetized. She kept thinking of the huge audience awaiting her in the auditorium. She knew it was huge because she'd seen the HOUSE FULL signs on the way in.

Mr McRae left her to order the tea, returning with a bespectacled man whom he introduced as Charlie, the pianist.

She shook Charlie's hand, noticing her own was trembling slightly, and handed over her music which he glanced at briefly.

'Just give me the nod when you're ready,' said Charlie. Adding kindly, 'And if you're a wee bit nervous don't worry. *I'll* be following *you.*'

'Thank you,' she said gratefully.

The tea came which she drank, glancing up at the clock on the wall every few seconds as she did so.

Charlie had gone off with her music leaving her with Mr McRae, who immediately became immersed in work at his desk. On the stroke of eight he looked up and smiled.

'Ready?'

Despite the tea her throat was parched dry. When she returned his smile her muscles were so tense she thought her face must surely crack. 'Ready,' she replied.

She followed him down the same red plush corridor that she remembered from her previous visit. Only this time instead of going into the auditorium he took her up some back stairs which eventually led them into the wings.

She stared up in awe at the enormous silver screen upon which the film's credits were rolling. Then the screen was blank and the red curtains were swishing closed.

'I'll introduce you, your cue to come on stage being when I turn to face you and start clapping my hands. Got that?'

'Yes,' she whispered in reply.

'Good luck then.' Leaving her he strode on to the stage.

'Ladies and gentlemen. Tonight I have a special treat for you . . .'

Panic was going to engulf her she thought. She suddenly wanted to turn and run. Jim was right, she was mad thinking she could do this. It all looked so easy from out front. But here, waiting to go on, it was a different matter entirely.

And the audience, they terrified her. They were

like some great animal waiting to pounce and devour her once she stepped on stage.

The insides of her legs had started to tremble and her heart was beating nineteen to the dozen. She knew with certainty that when she opened her mouth to sing nothing would come.

And then, suddenly, the moment had arrived. Mr McRae was clapping and smiling at her. Still she hesitated, completely terrified. He was beckoning to her now.

Forcing herself she put one foot in front of the other, she smiled fixedly as she headed for centre stage; she felt like she was walking to her own execution.

There seemed to be millions of faces staring at her. Some expectantly. Others bored. Others talking amongst themselves.

And the heat! It hit her like a wave. Perspiration burst on her head and back. She clasped her hands together so that the audience wouldn't see how badly they were shaking.

She glanced down at Charlie in the pit, giving him the nod that she was ready. She opened her mouth and, completely surprising her, words came out. She sang:

'I fetch his slippers,
Fill up the pipe he smokes,

Join up with gyppers,
Laugh at his oldest jokes;
Yet here I anchor –
I might have had a banker –
Boy! What love has done to me!'

She came off to find Mr McRae waiting for her.
'How was I?' she asked.

'Fine. Not bad at all.'

'Can I have the job then?'

'Let's go to my office and talk money.'

As they left the wings, the audience was still applauding.

That night in bed she couldn't sleep. At long, long last she had a job! And what she would be getting per week and for only working the Friday and Saturday nights, would be fractionally more than what she was getting now from the parish. Come Monday morning she would take the greatest delight in going round to see the buggers and telling them she didn't need their money any more.

She thought again of herself out on that stage, singing. Going on had been sheer murder but once started she couldn't remember enjoying anything more. Especially after the first number when she knew the audience was for her.

What had happened to her up on that stage was a

strange feeling to describe. Like love, almost. Yes, that was it. Love.

A shiver ran through her. She hadn't experienced those sort of emotions since . . . since Frank.

She couldn't wait for next Friday night to come round so she could get back out there again.

'Boy! What love has done to me!' she sang softly in the darkness.

5

The moment she'd first clapped eyes on Brownlee, which was only ten minutes previously, she'd thought him a hard-eyed sod. What he was saying to her now confirmed that opinion.

'I'm sorry, Mrs Biles, but that's it. A fortnight's notice as from tomorrow,' he said coldly.

Brownlee was sitting behind what, up until that week, had been Ronnie McRae's desk. Dear Ronnie who, three-and-a-half years ago, had hired her as an interval singer. Nor had she missed a Friday or Saturday since.

'I know you're very popular with the audiences,' Brownlee went on, 'but now that I've taken over, I feel it's time for a change. A fresh face and voice so to speak. I'm sure you'll have no trouble finding employment elsewhere.'

Ronnie McRae's transfer to the Odeon, Paisley, had been a surprise to them all, Ronnie included. But, as he himself had said, it was company policy to move their managers about and he had been at the Kingsway a long time.

He'd also said to Nellie that he'd happily give her a job at his new picture house, an offer she'd had to refuse as Paisley was just too far to travel.

The entire theatre staff had clubbed together to give Ronnie a going-away present. They'd all had enormous respect and liking for him. He'd been a gem.

'What about Charlie?' she asked. She was referring to Charlie Muchan, her accompanist.

'He'll be going as well,' Brownlee replied.

Nellie nodded to herself. An era had come to an end. Glancing up at the clock on the wall she saw it was time for her to get ready for her first spot. Muttering her excuses she left the room.

She went out onto the stage to rapturous applause. Over the years she'd become a great favourite. Later, when she came off, there were tears in her eyes.

'You got the bullet as well?' Charlie asked when they got together for their usual cup of tea between spots.

'Aye.'

Charlie offered her a cigarette and they both lit

up. They'd become very friendly since that first night she'd appeared on the Kingsway stage. A number of times she'd been over to his house to have tea with his wife and weans.

'So what'll you do now?' he asked.

The thought of having to go back on the parish made her cringe inside. But that was what she'd have to do unless she found another job. The pound a week the Masons paid Jim from their Benevolent Committee, the award being made shortly after she'd started work at the Kingsway, was hardly enough for them to get by on.

'Start chapping doors again,' she replied morosely. 'I've got a fortnight so I can hope and pray I'll land something in that time.'

'One of the other town picture halls might have an opening for a singer,' Charlie suggested hopefully.

Nellie shook her head. 'They're all happily fixed up at the moment, I know that for fact.'

Nellie thought of Big Jessie, married and moved away to another part of Glasgow. With Jessie gone from the Bastille she could always try there again. But she doubted that would be any good. She'd been branded a bad worker. And that sort of thing wasn't forgotten.

Thinking of Harrison's made her think of Babs, also married, and very happily, to Phil Drummond. They had a wee boy called Ian who was the spit of his da. She smiled to think how even yet Babs still referred to Phil on occasion as her *Fate*.

Charlie frowned and stroked the left leg of his spectacles, a gesture of his when thinking.

'I did hear something the other day which might interest you,' he said.

'Oh, aye?'

'Do you know the Palace Theatre down in Jamaica Street?'

She nodded.

'Well, they're opening a new show there shortly and I heard they'll be auditioning sometime soon for lassies who can sing and dance.'

'What do you mean by sometime soon?'

'Next week I would imagine.'

The Palace was a well-respected variety theatre which put on many of the country's best acts. Harry Lauder himself had played there.

Nellie had been to the Palace twice, both times years ago before she'd met Jim.

To go into the professional theatre was an attractive thought and one which very much appealed. The singing she could cope with, of that she had no doubt. But what about dancing? She had no experience of that whatever.

'What's the pay like?' she asked.

He shrugged. 'Fair I would think. Certainly more than you're getting here.'

Then that was another big plus in its favour. And her current wage at the Kingsway wasn't all that bad either. Ronnie McRae had upped her money four times since taking her on. Each time he'd done so, he'd said she was more than worth it as her presence nearly always guaranteed a full house.

She would certainly have a go she decided. After all, she had nothing to lose – and everything to gain.

'I'll make enquiries tomorrow,' she said, excitement in her voice. 'Now what about you?'

And over the rest of their tea they talked about Charlie's prospects.

She was nervous, but not to the point where she was shaking, as she entered the Palace's stage door. She was confronted by an empty cubicle.

What to do now? she wondered. Best wait. There was a board with papers tacked to it on the wall facing the cubicle, which she crossed to and idly started to read.

When there was a noise behind her she turned abruptly to bump into a tiny, bald-headed man who went spinning to crash against the cubicle.

She was appalled. 'Oh I'm awful sorry!' she said as the stage doorkeeper came dizzily to his feet having nearly fallen.

She put her arm round his shoulders – he was considerably smaller than she – and said, 'Are you all right?'

'I think so,' he replied, shaking his head.

'I am sorry.'

'Not your fault. Mine. I should have been looking where I was going,' he said, taking her in for the first time, his eyes brown and warm.

He was wearing some sort of cologne Nellie decided, finding it strange and amusing. She'd never met a man before who wore cologne. In Govan that would've been thought of as jessie. A man wouldn't have dared wear it, even had he wanted to.

Oh well, she thought. This was the professional theatre. She was sure a man wearing cologne wouldn't be the only strange thing she'd come up against.

'Are you here for the auditions?' the man asked.

'Aye. The Palace Ladies.'

Reaching into the cubicle he picked up a sheet of paper which had a list of names on it. Against some of these names were tick marks.

'Name?' he asked.

'Nellie Biles.'

He looked up at her, smiling. 'You're early.'

'Better that than late.'

'True,' he said, replacing the piece of paper in the cubicle. 'I'm on my way past the stage. Will I take you through?'

'Please.'

Blonde and marvellous green eyes, he thought. Unusual combination for this part of the country. Quite a looker, too. 'Follow me then,' he said, and led the way.

On arriving at wooden swing doors the doorkeeper stopped and, turning to her, said, 'Through these, through the doors facing those and if you go down left you'll find a boy called Sandy. He'll look after you.'

'Thank you very much.'

'Good luck.' Giving her a salute with his hand he went on his way.

The stage itself was far bigger than she'd imagined. There was clutter everywhere. And everything looked so grimy!

She made her way down left past several bits of scenery – and how tawdry they were up close – to where a young boy was standing beside some ropes which were tied off and running upwards to disappear behind a catwalk above. On stage, a girl was singing, but she couldn't see her because of the intervening scenery.

'I'm Nellie Biles,' she whispered to the boy.

He consulted a sheet of paper, a copy of the one in the stage doorkeeper's cubicle. 'You're early,' he said.

'Yes.'

He chewed on a finger before making up his

mind. 'All right, I'll put you on next. Although you really should wait your turn.'

'Sorry,' she replied apologetically.

'That's all right,' he grinned.

The singing stopped and a male voice could now be heard on stage.

'That's the stage director, Roderique Mansell,' Sandy said. He pronounced Mansell with the emphasis on the first syllable, *Man*-sell.

Roderique? Nellie smiled to herself. She'd never heard of a man being called that before. He must be foreign, Spanish perhaps.

'You done this before?' Sandy asked.

She shook her head.

'That's good. They like new faces.'

There was the sound of dancing from the stage which went on for about a minute. Then Mansell's voice said, 'Fine, dear. You'll do.'

'Thank you ever so much, Mister Mansell,' a female voice answered. The girl came off smiling gratefully.

'Next!' Mansell bellowed.

The girl gave Nellie an encouraging smile as they walked past one another. 'Good luck,' she whispered.

Nellie went through a door in the scenery to emerge blinking into harsh white light which shone from above and out front.

'Name?' Mansell snapped.

'Nellie Biles.'

'Tell me, *briefly*, about yourself.'

Help, Nellie thought as she spoke. What sort of man was this?

Beside Roderique Mansell, a little cologne was nothing at all. His hair was dyed, and his face made-up. He stood staring at her, one hand on hip, the other dangling delicately by his side. When she'd finished speaking he came up close to her. 'Let me see your legs,' he said.

She pulled up her skirt to above the knee. 'Higher, dearie. Don't waste my time,' he snapped.

She pulled her skirt up to mid-thigh.

'Hmmh!' he said, sounding none too pleased. There was something sly about him, something sly and calculating. And something else she couldn't put her finger on. Then, suddenly it hit her! Bitchiness. That was it. It was a look she'd seen on certain women but never on a man before.

Turning abruptly, Mansell jumped over the foot-lights into the auditorium. He strode up the aisle to a seat roughly halfway. 'Sing!' he commanded.

She didn't like him at all. And what's more, she was sure he didn't like her. But she put that from her mind as she sang, concentrating on where she was and why. When she finished she knew she'd never sung better.

Mansell sat staring at her for a few seconds, then,

coming to his feet, he strode toward the stage. When he was standing beside her he held out his arms, indicating she should come into them.

'Waltz. You lead,' he said.

It confused her to dance without music, and even more because she had never led before. She did her best, however, surprised that she finished as well as she had.

Mansell stood, posing, regarding her. Finally he said, 'No. You're quite wrong, darling. Sorry.'

She was dismissed.

Sandy smiled apologetically when she rejoined him. 'Too bad,' he said.

She watched a dark-haired girl enter the same door she'd just come through. She couldn't believe she hadn't got the job. In her mind she'd convinced herself – oh so stupidly she could see now – that she had. It was a terrible disappointment that she hadn't.

At the stage doorkeeper's cubicle she stopped to light a cigarette. She would stand here and smoke it, until she calmed down and the threat of tears had passed.

'Well, did you get it?'

She turned to find the wee, bald-headed door-keeper smiling at her. She shook her head.

His smile faded, replaced by a frown. 'Why not?'

'Mister Mansell said I was quite wrong.'

'And that was all?'

'Yes.'

He studied her afresh. She was a knockout. Mansell should have grabbed her. Not only beautiful but talented, too. He'd heard her singing from the back of the auditorium. He knew then why Mansell had turned her down. He simply didn't want someone around who was prettier than he was.

It was time Mansell was taken down a peg or two. He had been getting far too big for his boots of late.

Suddenly he wasn't so nice and cuddly anymore. His eyes glinted as he said in a steely voice, 'What's your name again?'

'Nellie Biles.'

'You come with me, Nellie.'

She wondered what the doorkeeper wanted with her, but she followed him unquestioningly. It hadn't been a request. It had been an order.

Sandy, who'd been sitting, jumped to his feet the moment the doorkeeper and Nellie appeared.

'Sorry. You're not for us,' Mansell's voice said on stage.

The dark-haired girl who'd followed Nellie through the set door reappeared to shrug. 'Can't win them all,' she quipped in a tired, dispirited voice.

'Stay here,' the doorkeeper said to Nellie, and strode on to the set.

'You didn't say you knew him. Did you tell Mansell?' Sandy asked in a whisper.

'Know who?'

'Him. Mister Spira.'

'You mean the doorkeeper?'

Sandy grinned. 'He's not the doorkeeper. He *owns* the bloody place.'

'Oh!' was all Nellie could think of in reply.

On stage, Roderique Mansell was glowering at Baz Spira. 'She'll unbalance the line,' he said.

'Nonsense.'

'She's too different from the rest. She'll stick out like a sore thumb.'

'Then put her in the middle. Make a centrepiece of her.'

'Baz, I know my job –'

'And I know mine. What's more, I employ you. And you'll do as I say.'

'And if I don't?'

'There's a train leaves for Liverpool every evening. You can be on tonight's.'

Mansell winced. Though he came from Liverpool he much preferred having people believe he came from London.

Roderique Mansell swallowed hard and thought even harder. This was a good job and well paid. Jobs like this, even with his vast experience, weren't exactly ten a penny. And it suited him to stay in

Glasgow for the time being. He'd found a 'friend' in one of the other shows whom he was dotty on.

'Well?' Baz Spira demanded.

'As you say, you're the boss.'

'And don't you ever forget it, Roderique,' Baz replied. 'That Biles girl is exactly the type to have in the show. She's got class, quality. A line consisting of a dozen like her would make the Palace Ladies the best in Scotland. Britain even.'

'I'll build the line round her then,' Mansell replied.

'Now you're talking.'

'She isn't a particularly good dancer.'

'Then teach her. What do you think I pay you for?'

Mansell nodded. 'I'll do my best.'

'That's what I expect from you, same as everyone else in this theatre, including myself. Their best.'

Baz Spira strode off set to find Nellie waiting for him, eyes shining. She'd overheard every word.

'Thank you,' she said.

'That applies to you too,' he said, his eyes suddenly twinkling mischievously. 'Your best.'

She watched Baz Spira waddle away, then turned her attention to Sandy who was asking her address.

A few seconds later Mansell, his eyes blazing, brushed past. The look he gave her told her she'd made an enemy.

*

'That's marvellous news, Nellie,' said Myra Finlayson clapping her hands together.

Jim looked out sourly from the bed. 'And what about me? Who's going to look after me?' he demanded. 'For I sure as hell can't look after myself all day while you're rehearsing. Or at nights even while you're doing the show.'

It was a problem Nellie had already given considerable thought to. 'Myra,' she said, choosing her words carefully, 'how would you fancy the job of looking after Jim on a permanent basis? I couldn't pay you very much, but I'll give you what I can. And of course you'll eat here as you'll be cooking for Jim.'

Myra's homely features broke into a smile. She enjoyed looking after Jim. It made her feel useful.

'I'd like that fine,' she replied.

'Jim?'

'It's time for my back rub,' he grumbled.

'I'll do it,' said Myra quickly.

Nellie put the kettle on. It was settled.

Her call was for ten o'clock which was an awful late start she thought. But she certainly wasn't complaining. At the stage door she found the real doorkeeper in his cubicle.

'I'm here for rehearsals,' she said.

'Name?'

'Nellie Biles.'

He checked her name against his list, grunting when he found it. 'Away through to the green room,' he said.

The green room wasn't green at all and she wondered why it was called that. There were a number of easy chairs, one of which she sank into after greeting the other girls.

By one minute to ten the full dozen girls who would be making up the Palace Ladies were present. On the stroke of ten Roderique Mansell breezed in.

He was dressed like something straight out of the pictures, Nellie thought. He might have been Ali Baba or Sinbad the Sailor.

Sandy was with Mansell. When he saw Nellie he gave her a fly wink.

Nellie was one of five new girls, the other seven having been in the previous show. Starting with a pretty, dark-haired girl called Liz, each of the dozen was asked to stand up and introduce herself. When that was completed Mansell spoke for a good ten minutes about the theatre, the forthcoming show and himself. But mainly about himself, continually preening and striking poses as he talked.

When he was finally finished he said, 'Right, we'll have coffee now and then up to the dressing rooms to change into rehearsal clothes. We'll be rehearsing on stage.'

Rehearsal clothes? Nobody had mentioned

anything about those to her. What were they?

'Mister Mansell?'

He gave her an irritated look. 'Yes?'

'I'm afraid I haven't brought any special clothes to rehearse in. I wasn't told.'

He waved one hand in the air. 'Of course you weren't told, darling! One presumes you know. I mean, it's absolutely basic, isn't it?'

'I'm sorry,' she mumbled. She could feel her face redden with embarrassment.

'I knew you were going to be trouble. It's written all over you.'

She wanted to snap back at him, but, wanting the job, decided to keep her mouth shut.

'Huh!' said Mansell, turning to the other girls who were milling round a tray of coffee that Sandy had brought in. 'Here's one doesn't even know enough to bring rehearsal clothes with her! Talk about amateur.'

Several of the girls tittered, and Nellie blushed even more. How could she not have thought of it?

Mansell was enjoying making Nellie squirm. 'If you didn't bring rehearsal clothes I don't suppose you thought to bring flats with you?' he asked maliciously.

She hadn't a clue what flats were. And seeing her expression Mansell guessed as much.

'Ballet flats, darling. For dancing.'

'No,' she said.

'Not much use to us then this morning, are you, darling?'

She bit her lip.

'It's all right, Mister Mansell,' one of the girls piped up. 'I've got a spare set of clothes upstairs and her feet look about the same size as mine. She can borrow my old flats.'

Nellie flashed the girl a grateful smile.

Irritation crowded Mansell's face. His sport had been cut short. Snapping his fingers he said, 'On the green in five minutes,' and signalling to Sandy to follow, sauntered from the room.

Nellie crossed straightaway to the girl who'd saved her further embarrassment, and perhaps her job even. 'Thanks,' she said.

The girl stuck out a hand. 'I'm Margo, as you probably heard when I introduced myself.'

'And I'm Nellie, as you probably heard.'

'We'd better get upstairs and changed. When Roderique says five minutes he means just that.'

There were two dressing rooms, each long and narrow. Nellie chose a place beside Margo. From now on that would be her dressing table.

The rehearsal clothes turned out to be black tights and an old sweater. The flats were black leather with a very thin sole. As they changed Margo told her where she could buy flats of her own.

'He certainly seems to have got his knife into you,' Margo whispered, not wanting any of the other girls to overhear.

Nellie told her about the audition and the fact she'd been hired at Mr Spira's insistence.

'Nice man, Mister Spira,' Margo said. 'Not like that Mansell. I don't think he's got a soft spot in his body, unless it's his head'

'What about the rest of the people in the show? When do they come along and rehearse?' Nellie asked Margo. It was lunchtime that day and they were sitting in a cafe having coffee and a sandwich.

'They don't rehearse. At least not with us,' Margo explained. 'They're all self-contained acts which come and go from week to week. You see, we, the Palace Ladies, are the only constant thing about the show. And even then we change our routines every month. An act will be booked for a week or a fortnight, perhaps, fulfil the engagement and then move on.'

'Oh, I understand.'

'The show will run for ten months and then the theatre will go dark for two.'

'Dark?'

'Close down. There's never any business in those two months which include the fair anyway.'

The Glasgow Fair was the fortnight when, apart

from insurance offices, banks and food shops, the entire city closed down and went on holiday. For those who could afford holidays, that was.

Margo went on, 'Mister Spira usually goes away for the first month. When he comes back a new show is put together and the whole thing starts all over again.'

'How many shows have you been in?'

'This is my third. And I hope not my last.'

It was the opening night and five minutes had been called. Nellie was trembling with excitement. She couldn't wait to get out there.

'Nervous?' Margo asked.

'A little. But I'm looking forward to it.'

A natural performer, Margo thought. She'd come to that conclusion in rehearsals as, grudgingly, had Mansell. Not only was Nellie a natural, but she was also different, special in some way. She stood out from the rest of the line, not only because she was physically outstanding but also because she had, as Ronnie McRae had once told her, charisma.

They were in the wings waiting for the curtains, or the rag as Mansell called it, to open.

Nellie noticed a small man in baggy trousers, wearing an old coat and battered hat, with a pipe stuck in his mouth. His eyes were droopy, as though he was half asleep.

'Who's that?' she asked, nudging Margo. She'd never seen this man around before.

'Who?'

'Him over there.'

Margo glanced across at the man who gave her a wave. 'He's the top of the bill,' she said.

'Will Fyffe?'

'The same.'

Nellie stared in awe at the man who was a household name in Glasgow. Only Harry Lauder was bigger.

'He always stands in the wings for the first few minutes of every performance,' Margo said. 'He does it to get the feel of the audience before going on stage.'

'Go curtains!' a voice said.

Nellie took a deep breath as the curtains swung apart. Then she was on stage dancing, smiling – all teeth and tits darling, as Mansell put it – at the audience.

One of the differences between this and interval singing was that here the auditorium lights were off so she was staring into a black hole. On cue she started to sing, her voice soaring above the others. She was in her element.

'Very good, girls! Very good!' Baz Spira said, coming into the dressing room. He was carrying two bottles of champagne.

Several of the girls squealed with delight as a popped cork bounced off the ceiling. The second one flew across the room like a bullet.

It was the first time Nellie had tasted champagne. She liked it. There was an elegance about it which appealed.

'You did really well tonight,' Baz said to her. 'Justified my faith in you completely. But then, I knew you would.'

He moved on down the row of dressing tables, congratulating each girl in turn. Then he was gone.

Nellie cleansed her face of the heavy make-up, 'slap' Margo called it, then changed out of her costume into her street clothes.

Margo kept her make-up on but toned it down a little. 'Going out on the town with my chap,' she confided.

'Where to at this hour?' Nellie asked. It was well past pub closing time, and other places, like restaurants, would be shut as well. Glasgow was notorious for going to bed early.

'There are places. Clubs and the like. If you're in the know,' Margo replied.

'What sort of clubs?'

'Drinking. Gambling.'

Nellie was surprised. It was the first time she'd ever realized that type of establishment operated in Glasgow. It just showed, she reflected, how naïve and innocent she was about certain things.

'What about you?' Margo asked.

'Och, I'm away home to my bed.'

'Well, you've got a man to go back to after all.'

Nellie slowly lit a cigarette. She'd told Margo about Jim, and the fact that he was paralysed, but not that their marriage was a complete bust and she could hardly stand the sight of him.

What a relief it had been, these last few weeks, to be out of the house and away from him. She felt like she'd been reborn after all those months of being with only Jim day in and day out, and all those nights in between.

'What does your boyfriend do?' she asked.

'He's a chartered accountant.'

Nellie was impressed. An accountant was awfully grand. 'Are you going to marry him?'

Instantly, Margo's face fell. 'We have a problem there. I'm a Catholic, you see, and he's not.'

That Margo was a Catholic surprised Nellie, she didn't look like one at all.

Involuntarily Nellie thought of Frank Connelly, experiencing the same dull ache she did every time she did so. 'Why don't you go abroad together?'

'We've thought of that, but it's not really possible. He's too well established here to give it up. And then there's the matter of qualifications wherever we went.'

Nellie took her friend's hand and held it gently. 'Do you love him?'

'Aye.'

'Then God help you.'

Later, at the stage door, Nellie met the boyfriend, a chap called Bob Copeland. He was in his late thirties and very well spoken. She liked him.

'Have a good time,' she said, waving them on their way.

Catholics and Protestants, she thought as she trudged toward the tram stop with her coat collar turned up against the drizzle. The foundation of all her own problems. How much heartbreak had that bigoted division caused? She hated to think.

Poor Margo, she could have cried for her.

It was one night several months later that she was standing at the tram stop when a car drew up. The window rolled down and a voice said, 'Nellie?'

'Hello, Mister Spira,' she replied in surprise.

'Can I give you a lift?'

'I'm going to Govan.'

The door swung open. 'That's not too far out of my way.'

She got into the car, which smelled deliciously of polish and leather. 'This is awful kind of you.'

'Nonsense. It's a pleasure.'

They drove toward Eglinton Street, turning right

for the Paisley Road. 'How are you enjoying being in the theatre then?' he asked, breaking the awkward silence.

'I'm loving it.'

'Aye. That comes across.'

'I take it that's a compliment.'

'Oh indeed!' he laughed.

'Have you owned the Palace long?' she asked.

'A little over twenty years. And to be quite accurate I don't actually own it. My wife does. The twenty years is how long we've been married.' He stared intently at the road ahead. 'The theatre was part of her dowry,' he added.

'Pardon?'

He smiled in the darkness. 'We come from old families and keep our old customs. We still believe in dowries and arranged marriages.'

Nellie was intrigued. 'Was your marriage arranged, then?' she asked shyly.

'Yes.'

'And didn't you mind?'

'No. Why should I? It's the custom. Besides, I was getting a theatre which was something I'd always wanted. I've always been in the theatre, you see. Started off backstage at twelve and graduated to about every job there is. Flyman, dayman, I've even operated the limes. I've also worked as a booker down in London to get to know that side of things.

Good job it was, too. I thoroughly enjoyed it.'

'You make your marriage sound so . . .' She stopped herself, thinking she might well be going over the mark.

'Go on.'

'You might think it cheeky, especially coming from an employee.'

'Go on anyway. I'm interested in what you have to say.'

She said hesitatingly, 'You make it sound rather clinical if you don't mind my saying so. A bit cut and dried.'

'And it is,' he replied. 'But as I told you, that's our way. At least for some of us.'

There was silence for a while and then he said, 'Are you really so shocked?'

'I suppose I am.'

'You believe the only good marriages are those based on love?'

'Yes,' she said.

He chuckled. 'Love's a transient thing. It comes. It goes. And when it's gone you may well be left with someone totally unsuitable. Our way, well . . . you work at it. To begin with you work at respecting your partner and with that respect love often comes later. A love built on solid, secure foundations that will endure to the grave.'

'And what happens if that love doesn't come?'

'Then you have the respect to fall back on. And that in itself can make a worthwhile marriage. Believe you me.'

She was dying to ask him if he'd come to love his wife, but did not dare. 'And if there's no respect?' she asked, thinking of Jim.

Baz shrugged, glancing sideways at her. 'Then you make the best of what you've got, I suppose.'

Nellie couldn't help wondering what Babs – and surely there was no bigger romantic than her with her *Mr Right* and *Fate* – would have made of this conversation. Been completely scandalized, no doubt.

Again they drove in silence, she lost in thought.

'A penny for them?' he said eventually.

She roused herself. 'Oh, no, I couldn't!'

'Come on. I won't be offended.'

'Are you sure?'

'Certain,' he replied, laughter in his voice.

'If you got the theatre as part of your wife's dowry, then what did she get in return?'

'Good practical question,' he said. 'You know, you Scots and we Jews have a great deal in common. We're both very practical people. What did she get? Two things. I come from a better family than she, although a poor one as opposed to her rich one, so she was improving herself and any family we had together. She was also getting someone who could run her theatre for her. And when I say run it, I mean make a success of it. As I've done, I think I might say.'

'So you have some families who have better –' she groped for the right word.

'Ancestry?'

'Yes. Ancestry than others?'

'That's correct. My wife marrying me was the same as, well, you marrying someone of the landed gentry.' He added suddenly, 'I hope that hasn't offended *you*?'

'Not at all,' she laughed. 'I'm working class through and through. Rough as they come.'

'Working class, maybe. But not rough,' he said quietly.

She smiled. And then started to give directions for her turning.

Baz Spira slipped into the back of the auditorium just in time to catch the end of the vent, or ventriloquist, act which he could tell right away the audience hadn't enjoyed.

It was a new act that he'd booked in for a week. Well, good as the act was, and he knew it was artistically good, it seemed Glasgow audiences just didn't like it. The man wouldn't be getting an extension or a return engagement.

Then the vent was off and the Palace Ladies were on. And immediately the whole atmosphere changed.

Where minutes before the audience had been muted, restless, they were now alive, leaning forward in their seats to hear and see just that little bit better.

The girls were good, Baz thought. But no better than previous lines. What was different about this particular line was one girl in particular: Nellie Biles.

No doubt about it. She had magic on stage. As soon as she stepped on the boards she lit up, creating an aura, an electricity about her. She had the ability that all great artistes must have, to draw the audience to her, to empathize with them.

She shone in the middle of the line like a jewel, her dazzle so strong, she completely dimmed the glamour of those around her. It was high time he promoted her. Brought her on a bit. Not too quickly – which could destroy her – but at the right pace.

He had a potential moneymaker here. He knew that with certainty. All his theatrical instincts and hard-won knowledge screamed it.

He would give Roderique Mansell his instructions after the show.

'I've never known any girl get as many flowers as you,' said Margo. The curtain was just down a few minutes and the line had returned to their dressing rooms to change into their street clothes.

Nellie shook her head in amazement at the huge

bunch of red roses she now held in her hand, which had been waiting for her on her dressing table.

'Who's it from?' Margo asked eagerly.

There was a card upon which was written: Please accept this small token of my esteem. Humbly yours, Edward Tallis.

'Never heard of him,' said Nellie.

'Well he must be worth a bit if he can send you red roses,' said Margo.

'I suppose I'll have to take them home,' said Nellie. There were already four bunches of flowers in vases on her dressing table, all handed in back-stage by admirers. She laid the roses to one side and started to remove her slap. It had started not long after the show had opened, flowers, presents, invitations out.

The flowers and gifts she accepted, but never the invitations. The truth was, she didn't really want to know about men. Jim Biles was more than enough.

Nightly she thanked God he was paralysed and unable to come to her. Just thinking of what she'd had to endure at those hands – those terrible hands – was enough to make her skin crawl.

She might have gone out with them if she'd thought it would have stopped at conversation, a few drinks, a meal. But men were never content with just that. They always wanted more. And so she refused them all.

A few catty comments were made about the roses by several of the other girls, the ones who were jealous of her popularity, but she ignored them as she always did.

When she and Margo were ready they made their way down to the stage door where, as was often the case, they found a number of men waiting for a chance to speak to the particular girl who'd caught their eye. Of the six men there, five wanted to speak to Nellie. One of them was Edward Tallis.

Nellie, as she always did, had a quick word with each of them.

'Thank you for these beautiful flowers,' she said to Edward Tallis, a tallish, handsome man in his early thirties. The cut and style of his clothes, not to mention his accent, confirmed what Margo had guessed. He wouldn't be worrying where his next meal was coming from.

'I was wondering if I could possibly take you out tonight? Or if not tonight another night?' he asked hopefully.

Nellie smiled shyly. He seemed a nice sort of chap – and for a second she wished that things were different. 'I'm afraid I'm married,' she replied.

His face fell. 'Oh!'

'I'm sorry,' she said softly, and with Margo by her side moved on, leaving the five men staring after her.

'He wasn't bad at all,' commented Margo. 'Now, if that had been me he'd been asking, I'd have been tempted.'

'Get away with you. You're happy with the man you've got.'

'Aye,' sighed Margo. 'I suppose I am.'

'Be thankful. Believe me, be thankful.'

Margo looked at her quickly, surprised by the passion in her voice.

They parted, for Margo's tram stop was a different one to Nellie's and round the corner.

'Nellie, like a lift?'

Baz Spira didn't always give Nellie a lift. Some nights he wasn't in the theatre or went home early; others he worked on after the show was over. But at least once or twice a week, he waited for her.

'It went well tonight,' he said when she was seated beside him and they were on their way.

'I thought so, too.'

'Our audiences have really taken to you, you know.'

She smiled. 'Thank you.'

'Credit where it's due. That's what I always say.'

She decided she would give the roses to Myra Finlayson. Myra would go potty over them.

And, thinking of Myra, sighing to herself, she wondered just how long it was going to be before she heard that Jim's turn had come up for an institution bed. Still, they had warned her it could drag on.

'I had a word with Roderique Mansell before leaving tonight,' Baz said.

Nellie roused herself from her thoughts about Jim. 'Oh, yes?'

'As you know, the line starts rehearsals Monday for the monthly change of routines. Well, I've decided I'm going to feature you.'

A sense of joy and jubilation – and even of vindication – welled through Nellie. Lately, being on stage had come to mean a great deal more to her than just a job. To begin with, there had been the sheer pleasure of performing, but now the first buds of ambition had begun to grow. She had just begun to worry about what her next step up the theatrical ladder should be. Well, it seemed that step had been taken for her.

'That's . . . that's just marvellous,' she managed to say at last.

'I knew you'd be pleased.'

And she was. Oh how she was!

'Will it mean more money?' she asked.

He laughed. 'I was right about you Scots. Always the practical question. I'll put your wages up to twenty-two-and-six a week.'

Nellie thought of the roses lying on the back seat and the countless other bunches of flowers she'd received over the past months. Proof of how popular, as Baz had said only a minute ago, she'd become. Now, a man like Baz Spira didn't give something unless he was going to get a good return on it. Twenty-two-and-six sounded a lot, and it was, but if she was bringing in people just to see *her* now, and she knew she was, then how many more might she bring in when featured? That was what Baz was counting on and was why he was offering to feature her.

He was no mug Baz Spira. But, then, neither was she. And anyway what did she have to lose? For it was most unlikely he'd sack her. Fee haggling was part and parcel of this game she'd come to learn.

'Make it thirty bob and we'll shake hands on it,' she said.

He gave her a shrewd look and then nodded his head. 'Done,' he replied, extending a hand from the wheel.

This would be only the start if she had anything to do with it, she promised herself.

Only the start.

'But I've told you, I can't sing in that key,' Nellie said through gritted teeth.

'Try, darling,' Mansell replied.

'It hurts my throat.'

'Nonsense. You're just being difficult.'

The rest of the line stood watching the interchange. It had been like this ever since they'd started rehearsing the new routines three days ago.

Nellie ran a hand over her forehead, which was slick with sweat. She was almost at the end of her tether and knew it. If only he'd give her half a chance. But no. Whatever she did was wrong. Whatever was natural to her he changed. And he was revelling in it. She could tell that from the occasional smirking glint that crept into his eyes.

She was shaking inside from rage, her stomach hot and sour, an iron band of frustration gripping her chest.

She tried not to glare at him. That wouldn't improve matters, but only antagonize him more.

'From the top, sweetie,' said Mansell, shooting her a smile that was in itself an insult.

She sang:

> 'Fantasy in olden days
> In varying and different ways,
> Was very much in vogue,
> Columbine and Pantaloon,
> A wistful Pierrot 'neath the moon,
> And Harlequin a rogue.'

'Stop! Stop!' cried Mansell waving his hands in front of him. 'My God, darling, you sound like some dreadful screeching cat in a back alley!'

She fought to keep her temper under control. 'I'm aware of that, Mister Mansell,' she said sweetly.

'Oh, you are, are you. Well at least that's something. And would you mind, if it's not too much trouble, that is, telling me what you're going to do about it?'

'There's nothing I can do about it while I'm forced to sing in this key.'

'Perhaps it's the piano that's at fault as well?' he asked pleasantly.

'I keep telling you. The key is wrong for me.'

He raised an eyebrow. 'Are you now saying you know more about this than I do?'

'Of course not.'

'Well I'm glad about that,' he replied, and laughed.

She threw a despairing glance at Margo who gave her a sympathetic one in return. The man was impossible!

'I shall decide what is the correct key for you, darling. I after all, have been in the business a considerable amount of years. And this is your first professional job, isn't it?'

'Yes.'

'And what was it you were before again? Do remind us. I, for one, have forgotten.'

The majority of the line, including several of the girls who'd occasionally been jealous of Nellie, failed to respond. Like Margo, they were entirely sympathetic towards her. Mansell's behaviour, always peculiar, had become totally outrageous. Not only that, but it was making life more difficult for everyone. They were having to spend far more time in rehearsing these new routines than they would have done normally.

'I was an interval singer at the Kingsway picture house,' Nellie replied, clearly.

Mansell snapped his fingers. 'Of course! How could I possibly have forgotten that!'

Nellie was seething, her hands clenched into fists, her nails jabbing into her flesh. Whatever happened, she promised herself, she wouldn't cry. God and all his angels would descend first before she gave Mansell the satisfaction of that.

Because that was what he was after – or at least one of the things he was after. To have her in floods of tears would delight him. If she broke down that way, then he'd be one step closer to what he ultimately had in mind: to break her completely.

Mansell went on, 'So, what little you know about singing you learned amidst the rustle of sweetie papers and scraping of ice cream cartons? Not to mention the constant hum of chat. Very illuminating, darling.'

'They didn't chat while I was singing,' Nellie snapped back hotly.

'Oh, you were that brilliant, were you? I see.'

'They just listened, that's all.'

'So you say, darling. So you say.'

'Are you calling me a liar?' she asked, her voice little above a whisper.

'Heaven forbid, darling! I'm sure every word you've told us is gospel.' Having said that, he turned his back on her and tittered.

'Mister Mansell?' she asked.

He put his hand to his mouth before facing her. 'Yes?'

'Are you trying to make a fool of me?'

'I don't have to, darling,' he laughed. 'You do it so marvellously all on your own!'

The end of the tether had suddenly been reached. She could take no more of this dreadful man. The anger rose from the pit of her belly to engulf her in a red mist. Reason fled as she advanced on him, her hands extended as talons. There were a few moments when it was Big Jessie's face she saw instead of his.

His laughter died when he saw the look in her eyes. Starting to back off, he had only gone several paces when she leaped at him. He shrieked as her nails raked his cheeks.

Catching her on the chin, he sent her sprawling. 'You witch!' he howled, frantically trying to staunch the flow of blood from his lacerated cheeks with a fancy cotton handkerchief. 'I'll have you fired for this!'

She lay, exhausted on the stage where she had fallen, knowing it was true. You couldn't do what she'd done and expect to get away with it. Despair replaced her anger. She should have been able to control herself, but the provocation had just been too great. She stared up at Mansell, contempt and loathing written across her face. She wanted to come up with some stunning reply. Some shaft of wit that would leave him completely speechless.

She couldn't think of a single thing.

'She just attacked me for no reason at all. The girl's completely mad!' Mansell said, his voice rising hysterically.

Baz Spira was sitting at his desk, where he had been doing some paperwork when Mansell burst into his office. He eased himself back in his chair to stare at Mansell. 'Go on,' he said quietly, a small frown creasing his forehead.

'We were in the middle of rehearsals and I had been telling her how dreadful she was when suddenly she launched herself at me. Doing this with her nails.' He came closer so Baz could get a better view of his damaged cheeks. 'Vicious bitch!'

'Nasty,' said Baz. This didn't sound at all like the Nellie he knew. 'And there was no provocation?'

'None at all. Just can't take direction that's all. Thinks she knows better than anyone else. And her not five minutes in the business either. I tell you, Baz, she's got to go, and today. It's either her or me.'

'Yes I can see that,' said Baz quietly. He sighed. 'Well, you'd better send her in.'

Mansell hurried off to the green room where all the girls were waiting. 'The big boss wants you,' he said to Nellie, smirking. Then, clapping his hands, 'Come on girls, back to work. The fun's over and we've a lot to do today if we're to make up lost time.'

'Enter!' Baz shouted when she timidly knocked at his door.

She came in to stand before him. There was defiance in her eyes and her mouth was set with determination.

'Sit down,' he said, and when she'd done so, offered her a cigarette. 'Now tell me about it, Nellie,' he said when they'd both lit up.

He listened in silence, his eyes never leaving hers. He was certain, even before she was halfway through her story, that she was telling him the truth: that Mansell had been making life hell for her in rehearsals.

Nellie ended up by saying, 'But don't just take my word for it. Ask the girls.'

'Good idea,' he replied. 'Verification puts it beyond doubt.'

'I'm sorry about this, Baz. I feel I've let you down.'

'Wait in your dressing room and I'll send for you again shortly. In the meantime, ask Bunty to pop along and see me.'

Bunty was the oldest girl in the line, and one of the best liked.

She found the line rehearsing on stage. Coldly she said to Mansell, 'Mister Spira wants to speak to Bunty right away.' Without waiting for a reply, she made her way to the dressing room where she sat morosely staring into her mirror and playing with the rabbit's foot Margo had given her to dust off facial powder.

Bunty confirmed everything that Nellie had told Baz. As did Liz, Hannah and Margo. He didn't see the need to interview any more girls; the evidence against Mansell was overwhelming.

Mansell entered the office rubbing his hands and smiling. Both his cheeks had plasters on them. 'Yes, Baz?' he asked breezily.

'You lied to me,' Baz said bluntly.

'I beg your pardon?'

'You've been riding that girl unmercifully ever since rehearsals started.'

'That's just not true! Are you taking her word over mine?'

'Yes,' replied Baz quietly.

'This is preposterous!'

'No, you are, Roderique,' somehow making the word Roderique sound completely ridiculous. 'You said yourself, either she goes or you do.'

Mansell's eyes were suddenly veiled. He hadn't expected this at all.

'I want you out of the theatre within the next fifteen minutes. And if you report to the stage door tonight at the half hour I'll ensure your money is there waiting for you.'

Mansell was rocked. He had fired people often enough, but this was the first time it had happened to him. It wasn't a pleasant sensation at all.

'You won't find a better stage director than me,' he said.

'Balls!' shouted Baz. 'My instructions to you were to polish Nellie's technique and you interpret that as trying to destroy her. You call that being a good stage director?'

'What technique?' sneered Mansell. 'She doesn't know what she's doing half the time or why she's doing it.'

'A good stage director would have tried to teach her. Not carry out a vendetta against her.'

'Is that what she said?'

'That's what *everyone* said.'

Mansell reached up to touch one of his torn cheeks. 'I should have known you'd take her side,' he spat.

'Please close the door behind you on your way out, Mister Mansell,' Baz said, managing to get a wealth of meaningful innuendo into the word mister.

Mansell slammed the door. Baz chuckled.

'You're wanted on the green,' Margo said to Nellie.

'Who by?' although she knew. It was time to be given the sack.

'Mister Spira. And guess what?'

'What?'

'Mansell's been given the heave-ho.'

Nellie's face lit up. That was something at least. She rose from her dressing table and slipped her arm through Margo's. 'Well come on, let's get it over with.'

Baz had decided he would take the rehearsals himself, continuing to do so until the new routines had been worked into the show. The replacement stage director would take rehearsals for the new routines the month after.

'Right,' he said when Nellie and Margo appeared. 'Let's get on with it.'

Nellie stared at him.

'Something wrong, lass?' he asked.

'Me, too?'

'Yes.'

If the other girls hadn't been present she'd have taken him in her arms and given him a big hug. God Almighty! At the sweetie factory even to lay your hands on someone, no matter what the rights and wrongs of it were, meant instant dismissal. She'd come to think very highly of Baz Spira since he'd hired her. But now she positively worshipped him.

'You were rehearsing this particular song, I believe?' said Baz, holding up some sheet music.

'That's right.'

'Then we'll take it from the top in the key Mansell wanted you to do it in.'

She stared at him, unable to believe her ears.

'Well? What are you waiting for?'

She sang, genuinely doing her best, but it was hopeless.

'Hmmhh!' he said thoughtfully when she'd finished. 'You know Mansell was right. You do sound like a cat wailing in a back alley. Quite dreadful.' He suddenly burst out laughing. 'So shall we do it properly then?'

Nellie joined in the laughter with the other girls.

For a moment there he'd really had her going.

On the opening night of the new routines Nellie and the rest of the line – but Nellie in particular – were a huge success. Baz Spira wasn't surprised at all.

Making his way backstage after the show had rung down, he was thinking that Mansell had been right about one thing. Nellie's singing was magnificent. But if she was to go further, she would have to have lessons. A natural singing voice was one thing, fine for occasional use, but if she was going to hammer it night after night after night, then she needed to learn how to use it properly so that she didn't damage it.

He was fulsome in his congratulations to the line. When he had a chance he beckoned Nellie outside into the corridor.

'You were absolutely splendid,' he said, holding both her hands.

'You wouldn't lie?'

'In your case, Nellie, there's never any need to because you're never less than excellent. Now listen to me closely. I have a proposition I want to make to you.' He put his arm round her shoulders and walked her a little further down the corridor. 'I've been giving a lot of thought to you since I took over the rehearsals,' he went on. 'And I've decided to offer you a three-year contract. Apart from the guaranteed work, the advantages to you are twofold: first, I'll pay you when the theatre's dark, the same wages as when you're working; second, I will pay for singing lessons with a woman I know in the West End. What do you say?'

'How about yes?'

He smiled. 'That's what I'd hoped you'd say. I have other plans for you, but those will come in time. When I think you're ready. All right?'

She kissed him on the cheek. 'Thank you. I appreciate this.'

He smiled at her with more than his usual kindness. 'You're going to go far, Nellie. I sensed it the first time you auditioned. And I'm rarely wrong about these things.'

She closed her eyes, thinking how marvellous it would be to be up there, top of the bill. That was something she was coming to want more and more. Top of the bill. Number one. The very thought sent thrills racing up and down her spine.

'Now,' he said, heading her back to the dressing room, 'how about you and I celebrating by going out and having a little supper together?'

She tensed instantly, instinctively.

'Why are you suddenly looking at me like that?'

Supper one night, and then another – and then what would be expected of her?

'I have to get home to my husband,' she mumbled, suddenly feeling gauche and awkward.

'It was only an invitation to supper. Nothing else, Nellie,' Baz said quietly.

'Of course. I didn't think otherwise.'

What a strange one she was, he thought. She must be very much in love with this husband of hers although, from what he had heard, the man never came backstage or to any of the shows. A complete mystery man by all accounts.

'Perhaps another night,' he said, and giving her a curt nod walked away.

Nellie bit her lip as she watched him go. She knew he'd felt slighted, put down. And after him being so good to her.

'Oh hell,' she muttered to herself.

She ought to have been on top of the world, but having had to rebuff Baz had somehow soured the evening for her.

She slid her hatpin into position and then patted a stray hair into place. She was off to Miss McLeish for her Thursday lesson. She went twice a week, Tuesdays and Thursdays.

'Everything's all right now, Myra?' she asked *en route* to the door.

'Oh, aye, Mrs Biles. You don't have to worry about me,' Myra replied cheerily.

Jim was sitting up in bed sipping tea. 'This you off gallivanting again?' he asked.

'I'm going for my lesson.' As well he knew.

'That's what I said. Gallivanting.'

'You wouldn't call it that if you had Miss McLeish putting you through it.'

'Nor would Miss McLeish,' he replied quickly. The look in his eye left no doubt about exactly what he meant.

She looked at Myra but it was way over Myra's head.

It amazed her that Myra could voluntarily put up with Jim, who with every passing month became more whining and petty. It was time to write about the institution again, she thought. Surely something must be coming up soon! She prayed it would, for she'd never rest happy in this house till Jim Biles was out of it for the last time.

'I'm off then,' she said, giving Myra a final wave.

Outside she made her way to the tram stop. She enjoyed her lesson days. She'd learned a great deal in the four months she'd been taught by Miss McLeish who was a thin, bony stick of a woman with iron-grey hair and a will to match.

To begin with it had been a rude awakening to learn there was a great deal more to singing than just opening your mouth and letting the sound come out. She was thankful to Baz for suggesting the lessons. She could see now that if she'd gone on the way she had been, she might well have had no voice left in a few years' time.

She hadn't seen all that much of Baz since the night she'd refused his supper invitation. He was pleasant enough to her when they did meet. Always a smile and a kindly word. But not once had he brought her home after the show in his car.

*

Nellie tapped Baz's door. She was presenting herself as instructed.

'Come in!'

She found him smoking a cigar, almost hidden by a pall of blue fug.

'Sit down, Nellie,' he said, half rising. When she was settled comfortably he offered her a cigarette.

'You've had me dying with curiosity all afternoon,' she said.

He laughed. 'I thought I might.'

'So what's this all about then?'

'Your featured spots are doing very well. But of course you know that.'

She sat studying him, waiting.

'I've been keeping an eye on you and I must say I'm impressed. You just get better and better.'

'Thank you.'

'Now, the thing is, we're coming up to the end of the season when the theatre goes dark for two months. Nellie, when the new season opens, how would you feel about doing solo spots?'

Slowly, she took a deep breath. It was exactly what she'd been praying for.

'Miss McLeish assures me you're up to it. And I think so too,' he said. He went on, 'What I envisage is this. In the past only the Palace Ladies have been the permanent fixture in the show. Right?'

She nodded.

'What I'm thinking of now are you and them, sometimes working alone and sometimes together, as two permanent fixtures. So, in some spots you would be on your own. In others with them. And in yet others they would be on their own.'

It was perfect, she thought. Absolutely perfect. 'What about billing?' she asked.

'Nellie Biles and the Palace Ladies,' he replied. Then grimaced. 'We're going to have to do something about Biles. It's a dreadful name.'

She couldn't have agreed more. 'That's all right as long as my name is in bigger type than Palace Ladies,' she bargained.

He pretended to consider that, but it was precisely the billing he'd always intended. 'Deal,' he said.

'What about my material?'

'You and I will choose it together. And I will rehearse all your solo spots with you. That is, if you don't object?'

'Not at all. I couldn't ask for better.'

'Now – money,' he said, chuckling inwardly when he saw the gleam come into her eye. 'Fifteen pounds a week and I won't haggle.'

Fifteen pounds! she thought. It was a fortune!

'And I mean it when I say I won't haggle. That's my first and final offer.'

'Then that's what it'll be.'

He sat back in his chair. 'Now, what about a

name?' he mused aloud.

'Thompson's my maiden one,' she suggested.

He shook his head. 'Too ordinary. We want something with a bit of zing, a bit of stardust in it. A name that's different, which makes *you* different.'

Nothing different was coming into Nellie's mind at all. The only names she could think of were very ordinary ones, the names of Glasgow folk she knew and had grown up with.

Baz considered all sorts of possibilities, rejecting each in turn. What he really needed he decided was something that fitted Nellie's own personality. Something instantly identifiable with her.

Blonde? Green eyes? A sort of wildness about her. Although often very placid in appearance, when on stage, or emotionally aroused, there was a wildness about her which was unmistakably attractive.

On the other hand, there was that childlike quality about her which made you want to protect her from the harshness of the world.

A curious combination, he thought. And suddenly he had it. 'Nellie Wildchild,' he said, puffing smoke at her.

'Wildchild? What sort of name's that?'

'Theatrically, a damned good one,' he replied.

'Nellie Wildchild,' she said aloud, tasting it in her mouth and testing the sound of it on her ears. Well, it was certainly different, she couldn't deny that. And it would look good up on a bill. The sort of name to make people stop and stare and wonder.

'I like it,' she said.

So did Baz Spira. It had a money sound about it.

The theatre had been dark for two weeks and Nellie was bored to tears. How she missed the Palace and the other girls. But most of all she missed the audience: the rapport she had with them; the love they gave her.

Baz was abroad with his wife and family and wouldn't be back for another fortnight. She was missing him, too, in a strange and unexpected way.

She was still attending Miss McLeish twice weekly, which made the only break in the long dreary days.

She stared out of the window. The sun was bursting the skies and Glasgow was sweltering. It was funny, she thought, Glasgow just never looked right when the sun was shining on it. Glasgow was a dark city, built for rain, smoke and bitter cold. Sunshine made it look unnatural, almost obscene.

'Here we go then,' said Myra, pushing a wheelchair through the door. They'd had the wheelchair a few months now, and Myra often took Jim out and about. They kept it in the hallway where Myra and Nellie were for ever falling over it.

Jim glared at the wheelchair. 'I'm not getting in that damned thing again,' he declared stubbornly.

'It's beautiful out,' coaxed Myra.

'I don't care.'

'It'll do you good to get some sun about you. Look at your face. I've never seen anything so peely wally.'

'The wheelchair hurts me,' complained Jim.

Myra glanced across at Nellie. This was an allegation he'd made before, but one which they could neither prove nor disprove.

'But you always feel so much better after, despite what you say,' Myra said reasonably.

'It's a torture device, that's what it is. A torture device,' said Jim, eyeing the wheelchair with hostility.

The patience Myra had with Jim continually amazed Nellie. Myra put up with a lot more than she'd have been able to. 'I'm having no arguments,' said Nellie in her best matter-of-fact tone. 'You're going out for a breath of air, and that's an end to it.'

'I hate going out! I hate it!' Jim protested.

'But why? You always come back in a much better mood.'

'Because –' he glared at her. 'You wouldn't understand.'

'Try me,' Nellie urged him gently.

'I can't stand the pitying stares and comments that are made,' Jim burst out sullenly.

Both women paused to look at him.

Jim wiped his forehead with his one good hand. 'I

mean, look at me, the state I'm in compared to what I used to be like. It's bad enough for me to have to see myself. But for them to see me as well is just too much. "Poor man", they say. And "Isn't it a shame?" "To think what he used to be like, such a big strapping fellow".'

'I know full well what it's like for folk to say things about you,' Nellie said softly. 'It's not nice at all. But you learn to live with it. You have to. What else is there?'

'For me there's an alternative. I don't have to go out.'

'Ach, why cut off your nose to spite your face? You enjoy being outside. I know that. So if they bother you just forget about the people out there. Ignore them if you have to.'

'And if they want to stop and talk?'

'Myra can tell them you're in a hurry, or that you're not up to it. You don't have to talk if you don't want to.'

His eyes took on a faraway look and he turned to Myra. 'Would you take me down to the river? I'd love to see the Clyde again.'

'Then that's where we'll go,' she said, getting his things ready.

'And can we stay there a wee while and watch the big ships go up and down. I'd like that fine.'

Nellie and Myra exchanged a look and a smile. So

much had she hardened her heart against Jim that it surprised her when he did or said something that moved her. 'You two have a nice walk,' she said as she left the room, brushing just the smallest trace of moisture from her eye.

'Baz, how are you!' she yelled, and rushed into his arms.

He responded by squeezing her tight and then planting a wet kiss on her cheek.

He pushed her out to arms' length and swept his eyes over her. 'The break has done you good. You look raring to go.'

'And I am! God, I've been so bored!'

'I also. But don't tell anyone. You're not meant to be bored with your family.'

She laughed. It was marvellous seeing him again, and being back in the theatre. Smelling once more the now so familiar smells. Greasepaint, paint, size, ropes; the hundred and one odours which combined make the one peculiar to the backstage of a theatre.

Arm in arm, they went through to the green room where the other girls and Robert McLaughlin, the new stage director, were waiting.

McLaughlin would be rehearsing the line for those routines it did on its own. Baz would be rehearsing those it did with Nellie, as well as Nellie on her own.

Everyone had coffee and chatted, the new girls in the line being introduced and made to feel welcome. Margo was back, which pleased Nellie, but Bunty had left to get married. Liz had decamped to try her luck down south.

'All right, girls, on the green!' called Baz. It was time to start work.

On their way to the stage, he said to Nellie, 'Know all your songs?'

'Backwards.'

He laughed. 'I'll bet you do.'

And in that mood they started rehearsing the new show, Nellie's second – and first as a solo artiste.

A few days later Baz sat halfway up the stalls, listening to Nellie go through one of her numbers which she was attacking with verve and gusto, his thoughts wandering. While abroad he'd missed her tremendously, spending much of his time daydreaming about her. By the end of the holiday he knew he'd come under her spell completely. Hook, line and sinker.

Through all the years of his marriage, he had never been unfaithful to his wife. He had toyed with the idea several times, but in the end no attraction had ever been strong enough to tempt him fatally.

Nellie, however, was a different matter. It wasn't simply her body that he wanted; it was her. The person inside. He actually cared for her.

Wildchild, it suited her perfectly he thought. His wild child. His. But that was only as far as business was concerned. Every night she returned to this husband to whom she was so loyal. So what chance did he have? A small, fat, balding middle-aged man? None at all. He was old enough to be her father – and that was the way he should think of her.

But he doubted he'd be able to.

Nellie had them in the palm of her hand and knew it. Her voice rose, soaring like an eagle. A crashing wave of sound one moment; a silken caress the next.

In this particular number the words were immaterial. It was the music that was important. A shrewd choice by Baz, she now realized, as it showed her off superbly.

Also something of a gamble as it wasn't at all the usual sort of fare for a Palace audience. But if the one on this opening night was anything to go by, that gamble was going to pay off: they were lapping it up as cats do cream.

When she came to the end of the number she raised her hands, holding that position for a few seconds while the thunder of applause grew, then very slowly curtsied, hands coming down to her sides as she did so. The applause became an uproar; people standing, whistling, shouting 'encore!'

She rose and blew them a kiss, then turning on her heel, ran into the wings.

But they wouldn't let her go. Again and again they called her back to take bow after bow.

Even the old pros said they'd never seen anything like it.

The opening show was over. Nellie sat numbly at her dressing table staring into the mirror. She couldn't believe what had happened tonight was real.

She touched her face. Was this the same Nellie who'd worked at the sweetie factory? Who'd lived for so many years in grey despair because she'd been unable to get a job? The same Nellie who was just like any other Glasgow lassie?

Well she was, and she wasn't. She was the same person, but only to a certain extent. For since coming into the theatre she had changed: imperceptibly at first; more so of late.

Tonight she'd stepped out from amongst the ranks to become somebody, somebody important. From now on Glasgow was going to hear a lot more of Nellie Wildchild. She knew that was a certainty; she could feel it in the pounding of her heart.

'Come in!' she called out when there was a knock on the door.

Baz entered, his eyes shining. 'What can I say that the audience didn't? You were superlative, Nellie.

Superlative! Real alpha plus.'

'It's thanks to you, Baz. It was inspired of you to choose the operetta number.'

'It pleases me I had a little hand in it. But that doesn't detract in the least from you, my girl. The talent, presence, looks are all yours.'

'Thank you,' she said softly, finding herself blushing.

He took her hand and kissed the back of it. 'To a long and successful working relationship together.'

Before Nellie could reply there was more knocking at the door. 'It's open!' she shouted.

In burst Margo and some of the other girls in the line, come to offer their congratulations and be congratulated in return. Bob Copeland, Margo's boyfriend, was with them, waving an opened bottle of champagne.

Thinking something of a party was about to develop Baz made his excuses and left. He had other people in the show to call upon.

During the space of the next half hour more people came and went, till finally Nellie was left on her own. Margo and Bob had gone on somewhere, as had several of the other girls and their boyfriends. Suddenly it was all very anti-climactic. The champagne bubbles had burst. The elation died.

Slowly she started removing her slap, staring at herself in the glass. When her face was clean, she slowly began to comb her hair.

Everyone else was out having fun with someone they cared for, making their plans and swapping their dreams. All she had to go home to was Jim. Jim and her memories.

She started when there was a tap on the door. 'Come in!'

Baz poked his head round the door. 'Still here? I thought you'd be long gone by now.'

'I usually am, but tonight . . . well, I just fancied a little sit on.'

Immediately he was concerned. 'Everything all right?'

'Fine. Couldn't be better.'

'Husband in tonight?'

'No.'

Queer he thought. Definitely queer. 'Aren't you going out anywhere?'

She shook her head, suddenly feeling tearful. Probably the aftermath of the evening's excitement.

He smiled kindly. 'Still all keyed-up. Is that it?'

'I suppose so.'

He looked undecided for a few moments, and then seemed to come to a decision. 'Rachel, my wife, was supposed to be coming tonight but had to cry off at the last minute with a migraine. Suffers terribly from them, you know.'

'No, I didn't.'

'She regularly gets shocking heads. Often has to

shut herself away in a darkened room for two, some-times even three, days and nights. A dreadful business. Anyway, the point is that she and I were intending to go out for a meal after the show. A little private club I know where I'm a member. Now the thing is, the table's booked. How about you joining me?'

She remembered the last time she'd rebuffed him. How upset he'd been.

And, in truth, she desperately wanted to go on somewhere. To complete the evening. Not just go home to Jim's whining and her bed by the window.

'Won't Rachel mind?' she asked.

'Not in the least. She'll be only too happy that I didn't waste the booking.'

'But shouldn't you be getting back to her?'

'When she's got one of her migraines no one's allowed near her. All she wants is absolute peace and quiet with no disturbance, and that includes me.'

Nellie laid down her brush, her mind made up. 'I'm game if you are,' she said. Then added quickly, 'One thing, Baz.'

'What's that?'

'No strings?'

'None at all, Nellie. You're just going out for a meal with your uncle Basil.'

'Basil!' she exclaimed. 'I never knew that's what Baz was short for!'

'Well now you know.'

'But why Baz? Childhood name?'

'No. My own invention. For survival.'

She frowned. He'd lost her.

'Could you imagine being called Basil in Glasgow? My life would have been a continual misery if I hadn't had the bright idea to disguise it.'

Nellie laughed, relaxing for the first time in weeks.

'How long will you be?' he asked.

'Give me ten?'

'You've got five.'

She took fifteen.

She had never been in a club like this before. It was extremely opulent, exclusive and discreetly expensive.

The table they were ushered to was lit by a candle in a crystal holder. The cutlery was King's and silver, the tablecloth crisp, creamy and best Irish linen. To say Nellie was impressed would be an understatement.

Baz ordered champagne, Krug, snapping at the wine waiter to go ahead and pour when the man asked if he'd care to taste it.

'Pretentious nonsense that,' he said when the waiter had gone.

'I thought it was the done thing to taste wine before accepting it?'

He smiled. 'You shouldn't have to taste. Your eyes should tell you what's what. First, look at the clarity of the wine. If it looks right then ninety-nine times out of a hundred it is. Secondly, when the first glass is poured look at its level. If the bottle's been corked you'll see bits of the cork floating around. That bottle you have a right to send back.'

Nellie was fascinated. 'Do the bits of cork make all that much difference?'

Baz laughed. 'Not really. But at the prices you pay in a place like this, you may as well get what you're shelling out for. At home, I wouldn't bother too much about the cork. Mind you, I'm only a simple imbiber of wine. The real connoisseurs I'm sure wouldn't agree with me.'

Nellie stared around her. She couldn't help but compare the sophisticated, genteel atmosphere of the room they were in with Govan where she'd been born and bred. Govan of the dirt and grime and violence which had a permanent smell about it. An unwashed, acrid smell.

Not that she was ashamed of Govan in any way. Not at all. She was proud to come from there. But a place like this showed her how much more there was in the world. What better things there were to be had than what she had been taught to expect.

She ordered a veal dish which came covered in the most gorgeous, rich cream sauce. Brought up on the simplest of cooking, she wouldn't have believed that food could taste like this.

'Like it?' Baz asked.

She closed her eyes. 'Hmmh!'

It pleased him that she was pleased. It also gave him a great deal of pleasure to be able to entertain her this way. It took no brains to guess that this sort of lifestyle was completely new to her.

They finished the champagne and he ordered another, despite her protests. 'I'm the one who's got to be careful because I'm driving,' he argued.

Nellie was relaxed and thoroughly enjoying herself thanks to a combination of the alcohol and Baz's witty, and very clever, conversation. He would've made a marvellous comedian. It had been a long time since she had laughed like this. Since she had had any fun.

'What's wrong, Nellie? You've suddenly gone quiet,' he said.

'Just thinking about someone.'

'Your husband?' he asked shrewdly.

She gave him an astonished glance. 'Do you read minds as well?'

'Not quite.'

She lit a cigarette while he trimmed and lit a cigar. He regarded her through blue smoke.

'Want to talk about it?' he asked quietly.

'He's paralysed down one side and he's lost half

his leg on the other. He was hit by a motorbike.'

'I'm sorry, Nellie. I had no idea,' Baz said, reaching across and touching her hand.

'I suppose you, like the girls, have been wondering why he never picks me up or comes to see the show. Well now you know.'

She saw the sympathetic look on his face and gave a half smile. 'Don't think I'm cut up about it in any way. I'm not. He's been a right sod all the time we've been married. He means nothing at all to me, Baz. Less than nothing.'

'You must have loved him when you married him, surely?'

'Love? No. He got me on the rebound, and I thought he was a decent fellow. I thought I could make something of a go of it. But it's true when they say you don't know a person till you're married to them. I found that out to my cost.'

She didn't know why she was telling Baz all this. Except that, for some reason, she wanted to. It felt right somehow to confide in him.

'And who did your husband get you on the rebound from?'

She told him then about Frank Connelly, although not mentioning Frank by name, and how her father had forced her to break off their engagement.

Her voice was low and level as she recounted how

Frank had then run off abroad before she'd been able to get word to him that she'd wait for him till he was time served and they could elope.

She told Baz of Jim and how he'd seemed such a decent chap. Till the wedding day itself when she'd found him with her cousin Marj. And how that night in the hotel room, filled with drink, he had raped her.

Baz sat very still while Nellie told him about herself. He'd known there was something. He'd sensed it. And now here it was all coming out. It hurt him deeply to hear what she'd been through.

'And when I saw it was Jessie he was with I just blew up and ran at them,' Nellie said a little later. 'She saw me coming and took to her heels. Jim stayed long enough to knock me into the gutter and then he went after her. But it was foggy and he wasn't looking where he was going. Neither was the motorcyclist.'

He wanted to take her in his arms and comfort her. Her eyes had taken on a hollow, far-away look that tugged at his heart. In that look he could see quite plainly the years of despair behind her.

She looked so vulnerable he thought. But he knew that underneath the vulnerability there was tempered steel. Forged there by herself for survival.

When she was finished he called for brandies which they sat drinking in silence.

Finally she said, 'Sorry if I've spoiled your evening.'

He shook his head. 'You haven't, Nellie. I'm glad you told me all this.'

'It just seemed the right thing to do.'

'I'm flattered. But tell me, won't this Myra worry that you're late home?'

'She knows I'll be all right. That I can take care of myself. She mind the extra time looking after Jim? She'd happily do it twenty-four hours a day if asked.'

He parked outside the grey, stone tenement where she lived. 'I enjoyed our little supper,' he said.

'I enjoyed it also.'

They paused to listen to seagulls screeching overhead. An unusual occurrence late at night. Something must have disturbed them.

'Good night, Baz,' she said, opening the door, but on an impulse, leaned back and kissed him on the cheek.

'Good night,' he said as she banged the door shut behind her.

He watched her vanish up the gas-lit close. A slim, blonde-haired figure, young enough to be his daughter.

He stared in distaste at the tenement, at the dirt and graffitti and greyness of it.

He was going to have to do something about where she stayed, he decided. She certainly couldn't go on living here. Although he'd seen worse, and lived in it. In the old days in Russia. One day the family had been rich. The next, all they had were the clothes on their backs and a few small items they'd managed to pick up as they ran. And they'd been the lucky ones. For they'd escaped with their lives.

Even now, and though he'd been so young at the time, he could vividly remember the Cossacks descending on their village. The screams, the shouts of fear, of agony. The fires, the milling horses, the man with no head. The woman speared to a tree. The mangled mess that was a child who'd been trampled to death. The long march out of Russia into Germany where they'd lived for a few years before moving on to Scotland because there was no work in Germany and his father had the promise of a job in Glasgow.

Dear Glasgow. In Russia they'd never even heard of it. But to Glasgow they'd eventually come and here they'd settled.

Although hardly the prettiest city in the world, he had come to have enormous affection for Glasgow. It had great character.

He put these thoughts from his mind as he brought his attention back to Nellie. Knowing her better now, he felt even more for her than he had before.

Nellie was approachable. He was certain of it. But

it would have to be done very, very carefully if he was going to succeed. She was repressed, frightened of men. He would have to nurse and coax her out of herself. A little at a time until the closed flower was fully open again.

She liked him. He knew that. But fancied him? Well he was certainly no oil painting but he did have a lot to offer, not the least of which was the power he held over her career. And, as he well knew, power is one of the greatest aphrodisiacs there has ever been.

Nellie found Myra and Jim playing snap. 'Sorry to be so late,' she apologized.

'How did it go?' Myra asked anxiously.

'Marvellously. Couldn't have been better.'

'Oh, Nellie!' said Myra clapping her hands together. 'I'm so pleased for you.'

'Where have you been to this hour?' demanded Jim.

'Mister Spira's wife was taken ill before the show. He'd booked a table to take her out, and as she couldn't make it he asked me instead.'

'That was nice of him,' said Myra.

'I thought so, too.'

'I'll bet he's after you,' snarled Jim.

Nellie swung on him. 'Don't judge everyone by your own low standards,' she replied coldly.

'I'll away, then. See you in the morning. Usual time,' said Myra, and hurried out of the house to run upstairs.

Jim watched Nellie while she undressed. 'I don't want you to go out with this Spira fellow again,' he said.

Nellie stopped to turn and stare at him. 'What did you say?'

'You heard. I don't want you going out with him again.'

'I'll go out with whom I please.'

'I'll have you remember you're still a married woman,' he hissed angrily.

The sheer hypocrisy and audacity of the man made her want to laugh out loud. She regarded him in amazement. 'Being married didn't stop you seeing whoever you wished as I recall,' she said.

His eyes blazed with both anger and frustration. His face had gone red and blotchy.

'Are you sleeping with him?'

'No. Not that it's any of your business.'

'I don't believe you.'

'I don't give a damn whether you believe me or not.' She turned her back to him.

Hungrily he stared at her, desperately wanting her.

He felt so useless lying here. So utterly and totally useless. What had happened to him just wasn't fair, he screamed inside his head for what might well have been the millionth time. God, to be doomed to be like this for the rest of his life. There could be another forty, even fifty years like this; trapped inside this paralysed husk. Still wanting, and capable of having, a woman.

Get a grip, Jim, he told himself. Just get by day to day. Don't contemplate the future. For there was madness in that. Insanity.

He stared at this woman he'd married. It was still difficult to believe that she'd gone on the stage; that she was making such a success of it. Who would have credited it? His Nellie.

He'd tried to imagine her on stage, but couldn't. The image just wouldn't come somehow. Perhaps he just didn't want it to.

And the money she was making! That was incredible. Way and above anything he'd have been able to bring home if he'd still been working.

Mind you, he might have been making something like it had he succeeded in getting his own shop. And who knows? He might have done by now. There was no telling.

But now he'd never own a shop. Or go to work again. He was reliant on her for everything: the food he ate, what clothes he wore, the roof over his head, the fire in the grate.

He should have been thankful but all he felt was resentment.

She was in her nightclothes now, turning her bed down, her hair a cascade of yellow dancing on her shoulders.

Going on the stage had changed her, he thought. Given her more self-confidence, assurance. Not only that but her tastes had changed. Clothes, make-up, conversation even, all altered. She'd also acquired poise to compliment her natural elegance, an elegance that was in itself greatly enhanced of late.

Nellie paused in the process of lighting her last cigarette of the day. His eyes were fastened on her, malevolent with hate. He'd come to hate her as much as she hated him.

'I'll suggest to Myra she take you out for a hurl in your wheelchair tomorrow,' she said.

'It's your wheelchair. You bought it,' he replied.

'For you.'

He turned his face away. 'I don't want it.'

He was becoming more and more petty, she thought, but what else could you expect with him cooped up like this day after day.

'I'll buy you –' she started to say.

'I don't want you to buy me anything!' he yelled back. 'Not a damn thing!'

She shrugged. 'Suit yourself. It's no skin off my nose.'

'The sooner you get me into an institution the better.'

'Well don't think I'm not trying. You'll be in just as soon as there's a bed available for you. I promise.'

'I can't wait.'

Me neither, she thought. When she'd finished her cigarette she put out the light and crawled into bed. She was just drifting off when he spoke again.

'Nellie?'

'What?'

'Please?'

She didn't reply.

'Nellie?'

She squeezed her eyes tightly shut. If somehow she could have switched off her ears she would have done so.

Suddenly Jim lost his temper, furious with himself and humiliated at having pleaded with her. 'You're a rotten bitch of a woman!' he roared. 'The worst woman I ever had. Why if I wasn't lying here like this I wouldn't even spit on you!'

He ranted and raved, his voice ringing round the room while she lay with her hands covering her ears.

In her cold, narrow bed, Nellie wept silently.

'And this, Nellie, is my wife Rachel.'

The two women shook hands, Rachel saying, 'I've heard so much about you, Nellie, I feel I've known you for years already.'

Rachel Spira was a short woman, although still taller than Baz, in her early forties. Her figure was plump and matronly while at her chin several jowls wobbled. The overall impression was one of flesh.

'It's a great pleasure to meet you, Mrs Spira,' Nellie replied.

'Rachel, please. We don't stand on ceremony in this house.'

'And this is my son, Daniel,' said Baz proudly. Daniel was a strapping lad of about nineteen.

'And my second son, Joseph.' Joseph was a few years younger than his brother.

'And my daughter, Sarah.' Sarah was about twelve with large, doe eyes and jet-black hair.

Nellie shook hands with all three of them, thinking to herself what good-looking children they were. The girl especially. There was no doubt she would grow up to be a beauty.

'Allow me to get you a drink, Miss Wildchild,' Daniel said. 'What would you like?'

Miss Wildchild. If only it was true. 'It's Mrs actually,' she replied. And was secretly amused to see disappointment flash across his face. It seemed she'd made a conquest. 'I'll have a glass of wine, please,' she said.

Baz had asked her to this party the previous week, saying she could come on after the show was down for the night. He'd sent his car with a driver to pick her up.

Trying not to be too obvious, she stared about her. What a beautiful place it was. Certainly by far and away the grandest home she'd ever been in.

The carpet underfoot was fitted and inches thick; the furniture covered in gold velvet. But what impressed her most was the chandelier that hung overhead.

Her entrance into the room had created a stir. Heads, mostly male, were turned in her direction.

'Baz tells me you are a big success in the show,' Rachel said, returning to Nellie's side, having been gone for a minute to receive another late guest.

'It's very kind of him to say so.'

'He says you have the most marvellous voice. I must come myself one night and hear you.'

'Introduce us, Rachel,' a man said, having strode over to join them. He was of average height, thin, with carrot-red hair. He wasn't nearly as smartly dressed as the other men present. His cheeks were gaunt, the bones above them prominent. There was an overall air of intensity about him.

'Nellie, I'd like you to meet Geoff Carson. One of Glasgow's foremost painters,' Rachel said.

'Not one of, but *the*,' Carson put in swiftly.

Nellie smiled. 'Modest with it, too, I see.'

'He doesn't know the meaning of the word,'

Rachel said, a mischievous glint in her eye.

Carson was staring at Nellie like a hungry predator. She found his gaze uncomfortable.

'What do you think of McIan?' he demanded suddenly.

'Never heard of him.'

'Ah!' he said and gave a brief, wolfish smile.

'McIan's an Edinburgh painter and Geoff's main rival,' explained Rachel.

'Rival! Nonsense! The man's a no-talented phoney. He doesn't even begin to compare with me!'

'Not McIan again!' another man said, joining their little group. 'You're obsessed with him, Geoff.'

Carson glared at the man who smiled back rather patronizingly.

'What would you know about art anyway?' Carson demanded. 'You're nothing more than a businessman,' saying the last word as though it were something disgusting.

'Nellie, this is Murray Ventre,' Rachel said.

Ventre gave the tiniest of bows. 'At your service, Miss Wildchild.'

She was about to correct him, but decided against it. Let them think of her as an unmarried woman. At least for the moment.

The evening progressed, during the course of which Nellie met a great many interesting people from all walks of life, including a knight of the realm, a charming man down from Perthshire, where he had an estate not far from Pitlochry.

Nellie was thoroughly enjoying herself finding all these new and interesting acquaintances absolutely fascinating.

She was coming out of the toilet when she was suddenly accosted by Geoff Carson who came straight up to her and pinned her against the wall.

'I've been looking everywhere for you,' he breathed. 'I wanted to get you alone.'

He ran his glance over her. It was obvious enough what was going on in his mind. 'I thought I might take you home when you're ready.'

There was something about the expression on his face which reminded her of Jim. 'I don't think so,' she replied, trying to keep the contempt out of her voice.

'I want to paint you. Will you come to my studio tomorrow?'

'I have a rehearsal.'

'The next day, then?'

'I'm rehearsing then also.'

'When you're not rehearsing, then?' he said, angry now.

'I don't want my picture painted, thank you very much,' she said. 'And now will you please let me pass?'

He came closer, his breath thick with alcohol. 'I

don't think you realize that it's an honour, a great privilege to be asked by me to sit.'

'Thank you for the honour, but I decline.' She tried to push him aside, but came up short when his hand covered her breast. 'What do you think you're doing?' she hissed.

'You're lovely. The best-looking woman here tonight.'

'Do you mind taking your hand off me?'

As though she hadn't spoken, he began to fondle her.

She was outraged and ashamed. But how could she get rid of him without creating a scene? Without cheapening herself?

'Geoff, I think you're wanted in the other room,' Baz said quietly, suddenly appearing behind Carson. His voice was low and full of authority. The voice of a man used to giving orders and being obeyed.

The hand was removed instantly. 'Just talking to Nellie here,' Carson said with a grin.

Baz looked from Carson to Nellie and then back again. Carson wilted a little as Baz's eyes bored into him.

'I'll go away through then,' Carson said, moving off.

'You all right?' Baz asked anxiously when the painter was gone.

'Yes, thanks. No harm done.'

'He's had too much to drink, I'm afraid. The old Glasgow problem of not knowing when to stop.'

She brushed a wisp of hair away from her face. Dear Baz, she thought, trust him to be on hand to sort things out. Just like him. Always there when he was needed.

'I wanted to have a word with you anyway,' he said.

'About the show?'

'No. Something else. I have a surprise for you.'

'What?' she demanded eagerly.

A smile turned the corners of his mouth gently upward. 'If I told you it wouldn't be a surprise.'

'Beast!'

'Can you spare about an hour, maybe longer, after rehearsals tomorrow?'

'Of course.'

'I'll take you to your surprise then.'

'Take me to it?'

'That's right.'

She frowned, desperately trying to work out what this surprise could be.

'You'll never guess so there's no use trying,' he laughed, knowing full well that would only make her try the harder. 'Now shall we join the others?'

'Baz –?'

'And no questions about it. Because I'm not saying.'

Nor did he, despite the many times she tried to worm it out of him.

'Ready?' he asked.

She had changed out of rehearsal clothes into her outdoor ones. A last check at her mirror confirmed that her make-up was satisfactory. She was bubbling with anticipation inside, dying to find out what the surprise was.

'Let's go.'

He took her by the arm and guided her downstairs. Once outside they made their way to where his car was parked.

It was a cold, crisp, clear day, the air sharp and stinging.

'I liked your wife very much,' Nellie said once they were underway.

He gave her a sideways glance. 'And she liked you. In fact the whole family did. Daniel in particular.'

'I think he fancied me,' she said in a mock stage whisper.

'He wasn't the only one.'

She thought of Geoff Carson. 'So it seemed.'

But Baz wasn't thinking of the artist.

'Where are we going?' she asked.

'Wait and see.'

'You're not giving anything away, are you?'

'Whoever heard of a businessman giving some-

thing away!' he replied, pulling a face as though horrified at even the suggestion.

Nellie laughed. She liked men who made her
laugh.

They drove along the Great Western Road until at
last the urban sore that was Glasgow was left behind
them. The countryside was beautiful, very green
with occasional purple and yellow splashes. It made
a heart-lifting contrast to the seemingly never ending Glasgow grey.

Nellie sighed and leaned back in her seat. 'This is
the life,' she said languorously.

A little further on Baz turned off the road to
motor along a leafy lane. Presently he stopped in
front of a largish house which was fronted by a wild,
overgrown garden.

'Come on,' he said, helping her from the car.

'Where are we?'

'Just outside the village of Bishopton,' he replied,
and opening the garden gate ushered her through.

'Who lives here?'

'A woman I know,' he replied mysteriously.

At the door he produced a key which opened it.
Smiling he beckoned her inside.

The house hadn't been empty long. She could
tell that from the excellent condition it was in. Why
there wasn't even more than a few days' dust on the
window ledges.

He showed her round downstairs where there were four rooms with a kitchen and adjoining w.c. Upstairs there were three more rooms, a toilet and bathroom.

Nellie stood in what was obviously the master bedroom, staring out of a large window. As far as she could see there was greenery, and there, between two clumps of trees, the glint of water which was the Clyde.

'Like it?' Baz asked.

'Marvellous,' she replied. Then turning to him, 'So who's this female friend of yours who lives here?'

'Her name's Nellie Wildchild.'

She blinked and stared at him. 'I beg your pardon?'

'The place is yours.'

She shook her head. 'I don't understand?'

'Nellie, you can't continue living in a Govan slum. It's just not on now that you're becoming a name.'

'But I can't afford this!'

'You don't have to. It's a gift from me.'

She stared around her in wonder. What a wonderful house. Precisely the sort she'd always dreamed about. 'I can't accept it from you, Baz,' she said sorrowfully.

'Why ever not?'

'It just wouldn't be right.'

'Look, it didn't cost all that much. I swear it. Not

that I bought it on the open market. It came to me in lieu of a debt I was owed. I was already looking for a place for you anyway and so when this came up I thought it ideal.'

'It is. It is,' she replied. 'But I can't accept it as a present. It's far too much.'

'Let's talk about it,' he said, taking her by the arm and guiding her back downstairs.

Nellie was in love with the house, just aching to live in it. She thought how lovely it would be to wake up every morning in the country as opposed to the filthy squalor of Govan.

Baz took her out to the back where they found many fruit trees and bushes overgrown and running wild.

'The previous owner didn't go in much for gardening it seems,' he said. 'But this and the front garden wouldn't take long to get back in shape. Especially if you got someone in.'

There was a garage which he said they'd look at in a minute or two. After the matter of the house had been resolved.

'It's absolutely perfect,' Nellie said, eyes shining, staring up at the rear of the house.

'Then accept it from me.'

'I can't.'

'I'll make you change your mind somehow.'

'No you won't.'

'You're a stubborn woman, Nellie.'

'I thought you already knew that.'

They strolled round the side of the house. She was thinking she could put Jim downstairs in a room of his own, and, next door to him, Myra. That would leave her the entire upper area for herself. Her heart leaped at the thought of the freedom that would entail.

'How much did the person owe you?' she asked.

'Three-fifty.'

She didn't know much about house prices but was sure it was a snip for that.

'Why? What are you thinking?' he asked.

'That I would buy it off you. If you'd let me pay it up weekly that is.'

'But I want to *give* it to you!'

She shook her head. 'I buy or nothing.'

'You're mad, woman!'

'No, Baz. Just keeping my independence.'

'All right, we'll work it out that I dock your wages every week. Two or three years and you'll have paid it off.'

Her head was suddenly full of plans for the place. There was so much she was going to need in the way of furniture and furnishings.

'It's a lovely surprise, Baz. Thank you very, very much,' she said, and, stooping, kissed his cheek.

'Now you're sure this is how you want to do it?' he asked.

'Absolutely positive.'

He clicked his tongue and waved his hands in a gesture of reluctant acceptance. 'So, if I can't give you the house will you take a house-warming present? It is traditional you know.'

'All right,' she laughed.

'Come then,' he said, taking her by the hand and leading her to the garage.

It was a bull-nosed Morris in black and maroon. It had been polished till it shone.

'Now don't give me any shtik about not being able to accept it,' said Baz. 'Living out here you'll need a car to get to and from the theatre.'

'But I can't drive!'

'*Yet*, Nellie. *Yet*. I'll fix you up with some lessons. You'll soon get the hang of it. It isn't difficult, I promise you.' He caressed the bonnet of the car with his hand. 'She's not new, but a lovely little machine none the less. You'll get a lot of good use out of her.'

A house and a car in the same day. It was too much to take in at once. 'It's beautiful, Baz, truly.'

He beamed. 'You being happy makes me happy. It's also good for the show. Now come on, sit in her. Let me see how you look.'

'A picture,' he pronounced when she was behind the wheel.

'How about you giving me a lesson right now?' she asked.

'Why not! I'd enjoy that.'

The next half hour was a mixture of laughter and curses as for the first time in her life she came to grips with the internal combustion engine.

'Live in the country!' exclaimed Myra. 'That would be wonderful, Nellie.'

'Wait till you see it, Myra. It'll bowl you over.'

'I can hardly wait. And I'm to have my own room?'

'*And* I'll put your money up, of course. That seems only fair.'

Jim glowered from the bed. 'I think the idea stinks.'

'Oh, Jim, you'll love it. Just think of all that good, fresh air,' Myra coaxed.

'I was born and bred in Govan. Leaving it is the last thing I want,' grumbled Jim.

Nellie sat by the fire, regarding him thoughtfully. 'You've no option but to come,' she said finally. 'You certainly can't stay here on your own.'

'I'll have Myra to look after me.'

'Oh, aye? And who's going to pay the bills then, if I'm not here to do so?'

'I wondered how long it would take you to throw your money in my face.'

'I'm not doing that at all, Jim.'

'Sounds hellishly like it to me.'

There was nothing she could do that was right.

'I won't go,' he stated flatly.

'You'll do as you're told, and that's the end of it.'

'Don't I have any say in the matter?' he demanded.

'None at all.'

'I would have bought a house one day if it hadn't been for the accident,' he said defiantly. 'My luck was on the turn. I was coming up to the winning streak to end all winning streaks. I could feel it at the time.'

Nellie didn't answer. She'd heard it all before. It had bored her then as it did now. She let him ramble on about all the things he'd planned to do with his winnings. When he'd finally finished she said, 'Another thing. I now own a car.'

Myra gawped at her. Only real toffs owned cars.

'You're buying a house *and* a car?' Jim demanded.

'I'm buying the house. The car was a present.'

'From whom?'

'None of your business.'

'Your boss, Spira, I'll bet. You *are* having it off with him!'

'I am not. I told you.'

'Men don't give you cars for nothing. He must be getting something in return.'

'He is. My friendship.'

Jim guffawed. 'Don't be so bloody naïve! He wants inside your knickers. Don't you kid yourself he doesn't.'

She regarded him with distaste. Trust him to put it so crudely.

She threw what remained of her cigarette into the grate. 'I'll make a cup of tea,' she said.

Using the sharp end of an orange stick she put a dot of red on each of the inside junctures of her eyes. The lights out front would pick up the red, making her eyes appear larger and brighter.

When that job was done to her satisfaction she sat back in her chair and studied herself in her dressing-table mirror. The curtain wasn't long up and she would shortly be called for her first cue.

She thought back to the party at Baz's house. She had enjoyed that. Tremendously. She'd been nervous beforehand thinking she might be out of place – the proverbial square peg faced with a round hole – but she hadn't been. On the contrary, she'd felt completely at ease and at home.

Such interesting people had been there. Civilized people used to gracious living. The good things in life. Well-mannered, if you disregarded Geoff Carson. Soft-spoken. Cultured.

She'd thought that they might look down their noses at her because she spoke 'broad', but that hadn't been the case either. Not once had she detected even a hint of condescension or patronage because of her accent.

Still, that was something else she'd have to see to. At the moment there were singing lessons and driving lessons. When the driving ones were completed she would replace them with ones for speech.

She used the rabbit's foot Margo had given her to smooth in some powder that had become a little streaked, and thought about what Jim had said about Baz.

Jim was right, of course, Baz did fancy her. She'd known that for some time. The question she had to ask herself was what she was going to do when he did something about it. There was no doubt in her mind that she'd become tremendously fond of him since coming to the Palace – his kindness, his thoughtfulness.

But could she actually bring herself to sleep with him? That was something else entirely.

What she mustn't forget was that he ran the Palace, and as such could exercise tremendous influence over her career. A career that was blossoming more all the time.

There was nothing to stop her going to other theatres and appearing there, once her contract with Baz had expired, but why make life difficult when she had everything she could ask for at the Palace – and more? For a management to be so totally on her side wasn't something that should be discarded, or even interfered with, lightly.

Her thoughts were interrupted by a tap on the door. 'Come in!' she called out.

Sandy entered. 'This arrived by hand after the half so I thought I'd bring it up to you personally. I was coming this way anyway,' he said, handing her a letter.

She thanked him and they exchanged some good-natured banter before he left. Then she ripped open the envelope.

What she read brought a smile to her face. The letter was a request from one of the daily newspapers asking if one of their journalists could interview her with a view to doing a feature spread.

Well, well, well! She certainly was coming on, she thought. A newspaper article all about *her*! The prospect was thrilling.

Nellie held the high note, pure and golden. On and on it went, seemingly forever, till at last she killed it to finish the song.

Baz sighed with pleasure, enraptured. Miss McLeish nodded her approval. Nellie's voice had improved beyond measure since coming under her tutelage. Now Nellie was the master of the instrument instead of the other way around.

A glance at his watch told Baz the lesson was over which disappointed him. He could have sat all day listening to Nellie sing.

Nellie and Miss McLeish had a last few words, then Nellie slipped into her coat. She and Baz were now off to the salerooms to look at second-hand furniture for the house at Bishopton.

'I think I'll come up and listen to your lessons more often,' Baz said when they were underway. 'And, afterwards, if neither of us was rushing off anywhere, we could take tea together. What do you say?'

'I'd love that. But, Baz?'

'Yes?'

'If you and I are seen too often together won't it get back to Rachel? For such a big city, you know how small Glasgow can be.'

His face clouded. It was a thought that had crossed his mind before now. 'It's not as though we were doing anything wrong, is it?' he replied with a grin.

'There's still bound to be talk.'

He *would* have to be a bit more careful. He loved Rachel, and though it was a different love than that which he felt for Nellie, he didn't want to cause her pain or upset.

It would be a lot easier when the house at Bishopton was habitable, for then he wouldn't have to be seen out with Nellie nearly so much.

'It's best you buy second-hand for the moment,' he said. 'And then you can replace with new, providing you want to that is, as you go along. There's some very nice pine on sale today.'

For the rest of the drive to the showrooms, the subject of themselves put aside, he told her what was coming up for auction, having been to view himself beforehand.

Nellie was dog-tired. It was Saturday night, the end of the week. A week that had been harder than usual, because of getting the new house into shape on top of the show.

She said good night to Myra and then put the kettle on for a cup of tea. Jim was lying in bed watching her, the morning's paper spread before him.

'Pretty picture of you,' he said.

'Oh, you liked it then?'

'And a good article. Fair tugs the strings of your heart, the bit about the husband lying at home paralysed.'

'Does that upset you?'

'No. Why should it? It's true after all.'

Nellie put the tea by to mask. She'd considered it carefully before admitting to the journalist that she was married and that her husband was paralysed. If she'd thought she would have gotten away with saying she was single she would have done so, but she was too well known in Govan. Somebody would have told the papers what she was trying to hide. It was better this way; open and above board.

Besides, as Baz had pointed out, it wasn't such a bad thing being a married woman. It lent you a certain respectability and 'weight'. And as for Jim being paralysed, nothing but sympathy would come her way because of that.

'So that's Baz Spira, your boss,' Jim sneered, holding up the paper with his good hand. 'A right sugar daddy he looks.'

'It's not a particularly good photo of him,' Nellie replied.

'Good or not, it doesn't hide the fact he's bloody ancient.'

'He's not *that* old.'

'Gordon Highlanders, he looks older than your da! And bald to boot. Not to mention the size of him. Tuppence ha'penny's worth right enough. He doesn't even come up to your shoulders.'

'He may be wee, but he's kind and considerate and all the things you never were!' she retorted hotly.

'I might have been more kind and considerate if you'd been the same to me.'

'What did you expect after our wedding night? And me a virgin? Can you even begin to imagine what it was like?'

'You made far too much of it.'

'What, my virginity?'

'No. Our wedding night.'

'You don't understand,' she said shaking her head. 'You just don't understand.'

'I was due my rights and I took them. That's all there was to it,' he said in a surly voice.

'You consider you were due *your* rights after what I'd caught you doing to my cousin Marj at the reception?'

'That meant nothing at all. I told you that after.'

'It meant something to me!'

'All those months of me wanting you, Nellie, and you saying no, not till the wedding night. If I was seeing Marj, then you've only yourself to blame for denying me. I'm only a man, after all, and you were driving me nuts with wanting you.'

'Oh, so it was all my fault, was it?'

'There are two sides to every story, Nellie. And you never took mine into account.'

There was a certain amount of truth in what he said. She had been denying him. But it had been so important to her – so important to her dreams of marriage and of love. And how could she possibly have given into him when she hadn't to Frank? Frank whom she'd so desperately loved.

'How can you do it with a Jew?' Jim went on. 'They're a filthy people, Nellie. Filthy.'

'There's nothing filthy about them.'

'They're even worse than Catholics. And that's saying something.'

She thought of Baz, always so immaculately turned out. Even when he was wandering around backstage in his old cardy, he looked like he'd just stepped from the bath. And as for his house, why it had been beautiful inside, so clean she felt he could have eaten off the floor.

'I'll tell you for the last time. I'm not sleeping with him.'

His look told her he didn't believe her.

She poured herself a cup of tea and lit a cigarette. She couldn't wait to move into Bishopton and not have to face Jim every night. In Bishopton he would be tucked out of sight and, as much as possible anyway, out of mind.

'Nellie Wildchild,' said Jim scornfully. 'It's a bloody daft name.'

She put out the light and sat in the darkness finishing her tea and cigarette.

When he spoke several times more she didn't bother replying. She pretended he didn't exist.

'That's just about it,' said Baz glancing around. Outside the van that had brought the last of the sale furniture was moving away.

They were in Nellie's bedroom. The double bed had been the last item brought up.

Nellie tucked the sheets in and then the blankets. She'd bought them new that very morning. From now on she didn't want to sleep in any of the bedding associated with the Govan house.

'You're bringing them tomorrow?' Baz asked, studying Nellie while she went about making the bed.

'Yes.'

He watched the shape of her backside press against her skirt. It was all he could do to stop himself from reaching out and touching her.

She came upright and wiped the hair from her face. Her cheeks were flushed and there were beads of perspiration on her forehead.

'I love you, Nellie,' Baz said quietly.

She stopped to turn and stare at him. The truth of his statement was written quite plainly on his face.

'I know,' she replied softly.

He came to her and took her in his arms.

'What about Rachel?' she whispered.

'Rachel's my wife and I'll never leave her. I wouldn't, I couldn't break up the family. And there's the theatre – I couldn't give that up either.'

He drew her head down to him and kissed her, a gentle kiss, full of feeling.

'The last thing I want to do is hurt you in any way,' he whispered.

She was trembling, a leaf in the wind. She'd wondered how she'd feel when this moment came. And now she knew. Secure. That was it. Secure.

She was nervous, all right, but she didn't have the urge to run away screaming as she had every time Jim laid his hands on her.

'I never thought this would ever happen to me,' said Baz, pulling her down to the bed so that they were both in a sitting position.

'You once said this sort of love was transient,' Nellie replied.

He frowned, regretting having spoken those words. But they'd been spoken by a man who'd never experienced what it was like to be physically in love. The way he was with Nellie. He'd babbled on about love arising out of respect – true as far as it went. But that was a love totally unlike the all-consuming passion he felt now.

She closed her eyes as he undid her buttons, shivering as the dress fell away from her. Baz stroked her hair, her shoulder.

'If we're going to do this, then let's do it properly,' she said. Rising from his half embrace she allowed her dress to slip to the floor where it was soon joined by the rest of her clothes.

'Promise not to laugh? I'm hardly a male model.'

'I won't laugh,' she replied, touched.

They lay down together and he took her in his arms. He could feel how tense she was, almost rigid. 'There, there,' he crooned, stroking her thigh.

She closed her eyes, trying to relax, but the spring inside her just wouldn't uncoil.

'There's no rush. No rush at all,' he whispered, all the while stroking and ever so gently massaging.

Ages passed before he moved on top of and into her. Despite herself she gasped. It had been so long, she'd forgotten what an intrusion it was. She put her arms round him and held him as he moved, curiously detached, as though it were happening to someone else. She was getting no sensation at all from what he was doing, but she tried to give the impression that she was.

When it was over they again lay side by side. 'Thank you, Nellie,' he said.

'Hold me close, Baz. Cuddle me,' she whispered.

And he did till it was time for Nellie to get up and make herself ready for the theatre.

The taxi driver helped Myra and Nellie get Jim out of the cab and into his wheelchair where Myra immediately covered him with a rug.

He stared up at the house and sniffed, his eyes rheumy and his mouth set in a downward, disapproving slant. 'So this is it.'

'It looks grand,' said Myra.

'Wait till you see the inside. And the view,' said Nellie.

'I'm cold,' Jim whined. He'd hated the journey.

Especially the degredation of being manhandled in and out of the taxi.

'Bring the cases,' Nellie told the driver, and led the way in.

Myra was thrilled with her room and effusive in saying so. After the taxi driver had been paid off and told to return later to take Nellie to the theatre, she and Myra got Jim into his new bed, a second cocoon affair that the hospital people had constructed for him.

She left Myra to get herself and Jim sorted out while she went upstairs to unpack those items of hers that had been brought in the taxi. The bulk of her wardrobe and personal effects had already been installed during the past few weeks.

She stood at the window, lit a cigarette, and stared out over greenery to that glint of the Clyde in the far distance. From now on there would be no more having to sleep in the same room as Jim. And the relief was profound.

She smoked her cigarette through to the end and then carefully stubbed it out. Then she lay spread-eagled on the bed where Baz had made love to her.

What a loving, gentle man he was, how considerate and kind. He'd taken infinite care not to hurt her or rush her.

She thought about Baz's body which had fascinated her because of its softness. Rather like a baby's, and so different to Jim's which had been lean, hard and rough. Being made love to by Baz wasn't going to be a difficult thing to endure at all. She liked the cuddles. That and the feeling of security that went with him.

She gazed round the room. He'd come back here often. They'd discussed and agreed that.

Jim would make a fuss, of course. But she'd see he kept his mouth shut and was out of the way when Baz was around. She held all the ace cards, after all.

For the first time since marrying Jim Biles she felt free.

6

Nellie heard the commotion on the stairs followed by the sound of raised voices, one of which she recognized as the stage doorkeeper's. Seconds later there was a thundering on her dressing-room door.

'Miss Wildchild, can I please see you?' a strange voice boomed.

She snatched up her dressing gown and put it on. 'Who is it?'

'Ian McIan.'

She didn't know anyone of that name. 'I'm not decent. And anyway, I'm going on in a few minutes.' Neither statement was true. It was a good twenty minutes before her first cue.

'I won't take up much of your time. I promise!' McIan shouted. This was followed by more scuffling noises.

'I'm sorry, Miss Wildchild. He burst right past me!' the stage doorkeeper called out.

She opened the door to be confronted by a giant of a man sporting a huge, bushy beard above which were ropelike moustaches. So big was he, she felt like a doll beside him.

'I'm awfully sorry, Miss Wildchild,' the stage doorkeeper repeated.

'I can see why you had trouble keeping him out,' she replied drily. Which caused McIan to roar with laughter. The stage doorkeeper was old, small and painfully thin.

'What can I do for you?' she turned to McIan.

'Can I come in and sit a wee while? I won't get in your way.'

'Are you safe?'

He looked shocked at the suggestion that he wasn't. 'As houses, I can assure you.' Then with a wink, 'At least till I get to know you better.'

She decided to leave the door open. Just in case. She told the stage doorkeeper she'd look after McIan whom she ushered inside, where he perched his enormous frame into a rickety wooden chair which squeaked its protest.

'I can see what attracted him,' McIan said, peering at Nellie's face.

'Attracted whom?'

'Yon idiot and charlatan Carson.'

Suddenly it all clicked into place. This McIan must be the same one she'd been told about the night of Baz and Rachel's party. The Edinburgh man who was Geoff Carson's main rival.

'You're a painter,' she stated.

'Aye, that's right. Or at least I like to kid myself I am. Turn your head a wee bit to the left, will you?'

She did and he grunted, running his fingers through his beard and then scratching underneath.

'I heard Carson asked you to sit for him and you refused. Is that right?'

She nodded.

'Why did you do that?'

'Because I didn't like him.'

McIan's face lit up in a smile. 'Well that's something we agree on anyway,' he said. He rose from his chair and prowled first to the left and then to the right, his gaze never leaving Nellie's face.

'I can well see what the attraction was. For once yon bampot's shown a bit of taste,' McIan said.

Nellie was fascinated by this huge man with the magnetic eyes and slight lilt of a Highland accent. When she asked him if he was born in Edinburgh he replied no, he came from up north. Edinburgh was his adopted home.

'They're all phonies though there you understand,' he growled. 'Would-be artists and would-be intellectuals. Phoney through and through.'

'So why do you live there?'

'I like the city itself. I get something from it. Rather the same way Gauguin got something from the South Seas.'

'You mean it inspires you?'

'You could put it that way, I suppose. Although inspire, or inspiration, aren't words I like to use myself. I think they're overused and abused. Especially in Edinburgh.'

'I take your meaning,' she replied with a smile.

'I'm going to be totally honest with you,' he said. 'I came up here the night wanting to paint you for no other reason than to spite Carson, whom I can't stand at any price. You turned him down so I thought I'd put his nose out of joint by asking you to let me do you. But now I've seen you to hell with Carson and all that bloody nonsense! I want to paint you because . . . there's something about your face that's crying out to be put on canvas. And I'm the man to do it. If you'll let me.'

Nellie wasn't sure. She'd never really thought of herself in this particular light before. Carson's request had been denied out of hand because of her dislike for the man.

'What happens to the painting when it's complete?' she asked.

'I'm having an exhibition through in Edinburgh

later on this year. I'll make it the exhibition's focal point.'

That idea appealed. 'How much of my time would actually be taken up in sitting for you?' she asked.

He gazed about him, taking in the dressing room, thinking. 'I'll want to do you in a theatrical setting because that's where I feel you belong. So I'll tell you what. How about if you don't sit for me at all in the conventional sense? Let me come backstage to watch you and sketch, and I'll do it all from that.'

'I'll have to ask Mister Spira's permission first. It's not usual for people to wander about backstage.'

'I won't get in anyone's way. I'll just tuck myself up in some wee corner. And as long as there's enough light for me to see by, I'll get down on paper what I need. Now, what do you say?'

Why not? It certainly couldn't do any harm. And she'd taken a liking to this big painter.

'Leave me your address and I'll drop you a line after I've had a word with Mister Spira.'

McIan beamed. 'It's going to be a work of art!' he declared.

'And now you must go. I've got to get into my first costume.'

He took her hand and with a great flourish kissed it. 'Your devoted slave, Miss Wildchild,' he said.

Nellie laughed after he'd gone. Slave indeed!

*

For a week McIan haunted backstage. Sketchbook and pencil in hand, he was to be found lurking in various well-lit vantage points from where he could observe Nellie when she was on. True to his word, he was never any bother and never got in anyone's way.

During the second week McIan never came near the theatre. Then on the third he reappeared to do more sketching.

On the Wednesday of that week Nellie went out to do her second solo, a semi-novelty number. Confident and relaxed, she began to sing.

She was about to launch into the second verse when a face in the front row caught her attention. At first she couldn't place him. And then the penny dropped. He would glance at her, and then his head would dip as though he were reading something on his lap. Not reading she told herself, sketching. The man in the front row was Geoff Carson.

She came to the end of the number, with an effort concentrating on the song. As usual, the applause was almost deafening. She made her curtsy while the audience rose to her. When she was finally allowed off she signalled McIan to follow her out into the corridor.

When she told him Carson was in the front row sketching her, his face suffused with anger. 'Of all the lowdown, underhand rats!' he exclaimed vehemently. He clenched his right hand and the pencil in it snapped in two.

'He must have heard you were going to paint me,' she said.

He nodded and tugged his beard. He glanced across at the stage where an eccentric comedian was doing his stuff. 'How long till the interval?'

'About fifteen minutes.'

He tugged his beard again. 'Right. I'll settle Mister Geoff Carson's hash for him,' he said ominously, his eyes flashing like two black diamonds.

Nellie shivered, saying it was best she got back to her dressing room. But once there she decided she couldn't leave matters as they were and sent for Sandy. When he arrived she told him what had happened and asked him to find Mr Spira and explain the situation to him.

The interval came and went.

When she came off she found Baz waiting for her and together they went up to her dressing room. 'What happened?' she asked eagerly.

'McIan got to Carson before we got to him and half-killed him.'

'You mean there was an actual fight?'

'More of a massacre, as McIan's twice Carson's size. The iron was no sooner down than McIan went storming into the auditorium to confront Carson. Words were exchanged, the outcome of which was that McIan took Carson's sketches off him and tore the things up. Then Carson took a swing at McIan who promptly floored him.'

'Is he hurt badly?'

'He'll live. Although he's going to have an awful sore face for a few weeks to come.'

'And what about the customers?'

'Oh, they loved it. Thought it was great.'

Nellie laughed. 'Trust a Glasgow audience. So what happened then?'

'The police arrived. Don't ask me where from. It was like magic. And off McIan and Carson went to the station, the pair of them arrested for brawling in a public place.'

Nellie had been changing her costume while they'd been talking. She now paused as a thought struck her. 'Baz? I wonder if we could use this?' she said.

'How?'

'Remember that journalist who interviewed me before? He might think this was a good story. And if he printed it, it would be more publicity for the Palace.'

Baz raised his eyebrows. She definitely had something. And why just the one journalist? Why not all the dailies? A glance at his watch told him it was ten o'clock. First editions of the morning papers would be being put together even now.

'I'll make a few phone calls,' he said.

It was the following night and Nellie and Baz were lying on her bed drinking champagne. Copies of the morning's papers lay strewn around.

Baz brought himself up onto one elbow to stare at her. 'You just couldn't buy publicity like that,' he said. He glanced across to the nearest paper where the page three leader was, 'The Woman The Scottish Art World Is Fighting Over'. Below was a photograph of Nellie followed by a fifteen-paragraph story about her, McIan and Geoff Carson.

'You know what this means, don't you?' he said.

'What?'

'You're not only a sensation. You're an overnight celebrity. From now on everyone in Scotland will know the name Nellie Wildchild.'

She closed her eyes and smiled. 'Do I get to be top of the bill now?' she asked.

He wasn't only in love with her. He was besotted by her. He knew the trouble she was having with their lovemaking but that would right itself in time. In the meantime, he would have to work at it; breaking down and erasing the damage her husband had done to her.

'Next season, top of the bill,' he promised.

'Oh!' she whispered.

'I've got half an hour then I'll have to go,' he said.

He reached out to fondle her, kneading her flesh, then caressing it. 'As you know the theatre goes dark soon. What are you going to do with your time off?'

She liked it when he touched her this way. It made her think of herself as a cat. 'I've nothing specific planned.'

'Then how about coming away with me?'

Her eyes snapped open. 'Say that again?'

'Would you like to go on holiday with me?'

'What about Rachel and the children?'

'Daniel and Joe have planned to go off on their own anyway. Sarah was going to come with us but now she can go with her cousins. She'll much prefer that to being alone with me.'

'And Rachel?'

'Has just discovered a place down in Wiltshire where they claim they can cure migraines. Apparently the cure is all tied up with diet and exercise. And the course lasts six weeks. She's already been in touch with them and the only time they can fit her in is when we were supposed to be going on holiday. So now I'm going on my own. Or at least, that's what she'll believe.'

Excitement bubbled in Nellie. This was tremendous. 'Where had you planned to go?' she demanded eagerly.

'France. Belgium. Perhaps up into Germany. We can go where we like, really, I'll be taking the car.'

Nellie had never been out of Scotland before and the prospect thrilled her. She thought about Jim and Myra. There was no reason she could think of why they couldn't get on on their own for a while.

'Well?' he asked softly, his hand moving slowly in a cupped position between her legs.

'I can hardly wait.' She accepted him into her arms.

While he made love to her she imagined, behind closed eyes, all the places she was going to visit and the things they could do while there.

'What are you thinking about?' Nellie asked, curious. She'd found Jim in his wheelchair out in the back garden where Myra had left him to get some fresh air while she got on with a few chores.

Jim's eyes swung slowly round to fasten on to Nellie's. 'Things, people, places,' he replied.

'What people?'

'Oh, the wifeys who used to come into the shop for their butcher meat. I used to have a good crack with some of them. One or two were right comedians.' His gaze left hers to stare at a nearby bramble bush. 'I never really noticed things until this happened to me. I mean, have you ever had a really good look at a blackbird?'

She shook her head.

'There was one here up until a few moments ago.

Absolutely fascinating. And caterpillars, I could watch them for hours. Truly amazing creatures.'

This was a side to Jim that Nellie had never seen before. She almost felt some sympathy for him. Almost.

'When the season finishes, I'm going on holiday for a few weeks,' she said.

'Oh?'

'You and Myra will be all right here on your own, won't you?'

He gave a lopsided, leering smile. 'And what if I said we wouldn't be?'

'You'd be lying.

'True. True. We'll get by, I suppose.'

'Right, then,' she replied, and made to turn away.

He stopped her by saying, 'Where are you going?'

'Abroad.'

'Very nice. No doon ra watter for our big star, eh? Nothing but the best for her.'

'I deserve it,' Nellie snapped in reply.

He smiled again, as though laughing inwardly at some private joke. 'Going alone?' he asked.

'Yes.'

The smile widened. 'I don't think so. Not you,' he whispered.

'And even if I was going with someone it's certainly none of your business,' she said coldly.

'I'm still your husband.'

'Which you were when you were sleeping with Big Jessie and God knows who else.'

'You're going with the Jew, aren't you?'

She bit off her reply.

'At least I always stuck with my own kind.'

'I find him a lot more my kind than you.'

His eyes became hard and vicious. 'Whore!' he hissed. 'I hate you.'

'Coooeee!' Myra called out, appearing at the rear of the house with a steaming mug of coffee for Jim.

'Not nearly as much as I hate you,' Nellie retorted.

'Go rot in hell!' he shouted after her as she strode away.

'Blackbirds and caterpillars!' she exclaimed out loud. Who would have thought it?

The last night of the show they had a party on stage. Baz laid on whisky, beer and wine together with a buffet of cold meats, sausage rolls and sandwiches.

After a while the musicians played and everyone danced with everyone else. Sandy got drunk and swore undying love for Nellie who, not unkindly, told him to come back when he was more used to wearing long pants.

Rachel was there, and she and Nellie had a long chat about the place she was off to in a few days' time down in Wiltshire. She could hardly wait.

Migraines had been the bane of her life since puberty. Nellie wished her well and said she would keep her fingers crossed that the cure was successful.

Since the night of the party in the Spira home Nellie and Rachel had met a number of times, and, indeed, had become fairly good friends.

Nellie was never quite sure whether Rachel knew or not about her and Baz. She suspected she did. But no hint was ever given.

Nellie had come to the conclusion that as long as things continued the way they were, which is to say the Spira family wasn't directly threatened, then Rachel would continue to turn a blind eye. On the other hand, she might be quite wrong and Rachel might know nothing at all about her relationship with Baz. But she was only too well aware that wives have a way of finding these things out.

The party lasted into the small hours and finally ended when Edith, one of the girls in the line, nearly killed herself by falling into the orchestra pit – only saved at the last second by the Great Zampato, Magician.

Nellie drove home alone. Parking her car in the garage she went into the house and upstairs where she found a small supper laid out by her bedside, as it was every night, by Myra.

On the tray containing her supper was a letter. Her stomach gave a little lurch when she read the letter's contents. At last, at long last it had come! A bed was now available for Jim in an institution situated on the outskirts of the city. She lit a cigarette with trembling fingers. Then she read the letter through again.

Jim stared at Nellie, aghast. The threat of being institutionalized had been hanging over him for so long that he'd been lulled into believing it would never actually happen.

'It's all settled,' Nellie said. 'There will be an ambulance here for you later on today.' She'd just come downstairs having made the arrangements by telephone.

Myra stuffed her pinny into her face and started to cry, her eyes wide with horror.

Jim was staring at Nellie but what he was actually seeing was what he imagined the institution would be like. And the vision his mind conjured up caused him to quake inside.

'You can't do this to me,' he bullied.

Nellie was about to reply when suddenly she remembered that scene she'd had with Jim long, long ago. She'd bumped into Mr Sanderson, his old boss at the butcher's shop, and confided in Sanderson, asking him to have a word with Jim. Only Sanderson had made a mess of it by telling Jim that she'd spoken to him, and that night, after work, Jim had come home and beaten her. And after the beating she'd said, just as he had now, 'You can't do this to me.'

His reply rang in her ears. He'd shown no compassion, pity or feeling at all for her then. She'd show none of these things for him now.

'Who can't? I've just done it, haven't I?' she said, echoing his reply of long ago.

He seemed to crumble in on himself, as though, at long last, his spirit had been broken. He hung his head to stare dully at the floor.

Myra came to him and gathered him to her breast, her tears splashing down on to his head.

'Oh God! Oh God!' he whispered over and over again.

Nellie stood fully framed in her bedroom window watching the ambulancemen carry Jim out on a stretcher to their waiting vehicle.

Myra walked beside the stretcher looking as distraught as a human being can. All morning she'd been alternately keening and wailing. She was silent now that the moment of parting had arrived.

Nellie had already decided that when Myra was more herself she would offer her the position of housekeeper.

The stretcher was loaded into the ambulance and the rear doors shut. One man had stayed with Jim.

The other now climbed into the front of the ambulance and started the engine.

In celebration of having finally got Jim Biles out of her life Nellie painted her nails an exotic shade from a new bottle she'd been saving for a special occasion.

Nellie and Baz spent three weeks in the South of France then motored north into Belgium. After a few days there they decided to go on to Germany where, he told her, he and his family had once lived for a few years after they'd fled from Russia.

Nellie loved the German countryside: the thick pine forests, the clear blue lakes, the golden sun which blazed down day after glorious day.

They drove westward to Leipzig where they turned south again heading for Nürnberg and beyond that Regensburg which Baz remembered from his childhood.

They arrived in Regensburg early in the afternoon, booking into a small *Gasthaus* where they were shown to a large double room. As they'd done since coming on holiday, they registered as Mr and Mrs Spira.

'Everything is so clean,' said Nellie sinking into a large chair by the window which opened out on to a small balcony.

'Makes a change from Glasgow, eh?'

She raised an eyebrow. 'You can certainly say that again.' Even the most fanatically loyal Glaswegian had to admit that the words dirt and Glasgow were synonymous as far as the city's inner areas were concerned.

Nellie was bronzed and, despite the constant driving, feeling very fit. She was eating well and sleeping a lot. Her holiday was doing her the world of good.

A maid brought them a jug of coffee over which they planned their evening. It was decided that after eating they'd go out and explore the town, going where the fancy took them.

For supper they had chicken, sausages and sauerkraut. They washed it down with an excellent Rheinwein, indulging themselves by drinking two bottles between them.

The meal over, they strolled outside into a warm, balmy night. Arm in arm they crossed a square and into a cluster of small streets beyond. For over an hour they meandered, gradually making their way in a circle which would bring them back to their starting point. Outside a *Bierkeller* they stopped to listen to the accordion music coming from within.

'Shall we?' Baz asked.

The *Bierkeller* was busy with many flaxen-haired waitresses dressed in traditional clothes flying hither and yon, serving tankards and steins of foaming beer. There was also food to be had but not too many people were eating. It was the beer the majority of the customers were interested in.

They sat at a wooden table and Nellie lit a cigarette while Baz tried to catch the eye of one of the waitresses.

When she spoke to Baz in English she was aware of curious glances being shot in their direction. She also felt a subtle change in the atmosphere, which wasn't as friendly any more.

The girl who finally condescended to serve them did so with bad grace. She was hard-eyed and unsmiling.

'*Juden,*' a voice muttered in the background, causing Baz to look up. His good-humoured expression faded a little when the word was repeated with more hostility.

Nellie glanced around her. The men she saw were big and fleshy, many with red faces and eyes moist from drink. '*Engländer,*' she heard. And then '*Juden*' again. Tiny prickles of fear raced up and down her back.

'When we've finished this we'll go,' Baz said, attempting a smile which didn't quite come off.

'Why wait?' she replied, and started to rise. She was stopped by him placing his hand on hers.

'We finish our drink, *then* we go,' he said.

There was a group of Brown Shirts over in one

corner. They wore jackboots and peaked pillarbox hats. On their left arms each sported a swastika.

Baz followed the line of her gaze. '*Sturmabteilung* or storm troopers to you and I,' he muttered. 'Otherwise known as the SA.'

One of the Brown Shirts caught Nellie staring at him and his companions. He smiled, no doubt mistaking her for a German because of the colour of her hair. The smile became a glower when he saw Baz.

The accordionist launched into another tune and as he did the Brown Shirts began to sing. A rousing number which they sang with enormous passion.

'"The *Horst Wessel* song",' Baz said very quietly so that only Nellie could hear.

The atmosphere was ugly now, jagged and shot through with undertones. The singing rang loudly and raucously bouncing off the walls and ceiling to reverberate round and round the room.

She and Baz were the only ones not singing. His lips were compressed into a thin slash of a line.

The accordionist again changed tune, the new one being '*Deutschland Über Alles*'. Several of the singers flashed looks of triumph, and hate, in Baz's and Nellie's direction.

One of the Brown Shirts jumped to his feet to raise his arm in the Nazi salute. Every one of his companions immediately followed suit. *'Heil Hitler!*

Heil Hitler!' they chanted, while the rest of the singers continued with '*Deutschland Über Alles*'.

The clamour was deafening as Baz coolly finished his beer. He took some marks from his wallet and placed them under the stein. 'Shall we?' he said to Nellie.

There was cold sweat on her forehead and the insides of her thighs were trembling as she came to her feet, but she kept her face devoid of all emotion as she followed Baz to the stairs.

Once outside in the warm night air she took hold of his arm. 'That was terrible,' she said, feeling faint now that it was all over.

Baz shook his head. 'Such hate. And why?'

'Let's head back for France tomorrow,' she suggested. 'What happened down there has sickened me of Germany.'

'Trust me to walk into a den of Nazis,' Baz said, chuckling. The next moment he gave a cry and pitched forward to the ground as he was struck from behind.

There were four of them. Nellie recognized them as the Brown Shirts from the *Bierkeller*.

One of them took hold of her and flung her against a nearby wall. The other three started punching and kicking Baz.

'Stop it!' she screamed. 'Stop it!!' She struggled, trying to break free of the Brown Shirt who was holding her against the wall. But he was far too strong for her.

Coughing blood, Baz tried to come to his feet. His intention was to make a fight of it but he had no hope against the three hulking men surrounding him.

A hand chopped to send him spinning again to the ground, where the feet and fists started in on him again.

And then, as suddenly as it had started, it was all over. Nellie found herself released as the four figures hurried off into the darkness to disappear around a corner.

She ran and knelt beside the moaning Baz. She helped him into a sitting position, sickened and pained by his blood-covered face.

Carefully, he prodded himself all over. 'I don't think there's anything broken,' he mumbled. He held out his arm for her to take hold of, and she helped him to his feet, where he stood swaying.

'We'll have to call the police,' she said.

He shook his head. 'No police, no doctor. I'll be all right.'

'But Baz –'

'No buts, Nellie. I know what I'm doing.' He laughed, low and cynically. 'What makes you think the police would be any different from that lot there? Once in their cells they might well have another go at me. It's my fault for being stupid enough to come to Germany.'

With her supporting him he limped down the road in the direction of their *Gasthaus*. 'And tomorrow we *will* head back for France,' he said, squeezing her.

In the *Gasthaus* they made their way up to their room without being seen by anyone. There Nellie stretched Baz out on the bed and stripped him.

His plump body was ripped in several places, a few largish gashes in particular down his back. She insisted they call a doctor, but he was emphatic that they didn't.

Using a flannel soaked in hot water and some antiseptic, she washed him, gently removing the clotted and dried blood from round the gashes and his face.

Already his body was beginning to discolour. By morning he would be a mass of black and blue marks.

When she had washed him as best she could, she patted him dry with a towel. Returning from the bathroom, having rehung the towel, she found him silently crying.

'Baz?'

He turned his head away from her.

She sat on the bed and gently stroked him the way he had so often stroked her.

'Baz?' she said again.

The tears ran down the side of his face to fall on to the pillow where they were immediately absorbed. His eyes were distorted with pain and rage.

'I feel completely humiliated,' he choked in a small voice.

'There were four of them. Far too many for you.'

'I didn't even get in one punch. Not one.'

She could see the hurt was far more than physical. His pride had been wounded, and deeply. Her heart went out to him. She wanted to take him to her and comfort him like a child.

'It's a wonderful thing being a Jew,' he said. 'It can also be terrible. Tonight, well there were nights like this in Russia. Dreadful things have been done to my people, Nellie. Dreadful. And tonight I saw it starting to happen all over again. I'm crying not only for myself, but for Jews everywhere. Especially those in Germany. God help us all.'

She was crying now, too, the tears streaming down her face.

Somehow, it was right to make love at that moment. She knew that with an absolute certainty. With the tears still rolling down her face she stood and stripped. Inside she was a jumble of emotions, but the dominant one was the need to comfort Baz.

She sat by him and used her hand to arouse him, then knelt across him and very gently lowered herself on to him.

Her hair hung down over her face and her breasts fell against him as she moved. After a while she could feel his senses rising to meet her.

Perhaps it was because for the first time when having sex she was giving rather than being taken, but she began to experience sensations where there had never been any before.

Her breath became short and laboured as these new-found feelings forced her to move faster and faster. Part of her mind was filled with wonder and surprise, part given over to the urgency of the moment.

Baz came, a hot gush that she could feel quite clearly shooting up inside her. 'No!' she moaned. And then it happened. A shock wave of sheer pleasure exploded inside her. She screamed, a tearing sound that came from deep in the back of her throat. Her whole body was alive, each nerve end tingling, for the first time in her life. She screamed again as a second shock wave radiated through her.

The walls built up by Jim came tumbling and crashing down. The chains that had bound her broke and were shattered. The damage Jim had done to her had at long last been vanquished and overcome. She was whole again.

It was the first day of rehearsals and they'd just been called on stage from the green room. Beside Nellie and the line, which had half as many girls again as in previous years, there were also a dozen acts which would be making up the bill. The fact that those acts were called for rehearsal was unusual in the extreme. As was the fact that they'd been booked for the entire season rather than the normal week or fortnight.

Robert McLaughlin, the stage director, was there, as were Sandy and Baz, who would be directing the entire show.

'Gather round, ladies and gentlemen, and I'll explain to you what this is all about,' said Baz. He waited for silence before going on. 'Up until now the Palace has presented the normal type of variety, or music hall as it's called in England, with acts coming and going with a continual change over. Then last year I introduced the idea of having something constant in the show, or I should say, someone. Nellie here was that person. And most successful she and the idea proved, too.

'Well, this year I'm going to take that idea a lot further. I'm going to build an entire show, which will remain the same till the end of the season, round Nellie. That show will be called the Palace Follies.'

He waited until the excited buzz had died down before continuing.

'As you know, this sort of thing hasn't been done

before in Scotland, so we're all going to be in at the start of something new. And I think very exciting. Any questions?'

'I always knew you'd make it big,' Margo whispered to Nellie, squeezing her arm.

Nellie awoke to find herself gummy-eyed and with a foul taste in her mouth. She swung her feet out of bed, but had to grab hold of the side of it to steady herself. Her head swam round and round and she felt distinctly nauseous.

Must be a cold or the flu coming on, she told herself. That was the last thing she needed slap bang in what were proving to be the most arduous rehearsals she'd ever known.

Baz was working her harder than she'd ever been worked before. But it was going to be worth it. There was no doubt in anyone's mind that the show would be a winner. It had had that feel about it right from the first day.

She'd gone with Baz to the workshops to have a look at some completed scenery. That in itself was going to be a knockout, being grander and far more spectacular than anything yet seen on the Glasgow, and Scottish come to that, stage.

And then there were the costumes. A fortune had been spent on those. Every penny worth it, Baz had declared on viewing the first ones ready. Her reaction had been one of sheer incredulity, followed swiftly by delight. She hadn't thought so much dazzle and sparkle possible.

The dry retch caught her completely unawares. Gagging, she stumbled through to the bathroom. She thought she was going to throw up, but, gradually, the feeling subsided.

She returned to the bedroom to sit on the bed. She had an hour before being due at rehearsals. She reached for her blouse and skirt.

The skirt wouldn't do up. Impossible, she thought as she tugged at it. The damn thing had fitted her perfectly before. Finally she gave up and crossed to the wardrobe where she had a skirt which had always been a little bit loose on her. When she put that on she found it tight round the waist.

Suddenly all the pieces clicked together. Reaching up she touched her breasts which tingled beneath her fingers. She could feel they were fuller.

'Oh my God!' She ran a hand over her face. Pregnant.

She didn't know why she should be so shocked at discovering she was pregnant. She'd never taken any precautions after all! Nor had Baz, or Jim before him.

Somehow, over the years, she'd come to believe she'd never get pregnant. That, perhaps, she was incapable of it. There was absolutely no foundation for her believing this, other than the fact that it simply hadn't happened.

Well, now she knew differently. She was pregnant. Up the spout. In the club. A bun in the oven. And the show, which was totally geared round, and dependent on her, due to open in less than a fortnight.

She put her head in her hands. What a mess! Beside this, flu or a cold paled into insignificance.

Keeping it, she knew without thinking, was completely out of the question. Not only because of her, but because of Rachel and Baz as well.

But an abortion. She'd heard so many stories about what could happen, and often did. Lassies bleeding to death. Dying of blood poisoning. Always remembering.

Shaking her head, she put these thoughts from her mind. She would have to go through with it: the sooner the better.

Without talking about it, or thinking about it.

She wouldn't tell Baz till it was all over.

Betty answered the chap on the door to find Nellie smiling hesitantly at her. 'Help, my God! Come away in, hen,' she said.

'Is he still at his work?'

'Aye.'

She kissed her mother on the cheek and went

into the kitchen. She stared around. Everything was more or less just as she remembered it.

'A long time, lass,' said Betty.

'Aye, Ma. It is that.'

'You're looking well.'

'And so are you.' Which was a lie. Betty was looking older, and there was a frailness about her that hadn't been there before.

There was a photograph of her brother Roddy on the mantelpiece above the fire. She wouldn't have recognized him, he'd grown up so much. He was in uniform.

'He joined the Army a few months back,' Betty said proudly. 'He's in the HLI.' The Highland Light Infantry was Glasgow's most famous regiment.

'Time flies,' said Nellie. 'I still think of him as a wee boy.'

'It's a long time since he's been that,' replied Betty, putting the kettle on and getting out a tin of shortie. 'I hear you're doing right well at the Palace.'

'I'm top of the bill in the new show.'

'Fancy that. Our Nellie top of the bill,' said Betty, shaking her head in wonder.

'If you want to come and see me sometime, I'll get tickets for you.'

'Does that invitation include your da?'

'The tickets will be for you, Ma. If you want to take him with you then that's your affair. Just don't bring him backstage to see me, that's all.'

'Will you never forgive him, Nellie?'

'Never,' Nellie replied grimly. Defiantly she lit a cigarette, remembering the countless times she'd been dying for a fag in this room and not been allowed to light up.

'How's Jim?'

'Ma, I'm pregnant and I need your help,' Nellie stated bluntly.

Betty stared hard at her daughter, then sat down at the table. 'It's not your husband's then, I take it?' she said.

'It doesn't matter whose it is. I need to lose it.'

'Are you sure, Nellie? Killing a wean is an awful thing,' Betty said softly.

A little of her bravado left her then. White-faced, she sat looking at her mother. 'I know, Ma. But it has to be done. There's no other way. Believe me, I'd keep this baby if I could. But it just isn't possible.'

'It's dangerous.'

'I know that.'

'And it's never certain that it'll work.'

'I know that as well.'

Betty sighed, rising when the kettle began to sing.

'Will you help me, Ma?' Nellie pleaded, her mother's little girl again.

'Aye, lass. I will. How far gone are you?'

'I'm not sure. Seven, maybe eight weeks. I missed

my last period and the next should've been any day now.'

'You're certain you're pregnant?'

'Positive. I've got all the classic symptoms.'

'It'll cost about a tenner, Nellie.'

'That's no problem.'

Betty laid a cup of tea and some shortie in front of her daughter. 'Come back the same time tomorrow and I'll let you know what's what,' she said.

'The sooner the better, Ma.'

'Aye,' replied Betty. 'The sooner the better.'

The abortion was arranged for three days later. Nellie met up with Betty and together they made their way to an out-of-the-way part of Govan where Mrs Gourlay lived. Mrs Gourlay was the finest in the entire south side, Betty had assured her daughter. Nellie prayed that it was so.

The tenement they arrived at was an old one, broken down and crumbling. On its roof a chimney pot had become detached and was whirring round and round in the fierce wind that had sprung up. Side by side, the two women went into the close and up the stairs. Stairs that couldn't have seen a scrubbing brush in years.

Mrs Gourlay was old with white hair and a friendly smile. She looked like a kindly, much loved granny.

'Come in, come in,' she said, ushering them

through to the kitchen where things were already laid out in readiness. There was a roaring fire with a blanket spread in front of it. There was a pan of boiling water on the stove with an assortment of instruments in it.

Nellie was suddenly very afraid. For two beans she would've turned and fled. She reminded herself sternly that she had to go through with it. There was too much at stake for her not to.

'Do you want to stay here, or wait in the other room?' Mrs Gourlay asked Betty.

Betty glanced at Nellie. 'You go through, Ma,' Nellie said.

Betty nodded, relief plainly written across her face. 'Good luck, lass,' she said gently.

'If you'll just take your coat, skirt and knickers off and lie down there,' Mrs Gourlay said, pointing to the blanket.

Nellie's hands were shaking as she partially undressed herself. She lay down as instructed, watching fearfully as Mrs Gourlay took the sterilized instruments off the stove.

'I'll have to examine you first,' said Mrs Gourlay squatting beside her.

'Will it hurt?' Nellie asked fearfully.

'Och, just a wee bit, hen. But I'll be as quick and gentle as I can.'

Nellie was in a cold sweat and her heart was

hammering in her chest. Her flesh was a mass of goose bumps. Her buttocks and stomach tensed as the instrument touched her.

'Easy, lass. Easy.' Mrs Goulay crooned.

Nellie chewed her lip to keep her mind from what was happening. From the bottom of her eye she could see Mrs Gourlay's white head bent over her.

Mrs Gourlay began singing in a cracked, reedy voice. She sang soft and low about a mining disaster. The sound of her voice sent prickles up and down Nellie's spine.

Minutes the length of years passed, until it seemed to her it would never end. She felt as though someone had taken their fist and hit her between the legs again and again and again.

The singing finally stopped and Mrs Gourlay rose to her feet to smile down at Nellie. 'That's it,' she said simply.

Nellie rolled on to her elbow and tucked her legs up under her. That position relieved the aching a little. 'Is it gone?'

'Not yet. That'll take a few hours. What I've done, hopefully, is loosen the foetus. The next thing is for the body to reject it. I suggest you go home and into your bed. Let it happen there.'

Nellie came to her feet. Then, sitting on a nearby chair, she started to pull on her knickers, stopping in horror when she saw one of the instruments which had been used lying on the blanket. A knitting needle! There was no mistaking it. She'd always believed that knitting needles used for abortions was an old wives' tale.

Betty entered the room white-faced, her eyes immediately seeking out Nellie's. 'How did it go?' she asked, her voice trembling.

'We'll know in a few hours,' Mrs Gourlay replied. 'But I'm very hopeful.'

Betty helped Nellie into her coat.

'Ten pounds,' said Mrs Gourlay.

Nellie paid over two fivers, and then, her mother giving her support, they made their way downstairs to where her car was parked.

'Are you sure you're all right to drive?' Betty asked.

Nellie nodded. 'She said you should come home with me. Can you do that?'

'Of course. Your da can get his own tea for once. Won't do him any harm.'

Halfway back to Bishopton Nellie felt her temperature start to rise. Soon she was sweating badly. By the time they arrived she was slightly delirious.

She didn't bother putting the car in the garage as she normally did, but parked it in front of the house. With Betty supporting her, she made her way upstairs to collapse on to her bed.

Betty stripped her and got her into a clean nightgown. 'Hold my hand, Ma,' Nellie whispered.

Nellie dreamt then. A series of nightmares, which, afterwards, she couldn't remember anything about, except that at the time they had terrified her.

For five hours Nellie waited for something to happen, all this time sweating profusely and replenishing the liquid by gulping down cupful after cupful of water which Betty fetched from the bathroom.

'It's going to come, Ma,' she gasped suddenly, as a new pain racked her.

'Jesus!' she whimpered. The pain was almost unbearable. And then it was over.

Betty had seen the garden out back. 'I won't be long,' she said, and left the room.

Nellie was filled with an enormous sense of loss. Difficult to describe, it felt as though part of her very being had somehow been taken away from her.

She was still crying later when Betty returned. Betty sat on the bed and held her close. Mother and daughter wept together softly, no words needed.

When Betty finally left, she had made a firm promise that from then on in she would be a regular visitor to the house in Bishopton. The horror of the abortion had rekindled the natural closeness that had always existed between them but which had faded since Nellie's marriage and her leaving home.

The next morning Nellie presented herself at rehearsal promptly at ten o'clock, her call time. She looked dreadful. She was drawn and haggard, and there were dark bags under her eyes.

'What's wrong with you?' Baz exclaimed when he saw her. He told her to sit down and shouted to Sandy to get some coffee.

She didn't want to tell him yet. She would do that later at a more appropriate time. 'Flu, I think,' she mumbled.

'Perhaps you should go home –'

'No!' She shook her head. Lying in bed thinking about what she'd been through the previous night was the last thing she wanted. 'If you just let me take it easy for a couple of days I'll get by all right.'

Baz wasn't so certain of that. She really did look terrible. But Nellie was adamant. She would continue with rehearsals.

She had never known an atmosphere backstage like it. Even the normally phlegmatic stagehands were looking nervous.

'Five minutes,' whispered Sandy, giving her a reassuring wink.

Normally she wouldn't have been ready and backstage this early, but tonight was extra special. Tonight was the opening night of the Follies.

'Good luck,' whispered Margo.

'And you,' Nellie whispered back.

They kissed each other on the cheek, then Margo

joined the rest of the line who were in position now, ready to go on.

Baz appeared, dressed in an evening suit, looking as nervous as any of them. He took Nellie's hand and squeezed it. 'You're going to be marvellous,' he said. 'Just do it as you did in rehearsal and you can't go wrong. I promise you.'

'Good luck,' she whispered in reply.

'Break a leg.' He patted her on the arm, gave her what he hoped was a confident smile, and then left her to cross to the line.

'Beginners!' Sandy called quite unnecessarily as everyone was already in position waiting for the rag to open. It was that sort of night.

Nellie went up on her toes, an old pro's trick that helped you relax. With one hand on her diaphragm and the other on the side of her ribcage, she did some breathing exercises the way Miss McLeish had taught her.

Out front the music struck up and the atmosphere became electric. Robert McLaughlin, who, for that night only, was running the corner, looked across at Nellie and smiled. He then gave her the thumbs up sign.

There was the swish of the curtains opening, followed instantly by a round of applause. 'Go line!' instructed McLaughlin. The applause intensified as the line danced on stage.

The line danced and sang its way through the number; then it was time for Nellie's first entrance.

She came on, atop a built-up level of platforms, to thunderous acclaim. The stage lights had been dimmed, the two limes from out front holding her in a cone of brilliant light. Smiling, she began to descend the flight of steps that would take her on to the stage.

She started to sing, and as she did so the applause faded to an absolute hush. The proverbial dropping pin could have been heard.

'Somehow by fate misguided,
A buttercup resided
In the Mandarin's Orchid Garden –
A buttercup that did not grace
The loveliness of such a place.
And so it simply shrivelled up
And begged each orchid's pardon.
Poor little buttercup in The Orchid Garden.'

McIan was in the front row, an enraptured expression on his face. Every few seconds his chest heaved in a silent sigh.

She'd been confident when she came on but that confidence grew with every passing second. Soon she knew she could do no wrong. They were hers. Every last one of them.

At the end of her first song they rose to her, cheering and clapping, McIan at the front like some giant conductor leading the applause.

It went like that all night. An entire half hour was added to the show's running time because of applause.

She got eighteen curtain calls and one man, quite overcome, tried to crawl up on stage only to be hauled off by McIan.

Glasgow had never seen the like before.

Nellie's dressing room, the largest the theatre could provide, was chock-a-block with other artistes and well-wishers. Baz had laid on two crates of champagne and McIan had appeared waving a jeroboam of the stuff above his head, most of which, thanks to his treatment of it, ended up on the floor.

'I'm going to do an entire series of paintings of you,' McIan declared, having finally managed to collar Nellie on her own. 'And when they're finished, we'll have the Nellie Wildchild exhibition. Every picture of you. Nobody else. Just you. A feast of you! What do you say?'

Nellie laughed. She was feeling marvellous. Absolutely glorious. The show had been a success beyond her wildest imaginings.

'Well?' he demanded, his face flushed with excitement and drink.

'Why not?' she said.

'Why not indeed!' he roared. 'Why not indeed!'

She was still in her slap and walk-down costume, not having had time to change before her dressing room had been invaded. She sipped champagne and then puffed reflectively at her cigarette. She wanted this moment to go on and on. Never to stop.

'Miss Wildchild?'

She came out of her reverie to find the stage doorkeeper standing beside her.

'A man asked me to give this to you. He said I should bring it right up.'

'Have you time for a drink?' she asked.

His eyes flicked across to where Baz was standing. 'That's awful kind of you, but I think not,' he replied.

She took two half-crowns from the top of her dressing table and gave them to him. 'Have a dram on me then when you get the chance,' she said.

'You're a right toff, Miss Wildchild,' he replied, making the half-crowns disappear into his trouser pocket.

Nellie was about to read the note when one of the acts approached her asking if he could intro-duce his niece. She laid the note on top of her dressing table, and promptly forgot about it.

It was a good hour later before the party started to

break up. Baz had already gone off to his office, having told Nellie he'd return to take her home. The rambunctious McIan, with one of the new girls from the line hanging on to his arm and his every word, was the last to go.

A little bit tipsy from the champagne, Nellie sat at her dressing table and carefully removed her make-up. Then she changed into her street clothes.

She was about to put out the light when she saw the note the stage doorkeeper had handed in earlier. Picking it up she glanced at its contents.

Dear Nellie,

Remember me? Thought you were terrific tonight. I'll hang around outside the stage door for ten minutes as I'd love to have a word. But if you're too busy to see me, I'll understand perfectly.

Frank Connelly

'Oh no!' At the sight of that signature her heart nearly burst. Her Frank had been to see the show!

Whirling she ran from the dressing room, frantically clattering downstairs as she raced for the stage door.

'Good night, Miss Wildchild!' the stage door-keeper called out to her as she went haring past him. She never heard a word.

Through the stage door, into the night beyond.

But the area was deserted, as she'd known in her heart of hearts it would be.

'Frank! Oh, Frank!' she whispered, her face suddenly awash with scalding tears. If only she'd read that note when it had been handed to her. And to think she was upstairs guzzling champagne while he was down here waiting for her.

She staggered and put her hand against the theatre wall for support.

'Are you all right, Miss? I thought you looked funny as you went past,' a voice said.

She turned to find herself staring at the stage doorkeeper. Why did his face keep going round and round? Somewhere at the back of her mind it dawned on her that it wasn't only him but the whole world.

'Oh!' she said as the blackness closed in and she pitched forward in a dead faint into the stage doorkeeper's arms.

She came to in Baz's office to find herself stretched out on his day bed. He was hovering anxiously over her, holding a glass of water. There was a wet towel across her forehead.

'You fainted,' he said, and putting his arm under her shoulders lifted her up a bit so she could swallow some of the water.

'Will I call a doctor?' he asked.

She shook her head. 'No. That won't be necessary.'

He perched himself on the edge of the bed and chaffed her hand. 'You haven't been looking at all well since you had the flu. I've been dreadfully worried about you.'

She didn't want to tell him the real cause of her fainting. 'It wasn't flu I had. It was an abortion,' she said slowly.

Baz blinked. 'What?'

'We were halfway through rehearsals before I realised I was pregnant.'

He rose and crossed to his desk where he kept a bottle of brandy, pouring himself a liberal measure, which he drank neat.

'You should have said, Nellie.'

'Would it have made any difference? The result would have been the same, Baz. There was too much at stake for both of us. At least this way I spared you the extra worry and pressure.'

She fumbled in her pocket for cigarettes.

'Our child,' he said, staring into his now empty glass.

'I suppose the excitement tonight, not to mention the champagne, was just too much on top of everything else,' she lied.

He came to her then and took her in his arms. And they remained like that for some time, neither of them speaking.

He was thinking of her and their lost child. She was thinking of Frank Connelly.

Eighteen months passed, during which the first Follies season closed – a resounding success – and the second one opened to just as much acclaim. Nellie was now firmly established as the foremost female Scottish star, fêted by the public, the newspapers and fellow artistes alike.

As he'd promised he would, McIan, who'd become a great and close friend of hers and Baz's, had been beavering away doing a series of paintings with her as the subject. For months he'd haunted backstage making interminable sketches. One night he failed to turn up, and word reached them that he was now busy in his Edinburgh studio, translating his sketches on to canvas.

One Tuesday morning Nellie left Bishopton to drive into Sauchiehall Street where she was scheduled to open McIan's Nellie Wildchild exhibition. Normally he exhibited first in Edinburgh, but in this case, because his subject was so identified with Glasgow, he'd decided to have the opening there.

Nellie was in a good humour as she drove into town. After all, it wasn't every day you had this sort of honour. She was thinking of the forthcoming speech she would have to make – the press were to be in full attendance – when, absentmindedly, she noted the vaguely familiar face of a passer-by.

She was a hundred yards down the road when she suddenly realized who that person was. Uttering a muffled exclamation, she slammed on the brakes and came to an abrupt halt. Swivelling in her seat, she saw the man's back disappear up a side street.

She whipped the car into gear and, nearly causing an accident, did a U turn. She gunned the engine to go screeching round the corner in pursuit. The man was halfway up the hill when she brought the car to a shuddering halt beside him.

He looked down in surprise and she saw that the face was a lot older than she remembered it.

'Hello, Frank,' she said.

There was a cynical, quizzical look on his face. 'Nellie.'

She swung the passenger door open for him. When he was seated she stared at him, drinking him in. 'You've put on weight,' she said.

'You've changed as well. But nothing that doesn't suit you,' he said nervously.

She wanted to reach out and touch him. To hold him. 'That night you sent up the note. I never got to read it till well over an hour later, by which time you were gone.'

He smiled, but didn't speak.

'I came the moment I did read it.'

'And how are you? Married?'

'Yes.'

'And you?'

'I never did. Lots of women, mind you. But nothing permanent.'

There was so much she had to explain. So much to say. All the misunderstandings that had to be cleared up. She was already late for the opening of the exhibition.

'I've got to see you and talk to you properly, Frank,' she said. 'But I have to rush off just now. Believe me, I wouldn't if I didn't have to, but I do. When can we meet?'

He shrugged. 'Name a time. I'm my own boss so I can fit in with you.'

She named a time and a place. 'Can you meet me there for lunch?' she asked.

'I'll be there.'

On a sudden impulse she leaned across and kissed him on the cheek. 'It's so good to see you again, Frank. You've no idea.'

He got out of the car and closed the door behind him. 'Till later then,' he said, and immediately continued on his way.

She tooted her horn as she passed him and he waved back. She watched him in the mirror till she turned out of sight.

She'd met up again with Frank after all these

years. He wasn't married. And she was having lunch with him.

She felt like shouting her exultation to the skies!

She might have been a young lassie going out on her first date. Her insides were fluttering and she kept having the most ridiculous urge to giggle. She'd also been to the toilet four times in the past hour, which was something of a record for her.

On arriving at the rendezvous point she found him already there standing staring into space. His expression was thoughtful, withdrawn.

'Hello, again,' she said, coming to his side.

'You're early.'

'So are you.'

The moment they'd sat down she blurted out the story she had been waiting so long to tell him. 'I never wanted to break off our engagement. It was my da who made me. He threatened to have you killed if I didn't do as he said.'

Frank rocked back in his seat, staring at her in amazement.

'I planned getting word to you later saying that I would wait for you till you were time served and I was eighteen. Then we could have run off together. But I didn't know where you lived to send a letter or who your friends were even. So by the time I did find someone who could've passed on a message for me you'd already gone abroad.'

The waitress came and they placed their orders, neither particularly interested in what that order was.

'I didn't go abroad,' Frank said quietly. 'I went to London.'

'Your mates at the Yard seemed to think you'd gone off to Canada or New Zealand. South Africa someone even said later.'

'Your da threatened to kill me?'

'He'd have *had* it done. He wouldn't have done it personally.'

'And you broke off our engagement to save my life?'

Suddenly there was a huge lump in her throat. 'Yes,' she whispered.

Frank ran a hand across his face and then closed his eyes. When he opened them again he said, 'What a fool I was.'

'I never dreamed you'd run away like that. The thought just never entered my mind.'

'And your da was listening to our conversation?'

'Through the plate-glass window. You probably never even saw him.'

Frank shook his head in disbelief.

'I never stopped loving you,' Nellie stated in a whisper.

'But you got married?'

She gave a bitter smile. Then she told him all about Jim Biles.

He listened grimly, occasionally interrupting to ask a question or to have some point clarified. When she was finally finished he said, 'And what about now, Nellie? Who's your man now?'

She hung her head. Somehow he knew that she had a man other than Jim. She wouldn't lie to him, nor would she keep anything back. 'He's made me what I am,' she said. And told Frank all about Baz and how Baz had built her into a star.

'Do you love him?' Frank asked at last.

'I'm very fond of him.'

'That's not what I asked.'

'No. I don't. You're the only man I've ever loved.'

Frank called the waitress over and ordered himself a large whisky. Nellie declined to have a drink.

'And what about you?' she asked quietly. 'What happened after you left Glasgow?'

'Well, to begin with it wasn't easy. As you can imagine,' he said slowly. 'I took the train down to London, arriving there knowing not a soul. I slept rough for a couple of nights and then landed myself a job in a Covent Garden café.'

'What did you do in the café?' she asked, fascinated.

He smiled at the memory. 'As you probably know Covent Garden is where the fruit and veg arrive in

357

London from all over England, and the world. The traders who buy there have to have their purchases back in their shops before normal trading hours begin so that means a very early start indeed for those who work in the Garden. My own start was half past three, filling the coffee urn and slicing bread for sandwiches. The door was opened at four, by which time I'd been joined by the couple who owned the café. The rest of the working day, which was till 1 p.m., I spent behind the counter, clearing the tables, sweeping up, washing-up, drying. I never cooked though, the couple insisted on doing that themselves.'

'Half past three start,' said Nellie. And gave a tiny whistle. 'And I used to think the sweetie factory was bad. But go on, what did you work at after the café?' She indicated the smart suit he was wearing. 'I take it you're not still there?'

'No, I moved on. I went to work for a couple of Italian importers, brothers called Giovanni, or Johnny, as he's known, and Carlo Maestri. They're a fairly large organization which I've worked my way up in to an executive level.'

There was a slight pause. Then she said softly. 'So what brings you back to Glasgow? Holidays?'

'I'm here on business, Nellie. When I came to your opening night of the Follies I was up for a week. I had various people to see and reports to compile. Now the Maestris have sent me up again.'

'How long for this time?' she asked, unable to keep the eagerness out of her voice.

'That depends. Could be a month, a year, for ever even. It all hinges on the decision they eventually take on whether or not to open up a Glasgow end to their business.'

'You're obviously doing very well for yourself.'

'As are you,' he acknowledged with a grin. He shook his head. 'That night I came to see the Follies, I had no idea you were Nellie Wildchild. I nearly died when I recognized you.'

'Were you alone?' she asked coyly.

'No, I was with a business associate. It was he who provided the tickets.'

'And you never married, Frank?'

'Nope.'

'Can I ask why?'

'You know why.'

Warmth engulfed her. She felt suddenly weak and lightheaded. 'Tell me anyway,' she whispered.

'I never found anyone to replace you. And perhaps I never really wanted to.'

She reached out and took his hand, holding it clasped in hers. 'All those years wasted,' she said.

'But *can* we pick up where we left off?' he asked, studying her face.

'I want to try.' She stared down at the table. 'Do you?'

There was a moment of silence. Then, from far away, his voice said, 'Yes.'

It was one of the nights Baz wasn't in the theatre, being home with Rachel and the family. When the show was over Nellie changed in record time, not even bothering with her make-up. She would attend to that at home.

She was one of the first out of the stage door – a most unusual occurrence as she normally liked to linger for a while. He was under a standard lamp, waiting patiently.

'We're down early. Have you been here long?' she asked.

'Only a few minutes.'

'Have you got a car?'

'I left it at the hotel, knowing you've got one.'

She put her arm in his and guided him towards where hers was parked. 'How about the Roxy Saturday night?' she asked.

He laughed. 'God, do you remember?'

'I've never forgotten a moment of any of those times.'

'And we used to come into town so we wouldn't be seen together,' he said.

'Going home in the same tram and you following me into the back close.'

'You had a friend . . . ?'

'Babs. She's married now. A nice chap. They're very happy.'

'Do you still see her?'

'Oh, aye. She and some of my other pals from the sweetie factory come over from time to time. I see Babs more than the others. We usually meet up in the town and have afternoon tea.'

'And what about your da?'

Her face clouded over. 'Ma thinks I should forgive him for what he did to me, and you, but I never will. Hell will freeze over first.'

'I'm sure he thought he was doing it all for your own good.'

'That's what Ma says, but whichever way you look at it, I was the one who lost you and then had to live with Jim. Small consolation, knowing it was for my own good.'

During the drive to Bishopton they talked, she occasionally reaching out to touch his thigh, as though to reassure herself that he really was there and not a mirage.

He stood looking up at the house while she parked the car in the garage. 'Very nice,' he said when she joined him.

'Bought and paid for. And everything in it. I earn quite a bit now since the Follies opened. And this year more than last.'

She took him inside and up to her bedroom.

There he produced a bottle of whisky from his coat pocket, saying he hadn't come empty handed. The usual tray of supper was there from Myra, but she wasn't hungry. Nor was he.

She put on the gramophone while he poured more drinks. Then they sat back to look at one another. Neither was in a hurry.

'Tell me about your life in London.'

'Do you mean my life, or the women who've been in it?'

She laughed. 'Both.'

'I have a small flat in Islington overlooking the canal. From my back window you can watch the narrow boats chug up and down. I like that.'

'And the women?'

'They come and they go. All sorts really.'

'But nothing serious?'

'No,' he smiled.

She sipped her whisky and studied him. He'd become very self-contained. There was a strength about him which she found exciting. He'd always had strength of character, of course – that had always been a feature of his – but he had grown considerably, matured, in the intervening years. Those same years had also added creases and crinkles to his face – and the tiniest of scars above his left eyebrow.

He got up and crossed to the gramophone and

changed the record. His movements were also different. Before there had been the slight awkwardness of the young man. Now he moved with a tightly controlled assurance.

'Dance?' he asked. He'd put on a waltz.

She came into his arms feeling as though she fitted there. That it was the most natural place in the world for her to be. Like coming home.

They waltzed slowly, bodies hard against one another. She knew he was wanting her just as badly as she was wanting him. They danced to four records and then she said she'd had enough. She lit another cigarette while he topped up her drink.

'To us!' he toasted.

'Nellie?'

'Yes?'

'Let's go to bed.'

He was already in bed when she returned from the bathroom. He was up on one elbow, drinking whisky. The look he gave her made her shiver.

She slipped in beside him and they stared at one another. She was suddenly nervous. Feeling terribly virginal.

'This sure beats the back close,' he said, as nervous as she was. Reaching out she drew him to her. Breast to chest, she could feel the thudding of his heart.

Their lovemaking was over fairly quickly. Because

it meant so much to each of them, they'd been a little shy, reserved. But it was true love they'd made, and because of that the experience was memorable. Forever etched in both their minds.

Nellie curled up against Frank holding him close; wishing it was in her power to melt her flesh into his.

Jim had debased and defiled her. Baz had made her whole again. But Frank had lifted her into an entirely new world.

When she heard the knock on her dressing-room door she knew who it was and why he was there. It was a moment she'd been dreading. 'Come in, Baz!' she called out.

The smile on his face belied the hurt, quizzical expression in his eyes. 'Can I sit?' he asked.

'Of course.'

The half had been called. She was in her robe, putting on her make-up, concentrating on making the black lines which swept across her lower eyelids like a bird in flight.

'What's wrong, Nellie? Have I done something?' he asked hesitatingly.

It had been ten days now since he'd been home with her. During that time she'd pleaded every excuse imaginable from headaches to period pains.

'No, you've done nothing,' she replied, sadness

heavy within her. She was about to hurt dreadfully this man who'd been so kind to her. Inevitable as it was, it was the last thing she wanted to do.

'Then why do you keep putting me off?' he asked.

She laid down her eye brush and looked at him in the mirror, feeling about two inches tall. 'Do you remember I once told you that my husband got me on the rebound?' she asked.

Baz nodded.

'And then I told you about the chap he'd got me on the rebound from. Well that chap's name was, is Frank Connelly.'

Baz sat very still, his eyes glued to Nellie's in the mirror.

'You've been marvellous to me, Baz. I couldn't have met a sweeter, nicer man. Patient, too.' She made a gesture that took in not only the dressing room but the theatre as a whole. 'Then there's all this. Nellie Wildchild, star of the Follies. I owe it all to you. Even the name was your creation.'

'Are you saying it's all over between us?' he asked slowly.

'Frank came back. And I love him just as much as I ever did. I wouldn't break us up for any other man, Baz. You've got to believe that. But Frank and I, well, it's something made in heaven.'

Baz took out a small leather case from which he extracted a cigar, taking his time in lighting it. 'Are you and Frank going to get married?'

'If he asks me. I'll have to get divorced first from
Jim, of course.'

'Will he ask you?'

'I hope so.'

'But he's Catholic, isn't he?'

'That doesn't bother me in the least.'

'And where will you live?'

'Glasgow, London, wherever his job takes him.'

'You'll give up the theatre then?'

She hadn't really thought that through and said
so, adding, 'But I will if I have to. He's more important to me, and always has been, than anything else.'

'I see,' said Baz behind a cloud of blue smoke.

'I'm sorry,' she said.

He smiled bitterly. 'So am I.' He rose and crossed
to the door. 'I've come to love you as much as you
say you love him.' Still smiling, Baz closed the door
behind him.

That night after the show Frank met Nellie and she
drove them back to Bishopton. 'Baz came to see me
just after the half. He wanted to know what was what.
So I told him.'

'How did he take it?'

'It cut him up pretty badly. He said he was in love
with me as much as I am with you.'

They drove a little while in silence, each with their

separate thoughts. 'Now that's sorted out, do you want to move in with me?' she asked suddenly.

He glanced at her, then reached out to place his hand on her shoulder. 'I can't think of anything I'd like more,' he replied. 'Besides, the Scot in me hates like hell having to pay out for a hotel room I'm only changing my clothes in.'

Nellie and Frank lay on what was now their bed, glistening with sweat.

Each time they made love it got better and better as they relaxed and learned how best to please the other. As Frank joked, practice made perfect. They believed in lots of practice.

They'd been four days apart while Frank had been down to London talking to the Maestri brothers. They'd been pleased with what he'd had to report, telling him to consider himself based in Glasgow indefinitely. Nellie had been ecstatic to hear that; she could now continue at the Palace.

Frank had only been home from London a little over an hour.

'Oh, I've got something for you!' he exclaimed, and, getting up, crossed to where his suit had been thrown carelessly over a chair. He fished in the pockets till he found what he was looking for, returning to Nellie with one hand behind his back.

'Close your eyes,' he said. He took hold of her

left hand and slipped a ring on to her wedding finger. 'You can look now.'

She opened her eyes to find herself staring at an engagement ring that was strangely familiar.

'Recognize it?'

'It's not – ?'

'It is,' laughing at the expression of incredulity on her face.

She touched the ring, remembering it from all those years ago when he'd first given it to her; when she'd returned it to him that day in the shop entranceway in Sauchiehall Street.

'You kept it all this time,' she said, amazed.

'I suppose, at the beginning, I thought I might give it to someone else eventually. But of course I never did. I never dreamed I'd be giving it back to you, though.'

She raised the ring to her lips and kissed it, her eyes gleaming with tears.

'I had to wait till I went back to London before I could pick it up,' he said. 'And now that you've got it, will you marry me?'

The tears became a flood. 'For the second time, yes,' she sobbed.

He held her and kissed her till the tears had stopped. 'Before you can marry me you'll have to get divorced,' he said.

'I can't think of anything I'd rather do. I'll see a

solicitor in the morning,' she replied.

'I'll come with you.'

'I'd like that. And you know what else I'd like?'

Her expression told him what it was she wanted. He was only too willing to oblige.

7

The next few months for Nellie were idyllic. Each day was an absolute joy to wake up to, now that she had Frank.

The Follies were packing them in and it was rare enough to cause comment when a performance wasn't a sell-out.

Baz had been the perfect gentleman in accepting the situation between her and Frank, and although he was deeply hurt, there was never any bad feeling on his part toward either of them.

It was getting on for the end of the season when Nellie received a letter from the Press Club informing her she'd been voted Scottish Personality of the Year and asking her to attend a party they were throwing in her honour.

The night of the party, Frank picked her up after the show and they drove to the Press Club in his new car, a sleek Riley. They were both in a frivolous mood as they entered the club where Nellie was immediately given a standing ovation.

Drinks were pressed on them, and, after a short while, they were led through to a large room where rows of tables had been set out ready for a meal.

After the meal speeches were made, the final one by Nellie which was short, very funny and consisted mainly of her thanking the press for being so kind to her over the last few years. That done, everyone retired to the bar where the beer and whisky were soon flowing liberally.

McIan, voted Personality of the Year himself in the past, was also at the function. His Nellie Wildchild exhibition had been widely acclaimed and, indeed, had a great deal to do with Nellie receiving that year's award and accolade.

McIan and Frank were at the bar treating one another when Nellie was approached by a suspicious looking, beady-eyed man who walked with a limp.

The man stopped beside Nellie, who was chatting to a cartoonist called Neil Mungo, and stared at her, taking her in from head to toe.

Aware of this, she was suddenly uncomfortable. There was something repulsive about the man.

'So you're Nellie Wildchild!' he said, interrupting her conversation with Mungo.

She smiled at him and offered her hand. 'That's

right. I don't believe we've met.'

He ignored the proffered hand. 'Well, I certainly don't think you're anywhere near as good-looking as you're reputed to be,' he continued.

Nellie's smile became strained. She glanced to Mungo for help.

'Robin Carson,' Mungo said. 'Writes for the *Daily Post.*

'I've seen you perform, or should I say I've had the *misfortune* to see you perform, and you certainly didn't get my vote for the award. As a so-called star, I think you're decidedly lacking in twinkle.' Then he laughed at his own joke.

'Well, you're entitled to your opinion,' Nellie replied quietly. 'But it certainly doesn't seem to be one shared by the vast majority of the people who come to see the show.'

The eyes became even beadier as they bored into Nellie, who had no doubts whatever that she was facing an enemy.

Those within earshot of this exchange had fallen silent causing a soundless oasis amidst the surrounding babble. A number of men glanced sympathetically, and a few anxiously, in Nellie's direction. But none moved to intervene.

'Robin has a reputation for acid wit,' Mungo explained. 'I'm afraid we've all suffered from it in the past.'

Nellie suddenly realized that Neil Mungo was scared of Robin Carson, as were the others listening in. And as for the name Carson, it wasn't a particularly common one in Glasgow. In fact she'd only ever come across it once before.

'Are you by any chance related to Geoff Carson, the painter?' she asked.

'My brother.'

'Ah yes!' she replied. 'I thought I saw a similarity. You've both got atrocious manners.'

Robin Carson bared his teeth. 'Coming from the gutter as you have, I'm surprised you even know what manners are,' he said, his voice dripping spite and venom.

'I'm sure the gutter is something you know a great deal about,' she retorted instantly.

One of the onlookers tittered, stopping immediately when Carson flashed him a filthy look.

'And how is Geoff?' Nellie went on. 'Is he doing well?' She knew from McIan that he wasn't.

'You're becoming impertinent,' Carson snapped.

'Then that's something we'll have in common.'

'Are you trying to make a fool of me?'

'I don't have to, Mister Carson. You do that admirably enough yourself.'

The oasis of quiet had widened considerably now. Somewhere in its ranks there was a sharp, barking laugh followed by a guffaw.

Carson glared but couldn't see who the culprits were. He brought his attention back to Nellie. 'I've heard you slept your way to the top. Any comment?' he asked.

'What sort of question is that to ask a lady?' she replied.

His smile matched hers. Only there was a nasty, razor-like quality about his. 'I wouldn't ask it of a lady,' he said.

She'd left herself wide open on that one, she told herself. Suddenly she wasn't so sure she could handle Carson.

'Who's the creep?' a voice said. She looked round to find Frank by her side.

'Robin Carson. He writes for the *Daily Post*.'

'I've read some of your muck,' Frank said, though he had never heard of the man before. 'And muck is certainly the right name for it.'

'I didn't catch *your* name?' Carson said.

'Frank Connelly. Miss Wildchild's fiancé.'

'Ah! And you imagine, I suppose, that you've come galloping to her rescue. Saving lady fair. Only, as has already been said, this one's no lady.' He swung his attention back to Nellie. 'Again, I ask you, have you any comment on the accusation that you slept your way to the top?'

'Take it easy, Robin,' Neil Mungo said somewhat half-heartedly. He was rewarded with a withering look which caused him to smile nervously and glance away.

'I'm waiting for an answer!'

'You really are a horrible little creep, aren't you,' Frank said, diverting his attention away from Nellie.

Carson tapped the floor with his rubber-tipped stick. The entire room had gone quiet now. 'You're beginning to annoy me, Connelly.'

'*Mister* Connelly to you.'

'Indeed!' said Carson, and laughed. He glanced around. '*Mister*,' he said sarcastically and with great emphasis. He laughed again.

'I suggest if you want an interview with Miss Wildchild then you write asking for one,' Frank said. 'That's the normal procedure.'

'Are you trying to tell me how to do my job?' Carson asked ominously.

Frank raised an eyebrow, but didn't reply.

Carson looked Frank up and down, the way he had done Nellie a few minutes earlier. Frank waited till Carson had completed his visual examination, then did exactly the same thing to Carson.

Carson was furious and showed it.

Frank smiled, a nasty smile that was both dismissive and full of contempt, to infuriate Carson further.

'Why don't you run along and play your silly games elsewhere,' Frank said.

Breath hissed from Carson's mouth. Slowly, he

brought the tip of his stick up to jab Frank lightly in the chest with it. 'Connelly,' he said. 'I'm not going to forget that name.'

'Let's go home Frank,' said Nellie.

'Embarrassed or scared to answer my questions?' Carson asked her.

'Not in the least.'

'I'd say you were.'

'There's nothing I've ever done that I'd be ashamed to admit to.'

'A paragon eh?' Carson said, and chuckled, having regained his composure.

'Hardly that –'

'Tell me,' he interrupted. 'Is it true you used to work in a sweetie factory?'

'Yes.'

'And that you once brawled in the street with a co-worker?'

Where in the hell had he got that from? Nellie wondered.

'No answer, eh?'

Frank decided this had gone far enough. 'I've met men like you before,' he said. 'Bitter, twisted men who've become as deformed in their minds as they are in their bodies.'

'How dare you!' Carson spluttered.

'And how dare *you*!' Frank retorted. 'Now hobble off, before I'm tempted to flush you away.'

With a screech of rage Carson flew at Frank, managing to strike him several times about the face and shoulders with his stick before Frank was able to get his arms round him and hold him.

Carson struggled in his arms, trying to get free. It suddenly came to Frank what he should do. If he couldn't hit the man, then he'd humiliate him. In two swift movements he sank to the floor on one knee, Carson over his upright leg. With great gusto, he began to spank him.

The laughter began slowly and gathered momentum. By the time Frank had finished, it had become a great wave of sound filling up the room.

Frank dumped Carson unceremoniously on the floor. Rising, he extended a crooked arm which Nellie slipped hers through. And like that, triumphant, they carved their way through a sea of thundering, clapping hands to the exit.

McIan jostled his way after them. Tears of laughter were still rolling down his cheeks when he joined them outside. 'That was the funniest thing I've seen in years,' he said slapping Frank heartily on the back. 'It'll be the talk of the Press Club for the next decade, if not longer.'

They walked round the comer to where the Riley was parked. Frank opened the door and helped Nellie inside. He was turning to walk round the car when McIan took hold of his arm. He stared up at the painter towering over him.

'You've made a really bad enemy though, Frank. Be careful. That one's the original viper.'

'I'll remember. Although it's not myself I'm worried about. It's Nellie. A man like him who goes in for muckraking could give her bad publicity.'

Nellie rolled down the window so she could be heard. 'I'm sure that was in his mind before he even spoke to me tonight. He wants to get back at me because of his brother.' She explained to them then about Geoff Carson.

'So we'll just have to wait and see what happens now,' Frank said grimly.

They were nearly halfway home when he suddenly let out a great roar. 'I'll never forget that till my dying day!' he spluttered.

Nellie joined in the laughter.

Two weeks later Frank and Nellie came down to breakfast, and found the papers laid out on the kitchen table by Myra, the *Daily Post* among them.

On page three Frank came across the leader, 'What Sort Of Woman Is This Glasgow Has Come To Idolize?' Underneath was Robin Carson's by-line. And underneath that a picture of Nellie.

The article was a long one, most of which consisted of an interview with Jim Biles out at the institution.

Frank read it through, then, wordlessly, handed it to Nellie. By the time she'd come to the end she was white-faced.

'Carson's made you out to be some heartless monster who's committed her adoring husband, while she's cavorting with a fancy man, namely me.'

Nellie glanced at the article again. 'The trouble is, there's nothing here I can prove is a lie. Most of it would be Jim's word against mine.' Then suddenly she burst out angrily, 'How can he say he worshipped the ground I walked on!'

'To read that, you'd think Biles was a saint and butter wouldn't melt in his mouth,' Frank said bitterly.

'At least there's nothing about Baz and me. That's something at least.'

'How will his wife take it if that comes out?'

'Not very well I shouldn't think.'

'And Carson knows about you two. That's for certain.'

Nellie bit her lip. She hated the idea of Baz and his family being hurt.

The telephone rang then and when Nellie answered it she found it was Baz.

'Have you read it?' Baz asked.

'A minute ago. Will it affect business?'

'I don't know. We'll just have to wait and see.'

'Baz. He knows about us. He said as much at the

379

Press Club that night although your name was never mentioned. He just kept asking me if it was true I'd slept my way to the top.'

There was a pause, the only sound the crackle on the line.

'Baz?'

'I'm still here, Nellie. Do you think he'll print about us?'

'After what happened at the Press Club I think he'll print anything that can harm me.'

'Damn!' Baz swore.

'What are you going to do?'

'Explain the situation to Rachel. I'd much rather she got it from me than him.'

'Baz, I am sorry.'

'You're not to blame. It's that dreadful man who is.'

'Does Rachel know about us, do you think?'

'I don't know. She's certainly never said, or even hinted.'

'Will you speak to her today?'

'I think that's best. I mean, he could print about us tomorrow.'

Softly she said, 'Come and see me before curtain up. I'll want to know how you got on.'

'I'll come just after the half. Bye for now, Nellie.'

'What a damn mess,' she said to a grim-faced Frank.

*

That night there was a full house at the Palace and Nellie was received as warmly as ever, taking nine curtain calls at the end, which was fairly average. According to Baz and the box office advance bookings hadn't slackened off any.

Frank was waiting for Nellie, as he always did, when the curtain came down, and after she'd changed and taken off her slap they made their way to the Riley which was parked close by the theatre in a side street.

He was just about to help Nellie in when a bottle came whizzing out of the night to smash against the windscreen, glass flying in all directions.

Frank went round the car at a run to grab hold of the figure who'd thrown the missile. The man yelled in terror as Frank lifted him off his feet and smashed him against a tenement wall. Frank drew back his fist to hit the man and in that instant a flashbulb popped.

Frank turned to see a second man rushing off down the street, a camera cradled protectively in the crook of his arm.

The first man squirmed, trying to break away, but didn't succeed.

'Who put you up to this?' Frank demanded. 'As if I didn't know.'

The man shook his head.

'Let him go, Frank,' said Nellie, coming to his side.

'I could punch his head in!'

'That would only make matters worse.'

He released the man and jerked his head in the direction the photographer had taken. 'Get!' he said.

Needing no second bidding, the bottle-thrower went clattering away.

'Are you all right?' Frank demanded.

She picked a few shards of glass out of her hair and coat. 'Shocked, that's all. That bottle gave me quite a turn.'

'A set-up,' Frank said between gritted teeth. 'A damn set-up. Well, they got the picture they wanted. I can imagine the article that's going to go with it.'

He surveyed the damage done to his car and shook his head in sorrow. 'I'll bet this isn't mentioned though,' he said.

With Nellie's help he picked up all the broken glass on the front seat and floor and threw it into the gutter.

The article appeared two days later and was headed, 'Nellie Wildchild's Boy Friend', and it was the picture of Frank hauling off to hit the bottle-thrower.

The article was short and basically a recap of the previous one. Without actually saying so, it somehow gave the impression that Frank was a thug. Jim Biles was again very much the aggrieved party.

'The bastard,' Frank said, referring to Robin Carson.

Nellie looked grim. When she tried to pour the tea her hand was shaking with anger.

'Good-bye then. Take care of yourself,' said Babs through the car's open window.

'And you. See you soon,' Nellie replied.

Babs waved at her close mouth, then vanished inside.

Nellie always enjoyed being with Babs. Although she was now famous, and rich by Babs's standards, that hadn't come between them. When together they were still the two daft lassies who'd worked at Harrison's sweetie factory.

It was Sunday afternoon and Babs had been over for lunch. Her husband Phil had also been invited but had declined, saying he had a number of jobs round the house that desperately needed doing.

Nor had Frank been present. He'd been out since mid-morning on business, saying as he left that he wouldn't be back in till early evening.

Nellie slowly drove away from Babs's close, passing, a few streets further on, the place where she and Jim had lived.

Thinking of him made her remember she had some papers in the glove compartment which her solicitor had forwarded to her for perusal and signature. They were concerned with the divorce, which was now well under way, and they would also have to be signed by Jim. On a sudden impulse she decided she would go out to the institution and hand them to him personally rather than send them back to her solicitor as she'd intended.

It was a grim-looking place. Large, grey-stoned and Gothic, it had narrow slit windows in the walls and turrets on the roof. The overall impression was of a medieval fortress.

Inside it was gloomy with lots of tile and marble. There was a smell of polish in the air, mixed with something else. Hopelessness, she wondered?

She stopped a stern-faced, middle-aged nurse who told her where she could find Jim. She climbed three flights of well-worn stairs to his ward.

She was about to enter the ward when three men came out, one of them was her father, Davey. The other two were cronies from the Masons who'd often come round the house when she was at home. And, indeed, Turk Crombie, a tall hook-nosed man now staring at her intently, had called on Jim several times after the accident. 'Nellie,' Davey said.

She stared at him wordlessly. He was opening his mouth to say more when she swept past him. He swore and, for a moment, she thought he was going to come after her.

She took a deep breath to gather herself. The chance encounter had left her strangely shaken. Then she spied Jim at the far end of the ward.

Jim looked up in surprise as she sat down by his bedside. 'It's you,' he said, eyes flashing malevolence. 'You just missed your da.'

'Does he come often?'

'Fairly regularly.'

She gazed around. It was a long ward containing about thirty beds. Like the rest of the building, it was gloomy and almost lifeless.

'No grapes?' Jim asked mockingly.

She brought her attention back to him, aware that a number of people were glancing surreptitiously in her direction. She'd been recognized.

'I read what you had to say in the *Daily Post*,' she said.

'Oh, aye?'

'Not quite the way I remember it happening.'

'Well, it wouldn't be, would it?'

There was a pause. Then Jim said, 'This Frank Connelly you're going out with, he's the same Frank Connelly you were once engaged to, isn't he? The Fenian?'

'Yes.'

'Your da said he thought it was.'

'He came back to Glasgow and we met up again. We're going to be married after the divorce.'

Jim looked at her contemptuously. 'Are you turning?'

'No.'

'Is he?'

'As neither of us is a practising Christian, the religious difference doesn't bother us. And speaking of the divorce . . .' she fished in her handbag to produce the papers she'd placed there from the car's glove compartment, 'I brought these for you. They require your signature. She placed them on his bedside table.

Jim glanced at the papers, then back to her. 'Why the personal service?'

Her eyes glinted. 'I was curious to see this place.'

'Nice, isn't it?'

'It could be worse.'

His lips thinned and twisted down into a cynical smile. 'I hope knowing it's a rat hole gives you some satisfaction.'

She smiled sweetly. 'It does.'

'You're really something,' he hissed.

She drew on her cigarette, the smile still playing round her mouth. 'When it comes to being mean and downright nasty, I had a good teacher. In fact, the very best.'

He glared at her, all his anger and frustration in his face. His one good hand opened and closed. He would have given anything to have been able to strike her.

'I'll give Myra your regards when I get back,' Nellie said.

His hand took hold of a corner of the blanket and viciously twisted it. He was imagining it was Nellie's throat. Like a pot boiling furiously with the lid on, he might explode at any second.

'Good bye,' she said softly. And without waiting for a reply she turned and walked down the length of the ward.

Whether as a result of her visit to the institution, or because it had already been planned, a few days later another article by Robin Carson appeared in the *Daily Post*, again an interview with Jim.

In the article Jim said that Nellie had climbed to stardom through the beds of various men, and named, as an example, Mister Basil Spira who owned and ran the Palace Theatre. He went on to say that she'd done this after he'd been paralysed and unable to do anything about it. And yes, he had kept on loving her after his accident. But that love had died the day she'd packed him off to an institution so she could live with her current lover, Mr Frank Connelly.

'You pig,' Nellie breathed when she'd reached the end of the article.

Frank had already left for his office, going in particularly early that day as he'd wanted to catch up on some paperwork.

Crystal tears were streaming down her face when she rang him and told him about the article. Frank said to hell with the paperwork, it could wait. He told her to put the kettle on, he'd be there as quickly as the Riley would bring him.

A few minutes past 11 a.m. on Sunday 3 September 1939, Nellie was glued to her wireless set listening to Chamberlain's historic words announcing that Great Britain was once more in open conflict with Germany.

She lit a cigarette with trembling fingers as the Prime Minister went on. War had been inevitable since Friday when Germany had invaded Poland, Britain having reaffirmed its pledge to Poland two months previously.

Still, she'd hoped, as had everyone, that somehow this calamity would be averted. That a way would be found to stop the German insanity.

There was an unreal feeling in the air. Nellie was certain that unreality must be covering Britain like a blanket, as though time itself had stopped. As though the entire country were holding its breath.

Her brother Roddy was in the Army. She'd never been particularly close to him but he was her flesh and blood all the same. Now he would be in the forefront of whatever was about to follow.

Because she always found comfort and solace in

singing, she started to do so now, a tune Betty had sung to her as a child.

But for once her singing didn't bring comfort and solace, instead a terrible ice-cold fear gripped her insides. A fear she was going to find would refuse to go away.

The following Wednesday morning Nellie and Frank were sitting round the breakfast table. Frank was reading the paper, the first few pages of which were crammed with war news.

On page four Robin Carson's by-line caught his attention. 'Jesus Christ!' he exclaimed after reading the first few paragraphs.

Nellie looked up. 'What is it?'

'Carson's at it again,' he replied tightly, reading on.

'What's he said about me this time?'

'It's not an attack on you, but an indirect one on me. He's insinuating that I'm a Fascist because I work for the Maestris.'

'A Fascist!' Nellie said, eyes opening wide. Leaving her chair she came round to stand beside Frank, leaning over his shoulder to read the paper now spread on the table before him.

She read, 'proof beyond question that the Maestri brothers of Covent Garden, London, have direct connections with the Fascist party of Italy. Weekly money is sent by the Maestris to the Italian Fascists for the furtherance of Italian Fascist aims and expansion.

'We would remind readers that it is only last May that Italy signed a pact with Germany. A country we are now at war with. And in April last, Italy seized Albania having by then conquered and cruelly subdued Abyssinia.'

'Oh!' Nellie whispered when she came to the bit which said, 'Mr Frank Connelly, Nellie Wildchild's close friend and associate, is the Maestri brothers' representative in Glasgow.'

Nellie read the article through to the end, then looked up at Frank. 'He doesn't actually say you're a Fascist.'

'No, but he bloody well implies that I am.'

'Do you think the Maestris are sending money to the Italian Fascist party?' Nellie asked.

'They must be, otherwise Carson would never dare state so emphatically that they are.'

Frank gathered the paper into his hands, screwed it into a tight ball, then threw it away from him. He barked out a loud laugh. 'You have to admire Carson. He just never gives up. I mean, just think of the time and effort that must have gone into digging up that sort of information. Even I, who work for them, didn't know the Maestris were Fascists, for God's sake!'

'You spanking him at the Press Club that night was funny at the time. But I regret it now. You lit a time bomb. A time bomb Carson is determined will blow my career to smithereens.'

'I'll put a letter of resignation in the post this morning. I can't go on working for the Maestris now,' Frank said.

But even as Nellie and Frank talked, the knot of fear in her stomach tightened yet further.

It was her last solo number before the interval and the cup of tea she was looking forward to. She threw out her arms when she reached for the high note, a note that came out pure and golden, sheer pleasure on the ear.

'Where's your Fascist china?' the voice yelled from somewhere at the back of the stalls.

She continued with the song, not sure she'd heard correctly, hoping it was a trick of her imagination.

'I said, where's your Fascist china the night?' the man repeated, this time in a roar, shaking his raised fist.

Immediately a murmur ran through the audience. Heads turned in the man's direction, but he didn't resume his seat. Instead he remained standing, glaring defiantly and aggressively at Nellie on stage.

Nellie faltered and then stopped singing. She was at a complete loss as to what to do. She could see Sandy staring at her from the corner. He was making a motion which indicated dropping the curtain. She shook her head. That was the last thing she wanted.

Slowly she walked downstage. 'Put the auditorium lights up,' she ordered. They came on as she reached the foots.

Her heart was thudding in her chest and suddenly her throat was dry as a desert.

The man who'd shouted was of middle height with dark hair and a sallow complexion. She could tell from his appearance that he was a working man, the sort of man to whom Fascism would be anathema.

The audience was staring up expectantly at Nellie. Nor were all the faces she saw friendly. Quite a number were openly hostile.

'What makes you think my friend Frank Connelly is a Fascist?' she asked the man.

'It said so in the paper,' he shouted back.

'No it didn't. That article said the people he worked for were, it did not say he was.'

The man glanced around him. 'All tarred with the same brush if you ask me,' he said.

'Tell me something, who do you work for?' Nellie asked.

The man stared at her. 'Black Lion brewery,' he

replied slowly. 'Why, what's that to you?'

'Isn't Black Lion owned by a Mister James Cameron?' Everyone knew that, Cameron was a well-known figure in Glasgow. He nodded.

'A wealthy man, Mister Cameron I believe. How do you think he votes?'

'Och, Tory of course. What else would he be!'

'So you're a Tory then, I take it?'

The man stared at her in disbelief. 'Don't be bloody daft woman!' he spluttered.

'But you said to me that Frank Connelly must be a Fascist because he works for Fascists. By the same token you must be a Tory if you work for one.'

It was a fat woman halfway up the stalls who started laughing first. She was joined by her husband, then nearly everybody else.

The man stared around him in bewilderment. For a moment or two it was touch and go as to what his reaction would be, then he, too, much to Nellie's relief, started to laugh.

Nellie held up her hand for silence. 'I give you my word of honour, as one born and bred Glaswegian to another, that Frank Connelly is not, and never has been, a Fascist. That article in the *Daily Post* was a revelation as far as he was concerned. He'd never even suspected that his bosses were Fascists or that they were sending money to the Italian Fascist party.'

Nellie paused to let the man and the rest of the

audience digest her words. She then said to the man, 'It's now up to you whether or not I go on.'

The man twisted his hands together. He cleared his throat and shuffled his feet.

'Well?' Nellie prompted.

'I believe you, woman. Let's hear you sing,' the man said suddenly.

The audience applauded, some people standing and shouting their approval, others whistling and waving their hands in the air.

Again Nellie appealed for silence. When she judged she could be heard she said, 'Let's *all* sing the curtains in for the interval. A song I think most appropriate for this time.'

She began softly, the audience joining her almost right away.

'I belong to Glasgow, dear old Glasgow town,
There's nothing the matter with Glasgow
But it's going round and round.
I'm only a common old working chap,
As anyone here can see,
But when I get a couple of drinks on a Saturday,
Glasgow belongs to me!'

When Sandy brought the curtains slowly ringing in there was hardly a dry eye in the house.

*

Nellie was beside herself with excitement. It was the following afternoon and Baz had just been on the telephone to tell her the news that Robin Carson was leaving town.

According to Baz a journalist from one of the *Daily Post*'s rivals had been in the audience the previous evening. As a result of what had happened, he had written a piece in which he'd attacked Robin Carson for conducting a personal vendetta against her and Frank.

Nellie heard the front door click shut and instantly flew downstairs. Frank had been in town having had to do something or other. That was him back.

She rushed into his arms. 'You'll never guess what's happened!'

Frank stared down at her in astonishment. 'Not until you tell me,' he grinned.

It came out then in a tumble of words. 'Apparently this journalist described in detail not only what happened at the Press Club, but the way Carson plotted and lied against us. He's been given the sack and has left town. Isn't that absolutely marvellous?'

'You're certain about this?' Frank asked in a strangled voice.

'Oh, yes. No doubt about it. Carson's gone out of our lives forever.'

Like a man in a dream Frank walked away from Nellie and through to where he knew there was a bottle of whisky. He poured himself a large one, drank it right off, and poured himself another.

Nellie had anticipated a jubilation to match her own. Not this stunned, withdrawn silence.

'The thought of everyone knowing that he'd been publicly humiliated, along with everything else, was too much even for him,' Nellie said.

'Yes.'

'Men being what they are in Glasgow, he'd have been a complete laughing stock from one end of the city to the other.'

'Yes,' Frank repeated.

'I thought you'd be waving your wooden leg in the air on hearing it's all over.'

He turned to face her then. 'I've just come from joining the Army.'

Nellie grinned. 'You're having me on?'

'No, I'm going into the HLI.'

Her grin wavered and disappeared. The knot of fear that had been in her stomach ever since the war had started was suddenly so acute she thought she might be ill.

'Why?'

Frank ran a hand through his hair. His complexion had gone pale and muddy, his eyes were dull.

'I thought it would help,' he whispered.

'Help! How could it do that!' she screamed, a sudden fury erupting within her. Whatever had possessed him to do such a thing? Had he gone completely mad?

Shocked by this turn of events Frank groped for the words that would explain. 'It was an awful thing that happened to you last night at the theatre. When we went to bed I couldn't sleep. I lay awake thinking about it, and Carson. It seemed to me he could possibly take this Fascist thing a lot further. Use it, along with Jim Biles, as a club to beat you with. You talked about time bombs; well, it seemed to me that by joining up I was very neatly defusing this particular one. How could he continue to imply I'm a Fascist when I've become a member of His Majesty's fighting forces?'

Nellie's fury died as swiftly as it had been born. Dear, beautiful, darling Frank – he'd done this for her. To protect her and her career. 'If only you'd waited a few hours more,' she whispered.

'If ifs and ans were pots and pans,' he said, shrugging.

'Oh, Frank!' She was back in his arms, smothering him with kisses, loving him.

Sniffing, she pushed a stray lock of hair away from her face.

'I have to report to Maryhill Barracks first thing tomorrow morning.'

'So soon?'

He nodded, 'I'm afraid so.'

Nellie took a deep breath. Get hold of yourself girl, she told herself. What was done couldn't be undone. She'd have given her right arm if it could.

She stood at the window and watched him get into his car, raising her hand in farewell as the Riley's engines burst into life.

He rolled down the window and returned her salute. Their eyes met and, for a second, they were as one again. Then the moment was over and the Riley was moving on its way.

She watched the car till it was out of sight.

'Oh, my darling,' she whispered, placing the palm of her hand against the bed, where his smell still lingered. Burying her face in the rumpled sheets, she wailed her grief.

8

It was fifteen minutes to curtain up when there was a tap on Nellie's door. She was already in her first-number costume and applying the final touches of her make-up.

'Come in!' she called.

The door opened and the stage doorkeeper popped his head round. 'There's a chap here says he's your brother and that he must see you.'

'My brother!' Nellie jumped up. 'Show him in.'

The door opened wider and a uniformed figure entered, his right arm heavily bandaged and in a sling.

'He *is* your brother, isn't he?' the stage door-keeper demanded. He'd known young men get up to all sorts of dodges to get into a female's dressing room.

'He is, indeed,' Nellie replied. Rising she took Roddy into her arms, careful of his wound, and kissed him on the cheek.

'You've changed so much, I swear I would have walked past you in the street,' she said.

'It's been a long, long time,' he replied.

She indicated the arm in the sling. 'Is it bad?'

He shook his head. 'Not really. I'm told it'll take a wee while to mend. They've shipped me home and now I'm on my way up north to a convalescent home. We weren't supposed to stop in Glasgow, but we had to change over from the Central Station to Queen Street and the train there's been delayed a couple of hours. I took the opportunity to sneak off and see you. If I'd had longer I'd have waited till after the show, but as things are I'm lucky to be here at all.'

'And how's Frank?' she asked eagerly. Frank had joined the same regiment as Roddy and had written to her early on to say the pair of them had become quite pally. He often mentioned Roddy when he wrote.

There was a pause, then averting her gaze, Roddy said softly, 'It's because of Frank that I'm here, Nellie.'

She turned away from her brother and sat. It surprised her to note that her hand was rock steady when she lit a cigarette. 'Wounded also?' she asked.

'There were four of us. Frank, myself and two other blokes. I can't say where it was, I'm afraid, I'm not allowed to do that. Jerry caught us unawares with an artillery attack. The first shell landed right beside us. I was blown off my feet and collected this.' He tapped his arm.

'And Frank?'

'The other three are dead.'

Picking up the rabbit's foot Margo had given her she pretended to dust off excess powder.

'He wouldn't have felt a thing, Nellie. I give you my word on that.'

'Was his body badly – well, you know what I mean?' She looked at Roddy in the mirror and he glanced away. That was answer enough.

'They contacted his next of kin, which was his family in Drumoyne. But I knew you wouldn't know. I was going to write when I got to the convalescent home. But when this train thing happened I –'

'Thank you,' she said, interrupting him.

'I'm helluva sorry –'

'I appreciate you coming.'

'Frank was a good man, Nellie. Well liked.'

She rose and, crossing to the bottle of whisky she always kept in her dressing room, poured out a large dram. She handed it to Roddy.

'What about yourself?'

'Not just before a show.' She screwed the top back

on to the bottle and slipped it into his pocket. 'For you and your mates on the journey north.'

He finished his drink and laid the glass down. 'I'd better be getting back.'

She took the hand of his undamaged arm and squeezed it. 'Stay lucky,' she murmured.

At the door he gave her a smile and bob of the head. 'Cheerio!' he said. Then he was gone.

'Five minutes!' the call was shouted along the corridor.

She scrutinized her make-up and hair one last time. In the opening number she wore her hair up, and as she walked to the stage, all she could think of, over and over again, was that Frank had always preferred it down.

Baz gave her a wave. She waved back, forcing a smile on to her face.

On arriving backstage she climbed down a flight of stairs to below stage. There, a stagehand was waiting to help her into a trap which would send her shooting into the air above the raked set now towering over her head.

When she was in position she thought of the letter she'd sent Frank only yesterday, telling him that the divorce had at last come through; that when they next saw one another they'd be able to get married.

And now that marriage would never be.

She heard the curtains swish open and the line go

on stage. For a split second she thought she wouldn't be able to go through with the performance. Then she pulled herself together. It might be a cliché, but it was true none the less: the show had to go on. There was a full house out there waiting to see and hear *her*.

The stagehand nodded to her as her music cue was played. He pulled the lever that shot her up through the set. Clearing the trap she threw out her arms and legs in an aerial spreadeagle.

'Hello there!' she shouted.

'Hello there!!' the audience thundered back.

As she landed the line turned in on her and clapped their hands.

Seats banged as the audience rose to her. 'Nellie!' they cried. 'Nellie! '

She blew them kiss after kiss, the adulation washing over her, then launched into the opening bars of her first song.

She always sang well, but that night she was better than she'd ever been. That night she was singing for Frank. Somehow, somewhere, she was sure he could hear her.

Jessie Gray

PART ONE

Star
1947–48

1

The first time she laid eyes on Tommy McBride was in mid-November, 1947. Miss Parrot was in charge of the assembly where classes 2A, hers, and 3B, Tommy's, were to practise their dancing for the forthcoming Christmas 'do'.

'Gentlemen, take your partners please,' Miss Parrot instructed, and the boys who'd been lining one wall moved towards the girls lining the wall opposite, a few of whom were sniggering and giggling.

Suddenly he was there in front of her, mumbling the appropriate words while looking at some spot in the cleft of her neck. His own neck was flushed. He clearly found asking a lassie up on to the floor acutely embarrassing, which amused her.

'Thank you,' she replied demurely, thinking to herself that she'd never noticed him before.

'A waltz,' Miss Parrot announced, and bent to the old phonograph on which a record had already been placed.

She went into his arms, and then they were off to the somewhat scratchy music. He was a terrible dancer, stumbling over his own feet and hers. Halfway through the dance it felt as though a ton weight had been dropped on her left big toe.

'Sorry,' he muttered.

'Don't worry about it, I've nine others,' she answered testily, but immediately wished she hadn't when she saw how her reply had hurt him. 'We all have to learn, and polish up our techniques, that's the purpose of these assemblies,' she added, giving him a smile.

For a brief second their eyes met, then he quickly glanced away, his entire face colouring.

This one really is shy, she thought, which she didn't

find at all unattractive. Many of the boys at Queen's Park Senior Secondary had far too big a tip for themselves, some cocky in the extreme. A shy lad made a pleasant change.

When the waltz was over Miss Parrot told them all to separate into their lines again, then proceeded to give a demonstration of the fox trot, Miss Parrot doing this with John Drumsheil who was almost as good a dancer as she was.

When the fox trot had been demonstrated to Miss Parrot's satisfaction, Miss Parrot instructed the boys to take new partners.

She wondered if the shy one would ask her up again, but he didn't, he asked Marcie Allen instead. It was Rog Hastie who presented himself in front of her, Rog who always smelled as if he never changed his vest or underpants. Reluctantly, she accepted.

She didn't see the shy lad again till the end of the week when their two classes had another dancing assembly under Miss Parrot.

'Gentlemen, take your partners for a polka, please,' Miss Parrot announced.

He materialized out of the milling boys to mutter his request in such a low voice she had to strain to hear.

'I'd be delighted,' she replied, and followed him further out on to the floor.

He didn't speak, just stood there looking everywhere but directly into her face. She noticed his neck wasn't flushed this time round, and thought that an improvement.

What hadn't improved was his dancing which was even worse than before. Within seconds he'd managed to kick her shin so hard she knew it would be black and blue before the day was out.

'Try to relax, it'll come easier to you if you do,' she said kindly.

He did his best to relax, but that was no help. She exclaimed in pain when his heel came scything down on two of her toes. Muttering his apologies, he returned to being rigid again.

'Sorry for being so clumsy,' he mumbled at the end of the polka, then reluctantly left her.

She saw his reluctance, and was touched by it. When later on he asked her up again she was pleased, though apprehensive. Miraculously, she escaped this encounter unscathed.

The following Monday morning she was coming out of Latin class when she found herself beside him in the corridor. 'Hello,' she said.

He gave her a startled look, not having been aware of her. 'Oh hello.'

She said she was on her way to South Building, and he said he was too. They continued on their way together.

As they walked, and talked, she discovered he'd only been at Queen's Park a few weeks. He and his family had just recently moved into the district.

'Where from?' she asked, curious.

He hesitated fractionally before replying, 'Govanhill.'

She knew Govanhill was a rough area, quite different to Battlefield where they were now. Govanhill was lower working class; Battlefield was upper working to middle class. Or, as some folks might have put it, in Battlefield the toilets were inside the houses, not outside on the stairhead.

'How are you settling into Queen's Park then? Are you making pals?' she inquired.

He shrugged his shoulders. 'It's not that easy. I suppose it takes time.'

Lizzie Dunnachie called out to her and she waved over. Lizzie made a gesture that told her Lizzie had been round behind the bicycle shed having a fly smoke.

She brought her attention back to the shy one, and suddenly realized that she didn't know his name yet. 'I'm Star Gray, what are you called?' she said.

9

He gawped at her. 'You're what?'

'Star Gray.' Then, seeing his disbelief, explained, 'I was christened Jessie but I haven't been able to abide that since I was wee. I'm Star to my friends.'

Star! He'd never heard the like. 'I'm Tommy McBride,' he grinned.

They reached South Building and went inside. She was about to say goodbye when the idea came to her. 'When you lived in Govanhill were you in the Boys' Brigade?' she asked.

He shook his head.

'There's a church only a couple of minutes away from here called Battlefield Central. I know for a fact they've a grand B.B. Company there who meet every Friday night at a quarter to seven. Why don't you go along? They're a right friendly bunch.'

Tommy didn't fancy the B.B., or the Scouts, at all. In Govanhill they'd laughed at both lots. And those daft pillbox hats the B.B. wore! Proper nanas they looked. 'No thanks, the B.B.'s not for me.'

'Pity that. I certainly enjoy my nights there.'

She had to be taking the mickey out of him. 'They don't have girls in the B.B.,' he said.

'True enough,' she replied, eyes twinkling mischievously.

'So how can you enjoy your nights there?'

'Come along and find out,' she retorted, and, turning abruptly, strode off leaving him staring perplexedly after her.

As she went into class she wondered briefly if he would come down to the Hall, but decided he wouldn't. As it turned out, she was wrong.

Friday night at eight thirty on the dot she went through the door connecting the manse to the church, and along the narrow passageway at the rear behind the pulpit. This took her into the musty corridor that led down to the Church Hall where the B.B. meetings were held.

10

Up until the moment she entered, Tommy had considered the evening a waste of time. Well, not a complete waste, several of the lads had made friendly overtures.

Then Star walked in, and his evening was made. But what was she doing here? That was the mystery. A mystery that was soon resolved when she seated herself at the piano in the corner and started to pick out a tune.

Star had been playing piano for the B.B. since the previous year, when Mrs Lang's arthritis had got so bad she'd had to pack in playing for them.

When it was discovered that no one else in the congregation wanted the job, Star had volunteered. Although she was no older than many of the boys, her father had been delighted, declaring it a good Christian act.

The Maze Marching, for which Star played the accompanying music, was always the last item on the evening's agenda, and lasted through till nine o'clock. After that the entire Company came together to be dismissed.

Captain Bell (inevitably called Ding A Ling by the lads) strode into the Hall and barked out the command for those taking part in the Maze Marching to get, as he put it, fell into line.

'Shortest to the left, tallest to the right, single rank, size!' Ding A Ling shrieked in his best parade-ground manner, his voice so loud it made Tommy jump right up off his chair.

Seeing Tommy looking uncertain, Ding A Ling came over and told him Maze Marching wasn't compulsory. Tommy immediately replied that he'd love to take part.

Actually, he couldn't have cared less about Maze Marching, or any other sort of marching come to that. What did interest him was that Star would be playing the music for it and he didn't want to risk being sent to any of the rooms adjoining the Hall to do some other activity.

11

Star suddenly saw him grinning at her, and grinned in return. She was delighted he'd come, but it didn't occur to her to ask herself why.

Ding A Ling told Tommy just to follow the chap in front and he couldn't go wrong. Convoluted and complicated as Maze Marching was, only a handful of the marchers and the Staff Sergeant at the front had to memorize the various movements and patterns. Everyone else followed like sheep. But sheep who followed smartly, Ding A Ling emphasized, *very very* smartly, with bags of swank.

'By the left quick march!' Ding A Ling screamed, and Star struck up as the line moved off.

The first ten minutes were easy, and quite enjoyable, going over what had already been plotted and learned. After that, though, new moves were given and it became excruciatingly slow and tedious for everyone except the Staff Sergeant, who had to do this new piece of memorizing.

Finally the Maze Marching finished. To Tommy's disconcertment, Star immediately slipped from the Hall. He was about to follow her when the entire Company was called to order for the final proceedings which consisted of a short speech by Ding A Ling, followed by an even shorter prayer.

Then it was all over, and time to go. Picking up his things, Tommy made a beeline for the door through which Star had vanished, convinced that she'd be well gone by now and that he'd lost her.

But she hadn't gone, she was in the kitchen adjoining the Hall, washing up the officers' tea cups.

Suddenly he was shy again, completely lost for words. He made a sort of strangulated coughing sound to attract her attention. She turned, and immediately her face lit up with a smile.

'I was pleased to see you out there. Are you glad you came along?'

He looked down at his shoes. 'Oh aye. But I must say I

12

was surprised when you actually did show up. I was certain you were having me on.'

'And I was surprised to see you. I didn't think you'd come.'

Silence fell between them as she dried the cups and saucers, then began putting them away.

Tommy couldn't think of anything to say. He'd never been so taken with a lassie before. There was something different about Star. All he wanted was to be with her.

He shyly gazed at the small oval face, and the deep brown eyes and dark brown hair. She was slim, skinny some might have said, but although only fourteen, she already had a womanly body. Aye, very womanly, he thought to himself.

'Stare any harder and you'll stare holes through me,' Star said as she dried her hands on the tea cloth.

Embarrassment flooded him. Thankfully, she had no idea what had been going through his mind. He made a gesture that encompassed the entire building. 'What's your connection with this place?' he asked abruptly. 'You must have one.'

'My father's the minister here.' Her eyes twinkled as she went on with mock solemnity, 'The Reverend Kenneth Gray.'

He was momentarily stunned. That was the last thing he'd expected to hear. Her father a minister! Bloody hell!

Star couldn't help smiling at his stricken expression. It was one she was used to seeing when she announced what her father did. 'The manse is attached to the other side of the church. That's where I live.'

There were voices in the corridor as a contingent of the boys went through the door that led to the outside. Their voices were replaced by others which Tommy recognized as belonging to several of the officers.

'Everyone's leaving. I suppose I'd better get on my way, too,' he said, reluctance in his voice.

She was about to make a crack about his marching being an awful lot better than his dancing, then decided

13

against it. She already understood that he could be easily hurt. As her mother would have said, he was a sensitive lad.

'Listen,' she said, suddenly inspired. 'I usually go round to the Fives Cafe in Battlefield Road after this. A few of us get together for a cup of coffee and a bit of a natter. Would you care to come?'

'Sounds smashing,' he instantly replied, leaping at the opportunity to be with her longer.

'Whereabouts round here is it you live?' Star asked as they headed for the Fives.

'Millbrae Crescent. Do you know it?'

Star nodded, slightly puzzled. Millbrae Crescent was one of the poshest streets in the district. It surprised her that Tommy's family should have a house there. Govanhill to Millbrae Crescent – a big jump indeed, she thought. It was the difference between fish and chips and fillet steak. Not that she had any first hand knowledge of fillet steak, with the war only two years over and the country still heavily rationed.

On arriving at the Fives, Tommy saw why it had been given that name. Its address was 555 Battlefield Road. On entering the cosy cafe, they were immediately hailed by Lizzie Dunnachie, who was sitting at a table with another girl Tommy recognized from Queen's Park, and a lad from the B.B. There were about a dozen members of the B.B. in all scattered round the various tables.

Star introduced Tommy to Lizzie and Catherine, while James Ledingham said that he and Tommy had already met at the B.B. meeting.

Tommy ordered coffee for Star and himself from the short, fat man who came to take their order.

'Talking about dead boring places,' sighed Lizzie. 'Isn't that just Glasgow on a Friday night?'

'There's the cafes and that's about it,' agreed Catherine.

Lizzie lit a cigarette, blowing out a long thin stream of smoke, in a way she thought was *très sophisticated*, and certainly better than Glasgow deserved.

14

Catherine asked Tommy where he'd moved from. As soon as she heard he was from Govanhill, Catherine lost interest in him. As far as she was concerned only neds came from there; neds, hooligans and roughs. It was clear from her expression that anyone from Govanhill was unsavoury and inferior.

Noticing Catherine's disdainful attitude, Star became angry. She could tell from the veil that had descended over Tommy's eyes that he'd caught it also.

Lizzie prattled on that there was only one really decent entertainment available in Glasgow at the weekend, and that was the dancing in the town. She'd have been there like a shot, she said, if her Dad would allow her. But the old man wouldn't entertain the idea, not until her seventeenth birthday when he'd told her he'd allow her to go to the wee dance halls over at Shawlands Cross. She'd have to wait till eighteen before being allowed to attend the town dancing.

'There are always church activities, you could try getting involved in some of those,' Star said innocently, knowing fine well that Lizzie would be the last person to get involved in such.

Lizzie knew she was being teased. Star was always doing it to her. 'You do the only activity I'd be interested in, if I could play the piano that is,' Lizzie retorted.

'You'll come to a bad end one day if you're not careful Lizzie Dunnachie,' jibed Star.

'I live in hope,' said Lizzie, raising her eyes to heaven, and making everyone laugh.

Things were just relaxing when Star glanced at the clock and said she had to get back. Tommy jumped to his feet. 'I'll walk you,' he offered. Adding as the perfect excuse, 'I have to go that way anyway.'

'Will you be going back to the B.B. next week?' Star asked Tommy as they arrived in front of the manse. It was a squat, Gothic building that looked like some cancerous growth on the side of the church.

'I'll be there all right,' Tommy said quickly. Wild horses wouldn't keep him away.

She touched him lightly on the shoulder, sending a shiver through him. 'I'm glad. Good night, then.'

'Good night.'

She flew up the gravel path to the manse's medieval-style wood and metal door, opening it with her own key. She waved to Tommy, then the heavy door thudded closed and she was gone.

As Tommy continued towards Millbrae Crescent his walking became a march, and he began whistling one of the tunes she'd played earlier.

The next Friday night Tommy bolted his tea, then polished his shoes for the B.B. meeting. Jeannie, his mother, remarked drily that if the B.B. could get him to polish his shoes with such enthusiasm after only one attendance then the age of miracles was indeed not past.

Tommy duly presented himself at the Church Hall wearing his highly polished shoes, gleaming brass and leather belt, and daft wee pillbox hat. From that point onwards, the evening went interminably slowly as he waited for the Maze Marching – and Star.

When she finally arrived he caught her eyes as soon as he could, and smiled. Her smile back made his stomach turn over.

Later, at the end of the prayer, he hurried from the Hall to the kitchen where he found her washing the officers' tea cups and saucers just like before.

He entered the kitchen as nonchalantly as he was able. 'I thought we might go to the Fives again, what do you say?' he asked.

'I was on my way there anyway, so we might as well go together,' she agreed.

He wasn't exactly chuffed with the phrasing of her acceptance. But she *was* going with him, that was the main thing.

On arriving at the Fives they were again hailed by Lizzie Dunnachie. Catherine was sitting beside Lizzie, and beside Catherine was a chap whose face Tommy had seen around school. Star introduced him as Alec Muir.

'How was the Scripture Union class?' Star asked Alec as soon as she'd sat down.

Glancing at the lapel of Alec's jacket Tommy saw a green and gold S.U. badge there. He listened while Alec eagerly expounded to Star all that had taken place in that evening's class.

After a while Star glanced over at Tommy. She could see he was clearly bored by this conversation, but he was also wearing a peculiar, intense expression whose meaning she couldn't fathom. Then Alec claimed her attention once more, and Tommy's strange expression evaporated from her mind.

Eventually Tommy started to chat to Lizzie. When he tried to speak to Catherine she only replied in monosyllables; it didn't take a genius to realize he wasn't quoted there.

Alec waxed long and passionately about the S.U. class. Religion intrigued him, and he was seriously considering the idea of becoming a minister himself. He was almost convinced that he had 'the calling'.

Alex bent down under the table to lift four fat tomes off the floor which he placed beside his now empty coffee cup. 'These are the books I borrowed from your father the other week,' he said to Star. 'I thought I might return them tonight.'

Tommy's ears immediately pricked up. It would spoil everything if this Alec tagged along when he took Star home.

Lizzie Dunnachie leaned across to glance at the title of the top book. She pulled a face. 'Yuch!' she said.

Tommy reached over and picked it up: *The Life of St. Paul*.

'He had a fascinating life. Quite fascinating,' Alec said to Tommy, mistaking his curiosity for interest.

17

Tommy could see that Alec was in deadly earnest. 'I prefer Edgar Rice Burroughs myself,' he replied in a friendly tone.

Lizzie made a gargling noise at the back of her throat. 'Naked men cavorting about the jungle. Lovely!' she hissed, eyes agleam.

Alec was the first to laugh. He might be religious, but he wasn't without a sense of humour.

'You'd better come on then if you want to give those to Dad,' Star said to Alec, starting to rise. To Tommy, starting to rise also, she added. 'I'll see you next week at school, no doubt.'

Tommy had already risen several inches off his hard wooden chair, he now slowly sank back into it again. He managed a weak grin. 'No doubt,' he echoed, pleased that the words didn't come out strangulated as he'd feared they would.

He watched jealously as they headed for the door, Alec bowed under the weight of the books.

'God Squad,' Lizzie said to Tommy after Star and Alec had left, and winked.

The Reverend Kenneth Gray was most distinguished in appearance, every inch a right and proper minister. His face was finely boned, his hair a glossy silver which he wore extremely short and parted at the side. He was a little more than average height for a Glaswegian, and walked with a stiff and upright carriage as though at one time he'd been in the Army, which he hadn't.

The Reverend was sitting in his favourite leather arm-chair in front of the small fire burning in the grate. He'd just sat down again, after going to the bookcase to get some more books for Alec to borrow and replacing the ones Alec had returned.

Jessie was seeing Alec to the front door. The Reverend Kenneth Gray liked Alec. He was such a nice lad that. And he came from a terribly good background, even

18

though his parents had no money. The family were minor Scottish gentry who'd been fairly wealthy up until the late twenties, when Alec's grandfather had lost nearly everything speculating on commodities.

He glanced over at the settee on which Alec and Jessie had been sitting, and wondered for the hundredth time if anything was ever going to come of that relationship. They would certainly have his approval if it did. He considered Alec a fine catch for his lass. A union between the Muirs and Grays would be a step up for the Grays, no doubt about it.

'You're looking gey pensive dear,' Alison Gray broke into her husband's reverie. She was knitting herself a new winter cardy from some excellent unpicked wool she'd managed to buy at the church's last jumble sale.

Before the Reverend could answer, Star came bursting back into the room. She went directly to the fire, squatting and holding out her hands to the flames. 'It's bitter outside, I wouldn't be at all surprised if we had snow before morning,' she said.

'I was just about to say to your mother what a grand couple you and Alec Muir make,' the Reverend said.

Star smiled into the fire. She was only too well aware that her father had hopes for her and Alec. Snob that he was, she knew why he fostered that hope.

'Aye, Alec's a fine lad, there's no disputing that,' said Alison. 'And what about that new boy from the school? Did he turn up at the B.B. again tonight? The one you were trying to help make friends?'

Star turned to look at her mother. 'He did. I think he's taken to the B.B.'

This was the first the Reverend had heard about Tommy McBride. A question to Star revealed that Tommy had only recently moved into the neighbourhood, which meant the McBrides might not have joined a local congregation yet. The Reverend Gray was always on the lookout for new members. He fingered the briar in his lap. He would have loved another pipe, but had already smoked his quota for the day. 'What's the boy's address? I'll send his parents a letter inviting them to morning service the Sunday after next.'

Star once more faced the flames. 'They live in Millbrae Crescent, but I don't know the number. I'll find out for you if you want.'

The Reverend's hand tightened over his briar. Millbrae Crescent! Only top-drawer and monied families lived there. A few new members from Millbrae Crescent would be a most welcome addition to his congregation. Most of the 'better' families preferred the bigger kirk over at Langside, which had several titles, including a Knight of the Thistle and an ex-Lord Provost, amongst its numbers.

'What does Mr McBride do?' he asked casually, thinking about future donations to the church fund.

Star shook her head. 'I've no idea. Tommy's never mentioned.'

'On second thoughts, rather than write I think it would be better, as you're already friendly with the lad, to call on them personally. And you can accompany me. Speak to this Tommy as soon as you can and ask him to ask his parents when it would be convenient for the pair of us to visit.'

'As you wish.'

The Reverend nodded his satisfaction, and hoped that Stanley Carrell over at Langside hadn't beaten him to it.

Star looked up at the McBrides' beautiful house. She guessed there were four or five bedrooms, which made it almost as big as the manse.

A glance at her watch told her it was one minute to eight; they were due at eight. Her father was a stickler for being punctual.

The Reverend was noting the thick velvet curtains hanging inside the window nearest to him. Those must have cost a fair packet when they'd been bought before the war, he told himself.

'Pull the bell handle dear,' he instructed Star, and hoisted a smile on to his face.

Tommy was on his feet the moment the first clang reverberated through the house. He almost ran to the front door in his eagerness. He'd been excited about Star's coming since she'd broached the subject two days earlier.

In what they called the parlour Jim McBride glanced at his wife Jeannie and whispered for her not to be nervous. He rose from his chair and she did likewise.

As soon as she stepped into the hallway Star knew she liked this house, it had a warm and welcoming family feeling about it. As she walked behind Tommy and her father her eyes were darting all around, taking everything in.

There had been a lot of fresh painting done, which surprised her. Paint was still hard to come by even two years after the war. And the carpet underfoot was new, another surprise for the same reason.

'How do you do. It's kind of you to have myself and daughter into your home,' the Reverend said on entering the parlour, and extended his hand to Jim to be shaken.

The Reverend's practised smile wavered fractionally when he saw that instead of a right hand Jim had a hook.

Jim was well used to this situation. In a twisting motion he took the Reverend's outstretched hand with his left one, and shook heartily. 'Pleased to meet you, Reverend Gray.'

By the time the introductions had been completed Star had already decided she liked the McBrides. As she'd taken to their house, she took to them right away.

'A cup of tea?' asked Jeannie McBride.

'Or how about something stronger? Whisky, or a drop of Amontillado perhaps?' Jim added.

21

The Reverend beamed with pleasure. 'I haven't tasted Amontillado since 1942,' he declared. 'I'd be delighted to have a glass. It's always been my favourite.'

Jim produced a bottle of finest Amontillado from a well-stocked drinks cabinet and poured three schooners for the adults. For Star and Tommy he poured out fresh orange juice.

'Welcome to Battlefield!' said the Reverend to the McBrides, raising his glass in a toast. His expression was one of deepest appreciation as he tasted the contents of his glass.

'Perhaps Star would like to see over the house,' Jeannie suggested to Tommy.

The Reverend Gray blanched. His daughter's chosen name always embarrassed him. 'Silly name that, but she flatly refuses the good Christian one given her by her mother and me,' he said to Jeannie and Jim. He'd done everything in his power to get her to stop using such a ludicrous name, but in the end he'd had to admit defeat.

Jim McBride stared at Star across the rim of his schooner. She had all the signs of a real looker. Give her a couple of more years, he thought, and she'd be a cracker. It seemed she was also a determined young lady, a quality he admired. He could well understand why Tommy seemed so attracted to her.

The minister sipped his sherry and tried to gain his usual composure. It had been a shock for him to hear how the McBrides spoke. Star hadn't told him they'd come from Govanhill. Why, their accent was so common! Broad Glasgow. He certainly hadn't expected that, not in Millbrae Crescent. *Nouveaux riches*, he thought, and inwardly sneered.

Jim switched his attention back to the minister. A right sanctimonious fart was how he summed him up. He knew, however, that being accepted by a local church would make settling into the area all that much easier, and so was prepared to play his own game with Gray.

Jeannie gave the impression of being totally relaxed,

but in reality she was churning inside with anxiety. It had been against her wishes that they'd come to Millbrae Crescent in the first place, where she'd said they'd stick out like a sore thumb. But Jim had been insistent. He'd always fancied living with the toffs, and now that they could afford to they damn well would. Anyway, he'd argued, it was to Tommy's advantage that they do so, as it would give him the opportunity to meet some decent youngsters and make some good connections for the future. She didn't want him to turn out a lout like the other lads in Govanhill, did she?

Star was hesitating, unsure whether or not her father wanted her to remain by his side. When he still gave her no indication either way she said to Jeannie, 'Oh I'd adore to see round the house.'

There were five bedrooms, as it turned out. Star admired each one in turn. They were all newly decorated. Tommy's, where they ended up, was done in an exceptionally nice, tasteful wallpaper.

Star stared out Tommy's bedroom window at the falling snow. 'How did your father lose his hand?' she asked in a quiet voice.

He came up behind her. 'In the war. He was badly wounded at the Battle of Keren in Abyssinia. Besides having his hand blown clean off he also took some shrapnel in his right leg. You might not have noticed downstairs but he limps rather badly.'

Star thought of her cousin Haldane who'd gone to the war, and hadn't come back. She'd been very fond of Hal who'd been ten years older than she. Hal and two of his pals had gone into the army on the same day; none of them had survived.

The war had played such a large part in her life that as a child she'd come to believe it would go on for ever. She'd asked her father how Gentle Jesus could allow such awful things to happen, but her father's answer had been completely unsatisfactory.

Standing only a few feet behind Star, the smell of her

was driving Tommy wild. He tried to imagine what it would be like just to touch her hair.

'Why did you choose the name Star for yourself?' he asked, his voice husky.

She roused herself from her reverie, and gave a little smile. That was a question she didn't always answer. It all depended on who was doing the asking.

'When I decided I'd change my name I considered hundreds, but none of them were really right. Then one day I picked up a book of Familiar Quotations and there it was. Have you ever heard of *Elmer Gantry*?'

Tommy shook his head.

'It's a novel by an American writer, Sinclair Lewis. The quotation is from the character Elmer Gantry himself who says, "*What is love? It is the morning and the evening star.*" I was so taken with those words that I named myself after them. And so Jessie became Star.'

The story intrigued Tommy. He'd never heard anything so wonderful, or beautiful. This is no ordinary girl, he told himself. This girl was very very special.

Meanwhile, in the parlour, the Reverend Gray was saying that it was time he and Star headed back home. Jeannie went and called up the stairs for Star and Tommy to come down.

'I'll look forward to seeing you on Sunday, then,' the minister said to Jim. It had already been agreed that the McBrides would be taking a section of a pew from now on. Jim had paid for this privilege with a cheque for a year in advance.

Jim had a sudden thought while they waited for Star and Tommy. Telling the Reverend he'd only be a moment or two, he hurried from the room. When he returned to the parlour he was carrying a bottle of Amontillado identical to the one from his drinks cabinet.

'Oh no I couldn't!' the Reverend protested, but only half heartedly, when Jim attempted to press the bottle on him.

24

'I insist. If for no other reason than as a token of gratitude for Star's kindness to Tommy,' Jim said.

'If you put it like that,' the minister replied, trying to appear reluctant, and accepted the bottle.

At the front door hands were again shaken, and hearty goodbyes made.

As soon as the Grays had gone Tommy rushed back upstairs to his room where he sat savouring the smell of Star that still lingered there.

'The morning and the evening star,' he said once to himself, and smiled.

Tommy lay wide awake in the darkness. He'd been in bed for ages but couldn't sleep for thinking of Star. How she fascinated him! He was drawn to her like iron to a magnet.

But, although he thoroughly enjoyed her company, he wasn't always totally at ease in it. She was so different to the lassies he'd been used to in Govanhill, so refined. She often made him feel downright uncouth. What could a boy like him offer a girl like Star? And yet there was that fascination, that magnetism.

He decided what he would do next. He would take her out someplace, a proper taking out, not just the Fives after the B.B.

He racked his brains. He could take her to a James Craig tearoom for a cream tea, or high tea even. Better the cream tea, he told himself. If there was one thing a lassie liked more than a gooey cake, it was two gooey cakes.

Then he had it. It was so obvious, it was amazing he hadn't thought of it before. It was far better than a cream tea. The school Christmas Dance – he would take her to that.

Excitement filled him at the prospect. Low lights, Star in his arms, the smell of her in his nostrils. He was a terrible dancer, it was true, but he'd make a special effort between now and then to get better.

He would ask his mother to work with him on his steps in the parlour. For Jeannie was a grand dancer, his Dad had always said so.

That decision made, he finally began to drift off. He dreamt he was Fred Astaire and Star was Ginger Rogers.

Star was worried about her Latin. Despite her best efforts, she was continuing to do extremely badly in it and dreaded to think what her end of term mark was going to be. It wasn't that she lacked intelligence. She excelled in other subjects. When it came to Latin, however, she found herself up against a stone wall of incomprehension.

She knew it wasn't the teacher's fault; no one could have been more patient than Mr Orr. But even he despaired when she constructed a sentence without a verb in it.

A smile turned her lips upwards when she thought about music. Now that was a different kettle of fish entirely. She was head and shoulders above most of her year when it came to that. Besides piano, she played violin and clarinet, and had even scored several compositions. Miss Hamill, the music teacher, said she was a natural. For her the music classes weren't work, they were sheer pleasure. The minutes of music class zipped past, while those of Latin dragged along on leaden boots.

'Star!'

She turned to see Tommy racing after her. She waved happily and waited for him to catch up.

It had started snowing again, and there was thick slush underfoot. When he arrived by her side his cheeks were red from a combination of the biting wind and his exertion.

'I missed you at the main gate,' he said, falling into step beside her.

'I left by the back one because I was coming from the Science Labs,' she explained.

A tram rattled by to stop at Battlefield Rest. It was a cream, green and orange coloured building, the Corporation's colours, where the crews changed over. They crossed behind the Rest and in front of the Victoria Infirmary.

They walked in silence. Finally he took a deep breath and said in a rush, 'I was wondering if you'd go to the Christmas Dance with me? I'd like very much to take you.'

She stopped and turned to him in surprise. The look on his face made her realize that their friendship meant something totally different to him than it did to her. How stupid she'd been! She should have realized before now what was happening.

Damn you for a fool, Jessie Gray! she thought. So upset that she called herself by her real name.

'I'm afraid I can't,' she replied lamely.

Tommy had never even considered the possibility of her turning him down. The scenario had been simple as far as he'd been concerned: he'd ask, she'd accept, and that would be that.

'Why not?'

She was going to hurt him again, she knew, but what could she do? 'I've already been asked by Alec Muir, the chap you met in the Fives that night,' she said softly.

'Oh!'

She went on, knowing she had to. Tommy had to be given the full facts, for his own good. 'You see, Alec and I have more or less been going out together for a while now.'

Tommy seized this slender thread of hope. 'What do you mean more or less?'

Star sighed inwardly, he wasn't making this any easier. 'All right, we've been going steady,' she snapped in reply, hating herself for snapping.

Tommy felt such an idiot. 'I hadn't heard round school. No one ever mentioned it.'

27

'I thought you knew. I mean, I just presumed you did, everyone does.'

'Seems I was the exception,' he answered, and tried to smile. The smile that came out as a grimace, and made Star want to sweep him into her arms and hug him tightly. He looked just like a wee boy. A wee boy who'd taken something precious out to play for the first time, and lost it.

Tommy fought to keep himself under control. Somehow, and it was an awful struggle, he managed to assume a nonchalant if unconvincing pose.

'Thank you for asking, though,' she said gently.

Emotion clogged his throat; the nonchalant pose disintegrated into drooping shoulders. 'See you then,' he mumbled, and walked hurriedly away, in quite the wrong direction for Millbrae Crescent.

Star stood watching his retreating back. She could kick herself for what had just happened. Why hadn't she seen he was getting sweet on her? She must have been blind.

She watched him till finally he disappeared from view, telling herself she'd lost a friend, and the Boys' Brigade their new recruit.

That Friday proved her right about the latter.

Jim McBride hummed as he drove. He always enjoyed being out in the Arrole Johnstone, which he'd bought only eighteen months before. During the last years of the war the car had been owned by an American Air Force mechanic stationed at Prestwick who'd converted it from an ordinary gear shift to automatic.

Automatics were still a rarity in Britain, and Jim had jumped at the opportunity of owning one when he'd heard about the Arrole Johnstone being for sale. Even with a hook he could still drive an ordinary gear shift, but for him automatic made life a great deal easier, and safer.

His humming ceased as he turned into the Candleriggs, a street he knew every stone and cobble of as his entire working life before the war had been spent in it.

Halfway down he drew the Arrole Johnstone into the kerb and stared across the street at the building on the other side. Murison's Carpet Factory, proclaimed the sign in faded letters – letters that had been shiny bright when he'd first seen them at the age of twelve.

He vividly remembered his start there; the terrible deafening noise, the huge looms that were awesome – at least to his inexperienced eyes – the weft and warp threads interlacing those looms that were being transformed into chenile carpet, the smell of linen and jute which had seemed such a stink to him at first. In time he'd got used to both the stink and the noise.

Then, years later, after Big Sandy Peggie and others had taught him his trade, came that glorious day when he'd been made a foreman. Oh that had been a day right enough! He'd been certain his heart would burst he'd been so proud.

Shortly following that Jeannie had come along, and the wee house in Boyd Street where Tommy had been born. Hard times, but good times, until that awful morning when war had been declared and he'd known he'd be going for a soldier.

When he'd left, old Murison had come down to the floor to say goodbye and wish him all the best. 'And rest assured your job will be waiting for you when you come back to us, McBride,' Murison had said. But it had been a different story after he'd been invalided out of the Army and returned, with his hook and limp, to confront the old man. It had been a different story then, all right!

There had been soft words of sympathy, and a large dram to go with them. Then the knife had been slid in. He couldn't resume his position of foreman, not when he was so badly disabled. And for the same reason operating a loom was quite out of the question.

He'd agreed about operating a loom, but argued that his disabilities wouldn't affect his work as a foreman. A foreman supervised, chivvied those under his control, saw there was no slacking and that all minor problems were resolved. How did his hook and limp affect him doing that?

But Murison, though apologetic, was adamant. That was the way of it, there were no exceptions.

So what position *was* open to him, he'd wanted to know.

Murison had poured more whisky, and considered that. The offer, when it finally came, was that of a nightwatchman's job, the wage a quarter of what he'd earned as a foreman.

He'd been outraged. How could he possibly keep a wife and kiddie on that sort of money, he'd demanded to know.

Murison's reply was brief but blunt. It was a case of take it or leave it.

He'd told Murison to stuff the nightwatchman's job up the arse, and gone stomping out past the now all-female workforce.

That night the real reason why Murison refused to have him back as a foreman dawned on him. It was because the foremen were now all forewomen, and women were only paid half what a man earned. He'd realized then how advantageous the war was proving for Joseph Murison, whose factory was now churning out various types of materials for the War Department. Full production, full order books, minimum wage outlay – Murison was coining it.

He hadn't been bitter after losing his hand, or learning he'd limp for the rest of his life, or even when it seemed certain that he'd lose his entire arm due to the continuing re-infection of his stump. But he'd been bitter then. Bitter, disgusted, and so angry at Murison he would happily have swung for the bastard if it hadn't been for Jeannie and Tommy who needed him.

Jim smiled wryly to himself, thinking it was an ill wind. For if Murison hadn't done the dirty on him he'd never have got tied in with Paddy Swords to become the wealthy man he was today, and getting steadily wealthier with every passing week.

If it hadn't been for Murison's greed he'd still have been a foreman and living in Boyd Street. Instead he now had his own set-up and lived in Millbrae Crescent amongst the nobs. In a way, he owed Murison, but, as the saying went, if Murison had been on fire he wouldn't have peed on the bastard.

He saluted the factory with his hook then headed off down the Candleriggs to the Trongate and the Docks beyond.

At Queen's Dock he made for the North Basin where the M. V. Swan was tied up. It had arrived earlier that day from Dublin. He nodded with satisfaction to see his lorry parked alongside the Customs and Excise shed. In the lorry were a driver and three others on his payroll. He brought the Arrole Johnstone to a halt beside the lorry, had a quick word with Matt, the driver, then went into the shed where he found Willie McAllister brewing up.

'A cup of java?' Willie asked.

'Aye, that would go down a treat.' He offered Willie one of his cigarettes. 'Ten crates this trip,' Jim continued, letting Willie know, as he always did, that he was aware of the exact number of crates in the consignment. It was a precautionary measure. He might trust Willie, but only to an extent. Mind you, it would have been downright stupid of the Customs official to doublecross him, kill off the goose that laid the golden eggs so to speak, but stranger things had happened before now.

Willie handed him a cup and saucer, then pointed to some forms lying on the desk.

Crossing to the forms Jim swiftly signed them, acknowledging receipt of the crates.

'Your bills of lading,' Willie said to Jim, and gave Jim ten further forms, these large and yellow. Each form stated that the crate whose stencilled number it carried contained specialist machine parts. Jim's business, situated in the Calton district, was ostensibly a repair shop. Which

31

it was, and made a nice profit, too. But that was only a front for the way in which Jim really made his living.

Jim tucked the bills of lading into his inside jacket pocket, then took out his wallet. He counted off a number of five pound notes and gave these to Willie.

Willie recounted the notes in front of Jim; at the outset of their dealings together Jim had insisted on this, another precautionary measure. With the money recounted in front of him Willie could never come back at a later time to say the amount hadn't been correct.

'On the button as usual,' said Willie, and tucked the wad of fivers away.

'Next consignment is a week tomorrow. It's arriving on the S.S. *Hercules*, again from Dublin,' said Jim.

Willie digested the information, nodding. 'The S.S. *Hercules*, a week tomorrow. I'll make sure I'm the one on duty,' he replied.

Jim finished his coffee, accepted the release docket from Willie, then went out to the lorry to hand over the docket and tell the lads to secure the release of the crates and load them aboard.

Willie watched Jim through the shed window. He didn't know what was really in those crates, nor did he care. All that concerned him was the bung he got every time he passed a consignment through.

He grinned suddenly, remembering he was taking the new bint out that night. Her name was Sandra and she was a smasher! He'd buy her the best meal in Glasgow, then suggest the second house at the Alhambra. When the show was over it would be coffee and brandy in his West End flat.

It was the sort of night out he could only have afforded once in a while on his pay from the Customs and Excise. Thanks to Jim McBride he now did it all the time.

Star was in the school toilet with Lizzie Dunnachie, the pair of them sitting in cubicles next to one another.

Lizzie was in the middle of telling a filthy joke, and already had Star in stitches long before the punchline. Lizzie was the best filthy joke teller in the entire school, and had a seemingly endless supply of them. It was Lizzie's close secret where she got her jokes from.

The punchline was finally delivered, convulsing Star so much that she nearly fell off the w.c.

'Here listen, what's that?' asked Lizzie, as their laughter subsided.

Star caught her breath, listening. Then she heard it too, a commotion outside in the playground.

Just then Maev Whiteford, another 2A girl, came dashing into the cubicle on the other side of Star. 'Jesus!' she gasped, 'I thought I was going to get caught short there.'

'What's going on outside?' asked Star.

'That new boy . . . Tommy whatever his name is . . . he's having a fight with Korky Niven. It's a real humdinger, too, from what I saw as I dashed past.'

Tommy in a fight! And with Korky Niven! Korky was huge and a brute who enjoyed throwing his weight about. Star reached the toilet door with Lizzie right behind her. A crowd had gathered in the centre of the playground, heaving this way and that like a rugby scrum.

'Teacher,' muttered Lizzie, and gestured to where Mr Apsley, the P.T. teacher, was hurrying towards the crowd, black cape streaming out behind him.

Star and Lizzie reached the crowd at the same time as Mr Apsley, following in his wake as he carved a passage through the throng.

Star caught her breath when she saw Tommy. Blood was gushing from his nose, and the top buttons of his shirt had been ripped away. His tie had been jerked right round to the side of his neck. But though Korky was far larger than Tommy, the fight hadn't been one-sided. Korky's right eye was so swollen it was almost shut. There were also teeth marks on the cheek below the swollen eye.

The instant Korky saw Apsley he fell back from Tommy. 'Please sir, he started it! He attacked me with no provocation whatever, I swear that's the truth.'

'It's a lie,' hissed Tommy.

Mr Apsley stared hard at each lad in turn. He knew Korky to be a notorious bully, but that didn't necessarily mean he was the instigator of this. Tommy was more or less an unknown quantity to him, and did come from Govanhill, a right rough area.

'Why would he attack you without provocation?' Mr Apsley asked Korky at last.

Korky looked out innocently from his good eye. 'Please sir, I think he wanted to show everyone how tough he is, make a name for himself like. I was only defending myself, honestly.'

Mr Apsley wasn't yet convinced. 'Did anyone here see what happened?' he asked, addressing the crowd.

Korky had an inspiration then. 'Alec Muir saw and heard everything,' he said quickly staring directly at Alec.

Mr Apsley rounded on Alec, who was one of the school's most upright pupils. Mr Apsley knew Alec to be sound and reliable, a veritable paragon of virtue. If Alec confirmed Korky's account then that account was true.

Alec wanted to break eye contact with Korky, but couldn't. He was the rabbit mesmerized by the snake.

'Well, Alec?' demanded Mr Apsley.

'What Korky says is right enough sir,' Alec replied in a low voice.

Tommy couldn't believe that he'd just heard what he had. Why? Why was Alec lying? Wrongly, he concluded that it had to with Star. She must have told Alec about his asking her to the Christmas Dance, and this was Alec's revenge.

'Right then, it's the Head for you, my lad,' said Mr Apsley, and gestured to Tommy to start walking towards the Main Building, where the Head's study was located.

Korky congratulated himself on getting out of that one. He didn't envy in the least what was going to happen next to Tommy. He'd been up several times in the past before Commando McGee, and shuddered at the memory.

Alec saw Star, but didn't cross to her. Instead he backed off into the crowd at his rear and disappeared. He felt sick, and thoroughly ashamed of himself. He wanted to run and hide somewhere dark, just as he'd used to when wee and had done something wrong.

Star watched Tommy and Mr Apsley vanish into Main Building as around her the crowd began to disperse.

'Your friend Tommy will be for the high jump, that's a certainty,' Lizzie said to Star, for it was well known that Commando McGee couldn't abide fighting amongst his pupils and punished it severely.

Star looked round for Alec, wanting to talk with him, but he was gone. That's strange, she thought, for she knew he'd seen her. It was unlike him not to come over. He must have had something urgent to go off and attend to she told herself.

The bell rang, and those in the playground began to make their way into the four buildings that comprised the school. Star's next period was a study one, supervised by a Prefect. Impulsively, she decided not to attend. It was unlikely she wouldn't be missed, for the Prefects didn't take roll in study classes. Instead she'd wait for Tommy. After a session with McGee there was no telling what state he might be in. Maybe she could be of some help.

Star walked over to Main Building, the largest of the school's four buildings. On another impulse, she didn't go in but went round the side to stand directly beneath the Head's window. She wanted to hear what happened, and perhaps learn why Tommy had attacked Korky. It didn't really seem like the sort of thing Tommy would do.

The Commando was a small man with tremendously

broad and powerful shoulders. He'd been given the nickname Commando because he'd been one during the war. It was rumoured in the school that he'd killed half a dozen Germans, though not all at once, in hand to hand combat. He'd never been known to raise his voice, but when he was angry that voice took on a terrifying tone. That was the tone he was using now.

Tommy's guilt had been proven, so Commando McGee, to Star's disappointment, didn't bother going into the whys and wherefores. Rather he lectured Tommy about the behaviour he expected in his school, and that, as far as he was concerned, fighting was one of the two most heinous school crimes there were. Cheating was the other.

'Right then, it's twelve of the best. Six on the hands, six on the backside,' Commando McGee pronounced sentence.

Star gulped. Twelve! That was the maximum punishment allowed, and rarely administered. Tommy must be getting it because his attack on Korky had been unprovoked.

Star could imagine the Commando taking the black leather tawse from the cardboard box in which he kept it. The tawse was about eighteen inches long, three quarters of an inch thick, and sliced into fingers at the hitting end. She'd heard it said that the Commando periodically soaked his tawse in vinegar which supposedly made a blow from it more painful than it would otherwise have been, but she didn't believe that.

'Hold out your hands and cross them,' the Headmaster instructed.

She hoped Tommy knew not to partially draw away when the strap came down, for if it was only a partial hit then the Commando wouldn't allow it, even though a partial hit could sometimes be more painful than a full one. Or so she'd been told, she'd never had the strap herself.

She heard the whistle of the tawse through the air,

followed by the crack of it landing. She winced at the thought of what that must have felt like.

At the completion of the third stroke her clenched fist was grinding into her mouth, and she was shaking. Six times the tawse rose and fell with not a sound from Tommy.

'Now bend over the desk, boy,' ordered McGee.

Star knew the next stroke would be given a sideways motion, similar to the way a housewife beats a carpet hung over a low-slung washing line. Instead of the crack of leather on flesh there was the thud of leather striking material.

When it was finally over, Star's stomach was churning and she was still shaking. Turning away from the window, she stumbled back to the building's entranceway where she paused to collect herself. Then, straightening her shoulders, she went inside.

Minutes ticked by but Tommy didn't appear from the direction of the Head's study. Finally she had to come to the conclusion he must have left the building by some other way.

She'd missed him.

The tenement where Alec Muir lived with his mother and father was made of red sandstone that was visibly crumbling away. The windows staring out into Overdale Street had a mournful look about them, like eyes lost in memory, thinking of far better and more prosperous days. The stairs in the close Star walked up were concave from use.

Alec himself answered her agitated knock. He led her through to the sitting room, explaining that his mother was out doing some late shopping and his father was of course still at work.

Star always enjoyed being in the Muir house, there was a grace about it that attracted her. Once the contents would have been stunning, but now they were faded and,

37

like the stairs in the close, well worn from use and the passage of time. Carpets, curtains, furniture, all mere shadows of their former glory, had been originally bought by Alec's great-grandfather when Queen Victoria was still on the throne. Today, however, she was too upset to take much comfort from it. 'I looked for Tommy coming out of school but didn't see him. I can't think what on earth possessed him to do what he did. Can you?' she immediately demanded. Her face was pale with concern.

Alec shifted uneasily from one foot to the other. He was still feeling wretched about the incident in the playground. He'd tried praying earlier, but for once that hadn't helped. 'No,' he mumbled so softly he was barely audible.

Star wondered what was wrong with Alec, he looked so hangdog. 'Are you all right?' she queried.

He nodded, wishing she hadn't come. Her presence was making him feel even worse.

'Well, what happened? Did Tommy just go up to Korky and belt him one? Was that how it was?'

Alec went over to the fireplace and leant on the mantelpiece. He was going to have to tell her; if he didn't then Tommy would when she saw him. He groaned inwardly, damn that Korky Niven! Damn Korky to all the terrible fires of hell.

'I've no idea,' he replied.

Star blinked. 'But you must have, you saw it all,' she said.

'I saw nothing. When I arrived on the scene the pair of them were already at it hammer and tongs.'

He was pulling her leg, he had to be. 'Of course you saw what happened, I heard you tell Mr Apsley you did. You said Tommy launched an unprovoked attack on Korky.' She didn't move her eyes from him.

He stared at the smooth marble of the mantelpiece. At that moment he couldn't have faced her if his life had depended on it. 'I verified Korky's story because I knew fine well what Korky would do to me if I didn't,' he said at last in a thick voice.

Star heard again the crack of leather on flesh, the dull thud of leather on material. Until this moment she'd always looked up to Alec Muir, thought of him as infallible, an inspiration to all around him. Now she was seeing him in quite a different light.

Alec went on. 'Korky would have made me pay for not backing him, he'd have given me an awful bashing. The truth is I can't stand physical pain, never have been able to, and Korky knows it. That's why, apart from the fact that the masters think a lot of me, he picked me out of that crowd.'

She was filled with distaste – and pity. Tommy hadn't made a single sound when being belted by Commando McGee, but she could now visualize Alec screaming the place down at the very sight of the tawse, long before he'd even been touched by it.

'Look at it this way, Tommy didn't suffer because of me, the Head would have given him the belt anyway for fighting. My backing Korky's lie only meant that Korky didn't get belted too, that's all,' said Alec desperately.

'That's not true, Alec. Because you said that Tommy's attack on Korky was unprovoked he got twelve of the belt. He would never have got that much otherwise. He's never been in trouble before. It's your fault he got so many.' She glared at him, breathless with rage.

Alex wilted. Twelve of the tawse! His own flesh crawled at the thought. 'I can't help being a physical coward, that's the way I was born and I can't change it. Please say you understand and forgive me. Please, Star?'

She was startled to hear him sob, her heart softening.

'What else could I do?' he whispered.

She wanted to retort scathingly that he could have stood up to Korky like a man, but she didn't. A coward, and weak, that was Alec Muir, and it was a revelation to her. But he was right. He couldn't have stood up to

Korky Niven. And she reminded herself, he did have his good qualities. He was gentle, considerate, and highly intelligent – and he was really very kind. Her distaste melted away. Hadn't she ever done things she'd been ashamed of? This only proved him human, with faults like everyone else, and not the saintlike figure he'd previously seemed.

Alec's body shook with sobs as the tears washed down his cheeks. He felt Star come closer to him till she was standing only inches from his back. He shrank fractionally away from her, but her hand came to lightly rest on his shoulder.

'It's all right, Alec,' she said quietly. 'I do understand.' She felt that she wanted to protect him, the way a mother might her child.

He whirled round and clasped her tightly to his breast, his heart soaring with relief.

They stood there for a while in silence. Star waiting for his weeping to run its course. When it finally did, she kissed him full on his wet mouth, not a passionate kiss, but a kiss that was warm and reassuring.

'I'll make a pot of tea, we could both use a cup,' she said.

As she went through to the kitchen she decided she'd go from here to Tommy's house in Millbrae Crescent, she had to talk to him after what Alec had told her.

Tommy wasn't home when Star called. Mrs McBride said she thought he might have gone down to Lovers' Lane, a path running alongside a section of the River Cart. It was the only part of the riverbank in Battlefield and Langside accessible to the public, and Mrs McBride added that it had become something of a haunt for Tommy of late.

Star had gone to the McBrides on her bicycle, so she now cycled down to the river, only a few minutes away, then slowly cycled along the path. There was only a crescent moon that night, and the secluded path was extremely dark and shielded by a screen of trees from the nearest houses. The opposite bank was on the edge of the Albert Park, a private park, so there was no illumination from there.

Star was nearly at the far end of the path, and thinking that if he had come this way she must have missed him for the second time that day, when suddenly her bike light picked out a solitary strolling figure.

'Tommy, is that you?' she called.

The figure stopped. 'Star?'

She dismounted by his side. 'Are you feeling sorry for yourself?' she asked, which wasn't at all what she'd meant to say.

Tommy stiffened. 'What can I do for you?' he asked coldly.

'I wanted to speak to you.'

'About what?'

'The fight.'

He started to walk away from her and she had to hurry to catch him up. 'What really happened between you and Korky?'

'You heard what your boyfriend said, I attacked him without provocation.'

In the darkness it was difficult to make out his face. 'I saw Alec after school, he admitted he lied because he was scared of what Korky would do to him if he didn't.'

Tommy laughed harshly. 'Feart was he? Well at least he admitted what he did, that's something.'

Suddenly Tommy was irritating her, making her cross. 'We can't all be tough and brave,' she said cuttingly.

Tommy stopped again, and she did also. 'You don't have to worry about Alec, I won't touch him for what he did, if that's what you're here for.'

It had never occurred to her that Tommy might want revenge. 'And what about Korky?' she asked to cover her confusion.

41

'By now everyone in school will know he made a fool of me by getting Alec to lie for him. Well, I can't have that. I *won't* have it. We'll have to settle it between us.'

'You mean another fight?'

'Yes, another fight.' Tommy's voice was the only sound in the darkness.

Apprehension gripped her. She must try to dissuade him. He'd been lucky once against Korky but it was unlikely he'd be lucky twice.

'You did all right against Korky today,' she said as coolly as she could. 'But that would soon have changed if the fight had been allowed to continue. Take my word for it, you've no chance against Korky Niven, he'll mollicate you.'

'Then mollicate me he will, because I'm going to fight him. It doesn't matter if he beats me, it's the principle of the thing that's important. I'll not be a laughing stock, no matter what it costs,' Tommy replied, thinking he was damned if he was going to let those toffee noses at school have a laugh at his expense.

Her irritation changed to something akin to admiration. What a spirit he has, she thought. He had more integrity than anyone else she could think of.

There was a soft plop in the middle of the river. Tommy turned towards the sound, thinking it must have been made by a fish. Rivers and fish were still new to him. After the dirty, narrow streets of Govanhill this spot along the river seemed like a paradise on earth.

'I wouldn't totally dismiss my chances against Korky,' he went on more calmly. 'He may be big lad, but he isn't a street fighter. I know that from today. But *I* am. I had to learn to be in order to survive in Boyd Street. And I can use it to survive here.'

He wasn't to be talked out of this thing, she could tell that much. His voice told her so. He wasn't at all like the shy, sensitive chap who'd asked her up to dance in Miss Parrot's assembly, this was quite another side of him. It was certainly her day for seeing the other side of folk, she said to herself, thinking of Alec and what had been revealed to her in the house in Overdale Street.

'You still haven't told me what happened between you and Korky.'

'He called me a name.'

'It must have been something awful for you to get so het up about it.'

Tommy stared grimly out at the gently moving river. 'It was.'

Star sighed in exasperation. 'Well *tell* me for goodness sake!'

Thinking about the name made Tommy seethe inside, just as when Korky had called him it. He knew that part of the reason for his rage was because it was true, he was what Korky had said – and, desperately, he wished it weren't true.

He liked living in Millbrae Crescent. He liked the beautiful house and the posh neighbourhood. He liked having money and not living around people who beat each other up all the time. For the first time, he felt that he mattered, that he had the same chances as everybody else. Of course, he and his parents were a bit like square pegs in round holes, but given time they could adapt, change, be accepted. That was what he wanted; what he'd planned.

'Korky called me a scruff,' he said so softly she only just heard him.

His voice told her how much the name had hurt him. She could hear him breathing beside her in the dark, but she couldn't find the words to tell him that it didn't matter.

He suddenly pulled himself together. 'I'll see you,' he said in his normal voice. 'And don't worry about your boyfriend, he's safe from me.' Before she could reply, he strode off into the night and was quickly lost to view in the darkness.

Star wheeled her bicycle round. There had been no need for him to be so cold towards her. And there had

43

been contempt in his voice when he'd repeated that she needn't worry about Alec. Who did he think he was, talking to her like that?

Part of her wished she hadn't bothered to seek him out, part of her was pleased she had.

And another part was sick at the thought of what Korky Niven would do to him.

The word quickly spread through Queen's Park that Tommy McBride had challenged Korky Niven. The fight was to be held directly school let out that afternoon, and was to take place in what was known as the wild ground.

The wild ground was exactly that, it consisted of rough grass, clumps of heather, stunted bushes and a scattering of trees.

It started two streets away from the school, and went all the way over to the long grey dyke, a distance about the length of six hockey pitches. Beyond it was railway land and the railway line.

In length the wild land was a little over twice its breadth, with dykes on every side. Two of these dykes fronted on to major roads, the last on to a quiet residential street. The lie of the wild ground was such that once into it it was impossible to be seen from the outside. Which made it the perfect site for a fist fight and was why Korky had suggested it.

Star's final period of the afternoon was music. Normally she was blissfully happy during music, but today she was fidgety and on edge, one eye forever straying to her watch. When the bell rang she and almost everyone else would be going to the wild ground to watch the fight. She was dreading it.

If Star wasn't her usual self it didn't show in her playing. Miss Hamill beamed at Star as she played, until a Prefect arrived with a message and Miss Hamill had to leave the room.

If Miss Hamill had been beaming before she was called away, when she returned she was positively aglow. The class, restless to be gone, didn't notice.

At last the bell rang. Instantly instruments were downed and begun to be put away.

'Star and Janet,' said Miss Hamill above the noise. 'Stay behind, please, I want a word.'

Miss Hamill had Star and Janet Carnegie, 2A's other outstanding musician, stand by her desk till the rest of the class had hurried out. Then she smiled at them, unable to contain her excitement. 'Girls,' she said almost breathlessly, 'I've had a telephone call from an old and dear friend of mine who's on his way here right now. I'd like you to meet him. His name is Solomon Goldman. I'm sure you're aware that he is Conductor of the Glasgow Symphony Orchestra.'

Solomon Goldman! Star had seen the great man only three months ago when her father had taken her to the St. Andrew's Halls to hear Jose Iturbi who was on a British tour at the time. Goldman was a conductor of international repute, it was an undreamed-of honour to meet him.

Then she thought of Tommy, and her excitement vanished. Although she was dreading the fight, she wanted to be out there on the wild ground, cheering him on.

'How do you know Mr Goldman, Miss?' Janet Carnegie asked.

Star tried to listen to Miss Hamill's reply, but her mind was on the wild ground with Tommy. Very shortly he would be squaring up to Korky Niven.

The recent snow had vanished thanks to a sudden warm snap in the weather. The ground underfoot was dry and hard, perfect for fighting on. Tommy scanned the loose ring of people surrounding him and Korky, but failed to see who he was looking for. He glanced in the direction from which they'd all come, but there were no straggling figures, all those coming had arrived – and Star wasn't one of them.

With a shrug, he put his disappointment behind him and started to concentrate on the matter in hand. He wasn't exactly nervous, apprehensive more like, and wound up like a clockspring inside. He removed his jacket and handed it to someone near him, then watched Korky remove his and toss it casually to a crony.

Korky was about two and a half inches taller than Tommy and a good two stone heavier. His fists were thick and square, and Tommy knew from experience that they were veritable piledrivers once they swung into action.

He reminded himself that he mustn't let Korky get him in a stranglehold or bearhug. With his extra size it would quickly be all over if that happened.

'Let's be having you then, *scruff*!' Korky jeered and moved towards Tommy.

Tommy went forward to meet him.

'Perhaps I could hear you girls play,' Solomon Goldman was saying to Star and Janet.

Miss Hamill happily clapped her hands together, pretending that this was a delightful surprise when in reality it was what she'd been angling for ever since Solomon had arrived, as well he knew.

Hell's teeth! Star swore inwardly. Up until this moment she'd been hoping she'd still be able to make the fight. Korky was the sort to continue ladling into Tommy even though it was obvious Tommy was beaten. And Tommy was the sort to keep fighting as long as he was still conscious. She prayed that someone would step in and stop the fight before it was too late.

'A little Beethoven I think,' smiled Miss Hamill.

★ ★ ★

It was only Tommy's experience from the streets of Govanhill that had allowed him to survive this far, but he was taking a terrible pounding and knew he couldn't last much longer. He was aware only of the pain and of Korky goading him on.

The onlookers were silent. They'd started off cheering and shouting, but that had died away as the vicious fight progressed.

Repeating what had happened in their first bout, Korky had landed several vicious punches on Tommy's nose causing it to bleed profusely, the bright red stain covering his chin and spreading down his shirt. Tommy had also badly scraped the back of his left hand, so that his left fist looked as though it had been dyed crimson.

One of Korky's eyebrows had been cut and blood from there dribbled down his face. Although he didn't know it yet, he had a broken rib and two cracked ones.

Exhausted but still angry, the combatants closed again. Korky's fists flailed while Tommy shuffled heavily one way, then another. Tommy got in a swift jab to Korky's face, and received a glancing body blow in reply. He tried to shuffle in a circular motion, but his legs no longer obeyed the commands he sent them. Against his will, he stopped and sagged where he stood. This is it, he thought. Now I'm really for it.

Korky, realizing his opponent was done for, moved in for the kill.

During the war years the Army bivouacked often on the wild ground. Probably that was why the iron rod had come to be there. As Tommy's hand closed around it he thought it was a miracle.

He'd been sent sprawling by a mighty punch from Korky who was now kicking him in the side. If Star had been there she would have intervened now, or attempted to. Despite her fervent prayer in Miss Hamill's classroom, however, no one did any such thing. They were all too terrified of Korky Niven to risk getting in his way.

The rod was about a quarter of an inch thick, and approximately a yard long. Tommy swung it in a back-hand arc. It hissed through the air.

More by luck than good judgement, the rod took Korky smack across the forehead, sending him pitching headlong to the ground beside Tommy. Painfully, Tommy struggled on to his side to stare at the still figure of his enemy.

'Fucking arseholes, he's killed Korky!' a male voice exclaimed.

Tommy gasped in breath after breath. Killed Korky? He kept staring at the apparently lifeless form.

'Jesus Christ!' Lizzie Dunnachie said, eyes popping.

Realizing he was still clutching the rusty rod, Tommy threw it from him. Bending, he caught hold of Korky and pulled him over so that he was lying face up. Korky's colour was waxen, except for the nasty red imprint across his forehead where the iron rod had caught him.

Stanley Munro, one of Korky's chinas, made a move towards him, but stopped when he saw the look on Tommy's face. '*Is* he dead McBride?' Stanley demanded in a shaky voice.

Tommy put his ear to Korky's nose. Relief flooded through him. Korky was still breathing. Then Korky groaned, rolled over, and was sick.

Tommy hauled himself unsteadily to his feet. Now that he knew Korky was all right there was no pity in him as he watched Korky continue to spew. He knew it was only luck that he hadn't been the one nearly killed. Korky deserved all he had got.

'He's all right, but he's going to have a bloody awful head on him for a while,' Tommy said to Stanley.

Tommy's chest felt tight and his legs were wobbly, but despite this he felt fine. Just fine. He was the victor, and that was sweet. Very sweet indeed.

He retrieved his jacket, had a last look at the still prostrate Korky, then staggered through the ring of people clapping him on the back and congratulating him, delighted that someone had finally beaten Korky Niven at his own game.

As he went, a pair of eyes filled with admiration followed his departure. The eyes belonged to one of the prettiest girls in the school. Her name was Eve Smith, and she was just deciding that Tommy McBride was for her.

When it came to the lads, Eve Smith always got whoever she set her cap at.

Always.

Margaret Muir, Alec's mother, was hunched in an armchair, watching her son get ready for the Christmas Dance. She had a cigarette in one hand and a glass of whisky in the other. She was indulging herself with a dram because it was the festive season. Normally, they couldn't afford to have drink in the house.

Her thoughts drifted to her husband Geoffrey, out at a Masonic meeting, and her lips twisted downwards into a thin, disapproving frown. It was Geoffrey she disapproved of, not the Masons. In fact, it had been at her instigation that he'd joined the Masons. She'd hoped they would help him in his career, as they'd supposedly helped so many others. But they hadn't. She was certain she knew why. As she had, the Masons must have come to recognize Geoffrey for what he was: third rate and a born loser. There was no point in helping someone who would only let you down.

She swallowed a mouthful of whisky, enjoying the harshness and pungency of its taste. She had always enjoyed things hurting her, as long as the hurt wasn't too great. With another man, this was something she might have introduced into their sex life. But Geoffrey was as boring in bed as he was out of it.

Her expression changed fractionally to one of contempt – contempt for her husband and for herself for being stupid enough to marry him in the first place.

49

Oh, he'd been handsome then. Devilishly so. She hadn't been the only one after Geoffrey. But she'd been the *lucky* one who'd caught him.

Her hero; Margaret thought scathingly. He'd dazzled her with the tales of the success he was going to be in the banking world. He was still only a lowly teller, he'd told her, but it wouldn't be long before that changed. He would be a branch manager before he was thirty; and after that, who knew! The sky was the limit. He might go into merchant banking, he might aim for a seat on the Board of the bank he was already with, and beyond that seats on the Boards of other banks.

Pipe dreams, pie in the sky, hopeless fantasies, that's all it had turned out to be. Alec had been five years old, and her figure long gone with the carrying and nursing of him, when it had at last come home to her that Geoffrey's big talk was just that, big talk and nothing else. Finally she'd understood that he would never amount to anything, that he would always be the lowly teller he'd been when they'd first met.

'Which tie, Mother?' Alec asked, holding out a choice of four.

She regarded the ties, then pointed to the grey with thin blue stripes as the one that was the best for his suit.

Her eyes narrowed as she watched her son finish dressing. He might be weak like his father, but, thank the Lord, he'd inherited her brains. She fully intended seeing they were put to good use. And although Alec wasn't nearly as handsome as Geoffrey had been, he was a good looking lad and he did have charm, when he wanted to use it.

All these were assets that she literally intended to cash in on. Alec was her last hope. It was her intention that he would rebuild the family fortune lost by his grandfather and restore them to their former glory.

The great idea had come to her a few years back. Ever since, she'd been busy scheming and making contacts, doing everything she could to further her plan. The

50

Muirs might be poor, but they still had standing in Scottish society.

She smiled to herself, thinking of the list of suitable girls she'd been steadily compiling. The parents of these girls had either become friendly with her or were about to.

Top of the list – because her family was the wealthiest – was Morag Hutchison. Second was Ishbel Doig, whose father was big in the grocery trade. Third was Juliet Abercrombie, whose family was in nuts and bolts. These three girls, like the rest on Margaret's list, had one thing in common; they would bring money and opportunity when they married. She was determined that Alec would eventually find his bride amongst them.

This religious nonsense Alec was going through was merely a phase which she would allow to run its course. If he didn't give up on it naturally, then she would see to it herself. Alec being a minister in the Church, with the miserable stipend they earned, didn't figure at all in her schemes.

'How's that?' Alec asked nervously, smoothing back his hair, a stray piece immediately popping up again.

Rising, Margaret crossed to her son and inspected him. 'You'll do,' she replied shortly.

'I'll be home about eleven, don't wait up.'

She brushed a bit of lint from his shoulder. 'Of course I will, I'll want to hear all about it.'

Alec pecked his mother on the cheek, so excited he could barely take the time to say goodbye. He was due to pick up Star in ten minutes, he'd timed it just right.

Margaret knew Alec was taking Star, and that he was fond of her. A puppy romance was how she saw it. Alec was only fifteen, just beginning to spread his wings. It would be a couple of years yet before she started introducing him to the girls on her list. In the meantime there was no harm in him going out with Star Gray.

No harm at all. If anything, it was good experience for him.

*　　*　　*

While Alec was getting dressed, Star was also getting ready for the school Christmas Dance.

She was delighted with her dress. It was a pre-war one of Alison's that Alison had remade for the occasion by cutting it down a little, and totally altering the sleeves, which hadn't suited Star at all, to mutton-chop. It was beige with a large bow on the left hip and tassly things round the collar and bust. The matching shoes were an old pair that had been newly soled and heeled before being dyed the same colour as the dress.

'You look a proper treat,' Alison said, admiring her daughter from a few feet away. 'That dress really suits you.'

Star looked at herself in the mirror. She was bubbling with excitement, it was going to be a marvellous night, she just knew it. Her hand strayed to her face – if only . . . 'Couldn't I wear just a smidgin of make-up, please?' she pleaded softly.

Alison sighed. Why was it young girls always thought make-up made them prettier. 'Even if I thought you needed it, which I most certainly don't, I couldn't allow you to put on any. Your father would go through the roof.'

Star sighed resignedly. Her father had a phobia about 'painted Jezebels', as he called them, and had even spoken on the subject from the pulpit. To him a painted woman was no better than a common prostitute. He was not a man to move with the times.

Alison was about to say that there was no make-up in the house anyway, then realized that if Star was asking to wear some there must be. Better not let your father catch you out my lass, she thought grimly, for if he did there would be Laldy to pay.

'And he'll want to see you and Alec before you leave. He's in his study writing Sunday's sermon.' Alison added, just in case it was in Star's mind to try and sneak some make-up on before going off.

Star peered into the mirror. 'A teensy weensy bit would

have been nice, though,' she said wistfully.

A few minutes later the doorbell rang. Alec had arrived.

A great deal of time and effort had gone into making the gym look as nice as possible for the Christmas Dance. There was a large tree at the rear with – a real novelty in 1947 – electric fairy lights on it in every colour of the rainbow. Paper chains had been strung from corner to corner and side to side across the gym. Some theatrical floodlights had been borrowed from the Citizens' Theatre and these provided the general illumination.

Star's eyes were everywhere, taking it all in – the music, the decorations, the smiling couples. She saw Lizzie Dunnachie arrive with James Ledingham, and a few seconds later Catherine with Bobby Douglas who was in his fifth year and coming up to take his Highers.

When Alec excused himself to go to the toilet, Star wandered over to where Lizzie and James Ledingham were standing to have a natter with them.

Lizzie was in brilliant form, her patter even better than usual, which was saying something. She told the filthest joke Star had ever heard, the joke made even funnier by James being so embarrassed at being told it by a girl. They where still giggling when Alec returned, looking serious. In a low voice, he told them that a group of lads in the toilet had a bottle of whisky and were passing it to one another. 'I think it's shocking,' he said in an outraged voice. 'I'm going to report them.'

'Don't be soft, that's the last thing you want to do,' Star said.

'But these boys are all in the first year, and drinking at that age is wrong,' argued Alec.

'Right or wrong it's none of your affair,' put in James. 'If that's how they want to enjoy themselves then leave them to it.'

God Squad! thought Lizzie, they could be a right pain in the bum at times.

Their argument was interrupted by a sudden comotion round the far entranceway. Star craned her neck to see what was going on. A couple seemed to be the centre of attention, though she couldn't make out who they were.

The band struck up a lively Military Two Step. Star was about to suggest she and Alec take the floor again, when suddenly the couple who'd been receiving all the attention emerged from the crowd surrounding them. Star's jaw fell open in amazement. Tommy McBride and Eve Smith! The pair of them were arm in arm, Eve staring adoringly up at Tommy as though he were a Hollywood god just stepped down off the Silver Screen.

'Well, well,' murmured Lizzie, having also caught sight of the couple. She glanced quickly at Star to see what Star's reaction was, for she knew that Tommy had asked Star to the dance.

Star was speechless with rage. Eve Smith, of all people! Why the girl was . . . *notorious*!

'I wonder when that happened?' mused Lizzie.

Tommy's left hand was still bandaged from his recent fight with Korky Niven, and his nose had a new, splayed look about it, but he looked better than she'd ever before seen him. He no longer looked shy or out of place; he radiated confidence and pride.

Star hadn't realized how much of a celebrity Tommy had become since beating Korky, but she did now. Every second or so someone called out to him, gave him a friendly wave, or punched him playfully on the shoulder. And Eve, the cow, was all over him, positively basking in the reflected glory.

Why was she so angry? Star asked herself the question, but couldn't answer it. Tommy McBride meant nothing to her. She'd tried to help him settle into school, and that was all. He was the one who'd been keen on her, for goodness sake!

'That suit he's wearing cost a couple of quid,' James commented. And it was true. Tommy's suit was the very best material, and beautifully tailored.

54

Star's gaze narrowed on Eve's face. Eve's lips were a crimson slash and her eyes were accentuated by a bold black line along the lids. Expertly applied shadow highlighted her cheeks. The overall effect – though it hurt Star to have to admit it – was quite ravishing.

Star's gaze dropped to Eve's dress, and her dismay turned to despair. Eve's dress was a simple black sheath that did for her figure what her make-up did for her face. In short, it was sensational.

Star's hand went to her own dress. Compared to Eve's, it was a rag. She realized now how over fussy it was; how dowdy and frumpish. And to think how chuffed she'd been with it at the beginning of the night! She bit back tears, and wished herself anyplace but where she was.

'She could be twenty-one or -two got up like that,' Lizzie said enviously.

All Star wanted was to go home, but it was far too early for that. If she left now it would only cause comment, perhaps even get back to Tommy, which was the last thing she wanted. And what could she give as an explanation?

Turning to Lizzie she said, a triumphant tone in her voice. 'Forget the rest. Look at her ankles, they're positively *fat*!'

Lizzie smiled to herself. If those were fat ankles then she was the Empress of China. 'Oh aye, they are that, regular treetrunks,' she agreed, aware of how jealous Star was. Now that, thought Lizzie, is very interesting, and amusing.

Time passed, but Tommy didn't once glance in Star's direction. He might at least have had the courtesy to say hello, she thought testily. At one point she considered going over and saying hello to him, but then she remembered how her dress compared to Eve's and decided against it.

Tommy was well aware of Star staring over at him from time to time, but he refrained from acknowledging those stares. After all, why should he bother about someone who didn't even care enough about him to come to the fight he'd had with Korky?

Eve squirmed in his arms. Jesus, she was sexy! Tons more so than Star, he bet himself; he was far better off with Eve. She was the lass for him.

'How did it go?' Alison eagerly demanded later, when Star got in.

'Oh, all right,' Star replied vaguely, then in the same vague tone said she was straight off to bed, she was dog tired.

Alison stared perplexedly at Star's back as she sauntered from the room. Now what on earth's got into her, she wondered? 'Young people!' she muttered to herself. You never knew where you were with them.

2

It was January, 1948, and Queen's Park Senior Secondary School had been back from the Christmas holiday for two weeks.

The other girls in 2A were getting dressed after P.T., and as usual the changing room was crowded and noisy. Star was tugging on her jersey when the door flew open and in streamed the girls of 3D who were about to get ready for indoor netball. The already close space became jam packed with girls either struggling to put clothes on or take them off.

By chance, Eve Smith and several of her pals ended up beside Star and Lizzie Dunnachie. Without so much as a look between them, Star and Lizzie immediately tuned in to what Eve was saying, and it was clear from the loudness of her voice that Eve didn't care who heard her.

'He's absolutely gorgeous. He's the best boyfriend I've ever had,' Eve practically purred as she undid her blouse.

Lizzie caught Star's eye. It had to be Tommy that Eve was talking about.

'What do you mean *had*?' Kirsty Cairncross teased.

A sudden hush fell round the vicinity, all eyes turned to Eve, all ears waited for the reply.

She raised an imperious eyebrow, looked down her nose at the owlish Kirsty, and said. 'You're old enough to know what the word "had" means.'

There was a faint chorus of gasps following this statement. To actually *admit* such a thing in public! It was unheard of, it was scandalous, it was the most exciting thing to ever happen in either 2A or 3D!

Eve grinned to herself, pleased with the reaction she'd got. She felt like a movie star surrounded by fans.

Star spoke before she'd realized it. 'You're disgusting,' she snapped, her face flushed.

Eve rounded on Star, fixing her with a hard look. 'Did you speak Miss Goody Two Shoes?' she asked in a voice of mock sweetness.

There were a few titters; Kirsty Cairncross laughed behind her hand.

'Yes,' said Star determinedly. 'I said you're disgusting, Eve Smith,' she repeated, matching the older girl's stare.

Eve already knew that there was a lot of truth in the cliché that the best defence is a good offence. 'I suppose you're just jealous because no real boy would be caught dead with you,' she said condescendingly.

Star went pale. She wasn't sure exactly what Eve was getting at, but she knew it wasn't going to be good.

'There's nothing wrong with Alec Muir,' she replied quietly, wondering why she had such a terrible urge to launch herself at Eve and claw her eyes out.

'There's nothing right with him, either,' snapped Eve. 'He's wet as they come. But I guess that's why you like him. You're such a perfect couple. He probably couldn't get it up even if he wanted to.'

Get what up Star wondered. Then it dawned on her what Eve meant.

'Not that I suppose you would know one way or the other being such a *nice* girl,' Eve was going on, making the word 'nice' sound like some dreadful disease. Then Eve delivered her final blow. 'I wouldn't be at all surprised if Alec Muir goes with you because he doesn't really like girls.'

Star went cold all over. Except for Lizzie, all the girls were laughing at her now. Eve's laugh was so harsh and strident it might have been a piece of broken glass being dragged along a stone wall.

Time to get out of here, thought Lizzie, and picking up the remainder of her and Star's clothes, she took Star by the shoulder and gently propelled her towards the door.

'Don't even deign to reply, it isn't worth it,' she said in a loud voice, giving Eve a sideways glance that warned, say anything smart to me and you'll get the edge of my tongue, and you know what that'll be like.

Eve got the message. Lizzie's tongue was renowned, and not even Eve wanted to get into a verbal duel with her.

Outside in the playground Star started to shake. 'What a bitch,' she said through her tears.

'Don't pay any attention to her,' said Lizzie. 'She just likes to hear herself talk.' Privately, though, she thought that Star had asked for that one. She should have had the sense to keep her mouth shut.

Star took a deep breath, then another, which stopped her shaking. She was angry, confused and bewildered. Goody Two Shoes, was that how people saw her? Surely not, she was nothing like that. She was bright and strong. She was going to be somebody.

'I'll say this for Eve Smith, she's got one hell of a brass neck. Imagine admitting she's no longer a virgin straight out like that. That takes some nerve.' Lizzie's voice was tinged with admiration.

Star frowned, unable to see what was admirable in what Eve had done.

'There's not another girl in Queen's Park Secondary would have made such an admission,' added Lizzie.

58

'There's not many could,' Star said.

Lizzie gave a knowing smile. 'There's a lot more goes on around here than I think you realize.'

Star was intrigued. 'What do you mean?'

'Just that. Most of the girls go in for no more than holding hands a goodnight kiss, but there is more than one has gone a lot further than that. Not that they'd publicly admit it, of course.'

'Yes, but . . . they don't actually go all the way, do they?' Star queried, her frown deepening.

'Of course they do. Particularly the ones who go steady. After a while it's more or less expected.'

Star was astonished. 'I never knew that.'

Lizzie gave her a funny look. 'So what about you and Alec, doesn't he ever try it on?'

'No,' she said slowly. 'No, he never has. Not once.'

Lizzie gave a long low whistle. 'He must be even more religious than I thought,' she laughed. 'I didn't think there were any boys like him left.'

They had time before the next class, so Lizzie suggested they go behind the bicycle shed so she could have a fly puff. Star, deep in thought, agreed absentmindedly. It wasn't until Lizzie had lit up that Star asked, somewhat coyly, her voice choked with embarrassment, 'Lizzie . . . have you . . . ?'

Lizzie cracked a grin. 'Just between you, me and the drainpipe here?'

'Cross my heart and hope to die.'

'Yes. It was Hamish McInstray, but it was more his idea than mine.'

Star stared at Lizzie as though she had just arrived from the moon. 'How often?'

Lizzie held up four fingers.

It was a complete revelation to Star. 'And you say lots of girls are . . . are doing it?'

The look on Star's face had made it hard for Lizzie not to giggle, but now realizing how serious Star seemed to be she got suddenly serious herself. 'Oh aye, but you

59

have to take precautions, mind. You mustn't let them near you unless they're wearing an Ef-El, or you'll be in the club before you know where you are.' Ef-Els were French letters, or condoms.

'Why didn't you tell me all this before?' Star demanded.

Lizzie looked away, and blushed slightly. 'I don't really know why, you being my best china and all. I suppose it's because your old man's a minister. It didn't seem right talking about all that sort of thing to a minister's daughter. Not even you.'

'Just because my father's a minister doesn't make me different from the other girls,' Star snapped, surprised by the force of her feelings. It was as though there had been a conspiracy to make her the only girl in the entire world who didn't know what was going on. Was there something wrong with her? Was that why?

They walked in silence all the way to Latin class, where Star did even worse than usual. On being asked to decline Amaveram she could only get as far as Amaverat.

Mr Orr's comment about that was caustic in the extreme.

The Reverend Kenneth Gray was in the middle of his sermon, and going great guns. He always thoroughly enjoyed delivering sermons. There was a lot of the actor in him and he revelled in having an audience.

Star was sitting with her mother. To her left were Alec and Mr and Mrs Muir, and on her right, near the front, were the McBrides. Mrs McBride was wearing one of the most ostentatious hats she'd ever seen. Star pretended not to notice Tommy sitting between his parents.

Star fastened her attention on to Alec and tried to imagine what it would be like going to bed with him. She tried to imagine Alec getting carried away with passion, and couldn't. Somehow images of Alec getting carried away like that just wouldn't come. But then it was so unlike Alec to get carried away about anything, except, possibly, religion.

She gnawed her lip. Could what Eve had implied be true? *Could* he be . . . queer? Of course he's not, she told herself. He's just reserved, that's all.

Her gaze accidentally shifted to Tommy. Suddenly, so clear it could have been happening right there in front of her eyes, she could picture him making love to Eve Smith. She had no trouble picturing Tommy carried away by passion. Her throat had gone dry, and a sensation had blossomed in her, a warm feeling that seemed to emanate from the very core of her being.

She tore her gaze away from Tommy and returned it to Alec. Why couldn't she imagine him making love to her when she could vividly imagine Tommy making love to Eve?

Was it just because of the type of person that Alec was, or was there more to it than that? Was it something to do with her? Not only had Alec never tried to touch her, *no* boy had. Lizzie said it was normal for them to, so what was wrong with Star?

Did boys merely like her to talk too, to be friendly with, but never to fancy? Was that it, that she didn't have any sex appeal? That she was so plain and prissy that she was unattractive?

There were such women, she knew. Women who were not particularly ugly, or different – just more or less ordinary, except that men never thought to go to bed with them.

Panic and self-doubt flared through Star. Was she herself like those women – a female who completely lacked sex appeal?

She was suddenly aware of Margaret Muir smiling at her, and she smiled back. She liked Mrs Muir. Now there was a woman with sex appeal. Even though she'd gone to fat, her sexiness was still there. Star was certain that a lot of men, given half the chance, would have fallen over themselves to get into bed with Mrs Muir.

61

Alec must take after his father, she decided. And yet Mr Muir had married Mrs Muir, so perhaps he wasn't as bland as he seemed. In which case, Star concluded miserably, the problem really did lie with her.

The Reverend Kenneth Gray wound up his sermon, thinking smugly to himself that it had gone well, as usual, and sat down. Immediately the congregation relaxed, some shifting on the hard wooden pews, others getting rid of the coughs they'd been holding back.

The organist gave them about ten seconds to get sorted out, then went into the opening bars of 'Onward Christian Soldiers', the next hymn on the board, and the Reverend's favourite.

Star got to her feet, still so preoccupied with her thoughts that she failed to grimace, as she would normally have done, when the organist inadvertently played a wrong note.

Jim McBride looked forward to his weekly drive through to Edinburgh, and the safety deposit box that lay at the end of it.

The box was registered in the name of Ronald McArthur, a pal of his who'd fallen in the war.

The reason he'd chosen Edinburgh was that he knew no one there. In Edinburgh he could be Ronald McArthur, and no one would ever know otherwise. Glasgow had been too dangerous for his purposes; it might be a large town in many ways, but it was awfully small in others.

Thinking of what lay inside his safety deposit box brought a smile to Jim's face, as it always did. Seventeen thousand and three hundred pounds, all in used notes, all his. Seventeen thousand and seven hundred and fifty pounds, he corrected himself, that's what it would be shortly, after he'd added the notes now nestling in his inside jacket pocket.

It would all have to end someday of course, that was

inevitable. But in the meantime he was making money hand over fist, and the sky above, no matter what the weather, was always blue.

As Jim McBride passed the Edinburgh City boundary marker, Jeannie McBride was alighting from a tram opposite her beloved Boyd Street where she and Jim had spent, as she saw it, so many happy years together.

Oh, but it was grand being back! She fair loved these visits, lived for them really, for Jeannie, unlike her husband and son, hadn't settled in Millbrae Crescent, nor would she ever.

There was Mrs O'Leary, the Irish wifie, leaning out of her window just as she'd been doing time out of mind, watching what was going on and hoping someone would stop for a chin wag; and there was Young's the wee newsagent shop which sold farthing ice lollies Granny Young made in the rear shop in that pre-war refrigerator old man Young had dug up from somewhere, and which had paid for itself a thousand times over with the number of lollies they sold.

Jeannie sighed. This was her place true enough, and it had broken her heart to have to leave. But Jim was right when he said Millbrae Crescent was a doorway through which Tommy could step into a whole new, and better, way of life.

She breathed in that well remembered smell, so different from Battlefield. Millbrae Crescent smelt quite antiseptic by comparison.

She spied Elsie Murtagh and hurried across the road, calling out to her as she went.

Elsie clasped her close. 'Look at you!' she exclaimed. 'You look wonderful! Life amongst the toffs must suit you.'

'Oh it's very nice, but not like it is amongst *real* folk,' Jeannie replied, trying not to sound as sad as she felt.

'I've heard the folks you're living beside now are so grand they don't ever have to go to the cludgie,' Elsie joked, her voice crackling with mirth.

'Oh they go all right,' laughed Jeannie. 'But they call it the toy-let, not the cludgie.' She pronounced 'toilet' in an exaggerated Kelvinside manner that had Elsie doubled over, slapping a heavy thigh with an equally heavy fist.

'Och, you always were a right one, so you were,' she grinned, straightening up and slipping her arm through Jeannie's.

Jeannie glanced fondly and longingly around. 'East west, home's best,' she said simply.

Elsie knew exactly what her friend meant. 'Toy-let,' Elsie answered, using the same exaggerated pronunciation Jeannie had.

Laughing fit to bust and holding one another up, they made their way down the street in the direction of Elsie's room and kitchen.

Sunday afternoons, prior to tea and evening service, and weather permitting, Star always went for a walk, to the Linn Park, a little over a mile from the manse.

This Sunday afternoon Lizzie Dunnachie was with her, for as Lizzie always said when she accompanied Star on these jaunts, what the hell else was there to do in Glasgow on a Sunday afternoon? Everything, but everything, was either closed or shut tight, even the childrens' swing parks, the swings themselves chained and padlocked.

In Glasgow on a Sunday there was one commandment, and one only: Thou Shalt Not.

Both girls were wearing the obligatory hat and carrying the equally obligatory umbrella. It was unthinkable for a decent lassie to go out without these badges of respectability. The only exception was the umbrella, which could be left home in high summer, but the sun really had to be cracking the sky before even that exception could be made.

They'd been through one extremely large section of the park, and were now leaving by the Snuffmill Bridge end, where a bridge crossed the River Cart as it roared and churned far below.

Deep in conversation, the girls were unaware of Tommy, walking up the road towards the bridge. He'd only just discovered the park, but already it had become his favourite place. The first time he'd come he'd stared in awe at the great cathedral of trees which seemed to stretch on and on forever. Now he came to the park at every opportunity. For him, it was a magic place.

Looking up suddenly, instinctively, Star noticed Tommy before Lizzie. She set her face into an impassive mask when she realized that he was coming over to them, a big smile on his face. Star was still not over the scene in the locker room. In fact, the more time passed the more horrible the whole thing seemed to her. She was sure that everyone was still laughing at her, and she wondered what Eve had told Tommy about the incident. She took his smile not as a friendly greeting, but as a sign that he, too, thought she was a silly fool.

'Well, hello,' he said when he finally came to a stop beside them.

Tommy was in a frivolous mood. When the girls did not immediately respond, he decided to have a wee dig at Star.

'I hear you and Eve had a bit of a run-in,' he said. 'Is it true she called you Goody Two Shoes?' He laughed.

Star coloured. So he did know. She could easily imagine what Eve had told him, prissy little Star Gray making a fool of herself in front of two classes, no wonder even her own boyfriend wasn't interested in her. 'I wouldn't call it a run-in exactly,' said Star softly.

Star's obvious discomfort spurred Tommy on to even more laughter. 'Eve can be quite a girl when she wants to be,' he grinned.

'Well, you'd be the expert on that,' snapped Star.

Something in her voice and the look in her eyes made the next joke die on his lips. 'And what's that supposed to mean?'

65

'You know what it means,' said Star, unable to control her voice or anything it said. She wished she were home, she wished she had never come for this walk, she wished she had never been born. She wished she would shut up and just go away. 'And by now the entire school probably knows as well.'

Tommy looked at Lizzie. 'What's she talking about?'

'I'm talking about the run-in, as you call it,' interrupted Star. 'Surely Eve didn't forget to mention the anouncement she made to 2A and 3D?' Having gone so far, Star's fears had been supplanted by contempt. She was so angry now, so angry and so disgusted, that she didn't give a fig what Tommy McBride or his cheap girlfriend thought of her.

Tommy stared at her coldly. 'What announcement would that be, then?'

'That you and Eve are sleeping together,' Lizzie said quickly, wanting only to get Star moving again.

Tommy felt as though someone had kicked him in the stomach. It would never have occurred to him to tell anyone about Eve, and he had assumed that the same went for her about him. 'She what?'

'She told everyone that you and she were having it off,' Lizzie said sweetly.

'That's a lie!' Tommy exploded. 'You're making it up!' He looked as though he was about to grab Star by the shoulders and shake her.

'It's the truth and you know it,' Star shouted back, shaking off Lizzie's hand which was trying to pull her away. 'Didn't she tell you what our fight was about? That it all started because I said she was disgusting when she started going into details?' The look of horror on his face made up for everything. Now she had the power, now she was the one in control. 'Don't tell me you're ashamed of her,' she laughed, taking an uncharacteristic pleasure in twisting the knife.

This time Tommy did grab Star by the shoulders, holding her so that she had to look him in the face. 'No,

66

Miss Goody Two Shoes, I'm not ashamed of her,' he said quietly.

'Well maybe you should be,' said Lizzie.

Tommy let go of Star and rounded on her. 'And just what do you mean by that?'

Lizzie gave him one of her sweetest smiles. 'Nothing much. Just that it takes all sorts.' Her tone made it clear just what sort she thought Eve was.

Tommy was as angry now as he had been when Korky called him a scruff. 'I'll not hear anything said against Eve,' he said to Lizzie but his eyes on Star. 'Not by you or anybody else. She's a first class bird and that's all there is to it.'

Lizzie, realizing that she'd gone far enough, took a step backwards and said nothing.

Star, however, was far beyond caution. 'First class,' she laughed. 'You call that first class?'

Tommy's fingers clenched and unclenched, but he made no more moves to grab Star. 'Yes, I do,' he said evenly.

'Well, all I can say is your standards can't be too high if you think that little tart is first class,' said Star. 'What I can't fathom is what you see in her.'

'You wouldn't understand,' said Tommy in a voice that was menacing because it was so controlled.

'Oh, I don't know. We're both females, after all.'

Tommy searched for the most cutting retort he could think of, and found it. 'Only she's a lot more so,' he announced in triumph.

As though he'd slapped her across the face, Star stared at him, speechless. All the nightmares of the past few days came back in full force, and she realized even more strongly that she was the outsider, she was the one who was the object of ridicule.

This time Lizzie physically stepped between them. 'Why don't you go and find a stone to crawl under,' she said to Tommy.

Tommy didn't move his eyes from Star. 'Because I'd

probably find you two there first,' he said, then strode past the two of them in the direction of the park. He didn't turn around to see the tears begin to stream down Star's face.

Star wiped at the tears with her sleeve. Her shoulders heaved, but she didn't make a sound. Everything in her life had been marvellous until the fateful day she met Tommy McBride in Miss Parrot's dancing assembly. Since then nothing had gone right, and everything that had always seemed so perfect now seemed wrong. And all through him, as well. Everything was his fault.

As soon as Tommy was out of sight, Lizzie put her arm around Star's shoulders, 'Don't pay any attention to him,' she soothed. 'His sort wouldn't know a first class girl if she came with a label.'

Star wiped the last tears from her face. 'I don't want to talk about it,' she said in a whisper. 'I just want to go home.'

Leaving Star and Lizzie far behind him, and feeling almost crazy with anger, Tommy hurried straight to Eve's house, in such a state that he barely noticed how he got there.

'Why, Tommy,' said Eve in happy surprise when she opened the door. If she noticed the expression on his face she pretended not to. 'I wasn't expecting to see you.'

He shook off the hand that reached out to touch him. 'I want to talk to you.'

'Well, then you'd better come in.' She called through to her mother that it was Tommy. 'We're going up to my room,' she added. He followed her up the stairs as he had done before, but this time with none of the touching and giggling of his previous visits to her room. 'Jill's gone out with some friends,' Eve explained, speaking of her sister who shared the room with her. 'So we won't be disturbed for hours.' She opened the door and he fairly shoved her through it. 'Hey! What's wrong with you?'

He shut the door behind him and leaned against it. 'Just what do you mean by telling everyone that we've been making love?'

Eve's eyes widened. So that was it. 'Making love, is it? Since when did you start calling it that?' she teased, her laughter sounding like tiny bells.

He leaned towards her, his eyes still hard with rage. 'I don't care what you call it. What I want to know is why you had to make a public announcement about it.'

'I didn't exactly make a public announcement,' she said, not moving an inch. 'I made a suggestion and let them come to their own conclusions. But even if I did, so what? Why are you so upset about it?'

'Because there are some things between people that you don't broadcast to all and bloody sundry. And as for going into details, that's the most offensive thing of all.'

Eve watched him with not the slightest trace of fear. He was lovely when he was angry. The power and violence in him made him all that more attractive. Just as he'd been the day he nearly killed Korky Niven, the day she realized that she wanted him for herself.

She laid a hand on his shoulder, bringing her body just that much closer to his. 'Who told you I went into details?' she asked gently.

'Star Gray. I met her and Lizzie Dunnachie up at the Snuffmill Bridge a little while ago.'

Eve slowly moved her hand along his shoulder till she was caressing his neck. 'All I said was you were the best boyfriend I've ever had. I hardly consider that going into details,' she whispered silkily.

The nearness of her made it difficult for him to concentrate on his anger. 'You wouldn't lie to me, Eve?'

'On my word of honour, that was all I said. She got so upset because I said I thought Alec was so wet I doubted he could get it up.'

Tommy couldn't help but laugh. That was just the sort of thing a Boyd Street lassie might have said. Perhaps it was that side of Eve that was so attractive to him. In some ways they were two of a kind. 'What else did you say?'

'That I wouldn't be at all surprised if her precious Alec didn't go with her because he wasn't really interested in girls.'

Tommy whistled under his breath. No wonder he'd received such a frosty reception from Star! If he'd known he wouldn't have teased her, but Eve had only told him they'd had a bit of a spat and hadn't elaborated.

'I don't like that girl,' Eve went on, her arms now around him. 'She's got such airs and graces. And as for that silly name she uses, how daft can you get? *Star*, indeed!

'She doesn't like you much either,' Tommy grinned.

Eve made a face. 'I don't want to talk about that pretentious little madam. She's as boring as that dreary Alec Muir she's so possessive about.'

'Are you possessive about me?' Tommy teased, his anger now completely gone.

Eve smiled with the realization that she'd won. Tommy's anger had evaporated. She'd wound him round her little finger, as she'd known she would. 'Yes,' she said simply, and drew him to her in a kiss.

'You're absolutely certain your mother won't come up?' he asked after a while.

'Absolutely.'

Star and Alec were on their way back from the Fives where they'd met up after her B.B. Maze Marching and his Scripture Union class.

Star had been brooding all week long, her mind filled with questions to which she desperately wanted answers.

They arrived outside the manse. 'Let's go round the side,' she whispered, and taking his hand led the way to where a wall returned, in the seclusion of which they'd be screened from all prying eyes.

Alec was intrigued. 'What's wrong?' he asked once

they were in the still darkness of the return. Her recent mood had made him think something had happened, and he assumed that she was going to confide to him.

She stood facing him. 'Kiss me, Alec,' she commanded.

'What?' That was the last thing he'd expected her to say.

'Kiss me! Or don't you want to?'

'Now?'

'Don't you want to?'

'Well . . . of course.'

'Then do it.'

This was most unlike Star. Giving a mental shrug, he pecked her on the cheek.

Her mouth set hard in disappointment, and secret fear. 'Is that the best you can do?'

'You mean you want a proper one?'

The secret fear began to grow inside her chest. 'Please.'

Clumsily and gauchely he took her in his arms and put his lips on hers.

It was not a passionate kiss. She might as well be kissing a dead mackerel, she thought. Or one that was almost dead.

And that was the way he always kissed. It had never bothered her before, but it did now.

'Now what's all this about?' he demanded as they pulled apart, asking his question lightly in an attempt to inject some humour into the situation.

Star scowled. She didn't see his tone as humorous at all, but as patronizing.

'Don't you find me attractive?' she asked at last in a faraway voice.

Alec gave a low laugh that only irritated her more.

Did he think this was a joke?

'Of course I do. I wouldn't go out with you otherwise, would I?' He took her hand in his.

'Are you sure you're not confusing liking me as a person with finding me attractive?'

71

Her hand was cool and limp. 'Of course not. I think you're one of the most attractive girls I know.'

She relaxed slightly. 'Then why haven't you ever tried to touch me?' she asked, her voice sounding desperate in the quiet of the night.

What was she going on about? 'But I have touched you,' he said, frowning in bewilderment.

He was being dense, she thought. Or else evasive. She found his hand and placed it against her breast.

Alec jerked back his hand as though it had been burnt. 'What the . . .'

'I mean touching me, not just when we're dancing or you take my hand to cross the street. Really touching me.'

She waited for his hand to come back to her breast, to actually *feel* her breast, but the hand remained motionless at his side.

Alec was completely perplexed. He couldn't understand any of this. What *had* got into her? This wasn't the Star he knew.

'Well?'

'That's dirty,' he said simply, oddly embarrassed. 'I think more of you than that.'

It was the reply she would have expected – but was it the truth, the *whole* truth?

'But if we were married, man and wife, would you want to then?' she pushed.

'You know I would.'

'I do nothing of the sort. If I did I wouldn't have to ask,' she snapped back.

He coughed, glad of the darkness that was hiding his inflamed face from her. 'I would like nothing better than to touch you,' he said in a whisper.

'You're sure?'

'Of course I'm sure.'

She took hold of his hand a second time and returned it to her breast. 'Show me how it would be. I want you to, I want to know,' she urged him.

This was ridiculous! 'I can't. We're not married.'

'Try,' she said fiercely.

Tentatively, he uncurled his fingers, and almost immediately pulled his hand away again. 'You've no bra on!' he exclaimed in shock.

His tone was so outraged she almost wanted to laugh. 'So what?'

'I can't touch a bare breast, I'm going to be a minister one day.'

'But it's not bare, my woollie's over it.'

'You know what I mean.'

Her questions were still unanswered, she told herself. 'I don't believe you find me attractive at all,' she said at last in a small voice.

He ran his fingers through his hair. 'Yes I do.'

'You say so, but you don't act as if you do. Any normal boy wouldn't have reacted as you did. Any one else would have jumped at the chance. And I don't think there's anything dirty in that.'

'I explained. I'm going to be a minister one day. It wouldn't be right and proper. . .'

'Oh, nonsense. Are you sure you're not just using that as an excuse?'

He stared at the dark space from where her voice had come, wishing he could see her face, could read her expression. 'Excuse for what?' he asked hesitantly.

Star took a deep breath. If she wasn't so desperate she would never have gone so far. 'At school they're saying you don't really like girls,' she said quickly.

His mind reeled. Don't really like girls?

She went on. 'There's something wrong between you and me. There's something not normal about our relationship. I want to find out what, and why.'

He tried to speak, but no words came. Were they saying there was something wrong with him? 'Who says I'm not interested in girls?' he croaked at last.

'That doesn't matter. What does is the answer. Are you a homosexual?'

73

'Of course I'm not,' he answered quickly.

'Perhaps you don't know yourself yet. Perhaps you just think you're normal when actually you're not.'

Normal? Of course he was normal, he assured himself. Then doubt assailed him. Was he? Could she be right, could he only *think* he was? After all he'd never sat down and considered the possibility of his being abnormal; he'd always presumed he was just like other boys.

His doubt deepened into the beginnings of panic. Like Star, he also had to find out, he needed an answer.

'What am I going to do?' he asked eventually.

Star told him.

Tommy, home from school, let himself into the house in Millbrae Crescent and headed straight for the kitchen where he expected to find his mother waiting, ready with a little something to tide him over until tea together when Jim got home.

But Jeannie wasn't there, nor was she in any of the other downstairs rooms. There was an unsettling quiet about the house.

He eventually found her in her bedroom, slumped in a green Lloyd–Loom chair, tears streaming down her face.

'Mum?' he said quietly, shocked to see her like that.

She gave a startled exclamation at the sound of his voice. 'Oh, Tommy,' she said, wiping at the tears. 'I didn't hear you come in.'

'The door was open,' he said gently. 'I thought you heard me.'

Jeannie tried to smile, but the tears refused to stop. Her face was pale and drawn.

Tommy had never seen his mother cry before. The sight was quite unnerving. 'Can I get you something?' he asked. And she nodded, 'I'd like a glass of water, thank you.'

By the time she'd had a sip from the glass he brought

her she was once more in control of herself. 'I'm sorry about that,' she apologized. 'I didn't realize it was so late and that you were due back.'

He took the glass from her and laid it on the mantelpiece above the fire. 'What's upset you?' he asked gently.

She looked at her son through eyes still misty from tears. He wasn't a boy any more, she thought, he'd become a man. At some point during the past weeks or months a transformation had taken place, and this was the first she'd noticed it. She studied him carefully. There was a lot of Jim about him – in his expressions and in the way he held himself. As he was now he reminded her a lot of Jim when they first got married. And he was determined like Jim, with that same streak of wildness that Jim had still.

'It's your father, I worry about him,' she said flatly.

'Is there something wrong with his health?'

Jeannie shook her head.

'Then is it the business, is it starting to fall away?'

She wondered what he would say if he found out what his father really did? Probably ask to get involved, she thought, which made her grin inside in spite of herself. Aye, that would no doubt be his reaction right enough. She hoped and prayed he would never find out what Jim was up to, a young man starting afresh from the likes of Millbrae Crescent shouldn't have such knowledge about his dad.

Not that she was ashamed of what Jim was doing. Born and bred in Partick, she was well used to shady goings-on of all sorts. But in the new life Tommy was leading such things were not at all acceptable. She had even worried that in the years ahead Tommy might come to despise his father for what he was doing now.

By Jeannie's lights, Jim was only trying to earn a living for his family. With that hook and limp of his, he might well be idle, might never have got back on his feet after the war. She respected Jim's guts and endeavour. Not only was he earning a living, he was earning a damn fine one at that, and giving Tommy the chance in life that neither of them had ever had.

'It's not the business, that's going from strength to strength,' Jeannie assured him. This was partly true, and partly a lie. It was the business that worried her, though not because it was failing.

'So what is it then?'

She made her face smile. 'I suppose I'm worrying about nothing at all. Anyway, we women love a good greet once in a while, we feel the better for it.' Then changing the subject, she said, 'I went down to Boyd Street the other day and saw some of the old neighbours. Do you ever miss it?'

'Not me, that place is a hole. As far as I'm concerned, we're well away. If I never clapped eyes on Boyd Street again it wouldn't bother me one little bit,' he replied, matching her smile.

Already he'd adapted, she thought. There was none of her sense of being an outsider in him.

'Now I'm here I can't imagine living anywhere else,' he went on, thinking this was what she wanted to hear. 'It's so terrific just being able to go to the Linn Park. Did I tell you I saw an otter last time I was there?' his voice rising with excitement.

As they went downstairs to the kitchen Tommy raved on about the Linn Park, and what an absolutely magic place it was, and how he must take her and his father there soon so they could see for themselves.

Ever eager to please Tommy, Jeannie said perhaps they could all go the following Saturday or Sunday, even though the image he conjured up of endless trees and flowers made her shudder. Jeannie McBride was strictly an urban creature – the thought of being amongst that lot made her flesh creep.

Jim McBride was in the largest of the four small warehouses he rented. Two of them were near his own premises in the Calton district, the other two in Springburn. This particular one was one of the latter.

The latest consignment from Paddy Swords in Dublin had just been unloaded and was now stacked in front of him. It consisted of fourteen crates, all the same size.

Jim prised open the nearest crate with a jemmy, adroitly manipulating it with his left hand. Even so, sweat was beading on Jim's forehead when, with a final agonized creak of protest, the crate's lid was finally undone.

Inside the crate were thick white sacks, each with the marking 10 lbs stencilled in black on its front. Each sack had been screw tied at its neck with baling wire.

Jim selected a sack at random, undid the wire at its neck, then spilled a little of its contents into his hand. Bringing his hand to his mouth he licked the white substance on his palm. He gave an approving nod. Best quality sugar, always the best, never any grit or additives, that was Paddy for you.

He knew the sugar was refined in the south of Ireland from beet, but who did the refining, and where the refinery was, he had no idea, nor did he particularly want to know. As long as Paddy was able to keep shipping the beautiful stuff to him that was all that mattered.

Sugar might not be exactly worth its weight in gold, but it did command a hellishly high price when you sold it outside the points system – hoteliers, restaurateurs, and the like were his chief customers; less than twenty-five per cent went for ordinary domestic use. With ration books in force, and all foodstuffs coming under the points system, any food, especially one like sugar which had been in such short supply since the war, realized a tremendous mark-up when sold on the Black Market.

Nine times out of ten what Paddy shipped to him was sugar, the tenth time it was clothes, another thing which rationing had made expensive.

He re-did the sack and put it back with the others in the crate. There were fourteen crates in all. He made a few mental calculations, and figured the profit coming to him. It would take him less than forty-eight hours to shift the entire consignment, and he'd paid cash in hand, the *only* way he did business. Not a bad few days' work, not at all. He smiled as he thought about Paddy, or Paddy The Mad Irishman as he'd first been introduced to him.

His right stump had finally been on the mend and he'd been sent to a large house on the outskirts of St. Andrews for a period of convalescence. Fresh Air House the inmates called it, and that's exactly what it had been with the wind forever whipping in off the Bay and the cold North Sea beyond. The windows only closed at night. By God, he'd been in tip top shape when he'd finally left, or escaped as the immates termed it.

He and Paddy had become fast friends during those four months. They had quite a bit in common, of course. They were both working class lads from tough city neighbourhoods. And they had both lost their right hand.

He'd just told old man Murison where to put that insult of a nightwatchman's job, when Paddy had turned up out of the blue wearing a flashy suit and driving an even flashier car with a crate of whisky in its boot.

He remembered only too well his disbelieving look when he'd been shown that crate, an entire bloody crate when you really had to be in the know, *and* pay through the nose, to get a single bottle.

What a pish up that had been! The pair of them had ended up completely legless, with Paddy being sick into Jeannie's best vase. And during the bevy he'd told Paddy what had happened at Murison's, and how he hadn't been able to find a job since. With a hook and limp no one wanted to know.

The next day, Paddy had taken him aside and brought the subject up again. 'Us right handed hooks should stick together, and help one another out when we can,' Paddy had said, giving him a fly wink. And then Paddy had asked him how he'd feel about doing something strictly illegal, but extremely lucrative.

78

He'd listened carefully to Paddy's proposition, asked a few questions, and the deal had been struck. They shook hooks on it, an old gag of theirs from Fresh Air House.

Paddy would fund him initially to set up the Glasgow side of the operation, capital he would repay in time, and they would be partners, splitting everything straight down the middle after expenses had been deducted. From that day to this he'd never looked back. The money, as the saying went, just kept rolling in.

The sugar and clothes racket weren't the only ones Paddy had going, he knew Paddy had other fiddles in operation throughout the Irish south. But he never inquired about those, they were none of his business. All that concerned him were the sugar and clothes that arrived in Glasgow.

Locking the warehouse Jim got into the Arrole-Johnstone and set off for the town. He had customers to visit and orders to take.

Alec Muir was petrified. He had never been so scared in his entire life. He gripped his legs to stop his hands from shaking, certain they could be seen even through the cloth that covered his front.

Alec was having a haircut. The barber, Max Kyriacou, was also the owner of the shop.

Max employed two other men. One of them was also cutting hair, the other was sitting on the bench by the wall waiting for the next customer to walk in. Alec kept glancing at them nervously.

He had never patronized Max's before, and was only there now on the recommendation of a school chum who'd assured him that the Greek's was the best place to go for contraceptives as Max sold them to anyone, no matter what the person's age.

For the umpteenth time Alec glanced in the mirror facing him, seeking out the image of the Durex box that was in a prominent position beside the till.

'Lotion sir?'

Alec roused himself from his reverie. 'Yes, please,' he answered, his voice quivering at the edges.

A packet of three, that was the correct way to ask for them, Alec reminded himself. A packet of three, a packet of three, a packet of three, he repeated over and over. Lines from a doggerel he'd heard years previously flashed through his mind causing him to give a sort of hysterical snicker: 'It's only me with a packet of three, Barnacle Bill the sailor!'

Anything less like a Barnacle Bill than himself he couldn't imagine.

He watched Max's comb move through his hair. The haircut was going to be finished any moment now, then it would be the short walk to the till to pay his bill *and* . . . *and* . . . He groaned inwardly. Was he actually going to have the courage to ask for them? Was he really going to be able to speak those words?

He suddenly wanted desperately to go to the toilet, an almost uncontrollable urge to urinate having taken hold of him. He wanted to go to the toilet. He wanted to be outside. He wanted to be anywhere but standing in front of that till.

'How's that?' Max asked, brandishing a mirror behind Alec's head so he could see what the haircut was like at the back.

'Very nice,' Alec choked.

Max Kyriacou was enjoying this. He knew exactly why Alec had come to his shop – Alec's repeated glances at the Durex box in the mirror had long since given the real reason for Alec's visit away.

When the scared young lads came in for contraceptives it was a long-standing game of Max's to bet with himself as to whether or not the boy concerned would have the gumption to make the request when the time came. In this instance, his bet was that Alec would funk it at the last second and leave without the condoms.

Max replaced the mirror on its hook on the wall, then

whipped the cloth from around Alec's neck. He smiled benignly as he shook the cut hairs on to the floor.

Alec's legs were leaden as he swung them off the chair. He stood rigidly still as Max dusted down his shoulders.

The barber on the bench glanced up from the newspaper he was reading and his mouth thinned into a tight grin. He'd also seen Alec staring at the reflection of the Durex box in the mirror.

The barber placed his newspaper on the bench beside him, folded his arms, and leant back against the wall. Like Max, he loved these little dramas, they made a long day shorter.

He was going to wet himself, Alec thought. He couldn't help it, it was going to happen right there in the middle of the barber shop.

Max strode to the till and banged up the price of the haircut, the drawer of the till shooting open with a ting! 'That'll be one and six please,' he said.

Alec fumbled in a pocket, bringing out the ten shilling note he'd previously put there especially. Going to the till he silently gave the money to Max.

Knew you wouldn't son, Max thought, taking the note and making change. He counted the change into Alec's sweaty hand. 'Anything else, sir?' he asked. Behind Alec, the man on the bench's grin turned into a smirk.

Alec didn't reply.

'A bottle of lotion perhaps?' Max suggested, extending the agony.

'A thracket of pee please,' Alec said in a rush.

The other barber quickly covered his mouth to stop himself from laughing out loud.

Max was taken aback. 'Eh?'

There was a waterfall of noise in Alec's ears. 'A thracket of pee please,' he repeated, only then realizing the muddle he'd made of the words. He felt his face start to go red.

Max was disappointed that he'd lost his bet, and

decided to make Alec suffer a little more. 'Sorry, son. I'm not quite with you.'

Alec's face was now as bright as a beacon. Lifting a hand he pointed at the Durex box. 'Those,' he stuttered, his whole body shaking.

Max took pity then. Anyway, further torment would cease to be funny, merely cruel. 'Certainly, sir,' he replied, and lifting a packet from the box laid it in front of Alec.

Alec handed over half a crown, and willed himself to wait for his change. As he accepted the coins he picked up the Durex packet with his other hand.

'Come again, sir,' Max said.

Alec nodded, and walked stiffly to the door. Back on the street he maintained a walk till he was out of view of the barber shop window, then broke into a mad run.

As he raced along the filthy pavement, its gutter running with litter and refuse, he was quite delirious with excitement.

Leaping into the air he punched at the sky, 'Yippeee!' he shouted, to the astonishment of passers-by.

When he finally collected himself he realized he'd never before felt so marvellous in all his life. Then it dawned on him what it actually was he felt.

He felt a man, and oh but it was grand!

Star was standing in front of the bathroom mirror, applying some of the forbidden make-up. After the dab of rouge and the trace of red on her lips, she intended to smooth in just a whisk of powder with a fat pink puff.

The make-up had been taken from its hiding place in her bedroom the moment her parents had left for Reverend Carrell's annual whist drive over in Langside. Although the Grays always complained that the Carrells' whist drive didn't measure up to their own they always stayed on to the bitter end, probably, Star reasoned, because it gave them that much more to complain about. It would be hours before they returned.

Star put a dab of scent behind her ears, gave herself one last critical appraisal, then stepped out of the rest of her clothes and slipped into her dressing gown. She was ready.

She quietly made her way down the hallway and stopped outside her bedroom door for a moment. Taking a deep breath to compose herself – this was a momentous step, after all – she went inside.

Alec was already in the bed, looking rather scared, the covers drawn up almost to his chin.

'Are you sure we're doing the right thing?' he asked as she came to the side of the bed.

'Shhh,' she said, shrugging the dressing gown from her shoulders in what she hoped was a provocative manner. 'Don't say anything.'

But Alec was staring at her with an expression on his face she had never seen before. 'You're lovely,' he said in an awed whisper. 'You're the loveliest thing I've ever seen.'

Star felt a chill run through her that had nothing to do with the temperature of the room. 'Do you mean that? You're not just saying it?'

He reached out to touch the swell of her hip. The feel of her skin beneath his fingers was like nothing he had ever experienced before. It was like touching satin, he thought. Warm, vibrant satin.

Star slipped into the bed beside him, trembling. Her stomach muscles were jumping as if an electric current was running through her.

'You're more than lovely,' Alex whispered. 'You're beautiful. You're the most beautiful girl in Scotland.'

Star's voice came like a sigh. 'Really?'

'Really.'

'But am I *sexually* attractive?'

'Yes,' he breathed.

'Then kiss me, Alec,' she urged. 'Kiss me now.'

His lips reached for the sweetness of her lips, and his hands reached clumsily for her breasts. He could feel her nipples rise against his fingers and hear her breathing quicken. But his mind couldn't forget that God was watching him, watching him with disapproval. The instant he remembered God a war between his body and his conscience began. He caressed and kissed her longingly, but the erection which came so easily at times when it was least wanted refused to come now.

'What is it?' whispered Star, sensing the tenseness in him.

'Nothing,' pressing himself against her with renewed force.

'There's something wrong,' she persisted, suddenly knowing what it was. 'It's me, isn't it?' she asked, pushing him away. 'You just don't fancy me like this.'

His voice, when it came, sounded far away. 'No,' he mumbled. 'It has nothing to do with you.'

Tears filled her eyes. 'You don't have to lie,' she said, disentangling herself from his desperate embrace. 'It's all right.'

But when at last she could look into his face there were tears streaming from his eyes as well. 'Oh, Alec,' she cried, tenderly brushing the tears from his cheek.

'I'm sorry,' he whispered. 'Oh, Star, I'm so sorry.'

Star hugged him to her, gently stroking his hair, her own tears trickling down her face. Could it be that Alec simply wasn't attracted to her in a sexual way? And if so, was that because she lacked sex appeal, or because Alec would never be attracted to a woman? Star sighed. This fiasco certainly hadn't provided any answers.

Still crying, Alec laid his head against her breasts, his hands unthinkingly stroking her smooth, soft skin. Like two lost children in a storybook, they clung to each other until their fears were forgotten.

With surprise, Alec suddenly realized that his arousal had begun. 'Star,' he whispered, almost afraid to speak.

'Star.' He took her hand and placed it on himself, feeling the heat rise in his groin. 'Oh, Star . . .'

An eternity later, they pulled apart, their hands still touching. Alec felt like crowing. Any doubts he'd had about his own masculinity were gone for good. He was a man now. A real man.

Star stretched like a cat in the sun. All of her doubts were gone as well. She had aroused Alec to a pitch she wouldn't have believed possible – to the point where he was no longer reserved, methodical Alec but a man possessed by a wildness she had never before seen. She was a woman now, a desirable woman, a woman with oodles of sex appeal. As much as Eve Smith – as much as anyone.

Pulling herself to a sitting position, she let her gaze run down his body. Instantly, the look of satisfaction turned to one of horror. 'Alec!' she said in a strangled voice. 'Alec, where's the . . . the thing?'

Alec stared down at his naked penis, where the Durex should have been. 'Oh, Jesus!' he whispered.

'You did put it on, didn't you?'

'Of course I did,' he snapped. 'You saw me put it on.'

'Then where is it?' she wailed.

They tore the bed apart and shook out the blankets. But when they did find it it was in the worst possible place of all.

'It doesn't matter,' Alec said when at last his speech returned. 'Nothing's going to happen after just one time.'

'You're right,' said Star, trying not to panic. 'The odds against it must be a million to one.'

'A billion more like!'

'Maybe as much as a trillion.'

Alec laughed, but it was a nervous laugh that crackled at the edges.

Star felt the tears burning against her eyes again. She wanted him to take her in his arms and comfort her, to promise her that everything *was* going to be all right.

But Alec wasn't thinking of Star, he was thinking only of himself. A voice in his mind was telling him that he deserved this, that it was God's punishment for the awful sin he'd just committed. He should have known better. He should have been stronger. He shouldn't have let his doubts tempt him. He could hear God himself berating him for his weakness – and right behind God he could hear his mother.

'We have to beg for forgiveness,' he said suddenly, jumping out of the bed. 'We have to pray to God that nothing will come of what we've done.' Grabbing hold of Star's arm, he dragged her to the floor beside him. Joining his hands in supplication, he began, 'Our Father in Heaven . . .'

Halfway through Alec's fervent prayers, Star realized that she was still holding the useless condom in her hands.

Margaret Muir finished reading the solitary letter that had come in the morning post with an enigmatic sigh. The news it had brought had quite taken her breath away.

Cosmo Dunbarr was home from Kenya! And he'd brought his and Ginty's wee girl with him. Not so wee, she corrected herself with a smile; Virginia was the same age as her Alec.

Cosmo Dunbarr, the Earl of Clyde, was what Margaret Muir considered a darling, darling man. Ginty, her best friend since childhood, had married him in Glasgow Cathedral in what had been the wedding of the year. Cosmo had been Scotland's most eligible bachelor at the time, as well as possessor of one its greatest fortunes. As for the Dunbarrs, they were among Scotland's oldest families, far older than the Muirs, as well as among its canniest. Over the centuries they'd accrued enormous wealth, always managing to hold on to and increase it, no matter what the political or economic situation.

Margaret sighed. Poor Ginty, dead ten months now from the awful asthma that had plagued her since childhood. It was because of the asthma that Cosmo had bought the farm in Kenya, and why he'd taken his beloved Ginty there to live. But the Kenyan weather hadn't cured Ginty, it had merely extended her life. But the extension had run out, and Ginty had passed away one night in her sleep.

According to the letter, Cosmo hadn't been able to bear remaining in Kenya now that Ginty was dead. Her ghost had been everywhere, and so he'd decided to return to Scotland. He'd taken up residence again in the family town house. No. 56 Lindsay Drive, Kelvinside. It had already been arranged for Virginia to attend Laurel Bank School for girls, beginning next term.

Margaret nodded her approval of the Laurel Bank School. There were some preferred Craigholme, but in her estimation Laurel Bank was superior.

Alec suddenly appeared to her thoughts. She'd always wanted him to go to Hutcheson's, but the money hadn't been available. Instead Alec had had to go to Queen's Park Secondary, a local school of no particular merit, either academic or social. Another black mark against Geoffrey, one amongst many.

Margaret brought her mind back to Cosmo's letter. He'd gone on to say that he was looking forward to renewing his friendship with her and Geoffrey, and that he hoped they would call at Lindsay Drive in the very near future.

Margaret remembered Lindsay Drive with affection. She'd spent some marvellous evenings there when Ginty and Cosmo had first been married. Ginty had adored giving small, intimate dinner parties. Invitations to them had been much sought after, but Margaret had always had one.

From Lindsay Drive her thoughts went to Bonny-dykes, Cosmo's family estate in Renfrewshire and seat of the Earls of Clyde since the 14th century. It was a magnificent estate, and the memory of it fired all of Margaret's old dreams.

Lindsay Drive, Bonnydykes – Ginty's life may have been a short one, but by God she'd prospered during it. And Margaret? What had she ended up with? A house in Overdale Street and a worthless husband, less than worthless, *useless*.

Strangely enough, Cosmo had always liked Geoffrey, though she'd never been able to understand why. It could only be some male thing she just didn't understand.

She decided to reply to Cosmo's letter immediately, suggesting that she and Geoffrey call this coming Saturday after lunch. Alec would go along too, of course, Cosmo would want to see how he'd grown up. Just as they'd want to see how. . . The thought hit Margaret like a bombshell. Lady Virginia Dunbarr, Cosmo and Ginty's daughter, would be Cosmo's heir now that Ginty was gone, heiress to one of the largest fortunes in Scotland, perhaps even the largest. And then there was the title itself which would go to Virginia's eldest son. Suddenly, Margaret could see it all as though God had written it on the wall for her.

To Hell with Morag what's her name, Ishbel Doig, Juliet Abercrombie and that upstart crew! It was Virginia Alec should woo and wed. It would be a match beyond her wildest dreams!

She was so excited she began pacing around the room. Was it possible? Was it really possible? She answered the question herself: Why not?

For the next half hour she walked up and down, thinking, planning, scheming. Finally, she wrote her reply to Cosmo's letter.

Margaret was shocked to see Cosmo after all these years. She still remembered him as the young and dashing man who'd had all the girls swooning over his charms. How he'd aged! His once handsome face was worn and lined, his hair had thinned to such an extent that the scalp shone through, and his fine physique had gone to fat. She could barely keep the shock out of her face.

'Margaret!' he cried, holding out his arms. She rushed into them, hugging him with all the old affection. Geoffrey stood behind her, smiling.

While all this was going on, Alec studied Virginia. His mother had been talking non-stop about her since *the* letter had arrived. She was attractive enough, he thought, although it was somewhat startling to see a girl so brown she could almost have passed as an Indian, if it hadn't been for that straw-blonde hair and those washed-out blue eyes, that was. She had a good figure, too, he noticed, and coloured a little. He hadn't been the same since his episode in bed with Star. Losing his virginity had opened up areas within himself that he would never before have guessed existed. And all the prayers in the world wouldn't change that.

Virginia, virginity, he thought, and smiled inwardly. He wondered if she still was?

'You've both got fat,' Geoffrey laughed as they finally pulled apart.

'Beauty is in the eye of the beholder,' said Cosmo unsmilingly. 'And as far as I'm concerned Margaret is still as beautiful as she ever was.'

Margaret simply scowled at her husband.

'And this is Virginia,' Cosmo went on, gesturing towards his daughter.

She was Ginty to a T, Margaret thought, except that the girl was clearly bursting with health. 'Lady Virginia,' Margaret smiled, slightly wary now, for the lass had a mind of her own, that was evident in the haughty way she was staring back at her.

Virginia extended a hand. 'I've heard so much about you, Mrs Muir,' she said politely.

Margaret took her hand and shook it. 'I was hoping it might be Margaret. That's what it always was to your mother whose dear and devoted friend I was,' she replied.

Virginia immediately softened under this combined entreaty and overture. 'Then Margaret it shall be. But you must call me Virginia, as my mother would have wanted.'

That was that hurdle out the way Margaret told herself with relief. Things weren't going to be too difficult after all. She introduced Geoffrey and Alec. Then they all followed Cosmo into what was called the Chinese Room for drinks.

As Virginia entered the Chinese Room beside Alec she was thinking again how she hated Scotland. It had turned out to be even worse than she'd expected. She hadn't been warm since arriving; even when every fireplace in the house was ablaze she was still freezing. Every night she dreamt about Kenya, and woke next morning wishing she were back there under the blue sky, with that soft, gentle wind that was like velvet on the skin.

Alec had been primed by Margaret to concentrate on Virginia, whether he liked her or not, and this he did, like the obedient son that he was. The last thing he wanted was to encounter his mother's wrath.

'The house is in a dreadful state I'm afraid,' apologized Cosmo. 'After lying empty for so long, it's going to take some time to get it back to what it was.'

Margaret gazed about her critically. If the Chinese Room was anything to go by, he was right. Years of neglect had taken their toll. Suddenly it reminded her of their own house in Overdale Street, and she shuddered inwardly. But then an inspiration hit her. A way of getting Virginia under her influence. 'Why don't I help by organizing a total revamp for you?' she asked. 'Virginia and I – if she'd like that is – could do it together before she starts school. It would be a good way of introducing her to Glasgow. We'd have to visit all the big shops.'

'Would you do that?' Cosmo was obviously delighted.

'It would be my pleasure. What do you say, Virginia?'

Virginia thought for a moment, then nodded assent. Things couldn't get worse.

'Excellent!' Margaret declared, and took a sip of her whisky.

'How big is your farm in Kenya?' Alec asked Cosmo, genuinely interested, but also tired already of talking to Virginia.

'A hundred and twenty-five thousand acres,' Cosmo replied proudly.

Margaret's eyes glittered. She'd forgotten just how vast the farm was. And that was only one of Cosmo's many assets.

'Who's looking after it now you've left?' asked Geoffrey, also interested.

'I've appointed a manager, a Welshman called Roberts. He'll be running cattle on half of it, and growing tobacco on the other half. We employ local men, a friendly bunch from a tribe called the Kikuyu.'

Margaret's gaze flickered over to where Alec and Virginia were sitting silently and slightly apart. Alec had done all the talking between them so far. Virginia's replies, at least those she'd overheard, were restricted to monosyllables.

She brought her attention back to Cosmo. He was repeating how marvellous it was to see her and Geoffrey again, after such a long time. 'It's only too bad Ginty couldn't be here to share this,' he concluded, but at the mention of his dead wife's name his face darkened in sorrow, and his eyes took on a faraway look. Margaret knew it was Ginty he was seeing.

After a while Margaret suggested that Alec might take Virginia for a walk. It was such a lovely day, the sort of day young people should be out and about, not sitting in musty drawing rooms listening to their elders talk about times gone by which must be boring for them.

Alec took up his cue. 'It'll be nice down by the Kelvin,' he agreed. 'There's a lovely walk along the banks.'

Virginia sighed. Better to be bored in the fresh air, than in this mouldering old house.

Shortly after they had gone, Margaret said to Cosmo, 'It must seem like the end of the world to you with Ginty passing away, but just because her life is over doesn't mean yours is. It's not impossible, although it might seem so at the moment, that you'll meet someone else, and get married again. After all, we may all be getting on but none of us are exactly beyond it yet.'

Cosmo shook his head. 'I'll never marry again Margaret, of that I'm absolutely certain. I'm strictly a one woman man, and Ginty was the woman.

Margaret's expression was serious and sympathetic, but she was jubilant to hear him say that. It meant the title was safe with Virginia. Grandmother to an Earl. The thought almost made her forget not to smile.

Later, when they'd returned to Overdale Street, she drew Alec aside. 'How did you get on with the lassie?' she demanded abruptly.

Alec had no idea of what his mother was up to. He thought she wanted him to get on with Virginia because Virginia was the daughter of an old friend. 'Well enough. She wasn't very friendly to begin with. Until I asked about Kenya that is, then she wouldn't stop talking. She misses the place like mad.'

'And you liked her?' Margaret pressed.

'Oh aye, she's extremely nice.'

Good, Margaret thought. Very good indeed. 'And do you think she liked you?'

Alec couldn't understand his mother's extreme interest, but it didn't occur to him to question it. 'I'd say she did, particularly after I showed interest in Kenya.'

Margaret had another brainwave. 'There's a picture about Africa on in town next week, why don't you take her to see it? You could go Friday night.'

'But Friday night is my Scripture Union class,' objected Alec.

Margaret shooed his objection away. 'To miss it once

in a blue moon won't hurt. Anyway, you can regard it as putting into practice what you've been learning about being a Christian.'

A film about Africa, he'd rather enjoy that he thought. 'What's it called?' he asked.

But Margaret was no longer thinking about him. She was wondering how to get him with Virginia on Saturday as well.

'Are you all right?' Ding A Ling asked Star concernedly. She'd just finished playing for the Maze Marching, and if he'd thought she hadn't looked too clever on arriving in the hall, she now looked positively dreadful.

'I suspect I've got a cold or the flu coming on,' Star replied in a tremulous voice.

'If I was you I'd get right up to bed, and I'd take some hot lemon if your mother's got any.'

Star rose from the piano and gently lowered its lid. She'd banged out a dozen tunes for the marching, and couldn't remember playing a single one of them. 'I'll away then,' she said distractedly, and slowly made her way from the hall.

Once into the corridor she forgot all about the officers' cups and saucers that she normally washed, dried and put away, and broke into a run, scalding tears streaming down her face.

She burst into the toilet at the far end of the corridor, slamming the door closed behind her and locking it. Collapsing on to the w.c., she held her head in her hands and wailed her fear and grief. Her period was a whole week overdue, and it had never been even one day late.

She just knew it wasn't going to come now, she just knew!

3

Spring was in the air, Star could smell it. Soon the buds would be appearing on the trees and the first flowers in the gardens.

Star and Alec were in Lovers' Lane at her request. She'd told him at school that afternoon that she desperately needed to have a word with him. She'd suggested Lovers' Lane because it was quiet there, a good place to say what she had come to say.

'I'm pregnant,' she stated bluntly.

Alec could only stare at her. With the passing of time he'd almost forgotten about the possible consequences of the condom coming off. Almost, but not quite. Every so often the worry had re-emerged at the back of his mind, but he'd pushed it aside. For some reason neither of them had talked about it, preferring to leave it there like a bad smell they both hoped would suddenly disappear. Only it hadn't disappeared and the secret nightmare had now become a horrible reality.

'Are you sure?' he asked at last, if only because he had to say something.

'I've missed three periods, and I've never missed one before,' she said in a choked whisper. 'I consider that pretty conclusive. Wouldn't you?'

His head had gone light; the inside of his mouth was dry as dust. He wanted to take her hand but he couldn't move. 'Have you told anyone else?'

She shook her head. 'No. You had to be the first.'

He would never be a minister now, he thought. That balloon had just gone bang. Never be a minister! Just for one lapse! It was a catastrophe!

'Well?' said Star, worried at his silence. 'Say something!'

'I'll stand by you,' he replied quickly. 'I'll do the Christian thing.'

'Don't do me any favours!' she snapped back.

He stared at her, his feelings a combination of affection and dislike. If it weren't for her, none of this would ever have happened. This was God's vengeance, he told himself. He really was being paid back for his moment of weakness.

'I'm sorry,' he said more gently. 'I didn't mean that to sound so bald. What I meant was we'll get married. I know we're awful young, but it isn't exactly unheard of for couples to get married at our age. A bit unusual in Battlefield perhaps, but there we are. People will talk of course, there'll be lots of that, but that can't be helped.' Once he'd started he could barely keep the words from tumbling out, he was so terrified.

A surge of relief went through Star. She hadn't really doubted what his reaction would be, but the worry had been there. At least the baby would have a father and the father's name. 'The sooner we get everything settled the better,' she said trying to sound brave.

He picked up a chukkie and threw it into the water. If only she'd been two months gone instead of three. They might have been able to explain the baby's early arrival as its being premature. Three months no one would believe.

'I wish you'd told me before this,' he said.

'I kept hoping I was wrong, that it would come next time round.'

The local gossips were going to have a field day, he thought bitterly. His mother would go daft!'

'It was bad luck as we only did it the once,' Star said miserably.

Bad luck! That was the understatement of the year, he thought.

'We'd better tell our parents right away,' she said. She wanted it over with as quickly as possible.

'I wonder if your Dad will lose his job over this?' Alec

mused, knowing this could be a distinct possibility. After all, a minister with a fallen daughter wasn't exactly the pillar of moral rectitude a *Scottish* minister should be.

Star paled. She'd been so concerned about herself she'd failed to consider that. If her father lost Battlefield Central he'd never ever get another kirk. A horrifying scenario, and her fault entirely.

Alec took her cold hand in his. 'We'll go to Overdale Street first because that's closest to here.' As ye sow, so shall ye reap, he thought, and wanted to be sick.

As they trudged in the direction of Overdale Street Star felt incredibly small, frightened, and vulnerable. She reminded herself it could have been worse. Alec might have left her in the lurch.

'What!' Margaret screeched, her features contorted with fury.

Geoffrey Muir stared at his son in total astonishment. What Alec had just announced was the last thing he'd ever expected to hear the boy say. It seemed there was more to Alec than he'd ever given him credit for.

Margaret, however, was so beside herself Alec thought she must either have a heart attack or a seizure.

'Get her a dram,' Geoffrey instructed.

Alec hurried to obey, pouring her a large one. The bottle of whisky was one of twelve, a crate which Cosmo Dunbarr had sent over as a small token of appreciation for what Margaret was doing at Lindsay Drive. With that crate had been another of best claret.

Margaret's gaze bored into Alec, but what she was seeing was a large black hole down which all her dreams and aspirations for him, and herself, were disappearing. Pregnant! Marriage! The words sizzled in her brain as if they were burning there in letters of fire.

She took the dram from Alec and tossed half of it down, paused for breath, then drained the glass. 'Give me another,' she ordered returning the glass to Alec. The stupid wee bugger, she thought, watching Alec's retreating back. What on earth had come over him? There was only one answer, of course, Star bloody Gray, that was who. It had to be Star who seduced Alec, she couldn't even begin to imagine it happening the other way round, not with Alec. Well, one thing was certain, she told herself, she wasn't going to let Alec marry Star, not when Lady Virginia Dunbarr, and all the Dunbarr money, was in the offing.

Alec handed his mother the second dram, noting her eyes had taken on that calculating, scheming look he knew so well. Margaret was at her most dangerous when she wore that look.

Geoffrey Muir thought of Star again, and suppressed a smile. If he were Alec's age he wouldn't mind a go with her himself. But then his attention went back to Margaret. God but she was in a right mood this time. She was going to make his life even more of a hell from now on. And as for Star . . . he could only pity the lass. He knew roughly what was bound to happen next. He wasn't privy to Margaret's plans for Alec, but he was aware there were plans, and that they were hardly likely to include Star Gray, fine lassie that she was.

In a flash of insight it suddenly dawned on Geoffrey that it was Virginia Dunbarr whom Margaret had in mind for Alec. That was why she had been pushing the two of them together ever since Virginia had come to live in Lindsay Drive. Why hadn't he seen it before? If that was the case then Star was really on a hiding to nothing. His pity for Star deepened.

'And you said Star is outside on the landing waiting to meet us?' Margaret asked at last.

Alec nodded. 'That was my idea. I thought it best I break the news alone. Will I get her in now?'

Geoffrey lurched to his feet and made for the whisky bottle. If Alec thought he'd defused the situation by breaking the news to his mother alone he was wrong, as the lad would shortly discover.

Star gave a tight smile when Alec opened the front door. 'You're to come on through,' he said.

She stood aside while he closed the door behind them. He squeezed her arm, a gesture of encouragement, then led the way to where Margaret and Geoffrey were waiting. 'We're here,' he announced quite unnecessarily when he and Star were in the room.

Margaret fixed Star with an unblinking look, but didn't speak. Nor did Geoffrey; at that point he wouldn't have dared.

The pungent smell of whisky in the room made Star want to sneeze, or perhaps it was only her nerves. She had imagined what Alec's parents might say, but Margaret's first words hit her like a brick.

'How do we know it's Alec's baby?' she asked abruptly, going immediately on the offensive.

Star blinked, completely thrown. 'Who else's could it be?' she whispered in embarrassment.

'That's for you to know, I'm sure. But it's something I can always find out.'

Star had turned pale. 'But . . . but Alec is the only boy I . . . everybody knows we've been going together . . . I . . .' her words trailed off as she stared into Mrs Muir's cold, hard eyes.

Margaret twisted her face into a disbelieving sneer. 'There have been more lads trapped with that lie than you've had hot dinners,' she hissed.

'But there is no one else,' Star repeated frantically.

Margaret drew herself up to her full height. 'Let me tell you this, girl. You may be a minister's daughter, but as far as I'm concerned you're nothing more than a common trollop.'

Star recoiled, feeling as though she'd been physically assaulted.

'Mother!' Alec exclaimed, shocked.

'Quiet,' Margaret commanded.

Star glanced over at Alec, willing him to continue in her defence. Surely he wouldn't allow his mother to accuse her of such things, such lies! He knew the truth, as surely as she did.

'There'll be no wedding, at least not with my boy,' she continued. 'You'd better understand that, and accept it here and now.'

'But he *is* the father!' Star wailed.

Geoffrey stared down into his glass. This was bloody, and getting bloodier, just as he'd known it would be.

Margaret took a step towards her. 'If you put it about that he is then I'll stand up in your own father's congregation and cry you whore in front of everyone,' she threatened.

Star staggered backwards. 'You wouldn't!' she whispered, her eyes wide in disbelief.

'Oh, but she would,' said Geoffrey quietly.

'I'll do more than that,' Margaret raged. 'With Holy Bible in hand, I'll swear Alec has never slept with you and that you're only saying he has in order to trap him into marriage and give your bastard a name.'

Star turned to Alec, who was transfixed by his mother's glare. 'Alec?' she pleaded.

But Alec was no match for Margaret. He could no more go against his mother's wishes, or orders, than he could have sprouted wings, jumped out of the window and flown away.

'Alec?' Star pleaded again.

He turned to her. 'I'm sorry,' he mumbled and dropped his eyes to the carpet.

Game, set and match, thought Geoffrey, disgusted at what had just taken place. Disgusted he might be, but it never crossed his mind to interfere. He and Alec were alike in that respect.

'Now get out of our house, and never set foot in it again, you little *slut*,' Margaret ordered.

Before Star had felt small, frightened and vulnerable. Now she felt completely and utterly alone as well.

She turned to go, then stopped in front of Alec. 'I

realized you were weak, but now I see I was wrong. You're worse than that, you're pathetic.'

Margaret was at the window watching when Star came out into the street below. 'That settles her hash. And good riddance,' Margaret said.

Geoffrey rose from his chair and poured himself another drink. Maybe if he got drunk enough he could forget what had just happened.

He could be a minister after all, Alec told himself, so elated it made him want to jump for joy. Later, in the privacy of his bedroom, he got down on his knees and thanked God for relenting towards him. Then he added a prayer for Star.

Lizzie Dunnachie was stunned by what Star had just told her. The pair of them had come direct from school to the Fives.

'Pregnant!' Lizzie breathed.

Star nodded.

'And it was only the once?'

Star nodded again, her face showing just how wretched she felt.

Lizzie gave a low whistle. 'So what are you going to do now?'

Star waited while their coffees were placed in front of them, then replied, 'Tell my folks, I suppose. What else can I do?'

Lizzie lit a cigarette and drew on it pensively. Trust it to happen to Star, she thought, and her only having done it the once. There was no justice right enough.

'Why don't you . . . you know, lose it?' Lizzie asked slowly, aware that her heart had suddenly started going thump thump thump.

Star stared at her friend in shock. 'But that's murder,' she replied in a whisper.

Lizzie knew that if it had been she who'd had the misfortune to fall pregnant she wouldn't have hung back.

'If you go ahead and have it you'll never get married. Glasgow boys won't touch unmarried mothers, at least not for marriage. You'll ruin your whole life.'

It was true enough. Unmarried mothers became outcasts in this town. Oh, she'd get plenty of proposals all right, but not for a ring and wedding lines. And there was her father and his job to think about as well. If she lost the baby he need never know and his job saved.

Star could feel herself relenting. It was a solution, if a horrible one.

'Look at it like this, it can't be murder in the true sense when the wean hasn't been born, when it hasn't been out in the world yet,' Lizzie argued.

'That's just playing with words,' Star countered. 'The baby becomes alive at conception. Killing it now is as much murder as if I was to pull out a gun right here and blow your head off.'

'Well I don't agree,' Lizzie answered, wanting to remain unconvinced in case there ever came a time when she had a similar decision to make. 'All I can say is, it's either it or you. And the choice is yours.'

Star looked at Lizzie's cigarette, and for once wished she smoked. She could have done with something to hold on to right then. 'Even if I did decide to have an abortion, how would I go about it? I mean, I don't know anyone.'

Lizzie didn't know anyone either, but she did have information on the subject. 'You don't need to know anyone, you can do it yourself.'

Star didn't like the sound of that at all. 'How?' she asked cautiously, the chill running through her body.

'A piping hot bath and a bottle of gin. You sit in the bath, as hot as you can bear it, and drink the gin. You then lie back and let Mother Nature take her course.

A hot bath and gin! That didn't seem too awful. The chill subsided. 'Are you sure that works?'

'I've heard it on good authority. But don't ask me whose, that's my secret.'

101

A bath and a drink and all her troubles would be over, Star thought. She could go back to being the Star she'd been before all this had happened. No more worries about a baby, not getting married, her father's job, the family being turned out into the street, the shame, the humiliation, the . . .

'How would I get a bottle of gin?' she said.

'If you can raise the necessary to buy one then leave it to me,' Lizzie replied obviously relieved.

It was *murder*, Star thought, but she was coming to realize that in life there are things worse than that.

'I'll give you the money tomorrow morning at school,' she told Lizzie.

Star smuggled the gin into the bathroom inside her briefcase. She'd sought out her parents before going to the bathroom, explaining the briefcase by saying she intended doing some homework reading while enjoying a good long wallow. After her bath, she'd said, she'd go straight up to bed and have an early night.

Outside the door of the room where she'd just left her parents talking, she'd paused to take a breath. With that breath she'd begun to shake.

She was still shaking as she turned off the taps and tested the water in the bath. Any hotter and she'd scald herself, she thought. Sitting on the w.c., she took her briefcase on to her lap and opened it, then she opened the bottle of gin.

She screwed her face up at the gin's perfumed smell. It was going to be absolutely ghastly to get down, but get it down she would. She had to.

Her instructions from Lizzie were to get into the bath before starting on the gin, so rising again she shrugged herself out of her dressing gown, then removed the flannelette nightdress she was wearing beneath. She stared down at her belly, thinking of what was inside there. A shudder ran through her.

She fought back the tears, if they came she'd never go through with this, she knew that.

The bath was so hot it took her all of ten minutes to get into it and fully sit down. On finally accomplishing that, she reached for the gin bottle and the toothbrush cup she'd placed beside it. She filled the cup half full, raised it to her lips, forced herself not to think what she was doing, and drank. She managed to drink off the entire contents of the cup in one go.

Normally she liked hot baths, but this one was torture. She might have been in a cannibal pot being boiled alive.

She poured more gin. It wasn't too bad once you got the taste of it, she thought, and drank that lot back, this time taking two goes.

Alec was a rat, a weak, snivelling, mummy's boy rat. She was far better off without him, he'd have been a diabolical husband, she could see that now.

'Alec you're a rat,' she said aloud, and sipped more gin.

She felt a stirring deep within her. It happened again, but this time the pain was so intense that it made her squirm.

The pain passed away. 'Bye Bye Baby,' she sang softly to the tune of 'Bye Bye Blackbird', and giggled. She was getting drunk, she realized, and thoroughly pleasant it was proving too.

She swallowed more gin, focused her wavery gaze on the bottle, and saw she'd already consumed more than half. She was doing damn well for a beginner, she thought, and giggled again.

The bath was beginning to cool a little so she let out some of the water and poured in a fresh stream of hot. The painful sensation returned with a vengeance, knotting her stomach and causing her to groan. Eventually the pain subsided, and as it did she found herself again wanting to burst into tears. 'Mustn't, mustn't, mustn't . . .' she repeated over and over.

She drank yet more gin.

It was well over an hour later that Alison Gray

knocked on the bathroom door. 'Are you all right, Star? You've been in there a gey long while.'

Star had used the entire tank of hot water and was sitting in a bath that had gone stone cold. She was nursing a head that was threatening to blow itself apart from the inside.

'I said are you all right, Star?' Alison repeated, knocking the bathroom door a second time.

'I'm all right,' Star replied miserably. 'Nothing's happened mother, nothing at all.'

It was the period of the day between evening and night which the Scots call the gloaming, a soft ethereal twilight that makes the world seem like a fairlyland.

Finding himself at a loose end, Tommy McBride had decided to go down to Lovers' Lane. He would have preferred a walk to the Linn Park, but it was too late for that.

Spring had arrived in the last week, wakening the earth from its winter slumber. The birds overhead were crying from the joy of it, and here and there crocuses had appeared to brighten the landscape with their yellows, blues and purples.

Tommy stopped beside a goosegog bush, visualizing it heavy with fat, succulent berries. He smiled at the picture, and promised himself he'd come back in the summer and pick a big bagful.

He was about to move off again when he caught sight of Star about a hundred yards ahead of him. She was standing on the side of the bank staring pensively into the slow-moving water.

He wondered where she'd appeared from, she certainly hadn't been there when he'd stopped at the bush. She shouldn't stand so close to the edge, he thought, the bank could crumble or give way. He'd heard it was notorious round here for that.

He stood watching her. God, but she was lovely. Eve

Smith wasn't a patch on her, he'd known that all along. Eve was great fun, and a laugh, but Star, well she was special – at least to him she was. Alec Muir was a lucky so and so, that was certain. He was still staring at her when, to his complete astonishment and horror, Star stepped off the bank into the water and began wading out into the murky brown depths.

For the space of a few moments he stood paralysed, as though rooted to the spot, but then the spell was lifted and he sprang into action.

The river bed squelched under Star's feet and the freezing water lapped its way up her thighs, but she was aware of none of it. She was thinking about her father. Time and again she'd tried to tell him of her predicament, but each time the words had died in her throat. Every time she looked at him her guilt overwhelmed her. Every word she spoke to her father brought home her betrayal again. There was no doubt in her mind that they would all be better off if she was dead.

Tommy had shouted several times, but she'd been oblivious to his cries. Seeing her tense to dive, he threw himself across the last few feet, managing to grab hold of her the second before she jumped.

'Let me go!' Star screamed, twisting in his grasp. 'Let me go!'

She struggled like a demon, hitting and scratching as though she meant to kill him too.

In the end he knew there was only one way to stop her insane behaviour. He punched her hard on the jaw. Then he half dragged, half propelled her to the bank, pushing her roughly up on to dry land, swinging himself up beside her. Gently, he brushed the wet tangle of hair from her face, then glanced round to see if there was anyone else in the Lane. He and Star were quite alone.

'You should have let me die,' she whispered at last. 'You shouldn't have bothered.'

'Shhh,' he said, taking her hand in his. 'We'll talk later. But first we've got to get you out of those wet things.' He got to his feet, pulling her up as well. 'We're going to my house.'

Star made no objections. His punch had knocked all the fight out of her.

Taking one of her arms in his, he supported her as they walked, at the same time making sure that she couldn't get back to the river.

As they made their way to his house, Tommy talked to her in a soft, easy voice. He told her about something funny that had happened in one of his classes earlier that week, and he told her how nervous his mother had been that first time Star and her father had come to tea. 'You'd have thought he was visiting royalty or something the way she carried on.' Star listened in silence as he rambled on, comforted more by the sound of his voice than the words he was speaking. She relaxed against him, suddenly not afraid any more. And then she realized, as they walked down his street and he described with great glee each neighbour behind each curtain, that she no longer felt alone.

Once inside his house, he took her to the room she and her father had been in on that day that seemed so long ago. He sat her down in the most comfortable chair. 'My parents won't be back for at least another hour,' he said as he poured them each a whisky. 'That gives us some time to dry your clothes and have a little talk. But first you've got to drink this,' and he thrust the glass into her hand.

'Oh, I couldn't drink this,' protested Star, trying to hand it back.

'Drink it,' he insisted. 'It'll do you good. At the very least it'll warm you up a bit.'

It was only when she brought the glass to her lips that she realized she was shivering. Obediently, she sipped at the liquid, instantly feeling its warmth flow through her.

'Better?' he asked with a grin.

Star nodded. 'Much better.' Before, she had thought that the difference between Alec and Tommy was that

Alec was serious and well-bred and Tommy was at heart wild and a ruffian. Now she was beginning to understand that that wasn't the difference at all. She wasn't sure how Alec would have behaved if he were in Tommy's place right now, but she was certain how Tommy would have behaved had he been in Alec's.

'The next thing,' said Tommy, putting his glass down on the table, 'is to get you into something dry. You can put on my mother's dressing gown and we can lay out your clothes by the hearth. I'll show you where you can change.'

Star put her glass down on the table beside his, and prepared to follow him out of the room.

'And then you can tell me what all that nonsense down at the river was about.'

'I see,' said Jim thoughtfully when Star had finished recounting her story. He and Jeannie had returned to find Tommy and Star waiting for them. Tommy had said Star needed his help, then told them about Star's attempt to commit suicide. Star, calm by then, had gone on to explain what had happened.

Jim was both shocked and horrified by her tale. Shocked to think how desperate she had been; horrified at the Muirs' – particularly Mrs Muir's – behaviour. He glanced across at Jeannie. Her face told him she felt all the emotion he himself was feeling.

'So what do you want me to do?' he asked quietly.

Tommy glanced at Star and took a deep breath. 'Arrange a proper abortion for her,' he said quickly.

Star looked down at the floor.

Jim turned to Jeannie, who gave an almost imperceptible nod.

'I don't know anyone you see,' said Star in a strained whisper. 'And I don't have any money, even if I did. The bath and gin were my only hope.'

A lump came into Tommy's throat. He wanted to

sweep Star into his arms and hug her tight. Instead, he looked at his father questioningly.

Jim took a deep breath. He didn't know anything about abortions or abortionists, but he'd find out. One thing was certain, it wasn't going to be some dirty old wifie with a knitting needle. It would be a proper doctor, in proper surroundings, no matter what the cost. 'It'll have to be done quickly, I suppose. Leave all the arrangements and details to me,' he said, sounding more confident than he felt. 'We'll have everything sorted out in no time.'

Jeannie rose as though on cue. 'I'll put the kettle on. I don't know about anybody else, but I could certainly use a cup of tea,' she said briskly. But then, just as she was about to pass Star, she suddenly stopped and embraced Star fiercely. 'No' to fash yourself any more lassie,' she said warmly. 'You'll be all right now, my Jim'll see to that.'

Star had been examined by the gynaecologist, and now she and Jim sat in a reception room, waiting quietly but impatiently for the results of the doctor's tests.

'We'll get a time set for this week,' Jim said reassuringly, 'It'll be all over and done with before you know where you are.'

Star smiled her gratitude. She had never met anyone as kind before in her entire life. With the McBrides on her side she no longer felt either guilt or fear.

Some time later the gynaecologist came into the room, looking extremely pleased with himself. 'I've got some good news for you,' he said, laying a hand kindly on Star's shoulder. 'You won't be needing that operation after all.'

Star regarded him blankly. 'What's that?' asked Jim.

'I was more or less certain after the examination, but I did a few tests just to be certain. The young lady is not pregnant, and never has been.'

Star stared at him in disbelief. 'But what about the three periods I've missed?'

'Going on what you've told me, it would seem that what's happened is a combination of guilty conscience and worry. Deep down you were convinced you'd become pregnant, so your body did its best to oblige you, though you weren't. It happens more often than you'd think.'

'But I feel pregnant!' Star exclaimed.

'I'm sure you do,' said the doctor gently. 'But it's all in the mind, I assure you.'

'Thank God,' breathed Jim.

Star put a hand to her forehead, suddenly lightheaded. Not pregnant! All that fear and despair – and all for nothing.

But then she saw the look of relief and affection in Jim's eyes. At least she had discovered who her friends were.

Outside the house Star stared up at the sky, feeling as though she'd been reborn.

'That's that, then,' Jim said with a sigh.

'That's that,' she echoed.

That Saturday, to celebrate the fact Star wasn't pregnant, Jim took her, Tommy and Jeannie to the Grand Hotel in Charing Cross for lunch.

The Grand Hotel, though now well past its prime, was one of the most impressive buildings in Glasgow. Inside, the once plush opulence had faded, but the ghosts of its grandeur remained.

Star was dazzled by her surroundings. Her eyes darted everywhere, taking everything in. This was the first time she'd been in a restaurant, and she was fascinated by all that was going on around her.

'Has Tommy told you that if he can get a good enough pass and land a place he's going to go on to university after school,' Jeannie said proudly to Star.

Star gave an exclamation of delight. 'But that's wonderful. What will you read?' she asked, turning to Tommy.

'I thought I might have a bash at botany. I've become really interested in it since moving to Millbrae Crescent.'

'Imagine, a son a mine at university!' Jeannie exclaimed, excitedly raising her voice so that it was overheard by those at the adjoining tables.

'Ma!' Tommy hissed in embarrassment. That sort of thing might go down all right in Boyd Street, but not in the Grand Hotel.

'And what about you Star?' asked Jim. 'Have you any plans in that direction?'

'I wish I had, but I'm afraid my father's stipend doesn't run to higher education. But if I could go on , it wouldn't be to university but to a music college. I'd give my eye teeth to go there.'

'She's a fantastic musician,' Tommy said enthusiastically.

Jim remembered Tommy mentioning something about this in the past. 'What do you play?' he asked Star.

'You mean what *doesn't* she play!' Tommy laughed.

'Clarinet, piano and violin,' Star answered.

'I'm fond of the piano myself. Though I suppose the sort of music I like wouldn't be to your taste,' Jeannie said.

'Puccini or Jolson, it depends on the mood I'm in,' Star replied truthfully.

Jeannie wondered who the hell Puccini was? She must remember to ask Jim when they got home.

'You'd choose a career in music if you could, then?' Jim persisted.

'Oh yes! If it was ever possible.'

'What about a bursary?' Jim asked.

'There are two available for music every year, but neither has ever yet gone to a girl. I'll try for them of course when the time comes, but I'm not holding out much hope. I think the powers that be consider it would be a waste of money to give one to someone who might pack in her career to become a housewife and mother.'

'Well, I can understand that point of view, even if I don't wholly agree with it,' Jim said.

Suddenly Star noticed that Tommy was staring over her left shoulder with a peculiar expression on his face. She turned in her chair to see what he was looking at. There was Alec Muir staring at her.

'See what the cat has just dragged in,' Tommy said in a hard voice.

Star transferred her attention to the girl at Alec's side. She was whispering in Alec's ear in such a way as to make it clear that she and Alec were good and close friends.

Well, thought Star, it hasn't taken him long to find someone else. One thing was certain, whoever she was her parents weren't short of a bob or two, the clothes she was wearing were foreign, and clearly expensive.

Margaret had asked Cosmo Dunbarr to meet her and Virginia that morning to give final approval on a number of fabrics they'd selected and which were being held for them. As Cosmo was joining them, it had seemed natural for Alec to do likewise – or so Margaret had thought.

Cosmo had been so delighted with the choice of fabrics (as he was delighted with everything Margaret and Virginia were doing for the house in Lindsay Drive) that he had suggested they all go on to the Grand Hotel for luncheon.

Margaret, chattering nineteen to the dozen, glanced round the restaurant to see if there was anyone there worth being seen by. Her chattering ceased abruptly when she spotted Star.

'Something wrong?' Cosmo inquired solicitously.

Margaret forced a smile back on to her face, and caught her breath. 'It's nothing,' she replied lightly. 'Now, what was I talking about?'

When it came time to leave, Star realized they were going to have to pass close to the table where Alec and his

111

party were sitting. Should she acknowledge them, she wondered, or ignore them? She decided that rather than let them bring her down to their level she would stop and say hello. Anything else seemed somehow petty.

Virginia was telling Alec another story about Kenya when he realized that someone had halted just out of his line of vision. Looking up he found Star looking at him. Immediately, he felt the colour rise in his face.

Star opened her mouth to speak, but before she could get out even one word, Margaret snapped in a threatening tone, 'Please move on, Miss Gray. My son doesn't speak to tarts.'

Star froze in embarrassment. Alec turned scarlet, looking from Star to his mother in horror.

Anger was raging in Tommy, standing behind Star. If Margaret had been a man, he would have punched her on the nose. As it was, he strode over to her and glared down into her scowl.

'You're a truly horrible woman,' he said. And then he picked up her almost full soup bowl and poured the contents into her lap.

Margaret screeched and leapt to her feet. Tommy took hold of Star by the arm and forced her towards the door. All around them customers were staring in either shock, amazement, or ill-concealed amusement.

Jim McBride managed to keep a straight face until they were outside the hotel. Then he nearly doubled over with laughter. 'That's the funniest thing I've seen in years,' he gasped.

Jeannie also began laughing, seeing again the expression on Margaret Muir's face as the hot soup landed in her lap.

Tommy's anger fizzled out, and he too started laughing. 'I wouldn't have dared do that if I'd stopped to think about it. And in such a swanky place too!'

Star, still stunned by Margaret's quite gratuitous insult, and Tommy's reaction, slowly began to smile. 'Did you see her face?' she asked. 'Even after it happened

I don't think she believed it.' The smile melted into a laugh.

The four of them continued laughing all the way to the car.

Star had just told her parents that she had broken irrevocably with Alec Muir. The Reverend Gray was furious.

'I had such high hopes for you two,' the minister fumed.

'You mean for your daughter marrying into the Muirs,' Star corrected.

'Don't be cheeky, Jessie!' Alison snapped. 'Your father only wants what's best for you.'

'Then he should be happy now.'

'I just don't understand how you came to fall out so badly,' he went on. 'You were such close friends.'

'Perhaps this is only a storm in a teacup and you and Alec . . .'

'No, mother, it's definitely finished between us for good.'

'I'm sure the day will come when you'll rue this decision, and your impulsiveness,' the Reverend said heavily. 'You won't find another lad like that very easily.'

'I certainly hope I never find another like him,' said Star. 'Once is enough.'

'You thought highly enough of him until now,' suggested Alison nervously.

'Aye, up until now,' Star echoed. 'Up until now.'

Willie McAllister was congratulating himself as he led Maggie Pettigrew up the stairs to his flat in Athole Gardens. He'd lumbered Maggie from a party he'd been to in Kelvinbridge.

Going into the kitchen for water for his drink, he'd struck up a conversation with the pretty red-haired lassie he'd found there, and after a few minutes offered her a dram from the bottle he was carrying in his jacket pocket.

Maggie had readily accepted, and gone on to match him drink for drink. He'd liked her sense of humour and the relaxed, easy-going manner she had about her. Not only that, but told him she was a Civil Servant. 'Snap!' he'd laughed. 'So am I. I'm a Customs and Excise official.'

Willie opened the front door to his flat and switched on the hall lights. 'Ta ra!' he cried, and made a flamboyant gesture indicating that Maggie should enter.

Maggie laughed as she went past him. She was high on more than alcohol. She couldn't believe her luck, meeting someone like Willie. He was a smasher, right enough, and it had been a long time since she'd met a man who attracted her in that special way. Willie had clicked with her right off.

Inside the lounge door he kissed her before switching on the lights. She responded eagerly.

'You promised me a dram?' she whispered when the kiss was over, trying to regain her composure.

Willie kissed her again, pulling away from her slowly. 'I'm promising you a lot more than that,' he said softly, 'but if the lady wants a drink then a drink she shall have.'

He crossed the room and threw open the drinks cabinet. 'Glenfiddich, Glenmorangie, Glenlivet, or how about a nice Armagnac, Salignac or vodka or gin even?'

Maggie blinked in astonishment. 'You're well stocked,' she replied slowly.

'You name your poison and Uncle Willie has it,' he boasted.

'My God,' she said. 'You've even got tequila. I thought it was impossible to get.'

He gave her a fly wink. 'Nothing is impossible for those in the know, and with the wherewithal,' he smiled.

While he went into the kitchen for salt and lemon, Maggie gazed round the lounge, taking in the deep pile carpet, expensive furniture, magnificent bakelite wireless set, and the dozen or so other items, including the lead crystal glass she was holding, that spelled out plenty of money. He must have private means, she thought, this set-up is well outside the pocket of an ordinary Customs and Excise official.

Rich as well as a smasher! She'd fallen on her feet here, she told herself.

Maggie felt ill as she stared at the dark green door through which she knew she was going to have to walk to say her piece on the other side.

She offered up a silent prayer that she might be wrong, but deep down she was certain she was right. God damn you, Willie McAllister, she raged inwardly. And God damn her job and the rotten suspicious mind she'd had to develop to go with it.

She'd been seeing Willie a month now, and during that time had established that there were no private means. And yet, on each occasion they'd gone somewhere he'd spent a small fortune. So where was the money coming from?

She sighed with frustration. She'd fallen hard for the charming Willie, and would have seen him as husband material if not for her fears.

She focused again on the dark green door, wondering for the thousandth time if she was doing the right thing. But it had to be done, she reminded herself, there was nothing else she could do.

Oh hell, best get this over with, she told herself, and, rising, crossed to the dark green door.

'Enter!' called out a male voice.

As Maggie came into his office Inspector Tom Beaton looked up from the report he'd been reading and smiled.

'I wonder if I could have a word sir?' W. P. C. Pettigrew asked her boss.

★ ★ ★

115

Jim McBride noted that Willie McAllister's hand was trembling when Willie gave him the release docket for the twelve crates that had arrived that morning on the M.V. *Kathleen*.

'What's wrong with you, then?' Jim asked, staring at the trembling hand.

Willie followed Jim's gaze, saw what had prompted the remark, and hurriedly stuffed the hand into his trousers' pocket. 'Too much of the cratur last night, I suppose,' he mumbled.

Jim had had the shakes quite a few times in the past. 'How's your head?' he grinned.

'Terrible,' lied Willie.

'I'd watch it if I were you. The booze can soon get hold of you if you're not careful,' Jim said in a fatherly tone.

'Aye, I'll do that.'

'I'll see you next Tuesday then when the *Orion* gets in,' Jim said.

'I'll arrange my shifts accordingly,' Willie replied, wishing this was all over. Judas goat, that's what they'd made him, and it wasn't a nice feeling at all. But the rock solid guarantee of a good word being spoken to the beak on his behalf was not to be turned down, not when it could mean a couple of years off his sentence.

A minute later Jim was outside the shed handing Matt, his driver, the release docket. Matt and the other two men that had come in the lorry went off to collect the twelve crates and load them up.

The eighth crate was being hefted over the lorry's tailgate when, out of the corner of his eye, Jim caught the unmistakable blue flash of a police uniform.

There were three bobbies, with truncheons drawn, advancing on the lorry.

Jim knew then what had been wrong with Willie. It had nothing to do with the shakes, it was because the bastard had fingered him and known this was about to happen.

Behind the now barred shed door Willie sat staring

vacantly into space. Filled with self-pity, he silently began to weep.

Jim glanced over at the main entrance to the North Basin, and saw two police Rileys parked there blocking the entranceway. Another Riley appeared behind the three policemen advancing on foot. Jim looked over at Matt and the other two lads, who were as yet unaware of the police closing in on them.

Jim's mind was racing furiously; he had a contingency plan all worked out for just such an eventuality. He would pick the money up from the Edinburgh safety deposit box, get himself over to Ulster, then sneak across the border where Paddy Swords would pick him up. He would simply disappear in the Republic after that. Paddy would fix him up with a new identity.

Of course, this meant leaving Jeannie and Tommy behind for the time being, but that couldn't be helped. Paddy would ensure they knew he was all right, and that money got through to them on a regular basis. Sometime later, when this had blown over, Jeannie and Tommy would join him in the Republic. From there they would go to another country, Canada, perhaps, or Australia.

But first of all he had to escape this police trap, and he knew exactly how he was going to manage that.

He dived into the Arrole-Johnstone, switched on the engine, and peeled away in a burn of tyres. The Riley behind the policemen immediately set off in pursuit.

Matt looked up in surprise when the Arrole-Johnstone went screaming off down the dockside, then he saw the three policemen who were on foot charging down on the lorry. He gave a yell of warning to his two mates, and all three of them scattered in different directions.

Each policeman chose a man and followed him. More policemen on foot emerged from behind the two parked Rileys.

Jim had noticed some time before that the wall of wooden planks that divided the North Basin from the rest of Queen's dock was extremely old and rotten, the wood so soft and spongy in parts that it fell away to the touch. He now headed the Arrole-Johnstone directly at this wall with the intention of smashing his way through.

He hit the wall with a muted bang, and, as he'd known would happen, the Arrole-Johnstone ploughed through the wood with no bother. What he wasn't prepared for, however, was the ancient rusty capstan that had been cut from the dockside and dumped on the far side of the wall where it was waiting to be taken away for scrap. The Arrole-Johnstone hit the capstan a glancing blow, which sent it slewing sideways.

Jim cursed his luck as he fought to regain control of the car. Of all spots in the wall he'd had to pick that one!

Jim pulled the steering wheel in the opposite direction to the way the car was travelling, then, at what he judged the appropriate moment, stamped hard on the accelerator. The Arrole-Johnstone came out of the skid as Jim had intended, but two things happened which he hadn't intended. The steering was gone and the accelerator was jammed to the floor. Jim's concentration turned to horror when he realized the car was headed for the dry dock filled with water.

Hastily, he fumbled at the door, proposing to open it and throw himself out, but just as the door began to open the Arrole-Johnstone left the dockside and sailed out over the dry dock.

'Shit!' exclaimed one of the officers in the pursuing Riley.

The Arrole-Johnstone hit the water in a downward angle, sinking immediately.

For Jim the world had suddenly turned into a watery nightmare. He managed to keep the car door open by wedging his hook in it. The moment it came to rest on the dry dock bottom he put his shoulder against the door and his feet against the edge of the front passenger seat. He pushed with every ounce of strength he could muster.

Despite the depth pressure, the door gave way, allowing Jim to wiggle out of the car. He kicked for the surface, but was barely moving upwards. He kicked harder, and harder still. Far ahead of him he could see the shimmering light that was the surface. But despite his frantic efforts he wasn't making any progress. And then came the awful realization of what was holding him back. His hook! His bloody solid steel hook. He clawed at the harness straps, normally so easy to undo, but immensely difficult now. He got one strap loose, and was working on the second, when suddenly the water got darker and darker.

With a sudden, terrifying rush the darkness closed in on Jim McBride.

Tommy stared in disbelief at the two large policemen who'd come into their house. His father dead. Drowned while trying to evade capture?

The policemen were both Highlanders, and each was trying to give the impression of sympathy – and finding it hard to do. It was obvious that they considered men like Jim McBride to be scum.

Black marketeer! The words rang inside Tommy's head. That's what these two were accusing his dad of being, a black marketeer!

'It's a fucking lie!' Tommy burst out suddenly.

'I'm afraid not, son . . .' Constable Donaldson began in his soft Highland lilt.

Tommy knotted his hands into fists. He didn't care if they were police, they weren't going to say such a dreadful thing about his father. 'You'll take it back and apologize to my ma,' he threatened.

Donaldson and McTaggart exchanged glances. It was clear the boy hadn't known what was going on.

'I'm afraid it is the truth,' McTaggart said gently. 'We wouldn't have said it if we didn't have the proof.'

But Tommy was beyond reason. He flew at McTaggart, and succeeded in getting in several solid blows to the huge Highlander before McTaggart pinioned his arms by his side.

'You'll take back your filthy lies!' Tommy screamed.

Donaldson looked at Jeannie. 'Missus?' he appealed.

'We don't want to book the lad after what's happened, but we will if he forces us to,' McTaggart added.

'Come here, Tommy,' Jeannie said, nodding to the policemen to let him go.

Tommy went to his mother's side. She clasped his hand in hers. 'You mustn't go to jail, you're the head of the family now,' she said in a voice that was choked with tears.

Tommy personally escorted the policemen to the front door – not to be polite, but to make sure they'd actually gone. When he returned to Jeannie he found her slumped against the mantelpiece, clutching an old picture of Jim.

'It was a lie, wasn't it, Mum?' Tommy asked.

Jeannie shook her head. She took a deep breath, then went over to the drinks cabinet. If ever she needed a hard drink it was now. Jim gone! Gone just like that! That was going to take some time to sink in, a long time.

Tommy's gaze never left his mother. 'I don't understand,' he said softly.

'Let's sit down and I'll tell you all about it,' Jeannie replied taking a large sip of her drink.

Jim's death was reported on page two of the next day's *Glasgow Herald*. It was there over breakfast, that the Reverend Kenneth Gray learned the truth. He read the article through once to himself, then aloud for Alison's and Star's benefit.

'A black marketeer!' he breathed, eyes gleaming. 'I always suspected there was something fishy about McBride. Well now we know.'

Poor Tommy, thought Star. And his mother, what a hell she must be living through right now.

The Reverend Gray had a sudden uneasy thought.

Would Jim having been a member of his congregation reflect on him? 'I shall denounce McBride from the pulpit,' he declared.

Star stared at him aghast. 'Isn't that a bit strong?'

'I'm sure your father knows what's right and proper for him to do,' Alison said immediately.

'But what about Tommy and his mother?' asked Star. 'You will go and see them?'

'I shall do no such thing. The man was a criminal. I'll have nothing further to do with those he's left behind.'

'You can't just abandon them,' cried Star. 'You're a minister!'

'Your father's quite right,' Alison stated primly. 'There are some people beyond Christian charity.'

'I thought it said in the Bible that we should forgive, so that we'll be forgiven,' countered Star.

'Don't try and be clever with me young lady!' her father thundered back.

Star didn't flinch, she'd heard that bullying tone too often before. 'If you won't go over there, then I will,' she said, rising from the table.

'You'll do nothing of the sort. And what's more, I absolutely forbid you to speak to young McBride ever again. Is that clear?'

'You can't be serious!' Star gasped.

'Oh, but I am. I won't have a daugher of mine associating with that sort of trash.'

She stared at her father's hard, unyielding face. Tommy McBride was worth ten of him. As for Tommy, he'd need a friend now, and she'd stand by him just as he'd stood by her. She wouldn't let him down.

She wouldn't go to Millbrae Crescent just yet, though. In the circumstances, it might be embarrassing to Mrs McBride. She'd wait until Tommy came back to school. When he did return to Queenie she'd be there waiting.

'I'd better get along or I'll be late for my first period,' she said.

121

'Mind what I told you now,' the Reverend growled.

'I won't forget.' Of course she wouldn't forget, it was just that she had no intention of complying with his orders, that was all.

'Say that again!' Tommy exclaimed.

'The money your Dad had is lost to us,' Jeannie repeated.

'*All* of it?'

'With the exception of twenty-two pounds I retrieved from the Calton office a couple of hours ago.'

'But how?' Tommy demanded. Twenty-two pounds certainly wasn't going to get them very far.

Jeannie ran a hand through her dull limp hair. It was three days now since Jim had died, three days of shock and grief. Then late that morning, when Tommy was out at the undertaker's, she'd suddenly remembered about Jim's 'special arrangements' as he'd called them.

She'd gone straightaway over to the Calton repair shop in the hope there might be a sizeable amount of cash in the safe, but there wasn't. Twenty-two pounds was all there had been.

'When your father started in the business he realized he couldn't bank the large sums he was making without starting people asking questions. So he hired a safety deposit box, and kept the money in that,' Jeannie now explained.

'Where is this safety deposit box, then?'

Jeannie gave a grim smile, shaking her head. 'I don't know. Your father never volunteered that information, and I never inquired. It is in a bank, but I couldn't tell you which bank far less which branch. All I do know is that the box was hired under a phoney name.'

'What name was that?'

'I've no idea. He never mentioned that either.' Jeannie took her teacup and held it in her hands to try and warm them. She'd been so cold since Jim died, she'd come to half-believe she'd never be naturally warm again. 'Even if I knew the name, bank and branch I still wouldn't be able to get into the box. To do that I'd have to produce a death certificate in the phoney name, plus identification proving I was his next of kin. All impossible, of course. That money is lost to us forever, we just have to accept that.'

But Tommy couldn't give up. 'What about the bank account Dad had for the repair shop, surely there's something in that?'

'Jim always managed to keep his legitimate business account in overdraft, so in point of fact *we* owe *them*.'

'There's always the house, you've forgotten about that,' Tommy said, brightening.

'The house was bought on a mortgage, again because of the tax people. When we default on the mortgage at the beginning of the month, as we'll have to, then the house goes by the board.'

'How about Life Assurance?'

This time Jeannie merely shook her head.

Twenty-two pounds! Despair filled Tommy. That wasn't even enough to cover the funeral.

'What about furniture, carpets and all that sort of thing? Surely they belong to us and we can sell them to raise cash?'

Jeannie had forgotten all about the household contents. 'Oh, aye,' she said in a dazed way. 'There's that.'

Tommy let out a sigh of relief. At least that was something. What was important now was getting his mother out of here and to a new life as soon as possible. It was only then, he knew, that she stood a chance of surviving her enormous grief. The prospect of the future was still bleak, but not as totally bleak as it had been a few minutes ago. They'd still lose the house, but hopefully they'd have enough money to keep the pair of them until he got a job, although a job at what he didn't know.

'I'll telephone the Crown Showrooms and arrange for them to pick everything up directly after the funeral,' he

123

said. The Crown Showrooms specialized in auctioning off household and office contents.

'I don't want you to think less of your da for what he did. Remember, he did it for us, you and me.'

Tommy forced a smile on to his face and took her hands in his. 'I know,' he said warmly. 'I know.'

Star walked down the hill that was Millbrae Crescent. It was the Monday of the second week since Jim McBride's death, and still Tommy hadn't returned to school. Worried, she'd decided to go to him and not wait for his reappearance after all.

The moment the McBride house came into view she knew there was something different about it. She was almost at the door when it dawned on her that there were no curtains showing in the windows any more. Every last curtain at the front of the house had been removed.

She knocked and waited. Even the sound of her knock seemed strangely hollow.

She pulled the bell handle, and its reverberating clang sounded hollow as well, as if it were being rung inside a drum.

She knocked and pulled the bell handle again, and still there was no reply. Lifting up the letterbox she gazed into the hall. Where was the hall carpet? And where was . . . Standing up, she peered into the nearest window. The room was empty, every stick of furniture gone. A look in the window on the other side showed only walls and floorboards.

She squatted and had another look through the letterbox. There could be no doubt about it, the entire house was empty.

Why hadn't Tommy contacted her to say they were going? Because he'd been so ashamed of what Jim had been doing that he hadn't wanted to face her? Or because he'd heard what her father had said about Jim in church and had assumed that her father's view was hers? And where would Tommy and Mrs McBride have gone? With Jim's story splashed all over the Glasgow newspapers, it seemed likely that they'd left the city for good.

All at once she realized that she was never going to see Tommy McBride again. He'd gone out of her life forever.

Suddenly she felt like the house, completely empty inside. With tears washing her face, she made her way back up the hill.

PART TWO

Jessie
1955–58

4

Lizzie Dunnachie lit a cigarette and sank back into the train seat. 'Whew,' she gasped. 'I almost didn't make it that time.' She'd been late as usual, galloping down the station steps to catch the 8.20 by the skin of her teeth. Unknown to her a male passenger from Burnside further up the line regularly made book on her.

'You'll be late for your own funeral so you will,' Jessie laughed.

It was October, 1955, and both girls were now twenty-two. Being off to work, they were both soberly dressed in the manner approved by business. Lizzie wore a grey costume, Jessie a dark brown skirt with matching cardy, and both sported the beehive hairdo that was all the fashion.

'So where's it to be the night?' Lizzie asked. It was Friday and Friday night was the first of the two traditional nights for going out.

'Whitecraigs, I suppose,' Jessie answered without any enthusiasm. Whitecraigs was the name of the posh tennis club on the outskirts of the city which held a dance every Friday night during the winter in support of the club. It had the reputation of being frequented by a 'better class' of person.

Lizzie wrinkled her nose. 'I'm getting right fed up with there. We're getting older and older, and the male talent is getting younger and younger. When they get me up nowadays I feel like their big sister instead of a potential lumber.'

Jessie laughed. It was true enough, though. The lads there were getting on the young side for them.

'How about the Plaza then?' Jessie suggested. The Plaza was a swanky dancehall down at Eglinton Toll.

Lizzie pulled a face. It's just the opposite there. When they come out with their patter you expect it to be about their exploits in the First World War, if not the one against the Zulus.'

'So much for the Plaza,' Jessie replied. At the rate they were going they would end up staying in.

Jean Semple, a member of the Croftfoot contingent, leant forward from the other end of the carriage. 'I couldn't help but overhear you,' she said quietly. 'Can I make a suggestion?'

'Fire away,' said Lizzie.

'Do you like Rockabilly?'

'Rocky who?' Lizzie asked. Jessie laughed. She knew all about Rockabilly, having listened to a number of records in the shop where she worked. She'd never heard it live though.

Jean rolled her eyes heavenwards. 'You two aren't just old, you're bloody decrepit,' she teased. Jean was seventeen, just.

'Many a good tune played on an old violin I'll have you know. And anyway, less of your cheek, Miss. Have a wee bit of respect for your elders,' Lizzie snapped back with exaggerated dignity.

'I went to a new dancehall a fortnight ago called The Black Raven,' Jean went on. 'Well, it's not actually new, it's the Trocadero tarted up somewhat and its name changed. But I had a smashing time there. The music was this really fab Rockabilly, and the male talent enough to make you drool.'

Lizzie was immediately interested. Droolable talent! That sounded just the ticket.

'What sort of crowd go?' asked Jessie.

'Mixed. Some students from the Uni, people who work in town offices, a few workies; all ages and all sorts like.'

Lizzie snapped her fingers. 'I think we should give it a try. What do you say, Jessie?' she asked eagerly.

Jessie wasn't so sure. It didn't really sound like her sort

of place. She enjoyed Rockabilly enough, but the people she associated it with were definitely not her sort. 'Well . . .'

'Come on, nothing ventured nothing gained,' Lizzie urged.

'Oh, all right. The Black Raven it is then,' Jessie decided, unable to resist the pleading look in Lizzie's eyes.

It was a decision that was to change her entire life.

Jessie saw him elbow his way through the crowd and instinctively knew who it was he was making for. Oh, God, she thought. She'd noticed him on the dance floor a while back, pawing and mauling the lassie he was with, the girl clearly too terrified to protest.

He was a rough looking Teddy Boy in a maroon drape jacket, black brothel creepers and a headful of grease. Jessie cringed at the thought of him holding her in his arms. A quick glance around confirmed that she was hemmed in. It was impossible for her to slip away before he reached her. She would refuse him, she told herself; there was no way she was going to let him get her on to the floor.

He stopped right in front of her, looking as though he thought he was doing her a favour. It's amazing how arrogant ugly men can be, she thought.

'Are you dancing?' he said, and, without waiting for a reply, reached out and grabbed her by the arm.

'Not this one, thank you,' she answered hastily, forcing a pleasant smile on to her face. She should have stayed home.

He blinked. 'You what?'

'Not this one, I don't feel like it.'

His grip tightened, making her wince. 'Are you refusing me?'

Jessie desperately wished for Lizzie. Lizzie might have been able to deal with him, but Lizzie was at the far end of the floor with a chap she'd danced the last three numbers with.

'To be honest, I'm not feeling very well, I was just about to go to the Ladies',' she said trying to look ill.

'You're a liar,' he scowled. 'You're refusing me, and no bird does that.'

Jessie'd heard how dangerous Teds could be and couldn't stop the fear that was beginning to grow. She drew herself up to her full height nonetheless and tried not to appear frightened. She was aware that a ring of silence had descended in her immediate vicinity. 'I don't want to dance,' she repeated.

His grip tightened even more and he tugged her towards him. 'I said. . .'

'She said she didn't want to gēt up, so why don't you just piss off, toerag,' said a male voice quietly.

The man who'd spoken was another Ted, dressed completely in black. There was an authority about him that even she recognized. Her eyes moved from one to the other, and it was obvious that the first Ted felt it too. He let go of her wrist and took a step forward, but there was a new look of wariness in his face. 'And just what do you think you're doing on my patch?' he hissed.

The second Ted reached out and brushed an imaginary piece of lint from the other man's collar. 'Just visiting. Why? Don't tell me you have some objections.'

Jessie had been about to simply fade away into the crowd and get out of here as fast as she could, but the sound of the Ted's voice made her stop and look at him again. That voice, she thought, trying to recognize the face beneath the waterfall hairdo. That voice . . .

The first Ted's eyes flicked this way and that, checking on his friends.

'There are six of yours here,' the other Ted said with a thin smile. 'I've already counted.'

Ken Young, the first Ted, stared into the insolent eyes of his adversary. Ken was good at pushing women around; he was even good at pushing his own boys around, but he was not good at pushing around men who were stronger and smarter than he was. It was too early yet for most of his boys to be here, and even he could understand that that wasn't by chance.

'To save you asking,' the second Ted went on, 'I'm here mob handed. I've got twenty-three of my boys with me, and they're all looking right at you.'

Ken was carrying a bicycle chain, but as much as he would have dearly loved to use it he knew that any move like that on his part would be suicidal. He glanced quickly around, but there wasn't even one of his men in sight. 'Don't think I'll forget this effrontery,' Ken said with as much menace as he could muster. 'Don't think I will. Another day and you won't catch me by surprise.'

Jessie was suddenly aware of the number of Teds who'd quietly materialized around the black-clothed figure during this exchange. They were as ferocious looking as the press always claimed, despite the bright colours of their drapes. Only her rescuer was dressed in black. She turned her attention to him again. There was something so familiar about him, something in the way he stood, something in the expression of his eyes.

The second Ted laughed. 'You were always a great one for the scintillating repartee, Young. Another day I'll catch you by a lot more than surprise.' He jerked his thumb. 'Get lost, or I may forget my manners.'

Ken gave him one more belligerent look, then did as he was told, disappearing into the crowd.

'I do want to thank you,' began Jessie to the black back. 'I mean, thank you, if it hadn't been for you . . .'

And then he turned, grinning like a school boy – like the school boy she used to know. 'Hello, Star,' he said. 'Don't you recognize me any more?'

For a moment she couldn't react at all – couldn't move, couldn't speak, couldn't even think. Tommy. Tommy McBride. She wanted to fling her arms around him, to make sure that after all these years it was really he and not a dream. Instead, she heard herself saying, 'It's just plain Jessie now.'

A Ted in a bright yellow drape leaned towards Tommy. 'Do we stay or go?'

'We go,' decided Tommy instantly. 'We've had our laugh coming here, let's leave it at that.'

Jessie could see Lizzie pushing her way through the crowd towards them.

'What do you say?' asked Tommy. 'Do you fancy a drink, just plain Jessie?'

She hesitated for a moment, thinking of what her father would say if he ever saw her out with a Ted, or what any of her friends would say for that matter, but then she looked into Tommy's eyes and saw the nervousness there, like the first time he had asked her to dance in Miss Parrot's class. 'I'd love a drink,' she said. Then added, unexpectedly, 'I never thought I'd see you again.'

At that moment Lizzie broke through the crowd. 'Are you all right?' she demanded. She hadn't been able to see much from where she'd been standing, but she had been told that the trouble was over a girl, and she'd assumed the worst. She was more than willing to take on a roomful of Teds in defence of her pal.

'I'm fine,' laughed Jessie. 'Look who came to my rescue.'

It was a rare thing for Lizzie Dunnachie to be at a loss for words. Like Jessie, however, she couldn't believe her own eyes. 'My God,' she said at last. 'It's Tommy McBride! What are you doing here?'

Tommy winked. 'I've come to take two old school friends out for a drink.'

Once outside, Tommy linked an arm through one of Jessie's and one of Lizzie's. 'It's just like old times,' he grinned as they made their way down the street, flanked on either side by his boys in drapes and beetle crushers. As they walked along, people quickly stepped out of their way.

When they got to the pub, Tommy whispered something to one of his boys, and the next thing Jessie knew Lizzie was being shown to a table well away from where Tommy was inviting her to sit. She could see Lizzie turn to her and wink.

Tommy placed their order with another of his Teds, and sat down across from her. The eyes were the same, the eyes and his smile, but everything else was hard and new. She might have passed him on the street a hundred times and never known it was him.

'Well,' he said, staring at her as though she might suddenly vanish, 'it's been a long long time.'

'No one knew where you'd gone,' she said, looking back at this stranger who seemed like someone from another world. 'I went to your house to tell you how sorry I was about . . . about your father . . .'

He played with the ashtray in the centre of the table. 'It was all a bit of a rush,' he said, lowering his eyes. 'I just wanted to get Mum out of there as fast as I could.' He stared at the table top for a few seconds, then shook himself from his reverie. 'Why Jessie?' he asked suddenly. 'I thought you hated that name.'

She smiled wrily and shrugged. 'I suppose I just outgrew Star. I thought it made me sound special, you know. But now I guess I'm old enough to live with reality.'

He looked up as a Ted approached with their drinks. 'I guess that's something we've all had to learn to do,' he said softly.

She moved her eyes everywhere – from the floor to the table to the people around them – but not to him. 'I thought that, after all that there was in the papers, and your father so well off . . .' She stared at a point just beyond his shoulder. 'I thought that you would have left Glasgow for good.'

He laughed, but it was far from a happy sound. 'Dad had money, all right. But none of it came to us. He had it so safely stashed away that we didn't know where it was.

So we moved back to Boyd Street, and I finally managed to get a job.

At last her eyes rested on him. There was a look in them that he couldn't quite recognize. 'So that's where you've been all this while.'

'Aye,' he nodded. 'Right back where we started from.'

'And what's your job?'

He shrugged, looking young again, almost like the boy she remembered. 'It's not much. I'm a packer in a china shop. The one underneath Highlandman's bridge.' He smiled bitterly. 'It's not a great achievement, but it's the best I've been able to do.'

Her heart went out to him. He'd been such a promising student – so full of dreams, so full of spirit. 'I always imagined you were a botanist somewhere,' she said softly. It had never occurred to her that he hadn't gone to university, as he'd planned; that he hadn't made those dreams come true.

His eyes took on a far-away look. How it hurt him even now to remember that dream, those plans he'd felt so sure about. In only a few years he had moved a lifetime away from them. 'And what about you?' he asked, bringing himself back to the present abruptly. 'What's happened to you?'

Not a damn thing, she wanted to say. Time had passed, but she had nothing to show for it other than the days marked off on the calendar – the days, the weeks, the months, and then the years. She'd drifted along as though her life hadn't begun, as though it were still about to happen, kidding herself that something would happen to change the boredom and blandness of her life.

'I applied and auditioned for those two bursaries at the Music College, but I got nowhere. Now I work in a music shop. It's not exactly the same as being a professional musician, but it seems to be the closest I'll ever get.'

'And are you happy?'

She looked straight into his eyes. 'Are you?'

But instead of replying, he said, 'Seven years . . . in some ways it's a life time, but in others it's just like yesterday.'

'Yes,' she agreed softly. In some ways it was just like yesterday, a yesterday she'd never forgotten, whose dreams and promises haunted her still.

'You never got married, then?' he asked, taking her ringless hand in his.

She shook her head. 'And you?'

'Not me,' he said airily. 'I'm too busy enjoying myself.'

'You mean playing the field?' she teased, wondering at the pang of jealousy that stabbed through her.

'That and being a Ted,' he answered slowly.

She took in his appearance again, what a transformation from the Tommy she'd known at Queenie! There was something frightening about him now, but something fascinating, too. 'Why did you become a Ted?' she asked.

His mouth twisted into a crooked grin. 'There's excitement in being a Ted,' he said with real enthusiasm. 'A packer's life, even a head packer's life, is never more than dull. There were mornings, before I became a Ted, when I'd wake up wanting to scream at the thought of the day stretching ahead, Becoming a Ted changed all that. It makes me somebody.' He took a deep breath, then went on. 'I was the first in Boyd Street. Then a few others became Teds, and that's how the Boyd Street Boys came into existence.'

She understood what he meant about boredom, about one day just melting into the greyness of the next. 'And the others elected you leader?'

He shrugged. 'There was no election, it just fell out that way.'

Jessie took a sip of her shandy. 'What about fights, do you get into many of those?'

Tommy gave her a sideways look. 'They happen now and then. When challenged you have to hold your own, you can't be a Ted otherwise. But I wouldn't believe everything you read in the papers.'

'And do you. . .' searching for the right word. 'Do you enjoy them?'

'And how!' he grinned. Something in his tone sent a cold shiver down her spine.

Tommy patted his pockets, took out a cigarette packet, and opened the packet to find it empty. He made a sign to one of the Teds at an adjoining table who immediately jumped to his feet and came over to offer Tommy one of his fags.

Power, Jessie thought. That was what Tommy had now. And he had all the charisma of a born leader as well. Another pang of jealousy lanced through her as she realized how attractive he must be to the lassies he now moved amongst. Suddenly, she felt confused. 'Lizzie is a shorthand typist with the Gas Board,' she said in a different voice nodding in Lizzie's direction.

'Good for her, but it's you I want to hear about.'

She smiled shyly. 'There's not much to tell.'

'What about the Fives, do you still go there?'

'Not a lot, a younger set have taken over nowadays. If I do go to a cafe it tends to be the one up at the top of Battlefield Road, the one facing the school dinner hall.'

He grinned. 'I remember. The dinner hall in the church basement?'

'That's it,' she nodded.

'And what about the Boys' Brigade? Still playing piano for them?'

'No, I gave up doing that years ago.'

'Aye, of course you're not still playing for them. Tonight's a Friday, you'd have been there if you had.'

An uneasy silence fell between them. She stared into her glass as though it might tell her something to say. One minute he was Tommy McBride, the friend she'd missed for so long, and the next he was a tough, aggressive young man, leader of the Boyd Street Teds.

'And boyfriends, I suppose you've had quite a few of

those since the old days?' Tommy leaned back in his chair, affecting an uneasy, unconcerned manner.

'Oh aye, stacks and stacks,' she replied quickly, and gave a nervous, self-conscious, laugh. There had been boyfriends to be sure, but not that many and none who'd mattered. 'What about you? You must have a girlfriend or two.'

Tommy shook his head. 'They come and go, you know what I mean.'

Was he sleeping with them? Had to be, she told herself, Teds didn't go in for holding hands and a chaste good-night kiss as her boyfriends had.

'What is it? What's funny?' he demanded.

She'd been imagining him kissing a girl good night. 'Nothing.'

'There has to be something!'

'Just a memory, that's all.'

He glared at her. 'About me?'

'No, not about you. You're not the centre of the universe, you know.'

He dragged on his cigarette.

Touchy, she thought. That was interesting. Perhaps he wasn't quite as hard as he liked to make out.

She swallowed more of her shandy. Lizzie seemed to be doing all right with Jack. The pair of them were engrossed in conversation.

'It really is smashing seeing you again,' she said on a sudden impulse, and just as suddenly reached out and squeezed his hand.

'It's good to see you, too.'

She could hear in his voice that he meant that, and it pleased her. It pleased her a great deal.

They reminisced some more, and then, catching sight of the time, she announced that it was high time for her and Lizzie to be making tracks.

She and Tommy led the way out into the street, Lizzie and Jack right behind them. The other Teds fanned out around the two couples.

As they walked, Tommy said quietly to Jessie, 'Funny how things happen. If I hadn't decided to go to the Black Raven tonight to have a laugh at Ken Young's expense, and if you hadn't picked this particular night to go for the first time, we'd never have met up. If you'd come in later, even, I'd have gone.'

'It must be fate,' she laughed trying to sound more light-hearted than she felt.

'Now that we've met up again we mustn't lose touch,' he went on.

She nodded. 'No, we mustn't.'

They walked a little way in silence, not so much as looking at one another. They turned a corner and Jessie and Lizzie's tramstop came into view. Seeing the stop, Tommy slowed his pace fractionally, and the others followed suit.

'There's our tram now!' shouted Lizzie, pointing.

'Och, let it go, there'll be another along in a minute,' Tommy said quickly.

Jack, who'd been about to make a sprint for it with Lizzie, came down off his toes, and, taking hold of her elbow, resumed walking slowly, forcing her to do the same.

'No hurry is there?' Tommy asked Jessie with a side-ways glance.

She continued to look down at her feet. 'A few minutes longer won't make any difference.'

The tram clattered by as they came up to the tramstop. Tommy drew Jessie a little way aside. 'It really is good to see you again,' he said awkwardly.

'You've already said that, and so have I,' she reminded him.

He flicked back a slickened lock of hair. 'I was wondering . . . uh . . .'

She waited, guessing what was coming next, but not knowing what her answer was going to be.

'Me and the lads have a dancehall we go to. It's in Govanhill. It's a bit rough, mind you, but interesting, oh aye, very much that. I was wondering um . . . if you had nothing planned for next Friday, what about me taking you there to see the sights?' He paused, then added. 'You might enjoy it.'

She pretended to be interested in something across the road.

He shifted from one foot to the other. 'It was only a thought. You probably have something else planned.'

She made her decision, not at all sure it was the right one. 'Where shall we meet?'

He froze for a second, then swiftly regained his composure. 'How about Battlefield Rest?'

That was too close to home; she didn't want to be seen by anyone who might report back to her father and mother that she'd been in the company of a Ted. 'Outside Pearson's, the big ironmonger's in Victoria Road,' she suggested.

'That's fine,' he replied, nearly laughing with relief. 'That's perfect.' A second tram came clanking along. He shook her by the hand, a strangely formal gesture for a young man of his appearance. 'Till next Friday night then.'

'I'm looking forward to it,' she replied. She hesitated for a moment, then disentangled her hand and stepped aboard the tram.

'Let's go upstairs so I can have a fag,' Lizzie said, and headed up the metal stairs.

They sat in the back seat. Jessie watched Tommy till at last he was lost to view, just as he, illuminated by the harsh white street light, stood watching her.

Jessie was in a quandary about what to wear. All her dresses and outfits were of the sort acceptable at Whitecraigs or the like, but they weren't suitable for a Govanhill dancehall full of Teds.

She heard her father moving about downstairs. Her parents believed she was going out with Lizzie that evening. She could easily imagine their reaction if they knew the truth – that she was going out with Tommy McBride, the criminal's son, and that Tommy was a Teddy Boy now and was taking her jigging in Govanhill.

Her father would have had a canary, she thought, and smiled. As for Alison, hysterics at the very least.

She suddenly remembered the day Jim McBride had taken them all to the Grand Hotel and how Alec had been there with his mother and the girl he eventually married.

The marriage had made all the newspapers, even the London *Times*. Lady Virginia Dunbarr, daughter of the Earl of Clyde, weds Alexander Henry Muir in a ceremony in Glasgow Cathedral. Not all that long after the wedding Alec and his wife had gone to Kenya where he was now managing the Family's huge farm. That had also been in the paper.

Jessie wondered what had become of Alec's ambition to be a minister. Lady Virginia must have changed his mind about that. It was a pity in a way. Alec would have made a good minister. As for his being a farm manager, she couldn't imagine how he was making out at that.

She brought her mind back to the present. What ever was she going to wear?

He was waiting for her outside Pearson's. She was early, which meant he'd been even earlier.

Lord! she thought, momentarily seeing him as a Ted and not as Tommy. His sideboards were thick and bushy, his D.A. brushed to perfection.

This time he was wearing a black waistcoat below his black drape, with a watchchain dangling between the waistcoat's two pockets. He had five rings on his left hand, each gaudier than the next.

'Hello,' he said when she came up beside him.

Going up on to her tiptoes she brushed her lips against a point just below the left hand corner of his mouth. 'Hello,' she replied, surprising even herself.

The Cameo dancehall had a crumbling facade that was extensively covered with graffiti, a lot of it about the Boyd Street Boys.

Tommy led Jessie through to the foyer where she left her coat with the attendant. She noticed him giving her green and white polka-dot dress the once over out the corner of his eye, but he didn't comment.

Inside the hall itself a band called The Bad Angels was playing a loud rock song. Jessie was startled to see that a Ted was doing a handstand on the piano, while others were standing nonchalantly on top of the side booths and tables watching the action taking place on the floor. She gasped when she noticed that one of the dancing Teds was naked from the waist down. She looked quickly back to Tommy when the dancing Ted whirled round to expose his front.

'You were right about there being some sights here,' she grinned weakly.

Tommy laughed. 'And it's still fairly quiet yet,' he said ominously, and laughed again at the horrified expression on her face.

Despite her shock, it didn't take long for Jessie to become fascinated by the dancing. She'd never seen anything like it in the clubs she frequented. The music had something raw and almost primitive about it, and the dancing couples had about as much to do with the lessons learned in Miss Parrot's class as lovemaking has to do with business etiquette. The blatant sexuality of the dancing nearly took her breath away.

By Jessie's reckoning, there were somewhere between 80 and 100 Teds present. A good half that number, Tommy informed her, were not Boyd Street Boys but 'friendlies' from round about.

And then there were the girlfriends, equally exotic in appearance though not quite as calculatedly menacing.

Ted after Ted gave Tommy a sign that expressed not merely acknowledgement, but fealty as well. She suddenly felt as though she were visiting a strange and ancient tribe.

Affecting enormous dignity, Tommy took Jessie round introducing her. Everyone he spoke to seemed enormously pleased at the attention of the head man himself.

The reaction to Jessie was not quite so positive. It was clear they weren't at all sure what to make of her. They'd all heard about how he'd taken her away from Ken Young in the Black Raven, and the whisper was already around that she was an old friend, someone from his past.

Despite Tommy's efforts to make her feel at ease, Jessie couldn't feel comfortable. She stood out like a sore thumb amongst this lot. So great was the difference between her clothes and her behaviour and theirs that she might have been someone dumped down in the midst of a group of beings from another planet. All eyes were on her, sizing her up. She wanted to go home, but didn't want to leave Tommy. He seemed oblivious to either her discomfort or the looks she was getting, especially from the other girls.

'Well, I don't think the bitch is anything special!' a female voice suddenly boomed out behind her.

Jessie turned to find herself facing a striking blonde, standing with her hands on her hips. There was no doubt in Jessie's mind who this was.

'Lena!' Tommy warned.

'He's screwing me you know, so don't get any ideas,' Lena spat the words at Jessie.

Tommy gave an exclamation of anger, and made to go for Lena, but Jessie grabbed his arm. 'For heavens sake, you can't go around fighting everyone,' she hissed.

Lena tossed her pony tail. 'I want to know what's what,' she said staring defiantly into Tommy's eyes.

'I do as I please. Nobody owns me, and that includes you,' Tommy said in a quiet, measured voice.

Lena coloured with anger. 'You're no' coming here with another bird and making me a laughing stock.'

'The only person making you a laughing stock is yourself.'

Lena glared at him, then sauntered over to Jessie. She fastened her gaze on Jessie's feet and worked her way up inch by inch, until finally she was looking Jessie straight in the eye. 'Like I said,' she declared, 'nothing special at all.'

Jessie was so sure that Tommy wouldn't let anything happen to her that she wasn't even slightly afraid.

Suddenly, Lena's palm cracked against Jessie's cheek.

Without thinking, Jessie threw a punch at Lena which took Lena right on the end of the nose and threw her backwards.

Jessie couldn't believe what she'd done. Nor, from the amazement on their faces, could anyone else, least of all Tommy.

Lena scrambled back to her feet, puzzlement and a grudging respect in her eyes. 'You couldn't do that a second time,' she challenged.

Jessie gave the blonde a sheepish smile. 'To be honest, I didn't know I could do it a first.'

As quickly as it had sprung up, the situation was defused. 'Och tae hell with it, I wanted a change as well,' Lena said, almost friendly. She turned to Tommy and gave him a long kiss. 'That's for good-bye,' she winked.

'Would you like to dance or sit down?' Tommy asked Jessie when they were finally alone again.

'Sit down, before I fall down.'

He guided her to a side booth whose inhabitants vacated it when Tommy made it known he wanted to use it.

He stared across at her in open admiration. 'That was really something,' he said with his lop-sided grin.

Jessie frowned. 'You should have warned me you had someone here.'

'I told you in the pub last week, there's nobody important in my life.'

'Lena seemed to think she was.'

'She was wrong, and she should have known better.'

Jessie glanced down at the hand she'd hit Lena with, still unable to believe she'd actually done such a thing. Two of her knuckles were grazed. What would her parents say if they found out she was in a place like this, brawling?

'She's very attractive,' she said at last, not taking her eyes from her hand.

'Who?'

'Your friend, Lena.'

'Oh, she's that all right. I do have taste you know.'

Jessie sucked the grazes, all at once feeling what a mistake this date was. 'I hope you don't regret having asked me here tonight.'

'Why should I regret it?'

'Me being so . . . so normal compared to your friends.'

'You're not so normal,' he laughed. 'Not with that right. Anyway, if I have a regret it's for what happened with Lena there. I'm sorry.'

'She's fond of you, I could see that.'

He shrugged.

'I wish . . .' she stopped herself from saying that she wished he wasn't a Teddy Boy, that he was normal, like she was, that he was more like he used to be.

'Wish what?' he prompted.

'Nothing.'

'Is all this. . .' making a gesture that encompassed the entire dancehall, 'is all this hateful to you?'

'No, no . . . I don't hate it – I just feel out of place. I really love the music, though.'

'There are nights I come here after a day's work completely washed out,' said Tommy thoughtfully, 'and then I meet these people, and hear that beat, and I feel life's worth living again.'

'I don't suppose you mind the way they all treat you either,' she teased.

'I'd be a liar if I denied it. During the day amongst the cups and saucers, the teapots and chanties I'm no one at all. But here I count.'

Jessie smothered a laugh. 'You don't sell chanties there do you? I thought they went out with Queen Victoria.' A chantie was a chamberpot.

'I'll have you know there's still a big demand for them. Why, would you like one? I can get you a nice bone china one with roses on the outside.'

'No thank you,' she laughed.

'That's what comes from living in a manse with inside cludgies, you don't know what real life's all about,' he said, not quite joking. 'If you stayed in a tenement you'd find a chantie very preferable, having woken in the early hours say, to going down ice cold stone stairs to a middle landing lavvy.'

She glanced down at the table. 'I take your point.'

'Fifteen minutes by tram from Queen's Park and Battlefield to Boyd Street, fifteen minutes that'll take you back half a century, from one world to another.' He took a deep breath. 'Here's me getting all intense and maudlin and it's the last thing I want to do. How about a dance? Do you think you could brave the floor?'

She stood up. 'I just hope your dancing's improved, that's all. You used to murder my feet in Miss Parrot's class.'

'Oh I think I've improved a wee bit since then.'

And he had. In fact, he wasn't just a good dancer now. He was terrific.

'I'll see you home,' Tommy said as they walked to the tramstop.

'You'd better not,' she said slowly, not wanting to hurt his feelings. 'For the same reason I didn't want you to meet me at Battlefield Rest. You know as well as anyone what my father's like.'

147

He nodded. 'I think I can remember.'

They halted at the tramstop, the only ones there. 'I enjoyed myself tonight, thank you,' she said softly, suddenly feeling awkward and shy.

Silence fell between them.

Jessie glanced at her watch. 'Shouldn't be long before a tram comes along.'

'No, they're pretty frequent,' making a show of looking up the road.

Suddenly Tommy laughed, startling Jessie. 'I'll never forget Lena's expression as she got up off the deck after you'd hit her. It was priceless!'

'One night out with a Teddy Boy and already I'm thumping folk,' she replied, and then regretted her words when she saw the expression on his face. 'I'm sorry, Tommy,' she whispered, 'I didn't mean it like that.'

'Well, as I said before, we do live in two different worlds, don't we?'

'Yes, I guess we do.'

He lit a cigarette, striking the match, viciously almost, against the box. 'What's that expression? East is East and West is West and never the twain shall meet?'

'Kipling,' she mumbled.

'Whoever, I suppose they're right. We're not kids any more, are we?'

She studied him in the glow of his cigarette. There was still something in him that reminded her of the Tommy of old.

'I don't suppose there's any point in asking you out again, you'd only refuse.'

Did she want to see him again? She looked into his eyes. She was being mad, she thought, he was a Teddy Boy! But he wasn't only a Teddy Boy, he was Tommy – the same Tommy who'd once saved her life, the Tommy for whom she'd had a deep affection. *Still* had a deep affection, she corrected herself.

'How about next Friday, same time same place?' she suggested.

He stared at her hard, then nodded. 'That's fine by me.'

'I'll look forward to it then.'

'Me too.'

When the tram came he kissed her quickly on the lips. It was a somewhat gauche kiss, which pleased her. She'd have bet a week's wages he'd never kissed Lena like that.

The tenements in Boyd Street were made of red sandstone rather than the usual grey. The street itself was long and lowering. Despite the time of year, wifeys were hanging out the windows, chatting to one another and watching the passing scene. A host of ragged children played on the pavements and in the gutters.

They came to Tommy's close and started up the stairs. It was early Saturday evening, and Tommy and Jessie had been going out together for a month now. She was on her way to have tea with him and Jeannie. It was the first time she'd been to his house in Boyd Street and the first time she'd met Jeannie since Millbrae Crescent.

Tonight Jessie was wearing a black knee-length skirt, a lilac blouse and black tinted nylons. It was hardly full Teddy Girl gear, but enough to help her blend in more easily with the Cameo crowd. She and Tommy were off to the Cameo after their tea.

The McBrides' room and kitchen was three stairs up and on the left of the landing. He let them in with a large iron key that was almost medieval in appearance. They found Jeannie dozing in a chair by the fire. An appetizing smell filled the tiny home.

Jeannie woke with a start when Tommy banged the door closed. 'Oh, there you are,' she said, quickly getting to her feet. 'I was just resting my eyes for a minute.'

'Do you always snore when you're resting your eyes?' Tommy teased.

She was about to protest, but then she saw the grin on his face. 'Ach, you,' she said fondly. And then she turned her attention to Jessie. 'Just look at you,' she said, taking every inch of Jessie in. 'What a handsome young woman you've turned out to be.'

Jessie found herself unexpectedly overwhelmed with emotion. The years dissolved away, and she was back in Millbrae Crescent with Jeannie's warm voice telling her that everything was going to be all right. 'It's so good to see you again, Mrs McBride,' she choked out at last. 'It really is . . . I . . . I . . .'

Tommy looked from one to the other. Both women were close to tears. 'Do I smell something burning?' he asked in mock horror, winking at Jessie.

'My stew!' cried Jeannie, rushing to the cooker. She was peering frantically into the pots on the stove when Tommy's laughter stopped her. 'All right, my joker,' she said, laughing herself, 'just for that you can help me get the table laid.'

'Oh, no,' interrupted Jessie. 'Let me.'

While she helped Jeannie get things ready she took in the McBride's new surroundings as surreptitiously as she could. It was a far cry from Millbrae Crescent, that was for sure. It was small and cramped and decorated not out of taste and money but out of necessity. If the house in Millbrae Crescent symbolized limitless opportunities and comfort, then the rooms on Boyd Street symbolized a lifetime of struggle and hardship. And yet, as she watched Jeannie bustling around the tiny room it came to Jessie that Jeannie McBride was far happier here than she had been in Millbrae Crescent. The nervousness and unease were gone, she was home at last. But Tommy wasn't. Although he'd never said a word to her, it was obvious from the way he'd strode down the street with her – obvious from the way he dressed and from the anger that was always there in him, just below the surface – that he resented being back, resented the stigma and the squalor.

They had a homey tea of stew and boiled potatoes and homemade scones. Jeannie made a few polite inquiries about Battlefield, but it was clear to Jessie that she wasn't at all interested, and had blocked out Battlefield and its memories as best she could. Then, when Tommy got up to rake the fire, she suddenly asked, 'And how are you getting on with Tommy's crowd? They're a bit different to what you're used to, I'd guess.'

'More than a bit!' Jessie laughed.

Tommy came back to the table. 'There's nothing wrong with them,' he said, frowning. 'They're good sorts, all of them.'

'I wasn't criticizing,' Jessie said softly.

'You better not,' said Tommy with a wink to his mother, 'or they'll be after you with chains.'

Jessie ignored him and went on to Jeannie. 'Let's just say that as long as I'm with Tommy they're prepared to put up with me.'

'Aye,' said Jeannie. 'I know what you mean.' Although she would never say anything to Tommy, she didn't approve of his winching Jessie. If living in Millbrae Crescent had taught her anything, it was that people should stay where they belonged. No good came, in her mind, in putting yourself above your place. As much as she liked Jessie, she couldn't see that anything would come of her and Tommy other than more pain and grief.

'And she puts up with *them*,' Tommy chipped in.

She leaned across the table and gave him a playful punch. 'It's you I put up with,' she laughed.

As soon as the table was cleared and the dishes done, Jeannie went off to visit a friend whose husband was working the late shift. 'She's expecting her fifth,' Jeannie explained, 'and she doesn't like to be alone all night.'

Jessie sat down in the chair by the fire.

'I'm just going to get washed and changed before we go out,' Tommy said, pointing at the sink. 'I'm afraid Boyd Street doesn't run to private baths.'

He boiled a kettle, poured the contents into the basin of the sink, and took off his shirt.

Jessie, who'd been chatting to him while he made his preparations, caught her breath. His body was marked

151

by four ugly scars, three cutting across his chest, and another along his left shoulder blade. Besides the old wounds, his upper arms were decorated with tattoos; a large spider on the left and crossed hatchets dripping blood on the right. It was the scars that made her shudder. She watched him as he washed, unable to take her eyes from his mutilated torso. At last, as he began to dry himself, she asked gently, 'How did you get those, then?'

'These here,' he said, pointing to his chest, 'were from a little argument with a fellow with a knife. The other one wasn't as civilized, that one was done with a broken bottle.'

Her eyes stayed on the jagged marks. 'It must have been very painful . . .'

He laughed at her concern. 'It hurt them a lot more than it hurt me,' he joked.

But instead of joining in his laughter, she got up and came slowly towards him. Very gently, she touched the scar on his shoulder blade. The hardness of it made her shiver. Slowly, almost delicately, she ran her finger along its length. 'Poor you,' she whispered, her breath warm against his skin. 'Poor you . . .'

Suddenly, she was in his arms, their lips meeting in a kiss that left them alone in the universe, their bodies pressed against one another in a yearning embrace. A passion she had never known before burned through her like a fever. All she knew at that moment was that she wanted his lips on hers, wanted his hands on her body – wanted him.

And then, just as suddenly, he gave a muffled exclamation and pulled himself away.

She stared at him in amazement. 'Tommy . . .'

He picked up the towel he'd dropped and ran it over his face. He was still breathing heavily. 'I'm sorry,' he mumbled from under cover of the towel. 'I . . . I forgot that you're not like the others.'

'What do you mean I'm not like the others? That I'm not as attractive to you? That I'm . . .'

He threw the towel onto the counter and laid a finger on her lips. 'I mean you're special, that's what I mean.'

'But I'm a woman, too,' she whispered, her voice close to breaking. 'I . . . I've never been with anyone since Alec. But you . . . with you . . .'

'I don't care about where you've been, Jessie,' he said, his fingers now tenderly stroking her cheek. 'But I do care about where you're going. You've always been special to me, you know. Always. I'm too close to having my dreams come true to want to rush things now.'

She held his hand still with her own. There was a glint of tears in her eyes. 'You're kind of special yourself, Tommy McBride,' she said.

It was New Year's Eve and the Cameo was in full swing. The band, new to the Cameo, was called the Rocking Quiffs. Their singer wore a drape with gold thread interwoven through it, and a Mohawk haircut, the entire head shaved except for a central strip of hair.

Jessie was sitting in one of the side booths with Tommy, watching the band, and thinking about the conversation she'd had half an hour before with the sax player during the break. She'd been surprised to learn how much money there was in rock bands. She'd never realized that a band could be more than a hobby, it could be a living as well.

Her thoughts were interrupted by a commotion at the main door. Excited and angry voices could be heard above the din of the band.

Tommy came to his feet as Jack, the same Jack who'd been at The Black Raven with Tommy when he'd rescued Jessie, was hustled towards him. Instantly his expression became grim. Jack's face was bright with blood, and his right ear partially torn from the side of his head.

'He's been whipped with a bike chain,' said one of the Teds who was holding Jack up.

'And had a couple of bad strokes from a razor,' added the other.

The band stopped playing. Tommy helped the others lay Jack down on the seat of the booth.

'He was dumped outside from a car, just like you see in those Yankee gangster movies,' a Ted called Vince said.

'A Zephyr. I saw it speeding off, but not who was inside,' Vince's girlfriend added.

Tommy leaned over his stricken friend. 'Jack! Jack! Can you hear me?' Jack moaned. 'Ken Young said I was to give you his regards,' he mumbled, and then he passed out.

Jessie guessed that the facial injuries weren't the only ones Jack had received. He'd probably been given a kicking as well. 'We need to get him to a hospital, and fast,' she said.

Tommy looked hesitant. 'Now, Tommy,' she urged. 'Right now.'

One of the Teds said he had a motor outside; he'd be glad to take Jack. Immediately, Jack was gently lifted and carried back out the way he'd just come.

Jessie could see from Tommy's expression what he intended to do.

'Tommy,' she said, grabbing hold of his arm. 'Listen to me before you do anything foolish.'

Tommy was white with fury. He barely felt her hand gripping him, all he could think of was revenge. His plan was to get Boyd Street Boys, and as many 'friendlies' who would come with them, and go straight to The Black Raven to have it out with Ken Young and his lads.

'Can't you see this is a set-up?' she asked, making him look at her. 'Strike back now and you'll be doing exactly as Young wants.'

Tommy blinked. 'What do you mean?'

'Go charging over to The Black Raven now and they'll be waiting for you. You'll be walking right into their trap.

Tommy forced himself to cool down, to think clearly

154

and rationally. She was right, of course. Doing over Jack and then dumping him outside the Cameo was a come on. It had to be.

Ken Young would have a host of Teds over at The Black Raven waiting the arrival of the Boyd Street Boys. Young wouldn't make a move like this unless ke knew he had them outnumbered. Well, he wasn't going to let Young call the tune. *He* would do that. When the Boyd Street Boys exacted revenge for what had been done to Jack it would be at a time and place of his own choosing.

He put his arm around her fondly. 'You can stop looking so worried,' he chided. 'You win. It would be suicide to do anything tonight. But Ken Young's going to be bloody sorry for what he did this Hogmanay.' His eyes were far away. 'Bloody sorry.'

That night Jessie lay in bed, staring at the ceiling. But it wasn't the shadowy ceiling she was seeing, it was a vivid picture of the forthcoming fight between the Boyd Street Boys and Ken Young's Teds. And there in the thick of it was her Tommy, the enemy swarming all around, each one of them trying to do his worst to Tommy. She shuddered to think what the bloody outcome might be.

If only she could stop the fight taking place. There had to be a way, some ruse or argument she could come up with.

Dawn found her still wide awake and wracking her brains.

Jessie and Tommy were in the Seaforth Bar, around the corner from the Cameo. They were having a quiet drink at her suggestion.

'I really don't understand why you feel you have to fight Young,' Jessie said, changing the conversation.

Tommy stared at her in astonishment. What was she havering on about now? 'Because of what has been done

155

to Jack,' he replied, his tone condescending at having to explain the obvious.

Jessie ran a finger round the rim of her glass. 'All Ken Young was doing was retaliating for what you did to him that night in The Black Raven. You were there for a laugh at his expense, and he repaid it by having Jack beaten. So why don't you just leave it at that. As it stands at the moment, the pair of you are quits.'

'And what about Jack?'

'Getting more of your boys cut up isn't going to change what happened to Jack.'

'No, but cutting up Young and his lads would.'

She laid a hand on top of his. 'You had your laugh, then Young had his. So now you're even. Leave it like that, don't escalate matters,' she begged.

'Young would have escalated matters by having us go to The Black Raven after Jack was done over,' Tommy persisted.

'But you didn't go, so nothing happened.'

There were times when Jessie infuriated him, and this was one of them. He gave a long sigh of frustration. Arguing with her was like arguing with a brick wall. 'You just don't understand,' he said, and took a swig of his beer.

She waited patiently till he'd put his glass back on the table. 'The trouble with you is you can't bear not to come out on top. A draw isn't good enough for you, you have to be a winner,' she said angrily.

Tommy glared at her. Her analysis was absolutely correct, but he certainly wasn't going to give her the satisfaction of admitting it. 'I can't call it quits, the others wouldn't allow it. One of us has been hurt, so we've got to hit back. It's as simple as that.'

'Since when do you take orders from them?' She knew she'd got through to him when she saw him colour. It might have been a beneath the belt blow, but it had worked. When he didn't reply she went on. 'Sometimes the hardest thing of all to do is nothing, Sweet Fanny

156

Adams. You've told me often enough how fond you are of the Boyd Street Boys, right?'

Tommy nodded slowly.

'You fight Ken Young and his Teds and how many of the Boys are going to end up in hospital? Broken arms, legs, mangled faces, gouged out eyes, maybe even some of them dead.'

'We're Teds, and Teds fight, it's part of the creed.'

'You may think it's manly to do that, but I don't. It would be far more manly not to force this fight, to have the strength and guts to say enough is enough, let's call a halt while it's all square.'

'I've told you, I can't call this fight off.' he replied stubbornly.

'So you're nothing more than a figurehead who takes orders from his own men.'

'I'm nothing of the sort!'

'Then if you're the leader, damn well lead. Save your friends from what's in store for them if they go up against Young.'

'I'm not a coward.'

Jessie leaned towards him urgently. 'Only a brave man will do what he thinks is right over what he knows is popular.'

Tommy stared at her. Could he convince the Boys to leave the situation as it was and not seek revenge for Jack? It was a hell of a challenge but the more he thought about it the more sense it made.

'You were aye God Squad Jessie,' he said after a while. Their laughter echoed through the bar.

It was early Friday evening and the Reverend Kenneth Gray was writing the first draft of his sermon for that Sunday. The theme was 'Man's Inhumanity to Man.'

Jessie was sitting over from him sipping a cup of coffee. When she finished that she intended going up to her room to get dressed. She was meeting Tommy in just

157

over an hour and a half. She was thinking about the new, bright pink lipstick she'd bought that lunchtime, and hoping Tommy liked it.

The Reverend paused in what he was doing to glance across at Jessie. She'd been different of late, a lot happier, and he wondered why. As he sat gazing at her a possible explanation came to him.

'Is it the dancing again tonight?' he asked.

'Yes, Dad,' she smiled.

'Seeing someone special, are you?'

She immediately became wary, what on earth had prompted him to ask that? Had she been seen with Tommy? Had something been said?

'Why should I be seeing anyone special?' she replied as casually as she could.

So he was right! The minister gave himself a mental pat on the back for his powers of deduction. He then explained how he'd arrived at that conclusion. It was a relief to know he was talking in the general, and not the particular. Her secret was still safe.

She faked a blush, then put on a coy look, giving the impression she was embarrassed to discuss the subject.

'Did you meet him at Whitecraigs?' her father continued.

'Yes,' she lied, mumbling into her cup.

The Reverend Gray nodded his satisfaction. If the lad went to Whitecraigs he must come from a good family, Jessie would be all right there. 'Perhaps you'd like to bring him to the house one day so your mother and I could be introduced?' he suggested.

She'd better get out of here before this went any further, Jessie thought. With a quick gulp she finished her coffee, and rose from her chair. 'I'll do that when I think he's ready for the third degree. If he's ever ready for the third degree,' she answered, making a joke of it.

After Jessie had left the room the minister wondered what the lad's name was, he'd forgotten to ask.

* * *

Ken Young was sitting in the Bluebird cafe moodily stirring his espresso. What was wrong with that bastard McBride? What did he have to do to get a reaction? When the Jack Gowrie business hadn't provoked McBride he'd engineered more proddings, but none of them had worked either.

He licked his spoon, and thought of how much he hated Tommy McBride. Partly it was a chemistry. He just had to be in McBride's presence to experience the almost overwhelming urge to banjo the bastard. But over and above that he hated McBride because Tommy was the only other serious contender for the position he saw as justly his, King of the Glasgow Teds.

He wanted McBride destroyed, and the Boyd Street Boys along with him, for he knew they would never give allegiance to any other than one of their own.

Ken Young's scowl deepened, as he recalled the time in The Black Raven when McBride had not only called him a toerag and told him to piss off, but stolen away the bitch who'd been refusing to dance with him, and whom he'd just been about to sort out.

To add insult to injury, McBride had not only stolen the bird away but had taken up winching her. From what he'd heard the two of them were now thick as could be.

Slowly, a smile spread across Ken Young's face. Now there was a thought, a right humdinger of one!

Jessie was re-stocking the sheet music when her boss came over. 'There's a personal telephone call for you in my office,' Mr Elvin said frostily. The receiving of personal calls wasn't forbidden, but it wasn't exactly encouraged either. The unspoken rule was that any calls had to be extremely important.

'Is it my mother or father?' Jessie asked anxiously, thinking that something might have happened at home.

'Neither. It's a *young* girl,' Mr Elvin replied crisply.

Puzzled, Jessie thanked him, and hurried to his office at

the rear of the shop. Could it be Lizzie Dunnachie? Lizzie's voice was hardly that of a young girl. Wondering, she picked up the receiver.

It wasn't Lizzie, but a lassie she didn't know who said she worked alongside Tommy. 'He can't come to the telephone himself, so he's asked me to ring instead. He says it's urgent he speaks with you before you go home the night, and he's given me an address where he wants to meet you directly after your work.'

The arrangement had been for Jessie to meet Tommy later on, to go dancing at the Cameo. Something must have come up and he was going to cancel their date, Jessie thought. She smiled, it was just like Tommy to want to tell her in person rather than have it done by someone else over the telephone.

'What's the address?' She jotted it down on a pad, and then jotted down the directions as well. It wasn't a street she knew.

She thanked the lassie and hung up, then seeing that Mr Elvin was busy with a customer, she made a hasty call to Battlefield to say she'd be late back and not to wait tea for her.

Jessie frowned. Linton Street was deserted, the tenements on either side were derelict. No smoke came from any of the chimneys, and many of the windows were boarded up. It was a condemned street waiting to be pulled down, she realized with a sudden rush of fear. Had she got it wrong? Was there more to this than Tommy merely cancelling their date? Was he in some sort of trouble? It was certainly a peculiar place for a rendezvous.

She hurried through the drizzling rain, her shoes resounding on the worn cobbles. She found the close number she was seeking half way down the street on the right hand side. The more she wandered in this deserted place, the more apprehensive she became. There was no name plate on the peeling brown door. The bell pull was long gone, either stolen for scrap or vandalized. She knocked and waited, convinced now that Tommy was in some sort of trouble.

She heard the tread of footsteps, then the door swung open.

'Surprise, surprise!' smiled Ken Young.

Jessie froze in shock. Only when Ken Young moved did she, but it was too late, and she was too slow. He grabbed her before she'd even got off the landing. She screamed as his strong arms encircled her, pinioning her own to her sides. With the struggling, still screaming, Jessie locked tightly in his grasp, Ken congratulated himself. His plan had worked a fair treat, and it was so simple. But then all the best plans were.

'You might as well stop screaming, there's no one to hear you. Except me that is,' he crooned sadistically. Lifting her up, he carried her into the damp and musty smelling house.

Jessie was propelled into the first bedroom they came to. He threw her right across the room to bang against the opposite wall. She fell to the floor and before she could pick herself up again heard the click of a padlock outside the door which had been slammed shut behind her. Seconds later the main house door also slammed shut. An eerie silence descended through the house. She knew it was useless, but tried the bedroom door anyway. The padlock she'd heard clicking closed held it fast.

The solitary window was partially boarded, but moonlight and street light streamed in through the unboarded part. A quick check showed that, four flights up and with a straight drop to the street below, there was no escape in that direction. Terrified, she looked around her. The bedroom was a ruin, the floor littered with old newspapers, rusty tins and other rubbish. Someone had defecated in a corner and covered the mess with a sheet of newspaper. The stink was nauseating. The only furniture was an ancient iron bed that had a couple of tattered blankets over its stained and ripped mattress.

161

After a while, Jessie sat on the bed, which was preferable to sitting on the floor, not allowing herself to imagine what would happen next.

Hours later, she heard laughing voices out on the landing. One of them she recognized as Ken Young's. She listened to the sound of the main door opening, then the scrape of a key in the padlock securing the bedroom door.

They'd been at the bevy, she could smell it the moment they entered the bedroom. Besides Ken Young there were four others, all Teds, all drunk, all loud, all menacing. Young held aloft a lighted storm lantern, casting weird dancing shadows around the room. 'And how are you hen?' he leered.

Jessie didn't answer. Fear was making her heart pound so loudly she was sure they could hear it.

'You're right Ken, she's not bad at all,' crowed one of the Teds.

Ken Young laughed without a trace of humour. 'I'm going to really enjoy this, so I am. Get her lads!'

The other four Teds swooped on Jessie and threw her backwards on to the bed, holding her down. She knew then, without a shadow of a doubt, what they intended next.

Ken Young sauntered over, ripping her clothes until she was completely exposed.

'Now that's what I call lovely,' he crooned, roughly handling her breasts. 'Don't you boys agree?'

This wasn't happening, it was a nightmare from which she was going to awake at any second. 'You're nothing but a pack of animals,' she screamed.

Young's hand lashed out to crack across her cheek, knocking her head sideways. Her head was knocked the other way when he hit her again.

'Watch this lads, I'll show you how an expert does it,' he boasted to the others. 'And then you can all have a turn.'

★　★　★

Lena McGurk was about to go into the Cameo when a Zephyr came screeching to a halt at the pavement. A door flew open, a bundle came rolling out, then the car was away again, peeling off down the road and out of sight.

There was a dull ache between Jessie's legs, and she felt as if every last ounce of energy had been drained from her body. Dimly, she became aware of Lena staring down at her, then Lena was kneeling by her side and talking, but she couldn't quite understand the words.

The girl from the cash desk came hurrying across, 'Go get Tommy, and hurry!' Lena ordered, taking off her cardigan and throwing it over Jessie's half-naked body.

Tommy was lounging against a pillar, watching the dancers, when the girl from the cash desk appeared by his side. One look at her face told him something was wrong.

He'd waited half an hour for Jessie at the tramstop where they'd arranged to meet. When she hadn't shown, he'd assumed she'd had to cancel and not been able to tell him, or else, for some reason or other, was going to be late, in which case she'd make her own way to the Cameo. Although nothing like that had ever happened before, it hadn't worried him. It had just never crossed his mind that something might have happened to her.

Tommy came thundering out into the street with a posse of Boyd Street Boys behind him. He stopped abruptly when he saw Jessie lying there, her head in Lena's lap.

He didn't have to ask her what had happened.

'It was Ken Young,' Lena said. 'I saw him clear as I'm seeing you. They dumped her from the same motor they dumped Jack from.'

'Have they hurt her?' Tommy demanded kneeling beside her.

Lena didn't say what she suspected. 'She's not been marked,' she assured him. 'And there are no bones broken.'

163

Tommy gently scooped Jessie into his arms and carried her to the foyer. The manager told him to take Jessie into his office where there was a fire and bottle.

By this time most of those inside had come crowding out into the foyer which was jam packed as a result. Tommy shouted to be let through, and followed the manager to his office.

Tommy heeled the office door closed behind him, then laid Jessie on the chaise longue that was drawn up beside the blazing fire. He muttered his thanks when the manager handed him a large glass of whisky for Jessie. 'I'll leave you two alone,' said the manager softly, and immediately left the room.

Tommy stroked Jessie's forehead. She was hot and feverish. He lifted her head and put the glass to her lips, but she moaned that she didn't want any. Well, he certainly did.

She was reviving quickly, thanks to the heat of the room and Tommy's presence.

'So what happened?' Tommy asked quietly at last.

She didn't want to tell him, knew she shouldn't, but the sheer horror of what she'd been through overcame her and the words came spilling out.

When Jessie was finally finished, she started to shake. Tommy, tears streaming down his face, clasped her to him and held her there.

'You mustn't retaliate, it's another set-up,' she sobbed.

'Aye, I know that,' he replied in a whisper.

He couldn't bear to think of what had been done to Jessie. There were no words to express the depth of his outrage. One thing he knew for certain, he was going to do his damnedest to make Ken Young pay for the violation of his Jessie, his Star. He held her tightly until she fell into an exhausted sleep.

Tommy covered her with a travelling rug that had been over the back of a chair and poured himself another large dram.

There was a sink in the corner where he washed his

face. When he'd towelled that dry he took another dram, after which he kissed Jessie on the cheek.

Then he went looking for Ken Young.

They came out of the night to descend on The Black Raven, forty-nine Boyd Street Boys and 'friendlies' with Tommy at their head, all carrying weapons.

There was music playing inside The Black Raven, but the music was muted, almost hushed. Outside the dancehall's front entranceway stood a lone figure, that of a wee boy of maybe ten or twelve.

'Which one of youse is Tommy McBride? I have a message for him' the wee boy's voice quavered.

Tommy stepped forward to stand towering over the small child. 'I'm McBride, what's the message?'

The boy licked his lips. 'I'm no part o' any of this, mister. Kenny gave me half a sheet to deliver the message, and that's why I'm doing it. I'm not involved.'

Tommy nodded that he understood.

'Not here, Kenny says it's too public. He says he'll be waiting for you and yours at Linton Street. Do you know where that is?'

Linton Street! Where Jessie had told him they'd taken her. 'I know,' Tommy replied evenly.

'That's it, then,' and the wee boy scurried away.

Linton Street, it was a fitting venue for what was going to happen, Tommy thought.

'Let's go,' he ordered, and he and the other forty-eight disappeared back into the night.

Jessie came awake with a start. She'd been dreaming she was in that awful bedroom again with Ken Young and the four others, only this time it *had been* a nightmare.

'Tommy?' she called out blearily.

'Tommy's gone, I'm to look after you,' said a voice close by.

165

Jessie struggled onto an elbow to discover Lena sitting on a chair by the chaise longue. 'Gone where?' she demanded, a new fear chasing the last traces of sleep.

Lena evaded the question. 'Tommy told me to take you home by taxi when you were fit enough to travel,' she answered instead.

'How long was I asleep?'

'An hour, maybe a little longer.'

'Has he gone alone or with the Boys?' Jessie asked. Lena's evasiveness had told her what she wanted to know.

Lena could see that Jessie had guessed what the situation was. There was no point in lying further. 'All of them.'

Jessie knew then what she had to do.

'You can call that taxi now,' she said, getting to her feet.

Ken Young stood directly in front of the house where he and his boys had raped Jessie. Every so often he grinned at the memory.

Young already knew that this time he'd been successful and that Tommy was on his way. Word had been phoned through from The Black Raven. Not long now and McBride and the Boyd Street Boys would be destroyed, leaving him uncontested King of the Glasgow Teds. He might even have a coronation, he thought. A coronation at The Black Raven! Aye, he liked that idea, King of the Glasgow Teds.

'They're coming!' a voice warned urgently

Ken Young reached for the bayonet he had tucked into the waistband of his drainies.

The night editor of the *Scottish Daily Record* was reading through copy about a small blaze in a bonded warehouse just off St Enoch Square when he was handed a note. A glance at the note, from a regular and thoroughly reliable outside source, caused him to raise an eyebrow in interest.

In two straight lines running down from his own desk were those of the reporters. Spying John Cameron staring off into space, he shouted to Cameron that he had an assignment for him.

A few minutes later John Cameron and photographer Fraser Tulloch hurriedly left the *Scottish Daily Record* building for Linton Street.

Tommy and his contingent stopped when they came in sight of the army of Teds waiting for them. They were well outnumbered, but they'd known they'd be.

'Just remember, unless I go down Ken Young is mine,' Tommy said in a loud, clear voice. He gazed down Linton Street. To actually see the place where Jessie had been raped further fuelled his already awesome anger.

Somewhere in the far distance a police siren sounded, its harsh wail rupturing the stillness of the night.

Tommy moved forward, and his people with him. As they neared Ken Young additional enemy Teds swarmed out of the closes nearest Young to swell Young's numbers even more.

'I'm claiming you!' Tommy yelled at Ken Young.

And with that battle was joined.

Jessie moved in her seat nervously as the taxi sped through Glasgow. Getting into the taxi, she'd told Lena that she'd left her purse behind in the manager's office, and Lena had immediately volunteered to return and get it for her. The moment Lena had vanished, Jessie had passed the driver five bob and told him to leave right away, and that their destination was now Linton Street, not Battlefield Central Church. It was Lena who'd found out where the big fight was to take place, although Jessie didn't know how.

As the taxi turned into Linton Street the driver swore and stamped on the brake, bringing the cab to a screeching halt. There were Teds fighting everywhere. 'This is as far as I go,' growled the man. 'And I'm not waiting.'

Jessie jumped from the taxi, handed the driver a pound note, and told him not to bother about change. He did an incredibly fast, reverse three-point turn, then roared off back the way he'd come.

Jessie recognized one of the Boyd Street Boys, Sammy McGlinchie, lying in an ever widening pool of blood that was coming from a knife wound in his side.

Another Ted, an enemy, was hunched against a lamp-post clutching his face that had been cut in ribbons, keening in agony.

But where was Tommy? That was all that interested Jessie as she dodged between the countless individual fights that were going on, too obsessed with finding him to be afraid.

Razors flashed, bicycle chains swished, lead pipes filled with cement thudded, and occasionally a bottle shattered. Some fought in silence, others howled and shrieked, and one of the combatants, his nose spread flat across his face, was actually laughing.

She raced on, interested in only one thing. And then there was Tommy, back to a tenement wall, Ken Young prostrate at his feet, fighting off three who were attacking him simultaneously. Tommy had a small hatchet in his right hand while his left was encased in bloody knucklers.

It happened quickly, one second Tommy was still upright, the next he'd lost his footing and gone down with a jarring thump.

No thought went into Jessie's reaction, no conscious decision. She saw her man in desperate trouble, and leapt to his defence. As she ran, she bent and snatched up a half brick that had already been used in the fight. Tommy was still fending off his opponents, though flat on his back. She took a deep breath and hit the nearest Ted on the head with the brick. To her surprise, he crumpled, senseless, to the ground.

The smaller of Tommy's remaining attackers whirled on Jessie, his flick knife raised in a stabbing position. Jessie's long nails desperately swept the length of his face, making trails of blood from forehead to chin. The Ted made a lunge with his knife, but she neatly side-stepped the descending blade.

A length of chain whistled towards Tommy's neck. He managed to catch it around the handle of his hatchet, and wrench it from the last Ted's grasp. A solid kick took the Ted full in the crotch.

Jessie's Ted, blood obscuring his vision, blundered after her, his knife hand lancing out again and again at the ever moving shadow he knew to be her.

Tommy despatched his Ted with a side blow of the hatchet, then he turned on Jessie's assailant, punching viciously at him with his knucklers. The boy pitched headlong to the pavement.

Jessie flew into Tommy's arms.

'It's all over. Drop your weapons, son,' a voice commanded.

Tommy looked up to find he and Jessie were surrounded by police, all with truncheons drawn.

Tommy gazed round him. There were Black Marias at either end of Linton Street, while the street itself was overrun with bobbies.

Tommy released his hatchet and knucklers which fell to the ground beside the stricken Ken Young who was still unconscious, badly wounded from the hatcheting Tommy had given him.

He brought his attention back to Jessie, who was clinging to him as though she would never let him go.

'I love you,' he whispered.

'And I love you.'

He held her close. She laid her head on a shoulder, closed her eyes, and thanked God that she'd been in time, that he was safe. She was filled with so much joy and love

169

that she felt she might burst with it. Nothing mattered. Not the police, not her parents, nothing mattered but them.

She looked up into his face, and he kissed her with all the passion in his heart.

A flashbulb popped. It was Fraser Tulloch taking their picture.

'You and I forever,' Tommy whispered when the kiss was over.

'Forever,' she agreed. Arm in arm, Jessie and Tommy were led to the nearest Black Maria. Ragged cheer after cheer from the Boyd Street Boys, still standing followed their progress.

'Who are they?' John Cameron asked one of the Boys.

'That's Tommy McBride, our leader and undisputed King of the Glasgow Teds.'

'King of the Glasgow Teds!' John Cameron breathed, already visualizing the words in print.

Jessie was sharing a cell with a prostitute and a middle-aged, middle-class woman held for shoplifting who kept saying over and over that it was all a horrible mistake.

The night had been long and bitterly cold. Jessie had done her best to sleep on the palliasse she'd been given, but thoughts of all that had happened had kept her restless.

There was a rattle of keys at the door, and a policeman appeared, bringing their dinner.

'About effing time, too!' snarled the prostitute, grabbing the first tray.

Jessie was not due up before the beak until the afternoon, but she knew that Tommy and the others had been scheduled for the morning session.

'Any idea what Tommy McBride got?' she asked the policeman anxiously.

'Two years,' he said shortly.

My God, Jessie thought. Two years was an eternity.

'You're famous now, quite the celebrity,' the police-man said suddenly, and handed her a folded copy of the *Scottish Daily Record* along with her tray.

Jessie laid the tray on the floor, then shook open the paper. The page 1 headline and the picture beneath it made her gasp.

The King and Queen of the Glasgow Teds screamed the headline in thick black type. Beneath it was a picture of her and Tommy kissing, Tommy's clenched and bloody fist draped around her neck. The accompanying story was a hair raising account of the fight that had occurred in Linton Street. Thankfully, no one had been killed, although apparently in several instances it had been a near thing. Ken Young, described as the leader of the North Glasgow Teds, a name John Cameron had invented, was reported to have multiple wounds and severe concussion.

Queen of the Glasgow Teds! Good Lord! She dreaded to think what her mother and father were going to say. The family didn't take the *Record*, but sure as eggs were eggs some 'friend' in the congregation would bring it to their attention.

The minister and his wife were on their knees praying when Jessie arrived home. As she entered the room, both glanced up to give her an accusatory stare.

After hearing Jessie's full story, it had been abundantly clear to the beak, an astute, wise, and widely experienced man, that she wasn't the wild Teddy Girl the *Scottish Daily Record* had made her out to be. In sentencing her he'd taken into consideration the circumstances which had both caused and brought her to the fight, as well as the fact that she came from a good family and had never been in trouble before.

However, regardless of the whys and wherefores, she had actually taken part in what the newspapers were describing as The Battle of Linton Street, and had been observed hitting an opponent with a brick. He therefore sentenced her to six months, sentence suspended.

She'd been overwhelmed with relief. Now, seeing her parents, she knew that her relief had been false.

The Reverend Gray got to his feet.

'Pack what you wish to take, then leave this house for all time,' he said, looking at her as though he didn't know her.

Jessie turned to her mother.

'How could you?' Alison whispered. 'After all we've done for you?'

'Tommy McBride of all people, a criminal just like his father,' he continued bitterly. 'You're no daughter of mine. You belong with the scum.'

In her mind's eye, Jessie saw a piece of string and scissors. The scissors opened and closed, and what had been one piece of string was now two. That was her relationship with her parents. Up until then she'd been part of the family, one with them. Now she was separate, for ever.

'I think you should know that I love Tommy,' Jessie said in a still voice. 'And he loves me.'

'How can you love someone who's no more than a common thug?' Alison asked scornfully. 'Don't you realize that your father could lose his job over this?'

What small people they really were, Jessie thought. When she was young, she'd seen her parents as giants, while in reality they were pygmies.

'There was a time I would have bent over backwards to save Dad's job, but not now. I know it's a strange thing to say after all the years he's been one, but I can't help wondering if he didn't make a mistake in becoming a minister.' And with that, she went upstairs to pack.

5

Jessie glanced at her wristwatch; it was only three minutes more to eleven a.m. Tommy was due to be released on the hour. He'd served eighteen months, with six months off for good behaviour.

Barlinne Prison was an evil place, you could smell it like some invisible, poisonous cloud.

She'd come alone, leaving Jeannie behind to cook the dinner. She'd been staying with her at Boyd Street since the day her parents threw her out. Jeannie had taken her in, given her Tommy's inset bed in the kitchen, and made her welcome. The pair of them had grown close over the long months of waiting.

Tommy was the last of the Boyd Street Boys to leave prison, but not the last of those who'd taken part in what was now widely known as The Battle of Linton Street, for there were still a handful of Ken Young's followers inside, those with previous records.

Ken Young himself had got out a few months back, a lot of the stuffing knocked out of him after his defeat by Tommy. Within a week of leaving the Bar-L, as Barlinne was often cried, he'd departed the city for London. Rumour had it he was running with a group of Willesden Teds.

Jessie frowned as she looked across to where half a dozen cars were parked. The Press had come in force to cover Tommy's release.

The small green door inset in the larger green one swung open, and Tommy McBride stepped out into the August sunshine.

He had a grey pallor, and was thin to the point of skin and bones. She hadn't noticed either of these things during the many times she'd visited him.

She walked hesitantly towards him, suddenly shy, although she couldn't think why that should be. Tommy was shy also, she could read it in his face, and that made everything all right somehow.

'Hello,' he said in a low voice.

Her answer was to move into his arms for the kiss she'd been dreaming of for so long.

He laid a hand against one of her cheeks, and momentarily closed his eyes. 'You don't know how good it is to be able to touch you again,' he whispered.

'Oh, but I do. You just wait and see.'

He smiled at her, a smile so warm and deep she felt she could have fallen in it and drowned.

His eyes flickered over her shoulder to take in the cars, and the reporters and photographers waiting expectantly by them.

'The Press have come to interview the newly released King of the Glasgow Teds, are you up to it?' she asked following his gaze.

'Do I have a choice?'

'I doubt it. They all appear the type that'd hound you till they got what they wanted.'

'Then let's get it over with. Then we can go home.'

Jessie waved to the pressmen, and they hurried over.

As soon as the photographers were close enough the flashbulbs began to pop.

The Boyd Street Boys had planned a welcome home party at the Cameo that night. They dressed in style for the party. Jessie, having decided to play the part she'd been given, had a brand new outfit she'd bought for the occasion. Tommy was wearing his best black drape, a gaucho string tie, and a thick black belt with a silver death's head buckle. Jessie a black pencil skirt, body hugging deep purple sweater, purple stilettoes and black mesh stockings.

She'd parted her hair down the middle, and combed it

to fall straight on either side. The other girls at the Cameo would have high, back-combed bouffants, but she preferred to be different. If she was a queen, she'd show it.

The Boyd Street Boys were standing in facing twin lines, with a corridor down the centre. The moment Tommy and Jessie appeared everyone began shouting, whistling, cheering and clapping.

Tommy and Jessie slowly made their way between the rows of Teds. Everyone wanted to shake their hands. After that, Jack Gowrie made a speech welcoming Tommy home. Tommy said a few words of thanks. Then the band struck up, and Tommy and Jessie led off the dancing.

It was about an hour later that the first strange Teds, from Balornock, appeared to offer fealty on their group's behalf. As the night wore on, though, more and more strange Teds arrived to pay fealty.

Perhaps they really were the King and Queen of the Glasgow Teds, she thought to herself.

The chimes of midnight found everyone well into the spirit of things. One of the band, guttered out of his skull, staggered off the rostrum to go and call for Ralph.

Tommy watched the sax player go, and had an idea. He turned to Jessie suddenly. 'I'll tell you what, if you'll play that saxophone up there I'll sing.'

Jessie stared at him in astonishment, wondering if he'd had even more than she'd thought. 'I didn't know you could sing.'

'I'm sure there are lots of things about me you don't know,' he answered, giving her a wink.

Jessie waited for the punchline, but none came. He really was serious. She glanced over at the saxophone; knowing how to play the clarinet meant she could also play that, but it had been so long since she'd had an instrument in her hands. She was bound to be rusty. The last thing she wanted was to make a fool of herself in front of all these folk.

'Are you scared?' Tommy whispered mischievously.

'I'm nothing of the sort,'

Tommy lurched to his feet and drew her to hers. 'Can you manage Rock Around The Clock?'

'Can you?'

His reply was to take her to the rostrum, jump onto it, and pull her up after him.

After a word with the band, Tommy faced the floor and gestured for silence. 'I've been saving my voice for the past year or so for an occasion like this,' he announced. 'And Jessie's going to be kind enough to drown out my mistakes with the sax.' The dancehall was filled with a veritable Hampden Roar of approval.

A wave of pleasure surged through her to be holding an instrument again. She didn't know why she'd given up playing since going to live in Boyd Street, she'd just never felt the urge. She did now though, the hunger to play suddenly revitalized within her.

A tapping of the feet, one, two, three, and they were away. Immediately, she felt herself take control, every cell of her body knowing exactly what to do.

The big surprise for her was Tommy's singing voice. Not only was it not bad it was better than good. It had character and sexuality, a rasping greyness that was Glasgow personified.

But, apart from his voice, what impressed Jessie was the way Tommy was handling himself, reaching out for the audience through his personality to grab them and make them listen. He was not only charismatic, he was a natural performer. What a transformation from the shy lad she'd first met at Queen's Park Senior Secondary, she thought with an inward grin.

The number finished to tumultuous applause, which only died down when Tommy started singing again, this time Johnnie 'Cry Guy' Ray's, 'Such A Night'. Jessie and the band went with him.

When it was finished Tommy moved over to Jessie who'd been standing a little apart from him: his eyes were glowing, as were hers.

176

'That was fab!' she said, and, realizing he hadn't heard because of the battering waves of applause that were reverberating round the dancehall, put her mouth to his ear and repeated herself.

He nodded, then put his mouth to her ear. 'I was going to ask you later on tonight, but why not here! Will you marry me?'

She was sure she hadn't heard him right. 'What?' she screamed.

'Will you marry me?' he shouted back.

In a million years she'd never have imagined a proposal like this. 'Yes,' she yelled. 'Yes, I will.'

Her acceptance was drowned by the noise, but that didn't matter to him, he could see what her answer had been.

Tommy faced the audience, held up his hands and kept them there till he finally had a semblance of quiet. 'I have an announcement to make,' he stated.

Jessie unhooked the sax and placed it in its case, then laid the lanyard alongside it. What a day it had been. Tommy out of prison, the party, and now his proposal! She felt lightheaded with joy.

'I first met Jessie here years ago,' Tommy was saying. 'And I think I knew even then that I wanted to marry her. Well tonight I've proposed, and she's accepted. We'll be getting wed just as soon as I can make the necessary arrangements.'

The cheering and applause was the loudest yet. Unable to help herself, Jessie burst into tears. It was hardly the thing for the Queen of the Glasgow Teds to do, but she didn't care about that. At last she knew that she'd been right to follow her heart. A new chapter in her life was beginning. A better chapter than any that had gone before.

Jeannie was already in bed, fast asleep. In the kitchen, where Jessie had been sleeping in Tommy's inset bed, some spare sheets and blankets had been put out. Jeannie had tactfully avoided any mention of new sleeping arrangements now that Tommy was back, and Jessie had seen no reason to bring them up either.

'I'll stick the kettle on,' Jessie said, suddenly feeling shy and awkward.

Tommy stood staring at the sheets and blankets, then nodded. 'Aye, that would be best. I'll make a bed up in Mum's room for myself,' he said.

'There's no need for that,' she said softly, her back to him so he couldn't see her face.

'We'll be married soon enough. After waiting for so long what's a wee while longer?'

She laid out the cups and saucers. 'Will you stop havering, Tommy? Do you love me or don't you?'

He blinked. 'Of course I do. I've told you!'

'And I love you, and we're to be married. We're already living in the same house together. It would be downright silly not to share the same bed.' She paused in what she was doing, her hands shaking. 'All right?' she whispered.

He came up behind her, his arms around her. 'All right.'

Jessie was on the tram coming home from work. Following The Battle of Linton Street, and her picture appearing in the paper, she'd been sacked from the music shop, Mr Elvin telling her sniffily that he had no place for the likes of her in his establishment.

It was Jeannie who'd come to the rescue. The job in the laundry was no great shakes, but it kept the wolf from the door, for which Jessie was grateful. She tended the counter with a woman called Jane Lamont.

As the tram rattled along Jessie was worrying about Tommy who'd been going to drop by his old place of employment that afternoon to find out if they'd take him back. He hadn't said anything, but she knew he hadn't been holding out any great hope, and in truth neither had she – not after the new pictures that had appeared in the newspapers the previous week, showing Tommy's release from Barlinne.

The trouble was that jobs were hard to come by, times weren't good in Glasgow, and hadn't been since the war. In some areas every street corner you passed had a gathering of lounging, unemployed men on it, just passing away the day.

Thank goodness she and Jeannie were grafting, even with Tommy to feed they could aye get by on what the pair of them brought in, but it would be far from a life of luxury, that was sure.

She'd bought a copy of that night's *Evening Citizen* and was glancing through it. An item on page 2 now caught her attention: 'Lady Virginia Muir, formerly Lady Virginia Dunbarr, and daughter of the Earl of Clyde, her husband, Mr A Muir, and young son Cosmo Muir, were murdered by the Mau Mau at their farm in Kenya. . .' Jessie read it through twice unable to believe her eyes. There were no real details, only that Alec, his wife and son had been the sole Europeans on their farm when the attack had occurred. They'd been buried on the farm where they'd died.

What a terrible thing to happen. She left the paper open on her lap. It was funny how life turned out so differently to what you'd imagined it would be. Everything had seemed so clear cut when she'd been young. Alec would be a minister; she, she'd hoped, his wife. Instead he'd married a titled lady and become an African farm manager, while she'd become Queen of the Glasgow Teds, living in a slum.

Who could have foreseen his death so many miles from home – or her new life a world away from her past?

Closing her eyes she offered up a prayer for the soul of Alec Muir.

★　　★　　★

She found Tommy sitting at home staring moodily into the empty grate. It was obvious what the outcome of his excursion into town had been.

'No luck, eh?' she said, giving him a sympathetic smile.

Tommy roused himself from his reverie. 'I thought the bastarding boss was going to shit himself when I strolled in through his door. He went green with fright.'

Jessie filled the kettle and put it on the stove. She always made the tea as Jeannie came in after her. Jeannie always washed and put away the dishes.

'You'd think I was Genghis Khan and Attila the Hun rolled into one,' Tommy muttered.

'That's probably how he now sees you,' Jessie said gently. This was just what she'd feared. She gave Tommy a sideways look. 'If he was so scared of you couldn't you have done a wee bit of not-so-subtle persuasion? Like cleaning you nails with a flickie as you requested employment for a second time?'

Tommy laughed. It was rich to hear Jessie suggesting such a thing. But then he knew she wasn't advocating he use violence, just hint that the possibility could be there; make his reputation work for him rather than against him.

'To be honest, I considered doing something like that, but what if it backfired and he called the police as soon as I'd left him? It wasn't worth the risk.'

'Aye,' she said. 'I know. Everything's harder now.'

'It's not that big a problem. I'll soon find a job elsewhere,' he said in a confident tone, but she could hear that it lacked conviction.

'Do you want to postpone the wedding until you get work?' she asked quietly.

In answer, he grabbed her to him, and sat her on his knee. 'Don't think you're getting out of marrying me as easily as that. A week on Saturday and it's down to Martha Street where it'll be ring and paper. It'll take The

Big Yin Himself to stop us getting spliced, I promise you.'

Later that night, they decided to treat themselves to a night out. They went into a pub for a couple of drinks and there decided to head for a club in the Broomielaw where they'd gone together several times before Tommy had been sent to Barlinne.

The Omar Khayyam – a pretentious name for a club Jessie had always thought – was a place where the arty set hung out. It served drinks and simple meals, and the babble of talk was usually about philosophy, literature or the theatre rather than music or sports.

At least that was how the Omar Khayyam had been the last time they'd been there, but in the intervening eighteen months all that had changed.

To begin with, the club had a new management who had gutted the premises from top to bottom. The mouldering Arabian décor had been replaced by Hessian wallpaper, a great deal of plastic, and spotlights that hung from the ceiling in clusters, making Jessie think that many-eyed monsters were peering down at her. The only thing about the club that remained the same was the name.

As soon as they went inside Tommy and Jessie were hailed by several Teds who neither Tommy or Jessie knew, but who recognized them instantly. Drinks were conjured up and pressed on Tommy and Jessie, and when those drinks were finished more appeared.

The music before had been modern jazz, which Jessie had a taste for, but that had also changed, as they now found out.

A nattily attired chap bounded onto the stage area, and a hush fell amongst the clientele who were as different from the previous clientele as the music was going to turn out to be.

'Ladies and gentlemen, I'd like you to put your hands

181

together for one of Glasgow's sons who's made a big success in the South. Down there he's taken them by storm with what can only be termed his own individual way of doing things. I am, of course, referring to the one, the only *Lonnie Donegan*!'

'Who's Lonnie Donegan? Never heard of him,' Tommy whispered to Jessie, who shrugged; she'd never heard of Donegan either.

Lonnie Donegan turned out to be a flat-faced young man with a shock of hair that gave the appearance of standing up from his head as though in fright. Donegan cracked jokes as his band formed up behind him. They can't be serious, Jessie thought, for they didn't have instruments – at least not the conventional sort.

There was a tea chest with a broom handle sticking up from it, and a gut string running from the top of the handle to the chest itself. It wasn't until they started playing that Jessie realized this was a primitive bass. Besides the tea chest there was an empty suitcase, a partially galvanized washboard, a seven-gallon Jug and a kazoo.

'What is this?' Jessie whispered to one of the Teds who'd been buying her and Tommy drinks.

'It's called Skiffle.'

Jessie recalled then that she'd read something about Skiffle being popular in the Twenties and a name, The Mound City Blowers, popped into her mind, but this would be the first time she'd either heard or seen it.

'Rock Island Line,' Lonnie Donegan announced.

It worked surprisingly well, Jessie thought as the number got under way and Donegan certainly had star quality that stood out a mile.

'Is he a real musician?' she asked the Ted who'd told her what it was they were hearing.

'I think he played with Ken Colyer for a while, banjo or something like that.'

That impressed Jessie. Ken Colyer was well respected, as was Chris Barber who also played with him.

'I like this,' Tommy said to Jessie, who agreed with him. She liked it too.

They got smashing weather for the wedding, but September often produced sunny days for Glasgow.

When they arrived at Martha Street in a hired car Jessie gasped to see the crowds, mostly Teds from all over the city, but there were a contingent of the press and spectators come to see the King and Queen of the Glasgow Teds at their wedding.

The Boyd Street Boys had gone on ahead of Tommy and Jessie, and now formed twin lines – just as they'd done in the Cameo on the night of the party – from the car to the door of the Register Office. As Tommy helped Jessie from the car the photographers went daft. So many flashbulbs popped it was like silent machine gun fire.

The reporters tried to get to speak to them in person, but were held back by the Boyd Street Boys who linked arms as if they were policemen.

There were policemen present as well, but they'd wisely restricted their presence to the fringes where it was their intention to stay unless trouble broke out. Which, thanks to the festive mood, it didn't.

Tommy, because it was expected of him, had insisted on wearing a drape for the occasion. Jessie had therefore decided that if she had to dress in Ted gear she'd do so spectacularly. She wore a cream-coloured pencil skirt with matching mesh stockings and four-inch stilettos. Her top was a man's cream-coloured shirt, with brass links at the cuffs, and old-fashioned brass bands on her upper arms. Round her neck she sported a cream-coloured tie done in a Windsor Knot. She'd combed her hair in the fashion now identified with her, hanging straight and parted in the middle. She had black shadow on her eyelids, and on her left cheek she'd painted a white butterfly which she'd outlined in black.

Tommy, in contrast to her cream, was dressed entirely in black, for once without rings or any other metal adornment.

Glasgow had never seen the like before.

When the ceremony was over they emerged to a cloud of confetti and cheers from the Teds. Then it was back into the car, a repeat of the silent machine gun fire, and off home to Govanhill and the Cathcart Road T.A. Hall where the reception was being held.

Invites to the reception had been restricted to immediate family – Jessie had sent an invitation to her parents but hadn't even received a reply – the Boyd Street Boys, the Boyd Street neighbours, and some 'friendlies' and other pals from the Cameo. All in all, 260-odd people crowded into the hall.

There was a large cardboard box at the end of the bar and into that went cash donations to help cover the cost of the reception.

At ten o'clock after a marvellous party, Tommy and Jessie decided to be off. Not that they were going on honeymoon, there was no question of that. They were headed back to Boyd Street where they'd be alone for the night as Jeannie had arranged to stay with a friend.

They left the hall surreptitiously, Jessie via a trip to the toilet, Tommy out a side exit. The reason they went in this fashion was because they didn't trust the Boys not to have some sort of surprise cooked up, and as they later found out, such a surprise had indeed been scheduled. So they escaped that.

Once home, Jessie kicked off her shoes and sank into a chair. Tommy produced a bottle of whisky that he'd lifted from the reception, but she didn't want to know about any more alcohol, it was tea for her. Tommy poured himself a stiff dram, and said he'd make the tea.

'Are you sure you know how to?' she teased. It was rare he turned a hand to anything round the house that came under the umbrella of 'women's work'.

'Go and raffle your doughnut,' he said indignantly. 'I can make a pot of tea with the best of them, as you will soon find out.'

While he was making the tea he said suddenly, 'It would have been nice to go doon the water for a couple of days, Largs or Dunoon maybe.'

'It doesn't matter to me,' she said, her eyes on him. 'I'm happy just being with you.'

He smiled, but he continued to feel guilty.

'We'll do it later, after you've got that job,' she suggested.

'Aye, and we'll make it a fortnight, not a couple of measly days,' he said with false enthusiasm.

She got up and put her arms around him. 'It was a grand wedding Tommy, I couldn't have asked for better.'

'Oh? And how does it feel to be Mrs Thomas McBride?'

'Lovely.'

'What happens if I never get another job?' he asked quietly, voicing the fear that had been growing daily within him since being released from jail.

'We'll cope somehow. We've got each other, and in the end that's all that really matters,' she answered softly, running a hand through his hair, and thinking how much she felt for this man who'd come to be so dear to her.

She was naked, held in a spreadeagled position by the four grinning Teds, and an equally naked Ken Young was leering down at her. 'First me, then the others, each in turn,' he crooned. She tried to scream, but for some reason no sound would come. She twisted her head this way and that, seeing the five faces watching her expand and contract, expand and contract, over and over. If only she could escape, if only she could jump up and run away from this terrible place, if only Ken Young and the other four would disappear, if only . . . 'And when we're finished we'll go back to the beginning and all do it again,' Ken Young laughed. She couldn't make a sound, no matter how hard she tried. No! she screamed in her brain. No! No! NO!

Jessie came awake with a start to find she was drenched in sweat and shaking. She hugged herself to calm herself down.

There were variations of the nightmare. In some of them Young and the others got as far as actually raping her. In others it was just the threat, over and over again.

She wiped the wet from her forehead using the sleeve of her nightdress. The nightmares weren't occurring as often as they once had, but she was certain that she'd never be entirely free of them, that they'd be with her for the rest of her life.

It would be a good hour before she'd get back to sleep, it always was. She lay in the darkness and thought about Tommy snoring by her side.

It was three months now since he'd got out of Barlinne, and he still didn't have a job, not even the sniff of one. He hadn't spoken since their wedding night about his fear that he never would find another job, but she knew the fear was still there, she'd seen it in his eyes when he wasn't aware she was watching him.

If only she could do something to help, but what? If she'd known an employer she could have approached on his behalf she'd happily have done so. But she didn't know any employers.

She was being as supportive and encouraging as she could, but it didn't seem enough. She wanted to do more; felt she should be doing more.

If only he hadn't been King of the Glasgow Teds, if only he hadn't received that publicity for The Battle of Linton Street and the huge amount of coverage that had accompanied their wedding. If only. . .

When she finally dropped off again she dreamt again. In this one Tommy was a successful botanist, who looked like everyone else, and he and she lived in a nice part of town.

That was a lovely dream.

It was Jessie's twenty-third birthday, and they were celebrating at the Cameo. Tommy was in great form, as he'd been all day. He'd been out in the morning after breakfast, returning with a bunch of flowers. She'd thanked him for them, then asked where he'd got them. His reply, delivered with a cheeky grin, had been, ask no questions, get no lies. She'd known from that he hadn't paid for them, and suspected he might have pinched them out of a greenhouse somewhere.

Tommy had a fair old skinful in him, though he wasn't drunk, just extremely happy. They'd been to the Seaforth Bar before coming in, and as was always the case there at the weekend they hadn't paid for anything, others being only too eager to buy for them.

Tommy excused himself and went over to talk to Jack Gowrie who, after a few seconds, glanced in her direction. Something was planned, she thought, that look of Jack's gave the game away.

Tommy left Jack and crossed to Sammy McGlinchie who was soon nodding vigorously at whatever Tommy was saying. So Sammy was in on it too. She hoped it was nothing that was going to embarrass her.

Tommy and Sammy disappeared into the crowd, and when she glanced back to where Jack had been it was to find that he also had done a vanishing act.

Minutes passed without either of that threesome reappearing, then the band completed their session and left the rostrum for a break, taking their instruments with them.

The lights suddenly went out, plunging the dancehall into darkness. A girl screamed, another was heard to say loudly, 'Keep your hands to yourself you dirty bastard!'

'What's going on?' a female voice demanded.

'Bugger if I know hen,' a male voice replied.

A single green light snapped on to reveal Tommy standing on the rostrum. Jessie could make out that there were others on the rostrum with him.

'As most of you know, it's my wife Jessie's birthday today, and to give her a bit of a giggle, because I know she likes one, me and a couple of the lads have organized the following. Jessie darling, this is for, and dedicated to you. A brand new band, folks! The Boyd Street Skifflers!'

The green light snapped off, and the normal lighting came back on. Tommy, Jake, Sammy and Jake 'The Rake' Stewart could now all be seen, and with them was the same weird assortment of instruments that Tommy and Jessie had watched Lonnie Donegan and his band play at the Omar Khayyam.

Jessie sniggered and put her hand to her mouth. Jack was on the tea chest and broom handle, Sammy the washboard, and Jake 'The Rake' the seven-gallon jug and kazoo. Tommy was the singer.

'Rock Island Line,' Tommy announced, and gave Jessie a broad wink.

There had been several times during the past couple of weeks when Tommy had gone off mysteriously in the evening, not telling her where he was going as he usually did. Now she knew that he'd been practising for this.

It might have been meant as a joke, but that wasn't at all how they sounded. They were extremely good, especially Tommy.

And that was when the great idea came to her. She sat there, forgetting everything around her, wondering why she hadn't thought of this before.

She said nothing to Tommy until they were home and getting ready for bed. The kitchen was lovely and warm as Jeannie had had a fire going all night.

Jessie sat curled in a chair, a shawl round her shoulders,

188

a cup of Ovaltine in her hand. Tommy was just getting into his pyjamas.

'I've had a thought,' she said as casually as she could.

'Oh, aye?'

'Tell me one thing, though, do you trust my musical judgement?'

He stopped and stared at her. What a funny thing to ask. 'You know I do. What are you leading up to?'

She took a deep breath. 'Just that I think you're a smashing singer. Not only that, but you put yourself across well and you know how to handle an audience.'

'Well, thanks very much,' he grinned, chuffed with himself. Such a compliment from Jessie was a compliment indeed.

But Jessie hadn't finished yet. 'The others who got up with you, can any of them play real instruments?'

'Sammy knows a few tunes on the mouth organ, but that's about it. Why?'

'So why did you choose them?'

'I put it to Jack and he roped in the two others. There weren't any special reasons. Does it matter?'

She shook her head. 'No. It's just that you all worked so well as a group.' She was watching him closely. 'In fact you were so good that I think you should try and make a go of it together.'

He stopped tying the cord of his pyjama trousers and looked at her sharply. What was she havering on about now? 'A go at what?'

Jessie was nearly jumping with excitement. 'A go as a skiffle band.'

'You mean do it properly. For real?'

'You're looking for a job, why not this? I'd bet anything your band would be popular.'

He sat facing her, dazed by her suggestion. 'Why should our band be popular?' he asked slowly.

She gave a wry smile, sometimes he was so naive. 'Because of you. You're the King of the Glasgow Teds, wherever you play the Teds in the area will flock to hear

189

you. And then the 'straights' will come to get a charge out of being in the same hall as an outlaw like yourself.' Her eyes were sparkling.

But Tommy didn't look delighted. He had a vision of all those 'straights' coming to gawp at him, and it made his flesh creep. 'That's what they did to Sitting Bull,' he said slowly.

'Sitting Bull?'

'They put him on show, made him no more than a circus clown. Is that what you want for me?'

'Of course not.'

'I'd be a laughing stock.'

'You'd be nothing of the sort. Once they've heard you no one will be laughing. I promise I know I'm right.'

Tommy didn't like the idea at all. It was one thing to get up at the Cameo, those were his friends and mates, but to get up in front of a lot of strangers was something else. Aye, and it frightened him, too. He'd rather fight a Ken Young any time.

'The whole notion's preposterous,' he said shortly, ready to dismiss it completely.

Jessie was beginning to lose her temper. Why did he have to be so obstinate? Here was the perfect solution to their problems, and all he could do was turn up his nose at it.

'Give me one reason, one *good* reason, why you shouldn't have a go?'

'I just have. It would be demeaning.'

'It seems to me to be far more demeaning to be jobless and living off your mother and me. Do you want to go on accepting handouts for the rest of your life?'

He went white as a sheet. How could she say such a thing? How could she be so cruel?

'I won't turn myself into a circus clown for you or for anyone else,' he replied.

'But you wouldn't be. You've got real talent.'

'No.' He turned away from her.

'Tommy. . .'

'I said no, and I mean no! Having a giggle like we did the night is one thing, what you're proposing quite another. And that's the end of it.'

'Silly bugger,' she muttered into her cup.

He whirled on her. 'What did you say?'

'I said you were a silly bugger!' she repeated loudly.

His gaze went to the wall. 'Sssh! You'll wake up Ma.'

'Good, then she can tell you you're a silly bugger as well!'

He stalked stiffly to the bed and got in, turning on to his side so that his back was to her.

She stayed in the chair till long after the fire was out and was so cold that she had to make a move.

She knew he was only pretending to be asleep.

What an end to her birthday! But that was unimportant. The real disappointment was his reaction to her idea. He so *badly* needed a job. As time passed he was getting more and more moody and ill-tempered.

Well she wouldn't give up her idea of the band, it was too good an idea.

'Jessie?'

Closing her eyes she pretended *she* was asleep.

Jessie was doing a bit of darning while listening to the Light Programme on the wireless, Jeannie was at a friend's and Tommy was out having a couple of pints with some of the Boyd Street Boys.

The socks she was darning were well past it, but she wouldn't be throwing them away, money was too tight for that. Despite the state they were in they'd just have to last a while longer.

She glanced up in surprise when she heard the outside door click open, she wasn't expecting Tommy back for at least another hour.

She leapt to her feet, the darning tumbling to the floor, the moment she saw him. There was blood all down the side of his face and his drape was ripped.

She rushed to his side. 'What happened to you?'

'Fight.' He collapsed into the nearest chair with a heavy sigh.

'Are you hurt?' she asked, kneeling beside him, her brow furrowed with concern.

'Just a bit. He nicked my cheek with his razor and he hit me on the shoulder with a hammer. That's fair giving me gyp. But I'm all right.'

The blood on his face had dried. As far as she could tell he was right, it was only a small nick about half an inch in length. She tried not to think what Tommy's face might have been like had that razor really connected.

She switched off the wireless, filled the kettle and put it on the stove. She wanted hot water to wash the blood away.

Returning to Tommy, she helped him out of his drape, then, being as gentle as she could, took his shirt off. 'Oh my God,' she whispered. His left shoulder was black and blue and swollen.

'I don't think anything's broken,' he said, flexing his fingers.

She had a feel of the shoulder. 'It's amazing, but it seems to be intact.' But it was a right sore shoulder all the same. She'd put a hot compress on it, that would help.

'How did the fight come about?' she asked, hunting in the press for the flannel for the compress.

'We were having a quiet drink in the Albion Arms when in comes this young Ted who announces he's been searching for me to challenge me for my title.'

'Had you seen him before?'

Tommy shook his head. 'Never clapped eyes on him till he walked into the Albion. He was from Garthamlock, pretty far out on the north side.'

Jessie's hands were shaking as she poured some of the hot water into a bowl, then put the kettle back on the gas. She'd clean up his face first, then tend his shoulder.

Tommy went on. 'So he and I went round the rear of the pub and got stuck into it. I'll say this for him, he was a bonny fighter, if he'd been a wee bit bigger or stronger he might well have had me.'

'Was he badly injured?' Jessie asked, gently daubing at his face.

'Jack rang 999 and told them to send an ambulance, so he'll be in hospital now.'

She knelt beside him, her hand on his. 'What future is there for you in all this love?' she asked softly.

'I didn't exactly *apply* to be King of the Glasgow Teds,' he snapped back.

She continued, 'Tommy, listen to me. You're on an eventual hiding if you go on as you are. You've been made King, but there will always be someone after your crown. Fight will follow fight will follow fight until one day you lose. You'll be the one coughing up blood or with a face razored to mincemeat. I can't bear the thought of that happening to you Tommy.' Warm tears sprang to her eyes.

'What can I do?' he asked in an agonized whisper.

'You know what I think you can do. You have two things going for you: your voice and the fact you *are* King of the Glasgow Teds.'

Tommy gnawed his lip. The skiffle band idea, they were back to that. It still frightened him to think of getting up in front of strangers, but it frightened him even more to think of being maimed or mutilated in some alley fight.

'You need an escape door from all this Tommy. The skiffle band could be that door. Will you at least give it a try, *please*?' she pleaded.

He stared at her lovingly, wondering what marvellous thing he'd done to be rewarded with his Jessie. 'You're wrong about me only having two things going for me, I have three, and the third, by far the best of all, is you.'

Her heart swelled with relief. She'd won him round, he was going to do it.

★　　★　　★

His singing was terrible, completely off key. The Tommy McBride Skiffle Band, due to open at the Yoker Palais the night after next, was in Jeannie's kitchen rehearsing their numbers, with Jessie supervising as Musical Director.

Jessie glanced at Jack who raised his eyes to heaven. If Tommy sang like this at Yoker it would be a disaster.

Finally she couldn't stand any more of it, and gestured them quiet. 'If I was outside listening in I'd think you were a chicken having its neck wrung,' she said to Tommy.

Tommy scowled at her, and stuck his hands deep into his pockets. 'I always said this was a bloody daft idea.'

'There's nothing daft about it!'

'Maybe Tommy's right,' Jake muttered.

Jessie ran a hand through her hair. There was no point in continuing with the rehearsal, she decided. The more it went on the worse Tommy became.

She told them that was it for the evening, and no, there wouldn't be another rehearsal the following evening, they were as ready as they were ever going to be.

Jack, Sammy and Jake took the cue and got ready to leave. Jessie saw them to the front door. 'Don't worry,' she whispered, 'I'll sort Tommy out. He'll be at his best at Yoker, you have my word on that.'

When she returned to the kitchen she found Tommy staring morosely out the window down into the back court. His hunched stance warned her that if she said the wrong thing he'd go off like a Guy Fawkes banger, and try to get out of the Yoker date.

'Can I get you anything?' she asked sweetly.

'I could murder a drink,' he muttered, knowing there was fat chance of that. Money was so tight it was some time since there had been booze in the house.

But he was wrong. Jessie had a large bottle of strong cider planked, and this she now got out.

He turned in surprise at the sound of the familiar chink, cider wasn't exactly a favourite of his, but it was a lot better than nothing.

'Now what's bothering you?' she asked, handing him a bubbling glass, half the contents of which he immediately downed in one swallow.

'Nothing.'

'It's obvious something is, so why not tell me?'

He shrugged and drank more cider.

Patience, she told herself, it would come, all she had to do was stand there and wait.

He finished the glass, and helped himself to more. 'Call it stage fright, nerves, or what you will, I suppose it's that,' he said suddenly, the words tumbling out in a rush.

Of course, she should have realized. He was terrified of what lay in front of him.

'I'm just worried sick that I'll make an idiot of myself,' he went on.

'You won't do that if you sing as you can, I promise you Tommy.'

'Just the thought of going out there makes me all tight inside, and if I feel that way now God know what I'll be like come the actual event.'

'A minute or two after you've started you'll be wondering why you were so worried,' she said reassuringly. 'It's just nerves.'

'Maybe so, but those first couple of minutes are going to be hell. What if my voice seizes on me like it did tonight? They'll laugh me off the stage, especially the 'straights' and I couldn't abide that.'

She topped his cider up yet again. If nerves did cause his voice to play up then they did have a problem. His singing career would be over before it had even begun.

'Don't forget that all the Boyd Street Boys and their lassies, will be there to give you support. It won't be all strangers, your friends will be there as well.'

Tommy began to relax a little. Jessie talked and talked, relaxing him even more. Their pals would be there when the doors opened, she assured him, she'd make sure word got round. She continued talking, but wasn't entirely satisfied with the result. What he still needed was an extra confidence booster to take him through those crucial opening minutes.

It was later when they were having a bite of supper that the answer came to her. She smiled at the memory of how the trick had worked on her and her class.

'Do you remember Mr Harrison at Queen's Park School?' she asked Tommy suddenly.

'Of course, he was a geography teacher.'

She went on to explain what she had in mind, and when she'd finished speaking Tommy was smiling, the first real smile she'd seen in days.

'How many do you think?' Tommy asked Jessie. They were in the wings of the Yoker Palais prior to the band going on stage. The Yoker Palais had a real stage that was at least three times the size of the rostrum at the Cameo.

Jessie peeked round the side of the heavy velvet curtain to see that it was already blue with fug in the hall which was nearly three-quarters full. That in itself was something – it was another hour till the pubs closed, the traditional time for most folk to come to the dancing.

It was gratifying to know such a large number had turned up, and so early, for the Yoker Palais had been doing rotten business of late. Tommy, as she'd predicted, was definitely a draw.

'Five, six hundred maybe,' she said to Tommy who, but it might have been the light, appeared to pale fractionally.

She squeezed his arm. 'You've nothing to fear, honest. Your voice was in cracking form when you sang for me this afternoon. Do Harrison's trick and you'll have them in the palm of your hand right from the off. It always worked for Harrison with a new class, so there's no reason why it shouldn't work for you.'

McLean, the manager, appeared. 'All set?'

Jessie glanced at Tommy, then Jack, Sammy and Jake. Jake gave her a cheery thumbs up sign.

'All set,' she confirmed.

'Good luck,' McLean smiled, and walked on stage to do an intro.

The band wouldn't be taking their instruments on with them, those were already behind the heavy velvet curtains. With the instruments was another little item that Jessie herself had put there, an empty biscuit tin. Harrison had always used a wastepaper basket, but she'd thought a tin box more appropriate to the occasion.

She was desperately nervous for Tommy, and trying not to show it. Everything depended on his confidence in those opening minutes.

'The Tommy McBride Skiffle Band!' McLean announced, completing his intro, and led the applause.

The curtains parted and Jack, Sammy and Jake 'The Rake' strolled on.

A buzz of expectation filled the air as the threesome took up their instruments, a buzz that became a questioning mutter. Where was the big man himself? Where was McBride?

Jessie let the tension stretch and stretch. 'Now!' she finally whispered.

Tommy made for the microphone, strolling as the other three had done. Just before the mike he encountered the tin box which was so placed that it looked as though it had been left there accidentally. He stopped to glower down at the box, as if furious that something was in his way. The audience stilled, wondering what was going to happen next.

With a snarl of pretended rage, Tommy lashed out with his right foot to send the tin box to the other side of the stage where it made a fearful clatter as it landed. He whirled on the watchers, his expression one that dared anyone to speak up against what he'd just done.

The moment was electric – and pure theatre.

'Aah!' gasped an ecstatic girl near the front, the only sound heard throughout the hall.

Tommy's nervousness subsided. He had them right where he wanted them. He was the boss in complete control. His reputation and Mr Harrison's little trick, had ensured that.

He completed his journey to the mike, stared out over the hall then slowly allowed his face to soften into a smile. 'Rock Island Line,' he said.

In the wings Jessie breathed a sigh of relief. Tommy would be all right now. And what a lovely piece of acting, he'd fooled even her, and she'd known what was going to happen.

She mentally thanked Mr Harrison, who'd used the trick to establish his authority with each new class. In the door he'd come, glower at the wastepaper basket in his path, and bang would go the basket, spilling its contents everywhere, and the class would be instantly awed into subjugation. None of the previous classes ever told the new class what to expect, or that Mr Harrison was in reality the sweetest man imaginable.

By the end of the opening set Jessie knew the Tommy McBride Skiffle Band was a great success. When those who'd gone to the pub prior to coming on to the dance-hall finally arrived they found the Hall Full signs out front, which hadn't happened at the Yoker Palais in years. Inside it was packed to bursting.

Jessie judged that about sixty per cent of those in the hall were Teds and their girls, the rest 'straights'. Both groups were quite clearly enjoying the music.

In the middle of the final set the manager appeared beside Jessie and asked her to follow him into the passageway outside.

'The lads have done well, I'm pleased. Do they have a booking for next weekend?' he asked.

'Not so far, but after tonight we shouldn't have any trouble in lining one up,' she said confidently, knowing what was coming next.

'How about them appearing here again then?' he proposed.

'Fine,' she said after a moment's consideration. 'But the fee goes up by half.'

McLean gave a small laugh. This girl was a born dealer, he'd realized that right from the beginning. 'Let's say an extra tenner because I think you're the prettiest lassie here tonight.'

Jessie ignored the flattery, he wouldn't get round her that way. 'It's half as much again or we go elsewhere,' she stated firmly.

'Maybe it's only a flash in the pan, maybe by next week the novelty will have worn off,' he challenged.

'If you thought that you wouldn't be standing here discussing them now.' she said shrewdly.

She had him there, and he could see she knew she did. 'All right, it's a deal. Half as much again it is. But with one provision.'

She became wary. 'And what's that?'

'You never forget it was me gave them their start,' he said.

Three weeks later, on a cold Wednesday night in February of 1958, Tommy was waiting at the tramstop for Jessie when she arrived back from work.

Her face lit up with pleasure when she saw him. His coming to meet her was a treat. 'Well, this is a surprise,' she laughed, hugging him.

'I've got something to show you,' he said mysteriously.

Right away her curiosity was aroused. 'What?' she demanded, hooking her arm in his.

'Wait and see.'

He led her along then turned into Allison Street, which ran parallel to Boyd Street.

'No hints even?'

'No hints even,' he laughed, delighting in her excitement and impatience.

Allison Street was older than Boyd Street and looked

it. It was also a far longer street, and wider, with shops dotted along its length.

The close he headed for was next to a newsagent's. Tommy took her to the second landing where he produced a yale key. With a flourish, he opened the door on a room and kitchen, similar to Jeannie's. It was empty now, but had been well cared for. She couldn't imagine why Tommy had brought her here.

'What do you think?' he asked eagerly.

'About what?'

'This.' His hand gestured around the room.

The penny dropped, and so did her spirits. 'You mean for us?'

He nodded. 'I heard on the grapevine that it was going, so I went straight to Meikle the factor and said we'd take it.'

Jessie gazed again round the room that overlooked Allison Street, but didn't reply. The wallpaper was hideous and the room itself seemed to speak of nothing but defeat.

'You don't seem pleased.'

She forced a smile on to her face. 'I am, yes. Of course I am.'

'It's a place of our own, Jessie.'

'Oh aye, another Buckingham Palace.'

'There's no need to be like that. I thought all that mattered was that we were together.'

'I'm sorry, it's just that it's so . . . so unexpected.'

He looked at her to say more.

After a pause she went on. 'I just thought we'd stay with Jeannie a while longer. Then, when we did move, we'd move right out of Govanhill altogether. I had dreams of us buying a house beside the Linn Park.'

His eyes gleamed. 'Do you really think that one day we could do that?'

'Why not? A year from now our lives could be entirely transformed.'

A house beside the Linn Park! 'I'll see Meikle again tomorrow and tell him we've changed our minds,' he said.

'No you don't. You were right to grab this house, we do need our own place. Just as long as we both know it's only temporary.'

'You really have set your sights high for me, haven't you?'

'I love you.'

'Well,' he laughed, 'There's going to be one big advantage of being in our own house, we won't have to wait till Ma goes to bed at night.'

'Is that the real reason you're so keen to take this place?'

'Can you think of a better?'

The Tommy McBride Skiffle Band was playing Logan's Dancehall in the London Road, and, as was usual wherever they appeared, the hall was mobbed with an appreciative audience.

Jessie was out front, mingling with the crowd. She liked to do that at least once a night to hear some of the comments made about Tommy and the band. One such comment now caused her to turn and stare at the speaker, for the truth of what he'd said was so blindingly obvious that she couldn't think why she hadn't seen it herself.

'Aye, you're right, Shughie, they should be doing their own songs,' a second Ted agreed with the first.

Their *own* songs, of course! So far, all their numbers were hits by, or closely identified with, already popular artists like Lonnie Donegan, the Vipers, Chas McDevitt and Nancy Whiskey, Johnny Duncan and the Bluegrass Boys etc.

If Tommy and the band ever hoped to join that group they could only do so playing original material. Therefore original material was the next step on the ladder. The problem was: who was going to write it?

'But where do we get original material?' Tommy asked. He was sitting in front of a roaring fire with a dram.

'London, I suppose. That's where the songwriters seem to be,' Jessie suggested.

Tommy sipped his drink, enjoying the heat of the fire washing over him. 'London!' London seemed a universe away.

Jessie was well away with her new idea. 'I could go next week and do the rounds.'

He didn't like the thought of her going to London on her own. On the other hand, he could hardly accompany her, the band was booked for four nights during the coming week and five the week after.

'What do you say?'

'I agree we should have our own material,' he said slowly. 'But I'm not so sure about you and London.'

She could read his mind. It amused her that he thought she might not be able to take care of herself. Men! Their egos made them forget how resourceful, capable women were.

Tommy's brow knotted in thought. He finished his dram and poured himself another from the bottle by his chair. Finally, he said, 'What you're proposing is to go to London and take pot luck at what you can find. Right? But it seems to me that it would be far better if instead of taking pot luck we had a number written specifically for the band.'

'You mean get a songwriter to come here from London, meet you, and then write his song?'

He shook his head. 'We could do it that way. But aren't there any Scottish songwriters around? If we're going to do new material, then it should be about us and the way we are. I don't want some Englishman telling me what my life is like.'

Jessie looked doubtful. 'I've never heard of any,' she said dismally.

The next thing Tommy said took her completely by surprise. 'What about you? Didn't you write music at one time? There certainly isn't anyone who understands me better than you.'

Jessie stared at him in astonishment. 'I have composed a bit, but that was years ago at school, and the sort of thing I composed was nothing like what you need.'

But Tommy wasn't to be put off. This time he was the one with the idea. 'Music is second nature to you, you know that. And you understand skiffle as well as anyone. So why don't you just see what you can come up with? We've nothing to lose, after all, except perhaps a wee bit of time.'

Write a skiffle number! Could she do it? But it had been so long . . .

'You told me to have a go as a singer, and that worked. So why shouldn't you have a go as a songwriter? You've certainly got more musical ability than I do.'

'What you're asking isn't as easy as you make it sound,' she answered, although it was clear from her expression that her resistance was weakening.

'Nothing worthwhile is every easy, you know that.'

'It's not just the music itself, there are also the lyrics, I've never tried my hand at those.'

'Well now's your chance,' he replied firmly.

She'd got herself into a proper pickle this time. How had her original idea come round to this?

'Perhaps a Glasgow theme, the local punters would certainly love that,' Tommy went on.

Jessie chewed on a strand of hair and thought about Glasgow. The docks, the shipbuilding, the heavy industry, the slums, the fierce pride of every Glaswegian. There was enough material, that was for sure.

'Well,' she said slowly, 'I could start working on something tomorrow night. But I'm not convinced I can pull it off.'

But she did. When her first number, 'King Of The Glasgow Teds', was introduced the following week it was the hit of the evening.

6

Jessie glanced at the clock on the mantelpiece, saw it was nearly 3 a.m., and groaned. She was going to be out on her feet at work tomorrow, but she wanted this new number finished so Tommy and the band would have a fair crack at rehearsing it before introducing it Friday night at the Locarno.

This would be the fourth number she'd written, and all of them had been extremely well received. The more new material the band had the better. The plan was that they'd eventually perform nothing but their own stuff, but that amount of songs was going to take a while for her to produce. She didn't want to churn out just any old rubbish.

Tommy was asleep in bed. They had spent the evening talking again about getting a disc cut, but that was proving a lot harder than they'd anticipated.

They'd had a demo made, reproduced, and sent off to quite a few London record companies, but so far they hadn't had a bite. It was becoming more and more apparent that talent and determination alone wasn't enough to get on, you needed contacts and that was one thing they didn't have.

But they'd come, she was sure of it. The thing to do was keep on building Tommy and the band as much as possible, eventually somebody would have to take notice.

If only they could get some wireless time, or on the newly popular television, either would be great.

The tune she'd been working on started buzzing again in her head, and her pencil flew. When she finally crawled in beside Tommy it was past four o'clock.

She was up again at seven.

*　　*　　*

The Locarno was crammed to capacity. There were Hall Full signs out front, as there had been every night Tommy and the band had played.

Jessie was in the dressing room while Tommy and the band were out on stage; from where she was sitting she could hear them performing her latest number. They'd done it twice already that night, and it had gone down a bomb each time. It was exhilarating to know that people could get so much enjoyment out of something she'd written.

She fell to thinking about the walk round inside the hall that she'd just had – or tried to have. Why, there must have been two and a half to three thousand people there, possibly even more. So how much did that mean the Locarno was taking in for the night?

She took out a pen and some paper, and made a calculation. The figure produced caused her to purse her lips in a silent whistle.

She compared that figure with what Tommy and the band were being paid, and the comparison was hardly a good one.

She decided this needed further thinking on.

Mr Bojangles wasn't only the largest dancehall in Glasgow, but the largest in all Scotland.

Ross Wylie was the manager. He was a wee, rat-faced man who twitched a great deal and smoked incessantly. 'The fee you ask is out of the question Mrs McBride,' he was saying. 'It's far far too high.'

Jessie smiled at him from across his desk. 'I admit it's a higher fee than anyone else in Scotland has been paid, but Tommy McBride will fill your hall for you, Mr Wylie, I can guarantee that.'

Wylie gave a thin, condescending smile. 'Tommy might have filled the Locarno, but Mr Bojangles is another matter entirely. We're double the Locarno's size.'

'I'm well aware of the size of your dancehall, Mr Wylie. But the sum I asked is what we want to play Mr Bojangles,' she answered, putting the very minimum of expression into her voice.

'Impossible, Mrs McBride,' Wylie said emphatically. 'Absolutely impossible.'

Jessie, keeping her face impassive, stared at Wylie. She knew he was keen for Tommy and the band to play Mr Bojangles, because they were rapidly becoming the hottest musical property in Scotland. The odds were in her favour.

The silence between Jessie and Wylie stretched on and on. She continued to watch him impassively, giving nothing away.

Finally it was he who broke the silence. 'If I do agree the fee you're asking, and Tommy fails to fill Mr Bojangles, then Mr Bojangles could be out of pocket. And that would be bad business,' he said reasonably.

That was a lie, Jessie thought, and a rather clumsy one at that. Mr Bojangles didn't have to be filled for the dancehall to make a profit on the deal, he must think her stupid if he imagined she'd swallow that.

'You're the one who came to us,' she said evenly.

'I'm a businessman, Mrs McBride,' he blustered. 'Not a patron of the arts.'

She counted twenty inside her head. 'Then I propose a deal whereby Mr Bojangles can't possibly lose.'

Wylie was immediately interested. 'And what sort of deal would that be?' he demanded.

'Put us on a percentage of the gross. That way you can't possibly lose on your fee.'

A percentage of the gross? He'd never heard of that being done in Scotland before. He knew some of the big stars, and particularly the Americans, arranged such deals in London, but London was London, and Glasgow Glasgow. 'It's novel,' he conceded.

'And fair. To Mr Bojangles as bookers, and to Tommy and the band as performers.'

He took his time about lighting a cigar while he thought about her proposition. 'What kind of percentage did you have in mind?' he asked at last.

She contained herself till she was out of the dancehall, and round the corner. There she let out a loud whoop of delight that startled several passers-by. A percentage of the gross was what she'd wanted all along, not the high fee she'd originally asked for. And what's more, she'd got a full percent and a half more than what she's had in mind when she'd walked into his office.

Now that the precedent had been set she fully intended that every contract from there on in would be on similar lines, and written down as a safeguard.

Ross Wylie might think himself a clever businessman, but she didn't consider him very clever, not very clever at all.

As was always the case on a Sunday, Glasgow was dead. It was a beautiful June day with the sun pouring down, making the area appear even more bleak, Jessie thought, as she stared out the room window into Allison Street.

Suddenly, she wanted away from there, if only temporarily. Maybe they could catch a red bus for the coast. They could go to Largs, or Dunoon, or Seamill. The day was just right for a bus run, and they both could certainly use a breath of fresh air after the amount of time they'd been spending in dancehalls of late.

And then she knew where she and Tommy would go. Not down the coast, but someplace far closer to home, and long neglected by them. A magic place.

She went into the kitchen where Tommy was sitting reading the *Sunday Post*. He never missed The Broons or Oor Wullie. 'Get your jacket,' she told him. 'We're going out.'

He demanded to know where, but she tapped her nose. 'Don't you mind where. You'll enjoy it, I promise.'

So as to keep him in suspense as long as possible, she

took him a way that was different to the one he'd used when he'd lived in Millbrae Crescent.

They got off the bus at Swanson's Garage in the Carmunnock Road, just below the blight of houses that was Castlemilk and crossed over into Simshill, a newly built private estate. Emerging from the far end of Simshill Jessie led Tommy to a hedged path that eventually dipped down to the golf course, the bottom end of which was adjacent to the southern boundaries of Linn Park.

Tommy stared out over the park, a crooked smile on his lips and the gleam of happy memories in his eyes.

'It's been an awful long time,' he said, a catch in his voice.

Hand in hand, they entered the park, stopping a few hundred yards further on to watch raucous rooks dart about a clump of horse chestnut trees, then moving into the small fir forest that went up one side of the brae, and down the other towards where the river twisted.

A young lad and his lass, out for a walk same as themselves, gawped at them as they passed one another, and it suddenly dawned on Jessie that she and Tommy, dressed in Ted gear, must look incongruous in these surroundings.

'Mind I bumped into you and Lizzie Dunnachie here once?' Tommy asked, laughing at the memory. Jessie remembered it well. She could visualize herself as she'd been then – the clothes she'd worn, the hat and umbrella, the hair-do. What a contrast to the way she was now!

'Whatever became of Lizzie?' Tommy went on.

'I've never seen or heard of her since I left the manse. I suppose I should have let her know where I'd gone, but I felt that she was part of my life as it had been, and Boyd Street was what it was now. I suppose I thought that if I tried to continue the friendship it would have gradually ended. It seemed better to stop it cleanly so that the good times we'd had didn't get lost in other things.'

There was sadness in her voice that cut right through him. He'd known it had been difficult for her to go and

208

live in Boyd Street, but until that moment he hadn't realized just what it had really meant to her.

He looked around. They were in Old Castle Road with the Snuffmill Bridge over on their left, the derelict castle up behind them. 'Let's look at these houses, then,' he urged. 'Just for fun. If ever I do make big money this is where we'll live. It's my favourite street in all Glasgow.'

There weren't very many houses in that part of the road. Those there were, sat amidst large walled gardens. Most had been built early in the previous century, but one or two were from the century before that.

One in particular caught Tommy's eye. It was made of grey granite and somewhat smaller than the rest. He and Jessie went to the wrought iron gate in order to get a better view. It was an imposing building with a regal look about it. A plate on the left hand pillar into which one of the gates was fixed bore the name GREENDAYS. Jessie's gaze moved across the garden. There were a lot of fruit trees, mainly apple and pear, and a row of gooseberry bushes at one side. It would be a marvellous garden in summer.

'This house is the pick of the bunch for me,' said Tommy. 'I'm not sure why, but it's special.'

Jessie giggled. 'I can't help thinking about our house in Allison Street, and you say you'd love to live in one of these houses here. Talk about going from the sublime to the ridiculous!'

Tommy joined in her laughter. 'Some day, though, perhaps. Some day,' he fantasized as they continued on their way.

Jessie had been waiting for the appropriate moment to spring her second surprise of that Sunday, and decided now was it. 'How would you feel about going on television?' she asked casually, knowing full well what his answer was going to be.

There was something in her tone told him this was more than an idle rhetorical question. 'What do you know that I don't?'

'The BBC programme New Talent is coming to Glasgow in August. They want the nine best new acts in Scotland for the show,' she explained excitedly.

New Talent! Why that went out at peak viewing time and was tremendously popular. 'If we could win that we'd be bound to get a recording contract with a major disc company,' he said, already making plans.

Jessie gave him a hug. 'That's how I see it, too.'

'You're not telling me we've already been accepted for the programme?'

'It's not quite as easy as that, I'm afraid. There's a small matter of an audition first. An I warn you now, when I spoke to the producer's office there had already been over a hundred applications, and the applications don't close for another three weeks.'

'Does that mean there's the possibility we may not even get auditioned?'

'You will if I have anything to do with it,' she answered with determination.

Jessie was at the piano Tommy had bought her the week before. A dozen of the Boys had bought it up the stairs, and what a to-do that had been. It had ended up with the outside door and the door to the room having to be taken off their hinges before they could get it where she wanted.

She had been worried that the folks up and down the close might complain about her playing late at night, which was when she usually worked on new songs, but they'd all said they weren't bothered in the least when she played. The truth was they were all very fond of her and Tommy, especially Tommy who was something of a celebrity in the neighbourhood.

Jessie frowned as she stared at what she'd scored. She had the music all right, but as always it was the lyrics that were giving her trouble.

A wee while later Tommy returned from playing

snooker to find her gazing glumly into space. 'What's wrong, love?' he asked with concern.

'I just can't write lyrics,' she said crossly.

'Let's hear the tune first,' he said, leaning on the piano.

She played the tune through. 'That's great,' he declared when she was finished. The tune had zest and style, and guts. He liked it and was certain the audiences would too. 'Now play it again, and this time sing the lyrics you have,' he instructed.

When she'd finished he was looking thoughtful. He could see what she meant by having trouble. The lyrics were nowhere near the standard of the music.

'Well?' she asked him.

It had never entered his mind to get involved in this side of things, but it was obvious Jessie needed help, and he was there, and her husband. It was up to him to give her what help he could.

'You want honesty?' he asked.

'Of course. Just don't be too honest.'

'It seems to me your trouble is that you're unclear about what you're trying to say. What you've written is vague and fuzzy. Soft, if you like. But it should be as sharp and hard as a diamond. Every word has to count. Now, what precisely *are* you trying to say?'

He was right of course. That was still unclear to her. She'd been hoping it would crystalize as she went along, but it hadn't.

With Tommy taking the lead they soon hammered out a story line, which they now had to transform into actual lyrics themselves. 'You're going to have to scrap what you've already done and start over.'

He brought a chair over to sit beside her at the piano. 'You play, we'll both suggest what we think should be put down, and as we agree I'll write it for you,' he said, taking up her pencil.

They started off suggesting equally, but it was very quickly evident to Jessie that Tommy was far better at the words than she. Before long she was merely playing while he spoke aloud, bouncing lines off her, she nodding, and he scribbling them over the previous lyrics.

It took them half an hour, and then they were done. Jessie played the tune through, and Tommy sang the lyrics. They were a perfect match.

'I sort of got carried away there,' Tommy said, realizing he'd taken command.

'Don't apologize, those lyrics are streets ahead of what I had. In fact, they're better than anything I've written,' she added ruefully.

'Do you really think so?'

'I most certainly do. You have a talent for writing lyrics, Tommy, that's plain as the nose on your face. From now on in, you're going to write all of them for us. I'll score the music, but you'll write the lyrics.'

He went over his lyrics again, they *were* good. Well how about that!

Jessie was puzzled. Tommy's talent wasn't at all raw as she would have expected, but appeared to have been worked at. But how could that be? Unless he'd been writing lyrics without telling her. 'Have you been writing songs on the side without telling me?' she teased.

'Not a one. It never occurred to me.'

'How about poetry, have you been penning some of that on the fly?'

He blushed, delighting her. Tommy McBride, King of the Glasgow Teds, blushing like a lassie! That was one for the book.

'Not for years now, but I did used to jot down the odd piece when I was at Queen's Park,' he admitted shyly.

'You've never said.'

He shrugged. 'There was no reason to. Anyway, only Crossmyloofs and English public school boys talk about poetry.'

'Do you still have any of it?'

He shook his head.

She was fascinated, who would have imagined

212

Tommy writing poetry! Although sensitive, he hadn't seemed quite the type. 'What was it about?' she pursued.

He blushed again and glanced away. 'A lot of it was about Lovers' Lane, the river, the Linn Park, that sort of thing,' he mumbled.

'What sort of thing?' she prompted.

'Animals, trees, fish and the like.'

He was holding something back, she could tell. 'And?'

'There were also some about you. Quite a lot in fact,' he replied reluctantly.

'Oh, Tommy! And you never said a word.' She was thrilled – Tommy writing poetry about her!

'You're not to laugh now,' he said.

'I wouldn't dream of laughing. I just wish I'd known before now how good you are with words, you'd have saved me an a lot of sweat and worry.'

'But most of your lyrics were smashing!' he protested.

'They were acceptable, and the people liked them, but they weren't in the same class as yours, believe me.'

Tommy was chuffed to hell to hear that. He'd never thought he had any talent.

'Listen, there's another tune been rattling around inside my head this past week, but I haven't actually put it on paper yet. If I do, will you have a go at doing the lyrics for it?'

'I don't see why not,' he answered, excited at the prospect.

It took her ten minutes to write down the tune. It took him twenty to produce the lyrics which were even better than the first set.

'This could be quite a partnership,' Jessie said, and to celebrate took her new found lyricist off to bed.

The BBC was situated in Queen Margaret Drive, the squat grey pile overlooking the River Kelvin.

The audition was for three o'clock, Jessie and Tommy McBride Skiffle Band arrived by taxi at quarter to, because she was terrified of arriving late and being told they'd missed their chance to audition.

The receptionist, a middle-aged woman dressed in twin-set and fake pearls, goggled when they presented themselves before her. She'd never seen the like in those hallowed premises. The poor woman recoiled when Jake 'The Rake' flicked his brylcreamed quiff and leered at her in a suggestive manner. Just for a laugh he almost propositioned her, but refrained from doing so knowing Jessie would murder him if he did.

Jessie intervened and told the receptionist who they were, and what their business was. Reluctantly, as if she feared they'd contaminate the upholstery, she asked them to take a seat.

Jack put down the tea chest he'd humped from the taxi. It was a brand new chest he'd bought specially for the audition; it had Made In India stencilled on every side.

Sammy, who played the washboard, not to be outdone by Jack's new tea chest, had purchased five new bright shiny thimbles for his strumming hand.

The receptionist rang an internal number, then called across that someone would be coming for them. Jessie thanked her. The woman was clearly surprised to be thanked. Good manners from Teds were the last thing she'd expected.

For the umpteenth time since it had arrived, Jessie re-read the letter stating the time and place of the audition. It was signed by a Mrs Baxter, personal secretary to Alan Hood the producer.

Jessie was amazed that they were apparently the only ones there for an audition; she'd been prepared for thousands all waiting their turn. And then she looked up and saw a face that struck a familiar chord in her memory. The woman was about the same age as herself, maybe a little older, wearing a blue suit and matching blouse that positively screamed money.

'Hello Tommy, hello Star,' the woman said, coming to stand in front of them.

It was Tommy who recognized her. 'Eve Smith!' he exclaimed.

'Eve Baxter, now. I'm married to a staff cameramen,' Eve smiled in reply.

Tommy kissed her on the cheek, saying how grand it was to see her again. Then Eve kissed Jessie.

Tommy *was* pleased to see Eve again. He had many fond memories of her. He could hardly credit her popping out of thin air like this, and after so long!

'I don't call myself Star anymore, I went back to Jessie,' Jessie explained coldly, still bewildered by this sudden turn of events.

Eve nodded, thinking to herself that Jessie was as good looking as ever – but those outlandish clothes! They didn't do anything for her at all. Eve thought with satisfaction of the suit she had on. She'd selected it for this meeting after great deliberation, wanting to look her absolute best. Alan had personally chosen it for her in London's Bond Street, and when he'd paid for it there had only been pennies change out of fifty pounds.

'So you're Mr Hood's personal secretary,' Jessie said.

'That's right. And I must admit this is no surprise to me, I knew it was you two when you applied for the audition. I've seen your pictures in the papers.' Turning to Tommy she said, 'Barlinne wasn't it?'

'Yes,' Tommy acknowledged. It didn't faze him to have his imprisonment referred to. It was something he'd long since learned to live with.

'Must have been terrible for you,' Eve said, relishing the shiver that ran across her belly. There had always been a wild, explosive, quality about Tommy McBride, Eve thought. It was a quality that excited her. Tommy was also the only man to ever ditch her. She'd never forgotten that, or forgiven it.

'I wondered why there was no one else here for the audition. Are we getting special treatment because of you?' Jessie asked in a whisper.

Eve gave Jessie a conspiratorial wink. 'What sort of a

person would I be if I couldn't help a couple of old school pals?' she whispered back.

Tommy introduced Eve to the lads. Then Eve said she would take them to the rehearsal room where they'd be auditioning. Alan Hood was already there waiting for them.

As they headed for the rehearsal room, with Tommy chatting to Eve, Jessie thought about how much Eve had mellowed since Queenie Park. This sophisticated, well made-up and exquisitely dressed young lady was completely unlike the tarty Eve Smith of those days.

But then she herself was also totally different to what she'd been then. Eve could hardly accuse her of being Goody Two Shoes now, you could hardly label the Queen of the Glasgow Teds as that!

Long forgotten memories came flooding back to Jessie. She recalled the barney she'd had with Eve in the changing room that time. How shocked and scandalized she'd been. She remembered saying Eve was disgusting, and Eve retaliating by calling her Goody Two Shoes.

Who would have thought the notorious school hussy would end up a svelte BBC television producer's secretary? Or the minister's daughter Queen of the Glasgow Teds?

Eve told Jessie she was living out in Bearsden, one of the poshest areas in Glasgow, she and her husband Norman had a bungalow there. She didn't ask Jessie where Jessie and Tommy were staying, she knew from the application for an audition that they were living in Govanhill. Down amongst the peasants was how she'd phrased it in her mind.

Eve recalled to herself the occasion she'd seen Tommy and Star's picture in the *Scottish Daily Record* after The Battle of Linton Street. What a mouth gaping shock it had been to realize that her old lover was now King of the Glasgow Teds – and that Miss Butter-Wouldn't-Melt-in-Her-Mouth-Goody-Two-Shoes was his queen.

Eve brought her thoughts back to the present as they

arrived at the rehearsal room where Alan Hood was waiting. Dear Alan, she'd had him under her thumb since shortly after becoming his secretary, a job she'd schemed and connived to get because it was one of the best positions for a woman in Queen Margaret Drive.

Alan was a non-descript man with red hair and very pale freckles, of medium height and medium weight. He lurched to his feet the moment Eve came through the door. As hands were shaken and introductions made he said how pleased he was to meet them all, and that he was looking forward to their audition.

Jessie didn't fail to notice how Eve controlled the situation. It was Eve who told the band to set up, and who suggested the most appropriate place in the room for them to do so. It was also Eve who organized coffee and jollied Hood – a bit of a cheek Jessie thought – into lining up the chairs for those who'd be watching.

Tommy had thought he might be nervous but wasn't. Hell, it was only Eve he'd be singing to, and as for Hood, the producer was about as frightening as a bowl of cold porridge.

Jessie learned from Eve that they were the only people auditioning that day. Eve had accorded them extra special treatment indeed, for which Jessie was uneasily grateful.

Eve was dying to hear Tommy sing. Word on the grapevine, for she'd made inquiries, had it he was good. How strange it was to think of him as a singer, so unlike the image of the Tommy McBride she'd carried in her mind all these years. Mind you, until seeing that picture in the *Scottish Daily Record*, that image hadn't been of him as a Teddy Boy either.

Tommy and Jessie had already decided he and the band would perform the two numbers he and she had collaborated on together. In Jessie's opinion those two numbers were by far the best in their repertoire of original material.

'Ready when you are,' Alan Hood smiled, and, hunching his shoulders, sank in on himself, a body posture he felt made him appear not only important but also extremely knowledgeable.

Jessie crossed two fingers for luck, and offered up a silent prayer. This was so important to Tommy.

Tommy tapped out the beat on the wooden floor, and they were off. Jack twanged the homemade bass, Sammy rattled on the washboard, Jake blew the seven-gallon jug, and Tommy sang.

What a hunk he'd turned out to be, Eve thought, her eyes glued on Tommy. He'd been fanciable as a schoolboy, but he was certainly not a boy any more. As for his singing – that definitely did things to her as well.

Alan Hood was greatly relieved to discover Tommy and the band had talent. It would have been a sod if they didn't and Eve insisted he put them in the show. He would have argued with her, of course, but the outcome would have been inevitable. Eve always got what she wanted.

Tommy's eyes met Jessie's, and she gave him a nod of encouragement, a nod that confirmed he was doing well, and to keep it up.

The band performed both numbers, then it was over. Jack and Sammy were grinning, for they were sure it had been a success. Jake 'The Rake' also looked highly pleased with himself, as if he'd just pulled the most beautiful doll in Glasgow. Tommy tried to hide how chuffed he felt.

Eve applauded loudly. Alan Hood not quite so loudly, but enthusiastically. Jessie didn't know whether it was right for her to applaud or not, and decided she might as well.

'So what do you say, Alan?' Eve demanded, knowing full well what he would say, for he always said the same thing to applicants.

'You'll be hearing from me in due course, but I want you to know I was most impressed, *most*,' Alan Hood said to Jessie, Tommy and the band.

Jessie glanced at Tommy. That sounded to her like it was in the bag. She could see he thought so, too.

Getting ready for bed that night Jessie put on the most seductive of her nightdresses and dabbed scent behind her ears and in the cleavage of her breasts.

Already under the covers, Tommy was still full of the audition, and didn't think he'd be able to sleep for ages yet. Because of this he'd brought a cowboy novel to bed with him to read.

Jessie had been thinking about Eve Smith, or Eve Baxter as she was now, ever since leaving the BBC. Eve had been so sophisticated and successful looking. And she'd been wearing the sort of clothes Jessie would have loved to wear, rather than the eccentric ones she did. Next to Eve, Jessie felt like a child. But to be truthful, it wasn't merely the clothes. Tommy was a one-time lover of hers. He must have noticed how attractive Eve was now. Must have noticed and wondered.

Tommy closed his eyes and pictured himself on television, losing himself in a fantastic dream. He suddenly realized that Jessie was talking. 'What did you say?'

'I thought the new Eve was quite a dish, didn't you?' she repeated.

He had indeed thought the new Eve quite a dish, a right cracker, but he had no intention of saying so to Jessie. There was a jealous streak in her, and her expression, which she thought was guarded, told him that streak was now very much to the fore.

'She was all right,' he shrugged, and pretended to begin reading his novel.

'I was wondering if you still fancied her? Couldn't say I'd blame you if you did,' Jessie went on.

'Eve could never hold a candle to you as far as I was concerned, you know that,' he replied without looking up from his book.

'Still?'

'Still.'

Jessie sighed. It was good to hear that, at least it relieved a little of her anxiety.

'So you *didn't* fancy her then, even though she was so much dishier than she used to be?' Jessie persisted.

Tommy gave an inward groan. Women! How they could go on when they got a bee in their bonnet about something.

'Not even a flicker of interest,' he lied convincingly.

'Jake fancied her.'

'Jake fancies anything that wears a skirt, as you know. Anyway, I don't see what you're driving at. Eve's clearly settled down now, in love with her husband, and living in happiness in posh Bearsden.'

Jessie snuggled up close to him. Using two fingers she walked her left hand over his thigh, and then down into the slit of his pyjama trousers where she took hold of him.

'How about it?'

'What if I don't feel like it?' he asked coolly, pretending indifference.

She gave a small, but sharp tug. 'If you don't I'll pull the bloody thing off,' she threatened.

'A very convincing argument,' he answered hastily.

Jessie put extra effort into her lovemaking. Just to be on the safe side.

Mid-morning the following Monday, as Tommy was brewing himself a pot of tea, there was a knock on the outside door. Opening the door he found a strange young man standing on the landing.

'Mr McBride?' the young man asked.

'Yes.'

'I'm a photographer from Auntie,' the young man said.

Tommy was baffled, what sort of gag was this: 'Auntie who?'

'Sorry, the BBC.'

Tommy shook his head, he'd never heard the expression before. Then excitement gripped him. A photographer from the BBC! It could only be something to do with the audition, the result of which he hadn't yet been notified.

'I've been sent by Mr Hood's office to do some photographs of you,' the young man explained, brandishing a camera.

Tommy immediately asked if that meant the band had been accepted for the show, but the photographer had no idea, he hadn't been given any information, only told to take a number of photographs.

Tommy ushered the young man through to the kitchen where he offered him a cup of tea, which the photographer refused.

'What about the other lads in the band, don't you want them too?' Tommy asked.

'Nope, only you.' The photographer produced a light meter. Squinting at it he asked casually, 'All alone?'

'Aye, the wife's at work.' Tommy decided he'd put on his best black drape for the photo session, the one he'd been married in.

The photographer muttered in exasperation, and said it was no use, there just wasn't enough light in the house. Would Tommy mind going out to a location? He had a car parked nearby.

Tommy answered that he wouldn't mind in the least, and told the photographer to wait while he got changed.

The photographer said he thought Tommy was fine as he was, there was no necessity to put on other clothes. Tommy considered insisting, but decided against it. He would have preferred the photos to have been of him in that particular drape, but there was no point in arguing.

The car, a Bentley, was parked around the corner. Its rear window blinds were drawn. As Tommy slid into the front passenger seat he realized there was another person in the back of the car. Turning round he found himself staring at Eve.

'The chap never said you were here,' Tommy said in surprise.

She smiled enigmatically. 'Drive on,' she instructed the photographer.

There was something fishy going on, Tommy suddenly thought. They didn't want the other lads in the band, only him. And now Eve had put in an appearance. 'What's your game?' he demanded bluntly.

'I wanted a chat, that's all. Knowing Star was at work I would have come up and knocked on your door myself, but you know what neighbours are like, always seeing what they shouldn't, and jumping to wrong conclusions. That's why I had Pete here do the knocking for me.'

'So there aren't to be any photos?'

'Sorry for the subterfuge. No photos, just a chat,' Eve said.

Tommy stared at Eve, not trusting her one iota. He remembered only too well the Eve of old. 'What kind of chat?'

'Relax, I just wanted to find out more about you and how you've been. Your plans for the future. Just a friendly interest in someone I used to be very fond of, okay?'

They drove to the Queen's Park, and swung into a side street, eventually coming to a halt adjacent to the bandstand.

Eve said they'd get out there, and waited for Tommy to open the door for her. When she was on the pavement beside him she hooked her arm in one of his.

'I thought we'd come to the bandstand,' she smiled. 'Not only is it the ideal place for a quiet chat, but you can see the school from there.'

At the bandstand Tommy looked in the direction of the school to see the spire of north building jutting into the sky about half a mile away.

'Imagine our paths crossing again after all this while,' she said softly. 'And you so transformed – King of the Teds and a singer.'

Something about her was making him uncomfortable. 'I haven't heard the outcome of the audition yet,' he said.

'You will,' she replied, lighting a cigarette.

They crossed to a wooden bench and sat down. Birds were singing and a warm breeze was gently blowing; it was a beautiful day.

'Tell me about being King of the Teds,' Eve coaxed.

Tommy didn't think there was any harm in that, so he recounted what it had been like for him since he'd been given the title.

Eve wanted to know all about the Battle of Linton Street, so he described what had happened, including the details of his fight with Ken Young. She listened with bated breath.

She asked about the reasons for the battle, causing Tommy to tense, wondering if she'd heard anything about what had happened to Jessie. That was something he never spoke of except to Jessie, and very occasionally to one of the Boys who'd been there. It was strictly private.

'There was a long standing grudge between me and Ken Young, that's all. One day it came to a head.'

Eve was satisfied with his explanation.

It gave Eve a thrill to have Tommy describe his exploits as King of the Glasgow Teds to her. She thought of Norman, her dull husband, and shuddered inwardly at how deadly boring he was. Any thrills Norman had once given her had long since vanished. 'And how did you become a singer?' she asked, coming out of her thoughts.

'It was Jessie's idea. She told me my voice was good enough for me to have a career in music.'

'I agree with her, it is.'

Tommy gazed off into the distance, but it wasn't the park he saw, it was his cell in Barlinne. If there was a hell hole on Earth it was that prison. 'When I came out of prison I discovered no one would employ me, so I was stuck without a job. Singing started me working again.'

223

'And you enjoy it?'

'Oh, aye. I was nervous at first, but soon got over that. Now I believe I can really go places, given the breaks that is.'

'You're ambitious then?' she prompted, watching him nervously.

'I am that. Jessie says I have it in me to go to the top, and that's where I'm going to do my damnedest to get.'

Eve smiled, he *was* ambitious, just as she'd hoped. Ambition made him vulnerable. 'So getting on the show really is important to you,' she said slowly.

'Winning it is even more important,' he replied with a grin.

She dropped what remained of her cigarette on to the grass and ground it underfoot. 'I can help you, you know,' she said simply. 'And not only with the show, but at the highest levels of the industry.'

He tried to hide his keen interest, but it shone through. 'How?'

Eve opened her handbag, took out a private card, and handed it to him.

'Come to lunch tomorrow at twelve. I'll show you then the power I have.'

He glanced down at the card, it was a Bearsden address. 'Shouldn't you be working then?' he asked quietly.

'I have an arrangement with Alan, and part of that arrangement is that I can have time off whenever I want. Within reason of course.' She got to her feet. 'And anyway,' she smiled, 'it is working.'

'And is the swish Bentley that brought us here also part of the arrangement?' Tommy asked.

Eve's eyes gleamed. 'Alan's a rich man in his own right.'

Tommy didn't have to ask Eve what her side of this arrangement was. He could guess.

*   *   *

224

Tommy had never been in Bearsden before. Walking down the street where Eve lived he decided he didn't like it. There was a sanctimonious air about the place which reminded him of Jessie's father, whom Jessie had never seen from the day she'd been chucked out to this.

The bungalow was painted beige with a red tiled roof. What originally had been a small garden out front had been concreted over. Sacrilege that, Tommy thought as he pressed the buzzer, wincing when a brassy scale of bells rang out.

Eve was wearing a light summer frock, no stockings and open-toed sandals. Her only make-up was scarlet lipstick. She looked a knockout. 'Right on time,' she laughed. 'Just like always.'

She took him through to the lounge where she poured him a generous whisky and herself a gin and tonic.

'Won't your husband mind you entertaining a man when he's not about?' Tommy asked, nervous now that he was actually here.

'I do as I please, Norman never complains,' she answered coolly.

Tommy glanced round, thinking there might be a photograph of Norman, but there wasn't. 'And what about neighbours, don't yours gossip?'

Her reply was to give him one of her enigmatic smiles, and sip her drink. He wasn't at all sure what to make of that.

'Did you tell Star you were coming here?' Eve asked.

Tommy shook his head. 'And she told you, it's Jessie nowadays.'

Still smiling, Eve crossed to an open bureau and lifted two sheets of paper from the desk. These she gave to Tommy. They were letters, both addressed to him, but as yet undated. He read them through.

One said the Tommy McBride Skiffle Band had been awarded a place on New Talent, the other was a polite rejection, saying the Tommy McBride Skiffle Band had failed to be selected.

'I decide which of those two letters gets sent to you. Not only that, if you do appear I can ensure you win,' Eve said.

'Hood?'

'As producer Alan names the winner. If I tell him to name you, then that's what he'll do.'

Tommy thought of the New Talent show. Winning it could make the Tommy McBride Skiffle Band a national name. It would be an enormous break for them.

'You mentioned the highest levels of the industry the other day?'

'I'll give you an example. You've heard of M.M.T. Records?'

Tommy nodded, M.M.T. was a top recording company, ranking alongside Decca in size and the number of first class artists they had signed to their label.

Eve gestured to a bright yellow telephone in the corner. 'I want you to do this yourself so that you know I'm not conning you in any way. Pick up that phone, ask for M.M.T.'s London number, then have the operator put you through. When they answer the party you want is Miss Grierson, the managing director's secretary, say you're ringing on my behalf. When Sally Grierson comes on the line you can then hand the phone over to me,' she instructed.

Tommy did as he was bid, handing the phone over once he'd been connected to the pleasant sounding Sally Grierson.

The ensuring conversation was about a big name star who would shortly be appearing on a BBC Glasgow Light Entertainment programme. Eve hung up, sat again, and stared at Tommy, that enigmatic smile on her lips.

'Sally Grierson is only one example of the contacts in high places that I have, there are dozens more. Being Alan's secretary I deal with these people every day. As a matter of course, and business, we do each other favours from time to time. It helps make life easier all round.' Eve

226

paused, then said slowly, and with emphasis. 'If I asked Sally to put in a good word for you at M.M.T. she would. It's a virtual certainty that a recording contract would follow.'

Tommy's heart jumped. A contract with M.M.T. would be an open sesame to the charts and playing the number one London venues.

'If for some reason it didn't, I guarantee I'd get you one with another top outfit,' she continued.

Now for the punchline, Tommy thought with dread. He was pretty sure he knew what it was going to be. 'What do I have to do for all this?' he asked.

'Agree to start sleeping with me again, and I'll do all the things I've just said. And more,' she promised. 'Lot's more.'

He stared at her, his eyes hard. 'Why?'

She treated him to one of her enigmatic smiles. 'Because I want you. It's as simple as that. I usually get what I set my heart on, and for now it's set on you.'

'What about Hood and hubby?'

She shrugged. 'Neither need know. And if they did it wouldn't matter, they're both broadminded.'

He found the whole thing disgusting. It told him a great deal about Alan Hood and Norman Baxter, that was for sure.

Eve played her ace. 'I might also mention the other side of the coin. I can pull strings on your behalf,' she purred. 'Or *against* you.'

He went cold all over, his mouth suddenly dry.

'Doing the dirty on you would be even easier than building you up. A dropped hint here, a little lie there, and soon . . . Well, you might continue to be booked by the Glasgow dancehalls, but you'd certainly never get any further than that. TV and radio would be closed to you, London wouldn't want to know. Tommy McBride, thug and ex-jailbird, and his skiffle band, would have a reputation that stank a mile high,' she said sweetly.

Oh you bitch, you rotten bitch, he thought. She'd certainly grown up.

Eve rose and smoothed down the front of her frock. 'Don't give me an answer now. Ring me at the Beeb, or here if you like, when you've decided,' she said, picking up the two letters from where she'd laid them and putting them back in the bureau. She turned to him with a smile. 'How about lunch? I'm ravenous.'

It was *coq au vin*, followed by raspberry fool.

It had taken Jessie thirty-five minutes to write down the music for their latest number. She'd finished that several hours ago, and Tommy had been struggling with the lyrics ever since.

She glanced over at the piano where Tommy was staring morosely off into space. It suddenly dawned on her that he looked pale and drawn, as if he was worried about something or ill. She hoped he wasn't coming down with something, for they had yet another booking for Mr Bojangles, opening the following night. They'd been lucky with health so far, none of the band having gone down with anything that had stopped them appearing.

Tommy was thinking about Eve's proposition, and feeling wretched as a result. She had him by the short and curlies, there was no getting away from it. He wondered if it would be any good reporting her to the BBC, but doubted it. Hood would back her up, and in the end if would boil down to his word against hers. He certainly didn't doubt that she'd stick the knife in him if he didn't comply, she'd stick the knife in and twist it, and smile that bloody enigmatic smile of hers as she was doing it.

With Eve against him it would take God alone knew how long to escape Govanhill, and being King of the Glasgow Teds, while every passing day increased the chances of his being involved in a barney he'd be carried out of feet first.

And then there was the fact that though he loved Jessie, if he agreed to becoming Eve's lover then the world was his on a plate. He'd win the New Talent show, there would be a contract with M.M.T., and from then on the sky was the limit – money, a smart car, all the luxuries you could think of. But most important of all, the escape from Govanhill that Jessie so craved, and his own escape from being King of the Glasgow Teds and his past. And if Jessie didn't find out, what was the harm?

'Are you all right?' Jessie asked, placing a hand on his shoulder.

He jerked away in surprise. 'I've got rather a headache I'm afraid,' he lied.

'Then you should pack this in for tonight, you're obviously struggling with these lyrics because you're not feeling all that hot.'

Abandoning piano and the few lyrics he'd managed, he crossed over to his favourite chair and slumped into it. 'Yes please,' he said when Jessie asked him if he'd like a cup of coffee.

As Jessie waited for the kettle to boil she saw that he'd closed his eyes and was rubbing his forehead. His headache must be worse than he was letting on, she thought.

Next morning he waited till the back of ten, he'd got the impression these people didn't go in for early starts, then walked along Allison Street to the nearest public phone box. From there he rang Eve at the BBC.

'Okay, I agree, but on one condition,' he said shortly.

Elation and self-satisfaction filled Eve. That, and a fluttering of sexual arousal. It wouldn't be long now before she had that gorgeous hunk in her bed. 'Which is?'

'On no account must Jessie find out.'

'She won't find out from me, you have my promise on that,' Eve replied.

They made arrangements for him to call at the Bearsden bungalow the following afternoon.

Eve answered the door in a clinging pale yellow silk dressing gown, a cloud of heady perfume hanging around her. Tommy slipped inside. She laughed at his furtiveness.

The truth was she didn't care what the neighbours thought about the various comings and goings at the bungalow. They'd long since stopped talking to her anyway.

She led the way to her bedroom where the curtains had already been drawn and a table lamp switched on. The bed's covers had been pulled back. On top of the vanity were two crystal glasses, a crystal decanter of whisky, and a plate of salmon sandwiches.

Eve stood with her back to Tommy, and undid her dressing gown, which fell in a whisper of silk to the thick fitted carpet. She was naked underneath. Going to the vanity, Eve picked up a sandwich and delicately bit into it. 'Help yourself,' she said to Tommy.

And gave him one of her enigmatic smiles.

Jessie slotted her key into the door lock, having just arrived home from work. It had been a tiring day with her never off her feet, and she still had the evening meal to make, with Mr Bojangles after that. She wondered about sending Tommy out for chicken and chips, which would at least give her time to have really good wash down at the sink.

Tommy was in the kitchen with a huge grin plastered all over his face.

'You look like you lost a tanner and found a pound,' she said.

He pulled a sheet of paper out from his inside jacket pocket and waved it at her. 'It's the New Talent show for us!' he exclaimed.

Jessie squealed with joy, throwing her arms around him. She kissed him on the cheek, the mouth, and the mouth again. Snatching the letter from him she hurriedly read it through.

'Have you told the others yet?' she asked excitedly.

'I wanted you to be the first to know. I'll tell them tonight at Bojangles.'

Her tiredness had vanished. She was now light as air, and full of energy. She felt as though she was going to laugh and cry at once. 'I can't tell you how pleased I am . . . I . . . oh, Tommy!'

She was so lovely, he thought, his beautiful darling Jessie. That look on her face made him feel that he'd done the right thing. Everything would be all right from now on. He wanted to take her to bed there and then, but he'd been with Eve nearly all afternoon and doubted that he could.

'Soon everyone's going to know who you are. Now we've been accepted for the show we've got to win it,' Jessie declared with determination.

Tommy took her in his arms. 'I've got a feeling about that,' he said.

Jessie was gathering their dirty laundry into a pile, as she did every week, to take it to work with her where it was done for nothing, one of the few perks of the job.

Her nose suddenly twitched at an unfamiliar smell. It was a nice smell, and one she couldn't place. She tried several of Tommy's shirts before she found the one it was coming from. It was a beautiful perfume, undoubtedly expensive, and quite different to the blue bottle she wore. Probably French, she thought, it smelled French.

Now how had Tommy got such perfume on his shirt? He didn't have another woman did he? Jessie laughed aloud at the idea, no it must have come from a fan, some lassie who'd rubbed herself up against him.

Another woman indeed, let him dare!

231

She thrust the shirt back into the pile and promptly forgot about it.

Jessie gnawed a nail, she'd already broken two others, and for the umpteenth time glanced at the wall clock. Twenty minutes till the show started and she wanted to be sick.

They'd been at Queen Margaret Drive since early that morning, the rehearsals culminating in a run-through that had finished an hour previously. The next run would be the real thing.

Jessie was in the dressing room allocated to Tommy and the band. Tommy and Jake 'The Rake' were chatting about snooker, while Jack and Sammy were off for their turn at make-up. She was expecting Jack and Sammy back at any moment.

Tommy was extremely relaxed, as if appearing on the box was a regular occurrence with him. Which meant there was one less thing to worry about. The more relaxed he was the better his singing would be.

She continued gnawing her nail and thought about the other acts. They were a mixed variety bag consisting of a juggler, a bicycle trio, a ventriloquist, a magician, three stand up comics, and a female singer. As far as she was concerned the singer was the main competition. The girl wasn't only exceptionally attractive, but she had a real belter of a voice, the sort of voice that could soothe you to sleep one moment and shatter glass the next.

'Come in!' Tommy called out in a reply to a rap on the door.

It was Eve, accompanied by a man about ten years older than herself. Snake hipped, dressed in casual clothes, he had a moustache and beard, and wore tinted glasses. The hair on his head was thin and balding. The eyes behind the glasses were small and sharp, reminding Jessie of a ferret. He had a thick gold chain around his neck, and a fankle of smaller gold chains dangling from the larger. He had three gold bracelets on his left wrist, a broad banded gold watch and another gold chain on his right.

He's queer Jessie thought.

'I'd like you all to meet my husband, Norman,' Eve said with a big smile.

Tommy was momentarily thrown, but swiftly recovered himself. 'Come away in, would you care for a hauf Norman?' he asked, indicating the bottle of whisky he personally had provided for after their performance and in case of visitors.

Norman replied he wouldn't, not just then anyway. He shook Jessie's hand, said he was delighted to meet her, then did the same with Tommy and Jake.

'I just wanted to wish you good luck,' Eve told Tommy.

Jack and Sammy arrived back from make-up, and were introduced to Norman by Jessie, who'd decided she didn't care at all for Eve's husband, he gave her the willies.

Norman made small talk by asking Tommy what the order of their appearance was in the show, and Tommy answered they were going on fifth. Eve said the fifth and sixth spots were generally considered to be the best.

The tannoy crackled into life, and the Production Assistant announced that there was now only fifteen minutes to go. He requested the acts to remain in their various dressing rooms, until they were called.

'Well, I'm going to take Norman out to his seat,' cooed Eve. 'Are you coming, Jessie? Your seat's next to Norman's so you'll be among friends.'

Jessie would much rather have sat beside total strangers than Norman Baxter.

'I'll be along in a minute.' She wanted to stay with Tommy for as long as she could.

Eve gave Tommy a big kiss on the mouth, wishing him good luck again. Jessie felt something stir at the back of her mind. She didn't know why, but that kiss annoyed

233

her. There seemed to be more to it than just good luck. She could, after all, have kissed him on the cheek. But then, Eve had always been a liberty taker.

When Eve and Norman were gone Jessie gave Tommy the once over to make sure he was as he should be and all in order, and then did the same for the lads. She insisted Jack do up his top shirt button, even though, he argued, he never usually did. That wasn't the point, she told him, he was going to appear before millions of people, and just because he was a Ted it didn't mean he had to look sloppy.

There was another rap on the door, and Alan Hood popped his head round. 'A quick all the best, I'm sure you'll do fine,' Alan smiled.

Tommy gave Hood the thumbs up, neither betraying to the other by even the smallest sign that it had already been decided that the Tommy McBride Skiffle Band was going to win.

At last she could find no more excuses for hanging around. She took one of Tommy's hands in her's and squeezed it warmly. 'Bring the house down,' she whispered.

'You can rely on it,' he whispered back.

She gave the lads a cuddle each, then fled the room for the corridor outside where she had to pause for nearly a full minute in order to collect herself.

Arriving in the studio she immediately caught sight of Norman Baxter who waved to her, then pointed at the empty seat beside him. She made her way across.

The stage consisted of a number of rostra surrounded on three sides by steeply banking seats. Jessie estimated there were about two hundred and fifty people in the studio which was already stiflingly hot.

When she was seated Norman gestured up into the gloom of the studio ceiling and there, on the side opposite, high above the hanging spots and floods, she could make out a pale green glow. He told her that was the director's box where Eve and Alan Hood were.

'How do you feel?' Norman asked, his eyes glinting behind his glasses.

Jessie gave him a weak, and very strained, smile. She wished he wouldn't keep talking, she would have preferred to suffer in silence.

Norman fumbled in a pocket to produce something which he slipped into her hand. 'Swallow that, it'll soon calm you down,' he said quietly.

It was a flat pink pill he'd placed in her palm. He was offering her drugs, she thought in a combination of disgust and alarm. 'No thanks,' she said quickly, trying not to sound contemptuous, or ungracious and returned the pill to him.

With a shrug he put it back into his pocket. 'I take them all the time myself,' he said. 'They're great when you need relaxing.

There was only a couple of minutes left now. Jessie squirmed in her seat, restless with anxiety for Tommy. She wondered if he was still as relaxed as he'd been when she'd left him. Oh, please, God, she prayed, don't let him lose his voice.

Then the P.A. was on the stage, welcoming the audience to the show, and cracking a few jokes to warm them up. He told them that at the end of the performances the V.T.R., the tape on which the show was being recorded, would be stopped and slips of paper passed amongst them. After they'd voted the slips would be taken away and counted, and when this had been done the V.T.R. would be restarted, and a decision announced, first, second and third, in the usual reverse order.

The lights shining on the audience dimmed, and died. 'Let's hear a large hand for our opening act, The Great McGregor, Magician Extraordinaire!' called the P.A.

The Great McGregor bounded onstage and right off produced a haggis from his ear. The audience, loving that, gave him a round of applause, and the show was off to a fine start.

Next up was one of the comics who'd clearly modelled

235

himself on Lex McLean who'd long been an enormous favourite with Glaswegians. By the end of his patter the feeling amongst the audience was that Lex wasn't in for any sleepless nights worrying about this particular competition.

The third act was the singer, a blonde girl in her early twenties, who had a magnificent figure as well as a magnificent voice. Somebody gave a wolf whistle before she began, another voice was heard to exclaim 'Wow!' The girl gave a charming smile, she was obviously used to that sort of attention.

When the singer was finished Jessie knew that Tommy and the band could be in trouble. She had been even better than the run-through, and she'd been damned good then.

The next act was the bicycle trio, which turned out to be comedic, although it wasn't supposed to be. The trio consisted of a father, mother and daughter, the father so nervous he repeatedly fell off his unicycle, at one point directly in front of the daughter who promptly ran over him.

Then it was the Tommy McBride Skiffle Band, who came to their instruments led by a scowling Tommy. The scowl and aggression were part of his act.

Jessie's heart was in her mouth. Without realizing it she'd taken hold of Norman Baxter's arm, clutching it so hard he'd have black and blue marks for a week.

She could hardly bear to look, and to begin with kept her gaze fastened to the rim of the seat in front.

The band's first number was the last she and Tommy had collaborated on, and their best to date. It was a raunchy, heavy beat number about a hard drinking dockie, out for a night on the town to drown his sorrows about his lost love who'd run off with his closest pal.

He reached out, took that audience by the scruff of the neck, and completely won them over. He'd had charisma before; now he knew how to use it.

The second number was poignant and bittersweet, and

Tommy sang it to perfection. The last note faded away, to be greeted with silence, a silence filled with emotion and pleasure. One person clapped and another, then they all were. Tears were rolling down Jessie's cheeks as she banged her hands together. That had been even better than she'd hoped. Tommy had surpassed even her expectations.

Norman Baxter leaned towards her. 'I'm very impressed,' he whispered. 'I think they have a good chance of winning.'

But Jessie didn't underestimate the threat of the blonde singer and her breasts. A lot of men in the audience would be voting for those breasts, it was the sort of thing men did.

The acts following seemed to fly by, then the P.A. was back on the stage saying the V.T.R. had been stopped, and voting would now take place.

The paper Jessie was given had the names of the nine acts on it, with a box against each name. Jessie's hand was shaking as she made her mark using Norman Baxter's pen. Throughout the audience pens and pencils were being passed back and forth.

The slips were collected, put into a cardboard container, and then the container given to the P.A. who disappeared off with it.

'How long do you think this'll take?' Jessie asked Norman. She was fidgeting with impatience.

'Not long. Eve will have it well organized, you can be sure of that.'

In the dressing room Tommy was pouring large whiskies, and congratulating himself on having done well. He didn't think he'd ever sung better, but then there had been no pressure whatever on him, as there had been on the other acts – he'd *known* he was going to win.

'Come on!' Jessie muttered, and glanced yet again at her watch.

In the director's box Alan Hood was finishing knotting his tie. He'd changed into a lounge suit, for he'd be going

237

onstage, in front of the camera, to declare the winner and runners up. The P.A. would run that last part of the show from the box.

Eve and Alan had personally, and in private, counted the votes and were surprised at the results.

Alan Hood made his way to the stage, where his appearance was greeted with applause. He held up his hands, gesturing for the clapping to stop. Hood made a brief speech about Scotland, the show, and the acts who'd performed that evening. Then he said, 'In third place, with forty-eight votes, The Great McGregor, Magician Extraordinaire!'

On hearing that he'd come third, the Great McGregor gave a whoop, and came bounding on stage to shake Hood's hand. When Hood had finally extricated his hand he found, to his own amusement as well as the audience's that he was holding a ring of black pudding.

So far so good, Jessie was thinking, bouncing in her seat.

'And in second place Roy Byrne!' Hood announced. Byrne was of the stand-up comics.

Despite the heat Jessie went chill all over. She'd thought first place was between Tommy and the female singer, in which case one of them should have come second. But they hadn't, Roy Byrne had! So either Tommy or the female singer wasn't placed at all, and she could hardly believe it was the singer, not with those sodding great tits!

Oh, Tommy, Jessie wailed inside. His big chance had ended in disaster.

'And in first place, with a hundred and three votes, the winner is . . .' Hood paused, drawing the moment out. 'The Tommy McBride Skiffle Band!'

They'd won! They'd won after all! Jessie leapt up and down with excitement and joy.

Tommy and the lads came onstage to shake Hood's hand, and give the audience 'thank you' gestures. Jake 'The Rake', so overcome by it all, was blowing kisses to every woman he could see.

Hood spoke into the camera, winding up the show. The P.A.'s voice boomed out from hidden loudspeakers saying that the show was over, and that the audience could now go.

Jessie left Norman Baxter, wriggling her way out to the aisle, and running down and over to where a beaming Tommy was being congratulated by The Great McGregor, Roy Byrne and Alan Hood.

She threw herself into his arms, and hugged him tightly. 'We did it! We did it!' she cried. 'You were wonderful!'

Tommy extracted Jessie and himself from the general confusion, and they returned to the dressing room where they toasted their success in whisky. Tommy confessed that he was also dumbfounded that the singer hadn't done better. Then he shut up about that, thinking the finagling of the votes he believed had taken place might well have accounted for the lassie's poor showing. The truth of the matter was, though, that it had done nothing of the sort. Eve and Hood had been just as surprised on counting the votes to discover the lassie had done so badly. As it had turned out, Tommy and the band had won fair and square, knocking the other acts for six. Eve hadn't had to do any finagling, something she never did tell Tommy. The figures Alan Hood had read had been exactly as cast.

Jack, Sammy and Jake arrived back in the dressing room, all three of them cock-a-hoop, and with another bottle of whisky which they gleefully declared they'd 'liberated'. Sammy, who'd been swallowing from the bottle as though it was lemonade, was already well on the way to getting paralytic, or 'deid mockit' as he would have put it.

Alan Hood appeared with a tall thin woman whom he introduced as his wife, Vanessa. 'I always take the winning act out for a meal after the show,' he said. 'You boys fancy a meal?'

During the drive to the restaurant Jessie snuggled up to

Tommy, she felt closer to him than she'd ever been, and so gloriously happy she must surely burst from it.

Tommy was still in bed the next morning, Jessie having long since gone to work, when there was a knock on the outside door. He'd been awake for a while now, but continued to lie there waiting for his muzzy head to clear. He'd drunk a lot the night before, as had everyone else. It had been a great celebration.

Getting out of bed he staggered through to answer the knock, to discover Eve standing on the landing. 'I've got news,' she said, and marched past him on into the kitchen. There she looked around in interest, though it was obvious from her expression that she didn't think much of what she saw.

'You're not on the phone, and there wasn't time to write, so I came in person,' she explained briefly.

'So I see,' he drawled, wondering what this was all about.

'I had a buzz about an hour ago from Sally Grierson at M.M.T. Daniel Silver watched you last night, and was most impressed.'

Tommy's ears pricked up. Daniel Silver was the boss of M.M.T., and, according to an article he'd read recently in *Melody Maker*, one of the most powerful people in the recording business. He was wide awake now. 'That's terrific!'

'It's more than that. He wants you and the others to fly down to London, at his expense, this afternoon to discuss your future.'

Tommy let out a yell, and punched the air. This was it, the big breakthrough. This was escape from Govanhill, and his past, and being King of the Glasgow Teds. This was the beginning of his dream coming true.

'My only worry was you might have a performance scheduled for tonight,' Eve said briskly. 'If so you'll have to cancel it.'

Tommy shook his head. 'We've nothing on, we're in the clear.'

'I've already booked you on the three o'clock plane. Sally Grierson will be meeting you at Heathrow.'

Tommy was fizzling inside, his hangover gone. He felt like he was walking on air.

'Do I deliver the goods or don't I?' Eve asked, standing right in front of him.

'You deliver,' he agreed.

'Then how about a little kiss of gratitude?'

He took her in his arms. 'Thanks,' he whispered. 'Thank you very much.'

Eve shivered. God but he was a hunk. The sense of danger he exhuded was an aphrodisiac that never failed to turn her on.

Their lips met, hers greedily on his.

Jessie sat down and clutched her head. Luckily they'd been quiet at work. She doubted she could have coped otherwise.

'Still bad?' Jane Lamont asked sympathetically.

'Worse if anything. It's a real blinder. I should have known better than mix grain and grape,' Jessie moaned.

Jane laughed. 'Always a mistake that.'

'It was a tremendous night mind, but I'm certainly paying for it now.'

Jane thought of the several favours Jessie had done her in the past. Here was her chance to repay at least one of them. 'Listen, I can see us being dead for the rest of the day, so why don't you hoof it? Way back to your kip and sleep. I'll manage here,' She suggested.

Jessie glanced up at her. 'Would you mind?'

'I wouldn't have mentioned it if I did. As you never take time off it seems to me you've earned the right of a skive. And to be truthful, you're not really very much help the way you are.'

Jessie gave a weak smile. 'I'd be eternally grateful.'

'On your bike, then. And don't worry, I'll see everything's all right here.'

Jessie left the shop a few minutes later, hoping Tommy was still in bed so she could cuddle up next to him.

Tommy was still in bed. He lay flat on his back with Eve astride him. He was paying the price for the news she'd brought. Not that it was all that difficult a price to pay, he'd have been lying if he said he didn't enjoy having sex with Eve.

He opened his eyes, and there she was staring down at him, smiling that damned enigmatic smile of hers. He gave a gasp of pleasure as she made a movement that was quite sensational. Then she did it again.

The fresh air had helped a bit, Jessie thought as she climbed the stair leading to the house. When she got in she'd have a nice cup of tea, and then get down underneath the quilt. A couple of aspirins, a few hours sleep, and hopefully she'd be right as rain again.

The first thing she noticed on going through the front door was that the lights in the bedroom were blazing, and then that the bedroom curtains were drawn. How odd, she thought. What was Tommy up to?

She snicked the front door shut behind her, then went into the bedroom. She came up short, blinking in disbelief at the sight confronting her. A naked Eve was on all fours, an equally naked Tommy crouched over her.

Tommy and Eve froze the moment Jessie entered the room. Tommy stared at Jessie in horror.

Whether it was a nervous reaction to the situation, or a manifestation of the nasty streak that ran all through Eve, was hard even for Eve to tell, but she started to laugh. It was a high, raucous laugh – and to Jessie's ears a triumphant and mocking one – that gutted Jessie where she stood. She gave a strangulated cry that was more animal than human.

Tommy, recovering his wits, threw Eve to one side, and tried to get to his feet. As he was doing that, Jessie spun round and fled.

'For God's sake, Jessie, stop!' he screamed, following her out of the house and down the stairs. At the close front, because of his nakedness, he was forced to stop. He watched in despair as Jessie ran up the street.

She ran and ran, not caring where to as long as it was away from the obscenity she'd just witnessed. She could still hear Eve's laugher, ringing in her head.

She found herself at a stop where a tram was picking up passengers, a tram that would take her back to work.

She jumped aboard.

During her return journey to the laundry, a strange intermingling took place in Jessie's mind. What she'd seen in her bedroom became mixed up with the rape she'd suffered in Linton Street.

Revulsion at what Tommy and Eve had been doing was as deep and profound as the revulsion she'd experienced then. She wanted to cry, to die, to be a million miles away. She stared out the tram window, but didn't see the passing scenery. Instead she saw herself spreadeagled, held fast, while Ken Young ravaged her, thrusting his flesh into hers just as Tommy had been thrusting into Eve. Then the picture changed, and now Tommy was one of the rapists, leering at her as he waited his turn.

He'd told her he loved her, he'd sworn it. The liar! THE LIAR!! If he loved her how could he do this to her? And in their bed; in their bed where they'd made love so many times. She heard Eve's laughter again, and cringed inside. She knew that laughter would haunt her for the rest of her life.

Suddenly, everything fell into place. She recalled the

expensive perfume she'd discovered clinging to his shirt, which she'd assumed had rubbed off from a fan. Fan indeed! It had come from Eve, she knew that as surely as she knew she had a nose on her face and five fingers on each hand. And that kiss in the dressing room last night . . .

'In the name of the Wee Man!' Jane Lamont exclaimed when Jessie stumbled into the laundry. Jessie's eyes were wild, her hair awry.

Jessie fled past the solitary customer, staring at her in amazement, and into the back shop where she flopped onto a wooden chair.

When the customer was finally gone Jane ran through to where Jessie sat slumped in the chair.

In a voice breaking with emotion, Jessie told her what had happened. Even though Jessie only hinted at the details, Jane was shaken. To think Jessie had walked in on the likes of that! No wonder the lass looked the way she did.

'I'll stick the kettle on, you need a coffee,' Jane said briskly, immediately suiting her actions to her words.

'In our bed, his and mine,' Jessie repeated. 'That was the worst thing of all.'

'Just forget about them for now.' Jane advised. 'You're getting yourself all worked up and it't not worth it.'

But Jessie couldn't stop torturing herself. 'I've been asking myself how often they've been there together. How often has he had her in our bed in the afternoon, then me at night, on the same sheets?'

Again, the scene she'd walked in on re-played itself in her mind, betraying everything her love for Tommy had stood for. 'I can never go back there, Jane. I'm leaving him.'

'Oh lass, be careful, don't do anything silly.'

Jessie shook her head. 'No I'm leaving him, my mind's made up.'

'I think you're making a bad mistake. If I was you, I'd fight for him.'

Jessie's eyes filled with tears. 'Why bother to fight for someone who can do that to me? He doesn't love me, he *can't* do. If he wants to replace me with Eve then let him, I'll make it easy for the pair of them by clearing off.'

'But where will you go? How will you manage?'

Jessie wiped away tears, but didn't reply. She was going to have to quit Glasgow altogether, that was something else she'd decided on the tram. She couldn't stay here, where everything would remind her of all she'd loved and lost.

In their own bed with another woman! He couldn't possibly love her to do that. No, she wasn't making a mistake, she was doing the right thing – the only thing.

Coming to her feet, she went to look amongst the parcels of laundry to search out her and Tommy's clean laundry, which she knew was there. When she found their parcel she opened it and separated hers from his. She regarded his pile thoughtfully for a couple of seconds, then picking it up heaved it into the garbage bin. There were three of his favourite shirts amongst that lot, which gave her some satisfaction.

She took a brown paper bag from the stock and put her laundry into it. It didn't amount to much, but it was better than nothing – at least she wouldn't be starting out with only the clothes she stood up in. As for money, she had cash in her purse that had been intended for several outstanding bills. She also had most of her previous week's pay left. Most importantly though, she had her Post Office book, which contained a fair amount as she'd been a regular saver since Tommy had started earning. Money, at least, wasn't a problem, at least not in the short term.

Taking a deep breath she turned to Jane whose face was drawn in doubt and concern. 'Don't worry, I'll be all right. Really, Jane. I know what I'm doing.'

'And what about your job here?'

'Apologize for me. Tell them I would have worked out

my notice had it been possible, but it's not. Make up any excuse you want.'

Jane broke down then, for she was terribly fond of Jessie. 'I'll miss you so I will,' she wept.

'And I'll miss you, too.'

They hugged one another, each squeezing the other tight. 'I love him more than life itself, and I believed he loved me,' Jessie whispered. 'That's why I never want to see, or be with him ever again.'

Disentangling herself, Jessie picked up the brown paper bag and left the shop. She turned once to wave to Jane standing in the window, then disappeared round a corner.

PART THREE

Mrs McBride
1959–62

7

Jessie gave the glass she was drying a final wipe, and stacked it with the other pint pots. A glance at the clock above the bar told her it was just gone half past eleven, they were done early for a Saturday night. At times it could be midnight, or later, before the last glass was put away.

'See to the staff drinks will you, darling!' Julian called out to his wife Pixie from the corner where he was sitting cashing up.

Julian was thirty-three, and had been to Eton. Jessie considered his aristocratic background a strange one for a pub landlord, but that was London for you.

Pixie, who Jessie thought a real sweetie, wasn't quite so upper crust, but good enough for Julian's family not to complain when he married her. At least that was what Pixie said, and Pixie wasn't the kind to lie about that sort of thing. In fact there was hardly anything Jessie could imagine Pixie telling a lie about, she was that type of person.

Besides Jessie there was another barmaid working that night in The Lonsdale Arms, a Cockney girl called Yvonne, who originally came from Hackney, but now lived in a flat across the road.

'I'll have a pint of bitter,' Jessie called. She'd developed a taste for beer since coming to work in the pub, and as far as her figure was concerned it was beginning to show. She'd put on more than a bit of weight since leaving Glasgow eight months ago. If she'd been interested in men it might have bothered her, but she wasn't, so it didn't. Men had become strictly past tense in her book. Since Tommy she hadn't wanted to know.

She lit a gasper, another bad habit she'd acquired. She'd

vaguely hoped that smoking might help her weight, but it didn't seem to make any perceptible difference.

The Lonsdale Arms was located in the St Mary Ward of the Borough of Islington. When Jessie arrived at Euston last September she booked into a cheap hotel in that neighbourhood, then the next morning started looking for digs. She hadn't fancied the Euston area, or the adjacent King's Cross one, so she'd hopped on a bus, getting off again in the next borough, which was Islington.

After several hours' fruitless viewing of rooms, all so bad she wouldn't have let a pig stay in any of them, she'd decided to give her feet a rest, and have a bit of a sit down. She'd headed for a cafe she'd passed earlier, but before coming to it had chanced upon The Lonsdale Arms and the sign in its window. Live-in Barmaid Wanted, the sign had said, which had set her thinking.

Inside, she'd ordered a drink and had a good look round. The pub hadn't been modernized with formica and chrome like many, but retained its original Victorian décor with highly polished wood and brass everywhere.

Julian had been behind the bar, talking loudly in that toffy voice of his (he always talked loudly she was soon to learn) and she'd thought he was a character.

She'd decided she liked The Lonsdale Arms. It had a good feel about it. You could just tell that the landlord and his wife were nice, and that the customers were nice, too.

She'd gone up and inquired about the job. 'Have you ever worked in a pub before?' Julian asked, taking her in without seeming to. Jessie didn't know how desperate she looked.

'Well, no,' she'd admitted. 'But I'm a quick learner, and I do need a job.'

Without blinking Julian had called Pixie out from the back where she was cooking, introduced them, mentioned what the job paid, and told Pixie to show Jessie the room that would be hers before Jessie made a decision.

Jessie had adored the bedroom. It had pretty floral wall-paper, a table covered by an old fashioned velvet cloth that had tassles on it, and there was even a continental quilt on the bed, something she'd read about but never seen. There was also a green painted hard backed chair, the same colour green as the cloth on the table. 'Oh, this is lovely,' she'd said enthusiastically, relaxing for the first time since she'd left Glasgow. 'Well, that's it, then,' Pixie had smiled, and they'd shaken hands on it, and Pixie had said to take that day to move in and get herself comfy, she could start work the next morning.

So she'd begun work at The Lonsdale Arms, and had been there ever since. She considered herself to have fallen on her feet. The job itself, the friendly chat and banter and camaraderie was exactly what she needed after the trauma of walking out on Tommy, and the enormous gap that had left in her life.

'How did we do tonight?' Pixie asked Julian, knowing without having to be told that business was down on the previous Saturday, which itself had been down on the Saturday before that.

Julian scrunched up his nose. 'Could be worse, I suppose, but I must admit this falling away of trade is getting me worried. And the brewery isn't happy about it either, not that they've said anything, yet, but I get this feeling every time I talk to them on the phone.'

'That big pub on Islington Green is packing them in,' Jessie said. 'I heard one of the customers talking about it the other night.

'It's because it's got that location. Being at the junction of two main roads is a lot different to being in an out of the way street like us,' Julian said sadly.

Yvonne sipped her gin, and looked thoughtful. 'You know what you want is a gimmick, something that will make this pub different, and have the customers wanting to come here rather than go elsewhere,' she said slowly.

Julian glanced at her with interest. Yvonne somehow gave the impression of being thick, but was anything but. When she made a suggestion it was always a good idea to pay heed.

'What sort of gimmick?' Julian asked.

'How about Morris Dancers?' chipped in Pixie.

'With their wee hankies and their jingly jangly bells?' laughed Jessie. 'Where would you put them all? And who would they attract?'

Yvonne sniggered into her hand.

'Then you come up with something!' Pixie retorted a little miffed that her idea had been received with such scorn.

Jessie racked her brain. What sort of gimmick would get folk into a pub? And the folk round here in particular, who were partly third and fourth generation working class Islingtonians, and partly the new young professional people who were moving in because it was relatively cheap, and they could affort to buy whole houses and do them up.

Darts were popular, of course, but lots of the pubs had that, many even ran their own tournaments. So darts were hardly a novelty.

'Live music,' Jessie said abruptly, remembering that in Glasgow you couldn't fail with live music, provided it was good. So why not here?

'Live music,' Julian mused, now there was a thought. There wasn't a pub in the district, as far as he knew, that had live music. The odds were high it would be a draw, especially with so many young people around.

'What sort of live music, jazz?' he asked Jessie.

Jessie made a face. 'Personally, I'd go for a modern group who would attract the young set, they're the ones with money nowadays. And they're the ones with few real venues.'

Julian turned to his wife. 'What do you say Pixie?'

'I think it's a smashing idea. It would liven things up no end.'

'Yvonne?'

'Should be fun, and I'm always in favour of that.'

Julian snapped a thumb and forefinger. 'Live music and a modern group it is, then. Jessie, take a gold star and go to the top of the class!'

Jessie laughed, top of the class indeed!

'This calls for another round on me,' Julian said, and got up to do the honours.

'I don't suppose you know any modern groups?' he asked Jessie, when he came back with the drinks.

Jessie gave a wry smile. 'Not in London,' she said softly.

'Then I'll place an ad in the *Gazette* and see what that produces,' Julian said. 'There must be lots of groups around dying for a place to play.'

They sat around for some time, making plans, then Jessie went up to her bedroom to get ready for bed.

Talking about live music and groups had brought on another bout of depression. She'd been suffering from recurring bouts since coming south. Jessie blamed beer for her weight problem, but that wasn't the whole answer. Her loneliness and unending unhappiness were also to blame. Part of her had simply given up.

When she was in her nightie, she went over to the old wind up gramophone she'd found in the pub basement which Julian had allowed her to bring up to her room to use. She'd bought a stack of 78s down Camden Passage, an antique market not all that far away, and she now selected one of these and put it on the machine.

Lavender blue dilly dilly,
lavender green.
When I am King, dilly dilly,
you'll be my Queen. . .

'*When I am King, dilly dilly, you'll be my Queen,*' she echoed, and started to cry, ending up sitting on the bed, rocking herself back and forth, while the tears cascaded down her face.

The band was called The Light, and Jessie thought them not bad at all. This was their first appearance in The Lonsdale Arms, and it was on a trial basis only.

The vocalist, and guitar player, was a tall, slim, flaxen haired young man; there was a young negro man on the drums, and a very intense looking fellow on the piano. They were a trio.

Julian sidled up to Jessie while the fair young man was in the middle of Buddy Holly's hit 'Peggy Sue'. 'What's your opinion of them?' he asked for once not talking at the top of his voice.

'I like. And you?'

He nodded. 'So do the customers I've chatted to. When they take their next break, give them a drink on me, okay?'

After 'Peggy Sue' the band played 'Love Is Strange', an Everly Brothers' hit, followed by 'Crying in the Rain', another Everly hit.

When they'd finished that the drummer gave a small roll, and the guitarist, apparently the band's spokesman and leader, announced they were taking a break.

Jessie caught the guitarist's eye and crooked a finger. He stood his guitar in a corner and came over.

'Julian says you're all to have one on the house, what'll it be?' she smiled.

'Three pints would be lovely,' he replied with a grin. 'I'm Phil by the way,' he added as she pulled the pints.

'I'm Jessie.'

'Pleased to meet you, Jessie.'

When she placed the final pint in front of him he leaned in towards her. 'Do me a favour and stick in a good word for us with the guv'nor,' he whispered.

Well, this one certainly wasn't shy in coming forward, she thought. But it was enterprising, and she liked enterprising folk.

'I already have,' she winked.

He stared at her for a second, and knew she was telling the truth. 'Do you have a favourite song?' he asked.

Her mind went back. 'Do you know "Rock Island Line"?' she asked softly.

It was the first number in their next set, and all the time

Phil was singing there was a dull ache in her stomach, a lump in her throat, and a blur before her eyes. Phil might be singing, but it was Tommy's voice she was hearing.

The evening was a success for The Light. Julian bought them another drink when they'd completed their final set, and asked if they'd play the following Saturday and Sunday, which Phil hastily agreed to.

Just like old times, Jessie thought.

Phil gave her a wave when the band left the pub, and she waved back.

This was the fourth weekend that The Light had appeared at The Lonsdale Arms, and they were proving popular, as Julian had been hoping.

His takings were up, a fact the brewery had seen fit to mention on several occasions. There had even been a hint of a bonus for Julian if the trend continued.

Earlier Phil had whispered to Jessie that the band had a surprise in store for that evening, and that surprise would be their closing number.

Jessie and Yvonne had been working flat out since nine, they were so busy Julian was having to do his own pot collecting, but he didn't mind that in the least. Pixie was upstairs with her two children, the youngest of which, Sally, was ill with the mumps.

Julian plonked some more glasses on the bar, then gazed around. This was the busiest yet, with many new faces to be seen.

'And now the last number of the evening, a little concoction of our own,' Phil announced, '"Why Fucking Not!" We hope you like it.'

Jessie nearly dropped the sweet sherry she'd just poured. Had she heard right? A glance at Julian's astounded face told her she had. A number of customers were gaping at the band.

It was the most astonishing song Jessie had ever heard, thundered out to a crashing beat it centred round the repetition of the line 'Why fucking not!' while Phil leapt up and down on the spot as if he was having a fit.

Jessie knew audiences, and she could feel this one respond with enthusiasm. The enthusiasm snowballed as the number gathered more and more momentum, until Phil was literally shrieking into the stand mike in a deranged manner.

When the number was finally over the customers gave the band a huge hand, some whistling and shouting, others pounding their feet in approval and appreciation.

In the ensuing babble of conversation that broke out nearly everyone was talking about the last number. Even the few who'd found it outrageous couldn't stop talking about it.

Phil, flushed and dripping with sweat sauntered over to Julian. 'I didn't tell you about that because I thought you'd forbid us to do it. But now you've heard it and seen the reaction, can we do it as a closer every night we play here?' he asked.

Phil was right, if he'd been asked beforehand he would have said no. But now Julian readily gave his consent. The song had gone down a bomb, and, despite its refrain it was strangely inoffensive.

'We think it's going to be a crowd puller,' Phil explained excitedly.

'Just as long as it doesn't pull the police as well,' Julian joked.

Jessie looked up from the sink where she was washing glasses to find Phil on the other side of the bar. 'Do you ever get a night off?' he asked casually.

He was going to ask her out, she'd known for several weeks that he would. She had already decided what her answer would be, and that was no.

'Every Monday,' she answered immediately.

'How about me taking you to the pictures next Monday, then?'

'I'd love to,' she said, and then realized with shock that she'd accepted when she'd fully intended refusing. Now what on earth had prompted her to do that? She wasn't interested in men any more, and yet it was as though the words had had a will of their own, not uttered as a result of a message from her brain.

'Seven o'clock then, I'll be in the bar here waiting,' Phil said, and, giving her a brief smile, returned to where Oscar and Len, the other two band members, were packing up.

Oh why fucking not! Jessie told herself, and shrugged.

They went to the Odeon in Upper Street where the picture was a real oldie doing the rounds for the umpteenth time, *Nanook of the North*, the story of an eskimo.

During the entire performance Phil sat enthralled, completely caught up. Jessie glanced at him occasionally, but his eyes never wavered from the silver screen. She might just as well have been there on her own, she thought.

When the picture was over they went out into the hot and sultry June night. Jessie didn't like this sort of weather at all, it was far too close and sticky for her taste, quite different to Glasgow where even when the temperature was high there was a freshness off the sea.

'I adore everything about eskimos and the north pole, I just find them fascinating.' Phil said, his eyes glowing with enthusiasm.

'So I noticed,' Jessie replied drily, but her sarcasm passed him by.

'The eskimo name for themselves is *Innuit*. It means The People,' he told her.

'You're not part eskimo yourself by any chance?' she said, and laughed, anyone less eskimo looking she couldn't imagine.

'No,' he said. 'I'm hundred per cent Jewish.'

She was flabbergasted. 'But you're so blond? I'd never have dreamt . . .' She trailed off, wondering if she was being rude.

'We don't all have huge hooters and need to shave twice a day,' he laughed. 'Some of us are fair and baby-faced and beautiful like me.'

'What's your last name, then?' she asked.

'Jacobs.'

Well that was Jewish enough, she thought. Phil Jacobs, it had a pleasant ring to it.

They walked towards Islington Green. 'It's early still, we could have a drink, or how about coming in for coffee? I live only over the road,' Phil said.

She was curious enough to want to know more about him, but didn't really want to go into a pub, six nights a week in one was sufficient. 'I'll have the coffee,' she answered.

They turned into St. Peter's Street, which ran down the side of the Camden Passage Antique Market where she'd bought her 78s, a long road of Georgian houses that were gradually being taken over and done up by the new people moving into the area.

He had a ground floor flat, a small reception doubling as bedroom, and an adjoining kitchen of the same size. He told her his bathroom was at the end of the entrance-way passage, where he had exclusive use of the bath, but had to share the w.c. with the nasty old biddy upstairs.

He closed the front curtains, having already switched on the lights, and went through to the kitchen where he started filling the kettle.

Jessie took the opportunity to look around. The walls and ceiling were painted white and on the floor was a fitted chocolate brown carpet that had seen better, and chocolatier days.

There were racks of bookshelves on either side of the chimney, each crammed to overflowing with books, mainly paperbacks. The original fireplace had been taken out and a gas one installed. The furniture consisted of a green moquette armchair, a pouffe, a single bed and a radiogram.

Switching her interest to the kitchen she saw there was

a pine table and two pine chairs there. The black and white squared vinyl floor didn't appear to have been acquainted with a brush or mop in ages, though the rest of the flat seemed clean and tidy enough.

'It's a nice place you've got here,' she said.

'Thank you. It's big drawback is the woman upstairs. I'm convinced she's quite mad. Would you believe she keeps a bucket upstairs which she pees in, and brings the bucket down once a week to pour its contents down the w.c.?'

Jessie screwed up her face in a combination of distaste and laughter. 'But why does she do that? Does she have trouble getting up and down the stairs?'

'Not her, she's as nimble as a mountain goat. I've no idea why, she just does, that's all. And I'll tell you this, it doesn't half pong after. She's no sooner back in her own flat than I'm out in the loo with Domestos.'

Jessie laughed at the picture of him chucking Domestos down the pan with one hand and holding his nose with the other.

He told her some more stories about Mrs Perkins which had her in stiches. She hadn't laughed like this for months.

'I've been wanting to ask, why do you call the band The Light?' she asked after a while.

'The light referred to isn't electric, but inner,' he answered seriously.

'Oh!' she exclaimed, taken aback by this new pretentiousness.

She judged Phil to be about twenty-four in which case he was a couple of years younger than herself. 'What do you do beside the band?' she asked, accepting a mug of coffee from him.

'Nothing, the band's it. I used to have a proper job, as the expression goes, but I gave it up once we got the band together. You see, I have every intention that the band will succeed.'

She was impressed; not only enterprising, but a man of

positive action and determination as well. 'And what was your so called proper job?'

'A stockbroker, as my father is, and his father before him. We're a family of stockbrokers.'

'It sounds as though your family is well off?'

He gave a thin smile. 'Stinking rich. We've got a house you could easily get lost in.'

'So what do your parents think about you breaking with family tradition?'

Phil laughed, and ran a hand in comb-like fashion through his shoulder length hair. 'Father gave me his blessing, but my mother! She had hysterics when I told her what I intended doing. She's round here at least once a week trying to make me change my mind and go back to the firm. She swears I've broken her heart.'

'Mothers tend to worry,' Jessie smiled.

'You can say that again.' Phil laughed. 'But she could let me be myself.'

'At least you've got a good solid profession to fall back on should you fail to make it in the music world,' she said.

'I'll make it, Jessie. Nothing, and no one, is going to stop me.'

She raised her mug in salute. 'Here's to your musical career then,' she toasted.

He acknowledged her toast by raising his own mug, then they both drank.

'I have some Bacardi if you prefer?' he suggested.

She was enjoying herself more than she'd thought possible. 'Sure,' she smiled. He poured them fairly large ones, topping the glasses up with coke, and they abandoned the coffee.

'How did you meet Oscar and Len?' Jessie asked once they were settled again.

'I heard about Oscar through a mutual friend, and Oscar knew Len,' he explained. 'It was as simple as that. Of course,' he continued, 'actually getting gigs isn't quite that simple. The Lonsdale Arms was our first.'

'What do you do the nights you're not playing The

Lonsdale Arms?' Phil told her they were managing two sometimes three, dates during that time, mainly private functions which they were getting through word of mouth.

'And "Why Fucking Not!" was that a joint effort?'

He grinned wryly, 'No, it was my baby, really. I wanted something completely different, something that would grab attention, make people sit up and take notice. "Why Fucking Not!" was what I came up with.'

'It's certainly different, I'll grant you that,' she laughed taking another drink of her rum.

'Now tell me about you,' Phil prompted.

The last thing Jessie wanted was to talk about her life up until then, so she gave Phil a much edited version. She told him she'd been married, that the marriage had failed, and that because of that failure she'd come to London to start afresh. She added that her parents were in Glasgow, but she wasn't in contact with them as they'd fallen out years ago.

Phil poured them each more Bacardi, and they talked about the current music scene, a subject he knew inside out. More Bacardi was poured, and more after that, then Jessie, feeling somewhat high by now, and unusually relaxed, excused herself to go to the loo.

When she returned Phil was waiting in ambush. She'd no sooner closed the door behind her than he'd taken her in his arms and was pressing an eager mouth against hers, a hand groping for her breast.

She pushed him away angrily. 'What do you think you're doing?' she demanded coldly.

He looked at her in confusion. 'I'm sorry, I got the impression you liked me. We were getting on so well together.'

'I do like you, but that doesn't give you the right to attack me.'

His face coloured. 'It wasn't meant as an attack. It wasn't meant that way at all.'

She took a deep breath, and told herself she was being

261

stupid, she should have seen how things were going, what had she expected? But she'd been enjoying herself so much that she forgot to pay attention.

'I'd like to go home now. You don't have to worry about walking me back, I'll be quite all right on my own,' she said softly.

Phil looked miserable. 'I've offended you,' he muttered.

She indicated what remained of her drink. 'Thank you for the Bacardi, I've really enjoyed tonight.'

He tried to insist on escorting her home, but she was even more insistent that he didn't. Finally she escaped out into the night, turning at the end of St. Peter's Street to find he was standing outside his flat staring after her. When he raised a hand in salute she waved in return.

She berated herself all the way home. She'd handled that extremely badly and felt guilty about being so cold and angry with him. It was just that he'd caught her so unawares, she told herself. For a while there she'd felt so much like her old self that she hadn't expected a pass.

Stupid stupid stupid, she told herself.

When she got back to the pub she went straight up to her room, and there got ready for bed. She looked at her naked body in disgust. She'd got so fat! She ran her hands over her thighs and hips.

How could Phil fancy someone so fat she wondered? And yet fancy her he did, even though she wasn't as pretty as she'd been less than a year ago – even though her own husband had found her so unattractive that he had wanted someone else.

Well, she thought as she climbed into bed. Phil didn't matter now, not after the way she'd behaved.

Much to Jessie's surprise, Phil asked her out the following Monday night, and to her further surprise she accepted. They went to the Upper Street Odeon again where, this time, there was a Cary Grant film on that was much more to her taste than *Nanook of the North*.

On coming out they went to a cafe for coffee, chatting over several cups before he took her back to The Lonsdale Arms.

Instead of trying to kiss her goodnight he shook her by the hand and said he'd found the evening a pleasure. She wasn't at all sure whether he was being polite and formal, or taking the Michael.

In the middle of the week he popped into the pub to say he'd like to see her that Monday, but he desperately wanted to watch a show that was on television, he'd just rented one he explained, and how would she feel about coming round to St. Peter's Street and watching it with him? 'I'll even throw in a home-cooked meal,' he grinned.

He was a perseverer, she had to give him that. 'That sounds great, Phil,' she found herself saying. 'I'd love to.' Then she moved off to serve a customer. When she returned to where he'd been he was gone.

Saturday and Sunday nights the pub was jammed to bursting. Everyone came to hear The Light, and this fantastic new number, 'Why Fucking Not!'

As Julian remarked to Jessie, The Lonsdale Arms was rapidly becoming the 'in' place in Islington. And not just Islington, either. Why, a couple he'd spoken to earlier had come all the way from Chelsea just to hear 'Why Fucking Not!'

On the Monday morning Jessie had the luxury of a long lie, after which, as it was a glorious day, she went for a walk down to a nearby leg of the Regents Canal where she watched the gaily coloured narrow boats chug past. She was feeling better than she had in a long time and then a boat which had thistles and bluebells on it went by, making her think of Glasgow and how much she missed it. Not Boyd Street and Allison Street and her being Queen of the Glasgow Teds, but the very essence of Glasgow itself that ran through its streets and its people alike.

She thought of Tommy, the Linn Park, the Boyd

Street Boys, they were all gone forever. She doubted she would ever return there, she could never go back to the source of her pain.

She thought about her parents and wondered; they could be dead for all she knew. And Lizzle Dunnachie, dear chain-smoking Lizzie, what had become of her? She thought of Battlefield, the Fives Cafe, and seducing Alec Muir because she'd been worried about not being sexually attractive.

And Eve Smith, now Eve Baxter, she mustn't forget Eve, and the image of Eve that was forever burned into her memory, or Eve's laugh, triumphant and mocking. A laugh that would haunt her till her dying day.

Putting a hand to her forehead, Jessie discovered it was cold with sweat. Going back to the pub she tried to sleep some more, but couldn't. Every time she closed her eyes she saw Eve and Tommy.

Tommy and Eve. . . .

Phil had cooked spaghetti bolognaise, and complimented it with the traditional bottle of chianti. They ate in the kitchen. The spaghetti was surprisingly good. 'I'm so impressed,' she laughed 'that I'll wash if you dry.'

When the bottle of chianti was finished, he produced a second, saying it was what posh folk called 'the other half'. With a full glass in her hand Jessie settled down in the green moquette chair while he turned on his new hired telly. When he had the channel he wanted he sat on the pouffe.

The show was called Espresso Coffee, and, as Phil explained to Jessie, was a forum for rock bands, both the well-known and the not-so-well-known. Jessie sat back in her chair, thinking to herself that she was going to enjoy this.

The first band were the Bepops, a coloured group who sang exceptionally well. Phil told her they'd just returned from a tour of West Germany.

'The next band this evening is the Tommy McBride Skiffle Band!' the compere announced, and a curtain flew away to reveal Tommy, Jack, Sammy and Jake 'The Rake'.

Jessie went very still, her heart thumping nineteen to the dozen, as she stared at Tommy. The band was already into their first number.

Phil glanced in her direction, about to say something, but frowned instead. 'Are you all right?' he asked concernedly. She looked as if she'd had a bad turn. When he got no reply he repeated his question with even more concern.

Jessie's mouth had gone so dry she had to consciously make an effort to speak.

'That's my husband,' she whispered, pointing to the box.

Phil brought his attention back to the set, as Jessie's surname was McBride she could only be talking about the vocalist.

He took in the black drape, black drainies, brothel creepers, gaucho tie, flamboyant white shirt and well greased quiff. 'Is your husband a real Ted?' he asked.

Jessie nodded. 'As real as they come. He's King of the Glasgow Teds.'

Phil pursed his lips in amazement, here was a revelation indeed. His barmaid, the shy and reserved Jessie, married to a King of the Teds. Who would have imagined such a thing?

Tommy hadn't changed since she'd seen him last, he was exactly as she remembered. She almost felt as though she could reach out and touch him, as though she could reach into the past and nothing would have changed.

'Tommy and I collaborated on the number he's singing,' she said just to hear herself say something.

Phil was further amazed. 'You write music?' he exclaimed.

'Only for Tommy and the band. I wrote some by myself, but the best were those where I scored the music

265

and Tommy added the lyrics. He has a feel for lyrics,' she said softly, her lips trembling.

The show wasn't from Scotland, but transmitted from Lime Grove, which meant Tommy was in London. Was Eve with him, she wondered? A jagged pang of jealousy shot through her so real that she almost cried out.

No doubt Eve was waiting for him in his dressing room even now, the pair of them intending to paint the town red once the show was over. She could see the two of them together, hear them laughing.

It suddenly hit Jessie that she was wasting what remained of her life because of Tommy McBride. If she went on as she had been she would be mourning him forever, afraid to ever trust another man, afraid to ever love again. And would Tommy McBride care if she spent the rest of her life lonely and unwanted? Would Tommy McBride care that she wasted her life, an old maid with a fondness for beer? Tommy McBride was obviously on top of the world, and Eve undoubtedly on top of it with him.

'Did you know this second number is in the Top Ten?' Phil asked eagerly.

It was another number she and Tommy had collaborated on. If it was in the top ten then she was due royalties from it, an amount which might even be substantial. Well, she might be due those royalties, but didn't want them. She didn't want anything from that past association. Her pub job paid what she needed, she had enough, she'd get by.

'The Top Ten? That's interesting,' she said drily.

When the show was over, they polished off what remained of the chianti. 'Did it upset you seeing your husband again?' Phil asked gently.

'Not in the least,' Jessie lied. 'He means nothing to me now, nothing at all.'

He watched her closely. 'You don't look like someone who'd be married to a Teddy Boy,' he said at last.

Jessie gave a soft smile, what clothes she'd brought

266

with her from Glasgow had long since been consigned to the dustbin, and the replacements she'd bought were all 'straight'. She'd even had her hair cut in a different style, now it was neatly cut and layered, the epitome of respectability.

'The last thing *you* look is Jewish.' She teased. 'And yet you are. Appearances can be deceiving.'

Rising, she crossed to the window and closed the curtains. 'Do you still want to sleep with me?' she asked, keeping her back to him.

Another surprise! She was just full of them tonight, he thought.

He came to her and placed his hands on her hips, taking a firm but sensual hold of them. 'Yes,' he stated simply.

Jessie trembled, the last male hands other than Tommy's to touch her that way had been those in Linton Street, hands of hated memory.

'Doesn't it bother you that I'm fat?' she asked quietly.

'You're not fat, just well covered,' Phil whispered. 'I think you're lovely.'

She places her hands on his. 'Have you any more of that chianti?' she asked, still without turning round.

'I can go out and get another bottle.'

When he returned with the wine he found her in his bed, waiting.

Tommy was sitting in the bar at the BBC Lime Grove studios with the rest of the band and some others who'd latched on to them. He knew he and the band had gone down well on Espresso Coffee, everybody had said so.

Jake 'The Rake', flanked by two make-up girls whom he was holding by their waists, delivered the tag line of a funny story he was telling, and the company burst into laughter.

Tommy's laughter died in his throat when he caught sight of a lassie who'd just come into the bar. Her face was in profile to him, and the likeness was uncanny. It might have been Jessie standing there.

267

Sadness overwhelmed him. In his heart was nothing but a terrible, aching loneliness. He thought back to that awful day when Jessie had discovered him with Eve, shuddering at the memory. He would have given everything he had to make that day never have happened.

For what might have been the millionth time he wondered how she was, and how she was doing. If only she hadn't bolted as she had, but stayed and let him try to explain. If only she had just talked to him. If only. . . The lassie he was staring at turned round so that she was now full face to him, and with that the spell was broken. Face on, she didn't look at all like Jessie.

'You all right, china?' asked Jack.

Tommy brought himself out of his reverie and smiled. 'Never better,' he lied.

Jake 'The Rake' launched into another story that was even funnier than the first.

Tommy pretended to listen, but really he was thinking, remembering.

Jessie lay smoking a cigarette while Phil snored gently beside her. It was impossibly cramped in his single bed, but she'd put up with it while she smoked, then she'd get dressed and return to the pub.

Being made love to by Phil hadn't been anything like being made love to by Tommy. The trouble was that when she'd been with Tommy their lovemaking had been exactly that, the making of love. At least it had been on her part for she'd been in love with him. With Phil it had been no more than sex, and the difference between the two was enormous.

She might not love Phil but she did like him – she liked him a great deal. If he wanted to continue seeing her she'd be agreeable, just as she'd be agreeable to their continuing to go to bed together.

It might have been sex rather than the true making of love, but it hadn't been that bad, and it might get better if she worked at it. At least her period of mourning was over and she'd found someone new, she was grateful for that.

Outside a bird sang, heralding the rising of the dawn.

She was about to slip from the bed when Phil, who'd been lying quietly awake for some time, pulled himself on top of her, and she discovered dawn wasn't the only thing that had risen.

The band was half an hour late, and as they'd never been late before Julian was fretting, glancing anxiously every other minute at the clock above the bar. Early in the evening as it was, the pub was already doing brisk business, many of those present there to hear The Light sing their notorious song later on.

Julian had had to increase his staff for the nights when The Light were appearing, those nights he now had three extra girls, besides himself, Jessie and Yvonne, working the bar.

Through one of the leaded windows Jessie saw Oscar's purple van draw up, and called out to Julian that the band had arrived. The van was used to transport their equipment, including Len's piano.

Phil came striding into the pub, glanced round as if looking for someone, then went to Julian who, much relieved, greeted him warmly.

'Sorry we're late, but Oscar and I had to take Len home again. He woke up with a dose of flu this morning which has got worse as the day's gone on. He thought he might make it despite that, but he flaked out on the way here. It's impossible for him to play tonight,' Phil explained.

'But you and Oscar can still manage something?' Julian asked, anxious once more.

Phil turned to Jessie who'd joined Julian during his explanation of what had happened. 'Of all nights to go ill Len couldn't have picked a worse one. I had a letter from Mick Marco of Vestal Records yesterday saying he intended dropping by this evening, I've been trying to get him here ever since we started, and now the bastard's picked this bloody night to come.' Phil said in despair, running a hand through his hair.

'How important is he?' asked Jessie.

'To us *important*,' Oscar said.

Phil looked like he might cry. 'Shit,' he swore.

'I don't think we should play as a twosome, we'd be completely out of balance and Marco might get the wrong impression of us,' Oscar said to Phil.

'That's what's been bothering me too. But if we let him down tonight there's no telling when he'll come back again, maybe never.'

Jessie felt for them, it was a case of the devil and the deep blue sea. 'Can I make a suggestion?' she asked hestitantly.

Phil waved his hand. 'Go ahead.'

'If Julian says it's all right, I'll play piano for you. That way Marco can hear you as a threesome, and you can explain to him after that I'm only a stand-in.'

'I didn't know you played piano,' frowned Phil.

'Well I do.'

'But can you play our numbers?' Oscar demanded.

'There's nothing you've ever played here that I can't play. And I've heard you so often now I know your style inside out.'

'If he likes us with Jessie then that might encourage him to come back soon and hear us with Len,' Oscar said to Phil.

'I won't let you down, I promise.' Jessie smiled.

She was the magician who kept pulling rabbits out of the top hat, Phil thought. 'Does she have your permission to become a member of The Light for this evening?' he asked Julian.

'Certainly,' Julian replied, calming himself by thinking he'd get Pixie down from upstairs as a replacement for Jessie behind the bar.

'Then let's give it a whirl,' Phil said, and with a word

to Oscar he and Oscar started back for the van to begin unloading their gear.

Jessie was suddenly nervous. Had she made a bloomer by volunteering herself? It had been a long time since she'd played after all. And there would be no sheet music, she'd have to play by ear.

Of course she could do it, she told herself, her ear was excellent, and as for the actual playing itself, playing a piano was like riding a bike, once you knew how, you knew for life. She might be a little rusty to begin with, but that would soon wear off as she got into the swing of it.

Jessie continued serving until Phil and Oscar were set up, then she went over and sat at Len's piano, a smallish instrument that had been reduced to a working skeleton to make it easier to be carted from place to place.

Butterflies fluttered in her stomach when she placed her hands on the keyboard, then Phil was blowing into the stand mike and telling the crowd that Len wouldn't be appearing that night because of illness, but that Jessie McBride, the barmaid they all knew and loved, would be tinkling the ivories in his place. 'How about a show of appreciation for Jessie, please?' he called.

Oscar gave Jessie a drum roll as she acknowledged the applause. Phil said what the first set would be, and the order it would be played in.

'Ready?' he asked her.

'As I'll ever be,' she replied, a smile wavering on her face.

And so, off they went.

Within minutes her nervousness had completely disappeared, and she was thoroughly enjoying herself, and surprising herself by playing as well as she'd ever done despite the time it had been since she'd last sat at a piano.

They played Presley numbers – 'Hound Dog', 'Blue Suede Shoes', and 'Heartbreak Hotel' – following these with Tommy Steele's 1956 smash, 'Rock with the Cave Man'. The audience shouted for more.

At the end of the fourth set, and relishing a pint sent over by Julian, Jessie said to Phil, 'Any sign of Marco yet?'

'He came in about ten minutes ago.' Phil replied softly out the side of this mouth, and went on to describe where Marco was standing and what he looked like.

Over the rim of her glass Jessie's eyes casually sought out Marco. He was a short, barrel-chested man of about forty, dressed in a very expensive Italian-cut suit. He was talking animatedly to a stunning woman half his age whose clothes suggested both money and class.

Announcing the fifth set, Phil explained again about Jessie standing in for the ill Len, this for Marco's benefit, and again Jessie was given an enthusiastic and appreciative round of applause.

Finally last orders were called, and it was time for the number everyone was waiting for. The conversation and general pub noise died down in anticipation.

Phil excelled himself, leaping about like a crazy man, while the crowd, as always, went wild. It never ceased to amaze Jessie how the public, and repeated, utterance of 'that word' could provoke such a reaction, but it did. Perhaps a psychologist could have explained it, but she certainly couldn't.

When it was over the crowd continued to cheer, shout, stamp their feet, and more or less act as if demonically possessed. 'Again! Again!' they cried to no avail, Julian was most strict about that, it was difficult enough getting them out at the end, and he knew the local police kept a watchful eye on his premises.

Mick Marco and his companions made their way over. 'Absolutely terrif!' Marco enthused.

'How about recording it then?' Phil put in quickly.

Marco gave a wry smile and shook his head. 'You know that's impossible, but I wish I could. If I could I would.'

Phil, who'd met Marco previously, introduced Oscar and Jessie, and Marco responded by introducing the girl with him whose name was Caroline.

When Caroline spoke Jessie realized she was very upper crust indeed, the sort whose daddy has a 'seat' in the country, and whose ancestors came over with Duke William.

Caroline had a beautiful figure and a face to match. Jessie, overweight and self-conscious as she was, felt dreadful beside her. There had been a time when she'd have held her own, she thought, but no more.

Marco listened sympathetically to Phil's account of Len's flu, then Marco said he thought Jessie had been an admirable stand-in, he'd been impressed with all of them.

'I'll tell you what, why don't I come back again next Saturday to hear the band as it should be?' Marco suggested.

Phil's face lit up. That was precisly what he'd been hoping for. Oscar was beaming fit to bust.

'That would be fab.' Phil grinned.

'It's a date, then,' Marco confirmed.

When a few minutes later the pub had finally been cleared, and the doors shut, Marco asked Julian if he could buy everyone a drink, to which Julian agreed.

After a while Marco and Caroline left, Marco repeating that they'd be back the following Saturday.

When Marco and Caroline had gone Phil told Jessie what a grand job she'd done for the band that night, she'd been marvellous, a sentiment Oscar seconded.

Oscar went to the loo, and Phil to the telephone at the far end of the pub to ring Len and tell him the good news.

Jessie lit a cigarette and took another swallow of beer. She was shattered, but high with elation. She'd enjoyed the evening tremendously, the more so because it had been so unexpected.

Stubbing out her cigarette, she began playing a tune that had been running through her mind lately. Going back, altering and re-phrasing as she'd used to do on her piano in Allison Street.

The tune had a haunting quality about it that appealed to her, it was a love-song, she decided, a sad love-song.

'I like that, what is it?' Phil asked coming up beside her.

She glanced up, unaware until he'd spoken that he'd returned. 'It doesn't have a name yet. It hasn't even been scored properly.'

'You mean it's one of yours?'

She nodded, and played it from the top as far as she'd worked out.

Phil took a stool and sat beside her. 'Can I ask you a favour?' he smiled.

'Ask away.'

'Will you write it for me? I've been looking for original material for some time, but so far I haven't come up with anything. I've tried Tin Pan Alley, but the decent songs there get snapped up by the established singers and bands with a name, not to mention their managers and agents.

Jessie broke into 'Bony Moronie' while she thought about Phil's request. Why not? she asked herself, there was no reason why she shouldn't help him, and he was right, he did need original material. Playing other people's numbers was okay to start out with, but if a singer and band were to progress they couldn't go on that way.

'Okay, I'll write it for you,' she said simply.

Phil leaned over and kissed her on the tip of the nose. 'You're smashing,' he whispered.

It was the happiest she'd been since finding Tommy and Eve.

It was good to get back to writing music, she hadn't realized how much she'd missed it. As usual the music itself had been easy; as usual the lyrics were difficult.

She picked up her pencil, and laid it down again. She picked it up once more, chewed its end, and this time threw it down. She hummed the tune through, willing images into her mind, but nothing came.

She lit a cigarette and topped up her glass of whisky from the half bottle she'd bought in the off licence a block away.

A love-song, she reminded herself, that's what this is, a sad, haunting, love-song. Picking up the pencil she hastily scribbled 'Totti'.

Totti, what on earth did that mean?

She smiled as the answer came to her. Totti was the name of the girl the man in the song had lost. It would have to be a man losing a girl as Phil would be singing the song.

Losing someone, when had she decided that was the subject? She didn't know, what she did know was that it was right. The lyrics would be about her losing Tommy, only the sexes would be reversed. It would be a man losing a woman instead of the other way around, but the emotions and sense of loss would be the same.

She wrote:

> I miss my baby,
> I miss her, oh,
> why, oh why,
> do I still love her so?

And the chorus:

> She found another,
> and I found them.
> Together!

> I miss my baby,
> each and every night.
> I cry sad tears
> when I turn off the light.

> She found another,
> and I found them.
> Together!

When they were finished Jessie knew them to be the best lyrics she'd ever written – perhaps because they came straight from the soul.

She drank more whisky, then changed the single word

Totti to 'Missing Totti'. That would be the title of the song.

Switching out the light, she began to cry, just as she'd done so often at night when she'd been thinking about Tommy.

Just as she'd written.

'And now folks, we'd like to perform a brand new number especially written for the band, called 'Missing Totti'. It's by our very own Jessie McBride. A big hand for Jessie, please!' Phil said into the stand mike, gesturing to where Jessie was pulling a pint behind the bar. Oscar and Len led the applause.

Jessie blushed, feeling her face go quite red with embarrassment. She gave a half-hearted wave in response to the clapping, and slopped a wave of beer on to the floor as a result.

The evening had been going well so far. Phil was in fine voice and the band in good form. Because The Light was appearing the pub was packed and had been since before nine. Marco and Caroline, as promised, were present, and had wormed their way into one of the better viewing positions.

Marco was now staring at the still blushing Jessie in surprise, a song-writing barmaid! Whatever next? Then he remembered how she'd been on the piano the previous Saturday, and thought that maybe it wasn't so strange after all.

'I miss my Totti, nearly drives me bad. I always loved that girl, never treated her bad. . .' sang Phil.

The audience quietened, even those who'd been clamouring for drinks at the bar. Faces began to register the emotions of the song. Suddenly almost everyone in the pub looked sad.

The penultimate notes were on the piano, the last one of all a twang on the guitar, a twang that reverberated softly, then faded away to nothingness.

There were a few seconds of total silence, then the applause exploded. There could be no doubting that 'Missing Totti' had gone down a bomb. Phil waited till the applause finally began to ebb, then broke into the next number, 'Stand By Me'.

Jessie glanced across at Mick Marco who gave her the thumbs up sign, then she was back to pulling pints as it became pandemonium at the bar again.

By quarter past eleven the last customers had gone, ejected by Julian, and Phil, Marco, Caroline, Oscar and Len were sitting around a table while Jessie put a fresh tray of drinks, compliments of Marco, in front of them.

'Do you mind if I have Jessie join us here?' Marco called over to Julian, who replied that was all right by him. So Jessie sat beside Phil while the other girls got on with the washing and drying of the glasses.

'I'll come right to the point,' Marco said. 'I'd like to record The Light doing 'Missing Totti'.'

'Hot damn!' Len muttered, and slapped Oscar on the back.

Phil wanted to give a loud whoop of delight, but refrained from doing so, thinking Marco would consider it juvenile.

'But, do you have another new number for the flip side?' Marco went on.

Phil glanced at Jessie.

'When do you want to tape?' she asked Marco.

He consulted a pocket diary. 'How about the week after next?'

'The Light will have a second new number by then, I promise you.'

Marco nodded slowly. There was more to this girl than met the eye. Her reply hadn't been boastful, but confident – the confidence of someone who knew exactly what she was doing. 'Something tells me this isn't new to you,' he said thoughtfully.

Jessie gave a small smile. 'It isn't.'

'Her husband is Tommy McBride of the Tommy McBride Skiffle Band,' Phil interrupted. 'She and he collaborated in the past.'

'Ah!' Marco breathed.

One of the songs they collaborated on is number six in the charts,' Phil continued, ignoring the look on Jessie's face.

'Well I'll be. . .!' Oscar whistled. Neither Phil nor Jessie had let on to him or Len about her connection with Tommy, or even that she was married. She didn't wear a wedding ring; she'd thrown that out of the carriage window during the train journey down from Glasgow.

'So it's a pro I've got here,' Marco smiled.

' "Missing Totti" is extremely good, it has quality,' Caroline said.

Jessie blushed. If anyone at that table knew about quality it was the aristocratic Caroline. 'Thank you,' she mumbled.

'What day the week after next?' Phil asked Marco.

Marco shrugged. 'Do you have a preference?'

'The Monday would be best. It's Jessie's day off and it's only right that she's there at the recording,' Phil explained.

Marco again consulted his diary. 'At the moment, that date is fully booked, but there's a switch I can make, so the Monday it is. Shall we say two in the afternoon at our studios in Foubert's Place?'

'Two it is, then,' Phil replied quickly.

Marco was pleased with himself. He had a feeling about 'Missing Totti'. As Caroline said, it had quality, and, as he saw it, wide appeal.

When the girls had finished washing up and drying Julian bought another round, which included the staff drink, and Marco another after that. Julian was delighted to hear the news that The Light would be making a record, but also a bit worried about it. He could see himself losing this band that had done so much for his weekend takings, and which had made his pub the 'in' place in Islington.

Later Jessie went with Phil to St. Peter's Street, where they celebrated the forthcoming record with Carlsberg Specials they'd brought from the pub, lying naked in front of the blazing gas fire.

Foubert's Place was in Soho, an area Jessie hadn't been to before. Strolling along the narrow streets with Phil and Len its bohemian ambience now delighted her. It didn't even smell like a part of Britain, but the way she imagined the Continent must smell.

The majority of the shops were foreign, and filled with things she'd never seen before. One shop window was crammed with more types of cheeses than she would have thought existed in the entire world. The exotic smells were almost intoxicating.

On arriving in Foubert's Place they saw that Oscar and his van were there waiting for them, as they'd arranged.

They all went inside together.

The pretty receptionist made an internal telephone call and moments later Marco came bustling out to greet them personally. He asked Oscar for the van's keys, which Oscar handed over, saying they weren't to worry about their gear and equipment, he'd have his people unload and set it up for them in the studio.

Jessie was thrilled with everything. It was all so tremendously exciting, and she could tell from the gleam in Phil's eyes that she thought so, too.

The studio itself was something of a disappointment, smaller and more cramped than she'd expected. Sound technicians were fussing around, testing and making adjustments to the various mikes overhanging the performing area.

Marco ordered coffee, which appeared almost instantly, and they all repaired to the producer's booth which could only be entered from the corridor outside.

'How do you feel?' Marco smiled at Phil.

'Raring to go,' Phil replied.

'What's the second number you've got for me?' Marco asked Jessie, who handed him her score of 'Lamplighter Rock', a number in complete contrast to the sad, haunting 'Missing Totti'.

'They go well together,' Len said.

Marco didn't have to be told that, for he read music, and could see for himself that was the case.

The band drank coffee and chatted till the set up had been completed for them, they went through to the performing area for rehearsal. Jessie remained in the booth with Marco and four console operators.

The band played each number through twice, then announced they were ready whenever Marco was. Marco told them the operators said they'd go in a minute. They'd get a red light for warning, a green for the off.

It didn't start well. Phil was so nervous he fluffed his lyrics during the first two takes, and Len sounded as if he was playing with ten thumbs, all of them bandaged.

Marco assured Jessie in a whisper that he'd been expecting this. It wasn't at all uncommon when bands recorded for the first time and they'd settle down eventually. Sure enough, after a while they did.

It was twenty to five when they finally laid down a satisfactory tape of 'Missing Totti' and Marco called a break for coffee and cigarettes. Len asked for a proper drink, and was refused. No booze in studio time; house rules.

As the band trooped back into the performing area Caroline slipped into the booth. She gave Marco a peck on the cheek, then came to sit beside Jessie.

'How's it going?' she whispered.

Jessie grimaced, and Caroline gave a sympathetic smile.

Phil broke a guitar string, and everyone had to wait while he fixed a new one. There was a further hold-up while he retuned the guitar.

'You learn patience in this game,' Marco said to Jessie.

After twenty-seven takes, Marco glanced at the console operators in turn. Receiving a confirmatory nod from each, he flicked a switch and spoke directly to the band. 'That's it, lads. I'm satisfied. We've got two good masters. You can have that drink now, Len.'

Jessie had been watching Marco's face. He wasn't ecstatic about the final takes, but on the other hand he wasn't disappointed. She glanced through the glass panels. Phil had taken off his guitar, and was stretching. There were dark stains under his arms and at the small of his back.

Marco asked Caroline to take Jessie and the band to the hospitality room. He'd be along in a few minutes when he'd finished in the studio.

'How do you think it went?' Phil whispered to Jessie as they followed Caroline.

'It was fine,' she whispered in reply.

'Was Marco pleased?'

'Well, he wasn't jumping about shouting eureka! But he wasn't throwing up in the corner, either. I'd say he got what he wanted.'

Phil took a deep breath, he was absolutely shattered. He wouldn't have believed that recording could take so much out of you. It took up far more energy than playing before a live audience, for him at least.

The hospitality room was decorated in a soothing shade of green. Along one wall there was a trellis table with a white linen tablecloth over it. There were so many bottles on the table that it seemed strange that it wasn't sagging under the weight of them.

There were other people dotted round the largish room, all talking in low tones, as if confiding secrets to one another. They were all men, and they all wore expensive business suits.

Jessie gazed about her, taking everything in, just as she'd been taking everything in since entering the building. Vestal Records might be a small company, but it certainly wasn't operating on a shoestring. There was money here, and a lot of it.

'Jesus Christ!' Phil exclaimed suddenly, his voice shrill with excitement.

She turned, startled. 'What is it?'

'Do you know who that is?' he asked, nodding in the direction of two of the business suits.

She'd never seen either man before. 'No, who is it?'

'The taller man is Larry Parnes, who handles Billy Fury, Joe Brown, Duffy Power and Georgie Fame, to mention but a few. He's a very big noise indeed!' Phil breathed.

Jessie studied the man in question. She knew of him by reputation, and Phil was right, he was a big noise, in pop music his name was about as big as it got.

Phil gripped Jessie by the arm. 'Seeing him makes me realize I'm really on my way. It won't be long now till I'm up there with Billy Fury and Joe Brown, as big a star as they are,' he said, his voice filled with longing and desire.

A star! What memories that word evoked. Star Gray – it seemed a lifetime ago.

What is love? It is the morning and the evening star.

She had to smile. How pretentious to call herself Star; she cringed now to think about it. Yet, then, she'd considered it the most sophisticated thing in the world.

She remembered the night in Tommy's bedroom, the first time she'd visited the house in Millbrae Crescent, when she'd explained her chosen name to him. She also remembered that it was because of him that, later, she'd dropped the name.

'What are you thinking about?' Phil asked, noticing the far away look in her eyes, as if she were watching something a long way off.

With an effort, she brought herself back to the present. 'I was just recalling a star I used to know when I was young, so very young,' she replied wistfully.

He wondered what she was talking about. A star, what star? But before he could get her to elaborate, Mick

Marco arrived and gestured him over to the drinks table. He promptly forgot about Jessie and her mysterious star.

Jessie was serving up a pint of Guinness when Phil came into the pub. Although it was nearly noon he'd just got up because the band had been playing a private function down in Godalming, Surrey, the night before.

If it hadn't been *the day*, he'd still be in bed. But it was *the day*, the day 'Missing Totti' was being released, so he'd forced himself to get up hours before he would have done otherwise.

Jessie served the Guinness, then went over to where Julian was chatting animatedly to a customer about rugby. Julian was a great rugby fan.

'Phil's here. Can I take my break now?' she asked.

'Is it straight to the record shop?' Julian smiled.

'That's the plan.'

'Then away you go.'

Emerging from behind the counter she slipped an arm through one of Phil's. 'Excited?' she asked.

'Can't remember when I was more excited,' he grinned. 'Not even when I was little.'

Jessie pulled herself closer to him. She'd been looking forward to this moment ever since the recording session. Marco had sent them free copies of the single, but they still wanted to go into a shop and actually buy it for themselves, to make the whole thing real.

The closest record shop was in Cross Street, just off Upper Street. Arriving there they stopped outside to stare in the window.

Norman Banks, the owner, and a Lonsdale Arms regular, hadn't let them down. Norman had made a display of 'Missing Totti' and 'Lamplighter Rock'. A hand-written card at the front of the display informed the public that The Light were a local band and that Jessie McBride, who'd written the numbers, was another local.

They entered the shop and Norman greeted them

effusively, gushing about what a fab disc he thought it was and how it was bound to sell a million. Then he asked them if they would autograph some copies for him, which could only help sales, and was a personal booster for the shop.

They ended up signing every copy there, with the exception of the two they bought for themselves and those in the window.

Outside again, and laughing with sheer joy, they collapsed in each other's arms. 'Come on,' said Jessie, 'I'm taking you back to the pub for a drink. A celebration is definitely in order.'

En route she stopped at a street kiosk and bought a copy of the *Glasgow Herald*, as she did two or three times a week, for she liked to keep abreast of the Glasgow news.

At the pub a surprise awaited them. Julian had set up a hi-fi on the bar, his own machine from upstairs. As they came in through the front door Julian switched off the music he'd been playing, and the entire pub broke into applause. Nor did Jessie have to buy that drink for Julian had already put double whiskies on the bar for them.

Julian called for silence. 'You are now going to hear the disc of a song that was first sung in this very pub,' he announced. 'And I'm expecting each and every one of you to go out and buy a copy of it.'

Julian then solemnly asked Phil for his copy of the record, which Phil, equally solemnly, handed over.

There was a collective hush as Julian placed the disc on the spindle, a hush that continued as he clicked the play switch, and the arm descended.

'I miss my baby,' Phil's voice sang in the silent room. 'I miss her, oh, Why, oh why, do I still love her so?'

It was quite impossible to honestly judge the record in these circumstances, Jessie thought, and anyway, for the moment she was too subjective by far. To her it sounded great.

284

Listening to the lyrics she couldn't help but think of Tommy. Every detail of him came back to her, as though she were flipping through the pages of a photograph album. When would the pain stop, she wondered for the millionth time. When would she be able to think about him without re-breaking her heart?

'Missing Totti' came to an end, and everyone clapped enthusiastically. Julian turned the disc over and played the flip side.

Phil's face was flushed with pride. He accepted another large whisky that was thrust on him, as did Jessie, telling herself that that would have to be the last if she was going to get back to work, which she'd have to do shortly.

'Missing Totti' was played again, and Pixie suddenly appeared from the rear of the pub, where she'd been cooking, to declare it the best thing she'd heard in years, a remark which raised a ragged cheer of approval.

The record was played non-stop for half an hour, then Jessie insisted they stop playing it before everyone was sick and tired of it and never wanted to hear it again.

Phil stayed on a little longer, then told Jessie he was going home to get some more sleep. She could see this was only partly true. His real reason for going home was to continue playing his record. 'You go get some rest,' she said understandingly. Having your first disc out was something very special she knew, particularly for someone like Phil who so hungered after success.

It developed into a pretty hectic lunch time session. When it was all over, the glasses washed and dried, and the floor swept, Jessie sat down with Julian and Pixie to have their own lunch. It wasn't until then, while Julian and Pixie were chatting about the children, that Jessie opened her *Glasgow Herald* and began to read.

Almost accidentally, she cast an eye over the obituary column. She had glanced over most of the list before she realized what she'd read. Slowly, she brought her gaze back to the name which now leapt off the page at her.

Alison Irene Scott Gray, nee Turnbull, beloved wife of the Reverend Kenneth Cranston Gray. . .

The words misted in front of Jessie's eyes. Her mother was dead. The funeral was in two days.

Tears trickled down her cheeks as the memories came back. They'd had some good times, she and her mother, before that last awful confrontation.

She remembered a picnic the two of them had once had at Fairlie on the Firth of Clyde, travelling there by red bus and picnicking amongst the dunes while the herring gulls screeched and squawked overhead. A fishing boat had sailed past while she was tucking into banana sandwiches and lemonade, a fishing boat with a single, beautiful, rust-coloured sail.

And the time her mother had gone out and bought her the bonnet she'd been longing for every time she passed the window of Miss Agnes's Millinery Shop for ages and ages, when, as a twelve-year-old, she'd read the lesson for the first time in church. She'd been petrified of getting up in front of the congregation, but had taken confidence from the bonnet, knowing how braw it made her look. As a result of that confidence, and her mother's thoughtfulness in buying her the bonnet, she'd got through the reading without any trouble.

And then there were the wee secrets they'd shared like the time Alison had connived and manipulated the minister into buying a Chinese style carpet she had wanted, which he had been adamant they couldn't afford. She could see Alison and herself standing side by side, laughing, the morning the carpet had been delivered.

Then, too, there was the patient, understanding way Alison had explained the workings of her body to her when she was old enough to need to know.

'What is it, Jessie?' Pixie demanded, having just that moment noticed Jessie's tears.

In a trembling voice Jessie told them about her mother's death. Julian immediately went up to the bar to get her a brandy.

She swallowed half of that, while Pixie made sympathetic noises and looked at her with anxious eyes. What should she do, if anything, she wondered. She decided to ring the manse.

When she said what she intended Julian replied she wasn't to bother with the pay phone, but to use the phone in their reception room upstairs. He added that if she wanted time off to go to the funeral then she could, of course, have it.

She went to her own room first to get a hanky, and put her copy of 'Missie Totti' beside the old wind-up gramophone. She then blew her nose, wiped her face and had a cigarette. Feeling somewhat better she went through to Julian and Pixie's reception room, heart pounding.

Her father answered the telephone. 'The Reverend Gray speaking,' he said in a quiet, distant voice.

'Father,' said Jessie nervously. 'Father, it's Jessie. I've just read about mother in the *Glasgow Herald*.'

There was a long silence. She began to think he'd hung up. 'She died of a heart attack, there was no pain,' he answered finally.

No pain, that was some consolation at least. 'Where did it happen?' she asked gently.

'At the Women's Guild. Alison was addressing them when she suddenly keeled over. The doctor said she was probably dead before she hit the floor.'

'I . . . I'm very sorry, you know,' Jessie whispered, her voice breaking. 'I . . .'

'Where are you speaking from?' her father interrupted, his voice sharp and impersonal.

'London. I live here now.'

If he was surprised to learn that she wasn't still in Glasgow he gave no sign. 'Oh, London,' was all he said.

'Do you want me to come to the funeral?' Jessie asked. His breathing suddenly became heavy and laboured, as if he were having trouble getting air into his lungs.

When he spoke again his voice was cold as ice, and hard

as Aberdeen granite. It didn't sound human at all. 'You're not welcome either in this house or at the funeral. Your mother and I disowned you years ago, I see no call to change that state of affairs because of what's happened.'

She felt as though she'd been punched in the stomach. 'I thought Jesus's creed was one of love and forgiveness,' she said. 'I think perhaps you should read the parable of the prodigal again, you seem to have forgotten its lesson.'

There was a click and then the disconnected tone buzzed in her ear. Her father had hung up.

Jessie shivered as she left the warmth of the pub. It was late November and the nights were now chilly and inhospitable. Hurrying round to St. Peter's Street, she rang Phil's bell impatiently.

When he answered the door she saw right away that he'd been boozing. Inside the flat she discovered that the floor round his chair strewn with empty beer bottles and cans.

He noticed her staring pointedly at the empties. 'Oscar and Len were round, they've just gone,' he explained, trying to appear more sober than he was.

He was clearly down and getting worse. 'How were the lads?' she asked casually.

Picking up *Melody Maker* from his bed, he thrust it into her hands. 'That's today's. After four weeks we're not even in the top fifty, let alone the top twenty,' he complained bitterly.

So that was it. She'd totally forgotten that *Melody Maker* came out that day, but Phil wouldn't forget. 'It's not the end of the world,' she replied cheerfully. He glared at her darkly – he obviously thought it was. 'Have you spoken to Marco about it?'

His lips thinned into a cynical smile. 'I've rung four times today, and each time I was told the same thing: out, out, out and out again. The message is crystal.'

He went into the kitchen, reappearing with two fresh bottles of beer.

'The message isn't at all crystal as you put it, Phil. Marco is a busy man, you know that,' she argued.

He repeated his cynical smile, and took a drink of his beer. The smile vanished as he slumped into the green moquette chair, which gave a squeak of protest. 'It was a good record, Jessie. It should have done better than it has, a damn sight better,' he complained.

She wished there were something comforting she could say. For some time now there had been something about the record that niggled her, something she hadn't been able to put her finger on. Over the past few days, however, she had listened to the record on her own and had figured it out. It was his voice. For some reason, it had a cold, alien quality about it. There was no emapthy or feeling in it. She realized then that when listening to the record she'd been hearing Phil's live voice in her mind, and not his recorded one. The two were as different as night and day. His live voice was rich and warm and haunting. Was Phil's coldness and lack of emotion on 'Missing Totti' and 'Lamplighter Rock' a fault of the sound engineers? Or was that simply the way his voice sounded on disc? It seemed to her, that there was only one way to discover the answer to that question, and that was to have a second record made.

'You must keep on at Marco, talk him into doing another record,' she said to Phil.

'Which means you now think this one's a bummer?' he replied quickly.

'Not at all, of course not. But if at first you don't succeed, try, try and try again.'

'Like your King Robert the Bruce's spider?' he asked, grinning suddenly.

'Precisely,' she grinned back, pleased to see she'd succeeded in snapping him out of his black mood.

'And *when* we get a second recording, it'll be one of your songs, I'll insist on that,'

He was lovely, she thought, if a little naive at times. 'You'll insist on nothing of the sort. If Marco wants you to record more of my songs, well and fine. If not, you'll record what he says, and not argue about it.'

He reached out and took her hand. 'You'll stay the night?' he asked in a new tone of voice.

She leaned her cheek against his hand. 'I'll stay the night,' she agreed.

Jessie was cleaning the St. Peter's Street flat. She was between pub sessions and waiting for Phil to get back from Soho where The Light was making a demo for Marco. Marco had insisted on it before he committed himself to a second record. The material being used wasn't Jessie's this time. Marco had shied away when Phil had broached the subject, and Phil, wisely heeding Jessie's advice, hadn't pursued the matter.

It was now seven weeks since 'Missing Totti' was released, and it had sunk without trace. Jessie didn't know if Vestal had pushed the record, but she suspected they hadn't. When she'd tried to quiz Marco about it he'd been evasive, muttering about the cost of promotion and the risks with new artists.

It was Jessie's guess, however, that other Vestal records coming out at the same time had been chosen to be pushed, and have money spent on them. If that was so, 'Missing Totti' had failed at the starter's gate.

She was in the kitchen, wiping down the soot ingrained Ascot, when Phil returned. 'How did it go?' she asked eagerly.

Phil took her in his arms and kissed her. 'I'm hopeful. Marco wouldn't give a decision there and then, he had to consult with other people before he did that, but I'm hopeful. It went well, I could feel it.' Phil was excited. It was the brightest he'd been in a long time.

She hugged him tightly. 'So how long before you hear?'

'Next couple of days, three at the most. Shouldn't be longer than that.'

'Then we'll just have to keep our fingers crossed,' she laughed and wished she was more hopeful for him.

In the event, Marco's verdict arrived by the next morning's post. It was only a few minutes past opening time when Phil, Oscar and Len trooped into The Lonsdale Arms, their gloomy expressions telling the whole sorry story.

'It's a bust with Marco and Vestal Records,' Phil said to Jessie, his face white as a sheet. Up until the arrival of the letter he'd been convinced Marco's decision would be in the affirmative.

'Three large navy rums, and a pistol if you have one,' Oscar ordered.

'Did Marco give you a reason?' Jessie asked as she poured the rums at the gantry.

Phil shook his head. 'Just that there wouldn't be a second recording with Vestel. But he wishes us all the very best for the future.'

If the demo session had gone as well as Phil had believed, then it had to be the way his voice came out on disc, Jessie thought. Later, when Phil played a copy of the demo record for her, this proved to be true. His voice was just as it had been on 'Missing Totti' and 'Lamplighter Rock'.

Jessie commiserated with the three downcast musicians, several times squeezing Phil's hand in sympathy. This was an awful blow to them all, but especially to him.

Len finished his rum and said they'd have another round. 'As we don't have a gig tonight,' he announced, 'I am going to get as drunk as the proverbial skunk.' Oscar and Phil cheered.

Julian appeared, and heard the news. Although secretly pleased, for he feared that a successful The Light

291

would leave his pub, he kept a straight face as he condemned Marco's action, saying Marco had made a big mistake. He then announced that a further round of rums was to be on him.

A little later, Pixie, dressed for town, came down from upstairs. Julian had informed her what had happened. 'As far as I'm concerned,' she said loudly, 'Marco is a horse's backside. Why, The Light is fantastic! Everybody knows that.'

Pixie hung around for a few minutes, until Yvonne came on duty, wanting to make sure Yvonne turned up before leaving, then said goodbye to everyone, she was off to Oxford Street to do some Christmas shopping. Christmas was less than a fortnight away. As soon as she was gone the brief euphoria she'd generated vanished.

Julian reappeared to tell Jessie he'd decided to do a spirits stock-take, and Yvonne was going to assist him by restocking the two spirits cupboards under the bar which were nearly depleted.

Julian and Yvonne disappeared down into the cellar leaving Jessie in charge of the bar, and pouring yet another round of rums for The Light who were now well on the way to getting drunk.

Customers came and went, and The Light continued drinking heavily. Jessie began to wonder what was keeping Yvonne. She hadn't brought a single bottle up yet. Another round finished the navy rum on the gantry, nor was there any more in the two cupboards under the bar.

Minutes later, Len was demanding another round. 'You'll have to wait until Yvonne brings some up,' she told him shortly, too busy to be polite. She served more pints, shooed a tramp out the door who'd come into the pub in the hope of being able to cadge a wet, and answered the public phone, which turned out to be a wrong number.

'Where's that bloody rum!' Oscar complained.

Jessie slammed a pint on the counter. She'd have to give Yvonne a shout. She and Julian were probably yakking nineteen to the dozen and hadn't noticed how much time had slipped by.

Jessie called Phil up to the bar and asked him to keep an eye on the till while she popped down to the cellar to hurry up their rum. 'I'll not be a moment,' she promised.

The cellar was a large one, rectangular in shape and the spirits' store was located at the area of the cellar furthest away from the stairs. All the lights were on, and the hoppy tang of beer hung heavily in the air. There were numerous stacks of wooden barrels to be seen, and other stacks of the relatively new metal casks which, according to Julian, were revolutionizing the beer trade.

Jessie was about to stride in the direction of the store when she heard a groan that made her pause. Then there it was again, another groan. There was no mistaking what it meant. And then she distinguished Julian's voice, murmuring words of endearment, and Yvonne's soft moans.

Jessie went cold all over, beginning to tremble. It was as though she were back in Glasgow, back in that bedroom of so long ago.

She took a sideways step, and Julian and Yvonne came into view, both turned away from her.

Jessie stared at them, frozen in time. It wasn't Julian and Yvonne she saw, but Tommy and Eve. She wanted to be sick, or to cry out. How could Julian do this to Pixie in what amounted to their own house? For the pub wasn't only their place of business, it was where they lived – it was their home.

Her disgust and horror were so great that her trembling turned into actual shaking. How *could* Julian do this to Pixie? Why, a sweeter woman never lived!

In the awful seconds she stood rooted to the spot, Jessie heard enough to realize this wasn't something that had happened on the spur of the moment. It had been going on for quite some time.

As quietly as she was able, Jessie tip-toed back the way she'd come.

*   *   *

293

The rest of the day somehow passed. She managed to be civil to Julian and Yvonne, and also managed to avoid coming face to face with Pixie.

When the evening session was finally over, and the glasses washed and put away, she made her excuses and fled without having her staff drink. She'd never done that before, but they assumed she was upset because of Phil and the band.

She ran round to St. Peter's Street, where she found Phil nursing a sore head and drinking black coffee. He told her he'd only woken an hour since, having been asleep since staggering back at lunch time. He sat in the kitchen with her while she made some coffee for herself.

Jessie had come to a decision. She was going to leave The Lonsdale Arms, and the sooner the better. She just couldn't continue to work and live alongside Pixie and Julian knowing what she did. She was genuinely terrified, feeling as strongly as she did, that she might let slip something of what she'd witnessed in the cellar. If Pixie was ever to find out about Julian and Yvonne, she didn't want it coming from her.

'Do you know of any rooms or flat shares going locally?' she asked Phil suddenly.

'Somebody in the pub asked you to look out for them?' he asked, going over to the counter for more aspirin. His head was unbelievable.

'No, it's for me. I'm quitting The Lonsdale Arms,' she said shortly.

He turned round to stare at her in surprise. 'This is rather sudden, isn't it? Why?'

'I have my reasons.' She had no intention of disclosing to Phil what those reasons were.

He tried to probe, but got nowhere. All Jessie would say was that she intended leaving, and that was that. 'What about a job?' he demanded.

'There's a barmaid's position going at The York. I'll apply for it as soon as I can get round there. I know the

294

governor, so if the job hasn't gone I should be all right there. The big drawback is it isn't live in.'

Phil listened thoughtfully. 'Can I ask you a question?' he asked somewhat nervously.

'Of course.'

'You do like me don't you? I mean *really* like me?'

'I wouldn't sleep with you if I didn't,' she replied gently.

'Then why don't you come and stay here?'

The thought had crossed her mind, but she wasn't at all sure about it. The trouble was that when she thought of herself living with a man it was always Tommy she imagined, and no one else.

'You don't fancy the idea?' Phil looked suddenly crest-fallen.

There were occasions when Phil looked such a little boy that all she wanted to do was to take him in her arms, stroke his hair, and tell him it was all right, the nasty bogey man wouldn't get him, not while she was there.

But she also remembered why she had begun to sleep with Phil in the first place. Tommy was gone. He was the past, and she had the rest of her life to live, and live it to the full she would. There was no use clinging on to what had been. Phil was here and now, today and the future; Tommy was yesterday.

'I've never lived with a girl,' he said miserably. 'And to be honest, you're the first I've ever asked to live with me.'

It was embarrassing him to be so open with her. Jessie could see the discomfort and pain in his downcast eyes.

She went over and put her hands on his shoulders. 'You can help me move my bits and pieces round tomorrow,' she said softly.

Phil looked up at her, beaming. 'I'm not doing so well at the moment,' he said, 'but I'll make good yet. I'll be up there with the stars, I promise you.'

She wanted to say to him that his being a star didn't matter to her, except for the fact that he wanted it so badly. What did matter was the quality of their relationship, that they were happy together.

Instead, she announced that she was suddenly ravenous. 'What food have you got? Eggs? Milk? Onions? Mushrooms?'

'You haven't even moved in yet and already you're taking over,' he laughed.

'I am going to make you the best omelette you've ever had,' she laughed back. 'No flat mate of mine's going to go hungry.'

Busying herself preparing the omelette, Jessie began to sing.

Jessie came awake, her eyes still closed, and stretched languorously. She sought out Phil's naked body with her hand, and snuggled closer. She felt absolutely marvellous. Despite the narrowness of the bed, she'd slept extremely well. Twice during the night he'd made love to her, and as a result she was filled with well being.

'What is the meaning of this Philip?' a woman's voice suddenly demanded.

Jessie was so startled she nearly jumped out of her skin. She hadn't heard anyone come into the flat. Her eyes flew open, and she found herself staring at a heavily built woman whose small eyes bored disapprovingly into hers.

'Hello, mamma,' Phil said in a small voice.

So this was the redoubtable Mrs Jacobs, whom she'd heard so much about. She should have guessed.

Mrs Jacobs was in her late fifties. Her clothes were expensive, but flamboyant and the pudgy hands were loaded down with rings.

'Pleased to meet you,' Jessie said as evenly as she could, attempting a smile that came out more as a grimace.

'Who is this . . . this *person* Philip?' Mrs Jacobs asked in a tone as heavy as her build.

Phil cleared his throat. He hadn't been expecting his

mother for another couple of days yet, and had been going to phone and explain. At least that had been his intention. As ever, though, he had put it off and was too late. 'This is Jessie McBride, mother,' he said, trying to sit up. 'She and I are living together now.'

Mrs Jacobs eyes narrowed. 'You're not Jewish, are you?' she asked.

'No, I'm Scots,' Jessie replied.

Mrs Jacobs sniffed. 'You'll never get him for good, you know,' she said. 'He'll never marry you. He'll only marry one of his own kind.'

Jessie was taken aback by the woman's vehemence. If only she wasn't naked under the bedclothes, she could get up and stand her ground properly. 'That's fine with me,' she said sweetly. 'I'm already married anyway.'

Mrs Jacob's expression as she stared at Jessie was one of contempt. Things were clearly as bad as she'd thought.

Jessie stared defiantly back, she wasn't going to let Phil's mother browbeat her, no matter what.

Mrs Jacobs' gaze moved to the cringing Phil. 'So this is what you've sunk to, living in sin with a married shiksa. I weep for you, my son,' she wailed, though Jessie could see no tears. 'I weep for what you've become.'

'Mother, please . . .' Phil began.

'It's still not too late, you can still come home with me and take up again where you left off,' she interrupted.

Phil shook his head. 'I can never go back to that world,' he said in a voice he hadn't used before to his mother. 'I hate it. I'm a musician, that's what I want to do, and this is the life that makes me happy.'

There was a moment of silence and then, giving up on that argument, Mrs Jacobs brought her attention back to Jessie. She stared at her briefly, and then gave a dismissive snort. 'Get your washing together for me Philip,' she said to her son, continuing to look at Jessie as though she were in a cage.

'Mamma does my washing for me,' Phil explained to

Jessie in a small voice. 'That's why she has her own keys.'

'Well now I'm in residence she won't have to bother any more,' said Jessie sweetly. 'I'll be doing your washing from here on.'

Mrs Jacobs turned her eyes from Jessie to her son. 'Philip . . .'

Phil looked from one to the other. 'I don't know. . .'

'I can always find another place,' said Jessie quietly.

'Philip doesn't have a washing machine,' argued Mrs Jacobs. 'It's never the same done by hand.'

Jessie smiled. 'There's a launderette down the road.'

Mrs Jacobs glared at her for a second, then again decided to change the conversation. 'Your poppa and I want to speak to you at home. Come and see us as soon as you can,' she commanded Phil. Then, without waiting for a reply, she stormed off, banging the three doors from where she'd been standing to the outside behind her.

'She's really very nice,' said Phil weakly.

'Make sure you get those keys back when you go home,' Jessie replied, and got out of bed.

It was St. Valentine's day, 1960, and Jessie was pleased because when she'd got up in the morning she'd found a card on the kitchen table from Phil. He must have stuck it there the night before. It was sloppily romantic with lots of hearts and cupids on it, she was delighted with it. Phil had penned in many of the old favourite rhymes and legends – everything from 'Postie postie do not falter, this may lead me to the altar' to 'Roses are red, violets are blue, I'm full of love and it's all for you'. He had even written 'S.W.A.L.K.' (Sealed with a Loving Kiss) on the back flap.

She'd been thrilled, not only with the card but with the effort he'd gone to. It had put her into a good mood for the entire day.

Jessie was bottling up with Clive, the governor of the

new pub she was working at, when the telephone rang. Thinking it was his bookie, Clive answered it immediately.

'For you,' he said to Jessie, offering her the receiver.

Must be Phil, she thought, for he buzzed her at the pub occasionally. But it wasn't Phil. 'Hello?'

'Jessie this is Caroline, Mick Marco's friend. How are you?'

Jessie blinked in astonishment. She'd thought she'd seen the last of Caroline, and Mick Marco.

They exchanged pleasantries, and Caroline explained that she'd rung The Lonsdale Arms first and been told Jessie was now at The York. 'I was wondering if you could have dinner with me tomorrow night,' Caroline said at last.

Now why should Caroline want to invite her to dinner. 'I'm afraid I'm on duty,' Jessie said guardedly.

There was a slight pause. 'It's not exactly a social meeting I'm proposing. Dinner could be to your advantage, in fact it could be very much to your advantage,' Caroline said mysteriously.

'Can you be more specific?'

'Mick and I want you to meet someone. A rather special person whose name I don't particularly wish to mention over the telephone,' Caroline answered cagily.

Very mysterious, Jessie thought. Of course she'd have to go now, wild horses wouldn't keep her away. She was intrigued. 'Hang on a mo',' she said, and laying down the receiver went to check with Clive that she could get the night off. 'All right, it's on. Where and when?' Jessie said to Caroline.

'Eight o'clock at the Savoy. I'll be waiting for you in the foyer. And . . . the invitation is for you alone. Please don't turn up with Phil,' Caroline said.

'All right,' said Jessie even more puzzled.

Jessie cradled the receiver. How tantalizing! she thought.

Who was she going to be meeting?

★　　★　　★

Nervous and excited, Jessie arrived at the Savoy at exactly eight o'clock and found Caroline waiting for her as she had promised. Caroline, as always, looked absolutely stunning in a beige dress that had clearly been made for her.

Jessie was content with her own outfit, a beaded and sequinned black Victorian dress that she'd bought from a junk stall in Camden Passage for the princely sum of five bob.

'They're in the bar having a drink before dinner, shall we join them?' Caroline said after greeting Jessie.

'So who am I going to meet?' Jessie asked eagerly, consumed with curiosity. She hadn't been able to think of anything else since the telephone call.

'Wait and see,' Caroline teased.

Marco and the man with him were in a booth. The man was a small, handsome Negro dressed in flamingo pink suit, with shirt, tie and socks to match. There was something familiar about the man's face, Jessie thought, almost feeling as if she'd met him before. But if she had met him before she would certainly remember it.

Marco and the stranger climbed out of the booth. 'How nice to see you again, darling, I'm so glad you could make it,' Marco gushed, kissing Jessie on the cheek.

'Jessie,' Caroline said. 'I'd like you to meet Marvin Leroi.'

Marvin Leroi shook her hand warmly. 'It's a real pleasure to meet you, Miss McBride,' he declared in an accent straight out of *Gone with the Wind*.

Jessie stared at him in amazement, her good manners totally forgotten. Marvin Leroi! No wonder he looked familiar. On the American rock scene there was only one name bigger, and that was Elvis himself.

'How do you do Mr Leroi,' Jessie replied in a shaky voice, trying not to appear as star-struck as she felt.

He flashed her a brilliant smile. 'Hey, let's forget all this formal Miss and Mr jazz. I'm Marvin and you're Jessie, okay?'

Jessie laughed. 'Okay,' she agreed, feeling herself relax under his charm. He was obviously not only one of the most famous singers in the world, but one of the nicest as well.

They all sat, ordered drinks, and then chatted about London and the States for a while. It was Marvin's last night in Britain, he was flying home next morning.

There has to be a reason behind all this, Jessie told herself, as the talk went on, and tried to be patient.

Finally they left the bar and went to the Grill, where a table had been reserved for them. Jessie tried several times to catch Caroline's eye, wanting some sort of sign from her, but Caroline was obviously enjoying Jessie's suspense.

It wasn't until the they were in the middle of the first course that Marvin dropped his bombshell. 'I'm interested in your song "Missing Totti" Jessie,' he said. 'I like it very much.'

'Very much,' Marco echoed with a broad smile.

Jessie was too surprised to speak.

'I do think however that the lyrics could do with a. . . a little polishing here and there,' Marvin went on carefully, toying with his avocado.

Jessie was suddenly aware that the three of them were staring at her, waiting for her response.

'Lyrics have always been my weak point,' she admitted.

Marvin looked relieved. Reaching into his inside jacket pocket he pulled out a folded score. 'I took the liberty, Jessie, of making a few alterations as I saw them. I'd like you to tell me what you think.'

She took the score from him and read it through. To begin with, the song had a new title, it was now called 'Together'. The other changes he'd made, though minor, tightened the song and made quite a difference for the better.

'I'm really impressed,' Jessie said, looking up at Marvin. 'You've made a definite improvement.'

'In that case,' he said, smiling, 'how would you feel about me recording your song?'

Jessie could only stare at him in disbelief. Could it really be true that an artist of Leroi's reputation wanted to record a song of hers?

'In Nashville,' he explained.

Marvin Leroi record *her* song? In Nashville? She was asleep and dreaming, she had to be! But she wasn't. Caroline and Marco were still sitting at the table, looking at her expectantly. Around the room, the other diners continued to eat and talk while the waiters threaded their way amongst the tables. None of them seemed aware that the world had stopped turning. And those brown eyes gazing into hers couldn't have been more serious.

'Well,' she breathed, finding her voice at last. 'Marvin, you've got yourself a song.'

8

It was August 1961, eighteen months since Marvin Leroi had recorded 'Together', and seventeen since he'd been tragically killed in an air crash along with several members of his band and another singer.

It had been a copper-bottomed certainty before Marvin's death that 'Together' would be a success, all his records were, but as a result of his untimely death 'Together' had gone straight to the number one spot on the American charts, and had stayed there for an unprecedented thirteen weeks. Altogether, it had remained on the charts for twenty-seven weeks. The story in Britain had been similar: nine weeks at number one; twenty-two in the charts overall.

Marvin's death had transformed him into an instant legend. 'Together', his last single, had become his biggest, and many said, his greatest.

All this had meant an amazing amount of money for Jessie, and she was, in fact, just coming from a meeting with her bank manager, who acted as her financial advisor.

After the quiet and coolness of the bank, the street outside was hot and muggy. Jessie pondered on what to do with the rest of the afternoon, she'd long since stopped working at the pub, and decided she'd pay Harrod's Food Hall a visit.

She'd buy some haggis, Scotch mutton pies. Scotch rolls, and a ring of black pudding. She called it nostalgia food. More and more lately, her thoughts were turning to Glasgow. Although well settled in London, she was beginning to miss it dreadfully.

She stopped at a phone box to ring Phil and tell him what she intended doing. He was at home, in the Georgian house she'd bought in Islington. It was a beautiful house, and she loved it, but half of her wished that when she opened the door it was a Scottish street she would come out on, and not an English one.

Phil grumbled because she'd woken him up. The Light had a gig that night at a party being thrown by a group of Fleet Street journalists and so he'd been taking a kip.

The Light was continuing to play local gigs and private parties, and The Lonsdale Arms at weekends. Phil was becoming gloomier and gloomier, and he was afraid it was a pattern which was never going to be broken. His dreams were further away than ever from coming true. There was nothing she could say any more to cheer him up. Her own unexpected success didn't help.

Emerging from the phone box, Jessie crossed to the kerbside with the intention of hailing a passing taxi. She was still waiting minutes later when there was an ominous roll of thunder and the heavens opened.

She took refuge in a cheap cafe-cum-restaurant just around the corner. She was already soaked, and the rain didn't look as though it was going to stop in a hurry. At least there she could have a warming cup of tea.

The cafe was typical of many to be found in central London: there were no frills, the accent, first and foremost, was on economy. Economy for the management, economy for the customers.

Jessie sat at a plastic topped table. A man, you could hardly give him the title of waiter, came over reluctantly and took her order. There were several other people in the cafe, most of whom seemed to be escaping the downpour as well. She looked around at the yellowed walls and the counter with its display of rolls and pastries. And then her gaze stopped at a neck behind the counter. It belonged to the man cooking on the large gas stove fixed to the far wall of the room. For a second, she couldn't catch her breath. She knew that neck and she knew the back of the head above it. She rubbed her eyes and blinked. Maybe it was just her memory playing her tricks. She craned around, trying to see the man's face, but couldn't. Come on, turn, she commanded silently. She looked away, then looked back. No, it couldn't be, she told herself, she was definitely imagining things.

Suddenly, he turned, slapping a plate of food on the counter.

Jessie must have made an exclamation, for the people near her turned in her direction. There, behind the counter was Tommy McBride.

He hadn't been back in the charts after that initial hit, but she'd imagined that he must be back in Glasgow, working the clubs there. It had never occurred to her that he might be in the same city as she. That she might bump into him at any time.

She quickly looked away as he glanced in her direction, pretending to be engrossed in studying the rain as it lashed against the street outside.

There was a tight knot in her stomach, and her heart was pounding so loudly she was sure everyone in the room could hear it.

She didn't want to talk to him. She had to get out of there as quickly and quietly as she could. It didn't matter that it was pouring cats and dogs, she couldn't remain in this cafe a second longer. She glanced out of the corner of her eye and saw that he was facing the wall again.

She fumbled in her handbag, found a two shilling piece, and then she hurried to the counter, put the coin beside the till, and raced out through the door. 'Hey,' called the man at the till, 'You forgot your change.'

She ran through the rain, looking neither left nor right, only intent on putting as much distance between her and Tommy McBride as she could. She broke a heel outside of Charing Cross Station, but she also finally found a taxi.

She wept all the way to Islington. He'd looked the same, exactly as she remembered. If she'd imagined that with time her image of him had faded, she'd been wrong. Very, very wrong. And if she'd thought that the pain had lessened, she'd been even more wrong.

When she arrived home she told Phil she wasn't feeling too well, and went to bed. There she resumed crying, and hid under the bedclothes, till she finally realized it was herself she was hiding from.

She thought Phil might bring her a nice cup of tea, or just come up to see how she was. But he didn't.

Finally, still sobbing, she fell into an exhausted sleep.

Jessie sat at her piano and began playing 'Together'. She'd been playing it every day since seeing Tommy a fortnight ago. He hadn't been out of her thoughts since.

There was a commotion in the hallway, then Phil and Len lurched in. It was clear to her right away that they'd been smoking marijuana. Phil always got a supercilious expression on his face after he'd been 'smoking', it was an expression she'd come to know well of late.

'That old song again? What about something new and exciting, another international number one hit!' Phil mocked, coming across the room.

She regarded him warily. He resented the success she'd

had with 'Together', resented it and was jealous of it, as though it was her success that was holding him back. With each passing day he grew more and more bitter about his own static situation. There was nothing she could do any more that wasn't wrong.

She'd written several numbers since Marvin Leroi had recorded 'Together', but they hadn't done much, staying low on the charts for a few weeks before fizzling out completely. And that had been the British charts, none of them had made the American. It might have been different if Marvin had lived, possibly he would have written the lyrics himself while she supplied the tune, but there was no point in wishing for what might have been.

'Beautiful dreams,' a totally spaced out Len said to no one in particular.

'Come on, Jessie,' Phil went on. 'Lets have another million-seller.'

'There are times when you can be such a bore,' Jessie said to Phil, sending him into a fit of giggles.

Jessie came to the end of 'Together', and reached for the whisky and lemonade she had sitting atop the piano. She stared at Phil over the rim of her glass. Only the other night he'd cried in her arms, making up excuses for his failure, begging her to stick with him, promising her the moon. Today, however, the chip was back on his shoulder and everything was her fault.

Maybe one day she'd write a song about Phil, she thought. If she ever did, she'd call it 'Lost Man's Rock'.

Phil and Len disappeared off upstairs where there was a second reception room, and soon the sweet smell of marijuana came wafting down the stairs.

Jessie started playing 'Together' again.

Jessie sat in the corner of the cafe, watching Tommy being busy at the stove. She'd been there for ten minutes and he hadn't noticed her yet. She wasn't sure what madness had driven her here, but it was too late to back out now. She chose a moment when the cafe was the emptiest it had been since she'd arrived. Steeling herself, she rose, walked over and paid her bill. She had to steel herself further to walk along the counter until she was directly behind him.

'Hello Tommy,' she said in a voice that almost sounded normal.

He didn't take in whose voice it was, he thought it was just one of the regular customers. He turned, the standard smile on his face, already saying, 'How are you?' before he looked up to face her.

She had put on weight, and there was little of the girl she'd been left in her eyes, but he would have recognized her anywhere.

'You've aged,' he blurted out.

'Oh, that's nice,' she replied sarcastically, but couldn't manage to say anything else.

'Well,' he laughed nervously, 'long time no see.'

'Yes,' she whispered. 'A long time.'

They stared at each other in silence. Now that she was meeting him again she didn't know what to say. In one way she knew so much about this man in front of her, in another he was a total stranger.

'I dropped in for coffee, and here you were,' she said at last.

Embarrassment crept into his face. He was acutely conscious of his greasy hands, his soiled apron and the stupid wee hat stuck on his head. 'Um. Here I am.'

'I didn't know you could cook,' she said, her voice sounding shrill in her ears.

He shrugged. 'The job was going, so I learned.'

Oh, Tommy! a voice inside her wailed.

'You look grand,' he said shyly.

'Grand but old,' she smiled 'You're not looking so bad yourself,' she went on. 'You're just as I remember you.'

'My hair's different,' he replied ruefully. 'And the clothes are less stylish,' indicating the apron and hat.

307

'Oh, but just as dashing,' she said instantly, trying to control her voice.

He cleared his throat. 'You didn't know I worked here then?'

'No, no. It was sheer chance that I came in.'

He cleared his throat again. He was finding this difficult. It would have been hard enough to know what to do if they'd been alone, but here it was impossible. After all these years, she was actually standing in front of him and he was making a fool of himself again. 'Are you living in London now?'

'I have been ever since . . . ever since . . . Yes, for some time.'

'I see,' he said, nodding. 'I see.'

She took a deep breath and decided to say what she'd come to say. 'Look we should talk, and we can't do that properly here. How about we meet?' she said in a rush.

He tried not to let his enthusiasm show. 'All right,' he replied casually.

Relief made her smile. 'When suits you? I can manage almost any time.'

He wanted to propose that night, but his pride restrained him. The last thing he wanted was to appear over eager. 'How about the evening after next? I knock off here at six and usually have a pint in the Globe across from the opera house before going home.'

'I'll be there just after six, then,' she said. 'Day after tomorrow.'

She smiled, and he smiled in return.

'Till then,' she said.

'Till then,' he repeated.

As she walked away from the cafe, she felt like a young lassie looking forward to her first date, and wasn't sure whether she was glad she felt so glad or not.

Jessie arrived outside the Globe at quarter to six; she'd been so anxious to get there that she'd left home far too early. She decided to go for a walk round about, she wanted Tommy to be waiting for her, not the other way around.

She'd been through Covent Garden a number of times, and always enjoyed it, for it was an interesting and colourful place. This time, though, it was completely wasted on her. All she could think of was that the minutes till her rendezvous with Tommy were crawling by so slowly each seemed like an hour. At eight minutes past, feverish with impatience, she decided to chance it. She charged through the doors of the Globe, relieved to discover him there, ordering at the bar.

She was nervous, but certain it didn't show. Tommy was thinking exactly the same thing about himself. He ordered their drinks and carried them to a table.

They sat, and looked at one another. 'How are Jack, Sammy and Jake "The Rake"?' she asked finally.

'Dandy, last I heard. Back in Glasgow, of course. The three of them caught the same train up when the band folded. Sammy's married now, to Cass McNulty. She used to go jigging at the Cameo.'

Jessie searched her memory. 'I remember her, she was very wee, and had ginger hair.'

'That's Cass,' Tommy grinned.

She pulled out her fags and he expressed surprise that she now smoked. A far cry from the upright minister's daughter he'd first met at Queen's Park School, she replied; and thought to herself, aye, a helluva far cry. He accepted a cigarette when she offered the packet.

'How come the band folded?' she asked when they were settled again.

Tommy made a face. 'After we won that talent show we landed a contract with M.M.T., and for a while things looked good. Then the skiffle fad began to wane, and M.M.T. lost interest in us. One morning, when it was three weeks since our last gig, Jack announced that he'd had enough and that he was off home to Glasgow.

309

And that was that – the end of the Tommy McBride Skiffle Band.'

He should have gone solo then, she thought. That had always been her plan for him. 'I'm sorry,' she murmured.

He drew savagely on his cigarette. The palms of his hands were sweating, and when he next spoke his voice had gone tight and husky. 'I can explain that afternoon in Allison Street,' he nearly whispered.

Jessie gave a dismissive shrug. 'There's nothing to explain. Eve was always attractive.' She had known this wouldn't be easy, but it was worse than she'd imagined. In a minute she'd be in tears.

'Oh, aye, she was attractive enough, I can't deny that. But that wasn't the reason why I was sleeping with her.' He paused his hand reaching for hers across the table. 'You've got to believe me, Jessie she was blackmailing me.'

Jessie looked at him sharply. 'Blackmail. Don't be ridiculous, Tommy McBride. I've heard it called a lot of things in my time, but blackmail's a new one.'

Slowly, and haltingly, he told her the whole story from start to finish. Eve propositioning him, her promise that the band would win the show, Sally Grierson and M.M.T., everything.

'You didn't *have* to be blackmailed, you could have said no,' Jessie said softly when he'd finished.

Tommy dropped his eyes to stare at the table. 'I won't try and excuse myself, I suppose all I can say is that the temptation was too great. Eve offered me an exit from Glasgow, to be able to break with the Ted scene once and for all, and so I went along with her proposition. And if I hadn't slept with her she'd have put the mockers on my singing career, and I'd never have broken away from the fix I was in.'

He looked up at Jessie, his eyes pleading. 'But I swear to God, if I'd known that sleeping with Eve was going to lose me you I'd never have agreed to it in a million years.

No opportunity, no big break, nothing was worth losing you. You've got to believe me. I've been living in hell since you left.'

There was a lump in her throat. He *had* loved her after all, that hadn't been a lie. That knowledge meant more than a lot to her – it meant the world.

'Me and the Boyd Street Boys scoured Glasgow for you after you'd run off, we tramped the streets for a week. I kept praying that one of us would stumble onto you, but, of course, you weren't there.'

Jessie wiped a tear from her eye. 'What happened to you and Eve?'

'I made her keep her side of the bargain. I promised her that if she didn't I'd razor her face so badly she'd be a monster for the rest of her natural if she didn't.' Tommy paused, then said quietly 'I never laid a finger on her again after you found us together. I swear that.'

Jessie took a deep breath. 'What a mess,' she whispered.

'If only I'd had the chance to talk to you after. If only you hadn't disappeared the way you did,' he said wretchedly.

How could she explain what had gone on in her mind, the profound sense of betrayal she'd felt? Life had been a bubble of love and happiness, then she'd walked into that room and the bubble had burst in her face.

'I didn't see how you could do what you were doing to her in our bed . . . and still care for me,' she said in a sob.

Tommy gazed into his pint. 'It was dreadful after you left. I did all manner of things I'm not proud of. In fact, I think it's fair to say that for a while I went a wee bit daft.'

She'd gone a wee bit daft herself, she thought. 'So why didn't you go back to Glasgow with the lads then?'

'If I'd done that I'd have had to have taken up where I left off, King of the Glasgow Teds and all that horror. By staying in London I was able to just be myself.'

He drank off what remained of his pint, and she went up to the bar where she ordered two more, and a couple of large drams.

He grinned when she placed his beer and whisky before him. 'The old Glasgow combination, heavy and 'the cratur', Rangers and Celtic, Protestants and Catholics,' he said.

'And what are you up to nowadays?' he asked after she'd sat back down. 'You look like you're doing all right.'

She'd wondered if he knew about her success, he clearly didn't.

'Remember Marvin Leroi's hit "Together"?'

Tommy nodded.

'I wrote it.'

He stared at her in astonishment. 'You?'

She nodded, laughing. 'It was recorded originally by a band called The Light, but that version flopped. Then Marvin heard it while he was over here on a trip, decided he wanted it for himself, recorded it in Nashville, and bingo!'

'That was one of the biggest hits ever,' Tommy whispered.

'An "all time great" it's been called,' she agreed. To hell with being modest. She wanted to impress Tommy, and maybe even rub salt in a bit.

Tommy was shaken. He didn't know what he'd been expecting her to tell him she'd been doing, but not that. 'I don't know why, but I never thought of you continuing to write songs,' he said at last.

'I hadn't planned to, I just sort of got caught up in it again.'

He looked at her sharply. 'How was that?'

She picked up her whisky and swirled it round in her glass. Did she tell him about Phil or didn't she? She decided she would. 'My chap is the singer with The Light, the band that recorded the song in the first place. It was he who asked me to write something for them. The old thing, desperate for new material,' she said quickly.

Tommy had gone very pale. 'Déjà vu,' he replied, giving a feeble grin.

'Déjà vu,' she agreed.

'You and this chap, is it serious?'

'We live together,' she replied, which didn't answer his question, but gave the impression it did.

'I see,' Tommy said.

'I've bought this house in Islington.'

He pretended to whistle. 'You must have made a fortune out of "Together".'

'A modest fortune.'

Rich and in love! Tommy was pleased for her, but at the same time he was madly jealous of this other man, whoever the man was. He reminded himself he had no right to be jealous, he had no claim on Jessie anymore. But claim or not, he was still jealous.

Then he had another thought. It would be dreadful if she went away from this meeting feeling *sorry* for him, he didn't want that at all. His pride couldn't take the humiliation. 'I'm over in Clapham, I live there with a friend,' he said casually, though it was clear from his voice that the friend was a woman.

'I don't know south of the river, it's a complete mystery to me,' was the only thing she could think of in reply to that.

Tommy grinned. 'And the north side, outside of central London, is a mystery to me.'

Jessie's emotions were in a turmoil, but the predominant one was jealousy. Another was anger, anger with herself at being jealous of this unknown woman Tommy had taken up with. 'What does your friend do?' she asked, trying to match Tommy's casual tone.

'Ania's on social security. She can't work because of the children.'

Jessie's heart skipped a beat. 'Yours?'

'No, their father was booted out by Ania shortly before I met her.'

'Ania's a pretty name,' Jessie said.

'She's a very pretty woman. She's got those high cheekbones that many Poles and Hungarians have. Her parents came over here from Cracow just before the war.'

Very pretty woman indeed, she was probably a bloody ravishing beauty! Jessie fought to control her features so that her jealousy didn't show. Or the black despair she felt to think how unattractive she'd become.

Tommy didn't want to say what he said next, but it seemed to him that with Jessie doing so well, and having fallen in love again, he was almost obliged to. 'I suppose we should talk about the divorce,' he said hesitantly.

She felt as though she'd been hit in the stomach. This wasn't at all how she'd planned their drink should go. It had started off so pleasantly, and now they were talking about divorce!

'I know you have to be separated for seven years in Scotland before you can file for one, but of course English law is different. We can probably go ahead and file right away down here,' Tommy rolled on.

'I imagine so,' Jessie replied reluctantly.

'Do you want me to initiate proceedings, or will you?'

She had the sudden urge to slap him silly. 'I'll file. If it turns out I have to cite someone do you want me to cite Ania or Eve?' she answered.

'Eve.' He wished he had kept his mouth shut. How had they gotten this far so quickly?

Protecting his lady, just like Tommy, he'd always been gallant, Jessie thought miserably. 'Right then,' she replied brightly.

'Right then,' Tommy echoed

Their conversation became static. They drank quickly and were soon on their way out of the pub.

'Can I give you a lift home, my car's parked nearby?' Jessie asked.

That was the last thing he wanted. Where he lived wasn't exactly a slum, but he was sure it would compare unfavourably with Jessie's home. 'That would be non-sense. I'm the other way from you entirely,' he said quickly.

She fumbled in her handbag to produce her card. 'That's my address and phone number, we'll have to keep in touch about the divorce,' she said.

'I'm afraid I don't have a card,' he admitted.

Jessie dived back into her handbag to bring out a small notepad and a pencil. 'Write it down,' she said, handing them to him.

When that was over neither of them was sure how to say goodbye, Jessie was about to kiss him on the cheek when he stuck out his hand. They shook as though mere acquaintances parting from each other after a night out.

Hands in pockets, and shoulders hunched, Tommy walked off down the street.

Jessie, feeling wretched and sick inside, watched him go. She'd been looking forward so much to their rendezvous. And now they were practically divorced!

Mick Marco switched off the hi-fi system he had in his office, at Jessie's request he'd been listening to the record the Tommy McBride Skiffle Band had got into the charts shortly after Jessie's arrival in London.

'You're right, McBride has got a good voice,' Marco nodded.

Jessie had come to Marco after a great deal of thought. She hated the idea of Tommy ending up as a short order cook, and had decided, if he was agreeable, to see if she couldn't give him a helping hand. Before speaking to Tommy, however, she'd come to Marco. She wanted him behind her before putting her proposal to Tommy.

'I always thought that he should go solo, eventually' she explained. 'The band was only a device to launch his career.'

Marco looked at her thoughtfully. 'What do you see him singing, rock or ballad?'

'He can sing either, but I'd prefer him to do rock. That's the market of the immediate future, and it's also what he identifies with the most.'

Marco nodded, she was quite right, of course. This boy wasn't just a good singer – when he sang you believed him. 'What about material? Would you like me to try and find something suitable, or are you intending to write for him yourself?'

'If he does want to make a comeback, then we'll team up as before. I'll write the tune, Tommy the lyrics.'

'Okay, then if he wants to go ahead, the pair of you get together and come back to me when you've got an A and B side. We'll make a demo and see what the reaction is within the company.'

That was precisely what Jessie had wanted to hear. 'If you do decide to cut a disc with him I want him promoted, the last thing I want is a repetition of what happened to "Missing Totti",' she said immediately.

'Promotion costs money,' Marco replied slowly.

'Money makes money, as you well know. I'll have Tommy and the record promoted even if I have to fund the campaign myself. But if I do that it's a completely different percentage deal. I want that clearly understood right from the word go.'

'Let's not cross bridges before we get to them. Let's just concentrate on the demo for now, and worry about promotion afterwards.'

She could see he was impressed she was willing to put her own money up front, which was what she'd intended. She wanted Marco to appreciate just how serious she was about this one.

The next night found Jessie and Tommy back in the Globe. She had rung him at home the previous evening. She hadn't specified why she wanted them to meet again other than it was imperative they do. He'd assumed it concerned the divorce – only he'd been wrong.

'A comeback?' Tommy repeated, quite stunned by her proposal.

'With us collaborating on the material.'

He drank some whisky, trying to collect his thoughts. He'd thought she was going to say everything was set for the divorce and they'd never have to see each other again, and she was offering a partnership!

'Are you suggesting this because you've taken pity on me?' he asked angrily. 'Because if you are, forget it, I don't want to know.'

The same old Tommy with his stubborn pride. 'You've got a damned fine singing voice, I've always said that, and Mick Marco of Vestal Records agrees with me.'

'Oh, yes?'

'For heaven's sake, Tommy, what future is there in being a short order cook?'

Tommy winced. 'That's exactly what I mean. You feel sorry for me.'

'What I'm feeling for you at this moment is not sorry,' she cried, exasperated. 'You've got nothing to lose Tommy, and everything to gain. So what do you say?'

He remained unconvinced. 'I don't need anybody's charity.'

She offered him a cigarette, and he snapped he'd have one of his own. 'Okay,' she snapped back, 'I'll have one of yours, too.'

'Look, Tommy, I'll be getting something out of this as well,' she said when she was calm again.

'What?' he demanded.

'Sure I had enormous success with "Together", but the finished version of the lyrics owed a great deal to Marvin Leroi. The tunes I've composed since have been just as good, but the lyrics haven't. I need a lyricist, and you're the natural choice. Your lyrics fit my tunes. If you agree to join forces with me you'll be helping me just as much as I'll be helping you.'

Tommy looked thoughtful. 'And this Mick Marco is definitely interested in me as a singer?'

Jessie nodded.

He thought of the cafe where he worked now, it was a dead end job if ever there was one. Jessie was right, so what did he have to lose? The answer was sod all. And she needed him, that was the clincher. She wasn't feeling sorry for him, or patronizing him. She *needed* him – him and his lyrics.

'You're on,' he said at last.

Jessie beamed. 'I'll get another round in to celebrate.'

'I'll get it in.' he said, already on his feet.

She watched him saunter up to the bar in that gallus way Glaswegian men have when they consider themselves cock of the walk. Tomorrow she was definitely going to start slimming she decided. And maybe see about having something done to her hair.

'But why do I have to go out? It's my home as well, you know,' Phil said angrily.

Jessie glanced at her watch. Tommy would be here at any moment to start their first session together as collaborators.

Tommy hadn't wanted to come to her house to work, but hadn't wanted her to go to his either. In the end, after some heated argument, he'd capitulated, although with bad grace.

Jessie had thought the reason he didn't want to come was because he didn't want to meet Phil. But that was only partly true. He didn't want to come because it was where she stayed with Phil, where she *slept* with Phil.

'I've already explained to you, I don't want him being inhibited by your presence. Say hello, give him a drink, then scoot off so he can relax and we can get some work done together.

'If anyone should be inhibited it's me, he's your husband after all, and I'm just the guy you're living in sin with.'

Jessie laughed.

318

'Anyway, I don't like the idea of you writing for him. If you have to write for someone write for me.' Phil continued petulantly.

Jessie sighed. 'First of all, I'm not writing for him, we'll be collaborating. And secondly I do write songs for you.'

'None I can ever get recorded,' he complained.

She'd been in a lighthearted mood up until then, now she began to get cross with him. 'Don't blame my songs for that,' she shapped.

If the bell hadn't rung then it would have developed into a blistering fight, of which they'd had so many of late. They seemed to be forever at one another's throats.

'Now you be pleasant,' she warned.

He raised his arm in the Nazi salute. 'Jawohl, Mein Führeress!' he barked out.

Phil was smiling, and the epitome of charm itself, when Jessie showed Tommy in. She introduced them, and they shook hands. Tommy replied he'd have a whisky when Phil asked him what he'd have to drink.

Tommy took in Phil's tall, slim figure as Phil poured the drinks. A good looking bugger, he thought. He glanced round the room, Jessie certainly hadn't stinted herself in the furnishings. The house and its contents must have cost a bomb!

The three of them chatted for a couple of minutes, then Phil announced he had to go out. Wishing them well with their work session, he took his leave of them.

Jessie was relieved to see him go, having feared he might say something snide or nasty to Tommy.

'Lovely place,' said Tommy, making a gesture that encompassed the entire house.

Jessie was about to remark on how different it was to Allison Street, but stopped herself, thinking Tommy might consider that to be a dig.

She refilled his glass, and suggested they go through to the music room, a room at the rear where she'd had the piano installed.

319

Tommy raised an eyebrow on seeing the piano was a Steinway Grand. Nothing but the very best for our Jessie now, he thought.

She sat at the piano, and he took off his jacket and placed it to one side.

They set to work.

Somewhere in the house a clock chimed midnight. Jessie was drained, and Tommy was the same. So far they'd failed to come up with anything that could be considered even half decent.

The outside door clicked shut, and a few minutes later Phil poked his head into the room. 'Still at it?' he said.

Jessie found his cheerful tone irritating, what was there to be so cheerful about! In the old days it had always been so easy for her and Tommy, but not now it seemed.

'Yes,' she replied balefully, 'we're still at it.'

'I'll away up to bed then,' Phil said to Jessie, rather pleased that it wasn't going well for them.

The word bed was like a shower of cold water to Tommy. The bed in question must be the one where Jessie would later be joining Phil. Where they made love together. 'I think we need a break, and another drink,' Tommy said, his voice suddenly husky.

Jessie agreed, they were batting their heads against a brick wall at the moment.

They returned to the lounge, and Tommy sank into a chesterfield while she poured out hefty drams for the pair of them.

'Do you want to ring Ania?' Jessie asked.

Tommy shook his head. 'She'll be in her pit long since. If I was to buzz her now I'd only wake her up,' he replied.

Tommy spied a framed blown up photo on the wall nearest him that he hadn't noticed before. The scene was a city street, the architecture unmistakable. Smiling in recognition, he went over to study the photo. The street

320

was in Springburn, the horse drawn tram in it belonged to the now defunct Glasgow Tramway & Omnibus Company. A date in the corner said the photo had been taken in 1890.

'When I came across it in a local antique market I just had to buy it,' Jessie explained.

Springburn had changed a lot since then, Tommy thought, and pictured Springburn in his mind as he'd last seen it. 'Do you miss Glasgow?' he asked softly.

'I didn't all that much to begin with, but I do more and more as time goes past.'

'I miss it, too. London's all right, but it's just not the same mind.'

She knew exactly what he meant. 'It's funny, mostly it's dirty and horrible, with so many problems, but I've never known a Glaswegian yet who didn't love the grey city, and if it came to the crunch wouldn't give his or her right arm for it,' she said.

'Aye, that's a fact sure enough,' Tommy agreed quietly. 'I'll never forget the Linn Park, my magic place.'

'How about Lover's Lane, that bit of the Cart river-bank where you used to walk?'

'I'll never forget there, either.'

Her face clouded. 'Do you remember . . . that time when I thought I was . . . and you . . .'

'Aye,' he cut in. 'I remember.'

'Star Gray, what a silly name.' She laughed, dispelling the sombre mood of the past few seconds.

'I thought it was great. It made you different, not that you needed a name to be that.'

Glasgow, once born there it was with you for life, she thought. She wouldn't have been at all surprised if when dead Glaswegians were cut open they were found to have the word Glasgow running through their insides as though they were sticks of rock.

'Will you ever go back?' she asked.

'Will you?'

Neither replied because it was a question they didn't

know the answer to. If the question had been, would you like to go back, they'd have answered yes without hesitation.

'Maybe that's where I'm going wrong,' Tommy mused.

'Wrong about what?'

'The lyrics I've been trying to write this evening. When I wrote before it was always about Glasgow, and the Glasgow situation, real things that I know inside out, and which are important to me.'

Jessie's interest quickened, he could well have put his finger on the problem.

'What I've been doing tonight is to write mid-Atlantic pap, froth and candy floss with nae guts or reality to it,' Tommy said slowly, thinking aloud.

'I'm not against you writing about Glasgow, but isn't it going to be limited in its appeal?' Jessie argued.

'Why should it be? Poverty, slums, hardship, hunger – they aren't just unique to Glasgow. They know all about them in Liverpool, Newcastle, London's East End, not to mention, New York City for example.' He paused, frowning in thought.

'Defiance, that's what I should make this song about. An individual's defiance against the terrible conditions he's been born into. It should be a great shout of fury, resolve to break free, to come out the dark into the light.

'It'll be pure Glasgow through and through, but folk the world over will understand, and I mean *understand*, what it's about.'

As Jessie had been listening to Tommy speak a tune had begun forming in her mind, a strident tune that matched the sort of lyrics he was talking about.

'Well?' he demanded.

'Let's get to it,' she replied, and led the way, almost at a run, she was so eager, back to the music room.

Dawn was tinting the sky outside when Jessie let herself into her bedroom having just seen Tommy off in a taxi.

She was filled with elation at what she and Tommy had achieved that evening. Both of them were happy with the song they'd finally produced.

She was slipping out of her dress when the bedside light suddenly snapped on, causing her to gasp in surprise.

'Sorry if I woke you,' she said to Phil who was leaning on an elbow staring coldly at her.

'You're like a bloody elephant the way you blunder round at times,' he grumbled.

Typical Phil comment of late, she thought. How loathsome he could be when he had a mind. She continued to undress.

'I wish I could say I liked him, but I didn't. To tell you the truth he struck me as a right yob,' Phil went on, and smiled.

She ignored that, at the same time feeling the elation begin to seep out of her. Trust Phil to spoil what had been a marvellous evening.

'But I was nice to him, wasn't I?'

She didn't reply.

'But then I had to be, those were your orders.'

Naked, she hurriedly reached for her nightie. She didn't want to be naked in front of him a second longer than she had to. He completely repulsed her when he was like this.

'And when you crack the whip I jump. I have to,' he continued, lighting a cigarette.

'You don't have to do any such thing,' she replied.

'Oh, but I do, my darling. And you know why? Because you pay all the bills round here.'

So that was it. Her paying all the bills was a subject he brought up periodically lately.

'I've told you before not to worry about that. It certainly doesn't bother me,' she said coolly.

He ground out his cigarette as she got into bed beside him. Reaching over to take hold of her.

'Not tonight, I'm far too tired,' she pleaded.

His hand moved under her nightie, seeking out a breast.

'A right yob,' Phil repeated, and gave a derisory laugh.

Jessie sipped her glass of Buck's Fizz and glanced about her. She and Phil were at Mick Marco's birthday party, which was being held in Marco's house off the King's Road in Chelsea.

There were about fifty people at the party, nearly all of them in some way connected with the music business. It was a very chic affair, and fascinating to observe as Jessie had been doing.

She looked over to where Phil was chatting up a pretty blonde, and recognized the girl as working for Vestal Records. She wondered idly if Phil was chatting the girl up because she was pretty, or because she worked for Vestal.

'You all right?' Caroline asked Jessie, joining her.

'Fine. Has Tommy arrived yet?'

'I haven't seen him. But that doesn't mean he's not in the house somewhere.'

Jessie glanced at her watch. He wasn't really late it was just that she was impatient for his company.

After a few minutes Caroline excused herself and moved on. An executive from H.M.V. came over to talk to Jessie, saying he understood she had written 'Together', the Marvin Leroi hit and how pleased he was to meet her.

Tommy arrived five minutes later, and Jessie's smile of greeting as he walked into the room died on her face when she realized he wasn't alone. A stunning brunette had hurried through the door after him, and slipped an arm through his. She had a sylphlike figure, and long, shapely legs. The eyes were wide, and vulnerable, the mouth a sensuous slash of red. She was Ania of course, the high cheekbones Tommy hd spoken of gave that away.

Jessie was glad the H.M.V. executive was still talking

to her, it would have been most embarrassing to have been seen by the pair of them to be standing on her own.

Out of the corner of her eye she saw Tommy steering Ania in her direction. Now what was the H.M.V. executive's name again? She was going to have to introduce him.

'Hello, Jessie,' Tommy said, giving her a shy, hesitant smile.

'Hello?' she smiled back.

'This is Ania Zumbach, Ania, this is Jessie.'

The hand that shook Jessie's was cool and delicate. Jessie could feel the bones under the skin.

'This is Clifford Grout who works for H.M.V.,' Jessie said, and Clifford shook hands with Ania and Tommy.

'I feel that I already know you, Tommy has told me so much about you,' Ania said to Jessie.

Jessie looked into Ania's face, searching for hidden dislike, contempt, amusement even, but all she saw was a genuine friendliness. The woman hadn't come to crow over a long fallen rival. What a relief. Jessie found herself, though jealous of her, warming to Ania Zumbach.

They chatted about records, and the music business in general, with Clifford Grout doing most of the talking. Then Clifford's wife joined them to say that Marco was going to make a speech shortly.

'Where's Phil?' Tommy asked Jessie.

'Oh, about somewhere,' she answered vaguely, hoping that Phil would come back soon and pay some attention to her so that Tommy could see him doing so. But Phil was no longer in the room, Jessie had already ascertained that, nor was the blonde he'd been chatting up. She hadn't noticed either of them leave.

Several minutes later Caroline appeared and in a loud voice, requested everyone to go upstairs to the lounge where Marco wanted to address them.

Caroline then came over to Jessie and Tommy, and said they were to stick with her, Marco wanted them close to him when he spoke.

325

'Why?' Tommy asked.

Caroline gave a conspiratorial wink. 'You'll soon find out,' she smiled.

Tommy glanced at Jessie, who shrugged. 'I don't know,' Jessie said. She was just as much in the dark as he was.

When everyone had crowded into the upstairs lounge Marco held his hands up and called for quiet.

He thanked all those present for coming to his party, and hoped they were enjoying themselves, for he certainly was. 'And now I'd like you to meet two people from Glasgow, Scotland, who've become friends of mine, and who are here tonight. The first is Tommy McBride whose brand new disc Vestal will be releasing in a few weeks time. Folks, Tommy McBride!'

Caroline propelled a startled, and momentarily nonplussed, Tommy forward to stand beside Marco who was leading the applause.

'Every so often a singer emerges whom you just know is going to make it to the top, and I, and Vestal, think that of Tommy,' Marco enthused.

Jessie saw that Phil had appeared at the back of the room. His features were contorted with jealousy as he glared at Tommy.

'Tommy's new single is called "Big City Shout", and was written by him in collaboration with that other Glaswegian I mentioned, the woman who wrote the all-time chart buster "Together", Jessie McBride!' Marco went on.

Jessie didn't wait for Caroline to give her a push, she knew what was expected of her. She went to stand at Marco's other side.

'Folks, I give you Vestal's next number one hit, "Big City Shout"!' proclaimed Marco, and punched the air with his fist, the cue for a copy of the demo to be played.

Everyone listened as the number thundered out, but none more intently than Jessie who was staring at the floor, not wanting the others to see her face in what was for her an highly intimate moment.

It was every bit as good as she'd thought at the recording session, she told herself. Slowly, she let her gaze wander to the room. Those present were responding positively, and with enthusiasm. Any lingering doubts were blown away: she and Tommy were on a winner.

Then the number was over and everyone was clapping again. Jessie glanced up to see Ania staring at Tommy in open admiration. He stared back proudly at her.

Marco said a few more words about 'Big City Shout', then concluded his speech by announcing that a buffet supper was now available in the adjoining room.

'You might have given us some warning about that,' Tommy said to Marco when Marco's speech was over, and the crowd had begun to disperse.

'I thought it'd be far more fun to spring it on you,' Marco laughed. 'You should have seen your face.'

'When did Vestal finally decide to go ahead?' Jessie asked; she and Tommy had been waiting anxiously for the decision since the demo had been cut.

'Just this morning,' Marco grinned.

'When do we do the actual recording?' demanded Tommy.

'Monday next.'

'And what about promotion?' Jessie asked softly.

'Vestal will be pushing the record hard, you have my word on that. Okay?'

'Okay,' Jessie nodded.

Ania joined Tommy as Caroline came over with fresh glasses of Buck's Fizz. The toast, proposed by Marco was to 'Big City Shout'.

After drinking Jessie glanced round the room, looking for Phil. But he had disappeared again.

Jessie picked up a sample of fabric and studied it. She and Tommy were in Gruman's Tailor Shop in Soho's Bridle

Lane. Solly Gruman specialized in show clothes which Tommy, at her insistence, was being kitted out with, and for which Vestal Records would be picking up the tab.

Solly Gruman was an old gentleman who still spoke with a heavy Russian accent, even though he'd been in Britain for sixty-eight years, having arrived from Russia at the age of nine. In show business circles his clothes were legendary.

Solly was in the middle of measuring Tommy when the telephone rang. An assistant informed Solly it was someone who wished to speak to him personally. Solly apologized to Tommy, and said he wouldn't be a moment, but he didn't ask the assistant to continue with the measuring. Solly always did that himself.

Jessie was bending over a box to pick up some more fabric samples when she happned to catch Tommy's reflection in a nearby full length mirror.

He, unaware she could see him, was watching her, his expression one she remembered only too well from the days when they'd been together. She called it his randy look. In the past when it had appeared they'd always ended up in bed shortly afterwards.

Seeing that look again, and directed at her, made her flustered. She could feel herself blush, for all the world like some virginal lassie.

Could he still fancy her, even though she'd become so unattractive? Then she thought of the beautiful Ania, and her spirits, which had soared, dropped again. She had no chance against Ania, not the chance of a snowball in hell. Whatever she thought she saw in his eyes was not for her.

As they were walking away from Gruman's, Tommy said he wanted to stop at the first newsagent they came to, he needed to buy a packet of cigarettes. The newsagent they went into had a large magazine rack, and Tommy surprised Jessie by not only buying cigarettes but a copy of *Town and Country* as well.

'I would hardly have thought that *Town and Country*

would have interested you,' Jessie teased when they were back outside again.

'If I'm going to be rich and famous I'll need a house to reflect my status,' he said in a posh voice. 'And *Town and Country* has an excellent real estate section.'

Jessie could see that, despite the joke voice, he was in deadly earnest. 'What's this, delusions of grandeur already?' she mocked, speaking in broad Glasgow, which made it sound even more mocking.

'And why the hell not!' he answered in a voice just as broad as hers.

They both burst out laughing.

'Big City Shout' was launched at Vestal Records with a drinks reception. A great many people in key positions crucial to the sales of records were invited, and most of them had turned up to be plied with as much liquor as they could drink and a free copy of 'Big City Shout'.

It was hard work for Jessie and Tommy who'd been primed by Marco that they were to continually circulate, and generally make themselves available.

'How are we doing?' Jessie asked Caroline, having taken Caroline to one side so the pair of them could have a moment's breather. She'd just been talking to an intellectual type whose conversation, thanks to the more obscure words in the English language he'd persisted in using, had been mainly way over her head. She'd just kept muttering yes, and no, and hoping she was saying the right thing at the right time.

'It's going great guns, Mick's pleased,' Caroline replied.

Jessie glanced over to where Tommy was standing. He was wearing one of Solly Gruman's suits, and looked extremely handsome. Very handsome indeed. It pleased her enormously to think she'd rescued him for that dreadful job. What a waste it would have been if he'd never gone back to music.

He suddenly gazed across at her, and their eyes met. She felt herself turn to jelly inside. She tore her gaze away from Tommy, and tried to concentrate again on what Caroline was saying.

'Jessie, I'd like you to meet Ron Bishop who handles our account at J. Walter Thompson,' said Marco, appearing beside Jessie and Caroline in the company of a small, smiling man.

Jessie shook hands, and plunged into yet another conversation about herself, Tommy and 'Big City Shout'.

Jessie sat on the edge of her bed staring at that day's edition of *Melody Maker* which had just been delivered to the house. 'Big City Shout' was at number twenty-five in the charts, only two places up on the previous week, and four on the week before that. It was now coming up to a month since the record had been released, and so far its performance in the shops had been unspectacular to say the very least.

Jessie worried a nail. Why wasn't it doing better? That's what she wanted to know. Marco had promised Vestal would push it, so why was it languishing so low down in the charts?

She decided to telephone Marco and demand an explanation. It was too early to ring him at Vestal, he wouldn't be there yet, so she'd contact him at home.

Caroline answered to say that Mick had just that minute left, then listened sympathetically while Jessie gave vent to her worries.

'It's a complete mystery to everybody at Vestal why 'Big City Shout' isn't doing better, no one can figure it out,' Caroline said.

'Are Vestal pushing it as they promised?' Jessie demanded.

'I can assure you they have been, Jessie. Really.'

'Hmmh!' said Jessie in disbelief.

330

'Vestal are doing all they can. But if it's one of those records that's just not going to go, then it's not going to go,' Caroline said bluntly.

Oh God, was it another 'Missing Totti'? And she'd come to be so sure about this song, a hundred percent certain. It was good, *it was*, she told herself. The only trouble was the buying public didn't seem to agree.

'There's still time yet for it to happen, and meanwhile everyone at Vestal will be doing their best to try and make it work,' Caroline reassured her.

Jessie eased off at that point, realizing that a slanging match with Caroline or Marco wasn't going to help matters. She spoke for a few more minutes to Caroline, then hung up, and got dressed.

She swithered about telephoning Tommy, decided not to, then changed her mind. Ania answered.

'Yes, he's seen *Melody Maker*,' she said with a sigh. 'You can imagine how depressed about it he is.'

'Maybe I can try and buck him up. Can I have a word with him?' Jessie asked.

'Of course.'

There was a pause during which Jessie knew Ania was still on the line.

'Jessie. . .' Ania said haltingly.

'Yes?'

There was a second pause, and Jessie got the distinct impression that Ania was debating with herself about whether or not to say something.

'Nothing, he'll tell you himself when he's ready. I'll get him,' Ania said in a rush, and laid down the phone.

Now what was that all about? *What* would Tommy tell her when he was ready, Jessie wondered, her curiosity aroused.

Although he tried to hide it Jessie could hear the disappointment in Tommy's voice when he came on the line. She did her best to cheer him up, but failed. When she finally rang off she was depressed as he.

331

Going downstairs, she found Phil sitting in the kitchen with a silly grin plastered all over his face and the cloying smell of grass hanging heavily in the air.

'I'm going out for a while,' she said, having decided to go to the shops and buy a new pair of shoes. Buying new shoes never failed to make her feel better.

Phil's eyes slowly focused on her, and the silly grin became a wide smile.

'You all right?' she asked.

'Oh, yes,' he whispered in reply. Then he laughed, a high pitched laugh that might have been a girl's.

Jessie was halfway down the street before it dawned on her why she'd been treated to the silly grin, wide smile, and funny laugh, as opposed to the supercilious expression that normally accompanied his pot smoking.

He'd brought *Melody Maker* up to her in the bedroom, but had looked up the charts before doing so.

He'd been celebrating the fact 'Big City Shout' was continuing to do badly.

'Bastard!' she hissed as she marched down the street.

The following day, a little after noon, Jessie was preparing a light lunch for herself – she'd taken off over a stone since starting on her diet – when the telephone rang. It was an ecstatic Tommy.

'Guess who's appearing on this week's 'Saturday Night Out''!' he cried jubilantly.

'Oh, Tommy!' she exclaimed. 'Saturday Night Out' was Britain's most popular television programme. There were millions who considered it an absolute must for weekend viewing.

'Marco buzzed just a few minutes ago. Apparently Stormy Waters was to top the bill on Saturday, but has had to drop out on account of laryngitis. Marco has persuaded them to book me in his place, although I won't get his top billing,' Tommy explained, having difficulty in keeping the excitement out of his voice.

Jessie felt almost as elated as he sounded 'That's absolutely marvellous news!'

'Will you watch me?'

'Of course I will. I wouldn't miss it for the world.'

'I'm totally bowled over, so's Ania. It's her favourite programme.'

Jessie's heart sank on hearing Ania's name mentioned. It had been on the tip of her tongue to suggest that she come to the studios with him, and sit in the live audience for the performance, but that was a suggestion she wouldn't make now. If he wanted anyone to go with him it would be Ania.

'Which of my suits should I wear?' he asked, sounding like a boy.

'I think you should let Ania choose. From the way she was dressed at Marco's party I'd guess she has excellent taste,' Jessie replied with no trace of the hurt she was feeling in her voice.

She'd also been contemplating asking Tommy and Ania over for a meal one night soon, but perversely decided that she wouldn't do that now.

'This might be just the boost the record needs,' Tommy said, unnecessarily, as that was obviously the reason Marco had fought so hard to get him booked as Stormy Waters' replacement.

'I'll have to go, I've got something in the oven and it smells like it's starting to burn,' Jessie lied.

'Oh, all right,' he replied somewhat put out by her abruptness. He'd wanted to talk with her longer.

'Good luck for Saturday, Tommy.'

'Thanks.'

She hung up. Frowning, she stared at the phone for some seconds. Maybe she should initiate the divorce proceedings, after all there was no point in being married to Tommy in name only.

Ania Zumbach.

She had nothing personally against the woman, in fact she liked her.

333

She just wished her parents had never bloody well left Cracow.

When 'Saturday Night Out' started she was so nervous for Tommy she poured most of a large whisky down the front of her dress rather than into her mouth.

'Buggeration!' she muttered, and refilled her glass. She would worry about the dress later, when the programme, or Tommy's part in it, was over.

The Light were playing The Lonsdale Arms, which meant she had the house to herself. She was pleased about that, the last thing she'd wanted was to watch Tommy in Phil's company. She had no doubt that Phil would have had something nasty and cutting to say no matter what Tommy's performance was like.

The master of ceremonies was a comedian called Dick Jones who told gags between the acts. He was a very funny man, and normally Jessie roared with laughter when he was on, but not tonight. Tonight she was far too wound up to pay attention to anything but Tommy.

The acts that came and went were all top class, for only the very best were booked for 'Saturday Night Out'. Then Dick Jones was introducing Tommy, and a curtain gauze flew away to reveal Tommy, holding a hand mike, picked out in spotlight.

Jessie crossed two fingers, and held her breath. She noticed that Ania had chosen the same suit for him that she would have chosen.

Tommy was in fine voice as he belted out 'Big City Shout'. More than the good voice, however, was his stage presence. There was not a second of his performance when he wasn't in control. When he was through, he got a terrific round of applause, louder and more intense than any of the other acts had received.

Jessie switched off her set, and poured a last large whisky. She'd already well broken her diet quota for the night, but it had been a special occasion after all.

She considered trying to ring Tommy at the studio, and decided not to. She'd ring him at home next morning.

Her own phone then rang and it was Marco asking her what she'd thought. She said that in her opinion Tommy and the song had come over very well indeed. Marco said that he and Caroline thought so, too.

She had a long bath which was so soothing and soporific she nearly nodded off. Coming out of it, she got ready for bed. She had no sooner turned off the bedside light than she fell instantly asleep, to dream of Tommy.

She awoke to find her shoulder being shaken by a flushed Phil, smelling of beer.

'We're on our way again,' he said excitedly.

She blinked in the sudden light. 'On our way where?'

'Not you and me, the lads and myself. The Light. There was a record producer in the pub tonight from Parlophone who was so knocked out by us he's invited us to make a demo for him.'

'That's smashing Phil, it really is,' she said, trying to come fully awake.

Phil jumped to his feet and began undressing. 'He thought "Why Fucking Not" was out of this world, but of course he can't record it for the same reasons Vestal couldn't.'

'So what are you going to record?' she asked, hoping it wasn't going to be one of the one's she'd written for him.

'He says he has a couple of numbers which are just right for us. He's sending them around by courier tomorrow morning.'

Naked now, Phil slid into bed alongside Jessie, his hand going straight to the hem of her nightie and pulling it up. 'Tommy McBride isn't the only one's who's going to get to the top, you wait and see,' he said.

She closed her eyes as he penetrated her, and conjured up in her mind a picture of Tommy as Tommy had been on television earlier.

She groaned as, still picturing Tommy, she had the first orgasm she'd had with Phil in ages.

As everyone connected with 'Big City Shout' had hoped, Tommy's appearance on 'Saturday Night Out' was a watershed for the song. Within days it had begun to sell in real quantity, and when the next charts came out it had risen to number nine. The following week it was at number three.

Jessie was in the process of painting her toenails blood red when she received a phone call from Caroline saying that Marco wanted to see her in his office that afternoon. When Jessie asked why Caroline said that she didn't know.

She's lying, Jessie thought as she hung up. But why would Caroline do that? It was all very mysterious.

Jessie arrived promptly at Vestal at the appointed time, to find Tommy waiting in reception. He said he didn't have a clue what this was all about, either.

Caroline took them up to Marco's office, and asked them to wait outside for a moment or two. When she reappeared, she was smiling. 'After you,' she grinned.

Marco and a number of other Vestal employees were grouped around Marco's desk. On the desk was a large cake with 'Big City Shout', Number 1 On The Hit Parade inscribed on it in pink icing.

'When the next charts come out "Big City Shout" is going to be Number 1, we have that on the q.t. from the very highest authority,' Marco beamed.

Jessie could only stare in amazement and joy. If a good fairy had granted her a wish, this would have been it. Well, one of two wishes, that is.

Champagne corks popped. The toast, proposed by Marco, was to Tommy, Jessie and 'Big City Shout'. "Long may it stay at Number 1,' he laughed.

'Let's hope it sells a million,' Tommy said after the toast had been drunk.

Marco raised a laugh all round by instantly replying he'd *certainly* drink to that.

Jessie was tipsy when she left Vestal Records, but quite sober again when she got back home. In the kitchen she found a letter from Phil.

He said he'd finally heard from Parlophone, the demo The Light had made for them had been rejected. This was the last straw, as far as he was concerned. He knew now he wasn't going to make it in the music business, at least not in the way he wanted.

He was getting out. Playing 'Why Fucking Not' at The Lonsdale Arms and other gigs had been great fun while it lasted, but he wasn't prepared to spend the rest of his life as a pub entertainer.

He was leaving her, and going back home to be a stockbroker. His mother had been right all along, that was where his future lay.

He was sorry, but goodbye.

Jessie put the letter down, and stared out the window. His leaving the music business, as a singer anyway, was undoubtedly the right decision. And as for leaving her. . .

Well they'd been all washed up for some time now, she'd known it, and he must have as well. She was pleased, and relieved, he'd gone before the situation had become any worse.

Now he would marry a good little Jewish girl, and keep regular nine to five working hours, just as his mother had wanted.

Throwing her head back Jessie laughed.

And laughed.

And laughed.

Then she went into the toilet and threw up.

'That's it, finished,' Jessie said.

She and Tommy, on Marco's instructions, had been

working all morning on a follow up to 'Big City Shout', which was now in its third week at the Number 1 spot. Tommy had titled the new number, 'Lonely Street Walk'.

Tommy picked the score off the piano, gave it a final glance through, then replaced it. 'I'll give Marco a ring, as he asked us to, to say we're done,' Tommy said, and stretched, yawning as he pushed his arms high above his head.

Jessie played the tune through again while Tommy was on the telephone. Her new tune was every bit as good as 'Big City Shout'; Tommy's lyrics were even better.

Tommy returned looking shaken. 'I'm off on tour, we open Norwich a week on Monday,' he announced.

'How long for?'

'Two months. Marco wants "Lonely Street Walk" recorded before I leave. And oh . . . I'm top of the bill.' His grin was as bright as the sun.

Two months without seeing him, it was a long time. 'That's marvellous. Congratulations,' she replied, doing her best to sound enthusiastic.

Tommy ran a hand through his hair. 'I've to close the first half, and the show itself. Marco says I'll need six numbers in all.'

'Don't worry about that, we'll do a song a day for the next four. You'll have your material.'

'Top of the hit parade, and a show in which I'm top of the bill, I couldn't ask for anything more, eh?' But to himself he thought that was a lie, there was something he wanted far more than either of those, something he would give his right arm for.

'This calls for a drink,' Jessie said, and led the way through to the front lounge where the spirits were kept.

'Slainthe!' Tommy said when she handed him a whisky.

'To the show!' she responded.

He sipped, and then sipped again, thinking for propriety's sake he'd have to ask Phil along as well. He's suggest a foursome. 'Listen, I've had an idea, why don't we all go out tonight and have a slap up nosh to celebrate? You and Phil, and Ania and I. If I give her a buzz now it'll give her time to arrange for one of the neighbours to come in and baby sit,' he said.

Jessie's face froze, and she dropped her eyes to stare into her glass.

'What's the matter, has Phil got a gig this evening?'

She swirled her whisky round and round till it made a miniature whirlpool. She hadn't told Tommy about Phil yet, she'd never volunteered the information, nor had the opportunity naturally presented itself to mention what had happened. Until now.

'Phil doesn't have a gig, he's not in the music business anymore. He's given it up,' she said.

'Since when?'

'The day Marco invited us to Vestal for cake and champagne. The Light had done a demo for Parlophone, and Parlophone gave it the elbow. That finished him. He went home to mummy and became a stockbroker again.'

For the space of about ten seconds the full import of what she'd said didn't sink in, then Tommy's eyes widened in surprise.

'You mean he's left you?'

Jessie nodded.

'For good?'

She nodded a second time.

Tommy mouthed a crude obscenity, and threw what remained of his whisky down his throat. 'Can I have another?'

'Help yourself.'

He poured himself a huge whisky while he tried to collect his thoughts. This was so unexpected . . . 'I got the impression it was all sweetness and light between you two,' he said at last.

'Not quite.'

'Are you sorry he's gone?'

'No,' she whispered.

Tommy took a deep breath, then another. 'Can we go out for that nosh up together? Just the two of us?' he asked quietly.

'Won't Ania object?'

He gave a laugh. 'There's something I've got to tell you about us.'

Jessie remembered Ania saying on the telephone that Tommy had something to tell her, which he would do when he was ready. This must be it she thought. He was going to tell her they were getting married.

'Ania's not my girlfriend, and never has been,' Tommy said in a rush.

Jessie stared at him blankly. What on earth was he havering on about? Of course Ania was his girlfriend!

'Are you trying to tell me you and Ania don't live together?' Jessie asked in disbelief.

'Oh, we do, but not as I've been pretending to you.'

Jessie stared at Tommy who looked like a wee boy who'd just been caught out in a lie. 'So in what fashion *do* you live together?'

'We're not lovers, and never have been. She's exactly as I first described her to you, a *friend*. She's also my landlady, I'm her lodger,' Tommy explained.

Jessie fought back the hysteria she felt mounting within her, Ania's lodger!

'When she kicked her husband out it left her very short of money, as you can well imagine. She put a card in a local newsagent's window. I was looking for digs at the time, and I answered her advert,' he went on.

'But why did you let me believe you were lovers? And why did she go along with it?'

Tommy returned to the decanter and refilled his glass. He wasn't enjoying this confession one little bit. He felt such a fool. What had seemed logical at the time now seemed only stupid.

'That first night in the Globe pub when I discovered you were rich, and successful, and living with a chap, I

. . . well, I didn't want my life to appear a complete failure compared to yours. And I was jealous. It was a case of, if you've got someone then I've got someone too,' he admitted reluctantly.

Jessie gave a high, brittle laugh. She understood perfectly now, and, knowing herself, realized that if the positions had been reversed, she'd probably have done the same thing. What a couple of prize chumps they were.

'Ania went along with the charade, against her better judgment, because I pleaded with her to.'

Jessie could feel that her hands were trembling. She felt curiously lightheaded, that strange, ethereal sensation that often follows the breaking of a fever. When she spoke, her voice sounded far away. 'When Phil asked me out I went because I told myself that even though I'd lost you my life wasn't over, and that I had to keep going and live what remained of it as best I could. I never loved Phil, although to begin with I did like him a great deal. Lately, though, I stopped liking him.' She paused for a brief second, then continued. 'I think, in truth, because he so resented my success with "Together", he stopped liking me before I stopped liking him.'

Tommy gazed fondly at Jessie, thinking how much they'd been through together – the spell at Queen's Park Senior Secondary which had terminated so abruptly when his father had been killed, their meeting up again, Ken Young and Linton Street, his period in Barlinne Prison, their marriage and being King and Queen of the Glasgow Teds, The Tommy McBride Skiffle Band, Allison Street. . .

'What I've never stopped doing is loving you, I want you to know that,' he whispered.

'Nor I you.'

Jessie read in his face what was coming next, and it was what she wanted also. For the first time since running away from Allison Street she felt whole again, complete.

'Ania's going to have to get herself another lodger,' she said as he came over and took her in his arms.

Tommy's tour had seemed interminable to Jessie. Each day might have been a week, each week a month, a month a year. But now the end was in sight. It was Tuesday of the last week.

Tommy had just been on the telephone proposing she drive up on Saturday and join him in Newcastle. She would see the final performance, and stay the night.

And on Sunday, well he had a surprise for her then, a real humdinger of a surprise that was going to take her breath away.

She'd done her best to winkle out of him what the surprise was, but he'd refused to tell her, saying adamantly that it would hardly be a surprise if he did.

Jessie then had a thought which brought a smile to her face. Two could play at this surprise business, why wait till Saturday to go to Newcastle, why not go tomorrow! There was nothing to keep her in London after all, nothing whatever.

Jessie had thoroughly enjoyed her drive north, the July weather had been balmy, perfect for motoring, and she'd had an absolutely splendid lunch in Chester-Le-Street where she'd stopped off for a leg stretch and leisurely meal.

Tommy was staying at the Royal Turks Head Hotel in Newcastle, but she had no intentions of going there directly. She'd see the show first, then surprise him after.

The Theatre Royal, where Tommy was playing, was directly opposite the hotel, so she parked the car round the corner, away from the stage door, and sneaked into the foyer where she ran into an unexpected problem in that the show was booked out.

She didn't want to contact Tommy and, as she saw it,

spoil her surprise, so, reluctantly, she asked for the Front of House Manager.

When Mr Inglis appeared she explained who she was, that she wanted to surprise Tommy after the show, and could he please find her a seat, and *not* let on to Tommy.

Mr Inglis was happy to oblige, and swore that no one would know from him that she was going to be at that evening's performance. Several house seats were always kept in reserve, and she could have one of those.

She had a couple of hours to kill before showtime, so she walked round the centre of Newcastle doing some sightseeing and window shopping, rounding that off with a drink in a pub snug.

Inside the theatre, and in a rapidly filling auditorium, she bought a programme, and sat back to enjoy herself.

And enjoy herself she most certainly did. The show was terrific. Tommy was better than she'd ever imagined.

Finally it was all over, the curtain ringing down for the last time to thunderous applause.

She went round to the stage door, where she expected to find a stage doorkeeper, but didn't. The man's cubby-hole was empty, of the man himself there was no sign. She asked a passing showgirl where Number 1 dressing room was, and was directed along an adjacent corridor. The first door she came to in the corridor had the figure 1 painted on it in gold, and beneath that a large gold star.

She tapped the door, and heard a muffled response. 'Surprise!' she cried as she stepped inside.

The scene that greeted her instantly transported her back in time to another door she'd stepped through to discover Tommy with Eve Baxter. This time, however, he was with a girl completely unknown to her, a girl stripped to the waist who was all over him like a rash.

Tommy's head jerked round to stare at Jessie in horror. 'Jesus!' he whispered.

Jessie reacted in the same way she'd done before. Turning tail she ran, the heels of her shoes rat-tat-tatting on the stone floor as she raced back up the corridor.

Tommy pushed the girl from him, and went after Jessie. This time, at least, he was fully dressed and didn't have to stop when he reached the street.

He caught her about two hundred yards from the theatre, grabbing hold of her arm and forcing her to stop.

'Go away! Just leave me alone!' Jessie spat, her face awash with scalding tears. She was mortified at this second betrayal of her love. And if there had been this girl how many others had there been while she'd been counting the long days to their being reunited!

'It's not what you think you've got it all wrong,' he shouted, holding her tightly.

'You had a half naked woman in your arms, are you now going to try and tell me you were teaching her to dance?' Jessie choked.

'I swear to you on all that's holy I've never seen that girl before. I came off stage, went into my dressing room, then there was a knock and it was her asking for my autograph. I thought she must be known to one of the other performers, how else would she get backstage? I bent over my dressing table to sign her book, and the next thing I know she's whipped off the top part of her clothes and is assaulting me.'

Jessie used the coat sleeve of the arm he wasn't holding fast to wipe wet from her face.

'If she's just a crazy fan I've no idea how she got past the stage doorkeeper, fans are usually kept waiting outside,' he went on.

Jessie remembered then that the stage doorkeeper hadn't been in his cubbyhole when she'd presented herself at the stage door. He hadn't been in evidence at all which had allowed her unchallenged access to the theatre. Was Tommy's explanation the truth then?

'The bird threw herself at me, and I was standing there wondering what the hell to do when you walked in.' Tommy paused, looked Jessie straight in the eyes, and added. 'What I'm telling you is the God's honest. May he strike me down dead here and now if it's not.'

Jessie sniffed. 'Just whipped half her clothes off?'

'While I was signing her autograph book.'

'No indication she was going to do it?'

'None at all.'

'And you'd never seen her before?'

'Never.'

Jessie sniffed again. 'You can let go now,' she said.

'I love you Jessie,' he told her, and kissed her. Then he let her go.

As they walked back to the theatre, she dabbed at her face with a hanky. She told Tommy about the stage doorkeeper's absence from his post, and he replied grimly the man would get a right telling off unless he had a damn good reason for not being there.

At the stage door they found the stage doorkeeper and several stage hands manhandling a group of shrieking girls, one of whom had been the lassie in Tommy's dressing room, out the door.

'Come on!' Tommy hissed to Jessie, and together they forced their way through the throng and into the theatre.

More stage hands came running to assist their mates and the aged, sweating, doorkeeper broke away to come over to Tommy and Jessie.

'I'm awful sorry Mr McBride, but that entire gang just burst past me and there was nothing I could do to stop them. They scattered in all directions trying to find you, and I did my best to go after them – but I'm afraid I'm only one man,' he explained.

So that was it, the poor old man had been backstage chasing the girls when she'd presented herself, Jessie thought.

'Some of these fans can be a proper menace,' the stage doorkeeper added sourly.

'All right?' Tommy asked Jessie.

She nodded.

They returned then to his dressing room where he changed out of his stage suit, and Jessie washed her face, and put on some fresh make-up.

'I'm sorry for jumping to conclusions,' she said.

'Considering what you saw when you walked in on Eve and me, I can't blame you,' Tommy replied, and kissed her again.

Jessie explained that her coming early to Newcastle was to surprise him, and he laughed, saying her turning up at the moment she had had certainly done that.

'So much for my surprise, now what about your surprise for me?' she asked.

Tommy's brow furrowed in thought. He'd planned this for Sunday, but he supposed he could advance the date. She could sleep going, he coming back, that way he shouldn't be too tired for tomorrow night's performance.

'You did drive up as I suggested?' he asked.

'Yes, of course.'

'Then come on.'

They left the theatre by the front entrance, just to be on the safe side in case any of those girls were still lurking round the stage door.

Tommy instructed Jessie to take them to where the car was parked, and on arriving at it asked her for the keys. After she'd given them to him he opened the driver's door and climbed into the driving seat. Leaning over, he opened the other door.

Jessie got in, an stared at him in astonishment. 'But you can't drive!' she exclaimed.

He grinned at her. 'I couldn't drive when I left London, but I can now. I've been going out every day with a chap from one of the acts who says I should now pass my test no bother.'

'Is *that* the surprise?'

He switched on the engine. 'A surprise, but not *the* surprise,' he said, and took the car smoothly away from the kerb.

He knew how to get where he wanted to go, having already mapped it out for that coming Sunday. On the outskirts of Newcastle he brought the car on to the Gosforth road, heading northwest.

'Where are we going?' Jessie demanded.

'Ask no questions, get no lies. Shut your mouth, and you'll catch no flies,' he replied.

'Be that way then,' she retorted, and pretended to be in the huff.

He was really looking forward to this, he thought, smiling in anticipation.

Jessie came awake to the chatter of birds. 'We've just this minute arrived,' Tommy said, and handed her a lit cigarette. Dawn had been half an hour previously.

She accepted the cigarette, took a drag, coughed, then glanced around, wondering where they were.

'It was with a shock that she recognized the street. 'Old Castle Road!' she breathed. They were back in Glasgow.

Tommy got out the car, then coming to her side helped her out.

Jessie stared ahead of them at the Linn Park which had meant so much to Tommy when he was at Queen's Park School, his magic place he'd called it. And there was the Snuffmill Bridge, she could hear the water rumbling below it.

Tommy led her over to a grey granite house that was somewhat smaller than the rest, though still a fair size all the same. A plate on the left hand pillar of the wrought iron gate bore the name GREENDAYS.

'This was the house you thought of as being special,' Jessie said, that conversation coming back to her suddenly.

'And this street way and far my most favourite in all Glasgow, and where I said I'd choose to live if I ever did make big money.' Tommy paused, savouring what he was going to say next. 'It's not finalized yet, but I'm in the process of buying GREENDAYS. For *us*,' he announced quietly.

Jessie caught her breath. 'But . . . how on earth did you know it was for sale?'

'Remember, looking for a suitable property, I started reading *Town and Country*?'

She nodded.

'Well I opened last month's issue and there was GREENDAYS on the market. I had already been swithering about my singing career, and as far as I was concerned that clinched it. Fate had intervened, and pointed the way.'

'I don't follow the bit about your singing career?' she said.

'Why did you get me to start singing in the first place? Because I didn't have a job. And in the second? To take me out of that rotten cafe. But from now on that's all over and done with, it's the quiet life for me. For us.'

'Are you saying what I think you are?' she prompted, wanting it spelled out.

'If you agree, we'll live in GREENDAYS and concentrate solely on writing songs together. No more recording or performing for me,' he answered.

'Oh Tommy!' she whispered, thrilled at the prospect.

'So what do you say, Mrs McBride?'

She threw her arms round his neck, and kissed him deeply. It had all come right at last. She had Tommy, a dream house in a part of Glasgow so loved by both of them, the rest was jam on the cake.

'It'll be heaven on earth, Tommy, I couldn't ask for anything more.'

He swelled with pleasure, and pride. There had been bad years, for each of them, but they were over now. In Jessie, and the house, he had everything he'd ever wanted and more.

'I love you, Mrs McBride,' he told her softly.

'And I love you, Mr McBride.'

He opened the wrought iron gate and they went into the garden. He didn't have the front door key, but that didn't stop them looking around the outside of the house.

As they strolled over the lush lawn, Jessie remembered something. 'If we're going to be writing for singers other than you, would we be interested in a telephone call I had the other day from a chap in Liverpool asking if we'd write a song for a new group?'

'Oh aye?'

'They're called the . . .' She racked her memory for the name, it had been a funny one. Then it came back. 'The Beatles.'

Tommy paused to ponder the name. 'Never heard of them,' he replied eventually, and led Jessie over to some tall sunflowers which he proceeded to enthuse about at length.

THE BLACKBIRD'S TALE

Emma Blair

From Glasgow on the brink of the Great War to the
cut-throat world of London publishing – the spellbinding
saga of three remarkable generations:

Cathy: A Glasgow factory-girl who experiences love, its
loss and a kind of victory in the space of two turbulent
wartime years . . .

Hannah: The daughter whose marriage enjoys the fruits of
undreamt prosperity. But her love must learn to endure the
turmoil of a very personal hurt . . .

Robyn: The product of her generation. Modern, extrovert
and vivacious, her heart is broken by the only man she'll
ever love. Yet she finally comes to control her destiny – and
that of the lover she never really lost . . .

This is the unforgettable story of three women united in
their love for books, for life, and for their men. A story
which began with the little bookshop that Cathy fell in love
with thirty years before. The Blackbird . . .

FLOWER OF SCOTLAND

Emma Blair

In the idyllic summer of 1912, all seems rosy for Murdo
Drummond and his four children. Charlotte is ecstatically
in love with her fiancé Geoffrey; Peter, the eldest, prepares
for the day when he will inherit the family whisky distillery;
while Andrew, gregarious and fun-loving, is already
turning heads and hearts. Nell, the youngest, contents
herself with daydreams of a handsome highlander. Even
Murdo, their proud father, though still mourning the
death of his beloved wife, is considering future happiness
with Jean Richie, an old family friend.

The Great War, however, has no respect for family life.
As those carefree pre-war days of the distillery fade,
with death, devastation, revenge, scandal and suicide
brought in their wake, the Drummonds are plunged
to the horrors of the trenches in France. Yet those
who survive discover that love can transcend class,
creed and country . . .

WILD STRAWBERRIES

Emma Blair

In the lush countryside of West Cornwall lies the small fishing village of Coverack and the warm welcome of the Paris Hotel. It is an appropriate name because the owner, Maizie Blackacre, finds her life changed forever by the arrival of a young Frenchman.

The Second World War has brought its own special turmoil to Coverack. When Maizie's husband Sam joins the Merchant Navy, she is left to cope with the hotel's dwindling trade and two young evacuees. Then the arrival of Christian Lee Gall, a French lieutenant recuperating from a war wound, lightens all their lives.

When Christian reports back for duty, Maizie is surprised at how sad she is to see him go – and how much she dreads the return of hard drinking Sam. Caught between loyalty for her unfeeling husband, and her growing affection for Christian, Maizie has to fight her own private war of emotions . . .

McADAM'S WOMEN

Evelyn Hood

The day her husband Kenneth died, Isla McAdam's life changed dramatically, irrevocably – and shockingly. Kenneth, twenty years her senior, has left her with two children, no money, and a shameful legacy. For just as Isla knew little about his business, she knew nothing at all about his other life – with another wife, another family, another existence . . .

And for a single mother in Paisley in the 1920s, it's not easy to make a living, particularly when Kenneth's duplicity catches up with her and forces a series of painful confrontations. But not all of McAdam's women are bent on destruction, and one of them helps Isla forge a new life for herself and her children. And although facing up to the past is a traumatic business, through the hurt comes the chance for a new and lifelong love . . .

'Evelyn Hood has been called Scotland's Catherine Cookson. Unfair. She has her own distinctive voice, never clearer than in *McAdam's Women*'
Scots Magazine

EVE'S DAUGHTER

Jeanne Whitmee

Eve and Jack Kenning have longed desperately for a child,
but when Jack goes off to fight in the war, the prospect
seems even more remote. So the news that Eve's flighty,
fun-loving lodger Sally is to have a baby as if it was her
own, even begging Sally to let her adopt the child. When
Sally is killed during an air raid, Eve is racked with guilt –
and happier than she feels she has the right to be.

Determined that the child, Carol, will grow up clever and
accomplished, Eve nurtures her natural talents. But Carol
wants a career as an actress and a life with the man she
loves – and her desperate bid for independence is now
threatened by a dark secret for the past . . .

BUTTERFLIES IN DECEMBER

Eileen Ramsay

It was her beloved father who first made the observation: that graceful, intelligent, independent women like Lucy Graham were as rare as butterflies in December. Lucy was determined to realise her ambition of becoming a doctor – but in one of the poorer districts of Dundee another bright young woman held on to the same dream. For Rosie Nesbitt, the path to her goal would be more of a struggle, demanding sacrifices from those closest to her and testing her resolve to the limit.

As pioneers in their field, it was perhaps inevitable that their paths would cross. And when they do, their chosen career isn't the only thing they have in common: the party at which they first meet is hosted by Kier Anderson-Howard – a potential husband of Lucy's – but whose attention is clearly centred on Rosie.

Lucy may have burnt her bridges with the man she had sacrificed to her career. But as the Great War approaches, Lucy's life encompasses further sorrow and joy with the re-appearance of a long-lost figure from the past – a figure she'd been resigned to losing forever . . .

Other bestselling Warner titles available by mail: